SHADOW OF THE SMOKING MOUNTAIN

The Chronicles of Hanuvar 3

**BAEN BOOKS
by HOWARD ANDREW JONES**

THE CHRONICLES OF HANUVAR
Lord of a Shattered Land
The City of Marble and Blood
Shadow of the Smoking Mountain
Daughters of the Silver Towers

To purchase these titles in e-book form, please go to www.baen.com.

SHADOW OF THE SMOKING MOUNTAIN

The Chronicles of Hanuvar 3

Howard Andrew Jones

SHADOW OF THE SMOKING MOUNTAIN

This is a work of fiction. All the characters and events portrayed in this book are fictional, and any resemblance to real people or incidents is purely coincidental.

Copyright © 2024 by Howard Andrew Jones

All rights reserved, including the right to reproduce this book or portions thereof in any form.

Earlier versions of some portions of this book have appeared previously in the following: "Discordant Factions" in *Heroic Fantasy Quarterly* issue 60, "Reflection from a Tarnished Mirror" in *Neither Beg Nor Yield*, and "Family Heirlooms" in *Paladins of Valor*.

A Baen Books Original

Baen Publishing Enterprises
P.O. Box 1403
Riverdale, NY 10471
www.baen.com

ISBN: 978-1-62579-985-2

Cover art by Dave Seeley

First printing, October 2024

Distributed by Simon & Schuster
1230 Avenue of the Americas
New York, NY 10020

Library of Congress Cataloging-in-Publication Data

Names: Jones, Howard A., author.
Title: Shadow of the smoking mountain / Howard Andrew Jones.
Description: Riverdale, NY : Baen Books/Baen Publishing Enterprises, 2024.
  | Series: The Chronicles of Hanuvar ; 3
Identifiers: LCCN 2024024519 (print) | LCCN 2024024520 (ebook) | ISBN
  9781982193676 (hardcover) | ISBN 9781625799852 (ebook)
Subjects: LCGFT: Fantasy fiction. | Novels.
Classification: LCC PS3610.O62535 S53 2024 (print) | LCC PS3610.O62535
  (ebook) | DDC 813/.6--dc23/eng/20240531
LC record available at https://lccn.loc.gov/2024024519
LC ebook record available at https://lccn.loc.gov/2024024520
Printed in the United States of America

10 9 8 7 6 5 4 3 2 1

Dedication

In memory of Karl,
creator of indelible horror and acid gothic tales,
and Mary, who brought Hannibal to life
so ably on the page.

Contents

3   Preamble

5   Chapter 1: The Voices From the Mountain

49   Chapter 2: Discordant Factions

77   Chapter 3: Monsters on the Shore

111   Chapter 4: Reflection From a Tarnished Mirror

153   Chapter 5: Issue of Malice

187   Chapter 6: Family Heirlooms

227   Chapter 7: The Heart of the Matter

271   Chapter 8: The Wonder Garden

307   Chapter 9: The People in the Stone

347   Chapter 10: The Cup of Fate

393   Chapter 11: Hillside Figures

409   Chapter 12: Death Grip

427   Chapter 13: Queen of a Nighted Realm

435   Chapter 14: A Time of Reckoning

491   Afterword

493   Acknowledgements

Book 3
Freely Adapted from
The Hanuvid of Antires Sosilos (the Elder),
with the commentary of Silenus

ANDRONIKOS SOSILOS (THE YOUNGER)

Preamble

He had crossed half a continent and ice-capped mountains to reach the heartland of his enemies, then dared to walk the streets of their capital. Aided by an invaluable few, Hanuvar reforged the broken links of his intelligence organization into the backbone of a liberation network. Thus had he brought Volani survivors by ones and twos and threes and dozens to freedom.

A brighter day had dawned for those hundreds, and for the empire as a whole, for a kindly young ruler had reached the Dervan throne. Hanuvar put his back to the politics captivating the capital and travelled to the Oscanus region along the southeast coast of Tyvol. There a small number of his people remained in the possession of intractable slave holders. The deliverance of each would have to come by clever stratagems, Hanuvar's specialty.

There too lay a makeshift boarding school owned by Hanuvar's old nemesis and firm friend, Ciprion, who had conspired with his wife, Amelia, to purchase all the Volani children they could at auction. Hanuvar hoped to find his niece Edonia hidden among them. And this was not the only relative he sought. With several companions, Hanuvar's daughter Narisia had escaped Dervan captivity into the countryside. Neither the revenants nor the praetorians nor Hanuvar's spies had found trace of her existence since.

Apart from worries, for his surviving family and many others, Hanuvar had much to be thankful for. Cured of a sorcerous malady, he was blessed with a handful of recovered years and a body healed of all but its most recent injuries. Further, he and Izivar Lenereva had not only forged a crucial alliance but also found solace in one another's company.

The roads we traveled felt incrementally safer. The new emperor had little love for the revenants and thus had decreased their funds and limited their domestic activities, blaming his father's assassination in part on their myopic focus upon tales of Hanuvar's survival. Enarius ordered them to center their efforts instead on the Cerdians who had not only engineered the old emperor's death but threatened Dervan western interests. Thus while revenants were occasionally to be glimpsed, large patrols led by their black-garbed trios became a thing of the past.

We did not yet know that the revenant legate had become obsessed with proving Hanuvar's existence to Emperor Enarius, so were more concerned that the scheming Metellus, whom Enarius had promoted to legate of the praetorians, held a trusted place at his side. At the time of our arrival along the Oscani coast, Metellus was still recovering from his recent injury, and was too busy basking in the benefits of his elevated status to be plotting much trouble, although the future was to show us just how right we were to have worried.

That a greater threat than either loomed over us all we had no hope of guessing.

Chapter 1: The Voices From the Mountain

I

Hanuvar knew some of the slaves applying shovels to the pastoral mountainside were Volani, but the figures were too distant for him to distinguish as he scanned the excavation site from horseback that morning. Antires, his friend and would-be chronicler, watched their activity from his driving bench on the carriage, but more for its novelty along this unexceptional road than for the condition of the workers.

Closer by, well-ordered tents half screened impressive mounds of soil that had once concealed the black walls of a ruined city curled around the mountain's base. A lone sentinel returned Hanuvar's scrutiny from beneath a shade tree on a hill overlooking the work. Rich landholders lived nearby, so a well-appointed coach was surely no rarity, and presumably the watchman's intense concentration centered on Hanuvar because he was the military escort, not because the man was suspicious of Hanuvar's true identity.

After all, even an eagle-eyed veteran of the last war would have to be exceptionally imaginative to see him as Hanuvar, or even guess his true age. Up to last year his dark hair had been well peppered with gray, but owing to a peculiar incident much of that gray had vanished, along with his scars and the accumulated weathering of the enemy general that Derva sought. His features were not dissimilar from the natives of this peninsula and his straight-cut bangs with clean-shaven face marked him as an upstanding citizen of the realm.

The sentry's attention shifted when a heavy crack, as of thunder, rumbled through the air. Birds and insects fell silent and the horses stopped in midstride with a nervous snorting and tossing of heads. The ground swayed as though a vast wave rolled beneath the earth. Hanuvar's mount stamped in alarm, and he forced its dancing into a tight circle. The carthorses whinnied and jostled in their traces.

The quake ceased as quickly as it had begun. Hanuvar searched the cone of Mount Esuvia rising above the piney slope nearby, knowing tremors sometimes portended eruptions. Thankfully, no new smoke rose from the old mountain, or from those of its two distant sisters,[1] just visible rising above the low green hills to the south.

A wide-eyed Antires sought reassurance, which Hanuvar provided with a nod. The ladies inside the carriage didn't offer comment but spoke in low tones to one another.

Hanuvar prodded his horse forward and continued his inspection of the camp. Antires could be heard shaking the reins and soon they all were in motion again.

The workers returned to their duties quickly, and their guard resumed his impassive consideration of the traveler, as if such tremblers were common and inconsequential. No matter Hanuvar's concern for them, the slaves excavating the ruin were a problem for another time. Their owner was disinterested in selling and those in his charge remained healthy as far as Carthalo's contacts could ascertain, and so getting them free remained lower on the priority list.

Hanuvar had a more difficult task before him today, one that would have him looking into the eyes of children who had witnessed the bloody end of their parents, siblings, and society. He had spent most of his own childhood in his father's army camp and most of his adulthood away from the comforts of family life so had little

---

[1] All three volcanoes had been quiescent in living human memory, although Mount Milenus had erupted four generations before, blowing its summit into fragments that rained inland. Old Turian murals can still be found displaying its original distinctive high, bent peak, but by this time squat Mount Delania stood hundreds of feet taller. —*Silenus*

experience interacting with youngsters. He wasn't entirely sure what to expect from them, and had relied on Izivar's advice for today's plans.

Antires swore from the driver seat as the rear carriage wheel struck a deep rut, and then the camp receded into the distance. They soon turned through an open wooden gate Hanuvar had been expecting and onto a dirt track barely wide enough for the carriage, where they passed a field of barley, and then patches of other grains and long rows of cabbages. A variety of rakes and sheers lay along the edges of the plots, but their wielders were absent.

Explanation for the abandonment became apparent soon after. While the tidy red-roofed villa stood intact, one small stone outbuilding had collapsed entirely and another was missing half its roof, the shingles of which had slid into a pile at its door. A small army of men, women, and children milled on the grounds outside the villa.

As Hanuvar's group approached he perceived more organization than had been apparent from a distance. A number of adults cleared rubble and a few bent to inspect the villa's foundation. Others kept knots of children well ordered: some sat in open-air teaching arrangements while others tossed a brown ball back and forth or played chase games. To Hanuvar's eyes the boys and girls appeared happy, ordinary even, and not for the first time he questioned whether uprooting them was truly the best choice. Amelia had promised they were being acculturated into their new society and learning trades so that they might prosper upon their manumission at adulthood. Few were likely to have living relatives and it might be a kind of cruelty to take them from this welcoming place, force them onto a ship, and send them to an entirely new land peopled by strangers.

Amelia herself was directing the attention of a gray-haired man to the villa's roof line. His were plain work clothes. Her dress too was unadorned, but clearly of superior fabric, a white short-sleeved stola of summer length over a whiter under tunic, and her dark hair was upswept with a spattering of tiny silver clips, which threw back the sun.

The track transformed into a bricked drive as it circled toward the villa's entrance. A pair of sun-browned attendants hurried to assist the carriage as Antires brought it to a halt. Amelia registered their arrival and started toward them through the well-ordered garden enveloping her stately residence. It still looked the impressive summer home it was designed to be, rather than the orphanage it had become.

Hanuvar dismounted, passing his reins to a servant, then opened the carriage door. Izivar Lenereva had no need of aid, but took his hand as she stepped down, then brushed travel dust from her light clothing, a stola in two layers, the inner deeper blue than the outer. A tall, trim woman with dark, curling hair, her sleeves were long and ornamented with clever oval gaps that showed her clear brown skin. She favored Hanuvar with a dazzling smile she quickly abandoned, remembering her role as his employer in this mission. She squeezed his fingers as if in apology for her pretense, and moved away. Hanuvar then offered his hand to Serliva, Izivar's gangly, sweet-faced maid. She stepped down with a bow of her head in thanks, and he relinquished her grip. A little taller than her mistress, she too wore a blue stola, though sleeveless, darker, and simpler.

Serliva ran fingers through her own locks then fussed with the shoulders of Izivar's garment.

Antires had already hopped down from the driver's bench and was patting down his green tunic. The handsome young man was one of those whose clothing always looked good on him, so he smoothed only a few wrinkles before abandoning the effort with disinterest. His dark, tightly coiled hair and his russet-brown skin instantly identified him as a Herrene. His chosen occupation as Hanuvar's chronicler was less obvious, although Hanuvar saw him sizing up the grounds with the approach of Amelia and imagined him working out what words he'd use for his descriptions.

Amelia stopped before them with a pleasant hello.

The villa's mistress was just as Hanuvar remembered; a stoutly handsome woman of middle years with a penetrating gaze and inborn aura of command. Apart from the pieces decorating her hair, she wore minimal jewelry.

The solemn, gray-haired steward waited at her left elbow. Coming up on her right was an aged Herrene with thin lips, a broad nose, and a gray beard cut straight across his chest as though he took grooming advice from ancient sculpture depicting philosophers. His long tunic was old-fashioned and formally pleated, and his curling hair was worn long and pushed back.

Owing to the others nearby, Amelia pretended not to be familiar with Hanuvar, and bowed her head instead to Izivar. "Welcome to our summer home, Lady Izivar. I hope that the little quake wasn't too alarming for you." Her voice possessed a slight rasp. Her husband had explained it had changed enduringly over the course of a long illness two winters previous.

Izivar bowed her head and addressed their hostess in lightly accented Dervan. "Thank you, Lady Amelia. The horses didn't care for it much, but we managed. Is everyone here alright?"

"The children are fine, only frightened or terribly curious, and my staff are all accounted for." Amelia gestured to the collapsed and damaged buildings with a sweep of her arm. "Fortunately those were just used for storage."

Antires had left the carriage in the hands of two old slaves who were driving the vehicle away. He cleared his throat and spoke from Hanuvar's left. "Forgive me, milady. Do these sorts of things happen often?"

Hanuvar was surprised by his bold address. Usually Antires was a stickler for remaining in character, and a cart driver would not ordinarily address a patrician out of turn.

Amelia replied easily enough. "Not at all, but still more often than I would prefer. Tremblors are the price one must pay for the lovely weather in Oscanus."

Izivar gestured to Antires. "This is my advisor, Stirses. I believe he may have assisted your husband upon one of his projects."

"I seem to recall the name," Amelia said with a polite nod. "And you look familiar as well," she said to Hanuvar.

"I just have one of those faces, milady."

His answer raised a sly smile from Amelia, quickly discarded.

"This is Decius, my steward and personal guard," Izivar explained, for the benefit of Amelia's staff. "He is fluent in both Dervan and Volani."

"A pleasure." Amelia gave the barest of nods to Hanuvar. She did not bother naming her steward, and gestured instead to the Herrene on her right, introducing him as the scholar Galinthias, hired as the chief instructor for the children. He exchanged greetings with Izivar, and Amelia resumed her address. "Normally I would invite you inside before we saw to the purpose of your visit, but I wish to make certain the roof won't fall in on us. Surely you would like refreshments, though." Amelia looked to her steward, who bowed his head and hurried off. She faced Izivar. "Or would you like to meet the children first?"

"The youth, please," Izivar said.

"Of course. Come with me." Amelia led them across the dense green sward and past its carefully trimmed bushes and ornamental trees, asking Galinthias to speak of his charges as they walked. In a slow, pleasant voice, he described how those seven and younger were kept together with their caregivers. Boys and girls eight to fifteen were housed separately. Their numbers Hanuvar had long since committed to memory but the Herrene mentioned them as if to emphasize the breadth of his responsibility.

"We bought all that we could," Amelia explained. "We were worried most for the young women of... marriageable age, but they were more expensive and we couldn't purchase as many as we wanted."

"If you had not protected those you did, who would have?" Izivar asked, voice rich with thanks. "I'm grateful to you."

Amelia bowed her head.

That the majority of surviving Volani children had been purchased by the kindly Ciprion and Amelia was one small mercy among innumerable horrors, and Hanuvar would be forever indebted to them for their generosity. They had gone so far as to buy Volani caretakers and tutors for the children as well, and to place a Herrene in charge of their education, recognizing that the traditions of Dervan schools would be anathema to young people used to Volani ways. The couple had even insisted the girls continue to receive instruction in writing and mathematics and natural sciences, although as they walked Galinthias was describing additional training the young women were receiving in comportment and weaving.

Hanuvar kept his reaction carefully masked, and Izivar nodded encouragingly. Serliva's expression was less guarded and betrayed her shock when she learned boys and girls were taught separately. How were they to be comfortable with one another when not allowed to interact from a young age? Before they had walked very far some of Hanuvar's chief concerns had already been made manifest. If the children were left here for much longer, even the oldest might be substantially different people from whom they'd have been if raised within Volanus, and the youngest might be indistinguishable from Dervans.

As they drew nearer, the children's caretakers halted their games or tutelage and separated the boys and girls further, grouped by age to await review. The littlest were made to sit. Older ones were told to stand in a line. Hanuvar already knew that there were more older girls than older boys, forty-four to twenty-one. The number of smaller children was fewer, and among those fourteen were three toddlers, minded by a young woman missing her left hand, another survivor, and likely another kindness of Ciprion and Amelia, for few would have much compassion for a one-handed slave.

Per their previous arrangement, Izivar and Serliva would handle the majority of the public interaction today. He meant to observe as unobtrusively as possible in case some sharp-eyed youngster recognized him even in disguise. His likeness had unfortunately been commonplace in murals and sculptures throughout Volanus.

A tall, graying tutor standing with the older girls watched Izivar with particular intensity, his expression shifting from caution to curiosity. When his inspection shifted to Hanuvar his gaze grew fixed. Finally his mouth gaped.

Hanuvar knew his observer. The man was Ahdanit, one of the leaders of the university faculty of Volanus. They had spoken many times during Hanuvar's years as a shofet, for Ahdanit had been an advocate of his institution's research projects, which frequently seemed to run over budget because of the scholars' tendency to discover additional lines of inquiry during their investigation, most of which Ahdanit had supported. Hanuvar had usually agreed with his reasoning if not his every request.

The slim academic's name hadn't been among the list of survivors, so he was clearly here under an assumed identity. Hanuvar met his eyes and shook his head ever so slightly. Ahdanit recovered with a tiny head bow and closed his mouth, confused but resolved to silence.

Knowing Hanuvar's hope for his niece Edonia, Izivar asked Amelia if they might meet the girls first, and Hanuvar readied himself for disappointment. He should be happy, he thought, that any of these young women had survived to be so well cared for. They and their clothes were clean, and they were well nourished. The youngest looked uninterested in their visitors, just bored or disappointed to have their activities interrupted, like any young people assembled before older ones.

Hanuvar had parlayed with more foreign leaders than he could quickly count, sometimes under very trying circumstances. And yet the thought of explaining to these children that they would be leaving here seemed a far greater challenge. They had good meals and decent bedding, familiar company, and routine. How would they react?

He was glad to yield lead in this matter to a more capable ally. Izivar would try to get a sense for how best to broach the topic and group the children during transport. For now, he confined himself to searching the faces of the dark-eyed girls.

Four years was a third of a lifetime for his niece Edonia. At seven, when he'd last seen her, she had favored her mother, sharing honey-brown eyes and pointed chin, though her unruly dark hair had looked more like his brother Melgar's. Temperamentally she had resembled neither of her fiery parents, for she had been focused and deliberative. Hanuvar's duties in Volanus left him too busy to frequently engage with his extended family, but he had known little Edonia because even at six she'd had the patience to sit down for games of draughts. While contemplating her possible moves and twisting her hair around her fingers, she had talked about her abiding interest in animals, and also about the great winged serpents who had made Volanus their home since the city's founding. She hoped to become one of the maidens at the temple of the asalda.

Hanuvar had enjoyed his scattered moments with her, wondering if she was what his daughter Narisia had been like as a little girl.

Izivar bade the children good morning in their own language, introducing herself by her given, not family, name. The children looked surprised to hear this elegant outsider speak their native tongue.

Edonia didn't seem to be present. But that short-haired girl there, or the one in back—no, her chin was too prominent. But her, on the left... It was unfortunate Hanuvar had to remain in a disguise he could not set aside. Surely, if his hair were parted and he wore a beard, Edonia would have stepped forward with a glad cry.

If she were here.

He turned to Amelia and addressed her softly. "Milady, might I visit alone with this instructor?" He indicated Ahdanit. He wished to make it clear to the scholar that he spoke with Amelia's permission.

She inclined her head politely. "Of course."

Izivar was already chatting to the girls about their daily routines while the Herrenic instructor looked on with some bemusement. Her grace and easy manner had them warming to her.

Hanuvar motioned Ahdanit aside and they walked apart, the scholar's eyes drinking him in. Probably he wondered if this were some trick. Even if the man hadn't seen Hanuvar's plummet into the sea he would have learned of it from his fellow prisoners or the Dervans themselves. He might also have heard wild rumors of Hanuvar's impossible return. But Ahdanit was an intellectual and a skeptic and would have judged those stories to be either fears or projected hopes.

Halting at the side of a myrtle twenty feet out from the children, Hanuvar spoke to Ahdanit in Volani. He got straight to the point. "It is me, and you and the children will be freed. But the boys and girls and the rest of the staff cannot be trusted with my name or our intentions until they are away from here." He did not add that children might talk, and servants overhear to spread gossip beyond the family holdings. Ahdanit was bright enough to understand.

The scholar struggled to sound normal as he replied. "Of course, Shofet. Freed? But how?"

Hanuvar dared not reveal specifics. "With few complications, and very soon. And do not bother with a title." Such honorifics were irrelevant here. He was glad he could offer further news. "Your wife lives. And your colleague Varahan."

Ahdanit blinked, and his eyes shown with moisture. He wiped at them. His voice was a hoarse whisper. "She lives?"

"Yes. I saw her myself only last week. She's free now." He did not add that she had been one of those on board a ship for New Volanus. He had spoken with the great musician only briefly, but had been delighted by her beaming smile.

Ahdanit could not help laughing in pleasure. "I thank you... this news is hard to take in. And so are you. Is Varahan all right? How are you doing this? How did you survive?"

"He's in good health. As for me... these are stories for another time. Now, tell me. Surely you're not the only one under an assumed name here. Are any of these young ladies Edonia Cabera?"

Ahdanit's expression fell. "I don't believe so. Not that they've told me. And we've talked a lot over the months." He took in Hanuvar's troubled look. "If you will permit me?"

Hanuvar didn't know what he was permitting but acquiesced with a head nod.

Ahdanit turned and called a girl's name, Esherah. One of the older girls asked approval of Galinthias, and then Amelia and, given it, stepped clear of the others, her expression tentative. Ahdanit waved her forward and she started toward them.

The scholar looked to Hanuvar as she neared. "What do I call you?"

"Decius."

The young lady stopped in front of them and sought reassurance from Ahdanit's gaze. Her thick hair was combed forward, likely in an attempt to hide the long white scar visible along her forehead. In her girl's stola and sandals she looked a proper young Dervan maiden, but as her eyes searched Hanuvar's own he was reminded of an entirely different young lady of about the same age who also had assessed him mistrustfully. He did not outwardly reveal the pang he experienced in recalling Takava, long since buried in the sands of a distant isle.

"Do not worry, Esherah," Ahdanit said in Volani. "Decius is a friend. Decius, Esherah is the clever young woman who warned children of the famous or those in training with coveted institutions to lie about their names. She's one of my best students."

Hanuvar supposed Ahdanit was teaching them mathematics. As far as the information he had shared about Esherah, Hanuvar understood Ahdanit meant it as a kindness to him in locating his niece, though he had little hope it would lead to anything useful. The scholar couldn't know how diligently Carthalo's people had already acquired the few Volani children outside this grouping from slave holders. Still, Hanuvar nodded his head politely to the girl. "Were there any such children among you?"

Her expression brightened in surprise to be addressed by a Dervan in such perfect Volani. She pursed her lips and gathered her thoughts. Hanuvar liked that she checked with Ahdanit a final time. The scholar nodded approval.

"I don't know, sir," Esherah responded respectfully. She glanced again at her instructor, as if asking for permission to provide more sensitive information.

"Speak the whole truth to him," he insisted.

"I've been told that some of them were maidens at the temple of the asalda. One of them is here."

The temple where Edonia had hoped to win a place, and where her mother had once served. Hanuvar kept rising interest from his expression.

"Why don't you ask her over?" Ahdanit suggested. Esherah turned and called another girl's name, waving her toward them, and that youngster sought approval from her minders, who then received permission from Amelia. Izivar and Serliva, meanwhile, talked animatedly with a now larger group of girls of mixed ages. The boys had been led aside, the younger playing fox and geese while the older were again seated before an instructor. Antires, standing with the ladies, looked longingly toward Hanuvar, but he had not been invited into the conversation and did not presume to intrude.

Soon a grave young girl with short, curling brown hair was standing closely to Esherah, her soft brown eyes searching. Hanuvar guessed her for nine or ten. She was introduced as Teonia.

Hanuvar took a knee and offered a smile. "Hello."

She would not meet his eyes. One of her arms was streaked with burn scars.

"Were you a handmaiden at the Hall of the Asalda?" Hanuvar asked.

"I was in training, sir," she answered after a long silence. Her voice was thin and remote.

"Do you know Edonia Cabera?"

She nodded; her expression revealed nothing more but she slipped further behind Esherah.

Hanuvar pretended calm. "Is she here?"

She shook her head no. Esherah took her hand, and the young girl clung tightly to her fingers.

That flare of optimism had been foolish. It would be painful, but another question was necessary. "Do you know if she survived?"

Teonia's eyes were grave as she finally looked at him. He could not read her meaning beyond shyness, or perhaps fear.

And then she nodded. Yes.

Hanuvar managed to keep intensity from his voice. He did not want to frighten the girl. "You saw her? You are certain?"

Teonia nodded vigorously. "She was in the pens."

"The slave pens in Derva," Ahdanit explained.

Suddenly Teonia was talking quickly, although her voice was soft. "They let her in back at Volanus. But they wouldn't let my cousin in even though he wasn't too badly wounded. He could still walk a little. The Dervans took him away and I never saw him again."

Some Dervan overseer must have decided there was little enough value to be had from a child, let alone one who would have to be nursed back to health. Young Teonia was fortunate that her cousin hadn't been killed in front of her.

Hanuvar fell silent in shared remorse for the lost child, and bit back his anger. That another had survived only to be culled by a Dervan like a sickly lamb all but shattered his composure.

He mastered himself with a breath and concentrated on the more positive aspects of Teonia's information: Edonia had lived to reach Derva, which meant she had to have been sold on. Hanuvar knew every name on the Dervan slave list, as well as those upon the supplemental lists of Volani purchased by citizens of other countries. Edonia's had not been among them. It might be that she had an assumed name, like Ahdanit. "Do you know what she was calling herself?"

"She said to tell everyone she was Betsara."

Edonia's grandmother's name on her mother's side. And one among those Hanuvar had seen, listed as sold with two other young women to someone listed only as a foreign national. His nostrils flared as he inhaled in frustration. He mentioned their names as well. "Did you know them?"

"They were all my friends," Teonia said. "The black-robed men took them. They led them away. They looked like wizards but weren't really, or they would have known that my brother and I had the touch but Edonia and Varina and Danae didn't. Not really."

Hanuvar wanted to make sure he understood what she meant. "What touch do you have?"

She suddenly found her sandaled feet of immense interest.

"It's all right," Ahdanit said. "Decius won't be afraid."

She hesitated. "But he's a Dervan. We're not supposed to talk to them about magic things."

Ahdanit addressed Hanuvar. "The comportment instructor has told them that civilized people don't tolerate such 'chicanery.'"

"It's wise of you to be careful what you say," Hanuvar told her. "But you can talk to me about this. Some of my friends have the kind of touch I think you mean, and pretending you don't have it is like pretending you can't hear. Who would want to do that?"

Teonia met his eyes then for the first time. She didn't exactly smile, but her expression cleared, and he recognized a spark of warmth in her eyes. "That's exactly how it is," she said.

She had just confirmed she was one of the rare few who were tuned to senses beyond the commonplace; such had been prized by the asalda because they found them easier to communicate with. The girl grew more comfortable as she continued. "I can feel things from far away. Like the magic from the man in the mountain. I can sense him from here. So can my brother."

"Teonia's brother is here as well," Ahdanit explained.

Hanuvar nodded his thanks and faced Teonia once more. "The man in the mountain?"

"He has many Volani voices with him, and he's using the voices to talk to the mountain and its old stones."

Hanuvar's interest quickened. Could she mean the scholar working in the ruins with the Volani slaves? "How do you know they're Volani?"

"I can hear them talking."

"What are they saying?"

"They are crying. They're lonely and scared, and he won't let them go. But he's lonely, too."

Hanuvar didn't care for the sound of that. His sources had told him the Volani under the thumb of this particular owner were reasonably well treated. "Do you know this man's name?"

She shook her head. "He came to speak to the Lady this week."

"She means Calenius," Ahdanit explained, confirming Hanuvar's suspicion, for that was the name of the scholar digging in the ruins. He had provided some sort of aid to the Dervan authorities during or soon after their campaign against Volanus. "He was there, at the siege. I remember seeing him wandering around the enclosures, and I heard his name called."

Hanuvar had heard that as well. "And he's a wizard?"

"That I do not know," Ahdanit said. "He's investigating some ruins south of here, on Mount Esuvia. I'm not sure what he spoke with Lady Amelia about."

Hanuvar smiled reassuringly to the girl and put his hand out, palm up. Hesitantly, she extended her own, and then he gently squeezed her fingers. "Thank you, Teonia. I am sorry about your cousin. And I'm sorry you have to hide."

Her expression was blank. Sorrow and sympathy were poor currency, so he continued. "But you have given me good news, and I'm grateful. Now I can try to find Edonia."

"Why?"

"So I can help her."

"Are you going to take us away?" Esherah asked. The older girl's eyes were suddenly piercing.

He could not tell her the truth, yet, but he could not lie to her. "Do you want to stay here?"

"I want to stay with my friends."

"I'm sure you will," Hanuvar said. He debated asking which of the girls were her favorites, the better to know which ones should be kept together during the wagon transport to the coast, but he didn't want to imply that any of them would be parted.

He doubted his answer fully satisfied her, but Esherah asked a different question rather than challenging him further. "Are you really a Dervan?" From Teonia's searching look it was clear she wondered the same thing.

"Does it matter? The important thing is that I'm a friend to Lady Izivar, and she's Volani. I will help her all I can."

They mulled that over.

Hanuvar climbed to his feet. "Thank you. Why don't you rejoin the others?"

They nodded politely to their elders, and then Esherah led the younger girl off by the hand.

"Your niece lives," Ahdanit said softly.

"So it seems." While Hanuvar struggled to adjust to this

welcome news, he was already considering the obstacles lying in front of Edonia's recovery. "Black-robed men" wasn't an especially useful description, but it was a start. The important thing was that Edonia survived, and she was among girls from her own people. If her owners thought her some kind of specialized worker that was all to the good, because that virtually guaranteed her better treatment.

After a moment, Ahdanit spoke with quiet restraint. "Shahara, she is well? She suffered no...hardship?"

Hanuvar understood Ahdanit's reluctance to mention terrible fates by name, as if doing so might give them the power to be real. And he realized he'd allowed himself to become too fixated upon his own worries, while this man had quietly waited for further word about the woman he loved.

"Forgive me. I should have told you more. She looked well, and she hadn't been treated harshly. She'd been working as a musical tutor. Her owners had even gifted her with a high-quality flute."

"My darling," he said softly. "She wasn't in the pens. She was visiting relatives in Elanthes when the Dervans came."

"So great was her renown that she was sold before she even reached Derva."

"I had no hope for her," Ahdanit said, his voice shuddering. "To have lost someone of such a talent..."

"She will ensure our musical heritage survives." Hanuvar thought of the fledgling academy in New Volanus, probably more advanced in the year since he'd seen it, but surely to benefit from Shahara's skill and passion. Hanuvar shifted topics before the scholar could ask for more details. "How well are you and the children being cared for here?"

He answered after only a moment of reflection. "The rest of the instructors and I have been very lucky. The children...They're doing so much better now than when we first came."

"They look healthy."

"Yes. They've been lucky, too, overall. When I think of all those who didn't make it, it's hard to complain, but—"

"Your honest assessment," Hanuvar said, striving not to sound curt.

Ahdanit gathered himself and stopped dithering. "They have

plenty of food, the company of their own people, even an education probably better than a lot of Dervans receive—it is nothing to object to. But Galinthias' lectures are wandering, like a comic imitation of a Herrenic philosopher, and the children have learned how to get him off on tangents so that he often isn't teaching them much. He could certainly be far worse, of course. He's never abusive."

Hanuvar nodded encouragement, and Ahdanit continued. "The Dervan language instructor is actually quite sweet, but completely oblivious about why any of these children would be disinterested in the finer points of Dervan society. The woman I mentioned who teaches the young ladies comportment is rigid and disliked, but the worst thing is that there aren't any real apprenticeship programs. Some of the older boys and girls were already apprenticed in Volanus. There aren't many crafting positions being offered here. And if you're a young woman, the only skills you're allowed to practice are the household arts. Young Esherah could be a world-class mathematician, and she seems to enjoy the academic pursuits immensely, but I think they intend her to be a ladies maid."

Hanuvar knew this to be a profession Dervans considered desirable for unmarried women from nonpatrician families. He happened to think a skilled assistant was invaluable to any enterprise, but he'd hate to see someone gifted in one profession forced into another. "If that's not what she wishes, that's not what's going to happen now," he vowed.

Ahdanit searched his eyes as if assuring himself Hanuvar's confidence was warranted.

Hanuvar hadn't paid particular attention to the bright chirping of orioles until they suddenly went silent. He knew another tremor was on its way a breath before the ground shook. The rumbling arrived this time with the shrill screams of young children. Adults called for calm, though some of them cried out in fear as well.

He spotted Izivar seated on the ground near the girls, far from danger, caught sight of Serliva and Amelia and Antires, then turned to scan Esuvia, as he had during the earlier tremor. The mountain's gray cone rose above its green-girt slopes just to the west.

But there came no smoke, nor even an avalanche, much less roiling ash plumes, and the cones of the old volcano's two distant sisters to the south were quiescent as well.

The shaking grew more violent. Behind him a louder crack of stone sounded, and he turned as a corner of the villa gave way. Red shingles slid from the roof to break in a clattering heap.

And then, only a few yards from himself, the earth was rent asunder. The grass parted and a gap of darkness yawned. Dirt and chaff mushroomed. Hanuvar struggled to keep his feet and threw out a hand to steady Ahdanit.

The quaking ceased just as suddenly as it had begun. Silence persisted for long moments, and then a few cautious orioles resumed their songs, joined quickly by the shrill whisper of starlings, angry about the disturbance.

Hanuvar again checked the children, and the volcano, and his friends. None seemed harmed. He strode for the gap that had opened, for he thought he'd glimpsed dark bricks within.

He had not imagined it. The earth had revealed a subterranean structure. Only ten feet down the crumbling slope lay a floor of incongruously shining black pavers, half hidden by mounded dirt, collapsed walls, and broken stone that was almost certainly a fallen ceiling.

Ahdanit came to stand at his side, peering with him. "What is that?"

Hanuvar didn't know. "A hallway, I think." Some fifteen feet of passage had been exposed. A few pavers were cracked or pushed diagonally upright, but the majority remained flat and even as a Dervan highway, stretching into lost darkness beneath the earth.

After a moment, someone smelling of clover and scented bath oils drew beside him. Amelia, who stepped fearlessly to the edge. Hanuvar kept at her side, ready to grab her should the ground give way. Divining his intent, she frowned irritably, as if to assert that she was perfectly capable of watching out for herself.

Antires and Izivar arrived a moment later, though neither ventured as close to the side.

"What do you suppose this is?" Amelia asked him.

"Something Calenius will be interested in," Hanuvar said. "I'm told he came to see you."

"He did. He wished to dig on our ground, if he could not buy it outright. He said he expected there were ruins beneath."

"Looks like he was right," Antires said dryly.

Amelia ignored him and continued speaking to Hanuvar. "Why does that interest you?"

"He holds Volani slaves that he will not sell. What did you tell him?"

"That our land was not for sale, nor was it currently for rent. He countered with the offer of large sums merely to explore, and I told him I would consider it. Now, I believe you've something in mind."

He did. There was little more he would be useful for here. He had satisfied his own curiosity as to the children's general health and the quality of their education, and learned more than he'd expected in that his niece was likely still alive, though probably far away. Izivar would carry out her strategy for evaluating the rest of the situation, and his part in it was very small. An opportunity like this couldn't be ignored. "Let me act as your negotiator. He's likely to offer more now that there's proof these ruins exist."

"And you will ask for the Volani slaves as part of the fee."

"If you would permit me."

Amelia hesitated. "It was my thought his excavators should not have close proximity to pretty girls just this side of puberty."

"A prudent precaution. What will you do with the land once the children are gone?"

She considered him gravely. "How soon are you planning to leave with them?"

"In a matter of weeks. Perhaps sooner, for their own safety."

"Safety?" Her expression darkened, and then she understood his meaning was not a rebuke for her standards of care. "Oh, this is nothing. The quakes happen from time to time. Esuvia just turns in her sleep. You do realize that the younger children have already grown attached to this place? And many are showing affinity for the skills they're learning. Wouldn't they be happier, here, settled and with a more certain future?"

Hanuvar kept his voice level. "The colony is settled. And they will be among their own people."

"I expected you would say that."

"Just as you would, if our roles were reversed."

No matter her intelligence, Amelia's blank stare suggested a mental block in conceiving a mirrored version of their fates. She recovered, returning to her central concern. "As someone who has many more years of direct experience with childcare, I ask for you to think not of the prior wrongs done to these children, but the benefits to them having a stable situation. Rather than displacing them. Again."

"It has given me some significant pause already," he admitted. "And I'll certainly consider your experienced counsel. But as to the matter of Calenius, I suggest you offer to have him inspect this tunnel. I can accompany his every move after you relocate the children far from view."

Amelia considered her reply only briefly. "Very well. I'll arrange things on this end. Tell him the price of examining the tunnels is the freeing of your slaves. If he wishes to do more, then he and I will have to come to an agreement. Size him up. I expect you to avoid bringing anyone back here that you can't protect us from."

II

Izivar's pleasure about Edonia's survival shown in her eyes the moment Hanuvar shared the news, though she refrained from extensive reaction with so many people nearby. Hanuvar had come to treasure her earnest compassion even more than her predictable competence. She had no hesitation in remaining with Serliva to continue her meetings with the children while he left to negotiate more releases.

Antires, however, insisted upon accompanying Hanuvar, who had him drive the carriage, the better to convey the slaves he hoped to free. Hanuvar preferred to take his horse, a reliable roan he'd invested a lot of hours training, and so once again rode at the vehicle's head. Antires shouted to be heard over the crunch of the carriage wheels on the dirt road.

"I'd like to point out again that this would all be simpler if you were just willing to acquire other slaves and trade them out for the ones Calenius bought. He only wants sturdy, reliable workers, doesn't he?"

"That's what he told Carthalo's agent. But I'm not buying anyone except to set them free."

"There are slaves all over the Inner Sea," Antires objected, not for the first time. He had been brought up surrounded by the societal distortions of slavery, and little understood Hanuvar's deep seated hatred of the practice.[2]

They retraced their route along the mountainside, noting the same sentry who took to his feet as they turned into the narrow dirt path leading to the tents and the excavation. Several dozen men were hard at work digging a trench with picks and shovels. Others trundled soil off in carts.

While Antires pulled the brake on the wagon and undid part of the harness so his horses could graze, Hanuvar left his trusted bay roan to join them and started forward. The sentry, rather than greeting them, retreated into the complex.

A few of the slaves looked up, but none halted their labors as Hanuvar and Antires walked to a portal in the field wall where they paused to take in the work beyond. The digging had exposed more than Hanuvar had anticipated, for the ground on the wall's far side had been extracted six feet further down, revealing an ancient street similar to those of Derva itself, complete with a bricked road and a sidewalk of shining black stone. Square pillars stretched skyward, the supports for some long-vanished pediment.

While they were taking in the sights, the beefy sentry rounded a corner to challenge them at last, two other guards at his heels. He declared the area unsafe and reminded them it was private property. His manner was unwelcoming and he moved as if he knew how to use the spear in his left hand. Hanuvar judged him a former gladiator.

Hanuvar affected the stiff demeanor of a servant on an uncomfortable errand and explained they had come to speak to the scholar Calenius at the behest of his neighbor, the Lady Amelia. After a calculating frown from the gladiator, they were conducted down steep stairs chiseled out of the dirt, then led into a maze of ancient streets.

Their guide was dour, a dark-brown man of likely Arbatean extraction, wearing a laborer's sleeveless tunic held up by a single shoulder strap. His well-made spear was honed to a razored point.

---

[2] Antires Sosilos actually seems to have understood the horrors of slavery and eventually advocated for laws protecting the welfare of slaves and preventing the worst abuses against them, but like many people of his time, it was impossible for him to consider how homesteads and entire economies might function without forced labor. —*Sosilos*

He did not offer a name nor inquire about theirs. The two behind were smaller, younger, and armed with the kind of short blade common throughout Tyvol; one appeared half Ceori and both seemed intent enough to die in the line of duty, should the need arise. Hanuvar was more interested in the surroundings but he strove to seem appropriately uneasy for the benefit of his escorts.

Several city blocks had been partially revealed, and Hanuvar studied the buildings they passed, fascinated that they had been fitted with stones that not only showed no mortar, but were perfectly smooth and symmetrical, as though all had been manufactured to incredibly precise standards. The interiors of most buildings were filled still with dirt, visible through ancient doorways and windows, but debris had been cleared from the streets and the building fronts themselves. There was something familiar in the sweeping lines and symmetrical archways, yet he could not identify the culture that had made them—it must be older than the Dervans and the Turians or Oscani before them.

Antires took in all of it keenly but said nothing.

Their guide halted finally where the street widened into an oval. The excavation ended at the far side, where human architecture stopped at a flat wall carved from smooth volcanic rock and rising forty feet into the air before the mountain's green slope slanted upward. Precisely etched letters decorated the stone every few inches, from a curving alphabet Hanuvar did not recognize. There were also fanciful images of men and women and beasts, and temples, and, towering over all, a mountain cone that must be Esuvia. To either side, a detailed relief of some kind of bull-serpent hybrid pointed a horned nose toward the height.

Hanuvar had heard rumors of ancient ruins dotting the southern half of Tyvol, but had little personal experience with them, aside from some old Turian fortresses, which, though formidable, had been much less intriguing.

While Antires advanced a few steps for a closer look at the images, Hanuvar watched the progress of the Arbatean sentry, who approached a taller man standing wide legged before the wall and speaking at a thin slave who made notes on a wax slate. The slave was a Herrene little older than Antires, dressed like the others in a work tunic with a single shoulder strap. The man addressing him, though, was almost certainly Calenius, whose memorable description from Carthalo's agents had still failed to convey the impact of his presence.

Even from the back this "scholar" was an imposing figure. Muscles corded the calves below his fine crimson tunic, and his arms and shoulders were immense. His hair was the red of burnished copper, worn long as Hanuvar's daughter's, when last he'd seen her, and in a queue no one wanting to blend with Dervan society would have dared. A long sword hung from his fine brown belt along the right side, as though he himself were left-handed. The belt also supported an axe, a wineskin, and a variety of pouches that would have made a smaller man look overburdened.

The precise nature of the advice Calenius had provided the Dervan government during the Third Volani War was not known to Hanuvar's sources, but the man had been awarded equestrian status as a result, and a plain gold band on his left hand denoted his position in society. It gleamed on his finger as he emphasized some point that his secretary nodded understanding about while writing.

Calenius held up a hand to the secretary as he was interrupted by the Arbatean. The scholar, who looked nothing like an academic, listened briefly to the sentry's words, then turned and walked toward Hanuvar and Antires, waiting with their silent guards. He moved with ease, radiating confidence. When he drew to a stop before them he towered half a head over Hanuvar, and his cool blue eyes were those of a seasoned killer. He used his gaze like a weapon, boldly peering at Hanuvar to assert dominance.

For a moment, Hanuvar was tempted to return that look. But he played a role, and so gave in to the unaccustomed discomfort he registered and glanced away towards Antires, who seemed to have no trouble appearing uneasy. The guards stood well back as if only awaiting dismissal rather than remaining alert to protect their employer.

"Welcome," Calenius said, cordial enough with his status established. His voice was rich and deep. His Dervan was smooth and faintly accented, but Hanuvar couldn't guess his native language. "What do you think of my excavations?"

Antires cleared his throat before answering in the nervous tone of a visiting tutor hoping for a permanent post. "I think you've exposed some lovely masonry. I don't fully recognize the style, although it looks a little like some work I've seen from Arbatea." His friend sought to draw the scholar out with appreciation; not a bad tactic given the circumstances.

A faint smile touched Calenius' lips. "An interesting observation. What makes you say that?"

"The sharp lines used to construct the figures themselves. They're stiff but still suggest motion; it's superior to typical work out of Hadira, although I'd warrant its even older."

"That's true. You've been to Arbatea?"

Antires shook his head no. "I've been in Cylene, and saw an exhibition of some of their tables in a temple there."

Calenius nodded and considered an image of men and women bearing produce-filled baskets down from the mountain. Hanuvar had still not managed to place his origin. Calenius seemed acutely conscious of power, but not in a Dervan way, for he, like his watchmen, hadn't bothered introducing himself, or asking their names. But then much of Dervan status had to do with generational landed bloodlines, and this man would not have those to lord over them.

"This work predates anything you'd find in Arbatea, or Hadira," Calenius said to Antires. "And you're right about the connections." He seemed to have grown bored with the interaction, though, for he changed the subject. "You're servants of Lady Amelia, I hear. What does she want of me?"

"There's been a collapse on her property," Hanuvar answered readily. "An underground tunnel has been exposed."

Calenius' absorption shown in his sudden stillness.

"The tile work's very similar to these streets," Hanuvar continued.

Calenius' left brow rose minutely. "Will she give me access?"

"She will permit you to inspect the collapse only. You will have to negotiate with her more specifically over excavation rights."

"I see." He studied Hanuvar intently now. "And is there a price for seeing what there is to see?"

"The award of several slaves."

Calenius frowned. "I need workers, and these meet my needs."

"Are they as hard to replace as this opportunity to see what's on the Lady's land?"

"This is about the Volani slaves, isn't it?" Calenius asked. "I thought it might have been her husband who sent those inquiries."

It had been the agents of Hanuvar's capable intelligence chief who'd approached Calenius, but Hanuvar saw no point in clearing up his confusion.

"Why do they want them so badly?"

"Why do you want these tunnels?" Hanuvar asked.

Calenius provided no answer but smiled indulgently as he swiftly made a decision. "Very well. I'll make a gift of my Volani slaves to the Lady Amelia so long as it seems worth my time when we get there. If it is, she must permit me to fully explore the material exposed, for the price I offered. I suppose she'll want something in writing?"

"I would be remiss if I did not request it."

"One moment." Calenius stepped away and motioned for the Arbatean watchman who'd guided them, patiently waiting near his fellows. When he came forward his employer spoke quietly to him, at length. As soon as the man acknowledged his instructions, Calenius sent him running, dismissed the other two, then called for the secretary. That man listened to his master's commands, then dug through his shoulder bag and quickly produced inkwell, stylus, and parchment. Calenius dictated while the secretary wrote.

Antires spoke softly to Hanuvar. "He's drawing up the sales document right now. This was easy."

"So far, yes."

"Why?"

"I'll explain later."

"You think he's listening?"

"Someone might be."

The answer was that Calenius was desperate to find something far more valuable to him in Amelia's tunnels than these slaves. Hanuvar was curious about what that might be but even more intrigued by the contradictions the seeker himself presented: he moved like a man half Hanuvar's age but commanded like an experienced general; he was clearly a foreigner, but radiated the assurance of someone at home; and he was no more attached to his slaves than a wealthy man to his spoon yet hadn't sold at an earlier and more remunerative opportunity.

Soon the secretary was scattering sand over the surface of the paper to accelerate its drying, and the Arbatean sentry was returning with eight able-bodied workers, a mix of rangy teenagers and seasoned men as old as forty. Most were smudged with dirt and sweat, and all carried shoulder bags. Hanuvar didn't see any he knew, but stepped into the shadow of a wall, for citizens of Volanus he'd never interacted with might recognize him, and Calenius would be an awkward audience to overhear that particular sort of conversation. He searched for signs of mistreatment but saw nothing obvious. Hanuvar thought that they looked troubled, but that could well owe to nervousness that this change in their routine portended some unfavorable shift in their fate.

"Your Lady's new slaves, provided I like what I see on her property," Calenius explained, and the men exchanged openly worried glances at that, though none dared speak. He motioned for the document the secretary had supplied him and popped it into a scroll case, then capped it. "Everything's ready for the Lady Amelia. I'll ride ahead on my horse."

"I'll join you," Hanuvar said.

"Well then. Your man can follow with the Volani."

Antires' expression fell in disappointment. He always preferred to be a direct witness rather than to hear summaries. Just because he often missed out on moments he thought likely to be interesting didn't mean he'd become inured to it, but Hanuvar gave him a meaningful stare after nodding toward the slaves and the younger man tightened his lips in acknowledgement. He'd provide the reassurance they needed as they left this place for good.

Hanuvar briefly wondered how Izivar would take these sweaty men riding in her carriage with its ornate decorations and delicate foot rests but decided she'd accept it. He hurried after the big scholar, mindful of his promise to Amelia.

At the road, another of Calenius' muscular slaves already waited with a burly black stallion. By the time Hanuvar was mounted, Calenius was under way. The man's self-possession in riding out alone seemed somehow more ominous than bringing a bevy of personal guard for "Decius" to monitor.

Calenius was focused forward, signaling his disinterest in conversation, but Hanuvar addressed him anyway as he urged his horse alongside, thinking his role as servant could permit a little inquisitiveness. "You're a student of history?"

"You could say that."

"But there's something specific you're searching for."

The scholar glanced sidelong at him. "We're all searching for something, aren't we? Power? Wealth? Many of us are searching for death, and never even know it."

Hanuvar decided any implied threat in that statement was indirect. Calenius sounded more like a philosopher than he looked. "Are you saying that's what you're doing?"

"I have, in the past. It never quite worked out." Calenius flashed a mirthless grin at no one in particular. "No, this time I happen to be searching for life."

"In cities of the dead," Hanuvar pointed out.

Calenius only grunted.

"Should Lady Amelia be concerned about what you're searching for?"

"My dig's not going to hurt her."

His slight emphasis on the second word caught Hanuvar's ear. "Is there danger from another source?"

Those piercing blue eyes shifted to him, seeming to reassess. "What are you to her, exactly?"

"A family friend."

"A friend of her husband's," Calenius guessed. "From the service."

"I advise them both."

"Well, an advisor should know that there are always dangers. The volcano's probably fine for the next few months but she might want to consider moving by fall."

"You know about volcanoes?"

"Among other things." Calenius feigned boredom once more. Hanuvar sensed he remained alert, however.

"Who built these ruins you're looking into?" Hanuvar asked.

"The culture was an ancient ancestor of the Turians. The Oscani." Calenius did not appear to care that it sounded as if he were lying.

Hanuvar supposed that these could be ruins of the fabled Vanished Ones. Their abandoned settlements were said to lay scattered throughout the Inner Sea and those who lived near routinely blocked openings to dank, subterranean passages worked into their weird temples, for legend had it unpleasant things crept out from them at night.

But he decided against pressing further. Despite his remaining questions, it occurred to Hanuvar that if that sharp intellect turned from its own interests Calenius could prove treacherous. Hanuvar shifted in his seat as if uneasy and instead devoted his thought to plans for securing the additional eight kinsman fortune had granted while keeping the children and his allies safe from the scholar's mysterious machinations. His silence appeared to content the big man, for Calenius neither volunteered nor asked anything further for the duration of the journey.

Ciprion's field slaves were still absent from their implements, which didn't surprise Hanuvar, for the buildings required substantial repair. Once beyond the gate, though, Hanuvar ascertained that some additional new and unwelcome event must have transpired in his absence. Instead of retreating to a back patio to enjoy wine or juices, both Izivar and Amelia frowned down at the crevice that had opened while a quartet of male slaves prepared a rope ladder and the lead instructor, gray-haired Galinthias, peered into the depths with a mirrored lantern despite the bright of the sun. The children were entirely absent.

Hanuvar urged his gelding faster, leading the way across the grounds toward the group, and Calenius kept pace just behind. There was no missing the brows furrowed with consternation on every head.

Amelia spoke before the two had even dismounted. "Good. You're here. Calenius, you are free to investigate this tunnel straight away. I'm certain Decius has arranged the price." She looked to Hanuvar for confirmation then proceeded. "But I must ask that you will keep alert for two of our children who've apparently entered it."

Calenius was terse. "You're sure of this?"

"Which children?" Hanuvar asked.

"One of the two you met," Amelia said, with a sharp look. "Teonia. And her brother Bannos. They tried to get others to go with them. They told their friends they heard wondrous music from down there."

Galinthias chimed in, "I have warned Geedis that hiding games should not be permitted." Amelia merely deepened her frown at this apparently repeated attempt to cast blame.

"We've heard no music." Izivar returned to the line of exposition Amelia had started. "And they took no light. Yet they went. And we're not sure how. No adults saw them go in but little Illia ran all the way back to get us. She was the only one they persuaded as far as the verge."

Hanuvar groaned inwardly. There might be no music that could be heard by those with normal perception, but that didn't mean Teonia and her brother hadn't sensed something magical. Had he inadvertently encouraged their exploration by reassuring the girl about her gifts?

The carriage rumbled onto the bricked road to the villa. Calenius looked toward it, thinking, then faced Amelia. "I will find the children, if they still live."

"I'll be going with you," Hanuvar said.

"As will I," Amelia asserted.

Calenius shook his head disdainfully. "This is no place for either of you. I have experience with the hazards these passages can present."

"Then I'll let you lead," Amelia said, breezily adding, "Decius and I will assist."

Calenius glanced at Hanuvar, not so much to verify that this was his name as to pin it to him. "The ground may have shifted. Old tunnels may not be safe."

"They seem to have held up quite well from ancient times," Amelia returned. "One of my men climbed down the side and shined a lantern along for a fair way. I've just sent him back to the villa for more."

Calenius glowered. "What would I say to your husband were he to ask how his wife and friend died beneath the earth?"

"You will have nothing of the sort to explain if you return us safely."

Calenius opened his mouth as if to object further, then waved his hand in a huffy acquiescence before striding off toward the carriage now pulling to a stop on the distant drive. The younger Volani that had jogged beside the conveyance stood attentively at his approach while older ones disembarked looking bemused. Antires hopped down to hurry toward his friends without seeing to the horses or the men.

Hanuvar spoke in low tones to Amelia as Izivar moved closer. "I don't like this—I've not been able to figure out what he's truly after, but it's old and powerful and there's probably something magical involved. Teonia and her brother are sensitive to such things."

Amelia's look wasn't so much blank as uncomprehending, and he realized that to her magic was the province of mountebanks. "They are children. With vivid imaginations."

"They are children, but they've probably been drawn by something quite real. If you descend with us, it's not just cave-ins we'll need to deal with."

"Monsters from myth?" She scoffed.

"Secrets, I mean, that Calenius may wish to keep hidden. Are you sure you want to go down there? If the situation becomes unfriendly—"

"Nonsense," Amelia interrupted firmly. "I'll help you keep an eye on the man. And besides, these children are still my responsibility."

Hanuvar recognized that she would not be swayed and fell silent, but couldn't suppress the image suggested by Calenius' protest about explaining her death to Ciprion. He was wryly heartened by the thought that such a scene would never play out because he'd be dead too.

Antires joined them, and a band of Amelia's slaves arrived with lanterns and rope and tools, so she stepped aside to organize what they'd brought. Hanuvar nodded to Antires, but spoke softly to Izivar.

"Don't tell me you want to go along as well?"

"No," she replied. "We all have our fields of expertise; I think you can manage this far better than I. And someone needs to keep an eye on things up here."

"Antires will help."

"You want me to stay here?" Antires scoffed. "Believe me, I'm not excited about going into another dark hole, but you need someone to watch your back. Calenius is dangerous."

"That he is. But we have eight newcomers here; they're going to be anxious about their new circumstances and two of them might have resentments toward the Lenereva family." He didn't have time to explain about the dispute the former shipwrights had brought to the council back when such things mattered. "You're needed here."

His friend sighed in resignation, but his frowning acknowledgment signaled he understood that the recovered men, for all that they were

Volani, were an unknown commodity. Hanuvar returned his attention to Izivar. "What's your assessment of the children?"

"The ones below? Or all of them?"

"All of them."

"Oh, they've been well cared for. There's no doubt of that."

He heard an unspoken qualifier in her voice. "But?" he prompted.

She hesitated briefly. "I never realized how much of my time in Volanus I'd taken for granted. There are greater divisions among these children than I remember from my youth, hierarchies with cruelties and resentments. I suppose the stress they've been under could account for some of it, but I can't help thinking that their time among the Dervans may be intensifying the conflicts. One of the boys actually accused me of lying when I told him I was Volani and free, and some of the girls treated me as if I were an exotic goddess."

"Understandable," Hanuvar said, though his tone was grim.

"I hate that there are no meaningful apprenticeships, virtually no understanding of cultures outside Tyvol, absolutely no instruction in self-defense, and an almost paranoid separation of the boys and girls most all the time."

"Ciprion and Amelia intended to make them a part of Dervan society," Antires said. "They had no idea we'd happen along. This is how things are done here."

"I thought I was prepared until I saw this," Izivar said. "The younger ones don't seem to remember Volanus and several don't speak the language anymore. We're going to have to get these children out sooner than I planned if we want them to do well in New Volanus. And I don't think some will be as happy up north. Amelia's right about that. I'd hoped to give them the rest of the summer here."

Calenius returned, leading the Volani to the far side of the crevice. After studying him, Izivar soberly held Hanuvar's eye and he understood that she was advising him to act with extreme caution. With a slow nod he assured both her, and the still troubled Antires, that he appreciated the risk.

The wizard and his group stopped at the point where one of Amelia's men had driven a pair of pitons into the ground. Robust ropes tied to them draped into the exposed tunnel. They joined Calenius in testing the knots.

"He's thorough," Antires said grudgingly.

It was almost time to leave. Hanuvar spoke again to Izivar, keeping his voice low. "Make sure the slaves we brought are the ones we're seeking."

"I don't have the list."

Hanuvar quietly recited their names, and she shook her head in amazement. "I still can't believe you memorized them all."

He had told her he'd done so because he'd feared he might have to destroy the list, for it was true and Izivar would understand that. But Hanuvar possessed an attention to detail others found remarkable, and that included precision memory for the written word, down to position of letters on a page. As a child he'd been surprised to learn friends and elders couldn't remember things the same way, and thereafter discussed it only rarely, for his only sibling with the same gift, after whom he had named his daughter, had said it was wrong to think yourself superior through some accident of birth. "You can be proud of what you do, not who you are," Narisia had instructed gravely. At twelve she had seemed incredibly wise, but then he had been six. "Use your gifts to aid your family, and your nation." Almost certainly she was repeating something their mother had said, but he had taken that advice to heart, for he had loved her, fiercely. He understood as he aged that she had been uncommonly perceptive.

"What's wrong?" Izivar asked sharply. "Beyond the obvious, I mean?"

"I was thinking about my sister."[3]

Izivar's expression gentled. She looked as though she wished to touch him, but wisely restrained herself. The person he pretended to be was probably standing in too familiar a way with his employer already.

"I would tell you to be careful..." Izivar said, affecting stiff formality. Her voice was still pitched just above a whisper.

"But you know he'll do whatever's needed regardless," Antires finished her thought quietly.

Hanuvar eyed both. "Take care of them."

---

[3] While Hanuvar had two sisters, the youngest died a few months after her birth, soon after her naming ceremony. Whenever he spoke of his sister, he meant Narisia rather than little Sonirla.
—*Sosilos*

Antires nodded solemnly and Izivar's lips thinned. The two understood this as a warning of what to do should he not return.

Amelia approached with a pair of slaves shouldering their own supplies.

Calenius waited impatiently at the top of the rope ladder the slaves had arranged, then took in Amelia's force. "You need these additional people?" His tone bordered on scathing.

"To help us search." Amelia bristled but did not otherwise show offense.

"Very well. But you must go only where I say. An area may appear perfectly stable, but you must trust my counsel. I'll examine the supports as we go."

"I shall rely upon your experience," Amelia promised stiffly.

The workers had transformed the twin anchored lines into a thick rope ladder with corded lattices. Calenius only climbed down part way before dropping and landed solidly on the exposed black pavers. He'd switched out of sandals to boots. Hanuvar would have done the same if he'd brought additional footgear.

The scholar inspected the exposed flooring and used lantern shutters to direct his beam down both ends of the tunnel, where it stretched into the darkness. Hanuvar told Amelia he'd await her below. He made short work of the descent, resisting the impulse to drop like Calenius. He had nothing to prove and was amused at his instinct to the contrary. He then held the ladder steady while Amelia climbed awkwardly down.

The Lady's two slaves came next. She had picked them well. They were athletic and watchful. And while it was generally true that Dervan masters kept weapons from their slaves, hers were apparently trusted with knives, which suggested both that they were loyal and that they knew how to wield them. He thought he could at least count on them to cry warning if things turned. One lit a lantern with practiced ease while the other used a shovel blade to test a nearby support pillar.

Scrapes along a set of exposed tree roots showed Hanuvar where the youngsters had climbed down.

There were stranger signs to note. Firstly, the cracks in the paving stones Hanuvar had seen earlier that day appeared smaller at close range, rather than larger, which went contrary to logic. Then, too, he remembered floor tiles thrust up at odd angles by the quake, including one that had jutted almost vertically. Now every paver lay perfectly flat.

He knew he had not imagined the floor's earlier condition. He contemplated the smashed roof tiles scattered among the dirt, half expecting to see them sliding slowly into alignment. They remained where they had fallen.

The second odd sign wasn't evident until Hanuvar and Amelia moved closer to the scholar himself, turning left into a cross tunnel with lantern shining. The place smelled of rich earth and cold stone and Hanuvar paused to adjust his eyes to the dimmer lighting. Untold centuries of dust lay thick on the floor here and two small pairs of sandaled footprints headed through it into the section of tunnel angling away from the estate, so close together that the children had likely been holding hands. They overlaid a set of clawed footprints broad as a bear's. The front and back legs revealed by those tracks were too far apart to be confused with a bear's, though, even had Hanuvar supposed one made these passages its home. The creature responsible for those prints dragged a long tail, the passage of which made a wavy line in the dust behind it.

Alarming as this was, at least the children obviously had come after the animal, for their sandal prints trod over the edges of some of the tail and claw marks.

Hanuvar halted. His voice was stern. "Before we go any further, you need to tell us what's crawling around down here."

Calenius answered without turning. "There are many beasts in the deep earth. One must have climbed higher due to the quake."

"Are the children in danger from it?" Amelia asked.

"We're all in danger." Calenius faced her and replied with gruff dignity. "This really isn't a place for noncombatants, my Lady. And I encourage you, again, to go back."

Amelia's lips firmed. "I think I'll manage long enough to find the children." Her slaves glanced at each other but said nothing.

Calenius shrugged his heavy shoulders and started forward. They went with him.

Hanuvar searched the ceiling for low points or cracks and saw an intact ribbed vault, carved of a greenish stone that had marble's gleam, though he had never seen marble of its kind. Every few feet scalloped columns rose, supporting black or green arches carved with whirling images suggestive of the foaming sea, or storm clouds.

The tunnel stretched on into the darkness.

"Who built this?" Amelia asked.

Calenius answered, though he did not take his eyes from the path. He was no more forthcoming to her than he'd been with Hanuvar. "An ancient people. Older than the Turians."

"Vanished Ones?" Amelia suggested, as if in jest.

Calenius did not dispute her assertion. "Some call them that. The legends make them sound wise and sinister. They were just people. Like you and me."

Amelia didn't ask how he had come to that opinion. "Why did they build these underground tunnels?"

"They tapped into the deep forces of the earth to power their works."

"And you're trying to figure out how to access that power?" Amelia speculated.

"No. I'm seeking lost information. A kind of book about their lives and customs."

"Will this knowledge help people?"

For the first time there was true passion in Calenius' voice. "More than you could possibly guess."

Amelia looked doubtful at this pronouncement. But Hanuvar could tell Calenius was saying something he thought was true.

"Perhaps you should call for the children," Calenius suggested to Amelia. "Would they come if you commanded?"

Amelia surely knew she was being directed away from her course of inquiry, but her chief priority here was her charges, and thus she shouted into the darkness for Teonia and Bannos. Four times she cried out their names, pausing for long moments after to listen. Only her echo returned.

Hanuvar looked over his shoulder. Amelia's slaves studied the ceiling and the walls as if expecting imminent collapse.

They arrived at a substantial subterranean crossroad. A wall to the left had given way, disgorging a small mound of black dirt, through which the children's tracks were clearly visible, skirting its edge and turning further left. The monster's passage had preceded the damage to the corridor, for there was no sign of its prints in the mound or the wide swathe of dirt scattered after.

Calenius bent beside the dirt pile, scooped some in a massive hand, and watched the drift of it slipping through his fingers. He then produced a yellowed ivory wand from one of his belt pouches, a stubby tool less than a foot in length. He crouched and applied it against the mound, indenting short, sharp lines. Hanuvar didn't recognize the language of the letters, though their construction reminded him of those he'd seen upon the walls of the ruins. By the time Calenius etched the seventh and final glyph, a slash with two intersection points and a curlicue, Hanuvar's arm hairs stood on end, as though clouds were about to birth a lightning storm. He wasn't the only one troubled by the sense of an ill wind. The man had openly worked magic, as if careless both of witnesses and the wrath of revenants. Both slaves gulped nervously and Amelia frowned.

"What was that for?" Amelia asked. "They've clearly gone this way."

"I'm just taking precautions." Calenius cat-footed forward.

"Precautious about what?" Amelia demanded.

Calenius didn't answer, for his lantern light had caught two slight bodies lying on a much larger dirt pile released from a collapsed tunnel beyond the intersection.

Hanuvar pushed past him and knelt by the children. So pale was their skin he was certain they were dead, and was surprised to discover the little girl's faint pulse. Her brother was even smaller than she, probably no older than seven. He, too, lived, and Hanuvar reported the information to Amelia.

She crouched at the side of the boy and spoke sharply to Calenius. "What's happened to them?"

The scholar hesitated, then answered brusquely, as if he'd decided the time for any evasion was over. "They heard the sound of the magic flowing here and followed it. They might even have detected the sorcerous emanations of the creature. It really depends upon what kind of gifts they possess. It found them and consumed their magics. And since their magic is interwoven with their life force, that left them weak. They may not survive."

Hanuvar had any number of questions about all their safety in present circumstances, but Teonia's breathing slowed to barely detectable. "What can be done for them?" His tone betrayed more authority and more urgency than he'd used with Calenius to this point—he sounded too much like the seasoned commander he was.

Calenius eyed Hanuvar with renewed interest. His finger wagged at him. "They matter even more to you than they do to her, don't they? The Volani children. The Volani slaves. Are they for her, or you?" He appeared faintly entertained, as though he were just beginning to understand a joke.

Hanuvar didn't care for his attention. "These children need help. They're fading."

Any suggestion of amusement passed from the scholar's face. "I understand you. I do. But I need my powers for when the beast returns." Calenius then faced Amelia. "I think these tunnels shall be of use to me. You can have the slaves." He lifted the scroll case with their sales papers. "Perhaps we can negotiate the price of full access."

"And the price of saving these children?" Amelia's voice was sharp.

"What happens if we simply carry them back to the surface?" Hanuvar asked.

Calenius looked doubtful.

"I demand that you help them," Amelia ordered.

That was the wrong tack. Hanuvar had briefly glimpsed fellow feeling in the eyes of the man beside them, but any hint of it vanished the moment Amelia's voice assumed an air of primacy. Calenius stood quiet as a figure of stone. In his absolute stillness there lurked a threat, something dark and ages old. Hanuvar thought to hear him issue a challenge, or even a warning, so he was surprised by the man's words. "I shall help them for my own reasons, Lady." He handed his lantern down to Hanuvar then took a knee before Teonia and her brother.

Hanuvar climbed to his feet, passed the lantern to Amelia, then briefly scanned the dark corridors around them. Amelia's frown deepened.

Calenius breathed out, then with surprising gentleness held a massive hand over each of the tiny forms lying in the dirt before him. His breathing altered; after a moment Hanuvar realized it matched that of the pale little bodies now in synchronization with the scholar.

Amelia's look to Hanuvar spoke volumes—she did not like the

situation and she did not like the man. Hanuvar stepped further from Calenius. The slaves shone lanterns of their own upon the wall beside a damaged pillar to the east, studying a large crack. One tested it gingerly with the blade of a shovel. Hanuvar walked past, seeing what he'd taken for a stretch of dirt beyond the north side of the crossroad was actually a yawning pit of darkness. He was reluctant to step too close to its crumbling edge. These tiles, at least, were too damaged to repair themselves.

Hanuvar returned to Amelia and the children, over whom the big man still leaned.

Calenius breathed heavily. Beneath his palms the children's pale skin took on the healthy flush of life. They shifted then, as if in sleep.

The scholar lifted his hands from the children, shaping them slowly into fists, then climbed to his feet. His magics must have wearied him, for his step was uncertain, though his voice remained steady. He addressed Amelia. "You and your people should take them back. Now."

"They're well?"

"They will be fine. I restored some of their magics, and that will speed their healing."

"I thank you," she said.

He looked sidelong at them. "I have worked directly for the revenants. They know of my magical expertise."

"Look to us for gratitude," Amelia said. "Not threats. My family has no interest in speaking with revenants, on any subject."

He weighed her words while Amelia called for her men to come up; she bent to retrieve the boy. One of her men set aside his shovel and scooped up the girl as a scuttling, scraping sound reached their ears. Something large drew near. It was then Hanuvar understood how the expenditure of Calenius' magic had served his purpose. Calenius had suggested the monster had been drawn to the magic it had detected in the children; probably his healing sorceries had called it back.

A glittering thing emerged into the intersection beyond, a shape so brilliant Hanuvar had to narrow his eyes. The creature seemed fashioned of sunbeams laced with diamonds.

Calenius drew his sword, a long, straight weapon suited for his huge hands, and shouted for them to run.

Amelia's men needed no encouragement and pulled their mistress back; Amelia barked for "Decius" to come too.

Hanuvar remained and freed his own sword. He'd seen Calenius was weakened and didn't have full faith the other man could stop the advancing creature. He thought he saw the animal waddling, lizard like, but details were a challenge. It was as though he faced into the sun.

The beast bore straight for Calenius.

The man had made no noise with his previous spell, but this time he chanted and stirred the air with his free hand. Hanuvar's neck hairs rose and a chill wind came.

Whatever Calenius' magic had done, it did not halt the monster, which accelerated to meet him.

Calenius' arm shook as he readied his sword. A dark spot appeared in the shining mass racing toward them, and after a brief moment of confusion Hanuvar recognized it for a black maw filled with sharp teeth. The beast had opened its mouth. Calenius leapt to its left and the monster turned with surprising speed. He slashed once, drawing a line of darkness with his blade tip along what might have been the thing's skull.

Hanuvar still had difficulty fixing upon its shape. Calenius, though, interacted without issue, which set Hanuvar guessing he'd thrown a spell to aid himself. He set aside his sword and picked up the shovel left by Amelia's slave, thrusting it into the nearby dirt. He sent soil raining down across the creature. Three quick throws and part of its side was better visible as a scaley body with four stubby legs and a large snakelike head even now snapping at Calenius. With it had come a wave of heat warm enough to raise sweat beads on Hanuvar's forehead.

The big man leapt back from the lizard's assault. Hanuvar dashed forward and drove the shovel blade into its side. The beast turned to hiss at Hanuvar, its tail slamming Calenius across the legs. The mage was flung backward. He landed along the pit's edge, and slid, scrabbling for purchase in the loose dirt. The creature spun to follow him.

Hanuvar snatched his sword and slashed at the lizard's tough, shining hide. It proved incredibly dense, for his second slice drew only a slim trickle of dark fluid.

Now the shining lizard turned its open maw upon Hanuvar.

Enough dirt had coated the thing that it could be looked upon, though many points of brilliance glittered through the gloom. It tasted the air with an enormous tongue then turned, irresistibly pulled toward Calenius, straining still to pull himself free from the pit edge. Hanuvar strove to keep the thing centered on him, slashing through the heat-distorted air with his blade, and wishing he carried a falcata. Not only was the blade of his people longer that the short sword he wielded, its heavy end would be far more effective at breaking through the creature's scales. His strikes succeeded only in annoying the beast.

It plodded after him, hissing with primordial rage, and pushing out heat like wind-driven flame and baring its fangs.

Only then did Calenius return. His earlier weakness had passed, and he leapt to land astride the creature's front shoulders. His long blade glowed an eerie blue, as if lit from deep inside. The great lizard turned its head but could not evade the blow, driven through its skull all the way to its questing tongue. Stinking ichor blossomed widely.

It should have died then, but writhed on, and Calenius somehow retained his position, striking twice more. Hanuvar did not think the man's manifest strength was responsible for slicing through hide and bone, but the sorcery shining within his blade.

Finally the beast sank to the stones and stilled. Calenius climbed clear. He stood panting beside the still bright length of body, its blood shining oddly purplish along his lit sword. As Calenius recovered, the blade's glow ebbed, just as the lizard's scales had begun to do.

Hanuvar wiped sweat from his brow and, breathing heavily, said: "Nicely done."

Calenius looked at the sword, then at Hanuvar, as if asking whether he wished to comment about the sorcery. When Hanuvar did not, he said: "You could have run."

"Then it might have had you."

Calenius appeared to have trouble digesting this explanation, for his stare was searching. "Who are you?"

"Who are you?"

Calenius smiled, then laughed, an open, expansive sound. Hanuvar had the sense it was not something he often did. The big man then turned to the creature, the glow of which had faded almost entirely. Once again the sword blazed beneath its coating of blood, and then he drove the weapon through its dull throat scales. Reeking gore burst upon the sodden ground. Calenius used his other hand to feel through the wound, at last withdrawing an orb of shining crimson hue, dripping with fluids.

He lay down his weapon, then wiped the orb on the bottom of his spattered tunic and stared into its depths. Hanuvar saw nothing within but swirling blackness, but decided to peer no more deeply. Being in the presence of the orb left him as comfortable as facing a battlefield's corpse wind.

Apparently the monster had carried whatever the sorcerer sought in these tunnels. Hanuvar wondered if the spherical object were the true source of magic that Teonia had sensed and pursued. Certainly it seemed to attract Calenius.

After a long moment, the big man dropped the orb in disgust. Whatever he'd wanted there was not within. There must be others. The object struck the old tile and chipped it, though took no damage itself. Nor did it roll. Calenius' eyes were hard as he considered Hanuvar. "Do you mean to cause me trouble?"

"If I wanted to make trouble for you, I wouldn't have helped you."

Calenius grunted. The answer seemed to satisfy him in one way, though he continued frowning. "True enough. You distracted it so it wouldn't come after me. And after you'd achieved your own objective. You had nothing to gain. You're not quite what I would expect."

Calenius then offered his hand to Hanuvar, who took it, surprised the other man gripped his fingers rather than his forearm, as was custom through most of the Inner Sea. Hanuvar returned the peculiar gesture.

"The children will live," Calenius said, with the air of a king making pronouncements. He released his grip. "Tell the woman I will search the rest of these tunnels, and I will pay what I offered when we first met. As for you, I will tell no one of your presence or your aims, Hanuvar, so long as your activities pose no interference with my own."

Sheer force of will prevented Hanuvar from gaping in surprise. He could not help the blood draining from his face, and this time, when he met the frigid blue eyes of the man across from him, he fully understood just how dangerous an adversary Calenius would be. He was larger and stronger, and at least as fast. A skilled and veteran warrior, he was also a sorcerer. And one apparently connected to the Dervan Revenants.

Hanuvar was not a complete stranger to being overmatched. There had always been stronger men, more accomplished warriors, and sorcerers, but never had he encountered a single individual possessing all three traits. Most disconcerting of all, Calenius' intellect was at least equal to his own. It was not that Hanuvar had never encountered others more clever than himself, but they had always been gifted in other fields. To see that level of perception in another warrior was more than disconcerting, it was frightening, and not just for reasons of pride—the depths of which surprised Hanuvar at some remove, for he liked to think of himself beyond such conceits—but because of the direct threat this man posed to the future of his people.

And against any other man, that danger would have prompted Hanuvar into immediate and lethal action. Those cold blue eyes bored deep into his own with a level of understanding that suggested Calenius knew that.

In the end, after taking a longer moment to consider his course than he was accustomed to requiring, Hanuvar said: "I see no reason for our activities to overlap, or for us to meet again. But I am not without resources of my own, should my plans be endangered."

"I would expect nothing less." Calenius' smile wasn't quite mocking; it was amused and strangely respectful, as if he had just heard the pronouncement of a gifted child.

They broke their grip at the same moment.

Hanuvar retrieved his sword, wiped it clean by driving it into the dirt, then sheathed it. He picked up one of the lanterns then nodded to Calenius. He did not bid him farewell before starting the long way back.

Antires saw Hanuvar just as he emerged squinting into the sun's light and comforting breeze. The sweet scent of barley and growing things was welcome as a lover's touch. The Herrene called out to him. Hanuvar blew out his lantern and was soon up the rope ladder where his friend waited with Izivar and Amelia.

Izivar's relief was palpable even though her expression remained subdued. Her shoulders relaxed; she breathed slowly but deeply then nodded politely to him. She was remembering to play a role in front of Amelia's servants. "I'm glad to see you're well."

"Thank you."

Antires was more demonstrative, and grinned, barely restraining himself from an embrace.

Members of Amelia's staff lingered just out of earshot, with a handcart holding pitchers and cups. Seeing them, Hanuvar realized how thirsty he himself was.

"Would you care for a drink?" Amelia asked. It was curious to find relief in her eyes as well.

He said that he did, and Antires promptly handed over a wineskin, although Hanuvar had one of his own. He drank deep, then capped it. "How are the children?"

"Weak, but awake," Izivar answered. "What happened down there? Where's Calenius?"

"We fought the guardian and he killed it," Hanuvar said. "It had something magical that he was after, but it wasn't the one he wanted. He's still searching for it." It no longer surprised Hanuvar that the sorcerer would proceed with his search unaided.

Amelia frowned and scrubbed at a spot of dirt she had noticed on her sleeve. "I will leave some men with refreshments for when he emerges. Thank you for your help."

"I'm grateful to you for yours." Hanuvar looked to Izivar. "How were the men Calenius turned over?"

"Astonished to be speaking with a kinswoman," Izivar replied. "They were the ones from your list. If they knew what Calenius was after, they were unwilling to discuss it."

"I don't think he's the kind who shares much." He faced Amelia. "But he said he'll pay you the rate he offered for access to the tunnels."

"I suppose that will do." She frowned. "I have changed my mind about housing the children here. It's not at all safe if there are... things wandering around so close that could turn up any time there's another quake."

"I'll have to return north to accelerate arrangements for their move," Izivar said. And simply from the way the two women stood it seemed clear invisible lines of tension between them had dissipated; they had found accord.

"Well," Amelia said, "let's get out of the sun and see you refreshed, Decius. My steward tells me he believes the villa is secure. Without a doubt the courtyard is. We have shade and some wonderful honeyed lemon juice, with mint. And a banquet. I can guess you'll want something to eat. I certainly do, and I didn't fight any monsters."

Hanuvar was hungry, and in need of a wash basin, although he was in little mood to be entertained. Still troubled by his exchange with Calenius, he'd rather have been on his way to Izivar's villa. But he recognized Amelia wanted to host them as she had originally intended, and had no desire to offend her. "It would be a pleasure." He gestured for her to precede him.

Instead, Amelia fell in at his side and they started across the grass. Izivar walked on his right. Antires trailed behind. Hanuvar didn't see Serliva, and supposed she was with the children.

"Do you have any idea what Calenius is truly after?" Amelia asked.

"Not much. I think he was sincere when he told us he meant to help people. I just don't know which ones. There's something he means to do, to right some wrong, and nothing matters to him more than that."

"You make him sound like you," Amelia said. "Although I do not see it. But then I used to say that about you to my husband."

"Oh?" Izivar inquired politely.

"Calenius is arrogant and rather rude. He seems like a man who takes what he wants without much regard for others." Amelia added, after a moment: "He is nothing like Decius."

Amelia had just complimented him doubly, admitting first that Hanuvar might be similar to her honorable husband and then implying an approval of the way he conducted himself. He'd never expected to hear anything of the kind from her lips. While he found both statements oddly touching, he did not embarrass Amelia by discussing them. "Calenius has warned that the volcano may erupt by autumn."

"How does he know that?" Amelia asked. "Do you believe him?"

"I think I do," Hanuvar replied.

"You sound as though you trust him," Antires suggested.

"No. I partly understand him, which is a different thing. But I hope never to cross his path again."

※ ※ ※

For a time it seemed Calenius would be a one-time acquaintance. We did not see him before our departure that day.

Izivar soon left our company entirely, returning to Selanto with the astonished former slaves of Calenius. If any bore animus against the

Lenereva family they never showed it. You may think the Volani who'd worked with the wizard possessed more details about his motives, but they had simply excavated where he pointed and followed his orders. That they might abandon digging and return to their trades of shipbuilding, cooperage, carpentry, and blacksmithing still felt a dream as impossible as their freedom. I spoke with them several times and could not believe that they had been crying out lonely and frightened while working for Calenius, as Teonia had described, for they all claimed the wizard had been a fair master to those willing to work. I dismissed the girl's account of fearful Volani voices as childish exaggeration, which proved a mistake.

As for Teonia and her brother,[4] both seemed to have no lingering effects after their experience, and their magical senses were restored, along with their health. They had never witnessed the lizard clearly, seeing only a shining thing that hummed with magics and put them to sleep. A few weeks later we were to learn they were troubled by recurring dreams of a strange power beneath the soil. Sometimes they spoke of tunnels linking dark cities clustered at the base of the mountains, fueled by that flowing light, and the bright lizards—pets or guardians—emerging at night to walk upon ebon-paved boulevards.

As for Hanuvar and myself, we took up residence in Izivar's villa at Apicius and began to oversee the challenging recovery efforts that lay before us. While I helped organize portions of the villa for a secret influx of children, Hanuvar left for an evening engagement in a nearby resort town. He had planned only to scout out the situation and get a sense of the man who'd refused to sell a trio of Volani singers. He always preferred to get the lay of the land before acting. This time, though, currents would sweep him into a situation that required immediate, and constant, improvisation to save not just the singers, but himself and an unexpected ally.

—Sosilos, Book Twelve

---

[4] When I spoke with Bannos many years later, what he chiefly recalled from the entire incident was the beauty of the melody. He had become a skilled musician, in part, he told me, because he wanted to find his way to the astonishing loveliness of the song he and his sister had heard. "I've not found it yet," he confessed with a wry smile. When asked why he and Teonia had felt compelled to journey into the dark, he told me that the tunnels were not dark to them. They apparently beheld a ghostly image of their former splendor, complete with rounded lanterns and shifting pinpoints of light upon the ceiling. It had seemed a wonderland, one of incredible allure. I could not help speculating that some of those said to have been lost to the darkness over the centuries were themselves magically gifted, and like Teonia and Bannos too young to recognize the hazards. —Silenus

Chapter 2:
Discordant Factions

The dark curling locks of the middle singer hid most of the red scar along the right side of her face as well as her missing ear, though a diminishing line of pink-tinged pale skin shone along the sun-bronzed cheek. Probably she remained in pain and would for the rest of her life, but this night she beamed, like the two singers beside her, as if delighted by her circumstance. All three wore traditional Herrenic dresses with tight waists, pleated skirts, and low collars. No matter their costume, all three were Volani, and raised their voices skillfully.

The dinner guests were too busy circulating under the garden's festive paper lanterns to pay the women any direct notice. For them, the masterful performance was no more than pleasant background noise, and likely few in attendance understood the Volani words about a boy's delight at the first spring flowers high upon the slope of frost-crowned Mount Keenai, towering still near lost Volanus.

Hanuvar had deliberately kept well back from the vocalists, concerned he might be recognized despite his disguise as a Dervan man of means, complete with citizen's ring and the lightweight toga praetexta draped over a yellow tunic. But he couldn't resist peering at them through a screen of foliage.

This villa was not far from the coast, and over the chatter of guests and the bustle of servants and the music itself he heard waves crashing against the shore, an omnipresent sound through much of the Volanus he had known. Almost, he could imagine himself at a party in his homeland. The lighting intensified the impression as a full moon peered out through the clouds. It was always easier to imagine the irrecoverable city by night, when dreams seeped halfway toward the waking world.

There were other entertainments underway as well, including a juggler who worked too hard to curry favor for his talents with handsome young men. He slunk away to try an eques guest after being spurned by one of the haughty, smooth-skinned Ilodoneans.

A handful of those distinctly foreign men wandered armed along the periphery, frowning and superior. Most were garbed in a uniform with blue capes and conical helms and oddly segmented dark red chest armor reminiscent of lobster carapaces. It was unusual to show weapons at a gathering of this sort so Hanuvar had readily elicited gossip that the four were bodyguards for a prince, although they were seldom near him.

Their apparent charge strode solemnly past Hanuvar to occupy an empty space directly before the Volani women. Unlike his guards he wore a strange mixture of styles, including an archaic bronze helm that afforded wide scope for his haughty black eyes but obscured the sides of his face down to his heavy chin. He surveyed the singers with a proprietary look before walking stiffly on, and their expressions briefly clouded.

After the prince passed, a Dervan man drew up on Hanuvar's left, working to use Hanuvar's body to block the Ilodonean's line of sight to him. Seeing that Hanuvar noticed what he did, the newcomer chuckled quietly, watched the prince depart, then shifted the white snack platter he held to his off hand while raising the other in greeting.

"Lartius Veritas," he said. "Some guests are just tiresome, even if you've invited them yourself."

"Julius Neponus," Hanuvar returned. "Very nice to meet you, sir. Thank you for having me."

Lartius waved off the privilege of the laboriously acquired invitation with a be-ringed hand, as though it were no great matter, his eyes still upon the hedge through which the Ilodonean prince had exited. Lartius was reedy and self-satisfied, with hair so precisely trimmed and arranged he looked to be wearing a fur helmet.

"Are the Ilodoneans a problem?" Hanuvar asked.

"Not so much a problem as a... point of contention. That was their prince, Xenxes."

"Why is his equipment such a jumble?"

Lartius eyed him in curiosity. "You really haven't heard of him? I've mentioned him in a number of my writings.[5] The Terror of the West?"

"I'm only newly come to your writings, sir. It was my esteemed uncle who was one of your devotees, and I'm afraid he's passed on. But he spoke so admiringly of your work, and the Zenith, that I had to beg an introduction when I was passing through the area."

"My condolences for your loss, then, and my welcome to you. Prince Xenxes is privy to a number of deeply consequential information streams from Ilodonea. But he simply cannot pull the data together properly, and his, shall we say, dogmatic conversational style was not apparent from the letters we have been exchanging."

"And his equipment?" Hanuvar persisted.

"Well, he's got the spear of Ikthos and the shield of Hundara and the helm of Iskandros himself. And that sword? That's the sword of Yriak the Great. The Cerdian conqueror." Though apparently annoyed by Xenxes, the patrician boasted about the prince's acquisitions, as though his own esteem were greater for having such a man as his guest.

Carrying the belongings of famous dead conquerors suggested Xenxes valued notoriety over expertise, but Hanuvar did not share that opinion with this audience, and instead managed to sound impressed. "He must be quite formidable."

"They say he's killed fifty men."

Hanuvar had never liked to enumerate, let alone advertise, the less savory aspects of his career, so this information further suggested Xenxes sought renown, for the prince was likely involved in spreading this figure. "He certainly looks dreadful."

---

[5] Lartius' writings were published monthly in widely circulated booklets that attracted a small but devoted cadre of readers, despite their promulgation of wild speculations lacking logic, internal consistency, or basic credibility. I spoke with former adherents later in life, and while some claimed they had only read his tracts for amusement, others still clung tenaciously to his "brilliant" insights about hidden connections that lay behind widely divergent incidents in our history.   —*Silenus*

Popping a honeyed walnut into his maw from the snack plate, Lartius expounded. "He tracked down a lot of those treasures himself over thousands of miles and all kinds of obstacles. He's something of a kindred spirit, although I'm far more interested in religious artifacts. Have you seen my collection?"

"I plan to," Hanuvar said. "I've heard it's impressive."

"The hardest piece to get was that Volani one, not because it's especially pretty, but because the bidding on it was so high. There won't ever be another one!" Lartius laughed shortly. "Do you know it stood in the temple of Varis for generations? That's Hanuvar's god," he added.

"Oh," said Hanuvar. "I didn't realize the man had one."

The singers had begun a song of the sea. The scarred young woman and the companion on her left had fallen silent apart from joining in the refrain, enabling the third to take the lead in a lilting alto. All swayed in time to the music, the pleats of their dresses shifting in perfect synchronization. He wasn't sure which of the names he'd memorized applied to which individual. "Are these young women Volani too?"

"Yes. They used to be temple singers."

Hanuvar knew that, but affected a polite interest, and Lartius continued. "Their coastal islands had women sing like this whenever the moon was full, and you could hear it all over the harbor of Volanus."

In point of fact, the choirs raised their voices at sunrise and sunset, although there were occasional nighttime festivals, but Hanuvar did not correct him.

"They're fetching, aren't they? The best one has been terribly marred, unfortunately. That's why we keep her hair swept forward. But not many of these singers survived, so we couldn't be too choosy. Caiax stormed the islands and stupidly crucified most of the occupants, trying to scare the Volani on the mainland, across the channel. Quite a waste of good performers, if you ask me. The man had no head for business."

Hanuvar raised his wine goblet to his lips, the better to mask the heat flushing his cheeks.

One of Lartius' followers spotted him and walked up to join them. Like the rest of the party guests, he was middle-aged and well-to-do.

He inserted himself into the conversation without an introduction. "I wonder what they're singing about," he said. "I can't understand a word of that gibberish."

"I couldn't tell you," Lartius said dismissively.

"They look so happy," the newcomer continued. "You suppose they're actually singing to us about their treacherous city, or that monster that led them to ruin?"

The word Volanus or his own name would be obvious but Hanuvar didn't bother pointing that out.

"Hanuvar's infiltrated the praetorians, you know," Lartius said to Hanuvar. The other man nodded and both watched him for reaction.

This was the last thing Hanuvar expected to hear, and he couldn't resist questioning the bizarre assertion. "He has?"

"Your uncle may have known, depending upon how deep into my writings he was."

"He didn't mention that. I'm sure I'd have remembered."

"The last emperor knew how dangerous Hanuvar was," the other man said. "Why do you think he destroyed Volanus?"

"I assumed it was because Emperor Gaius hated Volani opposition and wanted the city's riches." Hanuvar had some experience with the matter but his two companions smiled smugly at his apparent naïveté.

Lartius shook his perfect coif of hair and spoke with profound gravity, as if to convey a vital secret. "He knew Hanuvar was in league with the Vanished Ones to power their immortality magic, turning them to Dervan skins for his own purposes. Gaius was readying a counterstrike that would have eliminated the fiends, but Hanuvar had him killed, and is now shaping policy disguised as one of the emperor's top advisors."

"He's even more clever than I thought," said Hanuvar. He'd known this group of Dervans that named themselves "Zenith" held to peculiar beliefs, but hadn't guessed their doctrines were this strange.

Someone was advancing through the lawn to his right, and she spoke as she drew closer. "The Vanished Ones have a secret room under the senate, of course," she said, utterly serious. She slid a hand through the crook of Hanuvar's arm as he suppressed his discomfiture at finding her here.

He recognized Aleria's[6] voice, even though she adopted a sophisticated drawl, as of someone from Turian lineage, and she wore a stola of expensive sheer fabric with bared arms and silver accents. Her hair was elaborately styled and silver bracelets dangled on her wrists. She had always been attractive but the overall affect this evening was especially striking, and she carried herself with the confidence of a woman who knew it.

Lartius smiled. "Ah, the lovely Lucinda. She's well read on my work in this area," he said to Hanuvar. "Almost ready for the full initiation," he added.

"I hope to qualify next month." She patted Hanuvar's arm. "Have you seen Lartius' most recent update? I had no idea the Vanished Ones engineered the entire war with the Cerdians."

Hanuvar had no trouble managing to sound astonished. "Did they?"

"I'll tell you all about it." Aleria squeezed Hanuvar's arm, nodded her head toward Lartius, and led Hanuvar away toward the villa. Behind them, the singers were being moved off by a well-dressed house slave so that a trio of flautists could take their place.

Hanuvar spoke quietly to Aleria: "The Vanished Ones?" Earlier in the week he himself had spent time in some of their ruins and he had a passing familiarity with the folklore about them, but he'd never heard anyone claim the Vanished Ones were still in existence, much less involved in Dervan politics, or leaguing with Hanuvar.

She leaned toward him to answer, her voice low. "These people just lap this nonsense up. The crazier, the better." They stepped around a small knot of men and women discussing the impact of moon phases upon personalities, and made for a side entrance to the sprawling villa. "So what are you doing this time?" Aleria asked. "I didn't think you'd need another score this year. I'm starting to think you like to do this sort of thing for fun."

"What about you? Our last venture should have set you up for a long while. Yet here you are. And it seems like you're well known to their group."

"I've found I have expensive tastes. And it's not hard for a pretty

---

[6] Hanuvar first met Aleria during the course of the events described by Antires in the account of "The Autumn Horse," and recruited her to assist him in his theft of gold and information from the Dervan treasury detailed by Antires in "The Cursed Vault." —*Sosilos*

widow to get involved here. All that's needed is some reading time and a touch of sophistication."

"A widow," Hanuvar said. "How sad. Should I express my condolences?"

She pressed her free hand to her chest and spoke with mock sorrow. "My husband died at sea on the way to Hadira. I've been in mourning for the last year and was so shattered by his loss I have only now begun to circulate. This is my first time along the Oscani coast, and I am ever so eager for introductions." She fluttered her eyelids dramatically.

"I'm sure. I probably shouldn't ask, but I can't help wondering about Hanuvar's connections with the praetorians and the Vanished Ones."

She stopped just shy of the villa at the edge of the party, where a pair of women laughed loudly near the open door to the walled gardens attached to the residence. She guided him to a low stand of pines nearby and faced him. "Well, Hanuvar is disguised as Metellus, the new legate of the Praetorian Guard. He disfigured himself so no one would recognize him."

"I've seen Metellus. That's some commitment to a role.[7] Dare I ask what his plan is?"

Aleria adopted a limpid eyed expression of astonishing sincerity. "He's scheming to take the women of Derva to a hidden sect of Hadiran mystics in exchange for the secrets of the ancients."

"You're making this up as you go," Hanuvar suggested.

"I'm really not. How is it that you don't know all this? You're usually thoroughly invested in a part."

"I'm disguised as someone curious about Zenith but uninitiated. I'm scouting tonight."

"And what are you really after?"

"Several things."

She eyed him speculatively, then glanced over at the two women, still chatting animatedly before the garden's entrance. "I'm not opposed to us throwing in together, but I can't have you jeopardizing what I've worked for."

---

[7] By this point in his career, Metellus had lost an eye on one side of his face and gained three parallel scars upon the other. —*Sosilos*

"That's understandable."

He saw her shoulders relax minutely. "How could I forget how reasonable you are? But I need to know what you're here for."

"It's almost certainly not the same as your aims."

"How can you be sure? Is yours under guard?"

"Sometimes."

"Is it among the religious artifacts in the display room?"

"Part of it is."

"Do you have to be so mysterious? Or maybe that's a portion of your charm." She flashed him a smile then spoke before he could answer. "Let's go look." Aleria moved determinedly off, muttered a polite "excuse me" to the women inadvertently impeding access, then stepped through them, without waiting for Hanuvar to follow.

The walled garden beyond was extensively planted. A single wide path, illuminated with paper lanterns, ran along the side of the villa. Others led deeper into shoulder high lines of hedge, more sporadically lit. Curiously, one side branch was distinguished by unlit torches planted periodically along either side.

Several closed doors would have led into the manor proper, but only one of them was open onto a well-lit room. A handsome young man with a gladiator's heavy build sat on a stool just inside the doorway.

The sentry nodded politely to Aleria and Hanuvar both. On the floor beneath the waist-high first shelf on the left stood images of the peculiar animal-headed deities beloved of Hadirans. Central prominence was given to a leopard-headed goddess with bare breasts. A trio of gold and silver discs with complex Ilodonean pictographs stood in slanted plate holders on a shelf at shoulder level on the right, near a line of painted wooden figures of Ruminian horse and water spirits. A man-high stone carved with Ceori markings sat in one corner beside a closed door to the inner chambers.

Aleria's attention had fixed upon a row of tiny bejeweled figurines with oversized heads. They glittered in the torchlight. Not at all coincidentally they were positioned nearest the guard, who kept his eyes on Aleria when she drew close enough to touch them. His gaze was only partly admiring, for he had surely noted an acquisitive gleam in her eyes.

Hanuvar's own regard was drawn to the intricate stone carving from Volanus. Sitting in the corner across from the Ceori obelisk was a stone stellae of a bearded man with outspread arms, a thundercloud behind his head: Varis. This beautifully blue granite image had once graced the lectern of the central temple in Volanus. Hanuvar had been near it many times. He himself no longer felt much attachment to the gods of his people, but had to unclench his fists yet again before a dismemberment of Volani heritage for the amusement of rich Dervans. The piece looked heavier than he'd hoped.

He and Aleria pretended interest in the rest of the exhibit, then left the room.

She touched Hanuvar's arm and turned him down a path deeper into the garden. They passed a stone bench only a few paces beyond where the guard was posted, but kept on beyond a side passage where a tryst seemed underway, to judge by a throaty sigh and a giggle, and strolled for a far corner. Aleria led them behind a bronze dryad pouring water into a clamshell at her feet. The statue leaned out from atop a rock large enough to conceal them both as they took a seat behind it. Music swelled from beyond the garden. An entire cadre of performers played at once, which likely meant dinner was about to be served. They would most likely provide accompaniment through the first courses.

"We're going to miss the meal," Aleria said with a wistful look.

"I'm not after food," he replied softly to her. "And you're after the jewels."

"Was I so obvious? Well, they are the most valuable and most easily removed items here, of course. They're what you're after too, aren't they?" Her voice took on a peevish quality and in the poor light Hanuvar could see her bracing for an answer in the affirmative.

"No. I have a buyer for the Volani stone."

Her slim eyebrows arched in curiosity. "That's interesting."

"It's rare, now. Few who are left could carve such icons, or would be interested in doing so."

She grunted agreement, then added caustically: "The last emperor managed to create an entire rarified market. How are you planning to get it out?"

"I haven't advanced that far." Hanuvar was much more interested in the fate of the singers; they'd been sold through a chain of buyers prior to Lartius, who remained unwilling to part with them, owing to their scarcity. "Do you have something worked out?"

"I've discarded a number of more involved ideas," she admitted. "I've landed on a late night visit, with some tainted meat for the guard dogs they let loose."

"What does Lartius want with all these religious images?"

"He and his little 'Zenith' group believe these objects have been invested with power because people have worshiped them for so long. The theory is that possession transfers some of that power to their holder."

"But it's the power of other gods, isn't it?" Hanuvar asked. "I thought the Zenith was all about the hearth gods of Derva, and restoring them to prominence in households."

"So you *have* been doing some homework! Yes, that's a principle they promote, although the whole enterprise may as well have been designed to make itself money by spreading 'secrets.' I think Lartius is just one of those rich men who likes to collect rare things. He claims that the spiritual energy absorbed by his items can be channeled back into the Dervan hearths, which are all connected, to reinvigorate the righteous state. He's pretty convincing, too—when he talks I almost think he believes it."

"Interesting," Hanuvar said, and she laughed at the acerbity in his voice.

"He also thinks his estate here is the central access point for channeling the energy. He claims the grounds are over an ancient mystical site belonging to the Vanished Ones. The Zenith have secret ceremonies in an old cave nearby where there are some glyphs and drawings. There will be another one tonight, because the moon is high. A propitious time for magic. Surely you know that."

"I've heard it said. But I thought the Vanished Ones were villains in this play?"

"Lartius thinks he can use their own magic against them. The Vanished Ones are supposed to have left a great power hidden in the cave. Although I've no idea how, because I've been in the cave—"

"Of course you have."

"—and I've seen nothing but a dank play space for overactive imaginations. And how kind of you to assume that I am always well prepared. I'm frankly surprised at how little you know about this venture yourself."

"It's not a venture yet," Hanuvar said.

"My, my. You sound a little defensive." She patted his arm. "I heard. Just a scouting trip. You do know what's going to happen tonight, don't you?"

"A swearing in."

"In the cave," Aleria confirmed, and with a teasing smile, added more detail. "Tonight, when the moon's at its highest, Lartius' lot will be welcoming people into their innermost circle. You have to pay up through various rarified levels. It's a pretty inspired scheme, really. They typically invite new folks to their party to hear about the ceremonies, but not see them, so they'll want to be involved in later ones. I assume that's how you got in?"

"I'm a relative of an enthusiast pursuing a worthy investment in moral rectitude," Hanuvar said with mock gravity.

"You're great at that 'responsible member of society' look." She paused to appraise him. "What do you think, Helsa? Can we join forces?" She leaned closer. "This entire region is dripping with the foolish rich. You and I, working together, why, there's no telling how much wealth we could get ourselves."

"I could use more money," Hanuvar admitted. He knew he should not prolong the moment, but wanted to hear more about her plans, and was not entirely displeased by his proximity to this vibrant, clever, appealing woman.

"I'd like to see what you spend it on. How do you disguise yourself so capably? You look older than last time. Distinguished. But not so old as at first."

"That's a trade secret."

"So is this the real you?"

"Always."

"And what were you really doing in that no name village where we met?"

"You probably won't believe this, but I was just passing through."

She smiled and seemed about to inquire further before the thwack of the garden door slamming closed and the clomp of soldiers' hobnailed boots on stone made clear something troubling was afoot. Lartius' voice was raised against another, accented one; a debate about the number of initiates for ceremonies was growing heated as the men moved on toward the treasure display.

When they ascertained that part of the dispute entailed removal of "the treasures" Hanuvar and Aleria slipped out from behind the fountain and its interfering babble to better hear details, and they sneaked down a parallel inner path until they had arrived opposite the treasure room, crouching so as to not be observed.

Lartius stammered out a command to stand aside. The guard's answer was clearer.

"Master, are these men harming you?"

They then heard an outcry, a sudden shout, and a thud, of something heavy striking stone.

Even the sounds of the lovers quieted.

Though soft, the accented arrogance of a silky male voice was clearly audible. "He need not have died, Lartius. That was very foolish. Now I'll have to take more unpleasant measures to make sure there are no witnesses."

The next moment a soldierly command was given, and an affirmative response returned, though in a language Hanuvar knew poorly. He could not parse the Ilodonean words, but they were spoken with grim certainty. The tramp of soldiers rang out on the garden pavers as he and Aleria slid into deeper shadow. From the sheath hidden under his tunic Hanuvar palmed one of his throwing blades, at the same time drawing a short weapon from his belt. Its hilt was shaped like that of a standard utility knife, but its metal was finer, the blade wider, thicker, and sharper.

Aleria pulled a thin knife from her hair; her dark eyes were wary, but alert rather than frightened.

Hanuvar kept his weapons low as he backed away, the woman retreating with him along a wandering path of shoulder-high hedges. Hanuvar had to waste no words for Aleria to keep to the grass on the sides of the stone path.

He knew better than to return to the fountain once more, where he might be trapped in a dead end with no exit. He could likely kill one of these opponents, but not much more when he was armed only with knives and they carried swords and wore armor, and were allegedly skilled warriors besides. He couldn't tell if all four of the bodyguards he'd previously marked were here, but there were clearly more than two.

He and Aleria slid deep down a side path. Hanuvar glimpsed the top of an ornate arched gate at its end, another exit, but too far away, for one of the Ilodoneans could be heard jogging along the walkway and veered suddenly left, toward them. Hanuvar motioned Aleria to retreat further and back stepped just the far side of a bushy oleander. The soldier came to a halt. Hanuvar knew the man could not hear the slam of his heart, nor know that he was moments from having a knife to his throat. Behind him Aleria shifted slightly and the faint creak of her sandal seemed loud as an anvil strike.

At almost the same moment a male voice rose in pain. While it descended into a gurgle, the start of a woman shrieking was quickly cut off.

Their soldier turned and jogged off toward the noise even though the sounds of the party outside the hedge garden continued without interruption.

Hanuvar motioned Aleria back the way they had come, and down a little side path with a bench.

Now they could hear Lartius pleading with Xenxes, Terror of the West, for they were separated from him only by a single thick shrubbery row. The leader of Zenith had a tense and placating tone.

"—need for any of this. I won't even hold a grudge. If you really think the timing is off, we can hold the ceremony sooner—"

Xenxes cut him off in midsentence, his accented words heavy with contempt.

"So only now does my power convince you. You're so deafened by the sound of your own importance you can't hear anyone unless they're shouting. The timing is fine. The problem is the crowd, as I keep telling you. The secrets are for me, not for them. I want no other witnesses."

"Initiates grow the power—"

"You're an idiot. You hadn't even taught those females the right notes in the chord. Tonight they will sing as I have commanded before the gate. Do you know what will happen if even the slightest thing goes wrong? My ancestors are quick to take offense."

"I apologize—"

"Your apology is offered too late. But maybe I have a role for you, after all."

Hanuvar missed the precise details of what Xenxes intended, for the soldier returned. This time there was no missing his investigation of the path beyond the oleander and back to the wall. But thinking his previous search had secured the rest of the area, he did not venture again down the side trail where Hanuvar and Aleria hid. The assasin and his companion reported in Ilodonean to their commander. Hanuvar recognized the word for "empty," and Xenxes' acknowledgment.

"Come, Lartius," Xenxes said. "I sent Torlistes to gather the women. We'll meet him in the cave and then I will show you true secrets. Not the ones you've dreamed up to parcel out to your flatterers."

They headed deeper into the garden, then could be heard exiting through a door with a creaky hinge. Hanuvar and Aleria waited until their footfalls receded, then she returned the blade to her hair and led the way to the treasure room.

Aleria stopped at the body of the young guard prostrate across its threshold. She looked down at him only briefly, likely judging from the widening blood pool and his own stillness that there was no help for him. Lifting the edge of her dress, she took a long step over the blood to reach the tiny jeweled statuettes. She immediately wrapped them in a dark blue fabric belt she untied from her waist, knotting them in a bundle at the small of her back.

Hanuvar knelt near the guard.

"He's very dead." Aleria's complacency suggested she'd seen hard sights in her time.

He had already judged the man's condition. It was the sword that interested him. It lay a foot to his right, only a finger span from the advancing blood. He lifted it, reached over the body to cut open the belt, then slid the sheath off the leather, tucked the sword home inside, and slid it into a fold of his toga.

"All they took were those Ilodonean discs," Aleria said. "Now's your chance to get that stone you want."

It wasn't his chance, at all. Xenxes had plans for the Volani vocalists, and it sounded dangerous to them. He therefore had to be stopped. Hanuvar started for the door the Ilodoneans had left by.

"Where are you going?"

"Checking on my other commission."

He padded deeper into the garden to the thick door in the archway he'd spotted earlier. It was protected by a sturdy lock and emblazoned with a forbidding sign claiming Inner Circle Members Only were permitted beyond.

The Ilodoneans hadn't bothered pulling the door completely to, though, so he opened it a crack, peering out onto a line of young cypresses.

Aleria looked over his shoulder. "That's the path to the cave. Lartius is such a showman. You can walk right around the villa to get there too."

Hanuvar opened the door and passed through. Seeing that she meant to follow he held it for her then shut it carefully, frowning at the creek of hinges. He paused to listen for any other sounds, barely hearing the distant music over the sea thrashing the cliffs beyond the trees.

"You're after the singers?" Aleria guessed.

"My buyer collects Volani cultural artifacts. Like their songs. They'll be more valuable even than the old stone."

"It doesn't seem a good time. If I were you, I'd get out, now. Someone's going to find that guard's body soon, and besides, those Ilodoneans are planning to work magic with the women. Dangerous magic, from the way things sounded."

"The women won't be of any value if they're dead. You said this ceremony was going to be conducted in the caves. That's the trail, isn't it?" He pointed to a gap in the trees and she assented.

He slipped the toga off his tunic, strapped the sword sheathe around his waist, then started ahead.

She followed a pace behind, speaking softly. "Are you really sure this is wise? Your singers aren't just going to be involved with magic. They're surrounded by capable men in armor. With swords. Who've already killed this evening."

"It certainly doesn't seem wise," Hanuvar said.

"...but you're going anyway. There are safer ways to make money."

"There certainly are," Hanuvar agreed. "Wish me luck."

Aleria sighed in frustration. "I like you, Helsa, but I thought you were smarter than this."

"I understand your assessment and I wish you well." He nodded to her and hurried on down the grassy slope beyond the cypresses. After a moment he heard the soft whisper of her sandals in the path behind him, and he glanced back to see her shaking her head, either at him or her own foolishness for following.

The sound of the surf grew louder, the scent of saltwater stronger in the air. Hanuvar spotted a man in a conical helm standing sentinel beside a screen of scraggly juniper bushes. Moonbeams flared on whitecapped waves rolling across the vast dark water beyond and below him. The Ilodonean was staring idly off to the right, and Hanuvar motioned Aleria down. Probably they'd been lost up until now against the dark backdrop of hillside between them and the villa. The moon peeped through a break in the clouds, like a great eye peering through silver blue curtains.

Aleria spoke to Hanuvar's ear. "There's old stairs carved into the cliff. He's probably standing watch at their head."

"Excellent. Do me a favor and walk over that way, as though you're taking in the view."

Her eyes measured him. "What do you mean to do?"

"Use the advantage of your distraction. If you're in danger, run, and I'll handle it."

She mulled the idea over only briefly, then sighed without sound. "Just for you, Helsa."

Aleria sauntered left at a diagonal, putting a little sway in her walk, and the sentry noticed her after only a few steps. He called out but she pretended not to hear, passing within twenty feet of him before drawing up toward his right to stare out to sea.

The sentry trailed after, expostulating and pointing toward the villa, all but the roof of which was hidden by vegetation. She turned only then, placing a hand over her breasts in surprise.

Hanuvar came in from behind at a good clip, thinking his sound was hidden by the surf, but this sentry was no fool. He whirled when Hanuvar was eight paces out and drew a long blade.

Hanuvar's thrown knife caught the guard in an armored shoulder, for the veteran had noted the swift movement and swung away. Pulling his other knife free as he ran, Hanuvar was on him with the villa guard's sword, a sharp, well-balanced gladius.

The sentry struck first, for his reach was longer. Hanuvar caught the blow with his knife high in its swing, but the man slid back from Hanuvar's sword thrust.

What then followed was the swift, silent work of professional killers.

The sentry may have been keenly alert to Hanuvar's movements but let himself be steered too close to the cliff. They exchanged feint and counterthrust, well matched until Aleria dashed a few steps closer, waving her arms. The sentry was startled for only a moment, but it was enough. Hanuvar beat his opponent's blade out of line and then kicked his calf.

The sentry yelled as he dropped eighty feet toward the surf, crashing against sharp rocks. The sound was lost against the roar of the waves, and the sea swallowed him.

Hanuvar scanned the narrow stairway descending along the left, hugging the cliff until it reached a cave opening halfway toward the foaming sea. Light from within shone dully on the rocky lip before it. He saw no sign of other guards.

Aleria joined him. "Is that what you meant to do?" she whispered mordantly.

"I'd hoped to subdue and question him. You were a perfect distraction."

"I must be losing my touch," she said. "Or maybe I'm just not his type."

"He was probably just a good soldier." Hanuvar discovered the dead man's cloak draped over a boulder, and tossed it over his shoulders. "I'll handle it from here."

"You're really going through with this? Just for the singers?"

"I am. It's going to be far more dangerous here on out. You should stay. Take in some of that nice food."

He started down the steep, narrow steps, concentrating upon the terrain in the darkness, rather than the light illuminating the mouth of the cave. Meeting it directly would ruin his night vision. It was a shame the sentry had held onto his weapon as he fell, because Hanuvar would have liked a longer blade.

A shadow passed in front of the light source, throwing darkness across the narrow ledge where the stairs met the cave mouth. Though Hanuvar advanced with stealth, assisted by the roar of the surf, this guard, too, was unfortunately quite alert, and moved out onto the ledge just in time to see Hanuvar descending from four paces up.

The sentry called a challenge in Ilodonean. Hanuvar pointed a thumb over his shoulder as though he had something to report, then leapt the final flight.

The sentinel reached too late for his sword, only clearing half of his before Hanuvar's gladius slashed down through a leather shoulder guard and drove through bone. The sentinel's cry of pain was stilled when Hanuvar followed immediately with a punch to the throat. While the man put both hands up to his neck Hanuvar had time to reposition and drive the point of the gladius through his opponent's mouth. He caught the convulsing body and dragged it into the cave with him. While the soldier died, Hanuvar scanned the surroundings, struck by their unexpected gaudiness, then traded out his gladius and its sheath for the Ilodonean's better sword and scabbard, a twin to the one used by the first man to fall. He tried on the helmet, too, but found it too small. The shield and spear leaning a few feet inside the rocky passage were welcome, though. He slipped one over his arm and lifted the other.

A lantern well back from the door illuminated the entry way and a tunnel beyond. The passage appeared to have been broadened by human implements, for ancient pick and chisel marks were visible, though the stone itself practically sparkled with cleanliness. Lartius must have detailed a phalanx of slaves to scrub these walls regularly. Pointed glyphs had been recently drawn with yellow paint alive with lantern light. The symbols were reminiscent of those he'd seen in the ruined city Calenius had been excavating a day north of here, and Hanuvar frowned in recognition.

He heard Aleria whisper his assumed name behind him, informing him she was there.

"I thought you didn't want to come," he said without turning.

"There's that Hadiran line about cats and curiosity."

"About how it gets them killed? It's not safe here, Aleria."

There was a smile in her voice, and only the slightest hint that it was strained. "After seeing you in action, I'm inclined to think it's safer near you than anywhere else. I knew you had to have been a legion man. Maybe even some kind of elite bodyguard. That's it, isn't it?"

"I've been a soldier all my life," Hanuvar said. "There may be treasure here, but I wouldn't count on it. And if there's sorcery, I may not be able to stop it." He turned into the passage. She came after, as he expected. They moved quietly on and arrived at a roughly oval chamber covered in a wild profusion of carvings. These walls too had been carefully cleaned, so brightly polished they practically glowed, and these symbols had likewise been filled in with yellow paint. Two bright lanterns threw ruddy light from their crumbling niches out onto the walls and the sandy floor was swept clean and level.

A slender corridor extended further.

"That hall wasn't here before," Aleria said, and then, to Hanuvar's look, she smiled. "I'm thorough." She indicated a pair of the Ilodonean discs, each set into a round recess at head height to the sides of the tunnel's opening. "You recognize those, don't you? They were taken from the treasure room. This entry was flat stone before."

Hanuvar considered the discs and the wall, and searched the sides and ceiling above the passage, where a tiny lip of stone depended from the height. He saw no winch or pulley or hinge, but it appeared as though the stone had been taken up into the ceiling. Sorcery. He frowned.

"What do you suppose they're doing down there?" Aleria asked.

"They seek something worth killing over. But that doesn't make it valuable to you."

"You knew I was wanting you to suggest treasure. But they were talking about power and secrets."

"Secrets are only valuable to the right people," Hanuvar said. "Who might not like anyone left to know what they are." Sword sheathed at his side, spear ready, Hanuvar preceded her into the darkness and the steep, downward sloping tunnel. A faint point of illumination shone ahead. He walked slowly, senses stretched taut. The smell of the surf had long since receded, but he grew conscious of the scent of wet stone and salt water and algae. This passage must somehow connect with the waters of the coast. A hundred paces on, their way opened into an enormous cylinder carved out of the stone stretching above into darkness and below, where it terminated in a circular reservoir of still water. To Hanuvar's reckoning, this inner pool was lower than the sea outside. Stairs circled down along the smooth, curving wall to a wide ledge of stone beside the water.

The only light sources were two lanterns hung in slime-covered niches on either side of a wide recess. That light caught gleams in the still water and burnished points along the helms and armor of Xenxes and one of his crimson-clad bodyguards holding Lartius by the elbow near a square post of stone about as high as the lectern once graced by the carved image of Varis in the Dervan's trophy room. The three Volani singers huddled protectively nearby. Hanuvar could not find the other guard, who surely must be lurking out of sight.

While Lartius pleaded with Xenxes not to go through with it, whatever *it* was, Hanuvar headed down the stairs in the darkness. Algae and slick film coated the steps, as with long submersion, along with a profusion of barnacles.

Lartius continued addressing Xenxes. Hanuvar heard him whining about misunderstanding in the echoing place, before Xenxes cut him off. Here, the Ilodonean's voice was loud and certain. "Put your hands to the stone, or I will beat you."

Another voice interrupted him, speaking Ilodonean, and Hanuvar spotted what he supposed was the fourth guard stepping from an alcove in the wall beyond the lectern. This man had removed armor to don a dark tunic with silver filagree. He lifted a third Ilodonean disk, blazing with light the shade of blood.

"Prince," Lartius said. "Please accept my apology. Can't we get a slave for this? One of these women?"

"I need the women," Xenxes said. "I do not need you." He signaled, and the soldier gripped the Dervan's arm and dragged him to the pedestal, smacking him hard across the face when he resisted. The guard then forced both the aristocrat's hands onto the surface and leveraged something down across his wrists before stepping back. Hanuvar saw that a bar of stone seemed to have locked the Zenith leader's hands in place, no matter that he tugged.

"You said you wanted power," Xenxes cried. "Here leaders of old communed with the power of the deep! Together we shall see what secrets the ancients worked so hard to keep hidden!"

Only then did Hanuvar observe glyphs carved on these walls, too, for they took up a pulsing crimson glow as the robed Ilodonean placed the final disc on the pedestal's front. Its light repeatedly flashed down upon the water, a heartbeat across the inky deeps. The man in the robe pulled a hand drum from his garments and beat it in time with the pulse. The sound echoed tinnily through the vast space.

The noise concealed the scrapes of Hanuvar's descent. He was within good spear range now, but thought it best to wait so he could charge in the follow-up. So far the three Ilodoneans had other matters keeping them occupied.

Xenxes put a hand to his ornate sword hilt and faced the Volani women. "Now it's your turn. Sing and hold the notes I taught you."

The women shifted nervously.

"You heard me!" Xenxes' hand rose threateningly. "Sing!"

Weakly their voices rose, one by one, forming a dark chord.

Xenxes waved them on and they grew more certain they were doing as he wished, and so raised their volume, then at a signal from the prince shifted to a second chord that held unresolved and unpleasant.

Hanuvar thought himself finally close enough to act. The wall lay on his left side, leaving his dominant hand free. In it he grasped the spear. It was a little heavier than those he was used to, and designed more for stabbing than throwing, but having carried it and tested its heft as he walked, he thought he could gauge its capabilities.

He would liked to have dropped Xenxes, or the other warrior, but rather than risking a cast in the dim against men in armor, he sent it to a softer target and caught the robed man in his chest.

The Ilodonean cried out, clawed at the weapon's haft, then sank onto the stone. His drum bounced off the stone ledge and struck the water. The remaining guard shouted in anger and started up the stairs, spear in hand. Hanuvar closed to meet him.

Xenxes shouted at the women. "I didn't tell you to stop. Keep singing!" They instead backed as far along the ledge as they were able.

Like the other Ilodoneans, the approaching soldier proved aggressive and certain. As soon as he was within range he jabbed at Hanuvar's calves. Hanuvar slammed the spear blade with the long Ilodonean sword, planted a foot on a clear spot he'd noted on the stair below, and bashed the man's wrist with his shield.

The soldier stepped back, sliding on the scummy stairs, and Hanuvar caught him in the face with a kick. The Ilodonean slid off the steps, flailing for purchase, and struck the rocky lip with a cracking thud, helmet first. His body flopped into the water.

Hanuvar advanced with care even as Xenxes, frantic now, shouted at the singers with sword raised. The prince rightly feared a spell disturbed in mid casting.

The Volani lifted their chins in defiance and the shorter of the three insulted his ancestry, though the prince likely didn't know their language. Lartius struggled more furiously in the stone cuffs confining him, cursing at the women to help.

Xenxes let out what sounded like an oath and turned toward Hanuvar, almost in resignation. The dark steel of his blade caught the light of the blood-red wall glyphs, now pulsing ominously, as though governed by a monster heart. "Fool! I am Xenxes, Terror of the West!"

Hanuvar was generally disposed to be unimpressed by men who shouted their sobriquets, but the prince continued his apparently practiced self-introduction. "I wear the helm of Iskandros the Great! My shield was carried by Hundara when he advanced against his usurpers! And my sword is that borne by the matchless Yriak!"

Hanuvar left the final stair and emerged onto the curving stone ledge at last, slippery as the stairs. "But I have the sword of Hanuvar."

Xenxes' voice rose in fury. "You're a fool to mock me! That's one of the swords my men were carrying!"

He waited for a retort, but Hanuvar saved his breath.

"Prepare yourself! I am done with the preening arrogance of you fools from the young kingdoms! You shall see what it's like to face a warrior of best bloodline, wearing the finest armament in the world!" Xenxes raised the shield. A distinct ratcheting noise emerged from it as he advanced, and then a spray of tiny pebbles streamed out from an aperture high in its rim.

Hanuvar backstepped. Most of the little rocks fell short. The rest rebounded with a clang from his lifted shield. He slashed as he stepped forward.

Xenxes hopped back, sliding a little but not faltering, and Hanuvar came at him with a flurry of swings. Aleria shouted for the singers to hurry and climb to her. The scarred one spared a sympathetic look for Lartius, then urged the others past the combatants and up the stairwell.

Ominously, the shining pulse of the disc's ruddy light increased its tempo.

Xenxes retreated. A circular shape high on his helm tilted down and this time glittering dust spewed forth. Probably it was meant to blind but it was activated too far away; Xenxes in any case ruined the effect by shouting and charging.

Hanuvar ducked and slid left, taking the slash of Xenxes' sword on his shield. His back now was to the alcove so that he had a good view when a clawed white hand reached up from watery depths. It slapped the stone, and a second struck the verge a moment later, just as a spiny frill crested the still water and rose, dripping. It topped the head of a melded nightmare of ape and fish, with scales in place of fur, and staring bulbous black eyes. Lartius screamed as the thing climbed the rest of the way out of water with a croaking roar and straightened beside him. Only then was its true size made manifest, for it towered a full sword length over the Dervan, whose full-throated scream intensified until the thing reached out long spiny arms, cupped his face in taloned fingers, and casually ripped off his head.

Xenxes backed further off, shield upraised, sword warding. Hanuvar had nothing to gain either by pursuing the prince or attacking the beast, so retreated to the stairs. Xenxes addressed the corpse-colored monster as it raised the severed head and let blood drip into its fanged mouth. Hanuvar's Ilodonean was too poor to understand his words, but Xenxes' tone was tentative, which suggested the sea beast might have been unexpected.

Hanuvar reached the stairs and started up as fast as he dared, attention alternating between the drama below and the terrible footing.

Dripping a mix of water and blood, the thing raised its finned head and sniffed toward Xenxes, who jabbed his sword in Hanuvar's direction as his voice rose in command.

The thing turned and its protruding black eyes seemed to lock onto Hanuvar, circling above on the stairs built into the wall. It then turned once more to the prince. It snorted, then sprang at him. Xenxes swung to face the thing, sword pointed over the shield. It was a classic defensive stance, well executed.

The monstrosity cared not a whit. It grabbed hold of the shield of Hundara and lifted it into the air, the protesting prince along with it. The beast then flung both into the wall. The collision of armored man against stone produced both a smack and a clang. Xenxes cried out in pain, and then the thing lifted him by both legs and slapped him screaming again and again into the wall until he could make no sound.

It was then the red pulsing light ceased and the water level climbed. This was no steady creep, but a vast surge as though an immense pump was being worked. In a span of three of Hanuvar's steps it had risen ten feet, roiling as it came.

Hanuvar threw away his shield and dared to increase his speed. Multiple body lengths of stairs still turned above. He cast off the sword and his cloak but it was too little, and when he was ten feet from the top the water swept him up.

He fought just to stay afloat, striving to remain close to the wall even as the currents pulled him away.

Finally the seawater ceased its rise, just shy of the platform where a wide-eyed Aleria and the singers awaited him, frantically calling his assumed name. He struck out for them, felt solid ground beneath his feet and splashed up the final four stairs, submerged now by the waves.

Something grabbed his ankle in a vise grip.

Had he time to think he would have known that the strength of the thing that had come up under him was too great to fight. But he reacted with skills and instincts honed from a hundred battles, turning and sighting his target and striking at almost the same time. There was the finned head and its protruding fish eyes, there was the fanged mouth; stretched up ahead of it was an arm and a pale white hand, lightly scaled and elongated, but human enough in form he knew just where to drive his knife point before the grip on his leg tightened.

He'd struck the proper nerve; the hand released him and he scrambled to retain purchase on the tiny bit of land that represented life. A shriek rang out as a second clawed hand raked a blow across his thigh that nearly slammed him down. He struggled to his feet as the creature roared its rage, and pulled itself onto the stone surface while Hanuvar passed with Aleria into the long hallway, the two of them running at full strength. She'd already shouted the singers forward, and they were halfway down the hall. From too close behind came the pad of large wet feet, and bellows-like breaths.

The moment they reached the circular room, Hanuvar spun and yanked a shining Ilodonean disk from the side of the doorway.

Instantly a slab of stone grated down from the ceiling. Aleria pulled the second disc free but it did nothing to accelerate the slow fall of the curving barrier. The determined sea thing slopped on, the sound of its chase echoing toward them. Hanuvar saw one of its webbed feet sliding forward just before the door slammed home at last.

Only then did Hanuvar realize how heavily he himself breathed. He paused and leaned against the side of the wall, as blood and water stained the sand around his feet. He registered the sting of cuts along his thigh and various other scrapes he must have accumulated in the mad scramble for the ledge. Beside him, Aleria gasped too.

"No treasure," Hanuvar said.

Aleria patted his shoulder. "We've got these discs." Her eyes swept to the door, alert perhaps for signs of it opening behind them. Then she met his eyes, her look uncharacteristically serious. "I'm not sure I've ever seen anything braver than what you did tonight."

"Or as stupid," he suggested.

She chuckled.

"You're the brave one," he said, thinking of how she had continued to come after, for no good reason other than friendship.

"Oh, I was never in real danger. Those young women must really mean a lot to you."

"My client will pay a lot for them," he said.

"He'd better! Who is he?"

Hanuvar chuckled. "You wouldn't believe me."

"It's Hanuvar, isn't it? You're working for him, aren't you?"

"What makes you say that?"

"I'm no fool," she said. "And everyone knows he had spies all over the place."

"They must not be good spies, if everyone knows."

She looked sidelong at him.

They found the three Volani waiting at the mouth of the cave. The scarred one had picked up the gladius he'd left beside the body of the second Ilodonean he'd killed. Though tentative, they greeted Hanuvar and Aleria with relief, thanking both in broken Dervan.

"Oh, thank him, not me," Aleria said.

Hanuvar needed no thanks. He spoke to them in Dervan. "We can leave now."

Aleria peered around the corner at the stairs along the cliff. "Still clear," she said. "But we'd best get moving." She likely feared that the rest of the Zenith initiates might still intend to descend when the moon was highest. She started up at a swift pace.

Hanuvar gestured for the women to precede him. They eyed him in a mix of curiosity and apprehension. "Don't worry," he said, this time in Volani. "Things will be much better for you here on out. I'll get you into the household of a kinswoman, where you'll be freed. We must keep our plans to ourselves until we are away from my stylish friend."

They blinked in astonishment but didn't seem quite capable of digesting their change of fortune. Probably they had witnessed one too many surprises over the course of the last hour.

"Thank you," the scarred one said finally. "We can never thank you enough. Your Volani is excellent," she added.

"I've been speaking it a long time," Hanuvar said, and then the four of them advanced into the moonlight and up to freedom.

※ ※ ※

The three women were quiet and uneasy until they arrived at Izivar's villa early the next morning, where they were feted by the staff. In coming days they would be encouraged to sing as often as possible, but by then they already understood that Hanuvar's promises were reliable. Their presence helped to reassure the youngest Volani children and their caretakers, who soon arrived from Amelia's villa. I think Amelia would have preferred moving all of her charges at once, so careful was she of their safety, but we could not accommodate them in so large a group without drawing notice.

No one but us knew the true fate of Lartius. Many suspected agents of the state had led him away to hidden dungeons. Some thought he was on a secret mission with the Ilodoneans who'd vanished at the same time, though no one could adequately explain why one of their number had been found lying in his own blood within the initiation cave. Lesser hands took up the writing of Lartius' conspiracy booklets but his family divested themselves of its trappings, including the religious artifacts, which they sold in auction later in the summer. I managed to acquire the Volani piece for Izivar, and went down the steps to the hidden cave while bidding for other items was underway. So fine was the seal that I could not find the opening to the tunnel where the beast had chased Hanuvar and Aleria. I was studying the niches where the Ilodonean discs must have sat when a surly family retainer chased me from the site.

But as to the days immediately following the recovery of the singers, Izivar returned the next week from seeing to the preparation of quarters for the children in Selanto. After permitting her ship's crew a day of rest, she sent them north with their precious cargo and contacted Amelia to coordinate the transfer of the next group. I think that she and Izivar were too different to grow truly close, but I was to learn in later years that they became fond of one another. Amelia had apparently insisted Calenius close off the tunnels once he finished his exploration.

Amelia asked her son-in-law's family if she might stay at one of their villas along the coast near Apicius, thinking she might employ the place as another waypoint for the Volani children. Her grandchildren, she said, hoped to spend some time along the shore.

One of them was to do so very soon, although she was not to have the sort of beachside experience sought by most Dervan families.

—Sosilos, Book Twelve

Chapter 3:
Monsters on the Shore

I

Tens of thousands of the little crabs scuttled out of the foaming surf in the half hour before dawn, their hard white bodies radiant with phosphorescence. As they frenzied across the dark sands, their tiny glowing claws waved warning to rivals and enticement to mates.

Ciprion had never seen anything like it, and watched with interest greater than he'd anticipated, though it could not approach the awed regard of his granddaughter, nine-year-old Calvia, or of her young companion, Delmar, the son of her tutor. The two children gabbled at one another excitedly and stared and pointed to various features of the tableau that confirmed their previous learning or sparked new lines of inquiry. Even Ciprion's guards, who'd risen in foul spirits for the early hour walk into darkness, watched with undisguised curiosity.

This portion of the coast was reputedly home to monsters, and while Ciprion didn't have any particular anxiety about Oscani legends, his wife Amelia had insisted he be wary for any danger, including assassins, so he'd brought a quartet of sturdy veterans. Ciprion was glad for the extra eyes so he could appreciate the delight of his young charges.

Calvia and Delmar were on loan from his daughter Cornelia's household. Amelia had suggested Calvia visit them at the coastal property while the little girl's younger brother was on a trip with their father. Calvia had arrived with her tutor, Silenus, and a trio of large chests mostly filled with scrolls she frequently consulted. She didn't avoid her tutor like most children, instead treating him like a walking reference library she queried constantly. It was Silenus who'd proposed the morning's expedition, but a bad stomach had laid him low last night after dinner, probably owing to the immense number of oysters he'd downed.

Ciprion's granddaughter considered Silenus' amiable son an assistant scholar, and over the last two days the pair had inspected rocks to compare types of moist vegetation and waded into pools to examine the slippery or scuttley little creatures that dwelt there. The little boy was a surprisingly capable artist, and one of Calvia's chests was stuffed with his sketches of leaves and tree trunks annotated with her meticulous observations.

The curly-haired boy was staring off to the right while Calvia declaimed about the crabs in a rapturous voice. "Grandfather, look how the males' luminescence pattern diminishes along their echinated carapaces, enhancing the radiance of their smoother chelae!"

His granddaughter's fascination with large words had less to do with attempts to impress and more to do with her desire for precision. He approved of the latter. "The claws certainly are the brightest body part," he said. "Do you think the females prefer the little fellows with the greatest contrast?"

She nodded enthusiastically and leaned against the tall walking staff she'd brought with her. The staff was an affectation[8] of her tutor, but she had declared herself the scientific leader of the expedition in his place and he had indulgently waved his permission to take it as her sign of office as he shuffled back to his sickroom. "Silenus predicts their larger cousins will emerge from the estuaries later this week to burrow here. Can we come back? He said they sometimes attract larger sea predators. I should like to observe those too."

Ciprion readied himself to argue that idea down; he didn't wish to convince Amelia about the safety of a follow-up journey that would expressly bring the monsters that had worried her about this one.

Delmar wandered further to the right, near a heavy boulder just beyond the scurrying crabs.

---

[8] "Affectation" is inaccurate and somewhat unkind of Antires, given that he knew the elder Silenus and the unpredictable timing of his recurring foot pains. It is possible Antires sought concision over precision in this instance. —*Silenus*

"What's this?" he asked, and crouched down. He then let out a mouselike squeak and straightened.

A dark man-shape heaved up from the sand beside the boy. Fear must have frozen Delmar to the spot, for he could easily have sprinted clear. The figure's hand landed on his shoulder and tightened there.

Ciprion was already in motion, two men flanking him, hands on swords. "Easy," he told them. He didn't want the boy endangered. Calvia had stiffened anxiously.

It was hard to see much detail of the person who held Delmar; Ciprion made out a lean figure with long hair. It spoke with a woman's voice. Her Dervan had a thick Volani accent. "Leave me now," she said. "I don't want to hurt the boy."

"Let him go," Ciprion ordered, "and then we can talk."

Almost on the instant, the boy wriggled loose and dashed toward Calvia. The woman snatched after him, but her two steps were wobbly. Ciprion's guards started for her but he hissed them back, because they were drawing swords. "Hold!"

They stopped just out of weapon range. The stranger had brandished something as well, a small blade she shifted from target to target as she swayed. She was either drunk or injured, and her voice was not slurred, so Ciprion judged the latter.

"Lower your weapon," he ordered.

Whatever she said then was low voiced and he could not understand it. He trotted to Calvia, put hand to her walking staff, received her nod of approval, and took it. He returned to the woman.

Her attention shifted constantly between the two warriors, one to either side of her.

"I think you need help," Ciprion said. "But we can't help so long as you're threatening us."

She said something about Dervans in Volani that sounded like a curse, and waved her knife.

Ciprion moved toward her himself, imagining what his wife would say to see him walking toward a knife-bearing lunatic. But he had judged his opponent's condition aptly. She staggered as she tried to face him, and then he struck with the walking staff.

She saw his attack coming, but could not shift out of the way quickly enough. The blow slammed her calf, and, unsteady as she was, she dropped on the instant. When she hit the ground she lost hold of her knife, which flew backward to strike a boulder and ricocheted into the darkness.

In an instant his men were on her.

Ciprion urged them to be gentle. "She's wounded," he said, "and may be addled."

"She sounded Volani," Horatius said. He'd served with Ciprion since the invasion of Biranus.

"We'll see."

The woman offered no resistance as Horatius reached her and put hand to her weapon arm. She only groaned. It wasn't until they brought her nearer the lantern that he saw she was in her midtwenties, an athletic young woman in a sky blue garment more tunic than stola length, with soldier's boots. Her forehead was flush, though her limbs were icy, and her face was bruised. A blood-stained cloth bound one bicep.

"We'll carry her back to the villa to tend her. Calvia, I'm afraid the expedition's over. This woman needs our help."

His granddaughter watched the events too intently to bother with a response, although she accepted the return of the walking staff. Delmar stood stock still beside her, and Ciprion patted the little boy's head. "Are you all right?"

Delmar looked up with shining eyes. His voice was small. "Yes, sir."

"I don't think she really meant to hurt anyone," Ciprion told him. "She was just frightened. You were a brave lad."

"Is she going to be all right?" Delmar asked.

"Hopefully she'll be on the mend soon," Ciprion said. "We will call for a physician." And, he thought, for Hanuvar.

II

The woman lay on a pallet in a windowed room off the courtyard of a villa owned by an uncle of Ciprion's son-in-law. By the time Hanuvar arrived, evening was well on its way to night, and tapers lit the space. One burned in a sconce just to the right of her bed, throwing his shadow on the wall, where it merged with that of Antires, beside him so that they seemed one body with two heads.

She had been bathed and cleaned and combed and dressed in a simple sleeveless gown of the sort worn by many women her age across the Inner Sea. A nasty wound had sliced deep into her left upper arm. Ciprion said it had been cleaned, and that it was too late to sew it closed, though Hanuvar could see the latter from the swelling and bruising when he inspected the bandage. He had also seen an Eltyr tattoo upon her other arm, which identified her as a member of the warrior order even if he hadn't recognized her on sight.[9]

He would have liked to have asked her what she was doing here, but her eyes were closed and Ciprion reported she had not yet regained consciousness, at least not to do much more than mumble unintelligibly as she had been washed.

Hanuvar reached out to feel her forehead. The old Herrene who'd left when Hanuvar entered the room had lifted a wet cloth from her hairline, and it had left her moist. "She was alone?" Hanuvar asked.

"Yes. Additional footmarks would have been obvious on that stretch of beach." Ciprion had been watching him carefully. "You know her, don't you."

"I do."

"Who is she?"

"Elistala Laecanlis, an Eltyr officer." He took his hand from the wounded woman. "But she sailed with me to New Volanus before the last war. I haven't seen her since and she shouldn't be here." Though fairly certain they could not be overheard, as Ciprion had assured the young woman was tended in the most secure part of the house suitable for an invalid, he kept his voice soft.

Ciprion's heavy eyebrows drew together. He opened his mouth as if to speak, then closed it and waited. His health had improved since Hanuvar had encountered him in the provinces last year, when it seemed difficulties had prematurely aged him. His life was hardly without worries at present, for he was now one of the emperor's closest advisors. But the responsibilities seemed to have invigorated him. He even carried himself like a slightly younger man. His thick crop of dark brown hair and prominent eyebrows were only lightly dusted with gray, and he retained his athletic build.

---

[9] The Eltyr corps is often represented by the symbol of a half-circle above a horizontal line, contained within an arch, symbolic of an ocean moonrise viewed though the Volanus River Gate, where the Eltyr were originally stationed. —*Silenus*

Hanuvar glanced to the door, which remained closed, then shifted his attention to the sturdy latticed window permitting fresh air from the grounds. The sky beyond was fading to violet.

"What was she doing on an Oscani beach, alone?" Antires asked. He'd surely known Hanuvar would explain that, but unlike Ciprion, he hadn't been able to restrain his eagerness.

"I can only speculate." He provided details mostly for Ciprion's sake, for Antires knew much of what he was about to say. "I was on board a ship returning to Volanus when I learned the city was under attack. I went to help; I ordered the ship to turn back. It would have taken news to New Volanus of what our scout told us." He did not explain further that the scout had been Eledeva, the great asalda who had borne him through the air to their dying city while the vessel turned to reverse course.

Ciprion and Antires waited.

Hanuvar continued. "Long weeks passed before I sent the first ship of freed people back to New Volanus. I sent another vessel a little later, with a band of Eltyr. I instructed the crews of both to avoid the empire until I sent further word."

"You didn't want their help?" Ciprion's eyebrows rose.

"I needed far more help than they could give, and of a different sort."

Ciprion nodded. "You think this young woman returned on a ship trying to find you."[10]

"I doubt it."

Ciprion rubbed at the beard hairs stubbling his chin. "There's been an increase in pirate activity in the region. I don't know if you've heard. Some of their raids have freed slaves." He did not ask if Hanuvar was involved, although there was a question in his look.

"It's interfered with some of our own recovery efforts," Hanuvar replied.

---

[10] You will note that neither Ciprion nor Hanuvar speculated that Elistala's presence here had been prompted by either of the the two Volani ships dispatched to New Volanus earlier that summer. It would have been obvious to Hanuvar that not enough time had passed for this woman to have arrived from New Volanus in response to those more recent emigrees. He had not confided to Ciprion the coordinates of New Volanus, but their level of trust and the almost uncanny understanding between the two men—both of them geniuses in the same field—translated into an unspoken confidence in providing information necessary for, as Ciprion once described it to me, knowing the lay of a battlefield. Since Hanuvar did not offer that condition as a possibility, Ciprion apparently understood that it did not merit inquiry. —*Silenus*

Ciprion nodded in confirmation and said nothing more. He never inquired deeply into Hanuvar's activities.

"Do you think she was involved in those raids?" Antires asked. "Some of the ones who vanished were Volani."

Hanuvar thought it likely, but there was no way to know for certain. "It might be."

Ciprion frowned down at the battered young woman as if she were a puzzle he hoped to solve. It was not that he lacked compassion, but Hanuvar understood his friend was ever seeking answers to the next challenges that might arise, a quality they shared.

"I know the physician said she might not make it, but she looks like a survivor to me," Ciprion said. "I'd bet we'll have answers by tomorrow." The healer had actually given Elistala a fair chance of recovery, but conveyed that he would feel better about her odds if her fever broke.

"Good physicians never over promise," Antires said. It was a Herrenic saying.

"Do you think she might have something to do with your daughter?"

Hanuvar had wondered about it. There were various possible scenarios, but not enough information necessary to inform likelihood. "I'm not sure I can hope for that."

"We'll care for her as best we can," Ciprion assured him. "Why not guest with us tonight? Our conversation would have to be discreet over dinner; many of the staff here are my son-in-law's people. But we could speak more openly in the library after we eat."

"Fine company among fine books," Hanuvar said. "It will be a pleasure."

"Before we can move to more pleasant activities, I'm afraid I've bad tidings." Ciprion paused, and continued with regret. "Legate Aquilius of the revenants has grown obsessed with finding you. He means to restore Enarius' faith in his corps by proving the reports of your survival have been true. He's gotten hold of special hounds he means to use to track you."

Hanuvar didn't like the sound of that.

"How special?" Antires asked.

"He was smugly vague, and Enarius cut him off before I could learn any details. The emperor told him he'd see the revenants disbanded unless they focus their efforts upon the Cerdians, like he'd ordered, but I don't think Aquilius will heed him. Three young men in charge of a large dog were travelling south on the same ship with me. It didn't take much effort to get them boasting about its prowess and their honor as newly inducted revenants to be delivering the animal to their superiors here in the Oscanus region. I worried that the revenants might somehow have been alerted to your presence, but apparently such hounds are being sent to revenant groups throughout Tyvol."

Hanuvar would have liked to have learned more about the capabilities of the animals, but knew Ciprion had shared all he knew. "I thank you for the warning."

"This region's revenants lack a reputation for results, so I don't know that you'll have much trouble from them."

Hanuvar's own sources had reported much the same information.

"What brought you to Apicius, Senator?" Antires asked. "I thought you'd be helping plan for the war with Cerdia."

"I am. The emperor wants me to inspect our port fortifications here."

"Surely he doesn't think the Cerdians will try a sea invasion."

"He's not sure what they'll try, but our naval security has been neglected for the last decade as our forces scattered to the provinces." He didn't mention that their defeat of the great Volani sea power had diminished perceived need for strong maritime defenses.

"Will he be sending you to the front?"

"My wife has requested otherwise, through her own formidable channels, and for now the emperor seems content to leave Aminius in charge." Ciprion's mouth twisted dourly.

It was easy for Hanuvar to guess why his friend may be unhappy with that state of affairs: "Aminius will use any success to bolster his reputation with the army, and the people of your empire."

His friend bobbed his head in agreement. "I don't want to see Aminius succeed in any way, and neither does Amelia. But then we don't want the legions led to their deaths, either. My brother and my old friend Laelius are on Aminius' staff, and both have sound judgment. Laelius has a good head for tactics if Aminius is willing to hear him out."

"Probably he won't be," Hanuvar said. "Everyone knows how loyal Laelius is to you."

"Yes. But maybe the Cerdians will—"

Ciprion fell silent as sandaled footsteps drew close through the courtyard. He looked over to the door as he anticipated the loud rap delivered a moment later.

"Yes?"

Hanuvar recognized the voice of the house steward who'd conducted him into the villa. The man's tone was pressured. "Senator, some revenants are here. They're in the atrium."

"You let them in?" Ciprion's voice rose in approbation.

"They forced their way once I opened the door, Senator," the man objected apologetically.

"Keep them there." Ciprion scowled. "I'll be along shortly."

"Yes, Senator."

Ciprion listened to his retreating footsteps, then faced Hanuvar and Antires. "You should leave. I must have an informant in the household."

"An informant who knows who I am?" Hanuvar asked.

"Impossible. Amelia and I never speak of it."

"Then we should stay. Because if there's an informant, they'll tell the revenants we were here, and our departure will be more suspicious." His eyes dropped to Elistala. "They've come for her."

Ciprion's voice was clipped with anger. "They shall not have her."

Hanuvar appreciated his sentiment.

"Let's go meet the vipers." Ciprion opened the doors and strode through the courtyard for the main entrance.

Antires arched his eyebrows. Though he too appeared uneasy, it was easy to see that the younger man was excited to be present. He followed Hanuvar after Ciprion.

Three of the dreaded witch hunters stood inside the atrium facing the rangy, nervous steward, each garbed in their full accoutrements, with black lacquer breastplates over dark tunics. Skull-faced emblems shone on the front plate of their ebon-plumed helms, and a nearby lantern raised bloody glints from the grinning skulls on their signet rings. Short swords in black sheaths hung at their waists. Likely for dramatic effect they had placed the tallest and most broad shouldered member of their band to their rear, where he towered over the two average-sized men in front.

Neither of the giant's jowly companions would have looked

especially impressive or threatening without their uniforms. Hanuvar recognized the pair from his reports as Eprius and Casca, both said to rarely be glimpsed in their armor. He'd heard these two had little interest in their avowed duties and preferred to wax fat on food, guzzle wine, and loll about in a rent-free million sesterce villa with a sea view ostensibly provided by the magistrate in thanks for their service. They had to have known the gifts were bribes, but seemed perfectly pleased to return the abundant favors by rarely intruding into local affairs.

Apparently today was different. The two smiled effusively at Ciprion's gruff greeting.

"Ah, Senator, it is such an honor." Eprius' voice was almost lilting. His smile crinkled toward the black mole on his cheek.

"Indeed," Casca agreed. His lips were large, wide, and somehow frog-like, though his voice was smooth as a Ceori bard's. "We had heard of your recent arrival. It is truly humbling to be in your presence."

"We hope that you will convey our regards to the emperor." Eprius turned his smile to Hanuvar. "And who might you be?"

"This is a security consultant," Ciprion said.

"How curious," Eprius said, turning to his companion. "Don't you think it's curious that Ciprion requires a security consultant?"

"These are dangerous times," Casca allowed smoothly. "And who is this other fellow?"

"A secretary," Ciprion replied. "What brings you here today?"

Eprius' smile had not dimmed in the least. "We've grown aware that you have a prisoner in your household."

"I have no prisoners."

Casca chuckled indulgently. "Come, Senator. We've learned that your granddaughter was menaced by a woman speaking Volani, and that you subdued her."

Eprius lifted his hands as if offering a trophy. "How appropriate that the conqueror of Hanuvar be on hand to defeat another Volani threat!"

He and Casca laughed together. The third revenant was solemn as stone, and had not yet shown a single reaction to the conversation. Hanuvar kept his expression carefully bland. He trusted his friend to manage the revenants.

"The horse gains feathers and wings as it flees the stable," Ciprion said. To the blank look from the revenants he added: "It's a Nuvaran proverb."

"He's well read, too," Eprius said to Casca.

"Isn't he, though?"

"The incident has grown in the telling," Ciprion explained crisply. "The woman didn't menace my granddaughter; she could scarcely stand upright because she's ill. In her fever she has mumbled many times, with some utterances sounding like Volani. She is in poor shape, and may not live."

"All the more reason for us to take possession of her now," Eprius said reasonably. "While we might still get information from her."

Casca's eyes were suddenly cool. "If Ciprion wasn't concerned about her, what were you called in for, consultant? Decius, isn't it? My guess is that it's because you handle security for the emperor's Volani darling in Apicius."

Casca had expected to alarm with that statement, but Hanuvar was actually reassured that his cover identity as Izivar's security officer remained intact. The informer in this household might well have learned Ciprion had dispatched a messenger to Izivar's household. So Hanuvar answered as a Dervan who was unimpressed with the revenant's level of knowledge. "The senator told me his own Volani was rusty and asked for someone with a deeper knowledge of the language."

Casca addressed his companion. "It's curious he did not ask for Izivar Lenereva herself."

"Decius came with her recommendation," Ciprion said.

"That fact that you were curious about her words suggests that the woman spoke more Volani than you implied," Eprius said.

"She also addressed me in Dervan, and when she was more lucid," Ciprion said.

"She must not be one of the Lenereva hangers-on or the Lady Izivar would already have claimed her," Casca speculated. "Surely the woman would have noted if one of her household had wandered off."

"So that means she is most likely an escaped slave, or something worse," Eprius said. "Possibly an Eltyr."

"Perhaps noble Ciprion hadn't considered that." Casca's tone remained respectful but his eyes mocked. Hanuvar wondered how far they would dare to challenge one of the emperor's advisors.

Eprius spoke to his colleague. "I have heard he assumes the best in everyone because he is so honorable himself."

"Indeed. He was even kind to Hanuvar, I hear." Casca faced Ciprion. "Are you aware that Hanuvar's own daughter is alive and on the run?"

Eprius shook his head with exaggerated remorse. "Your prisoner may even be the Cabera woman. A matter of grave national security."

"I doubt that," Ciprion said. "And she's not a prisoner."

"Perhaps in your compassion you have missed some telltale sign of threat. Many of the Eltyr have a tattoo, you know. Sort of an involved half-circle thing, on the shoulder." The way Casca's eyes sparkled as he said this signaled his delight in knowing that Elistala possessed precisely such a marking.

Ciprion did not deny it. "I'm well aware that my guest possesses one. I look forward to finding out more about her connections to the Eltyr, should she recover."

Eprius shrugged. "We will take her with us and learn the truth, regardless of her condition."

Ciprion's heavy brows lifted quickly. He recovered, then shook his head gravely, with a faint air of disappointment in the man before him. "That's contrary to the standards of hospitality. I will not, in good conscience, allow her to be removed from my premises. I found her. I am responsible for her well-being."

"Did you know he was so old-fashioned?" Casca asked his companion.

But Eprius' expression had darkened. He was no longer playing a game. "I have personal experience with Eltyr." For the first time there was true passion in his voice. "They are treacherous, even for Volani, unwomanly snakes." Hanuvar had not yet heard steel in his delivery, but he heard it now. "We will take custody of her."

Hanuvar did not let his visceral reaction to this speech show in his demeanor, and merely watched Ciprion for reaction.

His friend did not yield. "She will remain. When I send my weekly dispatch to the emperor tomorrow I'm sure he'll concur with my decision."

Eprius shot his companion a look, as if to say he had predicted such a threat.

"The emperor would wish you to be safe," Casca said, a false pleading note evident in his delivery. "He has entrusted the revenants with seeing to all of the—"

"I do not require assistance to maintain my safety."

"Certainly," Casca agreed. "But surely you will not mind if we ourselves confirm the security of the situation. Come, Senator. It is only common sense. Let us see the woman."

Hanuvar saw Ciprion drawing in a breath, and his eyes narrowing, and knew the revenants were about to be forcefully expelled.

But anything his friend might have said went unheard, for a man deeper within the villa shouted "fire," and other voices repeated it frantically.

"Your doing?" Ciprion demanded of the revenants.

But Eprius' and Casca's surprise lacked the coy amusement so prominent previously. Their hulking companion's face wrinkled in confusion.

Eprius shook his head. "No, Senator."

The cry of fire continued, and a young Ceori slave ran forward, leading two children by the hand. One Hanuvar recognized for Calvia, Ciprion's perspicacious granddaughter, and she was protesting volubly about her papers and how they absolutely could not be abandoned.

Other household members dashed in, and Ciprion learned from one that a blaze had started in the rear garden, that his wife was organizing a bucket brigade, and that flames were spreading along the villa's back wall. The slaves already seemed to be caring for the children's safety, but Ciprion ordered them to see to their belongings and the scrolls in the library. He then instructed his guests to either help or get out, arching an eyebrow at Hanuvar.

He meant Hanuvar to see to Elistala. That brief glance had also communicated multiple layers of skepticism and a warning to take care. Probably he'd hoped that the revenants would leave, but they followed Ciprion across the courtyard, against the flow of slaves bearing chests of clothing, pottery, and bundles of scrolls both to the servant's exit and the front. A line of men extended from the large ornamental pool and on into the villa's back rooms. A scarred man of early middle age who had the haircut, hard-eyed manner, and musculature of a legion veteran was passing a bucket forward up the chain.

Hanuvar urged Antires on with Ciprion and the revenants and hurried to the right side of the courtyard and the guest rooms. He was only a few steps out when the shouting from the servant's exit resolved into something entirely different. Frightened slaves dropped household goods and fled before a band of weathered men waving swords.

The helmeted warrior in the lead shouted that no one would be harmed, and demanded he be taken to the woman. His voice had a pronounced Volani accent, and Hanuvar recognized it on the instant, though he could scarce believe it.

This was Bomilcar, one of the naval officers of New Volanus' tiny fleet. The young ship captain had accompanied Hanuvar to New Volanus, where he should have remained. In another reality, Bomilcar had become husband to Narisia, and father to Hanuvar's grandchildren.

Bomilcar brandished the long curving blade perfected by Volani, the falcata, and waved his people forward.

Hanuvar's sword, a gladius, was already to hand. He'd grasped it during the first glimpse of arms. He backpedaled as one of the invaders ran at him, parrying each deadly slash and ignoring an opening that would have killed his foe, for he recognized that squat, powerful form for one of the sailors who had manned the lead vessel he'd sailed to found New Volanus.

Even as he maintained a defense Hanuvar reasoned out his options. He could not speak in Volani to explain himself, for the odds were fair one of Ciprion's veterans or the revenants nearby understood the language.

Already the big revenant ran to the fight, and the other two were a few steps after. Against them were some dozen men in light armor of mixed Volani and Dervan make.

The big revenant charged Hanuvar's opponent, allowing Hanuvar himself to fall back and assess the environment. Ciprion's veteran and another much like him had set down their buckets to run forward with weapons of their own, stopping the momentum of the front rank of Volani even as their commander shouted orders, telling them to hold the line while detailing a trio to search the rooms.

Bomilcar faced the tall revenant. His falcata struck his opponent's cuirass with a splash of blood and the revenant staggered, then took a second blow to his helmet from the first Volani. The big man stabbed nonetheless; Bomilcar caught the ringing blow with the flat of his blade as he charged in, then kicked out the revenant's leg. Down the Dervan went, landing on his back. His companion revenants retreated, shouting for reinforcements.

Hanuvar snatched up a blue stola one of the fleeing slaves had dropped and lifted it high, then lowered it at same time he raised a second cloth with the other hand. The colors weren't quite right, for the second flag should be black rather than dark red, but Bomilcar's head turned toward him and froze; Hanuvar then dropped the garments.

Hanuvar felt the shock of recognition in Bomilcar's eyes almost as a physical force. Still, the shrewd young captain's reaction to the naval signal was almost instantaneous. "Fall back!" he cried out in Volani. "Retreat and regroup!"

He repeated his orders to his men, three of whom emerged from guest rooms without Elistala, who responded without hesitation.

"Stop them!" Eprius cried, pointing.

But neither Ciprion's two nor Hanuvar, nor Ciprion himself, wished to advance against twelve armored men now less threatening than the spreading fire. Bomilcar's raiders left through the servant's entrance.

Hanuvar would gladly have followed, but swallowed an oath and turned to shout Ciprion's countrymen back into line for the bucket brigade. Right now, he needed to help his friend save the villa. He would have to pursue the mystery appearance of Bomilcar later, though the explanation seemed clear enough—Bomilcar had journeyed from New Volanus either to seek him, or to strike back against the Dervans. He might even have come to do both things. Elistala had travelled with him, and now Bomilcar had come to rescue her.

While the revenants argued for men to follow and Ciprion snarlingly told them they would not, Hanuvar hurried to Elistala's room, only to learn why she had not left with Bomilcar's people. Her bed was to the wall, and the wooden grate within the window had been smashed out.

She had already made her escape.

III

Ciprion hadn't been carrying a blade of his own, and had decided to let the revenants take the brunt of the fight. He hadn't missed Hanuvar's signal, and was grateful it sent the Volani running. The revenants called for all able-bodied men to join them to pursue enemy raiders, but Ciprion overruled them and got his people back in line.

All three of the revenants hurried off, Eprius promising retribution. Ciprion knew Amelia was somewhere closer to the flames, probably orchestrating a second line of buckets from the well by this point. He hurried to find her. Hanuvar and Antires followed after a brief detour.

Against all odds the fire's starting point along the wall had been extinguished, but a tongue of flame had advanced up the back roof. Hanuvar climbed after Ciprion to the second story and then up an access ladder just shy of the fire.

The wind was with them, blowing the flames away from the house rather than deeper in, but even so it seemed to Ciprion they fought a holding action only, so little did the chain of buckets push back the blaze. Then two slaves turned up under Amelia's direction with an old water pump. While two of Ciprion's men provided the muscle below, Hanuvar sprayed hose water directly upon the roof. After a short while they were able, finally, to force the fire into retreat.

All that remained of the villa's storage room and its attic was blackened timber and ashes, but the living quarters were saved, and better news, no one had perished.

Fighting the fire had felt as though it had taken hours, but once they paused to catch their breath Ciprion was surprised to discover the western horizon still pale and the moon barely aglow.

Hanuvar stood beside him, face dotted with ash. Side by side they had worked to halt the flame, the Volani general first handing bucket after bucket to him and then taking charge of the hose. Now Ciprion nodded in thanks. He could not help thinking about the inferno that had engulfed Volanus and killed thousands of prisoners, certain that Hanuvar must have thought of it too.

His friend was too fine a man to speak of it.

The two climbed down from the roof where Amelia waited beside Antires, her white stola streaked with dirt. Her hair had tumbled messily along her cheeks. She looked lovely and vital and he was reminded again how fortunate he was to have her in his life, for it was she who had masterminded the winning strategy against the blaze.

She peered skeptically at Hanuvar, but before she could challenge him about his people's doings, the children returned with their tutor, Silenus, and a gaggle of other house slaves who'd carried valuables to safety. Amelia left to guide them to their places and arrange a meal for the hardworking slaves and retainers.

The courtyard pond was nearly drained already but Ciprion ordered a relief for his men and set others to pumping the rest of the water out, to protectively drench the regions beside the smoldering timbers.

After, Hanuvar motioned Ciprion to come with him for Elistala's chambers.

"She's gone?" Antires asked, seeing the empty bed and the forced window. "When?"

"She didn't leave with the raiders," Hanuvar said. "She must have sneaked away while we were talking with the revenants."

"Do you think she's found her people?" Ciprion asked.

"Let's see if we can tell."

Lantern in hand, they followed a few tracks in the dirt just outside the window. Neither Hanuvar nor his Herrenic friend were expert hunters, and Ciprion surely wasn't, but the few marks they could make out headed along the side of the villa rather than out into the countryside, and Ciprion realized they led in the direction of the stables.

The Eltyr apparently had a good eye for horseflesh, because she'd taken Ciprion's favorite white, Ghost, and galloped west.

"I'm sorry about the horse," Hanuvar said, then sighed. "And I'm sorry about the villa."

Ciprion held up a hand to halt any other words. He understood the Volani had meant to cause a distraction to more easily recover the woman they'd thought was being held prisoner. If they'd been aware of the presence of revenants they might even have been frightened about her safety. "I thank you for your help," he said, then nodded at Antires. "Both of you."

No matter a face and tunic dirt smeared and dampened, the Herrene sketched an elegant bow in response.

"I'm going to have to go after her," Hanuvar said. "I don't think we can count on her linking up with her crew."

Antires stepped away; he was already lifting a saddle to his little brown horse in the nearby stall. All the stable staff were in the house, having been called in to help fight the fire.

Hanuvar moved to his own animal, a sturdy bay roan.

Ciprion helped him carry the saddle. "You knew those men?"

"I did. They're from New Volanus. I've no real idea why they're here, because I passed on orders no one was to follow me." He stressed the last few words with some irritation.

"Not even the best subordinates obey every order," Ciprion said. "And they may have something important they've been wanting to tell you."

"I hope not. I have enough to worry about already." Hanuvar fitted the bridle to his mount, then slipped the bit between the gelding's teeth. He wiped his hand on his tunic edge, then offered his arm, and Ciprion clasped it. "I'm sorry for this. I will pay for damages. For now, I must ride. Please give my best to Amelia. Your family has already risked so much to protect my people, and this is the rudest form of ingratitude."

"She will understand when she has time to think it over." Ciprion turned to a more immediate challenge. "The revenants are off to hunt your people."

"And for Elistala. I need a lantern so I can seek her tracks."

"You think we can find them?" Antires asked. Ciprion thought it a good question.

"I mean to try. It's a lot easier to follow traces of horse movements, especially for one that's galloping. And I don't think she's going to get too far. She might have been pretending more weakness than she actually had, but she's still feverish."

Ciprion hesitated only a moment. "I'll come with you."

Hanuvar's features were drawn. "Are you sure?"

"I think you could probably use some more help."

"So could your wife."

"She has an entire household to assist. There are only two of you."

Hanuvar nodded once.

Antires chuckled. "Then let's ride, Senator!"

IV

Most of the time the Eltyr's passage through the sand and sparse grass was clear. If she had found a road, she could have lost them, but she headed for the coast, only a quarter mile away. They already saw the waters of the bay heaving into gleaming white peaks, shining in the moonlight before collapsing into dark troughs. Many miles on, the dark shape of a distant fishing boat struggled toward the shore, and Hanuvar, with the instinct of a seaborne people, wished them luck, for the currents were against them and the wind roamed wild and chill.

They found a riderless horse less than an hour after they began their search. Ciprion recognized his white. Elistala had fitted him with a bit but not bothered with a saddle. The animal now wandered, browsing along the way, in the general direction of home. He whickered in recognition of his fellows as they gathered him up.

The horse's recent course through the grass was clear enough, and led straight on for a little rocky rise. Nothing but the shore lay below, and they had no trouble finding Elistala's footprints in the sandy hill. Maybe she headed for a prearranged rendezvous point, should they become separated in some action. Right now, though, there was no sign that anyone else had come near it.

Hanuvar ground-tied his horse while the other two hitched theirs to scrub trees, then they started down the hillside, their cloaks belling in their wakes. Steep and initially rock studded, the slope terminated at a run of dark sand that stretched on for some forty feet before disappearing at the crashing surf. The scent of the sea was heavy in the air; salty, moist, thick with the odor of kelp and fish and lost things.

Though the Eltyr was not in sight, they were not alone, for a mass of crabs the size of breastplates scrabbled along the wet shoreline, their carapaces faintly glowing through some strange source of their own. Hanuvar had never seen the like and looked to Ciprion for explanation.

"Silenus said the big ones would not turn up to mate until next week," he said, his voice lifted to be heard over the surf. He'd explained how the Herrenic tutor had inspired him to take his granddaughter to see smaller ones that morning.

"There's much yet we don't know about the habits of animals," Antires remarked.

"Now you sound like Calvia," Ciprion said lightly. After a moment, he added: "Whoever marries her is going to end up taking a lot of nature hikes."

The cave at the bottom of the slope was invisible at first, but even in the moonlight they eventually spotted a line of greater darkness scarred into the hillside facing the beach. Hanuvar trod towards it and stopped. No fire shone within, and it came to him that the woman had fled with very little. She could not last long, and was likely to be feeling desperate.

He raised his voice and called to her, in Volani. "Elistala, we're here to help you. Are you inside?"

There was no answer. Scanning from right to left, Hanuvar advanced a single step into the dim recesses, waiting for his eyes to adjust. Ciprion and Antires remained outside.

It was the scrape of her sandal on a rock that alerted him to her charge even before her roar of defiance. He caught her sword arm as she raised the weapon for an overhead blow, then blocked a knee to the groin by raising his own leg. Her arm shook from fatigue or illness but she was not yet ready to give in. She punched at his throat with her balled left fist. He deflected but it still hit the side of his neck.

"Eltyr, at attention!" he barked.

She pulled at her weakening sword arm. When she saw Ciprion enter she tried hammering his throat again, but this time Hanuvar caught the blow with his hand, wrenched the sword away from her other, and dropped it to the cave floor. It landed with a clang against rock.

"Elistala," he said. "Stand down. It is your commander."

"It cannot be." Her voice was whisper soft. "You cannot trick me. That is the enemy. You would not stand with Ciprion."

"I would. He brought me to help you."

He felt more than saw her eyes upon them. She again attempted to free her arm, still held in his grip, so he released it.

"You're freezing." Hanuvar handed her his cloak.

After a moment, she took it, and wrapped her shoulders with it. "What's to be done?"

"I will reunite you with Bomilcar. But first we'll tend to you." He stooped to lift her sword, then passed it off to Antires and offered his arm to her. Hesitantly, she accepted his help, then fully leaned into him.

"You truly are the general?" she said. "This is no trick? I'm not dreaming?"

"It's me, Elistala. Come. We've a short ride, and then we'll get you taken care of."

They left together, Ciprion walking ahead. The wind was a low whistle now, and the waves rolled out at sea. The lumbering crabs upon the shore around them showed no more interest in their presence than that of the moon above.

But a huge black mastiff with shining eyes was fixated on them from the sands only ten feet off. Its ruff bristled and perhaps there was some strange quality of the light, but its fur seemed to emit a sheen of phosphorescence almost as bright as the claw-waving creatures that were giving it a wide berth.

The dog circled to their left, to higher ground. It growled.

Eprius and Casca emerged from the gloom, and the big revenant stood behind them at the head of three additional cloaked figures. Hanuvar was a little surprised to see the larger man moving around after the wounds he'd taken from Bomilcar, and was concerned he might be enhanced in some way by magics. The revenants did not just hunt sorcery to stamp it out. They also acquired and employed it.

"Ciprion and Decius!" Casca's voice cut through the wind. "You found the woman again! Who somehow escaped in your care!" He no longer bothered even to partially veil his sarcasm.

"We followed the horse tracks," Ciprion said. "It wasn't difficult."

"Is that what they did?" Eprius asked his companion.

Casca opened his arms as though lauding them. "However it was done, we owe you our thanks. We'll secure her now, and we then will find the pirates."

"Give me your knife, General," Elistala said in Volani to Hanuvar's ear, "And I will kill one before I slay myself."

"You will not die here," he vowed.

"It's strange that you're companionable with a man who's so obviously working with those pirates, Senator," Casca said. "Volani pirates." He turned a smug smile on Hanuvar. "Oh, we saw you signal to them. And we know the Herrene works with you. Strange, isn't it, Senator, that he works for a Volani? That you help an Eltyr? Why if I didn't know Senator Ciprion would never betray his people, I'd wonder if this might be Hanuvar!"

"Wasn't Ciprion always courteous to that murdering scum?" Eprius asked with mock curiosity.

Casca answered with exaggerated surprise. "You're right! Do you think this—"

At first the thing looming up from the sea seemed a cloud-cast shadow, or the dark prow of a ship. But as the dog wheeled and the revenants scattered Hanuvar saw an immense finned serpent's head at the end of a neck thick as an oak. It arched toward the large scurrying crabs a few yards away like a lightning bolt, then rose, masticating as little bits of crustacean fell away, the bulky creatures tiny in its huge maw.

There would be no better moment. Hanuvar sent a throwing knife toward the big man's throat. He swayed aside but it caught the face of the nearest follower. The man shrieked and fumbled with the hilt protruding from his cheek.

"I want Ciprion and Hanuvar alive!" Casca screamed. The junior revenant yelped in pain as he yanked Hanuvar's knife clear. The others pushed cloaks back as they advanced with drawn weapons.

"Kill," Eprius shouted, lifting his hand. "Kill the Eltyr!" An opal ring glowed upon it. The mastiff surged for Elistala even as Antires stepped in to intercede, slicing ferociously to keep the beast at bay. The thing danced side to side, snarling. The edges of its body were oddly blurred, as though it moved so rapidly that its image was sometimes left behind.

Hanuvar and Ciprion sprang into action at the same moment, one going left while the other went right. And as Hanuvar had suspected, Ciprion had no compunction about killing revenants, for his connection to Hanuvar, if exposed, endangered not just himself, but everyone he loved. His strike was swift and true and punched with such force that it split through one young revenant's cuirass. Blood spattered as Ciprion pulled his weapon free.

Hanuvar had no time to watch his friend's battle. Eprius fled behind the slim, wounded junior revenant and his pug-nosed, muscular companion. The wounded one had his blade only half drawn when Hanuvar slashed through his arm. He cut the scream off with a slice to his adversary's helmeted head, then pivoted and leaned away as pug-nose lunged. Hanuvar struck the weapon down and stabbed through his attacker's lower chest armor, twisting as he pulled his sword free. An explosion of stink wafted up when the man dropped gasping.

Intimidating hedge wizards and midwives was very different from engaging two of the world's finest generals.

A quick glance showed him Antires and Elistala back to back, each with a blade, the woman moving weakly but determined. The mastiff circled, growling and gnashing its teeth. The big revenant dueled Ciprion, who ducked a powerful flat-bladed strike for his head to drive his own blade into the revenant's side. The man seemed scarcely to note it.

Eprius, following behind, gleefully shouted: "Just wear him out, Septimus! He's already winded."

Casca had taken note that Hanuvar's opponents were dead or dying, and that nothing lay between him and the general's blade.

"To me, Eprius!" he cried, his voice rising in fear.

Hanuvar leapt pug-nose's body. Casca couldn't decide whether to worry about Hanuvar or the serpent, toward whom he backed. The wind was too loud for Hanuvar to hear the hiss of the revenant's blade, but steam rose from its edge. It had been drawn from a high-ranking revenant's sheath, which coated it in poison.

He lobbed his other knife underhand. Casca saw it coming and grunted. His wild swing caught it and sent it arcing away but left him out of line when Hanuvar leapt, sword borne high. The weapon tore down through Casca's neck and deep into his breast bone. He fell, screaming, the deadly blade falling from limp fingers.

He was still screaming as Hanuvar slashed down across the dying man's wrist. The hand plopped free from the spurting stump and Hanuvar lifted it, pointing at the big revenent Septimus. "Kill!"

On the instant the mastiff spun from Elistala and Antires and darted for the big revenant. The silent man turned at the last moment, and then the animal struck his side and bore him down.

He drove a sword into its side as he dropped, but the hound was not deterred, and buried its muzzle in his neck. Septimus thrust his blade into its side more and more weakly as the animal chewed through his throat. He stilled at last, arm going limp. The dog gnawed for a moment more then slumped across him, as though they were close companions down for a nap.

That left only Eprius. Even the sea serpent had retreated further down the beach, perhaps troubled by so many predators nearby. It had come for an easy meal, not a fight.

Ciprion flanked the revenant from the right, along the fringe of milling crabs, his expression determined and indomitable. His sword dripped blood.

"Spare me," Eprius cried. "I can keep your secret safe."

"I'm going to bet you haven't had time to write any report yet," Ciprion said.

"I have written one," Eprius admitted, "but it's not yet been sent."

"And it never will be," Ciprion promised.

Too late Eprius noticed a movement on his right. Summoning the last dregs of her energy, Elistala split the air with the ululating cry of the Eltyr. The revenant was only half turned when she leapt, driving her blade down through his helmet and deep into his skull. His body hit the sand with the thud a moment before she landed wobbily and sank to a knee.

After a long moment, she wrenched her sword free with a spatter of gore, then staggered upright, leaving a still body behind. She laughed softly from deep in her throat.

Antires swore in admiration.

Hanuvar tore the ring from the dead hand and pocketed it, then stepped to his friends. Antires' leg bled from a long claw scratch, and to Hanuvar's questioning look he shook his head. "I'm fine."

The Eltyr was winded, and covered with blood, but she smiled. "None of it's mine," she said. Antires was already advancing to offer Hanuvar's cloak to her once more.

Hanuvar eyed the serpent, leaning over the crabs further north. Closer crustaceans were already clambering over the dead. "What do you want to do about the bodies?"

"We're going to leave them to the tide," Ciprion said grimly. After a moment of contemplation he faced Hanuvar. "It won't be hard for me, with my position, to demand entrance to the home and offices of Eprius and Casca. I think I can arrange for a very interesting report for the emperor about their doings, as well as how their attempt to blackmail me turned violent."

Hanuvar imagined he could. After he recovered his knives, they cleaned and sheathed their weapons and left the beach and all the monsters, living and dead, in the darkness behind them.

V

They were nearly to their horses when a new band of figures stalked out of the night, closing from right and left. Ciprion lifted his sword even as a voice called out, addressing them in Dervan with a Volani accent. They were commanded to halt, and warned to lower weapons.

Hanuvar responded immediately in fluent Volani. Ciprion's own facility with the language had waned through years of disuse, although he was able to follow the flow of conversation and infer much of what was said. Hanuvar greeted the speaker as Bomilcar and told him to stand down, saying that Elistala had been recovered but was weak and still feverish and would need care. He also expressed pleasure in seeing the captain and his people.

In their turn, they clustered about Hanuvar, smiling with delight. Their leader removed his helm then contemplated his commanding officer with pleasure so profound it approached veneration. His hair was dark and tightly curling. His plain, square face was dominated by a strong brow ridge and thick nose that must have been broken more than once. Bomilcar then laughed and offered his arm, and Hanuvar smiled and clasped it.

After that the rest of the band lined up to greet Hanuvar, their words flowing so quickly Ciprion could not follow much of what they said. He was surprised to see a number of very capable-looking women in the group. They stayed close, ringing Hanuvar. They nodded genially to Antires, and embraced then tended Elistala, but seemed uncertain how to engage with Ciprion, an enemy Dervan. He understood that they knew his identity, for he heard his name on their lips.

Bomilcar regarded him even now with carefully banked hostility, like a guard dog waiting for an attack command. He half turned his head and asked a question of Hanuvar about revenants, though he kept his eyes upon Ciprion.

"No," Hanuvar said, and Bomilcar's brows rose questioningly. Hanuvar then spoke in Dervan, slowly. "Ciprion has risked his life for me, and you."

While Bomilcar puzzled that over and those who apparently understood Dervan explained to the Volani who did not, Hanuvar looked regretfully between Bomilcar and Ciprion. "For our joint safety, the less you two know about one another, the better." He faced the Volani leader. "There's something you must understand, though. Ciprion found Elistala and helped her. Without him she might already be dead. While you acted decisively to recover your soldier, you attacked the villa where Ciprion's wife and grandchildren are staying."

A glimmer of understanding at last reached Bomilcar's eyes. He frowned, then considered Ciprion again. His Dervan was halting. "I have heard the general speak of you with respect, but I did not guess your plans. When my scouts learned you had found Elistala, and then we saw the coming of revenants, I feared she would be questioned with pains. I had to stop watching, and act. Your family is well?"

"They are."

"If my actions harmed..." Bomilcar's voice faltered and his mouth twisted into a scowl. He spoke sharply to Hanuvar in Volani and Ciprion understood enough to parse that he demanded why he should apologize for damage done to a Dervan patrician's home when so many of his had been killed by Dervans.

Hanuvar's answer was brusque, and Ciprion could not follow the rapid-fire sentences, despite their brevity. When he finished, Bomilcar's head was bowed in discomfort. After he collected himself he faced Ciprion again. "I regret the worry I brought your wife and family, and yourself. I did not hope to cause them injury, and I am glad that they are well."

"I appreciate that," Ciprion replied gravely. "And I accept your apology."

At mention of the fire they had faced, he once again could not suppress the thought of flames racing through the buildings of the great coastal city, and the holdings where thousands of prisoners had been kept after its fall, and the screams as they burned alive. He had not been involved; he had spoken against the war, to his own detriment. But he was a part of the machine that had brought their city's end. How should he speak of Derva's war against a weakened Volanus, the destruction of its society, the death of its people? Words and phrases conveying regret tumbled uselessly through his mind but did not cross his lips, for they were hopelessly inadequate.

Hanuvar seemed to understand, for he again addressed Bomilcar, this time in Dervan. "Tell him about the steward."

"Your servant spied for revenants," Bomilcar returned with a heavy accent. "One of my scouts followed the revenants after my general ordered withdrawal, and the man came to find them. They meant to chase us, until your steward came and told them of our Eltyr escaped."

The steward was not Ciprion's, but that of his in-laws. "Where is he now?"

Ciprion's suspicion was confirmed by Bomilcar's dark look. "With his ancestors. My scout heard from him and ran to get us. We followed the revenants." He turned over a hand. "I was wrong on many thoughts. You fought them together didn't you?"

Ciprion nodded once.

"You know too much for Ciprion's safety," Hanuvar said. "Our connection must never be spoken of."

"It will not be," Bomilcar vowed. He then bowed his head to Ciprion. "I thank you."

Elistala, bundled now in a heavy cloak, had come silently up beside Bomilcar, and formally bowed her own head. "I give thanks as well," she said in Dervan. "Perhaps... there is hope if people of honor still work together."

Ciprion thought that a charming sentiment, though an unlikely one. "May your recovery be swift."

Hanuvar extended his hand, and he and Ciprion clasped forearms. "We should part," Hanuvar told him. "I thank you, for everything. Please convey my apologies to Amelia. I shall reimburse you for the damages as soon as I am able."

Ciprion shook his head. "I will not take money you need for your rescue operations. The emperor's always foisting rewards on us—I will accept one. I trust we shall meet again, and perhaps over that meal I had hoped for."

"I would like that," Hanuvar said.

There was much more to be said. There was always more that might be said between them, but now was not the time. Ciprion bade them all farewell, mounted his horse, and took the lead line of Ghost. He left Hanuvar, Antires, their two horses, and the Volani heading north along the coast.

VI

Bomilcar walked with Hanuvar at the head of the procession, so they could speak without being overheard by anyone but Antires. Hanuvar had introduced the playwright as his advisor, which seemed to startle and delight the younger man in equal measure.

The joy at travelling among so many of his own people was marred by Hanuvar's fear for them, and before even asking about Bomilcar's goals or their lives, Hanuvar asked where the captain was beached and how he'd avoided the Dervans.

Bomilcar snapped his fingers at the efficacy of the Dervan coastal patrols. "They're all landlubbers at heart. We're only about a mile north, in a safe little cove."

"And what are you doing here?"

"I'm probing the coast to assess its weaknesses. I'm in contact with Icilian pirates and some renegades east of Hadira and we expect to make things very tricky for the Dervans later this summer. Right when they need to trust the sea lanes to keep them supplied against Cerdia."

Hanuvar wasn't delighted to hear that, but at least Bomilcar hadn't been hunting him to report some dire news about the colony. "What's your objective?"

"My objective?" Bomilcar puzzled over the question. "To hurt Derva. To strike a retaliatory blow." He struggled to find the right words even in his own language. "Vengeance!" he managed finally.

Hanuvar understood. "The best thing you've done is free some of our people in your raids. How many have you recovered?"

"Eight."

"Well done," Hanuvar said. "But your presence here is going to stir up even more attention, and I can't afford it just now."

"No?" Bomilcar asked. "But our people require justice."

"No," Hanuvar insisted. "We can't be wasting our efforts on revenge. I'm trying to find and free all of our captured people, and nothing else matters half as much."

The sea captain did not seem happy about this disagreement, but his loyalty was unquestioning. "As you say, General, I will abandon the plan." He changed topics with a shift of broad shoulders. "We kept hearing rumors you were alive, but we couldn't really believe you'd escaped. Yet here you are! Deep under disguise in the Dervan countryside. What are you doing?" He drew in a breath. "Were you behind the emperor's death?"

The blunt inquiry returned him unbidden to the long months when he had feared his daughters' rage had warped her into a murderer of children, culminating in his discovery of the dying emperor, slain by a counterfeit Eltyr. A moment passed before he responded softly. "I was nearby, but no."

Bomilcar nodded soberly but did not ask for detail.

Hanuvar returned a question of his own. "How long have you been in the Inner Sea?"

"More than a year now. I left as soon as your ship came back from Volanus with the terrible news. And without you."

"So you haven't been back?"

"No, sir. I've been careful. It's taken some doing to set up the attacks you want me to cancel." He studied Hanuvar hopefully for signs he'd change his mind.

"It sounds like it would have been a very effective strategy for a more propitious time," Hanuvar said.

"Thank you, sir. We've also made contact with Volani enclaves in a number of provinces. Some of them have made the journey to New Volanus."

Hanuvar had eventually wished to reach out to the free Volani living in the provinces and beyond the borders of empire. But he'd hoped to finish his liberation campaign first. If the revenants learned there was a New Volanus, they might start noticing that all the Volani slaves were disappearing, and become more troublesome to Hanuvar's true aims.

There was nothing he could do now about actions Bomilcar had already taken. Assuming Hanuvar was dead and unaware of his plans, he had acted as he had thought best. "You've done well," Hanuvar said. "How are you? You and your people?"

"Fine, general. And we're in high spirits. It's felt good to strike back against Derva."

"How many ships do you have?"

"Three."

If Bomilcar had been busy in the Inner Sea seeking Volani, there was a faint chance he'd been successful with an important objective Hanuvar had so far failed to make any real progress toward. "Have you had any word of my daughter?"

The captain shook his head, speaking with grim forbearance. "Only that she had been captured. And presumably killed."

"Narisia escaped with several Eltyr and I have not found her."

Bomilcar sucked in a breath and blinked in surprise. Hanuvar knew he had always admired her.

Antires remained silent, listening, and Hanuvar felt his scrutiny intensify.

"Finding our people has to be the highest priority," Hanuvar said. "I applaud your efforts, but let's hold off on coodinated actions with the pirates until it can do us some greater good. Right now such raids would interfere with Derva's usual activities, complicate our ability to track the Volani left, and upend our efforts to recover all those sold into slavery."

"Yes, sir."

"Dispatch two of your ships to Selanto, where they can be deployed to transport the groups we've freed to New Volanus." Evacuating them sooner would decrease the risk of waiting for the purpose-built ships to return for them from New Volanus. "Have their captains report to Himli. He will provide you with paperwork to legitimize the vessels and their cargo. I want you to take your fastest ship to Surru. We've heard rumors of an underground Volani movement there, and think Narisia and the escaped Eltyr might have been in touch with them. Find them."

"We will," Bomilcar vowed. "But when I do, where shall I find you?"

It was a fair question. "I will tell you, but you must be exceptionally discreet. For the next few months I am hiding in plain sight, in the Apicius villa of Izivar Lenereva."

"The Lenereva?" Bomilcar spat.

"Her father is dead and Izivar has risked her life and her fortune to aid her people. She can be trusted. If you don't return before early autumn, seek me in Selanto, at the Lenereva holdings there, where we've expanded the port. Otherwise I'll be nearby Apicius."

"You can depend upon me. If Narisia's out there, I will find her."

"I know. Bomilcar, we have lost too many people already. Take great care of those with you. We need warriors and sailors to keep our new homeland safe." He felt the younger man readying objection, and cut him off. "These veteran lives are a resource we cannot afford to lose. Do you understand?"

"Yes, sir." While there was reluctance in Bomilcar's voice, Hanuvar thought he heard comprehension as well. The captain was far from stupid. He but lacked perspective. Hanuvar hoped he could be made to live long enough to gain it.

For the next quarter hour he visited with his people, asking after their health and their doings. One he was able to tell about a cousin rescued from a stone quarry, and another of a brother they hoped to free from a dye maker in the coming week. That there were lives still to be saved was solace to these brave souls, who had planned solely to drown their rage in blood. He spoke to them of the dream of New Volanus, and of how fragile it remained, and how much it needed skilled guardians.

Elistala thanked him again formally, telling him how honored she was to have gone into battle at his side.

"Rest up and heal fast," he told her. "Your captain will need help on his new assignment." Weary and sick though she was, the young woman's eyes shone in curiosity.

Hanuvar and Antires stopped on a hillock while the others descended to a sheltered cove where a little sailboat was beached. Bomilcar's larger ship was anchored among some islands a mile out to sea. The wind would be with them as they sailed east. Hanuvar and Antires stood with their horses as the Volani boarded and pushed off, and even watched awhile as the wind caught their sail and sent them skirting away.

The wind was cold, but he watched their silhouettes against the moon-brightened sea for a time, hoping they would find his daughter but hoping even more they would understand his counsel.

"What are you thinking about?" Antires asked him.

He would rather not have said, but he had promised to share his thoughts with the writer, and so he did. "I'm afraid for them." He'd found their adoration disconcerting and their hunger for revenge tiresome even though he understood it.

"Are you really going to send pirates against Tyvol some time?"

He shook his head no. "Bomilcar and his crew might claim that the shades of our people cried for reprisal, but their goal is fundamentally selfish, and self-destructive. A raid wouldn't attack those who'd guided the war or profited from it. It would kill hundreds of people who'd had nothing to do with it."

"That's what I was thinking," Antires said. "I'd hate to see anyone raid the Oscanus region—there are a lot of nice people here."

The thirst for revenge could blind a person to basic commonalities. Bomilcar's devotion to it had made him seem almost a different person than Hanuvar had known prior. And he and all of his followers had seemed very young. Younger even than Antires, though most had as many years or more.

And yet, once he turned his back upon them and rode into the dark countryside, he felt loneliness as he had not known for long weeks, as though he were soaked clean through by it. Even Antires' company was poor solace. Not until he lay warm in bed, Izivar's arm thrown across his chest, his left hand clasping her right, did he know a sense of comfort, and he counted himself fortunate to have any in a world where so many remained bereft.

※ ※ ※

In those weeks I found myself sometimes assisting the capable Izivar with either the transfer of the rescued or the management of her small shipping firm, for it must be remembered that her business had to prosper for at least a little while longer, both as a cover and because our monetary resources were hardly endless. At this remove I barely recall the daily challenges, and my notes are incomplete, for I sulked that I could not be involved in every moment of Hanuvar's own efforts. I remember the calm way Izivar addressed problems, and the day she discovered one of her ships had sent a huge cargo of fruit south rather than north to Ostra, and how she then had to scramble to find a different market or lose money upon the entire shipment. I recall the loyalty of her staff in the harbor office, and how quietly and efficiently they carried out their tasks. I think to them I must have seemed bumbling and overeager to prove myself, and probably I was.

Ciprion's report to the emperor on the doings of the revenants had the desired effect: the standing of the revenant legate himself grew even more perilous, and he was ordered in no uncertain terms to focus entirely upon Cerdia. He was forced to recall his hounds and redistribute his personnel to other duties, which he did, although he did not fully abandon his search, as we were soon to learn.

More and more Hanuvar deployed me as a scout, and twice I even handled the negotiations for some slaves all on my own. Successfully, I might add. I acted as his secretary, even suggesting the wording in some of the contact letters we sent landholders. And, under his tutelage, I had begun to refine my sword skill, practicing nearly every day, and often exercising with him. Unless in disguise in the midst of some assignment, Hanuvar never failed to perform his morning and evening drills.

On one memorable occasion I rode south and west with him into the hinterland, thinking we would return in a few days with a small band of Volani vintners. What we did not know is that the revenant legate had maneuvered Calenius into assisting him with a new scheme. Their actions were to have a lasting impact upon the entire region.

—Sosilos, Book Thirteen

Chapter 4:
Reflection From a Tarnished Mirror

I

The scents reminded him of a room he couldn't place, one with pungent spices where slim, brown-haired women walked among low counters. Gnaeus recalled a particularly pretty girl who'd smiled at him and then he wondered where he was. He'd thought he'd been telling his boys to hold the line. He was supposed to be getting them into formation, and he couldn't, not in this room that smelled of spices. He knew they had to be close and called to them. "Form up, boys!"

He was only vaguely aware of the beautiful wooden desk standing against the wall, a light brown oaken masterpiece carved with running horses, marred by a crushing blow to its right panel. A helm and some armor lay on a bench to the left, and in front of them were some vases that didn't look Dervan or Icilian, for a ribbony creature floated in puffy clouds above a fleet of ships, and there weren't any soldiers on any of the decks. Where were his men? "We have to form up," he said mostly to himself. His attention shifted to the fellow in the black tunic standing near the door. Maybe he knew where the lads had gone. He certainly looked like a military man. His straight, jet-black hair was cut short over a high, pale forehead, and a thin white scar stretched diagonally across his large, square chin.

The scarred warrior gestured at him to a companion now filling the doorway, a tall, powerfully built man with fiery red hair and blue eyes menacing as spear points. "Will he do?"

"Maybe." The big man advanced with an easy grace unlikely in someone so large and placed hands on either side of Gnaeus' face. His fingertips were cool, and their touch oddly soothing. After a short moment Gnaeus felt a pulse at their tips, almost like the drumbeat of a galley. That reminded him that he had to get the men into order. "Form on me, boys!" he called loudly. "We have to hold the line!"

The big man withdrew his hands and looked back to the other. "I asked for a blank slate, legate. There's still a personality in there."

The legate scoffed. "He took a blow to the head that laid open his skull. All he can do is shout to his nonexistent men. If he's not completely blank, then he's like a smeared old slate you can write over. Besides, I can't do better. I've accommodated you far enough. All of the rest of these things"—he gestured to the furniture and pottery—"were expensive."

"Not for you."

"For the state. What I'm saying is that you're going to have to work with it."

"I can't guarantee the results."

The legate snarled. "It had better work, wizard. The time and expense laid out demand more than a mumble and powder show." His dark eyes blazed warning no matter that the larger man topped him by a head.

The wizard shrugged, unfazed. "Oh, something will happen alright. But you may not like it. This kind of magic is unpredictable."

"Hold the line," Gnaeus shouted again.

The legate sneered and snapped at him. "Shut up, Centurion."

"Don't call him by a Dervan rank." The big redhead gripped Gnaeus' left arm and helped him rise from the bench. "It's time to put on your armor."

Gnaeus was accustomed to putting on his armor. When the wizard handed him the cuirass, old habits kicked in and he pulled it over his head.

"Is all of this theater really necessary?" the legate asked.

The wizard, tying up Gnaeus' shoulder tab, answered. "If this is really Hanuvar's armor, it is."

"It's from Volanus," the legate asserted. "All of it. Senator Apulius had it on display." He snorted his contempt.

Gnaeus looked to right and left. The boys were probably putting on their own gear somewhere nearby. This was taking too long. "We've got to form up."

"You're not quite ready." The big man held out a shining silver necklace, and bent his head as though in meditation, whispering words in a language Gnaeus hadn't heard before.

Gnaeus' gaze shifted to the helmet. He realized he wasn't wearing a helmet, and he needed one, though that one wasn't his. The armor wasn't his, either, was it? The colors were wrong, no reds. And the crest wasn't transverse. He started forward, but the big man put a hand to his chest almost gently.

"Hold up, soldier."

Gnaeus complied with that simple command, remaining still as the other slipped a chain over his head. It was a necklace supporting a circle of metal set around a honey-colored stone oval half again the size of a sesterce.

The wizard passed him the helmet with the green horsehair crest. "Put it on."

He obeyed the order. The moment the metal encased Gnaeus' head, the big man resumed his whispering and touched the stone hanging upon the breastplate.

Gnaeus gasped, for he'd seen a flash of light within the gem. More than that, something within him had cleared, though he could not yet have articulated what it was. He raised his hands as if contemplating them for the first time.

"Is it working?" the legate asked. There was no missing the strained excitement in his voice.

Gnaeus couldn't see out of one of his eyes and had to turn his head to observe both men fully. He lifted one hand to his face and discovered his eyepatch. He traced a line of tender skin that ran from his nasal bridge to his hairline.

"That's new," the legate whispered eagerly. "It's like he's more aware." He then pitched his voice at the man in armor. "Do you know who you are?"

"Where am I?" His voice sounded strange to him.

The legate smiled with feigned warmth and adopted a patronizing tone. "You're with friends, recovering from an injury."

"Who are you?"

The legate's smile deepened. "Who are you?"

He wasn't sure. He'd thought his name was Gnaeus, but another name loomed larger now, and it was one he dared not say, not when he was in the presence of someone who looked like he wore a revenant uniform. His thoughts were hazy. He fought off the recurring worry that he had to form up his unit. There was no unit here.

"Who are you?" the legate repeated insistently.

"It's likely to be a little while before it all takes effect," the big wizard cautioned, and watched Gnaeus with his eerie blue eyes.

The padding inside the helmet wasn't adjusted right, and Gnaeus took it off to examine the inside more closely. He'd worn this helmet when he was leading his army through Turia. But . . . he hadn't ever been stationed in the south, had he?

"Does it seem familiar?" the legate asked eagerly.

"Don't press too fast," the wizard cautioned.

The legate's lip curled at the criticism.

Wherever this was, he wasn't among men he could trust. He knew enough to judge that, just as he knew his perceptions were flawed and confused. He glanced down at the amber stone centered in his necklace. The shade reminded him of something. A woman's eyes. Yes, his sister Narisia's eyes had been almost this same color. But he didn't have a sister, did he? Much less one with a strange name.

The wizard indicated the amulet with a thick finger. The impact of those blue eyes was scorching. "Leave this about your neck. If you remove it, you'll be incapable of doing anything but telling your men to form in line. Do you understand?"

He nodded. Recent memories were fuzzy, but he had the sense he'd been walking in something like a permanent dream, from which he was only now waking. "And what do you want from me?"

The legate laughed, as if he meant to soothe or disarm his listener with bonhomie. He failed. "Your advice. That's all we want."

They wanted more than that. There was no missing it in the legate's hungry eyes, or in the other's penetrating stare. Of the two, he preferred the big man, who at least seemed to speak truth. "Why am I so tired? What's happened to me?"

The legate shot a probing look to the wizard, who said, "The spell may be taxing him."

"So what do you suggest we do?" the legate demanded.

"Let him rest. It will give a chance for the magics to settle in."

"How long before your spell starts working?"

"It's already working." The wizard at last betrayed a hint of annoyance at the constant challenge in the other's voice. "Unless you thought you could take any kind of advice from him before."

"But is he Hanuvar now?"

Hanuvar. Yes. He flexed his hands. They didn't look quite right. But nothing felt entirely right. He was on enemy ground. He had to find a vantage. No. He had to get away, to a place where he could learn the lay of the land and consider his options.

The wizard shook his head and spoke wearily, as if explaining something for the fourth or fifth time. "He'll never be Hanuvar. But for your purposes he may be close enough. You," he said to him, "should rest. Think about your past. Remember you're among friends. And leave the necklace on. We'll be back in the morning."

"The morning?" the legate asked sharply. "We have to wait that long?"

The big man spoke with an air of finality. "He should sleep with the amulet on. That will give the sorcery a better chance to root deep through him."

He didn't like the sound of that. But then he knew without the amulet he was...less than himself. "I will rest," he offered. "And then, hopefully, all this will be a little more clear."

The wizard agreed with an approving nod.

The legate frowned. "I can't help noticing that you're in a hurry to be out of here, Calenius. To be done with this."

"I've made no secret of that. I have my own projects. And this one has already proved more time consuming than I had hoped. But by tomorrow morning I think you'll be able to get some useful information out of him."

He set the helmet on the desk.

"I'll send a slave in to help you get the armor off," Calenius said.

"Shouldn't he leave all of it on?" the legate asked.

"No; he just needed it for the spell to start its work. Things Hanuvar had touched, things Hanuvar had used, or been near. To help focus the spell." Calenius spoke to him. "This was your desk, wasn't it?"

He nodded slowly as he drank in the elegant lines while memories and moments flowed through him. It was not until the two had left that true understanding dawned, though when the slave arrived he pretended to be muddled still.

The slave seemed surprised he was capable of conversation at all.

That night, he ate long and well. It was a three course Dervan meal, starting with hard-boiled eggs and ending with a nice selection of cherries, but he had to endure a fish heaped in their garum sauce in between. Then he pretended to be sleepy for a time before calling for the guard.

The next morning when the two returned, they would find the guard restrained with bedding in their charge's chamber and a tale of having been lured inside and subdued in the middle of the night.

He slipped away, with armor and a weapon taken from a fool who'd tried to stop him. He also had a name, and a purpose. Never again, Hanuvar vowed, would the Dervans capture him alive.

II

The summer sun hung only a dagger's length above the nearby hills when Hanuvar crossed onto the expansive farmlands owned by Minucius. Long years before, bearded and armored, he had ridden this same road at the head of troops. Today he was clean-shaven, his dark, gray-peppered hair straight cut in the Dervan manner, clothed in a fine blue tunic of the kind a well-to-do merchant or their representative might wear. His only companion this time around was Antires, a dark young man on an old white horse.

When they topped a ridge, the worn mountains that ribbed the Tyvolian peninsula rippled into view through the morning mist; he and Antires gazed down on a line of lower hills beneath which a villa sprawled, overlooking a stream pretty enough to have been painted on a mural. Sun-hatted slaves worked among the vegetables and tended leafy vines pinned to trellises. A vast warren of slave quarters stood open beside a long run of barns and outbuildings.

They found two older men repairing a wagon wheel in the shade of a laurel tree, one of whom guided them deeper into the grounds and presented them to Lucretius, the estate manager, sturdy and dough faced, clearly a hands-on administrator, for he too wore a sun hat, and while his tunic had sleeves, the cloth was worn, faded, and spotted. Lucretius recalled the letter he'd received last week from Fabius, Hanuvar's assumed identity for this enterprise.

"Ah, yes." Lucretius cleared his throat. "I'll have some refreshments set out. But I have bad news. I wrote you back—did the letter not come through?"

In point of fact it had, but Hanuvar pretended puzzlement.

Lucretius asked the slave to take the visitors' horses away for fodder and water, and to send a girl with snacks. Once the man was leading both animals off, Lucretius started down the road for the villa, Hanuvar and Antires at his side. He spoke quietly to Hanuvar. "I'm not at liberty to make any decisions about the slaves. That's the master's prerogative, especially expensive ones like this. So I'm afraid your trip has been for naught. I'm sorry about that."

For a man saying no, he remained quite welcoming. Hanuvar guessed the reason, but didn't want to assume too much. "Have you written your employer about my request?"

Lucretius inclined his head. "I have, but there's no telling when I'll have a response. He's ... distracted with other business matters."

Minucius, the villa owner, was actually busy gambling and drinking in Iskandria. Unlike the majority of problem cases Hanuvar's liberation network encountered while trying to buy up Volani slaves, this one had no active interest in his belongings while they were out of his sight. He was simply unreachable, and his estate manager remained unable or unwilling to make choices without him.

"My employer doesn't really need to purchase the slaves," Hanuvar said. "Merely borrow them for consultation. As I explained in the letter."

"Yes, yes. I understand." Lucretius nodded and led them toward the back side of the white-walled villa, where a pleasant shaded patio surrounded a reflecting pool. "And the offer of remuneration is quite generous. But I simply can't make such a decision without Minucius' involvement."

Food preparations must already have been underway, for a

quartet of slaves stepped into the roofed area and laid out platters as the three men walked up. "What a nice-looking spot," Antires said.

While Lucretius paused to praise the villa planners and previous manager, who'd apparently reworked the gardens, Hanuvar evaluated what he'd heard and decided how he would test his suspicion that Lucretius expected a bribe. Actual functionaries, like the two they pretended to be, would examine the merchandise before haggling. "Surely your master would not object to me speaking with your people here, at the villa?" Hanuvar asked.

"Of course not," Lucretius said reasonably. "But wouldn't they need to see the ground you mentioned, and evaluate the soil?"

They took the offered benches near a chipped statue of smiling cherubs.

"Of course," Hanuvar answered. "Before we discuss any other kind of arrangements for the slaves, though, we should verify that these three men are the experts they're alleged to be."

"That makes perfect sense." Lucretius clapped his hands. One of the slave girls trotted over and he asked her to send a runner to bring the Volani from the fields. She hurried off, and Lucretius swept a hand toward the repast before them. Gnats began investigating some of the grapes and salad greens. There was also a covered platter of what proved to be trout, the ubiquitous Dervan boiled eggs, and several bread loaves. Lucretius himself poured their wine, a lightly watered dry, robust red.

He then proceeded to tell them about his own role on the estate and the amount of time the job required for what amounted to very little money. He apparently took for granted the free use of skilled in-house cooks and ready access to Minucius' wine stock. As he spoke about his relative poverty it became all the more clear that he was setting himself up for a gratuity and Hanuvar decided that he'd liked the man a little better before he'd proved so obviously corrupt.

Hanuvar announced that he'd like to walk with the slaves when they arrived and see if they could demonstrate their skills. Lucretius said that would be fine.

"And if you don't mind, we'd like to talk to them alone. Without any input from any other learned agricultural men," Hanuvar finished with a smile.

"We want to make sure they're up to tackling our problems,"

Antires added. "These Volani vintners are supposed be expert with both southeastern strains and high-elevation growing?"

"I don't know about the latter, but they certainly know their way around vines in general, and all manner of exotic varieties. I'm sure you should be able to gauge their worth to you fairly fast." He smiled amiably. "Converse away. I'll sit here in the shade."

A small, ruddy-skinned man presented himself to Lucretius and announced that the Volani waited just beyond the decorative hedgerow. Lucretius addressed the rubicund slave. "Conduct our guests to them. Tell them they're to answer his questions."

Hanuvar allowed himself to be led to where three lean, disgruntled slaves stood in sun hats. They had the air of craftsmen called away from the midst of a project. They looked askance at Hanuvar, then at Antires, who'd followed a few steps behind, still holding a wine goblet.

The young slave conveyed Lucretius' instructions, which further soured the expressions of all three.

Hanuvar sent the slave off, then addressed the trio. "Your master's manager has given me leave to ask you a few questions about selection for better yields at higher altitudes. Walk with me." He started toward the vine fields and the three came after. Antires plodded silently at his side, sipping wine.

"Will this be long?" the oldest asked, his Volani accent thick. "We really must return to the work."

Certain now that they were out of earshot of anyone in the villa, Hanuvar spoke quietly to them in Volani. "Show no reaction as we talk. I'm working to buy your freedom and return you to other liberated people of your nation. The manager appears to be bribable; will you be prepared to leave on a pretend consult and not return?"

One of the men faltered in his walking even as Hanuvar pointed to the ground near a vine winding about a trellis, as if he meant to ask something about its quality. He was well informed about a multitude of subjects, but wine growing was not among them, and had only acquired enough information to pass muster.

"Who are you?" the second oldest returned, likewise speaking Volani. His close set eyes narrowed. "Why would you buy our freedom? Why do you speak our language?"

The elder raised a hand to him and spoke quietly. The deep brown eyes in his weathered face studied Hanuvar's features. "He is Volani."

As if by chance, Hanuvar had led them to a run of open storage sheds, where they were closed in from view both from the villa and the fields. There he stopped and let the others scrutinize him.

The youngest looked no more than twenty, and his smooth brow furrowed. "It might be a trick. Maybe Lucretius wants to test our loyalty."

The elder shook his head. "He's not imaginative enough to play tricks."

The young one, whom Hanuvar knew had been given the name Gisco by his parents, changed his thoughts on the instant and asked Hanuvar, "Can you free others, too?"

The one with the close-set eyes flashed a half smile and explained, "My cousin has a lover among the other slaves."

"We've friends here," the oldest told Hanuvar, his eyes searching for empathy. "People who deserve better than this."

There were always complications. Hanuvar wondered how to address the hopes of these people. To suggest the removal of any beyond the three Volani wine specialists before him would arouse the manager's suspicions.

Before he could formulate a counterproposal, Hanuvar heard a distant cry of alarm from somewhere near the villa, and then a shout of "bandits" from another point to the east. Hanuvar readied his knife just as a gang of men emerged from the vine fields on the right at a run; thickset, muscular spear bearers. The leader, startled to see Hanuvar's group, paused long enough to point four their direction, then continued on his way toward the house.

From their build Hanuvar knew them instantly for gladiators, some of the most dangerous man-to-man fighters in the world. The Volani vintners clustered together as the interlopers closed on them. One of the intruders remained at a distance as two of the burly young warriors flanked and a third advanced with spear low and ready, pointed at Hanuvar. His brows were furrowed over wary black eyes. "You'll stay quiet if you know what's good for you. You three are slaves?"

"Yes," the elder answered. He opened his mouth as if to say more, and gestured toward Hanuvar, but the lead gladiator's focus had already shifted to Antires. "And you?"

The playwright had cleverly dropped the wine goblet as the interlopers ran up.

"Of course," he said smoothly.

The curly-haired gladiator flanking from the left came then at Hanuvar, spear leveled.

Antires and the Volani cried out as one. "No!"

Hanuvar backed from the thrust, keeping just a foot away of the gleaming point. Another aggressor flanked from the right.

"No," Antires cried. "He's here to free these men!"

The Volani were shouting the same. The flanking gladiator paused to see whether his commander would order a change, but the first spear bearer came on with a scowl. Probably he'd fastened on the detail of Hanuvar's dress and haircut and seen him as an eques, one of the same class who paid to watch men like him fight and suffer and die.

Hanuvar retreated toward a shed wall where a broken-down vegetable cart sat, knife in one hand, weighing his choices. If he took his attacker down, the others would swarm. And that assumed he'd be able to kill the young man swiftly. He wasn't sure he could. But if he managed to stall, there might be time for cooler heads to intervene.

Antires and the Volani continued to plead for him, but the man with the spear came in, jabbing surely but not overextending. Hanuvar pretended overreach as he swiped a return, then jumped aside when his opponent charged. The point of the blade caught in a cart slat. Hanuvar sliced into the hairy extended forearm and got himself cuffed in the face for his effort, although his opponent released the weapon. Hanuvar slid to the right and the gladiator stepped back to draw his sword. The younger man flicked his thick arm so droplets from the injury sprayed, his gaze showing nothing but contempt.

There was no time to seize the spear. He retreated further toward a space between the sheds, where it would be harder to fully swing a sword.

One of the other gladiators shouted to stop, and Hanuvar spotted Antires dashing for the discarded spear.

Hanuvar's assailant heard his companion's command and partly turned, halting his advance. Antires started after.

"Drop the spear!" one of the other gladiators ordered. They were all moving in now.

And then another voice called out. "What's happening here? All of you, stand down!"

Warily, Hanuvar's opponent backed off, his eyes still showing hatred. Finally, though, the gladiator glanced over to where Hanuvar himself stared.

An armored warrior on a sturdy brown gelding had stopped before the shed with the broken cart. His grizzled hair was dark, and a patch covered his right eye. A scar shown pinkly from just behind the cloth and puckered into his hairline. As he sat rigidly on the horse, the stranger took in the field, and Hanuvar saw that the cuirass he wore was not only of Volani make, with dark green trim, but that it was one he himself had worn a lifetime ago. And then, upon further reflection Hanuvar realized the horseman looked very much like the version of himself he had conjured up in descriptions to frighten Dervans: a formidable one-eyed man with jet-black hair, with a confident, military bearing. Had that rumor taken living form?

III

He had only one eye left him, but Hanuvar saw clearly enough when his orders weren't being followed. Artus appeared to be at the forefront of the trouble again. He'd ordered Ennius to keep that one on a close leash.

"Report," Hanuvar demanded.

"This prisoner won't surrender." Artus pointed his sword at the Dervan man holding the knife.

Immediately a Herrene—holding a spear—objected. "That's a lie—this man with the sword has been trying to kill Fabius! But Fabius would have surrendered if he'd been given a chance. He doesn't own any slaves!"

The farm slaves in sun hats asserted this was true, tripping over their own words in their haste to defend this Fabius that Artus had cornered.

Hanuvar spoke to Ennius, watching with dejected expectancy. "Do these men have the right of it?"

Ennius held his companion's gaze for a moment, then faced his commander reluctantly. "It might be that Artus was a little too eager for the fight."

That sounded right. "You're done here, Artus. Join the sentries."

"These men drew weapons on me, sir! And he cut me." Artus then jabbed his sword in the direction of the Herrene. "And he's got my spear!"

"Give him the spear," Hanuvar ordered.

The young Herrene carefully laid the weapon in the grass with both hands, then stepped well back.

"Take your spear, get that wound cleaned up, and report to Olvus."

Scowling, Artus snatched his weapon and stomped away.

Hanuvar turned so he could take in the villa, where he heard a clatter and shrieks, and the occasional shout. Then he considered the man who'd been holding the knife. The Dervan patrician had sheathed it. Hanuvar beckoned him closer, and as he neared he sucked in a breath, for the Dervan's face was almost identical to the one he expected to see in the mirror when trimming his beard each morning, although this man was clean-shaven. His features were at least a decade older than they should have been, but there was no mistaking him for anyone else—not his father, nor even a sibling. It was him, Hanuvar.

The olive tinted face itself was weatherworn but unscarred, and somehow determined even at rest. His hair was dark, salted with gray, and his build was muscular and fit. Eyes the color of storm clouds searched his own.

Hanuvar could not help himself; he touched his eye patch, and the scar running down from his hairline. "Who are you?" he asked haltingly. He wanted to ask Fabius why he had Hanuvar's face, but knew that sounded mad.

"Who are you?" Fabius asked.

"I am Hanuvar Cabera."

Fabius addressed him in Volani. "That's curious. I've seen Hanuvar Cabera and you look less like him than I do."

Hanuvar understood the words, but they were hard work, and he touched his face again. He didn't remember taking the wound, but he thought it must have something to do with the strange turns his thinking sometimes took. He was able to reply in the same language, though the answer was labored and, he realized, awkwardly pronounced. "I do not remember meeting you. But...I was wounded during my capture by the Dervans and my memory is not what it was. Your name is Fabius?"

"Some call me that. What has brought you here?"

"I'm building an army to fight the Dervans," Hanuvar answered. "A lot of people don't want to suffer under the Dervan lash any more than I do."

A deep-voiced soldier called to him; he turned in his saddle, further than he was used to, so he could see him properly. It was Tafari, the resourceful Nuvaran he'd appointed third in command, jogging up from the villa. The dark-skinned gladiator came to a halt and saluted, then reported that the villa was secure.

"Good," Hanuvar said. "Casualties?"

"Eight. None on our side, sir."

"Prisoners?"

"Only a few. Most chose freedom. Laertes has a report for you. He's in the villa."

Hanuvar pointed to Fabius. "This one is to be our guest. He's to be well treated but watched. I'll speak to him in a little while."

Tafari eyed the stranger curiously. "Yes, sir."

"Put these with the others for questioning."

The Herrene objected, but Ennius told him to shut it and he marched them out. Hanuvar stared at Fabius and found his scrutiny returned. It left him strangely unsettled, but he forced the man from his thoughts. He had to learn what supplies Laertes had found and organize their withdrawal to more defensible environs.

IV

Hanuvar was searched and his knives were removed, though he was permitted to keep his coin purse. Tafari, a muscular Nuvaran with refined features and skin so dark it was almost ebony, directed him to a young oak and handed him a wineskin.

"Thank you. Where are all of you from?"

Tafari eyed him with cool contempt before answering in a low voice with a clipped Nuvaran accent. He deliberately misunderstood the aim of Hanuvar's question. "I am from Onatta. And I am a prince among my people, Dervan."

Hanuvar pressed on. "And you were captured, and sold to a gladiator school."

"I was." Tafari crossed muscular arms. "I fought many bouts before your people. Perhaps you saw them."

"No."

The gaze of those dark eyes would have withered another man. "Hanuvar freed all of us in Surobok's training school. That is what you meant, isn't it? It is like a Dervan to think our origin starts where you place us. But we are Ceori, and Nuvaran, and Tyvolian, and Volani, and Herrene. We are brothers, and we are free."

"May it last long," Hanuvar told him and settled into a reasonably comfortable seat between two roots.

The Nuvaran's skepticism of his sincerity showed in his frown. He retreated a few paces, then, like Hanuvar, watched the progress of the raid as outbuildings were systematically plundered. Men and women too ordinary to be gladiators carried off baskets of cabbages, grapes, bread, and other food. Others carted off pillows and blankets and fabric, and a few nervously emerged with armloads of glittering goblets, plates, or fine pottery. Horses were brought forth and inspected, and saddles were fixed across the best of them. Donkeys and oxen were hitched to wagons. Another line of raiders emerged from outbuildings bearing tools, and a third group, watched by a stern gladiator, left shouldering wine amphora.

For all that the looting was organized, it was folly. The Dervan legions would catch wind of this revolt and strike back mercilessly, crucifying the gladiators and every estate slave they'd freed in their march across the countryside. Hanuvar himself might be able to use the escapade to his advantage, particularly if this madman in his old armor were confused with him and killed, but the rebellion might just as easily draw too much attention to Hanuvar's secret war of liberation. And he didn't like to picture his noble Nuvaran guard, nor any of the other misused strangers here, nailed along the roadway to die in slow agony.

He'd been waiting in the shade for almost a half hour when a tall black-haired youth trotted up. He wore the same light brown sleeveless tunic as many of the gladiators, revealing the muscular build of his profession. A sword was belted to his waist and he carried a shield across his back. He stopped a few steps short of Hanuvar and scrutinized him, his expression growing more and more confused.

Tafari addressed the newcomer. "What are you doing here?"

The young man responded in Dervan with a pronounced Volani accent. "I have come to see the mystery man. I heard he speaks my language."

"I do," Hanuvar answered in Volani.

His young countryman eyed him keenly. "Who are you?"

"Does your friend understand Volani?"

The Volani gladiator shook his head ruefully, and quipped: "Most of my comrades barely speak Dervan."

Hanuvar glanced at Tafari, but the man showed no sign of comprehension. He climbed slowly to his feet, careful not to suggest he meant any advance. "I know you," he said. "You've bulked up and cut your hair short. You are Eshmun, a guard from the admiralty tower. We met when you were courting my secretary's daughter. And you recognize me, don't you?"

Eshmun's manner grew more confused, then almost frightened, as though he had seen a spirit. But he nodded slowly.

Tafari picked up on the tension. "What are you two talking about?"

Hanuvar ignored him. "This man who claims to be Hanuvar—why do you follow someone you know is lying?"

"He freed us," Eshmun answered. "And he speaks with authority. I'd almost convinced myself he was you somehow. But now... You live! What are you doing here? Is it true you were here to free these Volani slaves?"

"Yes. I knew some Volani were sold to the gladiator schools, but you've been hard to trace."

"I've been sold three separate times now." Eshmun's stare grew more searching. Hanuvar took note of the well-tended scars along both of the younger Volani's arms and wondered how many deadly stage appearances he'd already survived.

Tafari's tone had grown challenging. "What are you two talking about?"

Before either Hanuvar or Eshmun had to answer, the false

Hanuvar rode up and dropped down from his horse a few paces shy of the tree.

He nodded to Tafari, then greeted Eshmun with a question. "What are you doing here?"

The young gladiator politely bowed his head. "I heard that this man spoke Volani, and I came to speak with him." He indicated the real Hanuvar. "Do you know who he is?"

"He says he's called Fabius."

"He's you," Eshmun continued in Volani. "This is Hanuvar Cabera. Who are you, really?"

The false Hanuvar's brow furrowed. "I am Hanuvar Cabera."

"Then why do you speak Volani with a Dervan accent? Why can't you recall—"

"Enough!" the pretender said sharply, speaking Dervan once more. "You have your assigned duties. Or are you so unhappy with my service that you wish to leave it?"

Eshmun hesitated, then bowed his head and departed. The false Hanuvar then looked to Tafari. "Leave us."

The Nuvaran's eyebrows rose in disbelief. "Sir? Are you sure?"

"Yes. Go."

The pretender waited until the gladiator passed out of earshot, then felt the scar along his hairline before snatching his hand back, as if irritated at himself. He continued to study Hanuvar, his left hand shifting to stroke his necklace chain, the bottom of which was hidden beneath his armor. "I don't know what to make of you," he said. "You claim to be Hanuvar?"

"I made no claim," Hanuvar answered. "I was recognized by Eshmun. Who are you, really?"

The pretender's response was level and solemn. "I am Hanuvar Cabera."

"Are you. Where did you come from?"

"I am from Volanus," he answered impatiently. "What are you doing here? I spared you because I do not make war upon the innocent. But if you mean to sow dissension—"

"I mean to free the Volani slaves," Hanuvar interrupted. "And your actions are jeopardizing that. You're going to have legionaries pouring through this countryside just as I need it officially ignored."

"So I should fail to fight what is wrong because I fear reprisal?"

"You should look further than the struggle. If you're planning to build an army made up of fieldhands and gladiators, you'll have at most a few months of freedom and then you'll be crushed."

"We shall see."

Perhaps the pretender wasn't an opportunist, but a madman who believed his own lies. If so, Hanuvar might still play upon shared goals to reach his objectives. "I would like to leave here with the slaves I came for, and their allies. They have friends and loved ones waiting for them."

"They are free to do as they will."

"And am I?"

The other man didn't answer immediately, then acquiesced with a sudden head nod. "Of course. I will ask them if they wish to leave with you."

"I would prefer to speak with them myself."

"You will wait. Your presence has already disturbed one of my men, and may yet cause further trouble. If they want to go with you, they will be here shortly." The pretender's gaze lingered over Hanuvar's features in confusion. Then he turned away.

Hanuvar almost stayed silent. In the end, though, he could not hold his tongue. He had still not deduced his counterfeit's true motivation, although the man's sincerity was manifest. "You need to flee now."

The pretender stopped and turned. "We'll be pulling out shortly."

"I mean you have to leave Tyvol. Commandeer some ships. The Dervans will come for you. Even with a hundred times the resources you could gather here, they will overwhelm you and slaughter every man, woman, and child you protect."

The pretender clenched his jaw. When he spoke again it was in fluent Volani, with no hint of accent. "I will find a way or make one," he declared, in his delivery sounding so much like Hanuvar's father, Himli, that Hanuvar felt a chill down his back.

The pretender climbed into his saddle and rode toward the villa.

Hanuvar was used to quickly taking the measure of a man, but after a conversation with the pretender he'd grown even more confused about him. The false Hanuvar had acknowledged a head injury. While some who survived such wounds were forever changed in personality, capability, or both, he'd never heard of someone assuming another man's identity.

Tafari returned to stand guard, saying nothing, although his manner was more contemplative than before. A short while later Antires arrived, munching a peach. With him were Eshmun and the older two Volani vintners bearing their few belongings.

Eshmun handed over Hanuvar's knives. "You're free to go, General."

Hanuvar nodded his thanks and belted them back on. He addressed the vintners. "Where's Gisco?"

The eldest sighed in disgust. "The woman he loves wants to live free with the others. Our friends, too, did not wish to leave, though I told them I thought we'd be safer with you."

"They'll have no true freedom, nor a very long life," Hanuvar said. "They're being led to ruin."

"That may be," Eshmun said. "But we will die free."

His words astounded Hanuvar. "You're not coming with us?"

The young man shook his head no.

Hanuvar eyed him in disbelief. "You know he's not who he claims. There's something wrong with him."

"I owe him." Eshmun spoke like a man making a vow.

"Because he freed you? Thank him, then, and come with us."

Again Eshmun shook his head.

"Are there other Volani gladiators with you?"

"Yes," Eshmun answered. "Only one was in the same school as me. A wheelwright who took to the sword faster than many soldiers."

Hanuvar took a step closer to him. "Listen to me, Eshmun. The legions will come. I didn't stop them when I had an army, and allied cities behind us. How can your tiny force stand against them?"

"You didn't have an army of gladiators. We're getting more every week."

Eshmun surely knew he overvalued the skills he'd acquired in the arena, and the ability to quickly teach them to others. His gaze was briefly furtive, as if he recognized his reasoning was flawed, then he stiffened with resolve and tipped his chin toward Antires. "Your friend says you've freed whole families of Volani."

Hanuvar wished Antires wasn't so free with that information, because Eshmun might well be caught alive, and could spread that news to Dervans. He guessed Antires had shared the details because he'd hoped to convince the gladiator to come with them. "It's true," Hanuvar confirmed at last.

Eshmun swallowed, as if doing so gave him courage. "Do you know if my family is among them?"

"Come with me and find out. Bring the other Volani with you."

Eshmun considered it briefly. "I need to stay and fight."

"Our people need protectors like you. There are a lot of battles to win. We are all one family, now."

He thought he might have him then, for Eshmun wavered. But the gladiator shook his head a final time. "May Varis watch your steps," he said. And he strode away without another word.

Hanuvar's mood was dark as he turned to the others. "Come. We've a long way to go." He started away, his companions following. After a moment Antires walked at his side.

"They're keeping our horses?" Hanuvar asked. He was more than a little irritated to lose the roan he'd trained since he and Antires had begun travelling together.

"I asked about that. I was told they needed them more than we did. Who is that man, really? And why is he pretending to be you?"

"I'm not certain."

"Is he just fame hungry?"

Hanuvar shook his head. "That's what I thought at first. But... no. He's something else."

They passed through the fields and down to the main road with Antires questioning and speculating the while and Hanuvar barely speaking. They'd walked a good five miles before the cavalrymen rode up. Like many of the legion's horse-mounted troops, these were foreign auxiliaries, pale-haired Irimacians for the most part, led by an older veteran, a lean decurion possessing only a faint accent.

He and his entire patrol were hot eyed, alert for escaped slaves and ready for bloodletting, and it was only Hanuvar's patrician clothing and confident demeanor that stayed them. A few hours prior the same characteristics had nearly doomed him, but Hanuvar's guise as a well-to-do Dervan gave the decurion enough of a pause to examine Hanuvar's papers, which were perfect, for Carthalo himself had fabricated them.

He would have told the soldiers he'd seen no sign of the rebels, but the vintners reacted so visibly to the question that Hanuvar had to admit that they'd interacted with them. When asked how he'd survived, Hanuvar explained that the slaves with him were his own and had vouched for him as a kind master. The decurion ordered four of his troopers to escort them back to camp. Hanuvar tried to demur, but the decurion ignored him, and there was no convincing lower rankers after the order had been handed down, so before long they were conveyed to a small military camp. There were a few dozen cavalry troopers and their support staff within its boundaries, along with a handful of men in the somber black with silver death-head ornamentation of the revenant order. Hanuvar had occasionally experienced nightmares that unfolded like this.

Because the papers, appearance, and lack of accent showed that he, alone among his companions, was a Dervan citizen, the cavalrymen moved to separate them the moment they reached camp, saying that the legate would want to talk with him. Antires' look was tense, and Hanuvar tried to bolster him with a nod, silently willing all three to maintain their composure as they were pushed toward a fire at the outskirts where a few cooks were preparing large quantities of food.

"This way," the cavalry optio said, then bade Hanuvar follow him. They made for a larger tent on a little rise near the middle of the encampment but had to keep to the edge of the lane between tents when a disordered band of mounted revenants clomped past. Dusty and begrimed, many bore minor wounds. Others toward the rear proved far worse off, and had to be helped down from their saddles. There were calls for a medic even as a handful of tired corpsmen emerged to attend them.

Approaching the camp's center, Hanuvar concentrated on his breathing, counting his steps as he had on Narata. The loss of control and sense of impending doom in his chest was akin to that when and he and his friend Eledeva were plummeting hundreds of feet toward the sea after she had been struck from the air by a Dervan catapult stone. It was hard to think through.

The optio had mentioned a legate, and if he meant the revenant legate, whom Ciprion had said was desperate to prove Hanuvar's existence, then Hanuvar's situation was very dire indeed. Of all Dervans, the revenants were most likely to be aware of his true appearance. The murals and busts of him that had been visible in multiple points of Volanus would have depicted him with a thick beard, a Volani hairstyle, and dressed either in statesman's robes or armor, but those superficial differences might be easily discounted, especially if he conducted himself in his usual manner. He would have to depend upon more than a good command of the Dervan language, and channel everything Antires had ever taught him about losing himself in the performance of a role.

The optio bade Hanuvar wait while he conferred with the sentry before the largest and most ornamented tent to be seen. Even the tips of its tent posts, protruding above the red canvas cloth, were gilt with bright brass. The optio disappeared inside where he asked and received permission to report. The sentry, another of the Irimacian auxiliaries, gave Hanuvar a once-over but said nothing, more interested in overhearing the discussion inside than learning more about the stranger beside him.

The cavalry optio supplied information about the looting of Minucius' villa, the deaths of its overseers, and the exodus of most of the slaves, along with horses and supplies.

The angry officer demanded additional details, and the cavalryman suggested the legate might want to speak to the survivor they recovered.

"A survivor?" the legate said with a curse. "Why should I care about that?"

"He was travelling with some slaves. Says he's a merchant. His papers are in order. He says he met some of the rebels."

"Fine. Bring him in."

The optio pushed open the tent flap and motioned Hanuvar forward.

The command tent was large enough that it was subdivided and lit with a handful of strategically placed lanterns. Presumably a rest area lay beyond the canvas to the rear. The central area into which Hanuvar had been conducted was dominated by a campaign table across which a detailed regional map had been tacked, and a cloaked officer was frowning down at it.

He took Hanuvar in with a sour glance. He was a revenant in early middle age, of middling height, with short, jet-black hair, probably dyed. His skin was badly sunburned, and a thin, pale scar stood out along his heavy chin. From the gold-leaf gilt along his dark armor and the additional lightning pattern around the skulls upon his shoulder tabs, the man's high rank would have been apparent even if Hanuvar didn't recognize him from descriptions. This was Tertius Aetius Aquilius, legate of the revenants. That he was in the field hunting gladiators rather than sitting behind a desk in the bowels of the capital dictating to his minions was an ominous development in its own right. Hanuvar bowed his head, channeling his own fear into the natural nervousness any revenant surely expected as their due.

"Did you see the leader of the gladiators?"

"I think so," Hanuvar answered hesitantly.

"And he was healthy?" Aquilius watched him alertly.

Hanuvar stood with slumped shoulders, his expression blank with simple-minded dread. "I think so. I mean, he had an old injury. On his face. A scar. And he had an eye patch." Hanuvar sounded both frightened and foolish to his own ears. He kept his eyes wide and worried, the better to suggest he was someone completely different than himself.

"I'm referring to his mind," Aquilius said impatiently. "Was he clear, well spoken?"

Hanuvar thought this an interesting line of questioning. Either Aquilius had intelligence about the false Hanuvar, or he'd encountered him himself. He gulped. "I don't know. I didn't talk to him. Sir. Sorry."

The legate sighed and looked back down at the table. His eyes hadn't fastened on any of Hanuvar's more distinctive physical features, but then many men had a slight hook in their nose, and in the dull lighting his eye color would not be as obvious, and, as Antires had taught him, much of a man's character was revealed in how he carried himself. Presumably Aquilius had not imagined Hanuvar pretending to be a random, accentless, clean-shaven Dervan merchant of no great intelligence. And he seemed preoccupied with the pretender's uprising.

The tent flap was pushed open and a tall man ducked inside. He wore a massive dark bronze cuirass, and heavy boots rather than soldier's sandals. His red hair was pulled back in a tight ponytail and his eyes were a stark blue. Calenius. His right upper arm was heavily bandaged, and he smelled of soap and vinegar.

Hanuvar knew then that his time was up. He might be able to take out Aquilius, who would not anticipate the first blow, but the optio and Calenius would bear him down. He hoped Antires might be able to slip out in the noise and confusion—he'd have to draw things out as long as possible.

Aquilius saw the look of recognition that passed between Calenius and Hanuvar. "You've met this man?" he asked the wizard.

"I have." Calenius sounded reluctant to admit it.

"When?"

Hanuvar answered, putting a stammer in his delivery. "I arranged to buy some slaves this man owned." He watched Calenius, wondering if he would be contradicted.

But the big man seemed content enough with that simplified accounting of their interaction. And he had apparently decided to hold to his pledge to keep Hanuvar's identity secret, for he turned to Aquilius. "We need to get back out there."

"We need to regroup," Aquilius countered. Both men had miraculously decided to ignore him.

"It was a clever ambush. But that is what you would expect."

There was something in the big man's tone that raised a frown on the revenant's lips. "He's not even the real Hanuvar! If this keeps up, I'm going to have to send for an actual legion!" Suddenly Aquilius turned to the actual Hanuvar. "Was he still lying about that? Is this impostor still claiming to be Hanuvar?"

Hanuvar nodded earnestly. "He looked just as the stories say he does."

"It isn't him," Aquilius said curtly. "He's a fraud, just trying to stir up trouble." The legate sounded as though the false Hanuvar had acted out of spite against him alone.

"You have to press him," Calenius advised. "Keep after him. This was a screen because he knows he's vulnerable. He doesn't have enough men to do it again and again."

"You're sure of that?" Aquilius demanded. "Now that he has the manpower from this estate, he has even more men to keep watch and lay ambush."

"Which is why you should follow, now, instead of staying in camp," Calenius advised. "His new recruits won't have been trained yet to fight."

Aquilius shook his head. "My men need rest. I've got my cavalry following him. We'll pin him in place and then strike."

"You ask too little of your men," Calenius said.

The revenant stabbed a finger at the bigger man's chest. "You forget your place. I don't want your military advice. He keeps slipping away. You said you could track him."

"And I did. I need to recover before I can do that again," Calenius finished. Meaning his spell energy was spent.

Aquilius turned back to Hanuvar. "Did the rebels say anything about their plans, or where they were going?"

"Not to me. I'm lucky I got away at all."

The legate sighed.

"Um. I'd like to get back on the road to Rivona," Hanuvar said hopefully.

Aquilius snorted in disbelief. "Just because marauding slaves spared you once doesn't mean they'll do so again. I've no extra men to protect you."

Hanuvar wanted to be well away from Aquilius. "We couldn't possibly... I mean they took all our effects and I've already lost a week's sales and..."

"Fine. Go." Aquilius pointed to the door flap. "Optio, I'm done with this man and his slaves."

Aquilius didn't acknowledge Hanuvar's effusive thanks.

Hanuvar felt Calenius' eyes on him as he passed through the tent entrance. Though he had faced death countless times, the close brush with the legate had shaken him, and his heart still raced. While being escorted through the revenant camp he kept his face down, occasionally rubbing his cheek to better hide his features. No one looked at him more than once.

On the camp edge, Hanuvar found the Volani sitting nervously, listening to Antires tell a coarse tale to a pair of troopers while some rankers bustled to dole out rations to others.

Antires delivered a punchline about the goat not being his, the soldiers laughed, and the cavalryman with Hanuvar told him to stick to the north road and to not rest until they reached Rivona. While the Irimacians gossiped in low voices about the revenants and their terrible soldiering, he caught Antires' eye. It was clear how worried the Herrene had been. Antires opened his mouth as though to ask a question, his eyes betraying relief. Then his gaze swayed over Hanuvar's shoulder.

Calenius had followed from the camp and beckoned for Hanuvar. Neither the legate nor other revenants were near him, so he must not have intended betrayal, although Hanuvar doubted the visit was inspired by the wizard's sense of fellowship. Hanuvar pointed Antires to the vintners. "Get those two ready to march." He couldn't stand the thought of Antires and the two Volani remaining here any longer.

Antires stared at the big man in alarm, then checked with Hanuvar to make sure he understood.

"It's all right," he assured Antires. Hanuvar stepped away, hoping it was. He steadied himself for this new confrontation.

Calenius walked a dozen yards beyond the camp edge entirely, halting beside a spindly elm that blocked line of sight. He coolly appraised Hanuvar. "For a moment there, I thought he had you."

"For a moment there, so did I."

The big man regarded him at length, then addressed him bluntly. "I've had to go to greater effort than I anticipated to keep your identity safe. You owe me now. If anyone can take down this false Hanuvar, it's a real one."

"You expect me to kill him?"

Calenius shrugged. "No. All you need to do is take his necklace off."

Hanuvar had noted the chain the pretender had been fiddling with. "You made him." The truth and its implications clicked into place, and with it a clear-headed calm.

"Yes." Calenius answered Hanuvar's questioning look by providing more detail. "Aquilius wanted to find Hanuvar. I told him my magics didn't work that way, but he had this idea we could conjure up a simulacrum of Hanuvar that could tell us what he might be thinking. Apparently there were rumors that some other Dervan leader tried that."

"One of them tried something like that. Go on."

"It was a terrible idea," Calenius concluded. "This fake Hanuvar is enough like the real one that he escaped."

"Why did you help the revenant legate in the first place?"

"Aquilius threatens what I hope to achieve in this land."

The response intrigued Hanuvar. He'd expected that the answer would be money or resources. "I thought you were well regarded by the revenants, or you'd long since be dead in some grisly way for daring magic in Tyvol."

"He surely reminded me of that." Calenius' mouth twisted in a brief surge of anger, then his entire expression shifted into one of blithe carelessness. "Ordinarily I'd have killed him then and there, but I don't need such complications right now. Enough. Can you take care of it?"

"I want more information first. Who's the poor man you put the spell on?"

Hanuvar's interest in the assignment seemed to have granted the big wizard a modicum of patience, for he answered in detail. "A centurion from a legion posted in Herrenia. His men were so loyal they fought their way in to save him after he went down, then held a sword to the best Herrenian physician they could find, threatening to gut him if he didn't live. The healer kept him alive. But the man's mind is ruined. He could barely remember his name."

"What is his name?"

Calenius frowned. "Does it matter?"

"Yes."

"Gnaeus Calpurnius."

"How did you lay my personality over his?"

"Drawn from accounts, items you had in your possession when you were in southern Tyvol, and... other sources. Memories copied from other worlds," Calenius added. "You wouldn't understand."

Calenius underestimated him, but Hanuvar saw no point in correcting the assumption.

The wizard continued gruffly, "I could have more easily just pointed them to you. This has taken a lot more time than I wanted and now I want it over, tonight."

"What if I just get him to stop freeing slaves?"

Calenius' tone grew faintly mocking. "Feeling sentimental?"

"Maybe I'm being practical."

The big wizard eyed him for a long moment, then shrugged. "The magic will only last about seven more days. If you can get him to stop the raids until then, I guess I'm fine with that. Aquilius was planning simply to wait him out, but Gnaeus has kept causing trouble."

"And when the magic runs out, he'll be Gnaeus again?"

"And no threat at all. That shell of a man only has one idea in his head."

"Which idea?" Hanuvar asked.

"To get his men ready for the fight."

So. Even broken, Gnaeus Calpurnius tried to look out for his soldiers. "Perhaps I can use that to bring this whole thing to an end. Do you know anything else about him?"

Calenius' cold eyes searched Hanuvar's own, and then he opened a belt pouch, pulled out and unfolded some papyrus, and glanced through it as if to confirm its contents. Finally he handed it over. "Aquilius gave me a report on him."

Hanuvar nodded his thanks and took it. "I'll need a horse, and weapons."

"Very well. Wait here." Calenius turned and walked off.

Antires had been watching and hurried to Hanuvar's side the moment Calenius was gone.

"What were you talking to him about?" Antires asked. "What are you going to do?"

Hanuvar faced his friend and clapped his shoulder. "First, I'm going to thank you for your acting lessons, because they just saved us all."

Antires blinked in surprise, then grinned at the compliment.

"Second, I'm going to get you on the road with the Volani. No arguments. They don't know where to go. You must lead them. I'll catch up."

Antires never liked to be ordered away; it interfered with his ability to directly witness and record Hanuvar's activities. Moreover, they'd just been through a serious shock, and the Herrene would probably have felt a lot happier if they stayed together. There was a challenging note in his voice as he asked: "And what are you doing?"

"I'm going after our false Hanuvar. And do what I can for the men and women he has with him."

V

The lone hill commanded the best field of view in the area, steep on two sides so it was defensible, and was topped by a small screen of bushes and trees. It was such an obvious vantage point that Hanuvar set a band of his men to wait in the greenery upon one of the steep sides. When evening fell, an excited Artus brought him back to the site, gleefully saying that the lure had worked. A half-dozen cavalrymen, led by a decurion, had ridden up to the hill. Now each of them lay dead.

"These are good horses," Artus said, a glint of avarice in his eyes as he put his hand to the reins of one of the small black mounts. "And fine javelins." He patted the saddle, where a holster for the weapons hung.

Something about those javelins jarred a memory. Hanuvar had wielded weapons like those himself, many times. He remembered a black man laughing with him as they inspected the shoddy work on the points one of the green legionaries had sharpened—what was his name?

He started. Why would he have been laughing with a centurion, in a field he knew was in Herrenia? He'd never been to Herrenia, had he?

"Something wrong, sir?" Artus asked. There was doubt in his eye, and his gaze shifted to Hanuvar's hand, reflexively rubbing his necklace chain.

Hanuvar released his fingers and pulled himself together. He would have liked to have questioned a survivor, but he knew in the heat of combat obtaining prisoners wasn't always a reasonable option. Besides, Artus was clearly eager to be back in his commander's good graces after his embarrassment earlier. So Hanuvar commended him and told him and the others to be off to camp with their recovered gear.

It was twilight by the time he returned. Hanuvar personally checked with all the sentries, then made final arrangements for the predawn departure before returning to his tent, in a clearing above the forest camp. Two mornings before he had resolved to keep his bed a stone's throw beyond the others when he discovered he'd been crying out in his sleep for his men to form up. He didn't want his people concerned or having cause to question his guidance.

This evening he was glad for the distance, for there was loud laughter and raucous talk among the newly liberated. The gladiators had silenced their singing and kept the fires banked out of caution, but no one was in a mood to fully quash the high spirits that followed their recent string of victories.

He knew he should rest, yet he sat staring at the amulet, trying to remember exactly what the revenant legate and Calenius had talked about. His recollection was vague, like most of his recent memories until he'd donned the necklace.

His mind turned again and again to the man whom Eshmun had said was the real Hanuvar. He was Hanuvar, though! He knew it. He remembered the wide boulevards and the long quays and the scent of bread from the silver city's bakeries wafting through the morning air.

But if he was Hanuvar, why did he remember the men in a shield line with him, all in Dervan armor, fending off the line of Herrenic rebels? The ridge had to hold, and he had sworn that his boys would do that.

How then did he also remember seeing his brother's severed head on the camp outskirts after the sentries had called him over? He would never forget Melgar's sobbing anger, and how he'd feared he'd lose two brothers in one day, for Melgar had dashed off with only an honor guard and somehow sneaked behind enemy lines to recover the rest of Adruvar's body.

"Sir."

Tullus spoke to him from the tent entrance. Hanuvar tucked the amulet beneath his shirt and turned. "Yes?"

"Report from the sentries. There's a man with a lantern riding forward across the valley. He's calling for a parley with Hanuvar."

Hanuvar frowned. "Bring him to me."

"Should we blindfold him?"

"No. An astute enemy can guess our forces. And we will be gone from this place tomorrow."

The sentry saluted and left. Hanuvar fingered his necklace chain. The vocabulary he'd used to speak his orders felt right, and yet somehow the words were different from what he would normally have said, weren't they? Thoughts like this confused and unsettled him.

It was not long before Tafari and Ennius presented themselves at the tent, proclaiming that they had brought the visitor, and it was Fabius, from this morning.

Hanuvar went out to meet him, struck again by the sense he was staring at the face that should have been his. "Why have you returned?"

Fabius answered calmly. "Because the Dervans are coming, and I need to make you hear me."

Hanuvar held the tent flap open and bade his guest enter. He addressed his men. "I'll handle this. Stay within shouting distance."

"Yes, sir."

Hanuvar lifted the flap for Fabius and followed him inside. The tent didn't come close to the size of those designed for officers to hold strategy meetings, but it was the largest they'd recovered from their raids. There was enough room within both for a cot and a writing desk and stool.

He pointed his visitor to the stool and sat down on the side of the low cot. "I heard you the last time. You seem to think I have better options than the fight before me."

The other man's eyes were frank with concern. "You have had options all along. You escaped captivity. You decided to free the gladiators. You decided to have them free the farm hands."

Did his visitor think him a fool? "How am I to oppose the Dervans with no army?"

"You don't oppose them." The other man leaned forward. "Gnaeus Calpurnius. Do you remember that name? That's the one that defined you until eight days ago. Centurion Gnaeus Calpurnius. Of Savona."

He felt the blood drain from his face as a tide of memories washed through him. He spoke haltingly. "I remember a wide-hipped woman with freckled cheeks, brushing her hair. I remember my cousins, and my uncle, home from the legion in his uniform. I remember my legate, stern but steady. My best friend, Macro. I remember my optio, Quintus..." He was chattering to no good purpose, and frowned at the other man. "You're saying these are my original memories, but they're... embers in a dying fire. My memories as Hanuvar are so much more real."

"What all can you remember, Gnaeus? Do you remember standing with Gisco before the battle of Acanar?"

Yes, he did, with incredible clarity. Eight legions of Dervans had gathered in the plain below, an impossibly huge army, more than twice the size he himself had fielded. "Gisco remarked that it was amazing to see so many men numbered against us."

"And you remember what I said?" the other man asked.

"What I said," Hanuvar corrected, and slipped effortlessly into Volani. Should he know Volani? "'I'll tell you something even more amazing. In all that number of men there is no man named Gisco.' The laugh rippled through the ranks. And the fear of the men eased. I knew we were halfway to winning already."[11]

"Many men heard that," the other Hanuvar mused.

"You think I need to prove myself?"

"I know who I am. I want to see how much of me is in you. Do you remember our first words to Imilce?"

"I do. Do you?" He could not help but take umbrage.

Hanuvar and Imilce had met at the behest of parents more interested in cementing an alliance than building a romantic partnership, though Father had declared he thought the girl intelligent and pretty.

The man across from him spoke with surprising gentleness. "We will get through this together." He then breathed out slowly. "Do you remember her last words?"

He did not. It had not occurred to Hanuvar that she'd had last words, and he gasped. "She's dead?"

"Yes. Do you remember Melgar's last words?"

He felt the blood drain from his face. No. Not Melgar too. First Narisia, then Adruvar... Now Imilce and Melgar both. "How? What happened?"

"In the end I think he died of bitterness, although he'd been happier than I'd seen him in years. So many are dead. Even Volanus itself. Did you know that?"

"I..." Hanuvar's hands closed on the amulet chain and his eyes burned. "You're lying."

"Do you think so? Or do you just want to think so?" His visitor's voice grew more challenging. "Do you remember how you came into Dervan hands? What's the last thing you recall about being Hanuvar before you were imprisoned?"

"There was... a parade. No, a siege. Harnil was there—"

"Harnil is dead." The other man's speech was brutally terse. "The

---

[11] Gisco is a name so common among the Volani that it sometimes leads to confusion, but it is unused by Dervans. The jest, then, was found humorous by its listeners, but perhaps not to readers, for it is a sad truth that jokes that must be explained are rarely funny. —*Silenus*

armor you wear was mine almost twenty years ago. The spell is tied somehow to items that I wore then... among other things."

Hanuvar put hands to his head, and they came again to the scar. Why did he have that scar? He didn't remember, but he had a vague recollection of Calenius and the legate talking about a spell, and how he had to hold to the necklace if he wanted to remain himself.

Once again he fingered the pendant chain. He admitted then that his own reasoning was flawed, just as his memories seemed to be. The man before him was not lying. There were great gaps in his understanding of the world, and his time in it. Worse, he had avoided deep consideration of many troubling observations he'd made. He needed to study and evaluate all with logic, not just emotion, as his father had taught him... although it seemed more and more likely Himli Cabera had not been his father at all.

He could not believe that Harnil and Melgar and Imilce were dead. He wanted to ask about Ravella and his daughter, but feared what he would hear. But did any of that matter? As it turned out, he hadn't ever really met any of these people. None of these memories were his.

He massaged his forehead. "So... I am... Gnaeus." He met the other man's eyes. Hanuvar's eyes. "I think I knew that Volanus had fallen," he said slowly. "But not as... me. Hanuvar me, I mean. This other man, Gnaeus, knows. I can see some of his memories, but it's like peering through a heavy fog. And I recall what it was like, before I had the amulet. I think... I think he was worried about his men. I mean, I was."

"Like any good commander."

"So I am Dervan." It was hard to say. "And I should hate you, enemy of Derva." He looked across the tent at the man who had his face. Hanuvar's face.

"If you like. I don't find hate accomplishes much."

"I know that it's these memories that are keeping me going, even if they're not mine. I..." It was so confusing. Almost he ripped off the amulet. "But I need an army. I need to stop the Dervans! The Dervans must be stopped or they'll be the end of us!"

"They will not be stopped by you." Hanuvar spoke with weary sorrow. "You think you can outlast them, and you can't. You think you can reason with them, and you won't. The Dervans will not surrender. They drove me from their lands, and my resources were a thousand times grander than yours. And what is more, you are Dervan. You have no reason to wage this fight."

"I am neither you, nor Gnaeus," he admitted at last. "I think that man is lost. So who am I?"

"Right now you're a commander who's led his soldiers into danger. Because you thought you needed an army."

"I can make them one." He knew, with time, he could forge them into a force to be reckoned with, and that others would join them.

Hanuvar spoke slowly, with the air of a messenger bringing word of a loved one's death. "You do not have the time. Your necklace will stop functioning well before then."

"How do you know?"

"Because I talked with the man who made it, and he spoke truth, because he owes me a debt. But think. You have my memories. You must recall some of the magic in the war, on both sides, and how fragile and finite its effects were."

Gnaeus brought out the amulet and weighed it in his palm. "How long do I have?"

"A week at most."

"A week to be a thinking man." Gnaeus' teeth showed in a snarl. "And then I am once more a simpleton. You bring hard news."

"You are a soldier. We always live on borrowed time. Any day I could be caught and killed by the Dervans. I've already lasted far longer than I expected."

"You're freeing slaves, too."

"But not to build an army."

"Why, then?"

The real Hanuvar was a long time in answering, and Gnaeus guessed that he wrestled with sharing his mission. Finally, though, he did, his voice low, almost vulnerable, as though he revealed a terrible burden and source of shame. "To bring them to a life far from this conflict."

"All of them?"

"Yes."

Gnaeus slowly breathed out. He caught a blurred reflection of the lantern light in the stone at his neck. "I led them to this."

"Yes." Hanuvar's answer was blunt. "You did it because the

Dervans tried to make you into a different man. It didn't fully work, and your reasoning wasn't entirely sound."

He winced to hear it. "Why did they do this?"

"Because they wanted someone like me to reason out what I was doing, so they could find me. Whomever does will be celebrated, probably land a triumphal parade, unless I miss my guess."

Gnaeus nodded. That sounded right. He shook his head, trying to remember he was a Dervan himself. "Most of the people I freed aren't ours... yours. Will you help them, too?"

"Yes. If I don't get them away, the Dervans will crucify them. No matter that most haven't even lifted a sword. It's enough that they rebelled."

What he said was true. "It's my fault. I led them to this."

"And I will do what I can for them."

"Why?"

"Because no one else will, and because you and I are one, in a way."

Gnaeus smiled sadly. He understood. "And you can get them away?"

"There's a good chance."

He was no stranger to difficult circumstances. "Then I will explain the matter to them. And we will have to provide a distraction for our pursuers. Is it me or the slaves they're after?"

"Your pursuers don't want escaped slaves roaming the countryside. But it's mostly you. I'm almost certain their leader, Aquilius, created you without any official approval. If the emperor finds he accidentally let a new Hanuvar loose in the countryside, the rest of the legate's career will be very short."

Gnaeus liked the sound of that. "I'll rouse the men and tell them the truth. I'll need a few volunteers to stay with me, at least long enough to create the semblance of a large remaining unit."

"Good thinking," Hanuvar agreed.

Gnaeus felt a surge of affection for the man across from him, who so easily understood his reasoning. But then that was only to be expected, for sorcery had twisted him into this man's mental double. In Hanuvar's eyes he saw a flicker of that same regard, though it was overshadowed by sorrow. And pity.

He did not wish to look upon pity. Gnaeus pushed to his feet and stepped to the tent flap. He called for Ennius, told him to bring some refreshments for his guest, and then to assemble the men, because he was going to make an important announcement. Ennius hurried away.

Hanuvar stood.

"I want a moment alone," Gnaeus said. "To ready myself."

"Of course." Hanuvar looked as though he was considering laying a hand to his shoulder, then decided it might be unwelcome and passed from the tent.

Only after his visitor's footfalls receded did Gnaeus turn from the tent flap, hands to his face. Deep grief welled up from within. Harnil and Melgar both were dead... Imilce was gone. And what of his daughter, named in honor of lost Narisia? Tears tracked down his face and he wrenched out a sob. He had known none of these people, but could not help himself. He was a child, he thought, deceived by someone's chicanery. They had thought to make him a pawn. At least they had failed at that.

Even if he were not truly Hanuvar, he was not truly Gnaeus. He was some middle thing, and he would not even be that for much longer.

He heard someone slide into the tent behind him. He began his turn too late, on his bad side, and didn't see the object that struck his head. He staggered and dropped to his knee, hand falling toward his knife. He raised an arm and partly blocked a second blow that brought stars to his eyes. His knees folded and his senses swam. Someone reached around his shoulders and fumbled at his necklace chain.

He threw an elbow at whomever stood close, then was clouted in the face. "Guards!" he called weakly, then shouted again. "Guards!"

VI

Ennius, Hanuvar's escort, had set him up with a wineskin and moved away to pass along his commander's orders. When the weak cry for assistance came, Hanuvar paused in midswallow, then dashed toward the command tent in the small hilltop clearing. He was almost there when the gladiator staggered clear. Despite the darkness, Hanuvar recognized him as Artus, the curly-haired brute who'd been so intent on killing him at the villa.

A long necklace with an amber stone hung about his neck and Artus blinked, shaking his head, moving almost as if drunk. He paused, swaying after only two steps.

"What did you do with your commander?" Hanuvar demanded.

Artus stared at him. "How do you *see* so much..." he croaked. "How do you...the weight of it all...it *hurts*." His eyes were wild. He tore the amulet from his throat with a savage motion and dropped it.

"You'd best not have hurt him," Hanuvar said.

"Are you threatening me?" Artus asked with a sneer. "You couldn't take me before." He drew his sword. The arm he held it with was bandaged, but the wound Hanuvar had given him looked like it was causing no obvious trouble. "I knew there was something strange about him, and his necklace. And you. I was listening in."

"Then you know the amulet's going to wear out in only a few days."

"That's if I wear it all the time. I figure if I only put it on when I need a great battle plan, it will last a lot longer. I guess I'll have to get used to the rest of your nonsense, too. I never thought Hanuvar would be such an old woman. You're supposed to be fierce. Tough. But you're so worried about everyone. You love them so much," he continued mockingly. "I'll make a *better* Hanuvar." He trotted forward.

The gladiators had searched Hanuvar, but then he'd been expecting that. He pulled a throwing knife from the holster snugged along his inner thigh. He threw, a direct shot for the throat at close range.

Few could have dodged it, but Artus was a veteran. He deflected the attack with his blade tip then leapt forward with a chop.

Hanuvar ducked beneath a backhand strike and threw himself into a roll toward a pile of tinder. He came up with two thumb-width sticks.

Artus sneered and stabbed. Hanuvar slid clear of the strike, drove one of the stick ends into the nerve cluster along his opponent's wrist at the same time he jabbed at his throat.

The gladiator dropped the sword but snagged the second stick and tore it from Hanuvar's grasp. He pivoted and kicked Hanuvar's midriff, sending him sprawling.

Hanuvar had feared Gnaeus was already dead. Over Artus' shoulder he spotted him crawling from beneath the tent flap, calling his boys to hold the line.

Artus bent to grab his sword; Hanuvar rolled to his feet.

"You're slow." Artus leapt again, with another savage swing. Hanuvar slipped back. "Stand still, old man!"

The turning course of the battle had revealed Gnaeus to Artus, who swore.

Gnaeus lifted the necklace with shaking hands, shouting to hold the line. Tafari and Ennius arrived from the camp ringing the hill and paused to take stock of the commotion.

"That's mine!" Artus snarled at Gnaeus, and hurried toward him.

"Got to form up the men," Gnaeus shouted, his face glazed with desperation.

Artus reached him and lifted his sword.

Hanuvar heard the shout of the big Nuvaran, demanding to know what was happening. It was probably unwise to risk himself for the sake of Gnaeus, who had only a few days of coherent thought left him.

But Hanuvar threw himself for Artus' knees. He bore the gladiator to the ground.

Trained warrior that he was, Artus kept hold of his sword when he fell. He swore foully, rolled, and struck toward where Hanuvar had just been. He too had rolled, pressing himself flat so the blade just missed taking off his nose.

Artus scrambled upright. Hanuvar was up at the same moment. And Tafari, Ennius, and Eshmun had arrived. They warded Artus with bared blades.

Hanuvar stepped clear and bent toward the throwing knife he spotted winking moonlight in the grass.

Gnaeus climbed to his feet and addressed his people, his voice weak and strained.

"Artus attacked me."

Artus' voice rose in anger, and he stabbed a finger at Gnaeus while keeping his weapon ready. "He's a fake!" He waved the sword toward Hanuvar. "This one's the *real* Hanuvar, and he's just an old man. A weak old man with a soft heart!"

"Put down your sword, Artus," Gnaeus ordered.

Artus ignored him, his voice rising as he tried still to convince his fellows. "That necklace he wears? That's a spell. With it any of us can be as smart as Hanuvar. Better, even, because we're gladiators!" He seemed as though he'd go on for some time, but fell silent when Hanuvar's throwing knife caught him in the throat. Only blood spilled from his lips then. Soon, he was down to his knees, and then upon his side, writhing on the grass. Then he moved no more.

The gladiators looked uncertainly between Hanuvar and Gnaeus.

"Is it true, what he said?" Tafari asked.

Eshmun answered. "It's true. I've known since this morning."

Hanuvar added, "The Dervans put a spell on a man they thought would help them find me, but he escaped. And then he set you free. And he has led you again and again to victory."

Gnaeus spoke then, one hand pressed to the side of his head. "The spell's only temporary, and it's not going to last much longer. When it wears off . . . I'm useless to you. Or anyone. I didn't know."

The gladiators muttered among themselves.

"You need to go with the real Hanuvar," Gnaeus said. "He can get you out of this."

"What about you?" Eshmun asked Gnaeus.

"I've put all of you in danger. I'm going to distract the Dervans following us, but the rest should go with him. He'll get you away."

Tafari lowered his spear. He looked skeptically at Hanuvar. "There are more than sixty of us. How are you going to get us to safety?"

"It will be a challenge," Hanuvar admitted. "I can get you to a ship, but you'll need to shelter in the woods and stay hidden until I can arrange for it."

"Whose ship?" Tafari demanded. "Where is it going?"

"There are many choices," Hanuvar replied. "But it can take you to freedom."

The gladiators were startled by this news and a few spoke quietly among themselves until Gnaeus addressed them once more.

"I'll need a few to stay with me for a time. We'll lead the Dervans on a nice chase so the rest of you can get free."

"I'll arrange a rendezvous point for those in the diversion, once you've led off the Dervans," Hanuvar added.

The gladiators brought the rest of their number into the conversation that night, and Hanuvar and Gnaeus explained the situation and their plans in detail. The news wasn't easy for the freed slaves to accept, and some blamed Gnaeus for their plight. Most, though, remained grateful to him, regardless of his reasoning, and Hanuvar expected that Gnaeus' impending doom made them more inclined toward sympathy than anger.

After, the young Volani vintner, Gisco, and his lover and the dozens of others, some of whom Hanuvar recognized from the farm, readied themselves for departure.

Eshmun, though, said he could not abandon the man who had freed them, and took his place with Tafari and the other twelve who'd elected to stay with Gnaeus. To Hanuvar's objection he only shook his head. "If I can, once we know all of you are free and clear, we'll find our way to your rendezvous. If not, well, death and I are not strangers. I glimpsed her during the siege, and I've seen her on the arena field. If I go down by the sword, at least this time it will be a battle I've chosen."

Seeing that the young man had set his course, Hanuvar offered his hand to him, then, finally, turned to Gnaeus.

The man who was almost him had turned his blind eye away, to have a wider field of vision. "You will get them to safety?" he asked.

"If it can be done, I will do it."

Gnaeus nodded once.

Hanuvar pointed to the chain of the pendant, hidden behind Gnaeus' shirt. "You said you could barely function without the necklace. Yet you had the clarity to seek it."

Gnaeus' gaze was reflective. "I knew I was less than I wanted to be. I knew that my men needed help. And somehow I knew the necklace would aid me. I didn't really understand, but even lost as I was, I felt it was something that had to be done."

Hanuvar understood. He offered his arm, and Gnaeus took it. Their grip was long, and Hanuvar's words were heartfelt. "Good luck to you, Gnaeus. It has been an honor."

"Likewise." Gnaeus released his grasp, hesitated a moment, then spoke frankly. "I never had a brother. I suppose... this is what it would have felt like."

"Yes." Hanuvar wished there was something more that he could do. Some way to turn the course, and grant this man more time.

Gnaeus smiled sadly, sensing the line of his thoughts. "You said before that you never expected to live long. No soldier does."

"No."

"All we can do is live well for the moments we have, and die well, for the right reasons. Hail and farewell, Hanuvar."

When he had the collection of liberated slaves moving out ahead of him before dawn, Hanuvar looked back a final time from the back of his trusty roan, who had snorted appreciatively at their reunion. Gnaeus stood on the forested ridgeline, a tall, cloaked figure, head turned to one side, hand raised in parting.

Hanuvar lifted his own in response, thinking then of his final letter from Adruvar, and the hurried meal he'd shared with Harnil, never knowing it was to be their last, and the final hushed words with Melgar, at his bedside. This man wasn't his blood. He was more like an actor forced into a Hanuvar stage costume. And yet it had fit him well, and Hanuvar knew he'd reflect upon this moment with sorrow for the rest of his days. Thus he memorized the stance of that gray silhouette alone against the horizon, and breathed deeply of the piney scent, and felt the cool breeze. Only with reluctance did he turn away at last and follow his charges into the morning.

※ ※ ※

Gnaeus played cat and mouse with Aquilius and his cavalry for almost a week, laying traps and false trails and generally leading his pursuers in frustrating circles. And then, one day, when the Dervans crept cautiously up to a position, they found him lying dead with what was apparently a self-inflicted wound beside a letter in his own hand, laying out the crimes of the legate, though its exact wording may never be known, for it was swiftly burned and the cavalry man who'd found it met with an accident.

Of the twelve gladiators who rode with Gnaeus, three were dead. Ennius and the former Volani wheelwright turned up at the rendezvous point with two more. But Eshmun, Tafari, and the others melted into the woodlands, and were not to be found.

As for the youngest vintner, the farmhands, and the rest of the gladiators and farm slaves they'd freed, Hanuvar sequestered them in the wilds and sneaked them away by nightfall via boats out to one of our ships, and thence north to Selanto. The majority elected to make the journey to New Volanus when the ships returned, or the new ones were completed. Transport to other distant lands was arranged for the rest.

It should be mentioned that while Gnaeus still lived, Calenius claimed he had cast new magics to keep the man from further raids and slave recruiting, but with that he was done. Aquilius was little pleased with him, for the wizard insisted his power was spent and that he required time to recuperate. He withdrew to his mountain.

Once Gnaeus was found dead, Aquilius, still wroth that so many slaves had escaped, hunted for signs of them for another week, departing finally in grand dudgeon. He might have claimed to have found and slain the real Hanuvar, but he instead hushed that up, announcing he had merely destroyed an impostor. He hadn't even managed the little glory to be found in recapturing rebels. Ironically, gossip did spread to fuel Aquilius' reputation, for there were those who'd said he had hunted and hounded Hanuvar until the dread Volani had taken his own life. No one in positions of power believed it, but many commoners did, and that was to have repercussions in coming years.

Eventually we would learn that Aquilius blamed Calenius at least in part for the failure of his plans, but that did not impact Hanuvar yet for many weeks.

—Sosilos, Book Thirteen

Chapter 5:
Issue of Malice

I

The girl looked back only once when Hanuvar called to her, the wind throwing dark tresses across her face. Then she stepped into the air and plummeted from sight.

There was no point running any further, but Hanuvar didn't slow until he'd reached the ancient stone fence girding the cliff edge. Over the wind and the roll of surf and the cry of gulls he'd heard a piercing scream. It was incongruous, deceptive, for the girl herself could not possibly have survived to produce it.

A hundred feet below sailors stared out from their deck at the motionless thing in a pink dress twisted across the rocks. A group of figures huddled along the nearest of the harbor docks, among them Izivar in her green, hands to her mouth in horror while a slight figure in a stola beside her turned away. Julivar.

An ugly end for such a young life, and as Hanuvar looked down he thought back to what little he could guess about the stranger. She had appeared well kept. What could have driven her to take the irrevocable step? A troubled home life? A lover's betrayal? An unwanted child?

He was acquainted with a wealth of tragedies already, but this one did not leave Hanuvar unburdened, either emotionally or practically, for his rush in the girl's wake had been noted, and within the hour he found himself at the center of an inquiry by the local legionaries, wondering if he'd chased the girl to her death. He explained he was following Izivar Lenereva, there to meet her sister at the dock. After additional testimony from other witnesses who had gathered on the hillside, he found himself cleared.

The homely centurion from the local fort was dismayed by the entire incident, remarking darkly that there'd been a run of suicides this summer. "All young people," he said. He looked over the cliff. Below, a band of sailors had formed a human chain to pass buckets along to wash off the blood. The body had already been carried off.

"Any idea why?" Hanuvar asked.

The centurion shook his head. "These sorts of things happen in groups of youngsters sometimes. Like a terrible fashion. It's much better when they're competing to find the blackest horse or the most scandalous poem. They never think about the people left behind. I'm going to have to tell the girl's mother. I hear her father's out of town."

Hanuvar had passed along and received enough bad news over his life that he understood the soldier's discomfort. He nodded his sympathy and followed the centurion down from the overlook then left him at the side street where he'd spotted Izivar's carriage.

She sat under the awning of a counter restaurant further along the street, her elegant brow creased with worry. There was no sign of either her maid, Serliva, or of her young half-sister Julivar.

When she noticed him her slim shoulders eased in her stola, although she pretended no particular interest. She ran a finger through her curling dark hair and pushed off the restaurant stool.

When Hanuvar drew close she fell in beside him and the two started down the street for the carriage, past expensive waterfront shops.

"Where's Julilvar?" Hanuvar asked softly.

"I sent the carriage back to the villa with her and Serliva—and your horse—while I waited. It's had time to return and wait some more. You've been gone a while."

"Is she all right?"

Izivar frowned. "She saw the entire thing. She even knew that poor girl who died."

That only partly explained Izivar's discomfort; her continuing tension was surely related to her fear for Hanuvar during his interrogation.

"The questions were all routine," he said. "It's nothing to be worried about."

"No?" She did not say that she had feared for his life, and her own, as well as the lives of all those under their protection who would be arrested for harboring an enemy of the state if his true identity were discovered, as well as the fates of all those they'd be unable to save if they were led away in chains. Her sharp look conveyed the depth of her disquiet despite her outward composure.

Hanuvar opened the carriage door for her and she called to the driver that they would be returning home. She then climbed inside, and he followed, shutting the door.

Izivar sank into the cushions on the bench beside him. She reached for his hand and clutched fiercely to it for most of the ride. He let their physical proximity assuage any lingering fright. By mutual consent they spoke only of simple things, like the fine pheasant dinner Izivar had arranged for the evening to welcome Julivar's return home from their holdings to the north, and what Hanuvar would need for his ride west tomorrow. Upon arrival at the villa, Izivar announced that she wished to check on Julivar. The servants directed her to the outer garden.

Hanuvar went with her, both to greet the young lady and to assess her well-being after the tragedy they'd witnessed.

Julivar had abandoned her stola for a Dervan boy's tunic, so short it barely reached her knees, and had traded out sandals for sturdy riding boots. Holding the dulled sword Hanuvar had gifted her earlier that year, she advanced across a flat patch of grass, delivering a different cut to an imaginary foe with each step—right-side head strike, left-side neck strike, stomach thrust, right-side chest strike, left-side chest strike, right eye, left, overhead blow. It was a standard fighting drill, and Julivar executed the moves with an intensity beyond her years. Though her arms were lean, Hanuvar would not have liked to have been on the receiving end of those attacks.

Izivar frowned briefly at him as they stopped to watch. He pretended not to notice. She hadn't been thrilled by Julivar's interest in martial training, preferring her sister return to her earlier interest, ship design, and she hadn't liked Hanuvar offering instruction when he noted her stances and strikes lacked refinement.

Julivar glanced toward them, but did not interrupt her drill until she had finished two more complete patterns, reaching the end of the sward. She then turned, beamed at them, and waved her free hand.

She had not changed greatly since he'd first met her—she was a bright, coltish, irrepressible energy. She shared her sister's curling hair and small hooked nose, although her own eyes were a darker brown. Sheathing her sword with an ease that evidenced practice, she started for them.

"Decius!" she cried. She spoke in clean, unaccented Dervan, addressing Hanuvar by his assumed name, as did all of those in Izivar's circle. "Are you all right? Wasn't that horrible? I've been practicing every day. Can you tell? Are my stances long enough? And I've been running, too. These are great boots for that."

Hanuvar couldn't help smiling at her enthusiasm, and hugged her when she threw herself forward with arms outstretched. Fate was strange. He had never known his own child at this age, but he had come to cherish the daughter of the man who'd driven him from Volanus.

"Your stances are much better," Hanuvar said as they pulled apart. "And so are all of your inner strikes. Have you been practicing your blocks as well?"

"I have! Himli[12] sometimes pretends to strike at me and I parry. I've gotten pretty fast."

"And you remember to block on the upswing, not the downswing?"

"I try."

"It can make a difference, especially countering the blow of a stronger opponent." He did not add that most men would be stronger than her even after she filled out—if she filled out. One-on-one, the typical male soldier could bring greater power on a strike than the average female, which was best countered with greater skill. The Eltyr honed their accuracy with spear and bow and sling to legendary proficiency. "And archery?"

"That still needs a lot of work," Julivar admitted. "I think I need a better bow."

---

[12] The capable foreman and reliable manager overseeing Selanto whenever Izivar or Hanuvar were absent, not to be confused with the long dead father of Hanuvar and his siblings.—*Sosilos*

That reminded him very much of young Melgar's insistence that it wasn't his own lack of practice that was the problem, but the tools he used. He ruffled her hair as he had his youngest brother's. "I'll have to see how you're handling it."

Izivar cleared her throat, and both of them turned to her at the same moment. "I couldn't help noting today your stola looked a little worn, and too heavy for the summer."

"Oh it definitely is," Julivar agreed. "It's fine for up north, but down here I couldn't wait to get out of it."

"I thought we could go shopping this afternoon. There are some lovely summer fabrics in the square this year. And a new jewelry store with some fine pieces."

Committed though she was to sword work, Julivar hadn't abandoned a love of ornamentation, and her face brightened in interest. "Oh!" Then her expression fell and she turned to Hanuvar. "Can we look at my bow later? I haven't been able to go shopping at a real market in months!"

"Of course. Go spend time with your sister."

"Let me get changed." Julivar took a single step forward then turned as though she'd just remembered something important. Her countenance was suddenly somber. "You've seen a lot of people die, haven't you?" Typical for her, she didn't wait for an answer to her first question. "I've only seen a few," she added, mouth twisting in displeasure. "How common is it to see something... waft up from the body?"

"It's not," he answered. "What did you see?"

Julivar looked to her sister, apparently just as puzzled as Hanuvar, then gathered her thoughts before answering. "It was a kind of sparkly shimmer after Atolia's body struck the rock. I was looking right at her when it happened, and I didn't imagine it. Have you ever seen anything like that?"

"No."

"I thought maybe it was just something that happened, when a spirit left a body, and that you might have seen it a lot."

He shook his head. "I've never seen that."

Julivar's mouth twisted thoughtfully.

"It was probably just the sun shining off the water," Izivar suggested. "Why don't you run and get ready? I'll go freshen up."

II

Phrenius still couldn't decide whether the drop or the landing had been funnier. Atolia had actually flapped her arms a bit on the way down, as if she thought to take flight, and then thrown her hands out in front as though she could shield herself from impact. He was still chuckling at how dumb that was.

When she'd landed, one of her thumbs had popped off and bounced straight up from the rocks to land with a splat on the plank of a transport ship. The horrified cry from the old Ruminian who'd just missed getting struck by it had been almost as laughable as the screaming girl on the dock.

Now, though, his mood was glum, for he was almost back to his aunt's villa. He hated the sight of the place. Many a merchant or tradesman had finer accommodations than the crumbling home behind its tumbledown stone wall. Phrenius preferred always to come through the side closest to his room. The front would take him through the central courtyard, where his slug of an aunt lazed about with her fat old friends and their smug slaves. He scowled at the bent old one sweeping the walk.

Once back to the tiny little room his aunt had given him, he slammed his door then pushed yesterday's clothes off his chest and set down the dark wooden box he'd carried, long as his forearm. He'd opened it once on the way back, but just to be sure he undid the bronze clasp and opened it a second time. The old brown tunic still lay within. And the spirit was there again. He could feel it, loosely anchored. The thing was never fully sated, but always experienced a brief diminution in intensity after it secured prey. He sensed its regard brush against him. "Ah, ah, ah," he cautioned, and closed the lid, his hand tracing along the swirling marks carefully burned into the wood.

The spirit had no sense of loyalty, no matter how much satisfaction he'd brought it. "You ought to know better by now. I'll find you someone new, but it won't be me."

He set the box on the bed, then walked to his smaller chest in the corner, flipped it open, and reached for the incense bag.

But his fingers clutched only emptiness. Cursing, Phrenius rooted around in the chest some more, but it wasn't beneath the new undergarments his mother had insisted on sending with him, and it wasn't under the other items. The incense was gone.

And then, glowering, he realized what had happened. He stalked to the door and threw it open. His voice rose in a screech. "Aunt Galla! Where's my incense?"

"What?" Her answer, from the distant courtyard, drawled out the vowel in a long slur.

She was impossible. He raised his voice. "My incense! Did you take it?" He glared daggers at the frowzy-haired slave who glowered at him from around the corner.

"Yes!" she cried, with savage delight. "It stinks! I told you not to burn that awful concoction in my house, so I had it thrown out!"

He cursed her foully.

"You watch your tongue, you grubby little reprobate, or I'll send you back to your mother! I told you to get rid of it!"

He cursed her some more, under his breath, and gave the watching slave a few choice instructions about what he could do with himself.

"Did you hear me?" the old bag shouted again. He knew she hadn't bothered to push off the couch where she lay. "You keep a civil tongue in your head, or you'll be punished!"

He screwed up his face in a mockery of hers and mimed her threat in an undertone, then retreated to his room and slammed the door. He knew her slaves hated him almost as much as his aunt did, and had considerably more stamina, which is why he congratulated himself on having the foresight to set some of the incense aside in a more secret place.

He pushed the heavy chest away from the foot of his bed and felt around for the loose floorboard. He swore again as his efforts jabbed a splinter into his finger. Gods! Why was everything against him? He saw the end of the splinter but couldn't grasp it. He'd have to have one of the slaves pull it free later.

Now, though, he reached inside the dark cavity he'd revealed. He knew there weren't likely to be snakes, but a neighbor had once told him about poisonous centipedes, and scorpions, so he snatched the tiny pouch and lifted it up, whining his fear while he tossed it down.

He nudged it into the light with his sandal. Nothing was crawling on the brown cloth on one side, so he grasped it with the tips of his fingers and turned it over, breathing a sigh of relief when there was nothing clinging on the other side, either.

Organization was not among Phrenius' strengths. Once he had the extra supply, it took him nearly a quarter hour to round up the incense plate, steel, and flint. His aunt and her nasty old slaves hated the stench of the incense, so it would never have occurred to him to admit that the dark red and gold powdery stuff made him wrinkle his own nose. There was only enough for one good dosing, and Phrenius deployed his favorite curse word a few more times when he saw that, because he'd have to pay the extortionate price to that snotty boy at the temple to get more. Then came the trial of getting a good spark from the steel and flint, because he'd forgotten to grab a candle and he wasn't about to get up to fetch one now.

Finally, though, the smoke was streaming up from the incense plate, and Phrenius brought his stringy naked body close to it, especially his face and hands, which he'd been told were most important. While there was a faint sweetness to the scent, the more prominent notes were swampy with a hint of rotting fruit. To best protect himself he had to sit naked by the stuff and keep his clothing wadded up next to it so that the fabric thoroughly absorbed the smell.

While he performed his ablutions before the incense he thought of flat-chested Atolia and how she'd had it coming for asking him why he always smelled like a funeral. She'd always seemed so prissy and certain of herself it had been a true delight when the spirit showed him how deeply rooted her own doubts about her appearance ran. She had spent most of her time worrying whether that clerk at the market actually liked her. She'd been a pointless waste of flesh, and he was glad she was gone.

He'd have to find a new target for the spirit, though, and soon. Once again he put aside the temptation of choosing his aunt, because he didn't think she'd leave the villa to him or Mother in the will.

He redressed when the incense was spent, conscious of the echo of new voices in the home. More of his aunt's ugly friends had come.

Phrenius slunk away from his room and was making for the kitchens when he overheard one of the women in the courtyard talking about Atolia's jump.

He crept to the courtyard doorway and crouched to one side, peeking out past the shaded walk and through a fern leaf to where meaty redheaded Maia sat on a cushioned chair. She was in midsentence.

"...dreadful mess. And do you know who should be on the dock but that Volani woman, Izivar Lenereva, and her little sister—that girl screamed so loud that some legionaries ran out from the fort. The Lenerevas saw the poor young thing land on the rocks not more than a few feet away from them."

So it was a Volani who'd seen the fall? Phrenius still didn't understand why there were any Volani alive. Hadn't the last emperor gone to war to kill them all?

Aunt Galla cooed meaninglessly. She sat in the shade, his view of her screened by bushes. "Does anyone know why Atolia jumped?"

Phrenius sneered.

Maia nodded her plump chins. "At first people were suspicious of a man they spotted right up next to where she leaped, but it turns out he saw her climbing over the fence and tried to get to her in time."

"Probably mad for sex," Aunt Galla said. She suspected that all men probably were, or perhaps hoped it.

"Well, the legionaries didn't think so, or they wouldn't have let him go."

Aunt Galla sniffed to let her doubts be known. "Has anyone gone to Atolia's family yet?"

Maia had nothing to offer in response but speculation, so Phrenius lost interest and crept away. He hadn't decided on who he'd introduce the spirit to next, but figured he'd find some likely prospects at the town square. He filled up his coin purse, dreading the inevitable haggling with the temple boy, tucked the spirit's box under one arm, and slunk from the building.

He took his lunch from a counter restaurant. Fish stew. He was so tired of the fish that the Apicians seemed to put in every meal, and he hated the way the sailors came to the restaurant and flirted with the big-breasted girl behind the counter. He didn't like the way she flashed her eyes at them, either. She'd never looked at him that way, and men of his family were a lot more important than those sailors who couldn't even afford to wear different tunics day to day.

He'd about decided to single her out for the spirit, except that it would be hard to get her alone, and getting his targets alone really helped.

While he hunched over the counter, chewing and mulling over his approach, an older woman in a green dress, with dark hair in long ringlets, passed without looking within. Phrenius didn't realize why he recognized her until he noted the skinny girl walking with her, ahead of a young female slave. These were those Volani his aunt and her cow friend were talking about.

Phrenius chuckled. The gods themselves had given a sign, just like they'd done when they sent the white boar for Ention to prove his might. He swallowed a final bite of his food, and was so eager to get moving that he tripped over the leg of his stool as he grabbed his spirit box. The sailors laughed and pointed; the waitress looked his way, lips twisting in amusement. He whispered his favorite word again at the thought of her. She'd be next.

Beyond a pair of eateries the street broadened into a square. Merchants sold goods from carts around a fountain with a central porpoise spewing water into a shallow pool shaded by well-pruned elms. Several of the mobile establishments offered dessert breads and candied nuts, others carried selections of wooden toys, hats, and umbrellas.

None of these products interested the Volani, though. The woman and her slave poked through the colorful fabric in front of a cloth merchant's store. The slave with them held up material to the light and laughed, seeing how transparent it was. The girl appeared taken with some yellow linen, then flitted off to stare at some shining chains hanging in the front of a neighboring store. The wispy clerk looked as though she wanted to engage her, but was being monopolized by a graybeard loudly vacillating over what necklace he ought to buy his granddaughter.

Phrenius slipped up beside the girl. She glanced over at him, sizing him up and dismissing him as unworthy of notice in the same instance, and returned to her inspection of the necklaces.

He felt sweat bead his forehead. She didn't know how much power he had. If she'd been nice to him, he might have been merciful, but she'd pay now.

"You're a skinny little skinflint, aren't you?" Phrenius hissed.

"What?" She turned to him in surprise, dark brows lifting. Probably she wasn't used to hearing the truth.

"You Volani are always greedy for a better deal, aren't you?" he asked. "It doesn't matter how many jewels you pile on. No one will want that scrawny body of yours. There's more cleavage between your toes than on your chest." He felt the spirit's interest rise—it had liked that particular insult.

Something seized his shoulder in a vise and he stumbled as he was forcibly pulled around.

The Volani woman in green glared down at him. "WHAT is wrong with you?"

"I don't like Volani, you harlot bitch," he said. She gasped and he wrestled out from under her grip. He turned to sneer at the girl, watching openmouthed. "You've got a man's nose, too, you ugly piece." He laughed as he walked away. The spirit never laughed, exactly, but his tenuous connection with the thing vibrated in anticipation.

He heard the slap of sandals race after him and turned. The young slave woman had her hand up and ready to hit him, eyes blazing.

"Serliva!" the woman in green called. "Leave him be. He's not worth it."

"Yeah, leave me be, slave," Phrenius said. "Or I'll buy you and beat you."

"I'm no slave." The woman delivered a stinging strike to his check that sent him reeling. "And you reek."

He cursed at her as she stepped away with a grimace. Head high, she strode back to her mistress and the girl.

Phrenius shouted after her, letting her know what he thought of them. The hat merchant told him to take his mouth and get off the street, and the woman selling umbrellas glared at him, but he put his hand to his reddened cheek, cursed at them all, and made for a bench in the shadow of a tree on the fountain's far side. He could see just how upset the girl was, for her shoulders hunched in protectively and her head was bowed. She shielded her weedy frame by crossing her arms.

"She looks like she's going to cry," Phrenius said mockingly. And then he opened the box lid a tiny crack. The spirit had sensed her now. It wouldn't take long for it to root into her. It never did.

III

The ten young men lined up before Hanuvar were handsome and healthy. Of average and remarkably similar height, each wore a clean gray tunic and sturdy calf-length brown boots. Though they exuded the odor of horse flesh and manure, they were scrupulously shaved and their hair had been styled with the care usually only accorded the very rich. All but one had the same medium cut, their locks fluffed and trimmed and combed to perfection. Two fellows of Ermanian extraction possessed reddish brown tops. The pair beside them, identifiably Birani, had jet-black locks, and next to them stood two with the distinctive long chins of Irimacians, crowned with whitish blond hair.

Hanuvar happened to know that every one of these grooms had been purchased to better match the horse they cared for. As he advanced down the line, it was easy to imagine that pair matching some duns, that pair tending some whites, and so on.

He stopped, frowning, in front of the man at the end whose scalp was almost completely barren, apart from some scabs and uneven tufts. Hanuvar balled hands on his hips. "Are you sure you can't part with one that isn't bald?" he asked petulantly.

"I'm afraid not." The slave holder's chief steward, another slave, had kept a few paces behind Hanuvar. He was dressed even more extravagantly than Hanuvar himself, in soft doe-leather sandals and a billowy white tunic. An immaculate white band kept curling yellow hair from his eyes. He had the air of a handsome man who knew it, although he must have likewise known he was ten years too old to pull off his boyish haircut. Hanuvar wondered if that was his master's preference.

Hanuvar wore travelling clothes that were only a step down in flowy froth from the steward, and a multitude of shining bracelets decorated one arm. Several were on loan from Izivar. "Why did you bring all of them out, then?" he asked peevishly. "Several of these are much better looking."

"I wanted you to see just how fine a set they were," the steward protested. "They've been well kept, as you can tell. The master wouldn't have wanted to part with any of them, but, well. Gaius there just can't present very well anymore, can he?"

The steward indicated the man with missing hair. Gaius' actual Volani name was Aspar, and the profession given on the record of his slave sale was pharmacist's assistant. But the Dervans had given him a new profession and renamed him after the emperor responsible for the genocide of his people. Hanuvar glanced briefly at the man beside the Volani. A close match in skin tone, he looked to be from the tip of Tyvol, with locks a dark shade of brown near to black, not too different from Hanuvar's own, except where the gray was showing.

Hanuvar frowned and pointed at Aspar. "How is his health otherwise?"

"Heathy as a horse," the steward said, then laughed at his own joke. Hanuvar joined in as though the comment had been very clever.

"Go on, Gaius." The steward stepped up to Aspar. "Show the man your teeth."

As Aspar complied, the steward beamed, and Hanuvar pretended great interest in the strong even smile.

"You see?" the steward asked. "They're not only all in place, they're all straight and clean. I made sure I acquired only the best men for the master."

Hanuvar peered for a long while, then stepped back. Aspar, watching glumly, closed his mouth.

"And what's happened to his hair?" Hanuvar asked.

"No one knows!" The steward threw his hands up in consternation. "We had the master's physician check him over, but he can't figure it out. Maybe this is how Volani men go bald." He chuckled.

"He's not as pleasant to look at as I'd hoped," Hanuvar mused.

"Oh, he's fine. Just shave the rest of the hair off and slap a wig on him. That's what Hadirans do. No one will know. Maybe your mistress will even like having him topped differently for various occasions."

Hanuvar grunted doubtfully. "What she won't like is if I pay full price for damaged goods."

The steward must have known there was no way past that problem, and let out a breath in acknowledgment. "I know, I know."

They haggled for a bit, and then Hanuvar sighed dramatically at the agreed upon sum and motioned Antires forward. "Pay the man and take his papers."

Antires, dressed in a comparatively sober but well-tailored tunic, bowed and pulled the correct count of currency from a satchel while the steward motioned for his own assistant, who whistled. At that signal a boy trotted out of the stable office with a little platter holding cups.

"Oh, what's this?" Hanuvar asked perkily.

"I thought it fit to celebrate after the sale," the steward said. "And if you didn't want to buy, well, then there'd be two drinks for me!" He laughed and Hanuvar joined in.

The cups contained a spiced mix of wine and honey that was rather pleasant on a warm day, for it was chilled. "Exquisite!" Hanuvar said.

"I thought you might enjoy it." The steward watched the rest of the slaves being led off. Antires guided Aspar down the track to where Hanuvar's carriage sat. "Tomorrow I'm going to have to start scouring this whole peninsula for a man with hair just like the master's favorite bay. It shall take forever. It's not just about the hair color, you know. Their height, musculature, and even their disposition must harmonize. Finding the replacement shall require weeks of trudging all up and down the coastline." The steward lowered his cup with a sigh and swirled the remaining liquid inside. "These sorts of dire situations always fall upon me."

"It sounds an incredible trial."

After a few more moments of chitchat, Hanuvar bade the steward farewell, handed the goblet off to the boy, and walked down the lane to climb into the carriage. Aspar was seated on the bench in front with Antires, whom Hanuvar directed to get under way.

Two miles out from the villa, a figure climbed down the hill from a shady oak and waited along the empty country lane.

Antires drew to a stop.

Hanuvar opened the door and welcomed in both Aspar, warily hopeful, and Carthalo. The chief of his spies wore a plain brown travelling tunic and ankle boots. A sturdy man with receding dark hair, he possessed a pleasant though unremarkable face, one that might be glimpsed and easily forgotten.

"You look terrible," Carthalo said to Aspar in their native Volani, although his tone was approving. "How do you feel?"

"Strange, I guess." The younger man's dazed expression clouded with an anxiety he hadn't spoken of until then. "Will it grow back?" As instructed, he had been carefully pulling hairs off his head nightly for weeks.

"Probably," Carthalo answered levelly. "But the freedom's permanent."

Bemusedly putting a hand to his head, Aspar looked across the seat to Hanuvar and continued in the same language. "I'm really going to be free?"

Hanuvar nodded gravely, but this didn't satisfy Aspar, who returned his attention to Carthalo. He'd been the one who'd arranged the scheme after the owner had refused all sales inquiries but couldn't deal directly by then because he'd been seen.

"You surely are," Carthalo said. "You won't ever have to groom another horse. Unless you want to."

Aspar stared at them both as though he had heard the word of a phantom, whose promises were untrustworthy at best.

"You are both Volani," the man said, the faintest hint of a question in his delivery.

Hanuvar nodded encouragingly. "You're among friends."

"What are your names?"

"For now," Hanuvar said, "it's best if we just keep to our Dervan ones."

Aspar shifted to another topic without shifting his gaze. "Have you freed other people?"

"We have."

"Have you freed my sister?"

"Did you see her in the slave pens?" Hanuvar asked. He expected the answer to be negative, but Aspar nodded enthusiastically.

"Yes, yes, I did. But we were separated."

The odds then were much better for her, though her fate might still be problematic. "What name did she give the Dervans?" Hanuvar asked.

"Her true name," Aspar affirmed. "Sonispa. Sonispa Etlaniva."

Hanuvar nodded once. "She lives. She has already been recovered. She had been assigned as a handmaiden to an old matriarch in Utria."

He did not add that she was now nervous and uncomfortable in the presence of men, even those of her own people. The important thing was that she lived. Healing might yet take place.

Aspar looked more anxious than ever. "She's free? Is she all right?"

"She's fit and free," Carthalo answered. "And you'll be able to see her in a week or two."

The younger man put hands to his face. Very softly he began to weep.

Hanuvar looked politely away. Carthalo met his eyes, his own gaze morose and heavy with sympathy. There was a message there, as could only be communicated by two who knew each other well.

By carriage their journey back east took almost two full days, and it was with great relief that Hanuvar climbed down in front of Izivar's stables. He left Carthalo to settle Aspar into place and headed in through the servant's entrance, spirits lighter at the thought of seeing Izivar.

She had heard the carriage roll in and was waiting tensely for him in the little vestibule past the servant's door. She wore her favorite green stola with matching earrings, and her dark hair and skin were rich with the perfumed scents he had come to love. Her servants were absent, so she embraced him fully then stepped back. Though her eyes were warm, the anxiety in them reminded Hanuvar of how she had appeared when he'd returned from the questioning by the Dervan soldiers.

"Your trip went well?" she asked. "You got Aspar away from the Dervans?"

"Yes. What's wrong?"

"Oh. There are a lot of worries." She glanced away as if she might change the subject, then came to a decision and looked at him directly. "I'm worried about Julivar. She hasn't been the same since you left."

Hanuvar quirked an eyebrow.

"I think it was whatever the terrible boy said. The one from the marketplace." She needn't have clarified. She'd relayed the entire incident to Hanuvar the same evening it had happened.

"Boys want attention," he said, "and some are foolish enough they think insults—"

She cut him off. "That's not it. He wasn't wanting her attention. He wanted her dead. And I swear she's acting like she wants herself dead too."

"That doesn't sound like Julivar."

"I can't make any headway with her, at all." Izivar's hands fluttered uselessly. This, too, was uncharacteristic. She usually had very firm opinions about proper courses of action, and little hesitation in taking them.

"Do you want me to talk to her?" Izivar appeared to be implying that, although he felt compelled to verify. The emotional turmoil of young women was not his particular field of expertise.

She understood, and explained. "She respects you. We both know the chief reason she came south was to learn more of your sword moves."

"Sword moves," he repeated, but she wasn't in a playful mood and simply looked back. "I thought you disproved of her interest in martial studies."

"Well, now I'm more desperate to see any spark of enthusiasm, even if she wanted to take up chariot racing."

His first thought had been to read any correspondence then bathe and eat. But Izivar was not one to be idly nervous. "Have any important reports come in?"

"Some letters. None with the mark." Izivar was referring to the special note signifying highly urgent material hidden in the coded language Carthalo had devised.

He asked where Julivar might be found.

She had taken up residence in the courtyard, but she wasn't practicing sword work. She sat on the stone border of a raised garden bed, knees pulled up to her chin so that her legs were completely hidden by her dress. Only her sandaled toes were visible. She looked as though she hoped to hide under her clothes completely, as if by working hard enough she might entirely disappear.

She didn't react to Hanuvar until he was right in front of her. He expected she might have been crying, but her eyes were dry and deep with loathing, though it did not seem especially directed at him.

"Do you mind if I sit?"

She shrugged, and he took the stone beside her.

"Have you been practicing your steps?" he asked.

Her only response was a second shrug.

"Your sister told me about what happened in the market. Why do you care about what some rude young man says?"

"I don't want to talk about it." Her voice was so soft he barely heard her.

"Any blow hurts more if it strikes a weak point, or finds an unhealed wound. Is that what happened?"

She shifted; from that he gauged that he might have scored a point, though he was still uncertain of this game's rules.

"I don't know who he is," Hanuvar continued. "But I know who you are. The Julivar I know would snap her fingers and tell that boy what he could do with himself."

She interrupted him. "You don't. Not really. You've only known me a few months."

"We went into battle together, Julivar," he reminded her. "That is a bond between us no one can break."

"It wasn't a real battle."

"Lives would have been lost if we hadn't acted. Maybe our own. And if the emperor had died in your halls? It might have been the end of all the Volani in Tyvol."

He had won the ground, so she changed it. "You're just here because Izivar told you to come."

"She asked me," Hanuvar conceded. "But I wanted to see you."

"You've seen me. Tell her I'm fine."

"Are you?" He paused and decided to try a different approach. "I'm going to eat." He patted the side of the bench in conclusion. "Change into your athletic gear and meet me out here in an hour."

"I don't want to."

"You don't look very busy."

"I don't feel well."

"You'll feel better with some exercise."

"I said I don't want to." Her voice took on an uncharacteristic peevish tone. "And the last I heard, you weren't in charge of me."

This young lady sounded so different from the one he knew it was difficult to believe her one and the same. Apparently the young man's words had injured her deeply. "Wounds fester if they don't get aired out. And a body needs exercise if it's to heal properly."

"I'm not really any good. I'll never be an Eltyr."

"You have aptitude. With practice you'll be even better."

"It's easy for you to say. You're good at everything."

He sighed. "I'm well practiced with what's actually a small handful of skills, and those are dwarfed by all the things I don't know how to do. You could be as good if you wished to devote the same amount of time to your own interests, although I hope you'll be more balanced than I am."

"I'm going inside." She slid off the bench and slouched away from him, eyes low. Troubled, he watched her leave.

He found Izivar seated with Antires on the back patio. A meal had already been laid out, and Antires was thoughtfully tapping the side of a half-full wine cup while munching. Both he and Izivar looked up at his entrance.

Hanuvar poured himself a cup, then drank it down. The watered wine was sweet and cool and fresh, but it did not restore him.

"I spoke with Julivar," he said. "I understand why you're worried. She's not acting like herself. I can't tell why she hasn't shrugged this off." He poured another cup and sat down across from Izivar. There was bread and cheese, and a welcome soup with greens that smelled faintly of lime, a Volani specialty known as mulinest.

Antires swallowed and reached for more bread. He rubbed it into olive oil and then gestured with it, the crust glistening in sunlight. "I've been talking to Izivar about it. Do you know, this whole thing reminds me of a Herrenic legend."

Nearly every incident reminded the Herrene in some way of an existing story. But he offered his thoughts this time without the customary sparkle in his eye.

"What legend?" Izivar asked.

"There's a kind of ghost that feeds on bravery, reducing men to fear. It comes up in some of our plays, in battle scenes. You might have heard of it."

Izivar, waiting tensely, said nothing.

Antires continued his thought. "There's another, that feeds on joy and leaves people empty and disconsolate."

Izivar's expression grew sharp. "What does it look like?"

"Like nothing. It's a spirit." Antires sounded almost defensive.

"Julivar saw something leave that girl's body," Izivar said to Hanuvar.

"You said it was probably sunlight."

"What if I was wrong, and Julivar was right? There have been a series of suicides this summer, right here. All young people."

"So the centurion said. What do you propose we do?"

"What do the Herrenes do?" Izivar looked to Antires, who had stuffed more bread into his mouth, and held up a finger as though it were not already evident he had to chew and swallow before answering.

Even after finishing, Antires hesitated with the air of someone about to announce bad news. "It never ends well in myths," he said. "But the old stories exaggerate everything, don't they? If someone suspected there was a malignant spirit involved, I suppose they would make a sacrifice at the local temple to Hereptus and consult a priest there. That would be the equivalent of Lutar for Dervans," he added.

"There's a small temple to Lutar on the town outskirts." Izivar was starting to rise before she took note of Hanuvar's plate.

"I'll eat quickly," he promised.

He'd been looking forward to a good soak as well, not just because he was dirty, but owing to the stiffness of being on the road for most of the last week. But seeing the extent of Izivar's worry, he put his plans aside. Julivar was her last surviving sibling, for another sister had died years before and her younger brother had been slain last year. More than that, owing to the difference in their ages, Izivar's oversight of Julivar was more than a little maternal.

Hanuvar wolfed down some food and then he and Antires and Izivar headed out.

Just beyond the town's western gate stood the building they sought, a small square structure the size of an overgrown shrine, not much larger than a hermit's shack rendered in stone. A cemetery stretched on to the west, its disorderly rows of variously carved stone monuments desolate and abandoned but for creeping ivy and moss. Some of the forbidding crypts beside the road were far larger than the little temple to Lutar.

The twin pillars supporting the temple's pediment climbed only a little over eight feet, and the interior itself proved tiny. Hanuvar glimpsed the suggestion of carved relief along the walls, but the only proper lighting emerged from a brazier beside the altar, where a short youth adjusted mistletoe.

He turned at their footfall, his pimpled face marred by an irritated expression, as though their presence was something that must be endured rather than welcomed. His clothes were the traditional charcoal gray of Lutar's robes. Almost certainly he was an acolyte. "Have you lost someone?" he asked. He sounded as though a discussion about death and funerals might be inconvenient for him today.

Hanuvar was already searching past him for someone more useful. This being a minor temple, there was no actual statue to the Dervan god of the underworld, merely a representation of his sober, bearded countenance carved in stone on the back wall behind the sacrificial altar. A pair of slim dark doors were hidden in the shadows to either side.

"Where is the temple priest?" Izivar asked.

"He's not here at the moment," the boy said. "I am prepared to help you." He bowed his head.

Izivar ignored his invitation. "Where is he?"

"He is resting in his chambers. I assure you—"

"This is the Lady Izivar Lenereva," Hanuvar interrupted, "a close personal friend of Emperor Enarius. She needs to speak to the priest. Where are his chambers?"

"His home lies just behind the temple," the boy said. Inspired by the mention of Izivar's proximity to power, the boy grew briefly more engaged. "But he is in mourning and hasn't welcomed company in a while."

"Who died?" Hanuvar asked.

"His wife."

"How long ago?"

"This spring. He's been taking solace with every meal." The boy smirked and mimed tipping a bottle towards his mouth.

Hanuvar was glad to leave him. Beyond the temple, a humble villa lay behind high stone walls and an iron gate someone had forgotten to fully close. The door was answered by a stooped old slave who was either incapable of speech or inclined against it, for he listened to their wish to speak to his master, grunted, then beckoned them inside.

They passed through the little house and into to a small courtyard with an immaculate garden. The doorman gestured vaguely toward the rectangular pool surrounded by stone in the garden's center, and left, wordless.

Another gray-haired man tended the edge of the pond, in which water lilies grew. His back was to them as he plucked weeds from between stone slabs.

Hanuvar cleared his throat as they approached, but it wasn't until they came into the weed puller's line of sight that the man looked up. He appeared to have grayed prematurely, for his face wasn't heavily lined. His tunic was old, but well laundered. Brown, yellow-flecked eyes that were sunk into some inner world regarded them diffidently.

"Forgive our intrusion," Izivar said. "Are you the Priest of Lutar?"

"I am." The man glanced down at a fringe of dandelion poking out between the slabs two stones ahead.

"We've come to you for help. I'm Izivar Lenereva. I'm concerned that my sister is being tormented by a kind of spirit."

"In Herrenia we call it a sulisima," Antires supplied helpfully.

The priest weighed this information. He raised a tarnished metal cup to his lips, then eyed it with distaste and lowered it without drinking.

He listened despondently as Izivar described how her sister's character had changed. Hanuvar watched the priest's face, noting that while the man was bleary, he wasn't really drunk. Perhaps he wanted to be. The priest's expression fell further when Antires repeated the number of suicides among the Oscani youth over the summer. "No one has told me of this," he said.

"Your acolyte said you've been in mourning."

"I have still managed funerals." He massaged his forehead. "Wait. There was one young woman... Were the others seasonal visitors?"

Hanuvar looked to Izivar for confirmation.

"I think so," she said. In which case their wealthy families would almost surely have had the bodies transported by sea back to family plots elsewhere.

The priest pushed to his feet, then adjusted his tunic. "Spirits from without are often less dangerous than those from within. Your sister may simply be suffering from the insecurities of youth, and the society of troubled people her age. Is she betrothed?"

"She is not."

"Should she be? Are her friends all wed?" When Izivar frowned, he tried a different line of inquiry. "Did she know any of the others?"

"She saw one of them die, and recognized her from a visit last year. I don't know about the others."

Antires seemed to be interested in checking the man's credentials. "Have you dealt with any malevolent spirits around here?"

The priest scratched his head. "In early spring I drove a specter away from a woman near Edanalla, only a day's ride out. A relative had passed, a bitter man who wished to squash the joy of his fellows in life and meant to keep doing it in death. A specter. Or sulisima." He nodded to Antires, then turned to Izivar. "I'm not saying that one of them's bothering your sister, Lady. But there will be no harm in me speaking with her, if you wish."

"If it is a spirit, how can it be stopped?" Izivar asked.

"Well, there are rituals, of course. But the crucial thing is that you know from where the specter came. You find something important or familiar to it. A sandal or tunic or knife if it was a man. A dress or jewelry if it was a woman. Maybe the lock of a child's hair. You draw it in with this familiar thing, and then enclose it in a box with a seal mark. You then consign the box to a fire, after you prepare some rituals."

The priest was refreshingly forthcoming. At no point had he implied a temple donation might be necessary, or offered an unctuous condolence.

"What if you don't know where the specter came from?" Izivar asked.

Hanuvar had been wondering the same thing.

The priest nodded slowly. "You can try kenentari incense. Hadiran stuff. I think there are some Turian herbs that may work as well. The problem with the Turians is they never actually want to share their knowledge, and you can't count on them to sell you the real product. The Hadiran stuff is more expensive, but more trustworthy. I have some," he added.

"I am most grateful for your offer to speak to my sister," Izivar said resolutely. "We would be pleased to accompany you to our home. Today. With some of this incense."

The priest considered this and ran a hand back through his unruly hair. "Yes," he said. "Permit me a moment to change. Perhaps I could offer you refreshments?" he asked belatedly.

They declined, and walked about the little island of greenery, admiring the carefully tended plants, and a row of vases with blooming violets.

The priest returned in a formal charcoal tunic and better sandals. He had run a brush through his hair. Seeing their contemplation of his sanctuary he said: "It's lovely, isn't it? This was my wife's work. We could not have children, and I think she took comfort in the life she nourished in this space. I am glad to be able to say that I complimented her hand here while she lived, but I find myself wishing I had done so more regularly. And paid more attention to what she did, for no matter how I work, it does not bloom as well under my fingers." At that thought he glanced down at his hand and ran it again through his hair. "Enough. Come."

Hanuvar did not ask how she had died. The man's quiet reverence for his lost love touched him.

The priest led them back to the temple and opened the narrow doors on the left Hanuvar had noted while the acolyte watched alertly. A small pantry was revealed, into which the priest advanced, lifting his lantern to a storage shelf. Before very long he returned to the main chamber of the temple, his expression troubled. He spoke to the acolyte. "Atticus, where is the Hadiran incense?"

The boy's eyes shifted. Not with uncertainty, but discomfort. "Don't you remember? You said we had run out."

"I said no such thing." The priest was unflinching. "There was a fair bit left."

"No, sir. There really wasn't. I remember you commenting on it just last week when you wandered through."

"Did I?" The priest's certainty faded. Perhaps he remembered visiting while drunk.

Hanuvar advanced on the boy until the youth had backed into a wall. He put a hand to his shoulder. "I think you've done something with it."

"What would I want with Hadiran incense?"

"I think you might have been selling it," Hanuvar suggested. It hadn't been a difficult guess, given that the priest had told them it was expensive. He saw he'd judged rightly because of the sudden stilling of the boy's roving eyes.

"I wouldn't do that," Atticus said.

Hanuvar's hand tightened on the boy's shoulder. He pulled him forward and turned him to face the priest, whose brows had drawn sternly together.

"I'm very disappointed," the priest said. "Where is it?"

Atticus confessed on the instant. "Phrenius Apernius has it. I don't know what he wants it for, but he's been mad for it. Threatening, really. I was afraid what he'd do if I didn't sell it to him."

"If you were really afraid, you've have told me. Who is he?"

"Just a boy in town."

"You're bad at this," Hanuvar said, and tightened his grip on both of the young man's bony shoulders from behind. "Why does Phrenius want this special incense? He wouldn't know about it unless you'd told him."

The boy nodded to the priest. "He knows him, he just doesn't remember."

"I don't know him."

"But you do!" Atticus protested. "He's the one who asked you all those questions about the specter in the spring. Remember?"

The priest's expression cleared. "Yes. But that was in Edanalla. What's he doing here?"

"I don't know. But he's living with his aunt now."

The priest looked thoughtful for a moment. And then his eyes sharpened and turned fully upon Atticus. "What did you do with his uncle's box?"

"I burned it, just like you instructed."

"Did you?" The priest scowled. "It strikes me now that Phrenius was asking an awful lot of questions about specter boxes and disposals, and the rituals."

"What does this boy look like?" Izivar asked. "Is he skinny, about this tall, and sneering?" She raised her hand to a height near her nose. "With shifty eyes and a foul mouth?"

"That's him measured to the ounce," the boy agreed.

Izivar turned to Hanuvar. "He's the rude one at the square. And he was at the dock, watching when that poor girl jumped. I heard him laugh. He tried to stifle it, and I thought it was just one of those strange reactions people sometimes have..." Her voice trailed off, and she turned to the priest. "Are you saying that the boy's controlling this spirit somehow? With the incense?"

The priest shook his head. "He's protecting himself from harm with the incense. You can't control a spirit like this, but I suppose you might be able to direct it in some limited ways."

Hanuvar addressed the acolyte. "Where does this boy live?"

Atticus gulped and told them.

The priest's[13] voice was stern as he addressed Atticus. "Because of you, five girls are dead. And a sixth is in danger. I hope you enjoyed your money. Leave my sight and never enter it again."

IV

For a few days Phrenius wasn't certain the specter really had hold of the girl, for the skinny Volani bitch didn't respond the way the others had, even when he prodded with more cogent observations about her obvious faults. But eventually he felt its malicious delight growing and through the link he'd even glimpsed her imagining the ends she envisioned for herself. Before much longer he knew which one she had chosen, and when his gut tightened with resolve he understood he'd have to run. Like a lot of them, once she had decided she hurried out to get things over with, probably because she was afraid she'd change her mind. All females were cowards at heart. He sped out from the villa and raced down for the tide pool northeast of town.

Pleasant beaches, along with convenient natural harbors, were a rare commodity throughout most of the Tyvolian coast. The majority were accessible only via descents along steep cliff sides. Hidden shoals and sandbars jeopardized shipping; sharp rocks and treacherous currents endangered swimmers. From some previous visit the girl had learned of a tiny, bowl-shaped inlet that was deceptively inviting to bathers when the tide was low and a lethal trap when high. Despite warnings, people died there almost every year. And the Lenereva girl planned to be another of them.

Phrenius wondered just how much of her drowning he'd be able

---

[13] Astute readers will have noted Antires never directly named the priest of Lutar, and he confessed to me in a letter that is because while he noted his name, he had accidentally smudged the letters and by the time he set the story down had no easy way to learn the truth. He wrote further that he had considered inventing a name, but that he had respected and rather liked the fellow and thought it would be even less honorable to assign him the wrong name than to refer to him by his title. When I sought him out he was several years dead, but the community still spoke well of Silus Delnian. —*Silenus*

to see. How quickly would the waves overpower her? Would she struggle much? Or would she just sink under the way that idiot Marcella had when she swam a few dozen feet out from the shore?

He navigated around the bushy headland and onto the worn track that led down a steep slope, arriving finally atop a natural wall above a swirling cauldron of sea and foam contained by the outthrust arms of the cliff. The wall had a single small break facing the sea, no more than a dozen paces wide.

Julivar Lenereva stood at the elevated base of the rocky bowl, staring out at the gap. She must have made her way along the rough trail at the height rather than walking down the more worn path leading into the churning surf. She looked as if she were going to jump and at only twenty feet up she was sure to survive the drop. Probably she'd panic, and try to swim, and thus be thrown against the rocks repeatedly. She'd end up a battered, bloody mess and he had timed his arrival for the show almost perfectly.

Grinning, Phrenius crept carefully along the top of the encircling walls, moving between craggy boulders to maximize his view while keeping out of sight.

Julivar took a deep breath and leapt out to plunge feet first into the dark gray roil. For a heartbeat or ten Phrenius wondered if she'd already been swept away. Then her black wet head broke free, and she gasped from the cold, spitting water and struggling as a surge slapped her face.

He smiled, relishing the fight to come.

Phrenius didn't hear the clattering down the path until it was very close, and the sound of sandals on stone startled him. He whirled, heart pounding, and discovered an older man in ordinary travel clothes hurrying onto the wild rampart. Gray strands flecked his dark hair and his expression was grim. Limned by the sun were other figures on the cliff behind; Phrenius started in surprise, then fear, for something about the set of the stranger's face and his implacable advance scared him. Phrenius felt for his knife before realizing he could move further behind the boulders to hide. Though his view would be spoiled, he should still be able to savor the shrieks and general commotion.

Below, Phrenius felt the specter's hold on the Volani wretch loosening. That was strange—sometimes the girls fought for control in the earlier stages, but not so late, not with any real strength.

The man shouted for Julivar to hang on. Phrenius heard shuffling and a larger body hitting the water as well as some more scrambling along the ledge only a few feet from where he sheltered. He could not resist a look, and spotted a Herrene walking cautiously along the cliffside while scanning the water, a long rope in hand.

V

It was Izivar who'd guessed Julivar's destination, remembering how her sister had been horrified by an account of a drowned beach party there years previous.

Hanuvar feared the girl had run somewhere else to die and that they wasted their efforts toward the wrong direction. He'd even hoped that they were all wrong and that Julivar was less troubled than she'd seemed.

Close as he'd been to his siblings, Hanuvar had never understood why he hadn't sensed when they, too, were endangered, or dying, for he'd known men and women with such connections. It seemed Izivar and Julivar possessed one, for Hanuvar found the young lady exactly where Izivar had feared, in a high-sided, bowl-shaped cove with a narrow opening to the sea. The murderous boy was nowhere to be seen. Julivar floundered in the lethal waters below.

Somewhere behind him Antires hurried with a rope. And that would be the safest way to secure Julivar's survival. But he'd outpaced his friend and he wasn't sure there was time to wait.

He shucked off sandals and sword belt while he eyed the churn to get a sense of its flow. With each new wave sweeping in through the rocky gap, the surface water gathered power in a chaotic dance, funneling along the sides until it slammed the rear wall in a thunder of spray. Presumably an equally powerful force shifted the water beneath out to sea.

He leapt out from the wall, striking the cool waves feet first. He sank down until the lower currents spun him so he faced the opening.

He kicked up and his head cleared the spray, far to the left of where he'd expected. The water pushed him inexorably toward the gap. Julivar fought it with a solid effort but each new wave sent her spinning.

He flung himself toward her, laboring with every stroke and kick against the ocean's might. The seawater was constantly in his eyes so that when he finally reached Julivar it was more by accident and the current's pull than actual design.

Her face was a mask of anguish.

He shouted to be heard over the crashing surf. "Hold your breath. Focus on floating—" Then a wave stole his voice. She clung to him with one arm as he pulled her tight.

He allowed the flood to slosh them until a brief lull and then shouted: "Now! Deep breath. Under together." He sank with her and found nothing but sand with his feet. Pushing off and sliding along the undercurrent brought them nearer the sidewall. He kicked with powerful legs and pulled water with his free arm. The girl he held in the other fluttered her feet and moved her arms but progress was minimal. He thought he heard someone shouting, but the surf's roar was so great he couldn't be certain, and he had no way to gauge from where it had come.

Sheer stubbornness coupled with titanic effort got him within grasping distance of a rock near the steep upward slope, then the waves slammed them into it. He managed to twist so his back took the impact's brunt, but his shoulder and waist were scraped badly. Julivar cried out as a swell flung one of her arms into an abrasive fluted stone and drew blood in a long row of jagged scratches.

A rope dropped from above and Hanuvar lunged for it, abrading his calf on submerged rock. His hand closed on the lifeline. He knew a brief moment of panic as he lost hold of Julivar, then she clutched his tunic and he guided the rope into her hands.

"Go," he called, and she somehow found the strength to pull herself hand over hand up the humped stone and out of the water. She paused at the bottom of the rocky trail and looked back at Hanuvar, water dripping from her hairline into her eyes.

He had braced himself against the eager current by clawing to the uneven cliff wall. "Go on!" he called. A further wave swept over his head, then cleared away in time for him to see her using one hand on the rope while she dragged herself up the arduous slope with the other.

Hanuvar was watching Julivar's climb for safety when loneliness stabbed him. Something cool and coruscating passed across his face. It felt at first as though a light net had crossed him, but when he brushed his free hand over his eyes there was nothing there... apart from the weight of his own failures.

You have rescued this girl, a voice seemed to say, *but it was the wrong choice. You always make the wrong choices. You're my last child, and you save the daughter of our enemies?*

Somehow his father was there in the water with him, his expression caustic and disproving. *You failed us. You brought our people to doom. What did you think you would find? Glory? Peace? Do you think the Dervans would have struck back with such hatred had you not fought so hard?*

He wiped salt spray from his eyes, but the vision persisted, even as he was jostled against the jagged stone. *I would have done it better. You were rash, and young. I could have told you the Dervans would never yield. And you should have known southern Tyvol would never give you the men you needed. Nor would Volanus, not with the Lenerevas guiding the assembly. They were ever against us. And now you're literally in bed with them.* His father's lips twisted in a scathing sneer. *You should have killed yourself in shame long ago.*

Hanuvar was no stranger to doubt, and the sense his father might well have managed many things better than he, but he had long since schooled himself to make the best choices he could, and to reexamine mistakes only to avoid them. Sleepless nights of recrimination did no good for an officer or the men he led.

Yet he was weary, and alone, and reminded that he had survived when so many others had not. From out of nowhere the thought of Julivar's tormenter rose in his mind. He even imagined his features, though he had never seen him, for he could perfectly picture a narrow face twisted in mockery. And then he perceived that the boy was somehow connected, through this thing that tormented him with his father's image.

Hanuvar eyed the vision, grief and sorrow and all his hates welling up within him. Though it be twisted, there was truth in the searing words.

He shook his head. The wise learned from failure, they did not succumb to it, and life still offered many joys. The people he loved deserved better from him than self-pity and resignation.

"You're not real," he said aloud. "Do not look to me or mine to work your miseries."

The specter shouted in his face. "Let go! Open your mouth and breathe deep!"

But Hanuvar turned from it and pulled himself free from the water, then, one hand on the rope, the other braced on the steep slope, started toward his anxious friend, legs shaking with exertion. Julivar leaned against Antires, breathing heavily, eyes closed. He heard the specter shout at him even above the pounding surf, then caught movement out of the corner of his eye. A screaming figure plunged from the cliff. At the same instant the spirit was gone, taking its miasma with it.

Fearful for Izivar, Hanuvar twisted toward the churning water, and after a moment caught sight of a boy's head bobbing in the current. He even heard a choked scream for help. It was soon followed by others, garbled by the waves.

Hanuvar climbed until he had both feet securely under him, on the steep slope. He clasped the arm of his loyal friend, his eyes conveying his thanks.

Beside him, Julivar looked weary and small. Water dripped steadily down her bedraggled hair.

Antires thoughtfully contemplated the surf, where the boy still cried feebly. "Should we help him?"

Hanuvar answered between deep breaths. "No."

The playwright seemed only a little surprised. He undid the rope he'd braced against an outcropping.

Julivar paused once to watch the boy rocked by the wave swells, then turned away, leaning against Hanuvar as they walked to Izivar, waiting where the encircling arms met the cliff. She enfolded Julivar in a deep embrace and pulled her further inland. Hanuvar looked back to where the boy had been and saw only the crashing waves and rocks.

Twenty paces back from the cliff, near where their horses grazed, the priest had placed a rectangular wooden box amongst some scree and now sprinkled dark powder about it in a tight circle. He tossed tinder down on it from the pack he'd brought with him, struggled briefly with some flint, and soon had a low fire underway. It swept hungrily upon the box. Wordless and grim, the priest watched it burn. He met Hanuvar's eyes only once, then stood and watched the fire, like a sentry sworn to hold a post with his life.

"We should get closer to the fire," Izivar suggested.

"Not that fire." Hanuvar was chilled himself, especially with the full force of the wind off the headland beating into him, but he wanted no closer to magics than he already was.

"I kept thinking of him," Julivar said, breath ragged as she sank onto a patch of grass. Her gaze was piercing as an arrow. "The whole time. But it wasn't until I saw him again that I knew that I'd been feeling his hate. That sometimes the voice I'd heard was his."

Hanuvar brushed a lock of cold wet hair from her forehead. The shy smile she gave him was embarrassed and apologetic. She took his hand when he offered and let him help her to her feet. He squeezed her and kissed the top of her head.

Izivar watched approvingly, rubbing her back the while, then, when Julivar leaned back toward her, hugged her tightly.

"How do you think he ended up like that?" Antires asked. "Was he mistreated? Spoiled? Abused?"

Hanuvar didn't much care. "There's a host of possibilities. But others who come from terrible situations grow into perfectly fine human beings. Put him from your thoughts." He spoke to Izivar. "How did the boy happen to fall in?"

She was a moment answering. When she did, it was with cool disdain that brooked no challenge. "I had to get the box from him. And then he slipped. Julivar, let's get you home."

※ ※ ※

Julivar's improvement was gradual. By the next week she was nearly her old self, although was ever after slightly more reserved. Certainly she had become even more fixated upon improving her fighting skills. Hanuvar enjoyed instructing her, and I joined in the training.

Izivar did not entirely care for her sister's relentless application of Hanuvar's exercise regime. For all that, Izivar often came to watch us during even the simplest training, moments that she would have been expected to excuse herself from, and I knew then she understood how different that garden would have been if her sister had never again been there to pace across its stones and strike imagined enemies.

We had made great inroads into our efforts to liberate the Volani held in the Oscanus region. Hanuvar deployed me to make initial contact with some laboring at a sort of resort for vacationing Dervans, but I found the matter challenging in a number of unique ways. When

I returned to report to Hanuvar I discovered him absent and Izivar more pensive than usual.

For Carthalo had learned of a mad new plan hatched by the revenant legate. And he and Hanuvar had set upon a dangerous course of action. If successful, it might finally lead them to Narisia herself. But it would require them to work for long days under assumed identities with men paid to hunt down any they could find with the blood of the Cabera family.

—Sosilos, Book Fourteen

Chapter 6:
Family Heirlooms

I

Killian had come to hate being seen with the blade. It was a gladius, the short, stabbing sword worn by most in the legion, manufactured to a high standard by an old Birani smith. He'd purchased it from a retiring centurion when he himself had been appointed optio, and he'd treated it well from that day forward. Any smart soldier took good care of his weapons. That he'd wielded it to deliver Adruvar Cabera's death blow should have been happenstance, but his companions had made more of the weapon than they had his own prowess. So had his commander, Flaminian Marcius, who had borrowed the sword and then "restored" it with fine new wraps and a gem encrusted hilt, thinking to please Killian with the gift.

From then on it had been too beautiful to wield, and Killian had to purchase an unadorned replacement, consigning Adruvar's death weapon with its ridiculous jewelry to his campaign chest until the end of his service. Then it had hung on pegs in his study near the books he'd never gotten around to reading.

He would rather have left it on the wall for the rest of his life. Now, though, the weapon swung on his belt, and owing to the damnably pleasant weather there was no need for a cloak, which meant everyone spotted the gaudy hilt. If those who noticed hadn't happened to have heard what he'd done with the sword, his comrades obligingly told them.

The soldiers with him were fools and he'd long since tired of them. All eight were legionaries, but four had never been deployed beyond

Tyvol and all had spent the bulk of their service posted in Derva itself until reassignment with him. The route to their destination required them to travel mostly through tiny farm villages, where they took meals from roadside taverns. Once the novelty wore off, the common fare and the dearth of female company left the men ill-tempered. They were too used to the capital's luxuries.

In addition to these complainers, the revenants had saddled him with a wizard, and a green one at that. Publius was a thin young scholarly sort lacking the arrogance of his order, quiet unless someone made the mistake of asking him how his sorceries worked. Killian had committed that error only once, and been deluged with a wave of words that might as well have been a foreign language. He'd had to order the boy to shut up. The only thing Killian cared about the young man's magics was whether they worked. Thankfully Publius mostly kept to himself, pouring over scrolls in the evening and even sometimes during their travel breaks. He had claimed to be glad he was away from the revenants, and it might even be true, for he didn't speak to anyone about bloodlines or witches or the heresies of barbarians.

The revenant legate had the sense not to place the boy in charge of the expedition, even though the legate claimed it was the young wizard's powers that would get them to their goal. He'd selected Killian to lead and had wanted to supply a guide as well, but Killian insisted on bringing his own, an unassuming fellow who had once been a wine merchant and knew much of the Turian countryside. Though Killian didn't know him well, the man had a quiet competence which reassured him that at least one aspect of this assignment would succeed—they would get where they needed to go.

It had been a long, dull, irritating trip by horseback so far, but Killian forced them on. Life hadn't been easy after his army days. He had generally failed as a farmer and even his generous pension had run through his fingers. Still, this commission could set things right. Maybe he could finally hire an overseer to manage the slaves so he and his nephews could spend their time hunting in the woods instead of fighting the soil.

He thought about that future as he led the way across the countryside, consulting sometimes with the guide. A day out from Turian lands, they reached a sizable roadside inn and Killian announced they'd stop for the evening. This cheered the legionaries, who'd had to camp out the night before. They anticipated not just wine, but women, and traded boasts about their stamina with both in phrases ages old.

Publius seemed delighted for reasons of his own and immediately requested he have his food served in a private chamber, so that he might study in peace.

Killian made the arrangements and passed over some coins to the innkeeper before settling into the common room in a corner far from the locals, some of whom bet on arm wrestling, and distant from his own boys, who thought themselves charming and amusing as they joked with the local harlots. He ate a decent meal and watched. Surely those soldiers weren't so young that they didn't know whores were predisposed to laugh at their jests, but then they *were* idiots.

The guide disappeared somewhere. Killian didn't mind. He liked to be alone, which is why he wasn't especially happy when an old man in a worn gray tunic came to his table and stood across from him.

Killian fixed him with a glare before returning to the mutton and lentil pottage. "Whatever you want, I'm not interested."

The old fellow placed his brown knapsack on the table, then rested his hand on it as he sat down at a bench on the other side of the battered wooden surface. The man's face was seamed with sun and dirt. The hair was shaggy. The nose was slightly hooked, the eyes a bluish gray. A scraggly beard hung down from his chin but his face was otherwise clean-shaven.

"I have been waiting for you," the fellow said ominously. His voice was less weathered than his attire.

Killian's sigh was more a growl. "I'm really not in the mood."

"You're hunting Caberas, aren't you?" The old man leaned forward. "You are the man I foresaw. You bear the sword."

While Killian was processing that, the stranger whipped a dark brown object from his bag, displaying it with a flourish. Strange symbols and wandering lines and a mystic Hadiran eye all drawn in black decorated the top. Killian didn't recognize the grisly thing for a skull until the old man turned its empty sockets to him and planted it on the table.

Killian pushed back, snarling. "I'm eating! Put that away!"

"Adruvar Cabera can't hurt you," the man said with a chuckle. "You already killed him." But he slipped the skull back into its bag.

"How do you know what I'm hunting?"

"I could tell you I have dreamed of it. I do have dreams, Centurion. But there's a simpler explanation. I know someone high among the revenants, and word was passed along to me."

"And who are you?" Killian took a second look at the old man's stained tunic, coming to the belated realization that he spoke with a priest of Lutar, lord of the dead. Between that and the skull, Killian felt his annoyance ebb before a sense of foreboding.

"I am Brencis. And I, too, hunt Cabera. I'm told you have a tracker in your midst, but all I saw when you came in were these soldiers and the reedy one. Surely he's not your tracker?"

"I don't see what business this is of yours."

"Those with you may be good soldiers but it takes no skilled eye to see that they are Dervan boys. Do any of you speak Turian?"

"Our guide has some," Killian admitted. "You don't look Turian."

"But I speak it. Well. And I can help you locate the Cabera."

The man's abrupt approach surprised him, but Killian had met clever con men in his time. "I assume you want pay?"

"No."

"Attention, then."

"I want blood, Centurion. It's as simple as that. I have seen Narisia Cabera. I know what she looks like. Can any of your people say that?"

The old man spoke with such an air of conviction that Killian studied him anew. "You have dreamed of her?"

"Yes. But more than that. I have seen her with my own eyes. You know the docks in Ostra where the Volani slaves were first delivered? I marked her well."

Killian grunted at this news. On hearing it he wondered why Legate Aquilius hadn't sent someone on this quest who'd recognize its main target. It seemed a foolish oversight.

"You might have started with that, instead of the hoary skull," Killian said. "What's the point of carrying it around?"

"The point of the skull is to bring me closer to anyone of their bloodline. This skull was bathed in that blood. It can help me find others who bear it, living or dead."

"My wizard says he can do something similar." Killian nodded his head toward the staircase up which Publius had retreated. "If you can find Hanuvar's daughter or any other Cabera with your skull, why haven't you?"

"I have limits. Bring me within a few miles and I can feel them. Bring me within a few hundred paces and I will single them out of a crowd."

Over the course of their conversation, the man's words and quiet intensity had convinced Killian he was an unlikely charlatan. He put down his spoon. "You say you want blood. Why?"

"My brothers died in Hanuvar's wars." Brencis looked as though he might have said much more, but his mouth thinned and he fell silent.

Killian had heard enough to take a risk. "I'm charged with helping the boy find Narisia or Hanuvar Cabera himself. Or both. I'm told my tracker has the best chance the revenants can muster. But I'm always willing to improve my odds."

"Do you want them alive or dead?"

Killian concluded the eager old man would prefer the latter. "I get paid more if alive, but I'm sure they won't be that way long no matter what condition we bring them in."

Brencis' mouth thinned disapprovingly, but he acquiesced. "Fine."

"We travel light, and we travel fast. Have you a horse? Travel gear?"

"I do."

"We leave at dawn, on the morrow. Ride with us if you will. If you trouble me, I'll dismiss you. If I find you're a spy, I'll cut you down."

"I will be there." The old man bowed his head to him and slipped away. Killian watched him go, wondering why there was something familiar about him. He then realized the intensity in his eyes was reminiscent of the kind of hunger for vengeance he'd seen on some old veterans.

At the least, it would help to have someone else along who knew how to talk with the Turians. And if the priest should prove untrustworthy, well, Killian was no stranger to eliminating problems.

II

The previous winter Hanuvar had observed the revenant mage from a rooftop while the young man labored over a kind of portable wooden platform holding spell ingredients, carried through the streets of Derva by a pair of assistants. Unlike the vast number of those claiming magical provenance, Publius' powers actually worked, and he had doggedly pursued two men Hanuvar had freed from captivity, up until Hanuvar's snowball had disrupted the mage's tracking spell.

How Publius now planned to locate Narisia, Hanuvar had not yet learned, but he wished to be on hand when the mage threw his spells. Apparently the sword that had dealt Adruvar's death blow was to be somehow instrumental in the spellcasting, though Carthalo hadn't yet learned the details.

In his identity as a guide, Hanuvar's chief intelligence agent had worked partly into Killian's trust, and was consulting with him that morning in the predawn glow while each held the reins of their mounts. Carthalo pointed south along the road, his finger moving as though delineating points ahead. The rest of the men stretched and complained and tightened saddle girths while their horses snorted. No official introduction was passed along about Hanuvar's position in their party, but word had been disseminated, for the soldiers took him in, and he noted the surreptitious inspection the skinny young mage gave him.

Killian got them moving with a minimum of words. He led the way, with Carthalo riding along side. After him came the scholar, and then, in four pairs, the legionaries, though they had dispensed with leg greaves and heavy armor. Hanuvar brought up the rear, eating their dust.

Riding to the rear was a necessary evil. Hanuvar wished neither to be examined closely nor to appear particularly clean. The dirt would continue to disguise both his appearance and his age, for it emphasized his creases.

On they rode through the green lands south of Derva. Little of the Tyvolian countryside was flat, but this rolling farmland was more level than usual, and they occasionaly viewed tenant farmers and slaves working the fields for rich families ensconced in country villas beyond the road or absent entirely. The green bulk of the worn-down Acanthes rose to the west, usually blocking sight of the more rugged and distant Vertigines. The sun was warm against his neck and shoulders, and he smelled of his own sweat and that of his mount.

The road they traveled had been old when Derva was just a little hill village and Turia waxed mighty from the coast to the rugged western highlands. Later generations had bricked the road with great care, but the route was unchanged. Hanuvar himself had traveled it more than once, long years before. Had he been inclined to do so, he might have maundered on about the changed circumstances of his life, or the irony that he should be travelling in the company of Dervans to hunt for his own blood.

Instead, he was watchful. From time to time one of the soldiers would glance back, and he hoped all that they would ever see was a strange old priest of Lutar. He dreaded them growing more inquisitive and dropping back to ask suspicious questions of him.

It was not the soldiers who eventually fell out of formation to join him, but Carthalo. The spy would never deliberately draw a connection between them, so Hanuvar knew there'd be a reasonable explanation.

Carthalo coughed a little and waved his hand in front of his face. "You seem to have found all the road dust, old man," he said.

The spy had an astonishing ability to blend into his environment. He was sturdily built and ordinary, and his appearance could be affable and unassuming, or stern and certain. Under the identity of a guide, he looked more the latter, a seasoned man of middle years. He'd chosen a tunic that emphasized his powerful arm muscles and chest, the better to suggest fitness for work, then topped off his dark head with a straw hat, worn and stained from much use.

"Brencis, is it?" Carthalo asked.

Probably the others could not hear, owing to the clop of the hooves and the low mutter of conversation from some of the soldiers, but Carthalo liked leaving nothing to chance.

"That is my name," Hanuvar answered coolly.

"I'm your guide, Silvio. I'm told you speak Turian." Carthalo then switched to that language. Hanuvar had a good grasp of it, having spent years in the lands south of Derva, though it was haunted by an accent that wavered toward Dervan. Someone truly astute might have been able to detect the ring of Volani among certain words, but recognizing one accent in the speaking of a foreign language was likely beyond their companions. "Killian sent me to speak to you in Turian and gauge how much of a liar you are."

"I am a grand liar, as you well know," Hanuvar answered quietly.

Carthalo smiled tightly.

"What would you report?" Hanuvar asked.

"Two of our soldiers have served on the Irimacian border. They've been in a few skirmishes, but aren't what you'd call truly seasoned, although they like to pretend it. The others are more recent hires, who've won various awards for horsemanship and target spearing, but haven't ever seen combat. I think the esteemed legate evaluates the worth of these men by how much they brag."

Hanuvar had encountered other commanders like that—usually men without much experience on the front line themselves. "There's a kind of soldier that usually travels in threes." Like Carthalo, Hanuvar did not use certain names or titles, the better to disguise their topics of conversation.

"I've been watching for that. None show the mage particular deference, and all of them are a little arrogant. But I've got my eye on one who's more outspoken. He's younger; his self-assurance could just stem from his upbringing."

"But it might be from the order, and the company he keeps."

"Yes."

"What have you seen of the wizard?"

"He's studious and dedicated. Ask him about his craft and he'll spout a bunch of esoteric things he seems to believe."

"Trying to impress?"

"A little, but he's mostly a lonely enthusiast eager to talk shop."

"And what of our leader?"

"I don't think he wants to be here. I don't think he likes the job, but he's determined to see it done. He's a professional."

"What are they using to track the daughter of the dread general?"

Carthalo shot him a wary look. "We're not supposed to know that, but the mage talked a little in my earshot."

"And I'm not going to like it," Hanuvar guessed.

"I don't like it either. Part of the scalp of the general's father."

The general meaning him. Hanuvar stared into the distance, trying to keep the terrible detail remote from him and not quite managing it. He remembered his brother Melgar saying in his later years that the Cabera family line had only bad fortune, starting with their mother's death, then their sister's, but that their father had been the unluckiest of them all, dying with so many plans unfulfilled, most of his children half grown, and then having had his body lost for months before again being stolen.

"I haven't seen it," Carthalo added. "Is that even possible?"

"Yes. Yes, it is." Himli Cabera's body had been so badly treated by his murderers there had been almost nothing left to recover. Part of his scalp could well have been shorn free as a grisly memento and passed on to Dervan hands.

"What do you want to do about all of this?" Carthalo asked.

Tempting as it was to shut the entire expedition down, Hanuvar had already made his decision. "I've seen this mage at work. He actually can track people. He might well direct us to my daughter at last, and then we will improvise. If not, we will simply have spent some time in the Turian countryside."

"A relaxing vacation amongst the men who hunt for your blood," Carthalo said darkly.

He had confessed that when his agents had gotten wind of the revenant search he had hesitated to present Hanuvar with the information, fearing what he might do. In the end, Carthalo had agreed that this might be their best chance for finding Narisia, risky as it was, and that in any case the mission had to be disrupted. He had not liked the idea of Hanuvar being personally involved from the very start, and his warning look now was a reminder of it.

Hanuvar understood his worries, but he had made his choice. "Now we should briefly cover what you'll tell our leader we spoke about, so our tales agree."

"Of course."

That they did, and then Carthalo bade him farewell, cantered up past the string of soldiers, and fell in beside Killian. Hanuvar was left alone to contemplate the existence of a final physical remnant of his father, dried and held like a prize by a Dervan sorcerer for the purposes of hunting Himli's son and granddaughter and bringing them to their enemies for exhibition and execution. Hanuvar's hands tightened on the reins even as his father's words echoed in his ears. *Emotions should be mastered, lest your foes use them against you.* From an early age Hanuvar had been taught that those who let themselves be ruled by their reactions might as well turn control of their life's path to a wild horse.

He had thought his father an old man, and it was strange to think

Himli had been younger than Hanuvar was now on the night of his betrayal. He wondered how old he himself would be before his father no longer seemed more seasoned and wiser.

Never, he thought.

At midday they halted in the shade of some oaks. To judge by ashes and blackened ground and stones gathered about makeshift firepits, the stopover was put to frequent use and sometimes doubled as an overnight camping spot. It even came with a designated waste area about thirty paces beyond the oaks themselves, where flies and stink were thick.

Hanuvar sat apart from the others on a weathered log. He was halfway through his hard roll and dried meat when Publius sidled over.

Up close the mage's thin face was dotted with freckles. His eyes were dark and strangely hopeful. "I'm Publius," he said. His voice was mild, and betrayed the same eagerness visible in his gaze. "Do you mind if I join you?"

"As you like," Hanuvar said coolly. He drank from his wineskin and the young man sat down, studying him.

"It's Brencis, right?" the mage asked. He didn't wait for an answer. "A priest of Lutar."

"Yes."

"Killian says you're a magical tracker yourself. Are you an astronomer? Or are you a sympathetic magic user? Or a talismanic one?"

"I have some knowledge of many different schools," Hanuvar answered mildly. "I understand that you're a talismanic practitioner."

"Yes. Killian said that you had a talisman yourself, and that there were symbols upon it."

"It is true."

"I wondered if I might—"

"No."

Publius' expression fell, like a puppy denied a treat. And like a pup, he swiftly resumed his begging after a brief delay. "You mustn't think I'm after your secrets. I wish to share—"

"You would be wise to share nothing," Hanuvar said. "You may understand that when you're older."

"I'm more skilled than you think," the young man said. His cheeks were flushed. "What symbol system do you use to draw your power?"

"I use a blend of them. But mostly I focus through my connection with blessed Lutar and the moon and stars."

"Not the planets?"

"Only as they are conduits for the power of Lutar himself."

"We should be allies."

"I should trust revenants?" Hanuvar asked. "Who lure sorcerers in for advice, then try them for crimes once they steal their secrets?"

"I'm not like that."

"I don't intend to chance it. I know too well what your side is like. You think I'm foolish enough to court my own death by gifting you access to my life's work? Begone."

The boy opened his mouth to say more. He pushed angrily to his feet, hesitated as if debating saying something more, than stormed away.

Hanuvar understood he had not made a friend, but he knew his façade would almost surely crack if Publius were permitted to examine the alleged skull of Adruvar and its particular symbols. The browned bone was a tool for a single purpose, and its time had not yet come.

III

When the sentry came to wake him at the start of second watch, Killian was already upright and putting on his boots. Mazentius, the youngest and burliest of the soldiers, tried to make a joke of Killian's readiness. "You have a date, sir?"

Killian grunted. "I'm going to check the perimeter. Keep an eye on things while I'm gone."

The younger man didn't know what to make of that, and retreated to the fire, moving a little stiffly, as if irritated Killian hadn't smiled at his jest.

Killian stood, shifting shoulders and neck. He buckled on the sword belt, listening to the chirrup of crickets in the cool night air and the snuffle of one of the horses, hobbled with the others in a dark group.

The rest of his men lay twisted over their blankets about the fireside. Some were bundled against the night like children, and others slept without covers, pillowed on their rolled up cloaks. He wished some men from his own unit were with him. If this lot had to rouse in the middle of the night to fight, could they even find their swords?

He shook his head in disgust. His eyes strayed over to where Brencis lay, curled far to one side of the camp, then he looked up to where the stars shown brilliantly through the clear heavens, including the great shining bridge of them in a band above the moon, halfway to full.

There was no sign of the guide, but that didn't surprise him.

Mazentius frowned at Killian as he headed out. Probably he wondered who would bother walking their perimeter in peacetime, in friendly territory, when they had an armed and good-sized party. Killian didn't care enough about the man's good will to explain.

He strode away from the hill and into the rolling fields and brush surrounding them. After a quarter mile a figure slid out of a copse and lifted a hand. Killian grasped his sword hilt until he was certain it was Silvio.

"Anything?"

"Not so far. Did you expect anyone in particular?"

"No."

The guide had claimed to have scouted for the legions in Herrenia, and watching him at work as they explored the surrounds reassured Killian that he'd spoken the truth. The man knew how to move, what to be alert for, and how to approach hilltops. After a half hour circling, Killian stopped the guide by the little stand of trees where they'd rendezvoused. "You talked with the priest for a while. What was your take on him?"

"He knows Turian fairly well, though he speaks it with an accent. Like me," Silvio added. Killian appreciated that he was an honest broker, and not a man trying to impress. The guide seemed to think out loud. "What to make of him . . . well, he's a priest who doesn't like to talk much about magics. He's protective of what he knows. He doesn't want to share it."

"Did he say where he got the skull?" The head of Adruvar Cabera had been tossed into Hanuvar's camp, and then his body recovered by another of the Cabera brothers. Killian had assumed the body parts would be interred in the Cabera family crypt, or buried in the lands they were occupying in Tyvol at the time.

"It didn't come up. I can ask him directly, if you want."

"I may." It didn't really matter. "If he didn't talk about the skull or his magics or his past, what did he talk about?"

"Phases of the moon and signs from Lutar. I don't pay much attention to that kind of thing. I'd rather not know about the lands beyond death. He also talked about his brothers, and how they'd been killed by the Volani. I've never heard a priest so obsessed with vengeance before. Is that common?"

"They're as human as the rest of us, I guess," Killian said. "To me they always seemed most interested in the quality of the meat they can get off the sacrifices."

"Or arguing among themselves about signs and scriptures," Silvio suggested.

"Exactly. But priests of Lutar tend to be kind of loners anyway. Especially country ones."

"Loners are good at nursing grievances," Silvio observed.

He had a good point, but Killian wasn't worried about it. "So you think he can do what he says?"

Silvio fell silent.

"What, you don't want to say?"

"I'm just trying to decide if you want a real answer, or if you've already decided, and you're testing me."

Killian frowned at that.

Silvio looked sidelong at him. "I think he's a lot more interested in finding Caberas than your mage."

"You doubt the mage? The revenant legate himself sent him. We're lucky the boy's not in charge."

"I just think that one's like a young tribune in love with his own armor. Publius doesn't give a damn about the battle, he just wants to look good."

Killian nodded to himself. He knew the type.

Silvio asked a question of his own. "Do you really think this magical stuff is going to turn up Hanuvar or his daughter?"

"You were in the legion," Killian answered, saying nothing more.

"I've spent most of my life not getting paid to think," Silvio said. "I guess I can do it a little longer."

"Oh, I want you to think. I count on it. But that part's above our pay grade. If the magic works and hunts us up some fugitives, we get covered in glory." He felt his mouth twist. "It's overrated."

"So you're just here for the coins. But you want to see the job done right."

"Habit. Come on, I've seen enough. Let's get some sleep."

Silvio nodded, and they headed in together. Killian fell silent, thinking about his little troop. He didn't like them very much, but if they found a Cabera he'd have to count on them to watch his flanks. Probably he could stand to work harder to win them over.

At least he knew he could count on Silvio.

IV

Hanuvar woke before the dawn, though he did not rise until the camp stirred. By this, the third morning of travel with Killian in command, he was used to the man's routines, so he was surprised when the taciturn leader stood before his team at breakfast.

"We'll reach Turian lands before midday, and not long after that we'll close on the last reported point anyone saw Narisia Cabera. That's when our mage is going to throw his spell. If we find a living Cabera, do you realize how famous you're going to be? No door will be closed to you. You'll be getting free drinks in taverns for the rest of your lives."

The soldiers had been talking about varied permutations on an idyllic future where they were showered with money and affection, and their eyes shone to hear an aspect of it specified by their leader. His discussion of their potential prestige seemed to have made it more real for them. Killian thumped his chest. "I know you all long for the kind of glory I've had in my career. Well, you lot are lucky. Most people don't get a chance at the kind of prize we're after."

One of the soldiers muttered a fervent yes, and the others nodded vigorously.

"I don't know what we're going to find, but if there really are Caberas out here, it's not going to be simple. They'll have had months to prepare. You can't count the men who thought they were better than Hanuvar. They overflow the graveyards. And he may be old, but you ought to know there're some centurions old as him still in service, and they're hard as nails. You can bet he'll be just like them."

"Hanuvar's really alive?" The voice of one of the legionaries came close to trembling. "I thought we were just after his daughter."

"The revenant legate says he is. And even if he isn't, the daughter's probably no pushover. She's an Eltyr. They're fast, and deadly, and they go down hard. Some of the worst fighting of the war was at the Volani River Gate. The water foamed red with the blood of our men." Killian surveyed them. "So you scared yet?"

"No, sir," Mazentius said.

"I can't hear you!" Killian growled.

The men got it then, and answered as one, a crisp shout. "No sir!"

"That's better. You're Dervans. And you're tough, and you're trained, and you've got me. But take off your dresses, boys, and get your eyes and your swords sharp. Vacation time's over. If we're going to stay alive, we need to stay alert." He sucked in a breath and gave them a final once-over. "All right. That's all I've got. Let's get packed and get hunting."

After their leader's speech, the men's spirits were high, and they were eager to be on. The horses sensed the excitement and even they moved with more energy.

Shortly before midday they reached the little river Elathri and crossed a worn stone bridge over the ancient border into Turian lands. Roadside villages here looked little different from those to the north, save that occasionally ancient walls were incorporated into buildings, and the tired old hills that rose beyond the towns were studded with old white stone mausoleums and cliffside tomb doors.

Long centuries had passed since the Turians had been the dominant culture of the region. Many nationalities walked their lands now. Despite the introduction of people from across the peninsula and beyond, many the travelers saw still possessed the distinctive black eyes and wavy dark hair and clear, pale olive skin so often seen in ancient Turian mosaics. The people looked out from their shops or up from their plows, observing Killian's expedition with little warmth, as though the Dervans were interlopers even after all this time.

Despite their antipathy for the Dervans, Turian support for Hanuvar's invasion had never been as overt as those from southernmost Tyvol. But many Turians had joined his ranks as informers and scouts and even infantrymen. Some walled towns had opened their gates to his forces. Hanuvar doubted any of his former allies would have survived a Dervan purge, but he kept his head bowed as if in weariness whenever passing through settlements here, hoping no one would look close at a dirty old priest.

Two hours after midday they arrived at faded green hills scattered with abandoned walls built from the gray volcanic stones common to this area. Decrepit archways that must once have led to garden paths or mansions now fronted only dark forests. The wind was light, but often thick with the scents of lavender and rosemary.

The road wound in and out of ruins for another hour until Killian led them to a hilltop overlooking a valley. Here, he said, a patrol had followed Narisia Cabera and her two companions before the three disappeared into morning fog more than a year ago. A rainstorm had swept up and obscured their tracks and no Dervans had seen the women since. Nor, so far as Hanuvar had learned, had anyone else.

With some eagerness, Publius went to the goods secured on one of the pack horses, carefully unwrapped the contents, and began to assemble them. Hanuvar pretended to perform his own spell preparations, and drew a circle of charcoal that he filled with moon phases and images of eyes and open hands. He then lit a nub of a candle and placed it within the brown skull, festooned with images the more artistically gifted Izivar had drawn upon it. Carthalo had recovered it from a big revenant that they'd had to make disappear.

Hanuvar sat down within his circle, put his hand upon the skull and began to mutter, his gaze mimicking inward absorption. In truth he carefully watched Publius. Carthalo lingered near the mage, as if curious, though he was ready to strike. If Hanuvar's preparations failed, then they would be outnumbered by enemies very quickly.

Nearby, Publius finished assembling a small portable table, an improved design over the last one Hanuvar had seen him with. It had been crafted not only with high ridged sides, but walled compartments for a variety of dark powders that Publius arranged before carefully covering them with squares of finely cut glass he removed from leather holders. Some symbols he drew upon the wood in dark charcoal; others had been burned into the platform's surface.

Even with some of the work prepared beforehand, it took the scholar almost half an hour to arrange all of it to his liking. When finished at last he mumbled over Killian's sword for a time, then opened another leather container and reverently removed what looked like a small dark-brown wig.

Hanuvar's chest tightened at sight of his father's hair, and he continued to observe through slitted eyes.

Publius placed the scalp in the center of his legless table, sprinkling it with red powders and dried green herbs he had to lift one of his glass panes to procure.

Finally he slid the table about on the ground with great care, eying the angle of the sun, reached within a pocket of his robe that lay just over his heart, and produced what Hanuvar first took to be a gnarled stick suspended by a black thread.

Most of the soldiers were watching, though they were supposed to be standing guard, and three of them gasped. Their proximity enabled them to understand more swiftly than Hanuvar that Publius had produced a mummified human finger. Once, twice, three times Publius dipped it against the scrap of Himli Cabera's scalp, then he whispered to it, sprinkled it with blue powder, and held it just above the table's middle.

Hanuvar rose to a kneeling position, the skull facing him in his left hand, as though he were engaged with it in silent dialogue. If he had to move fast, he could spring and strike in a single blow.

For a long moment the finger was still. It swung a little to the left, though Publius seemed not to have touched it at all. And then, of its own volition, it turned half its circumference and pointed unwaveringly at Hanuvar.

"It works!" Killian cried.

"I shall have to adjust the spell to ignore the nearest Cabera," Publius said, his smile revealing that he was not irritated but pleased. Hanuvar then understood the mage himself had doubted whether the spell would work. Possibly he'd been hoping that he would detect the nearby skull purported to be Adruvar's.

And then Publius said something that tensed Hanuvar once more. "There is a pull beyond the close one. A Cabera is somewhere along the road, beyond Adruvar's skull."

Hanuvar's own pulse leapt at this news, though he betrayed no outward sign of his excitement. He lifted the skull to his ear and narrowed his eyes in concentration.

Killian grinned. "Then get your finger more certain, mage. What does your skull tell you, Brencis?"

"He whispers that it is not Hanuvar who lies ahead."

"No?" Killian's hard eyes were alight with interest. "Does he say who's up there?"

"He taunts me," Hanuvar said. "He does not want to aid me."

Carthalo still waited near the mage, hand on sword hilt.

But Publius either couldn't perceive their trickery or wasn't wary enough of him to probe more closely. He bent and whispered to the finger. Once more it swung and pointed left, down the road.

"So a Cabera is here? A living one?" Killian prompted. He sounded excited in spite of himself.

"I can't tell if she's living or dead," the boy admitted. "But I can tell she's within an hour or two of us."

Killian frowned and turned to Hanuvar. "What about you, priest?"

Hanuvar set aside worries for his daughter, and freely improvised. "Adruvar worries, though it is the sleepy, wormy worry of someone who thought themselves beyond cares. And I think then that a Cabera must live."

"All right. You two—help Publius get that conjuring table up on his saddle like we talked about. Stop staring, boys! Glory's coming your way!"

Hanuvar rose and wiped away his circle before the mage could pay its pictures any mind. He then put the candle flame out with his fingers, and pressed the smoking wax to his head and his heart. All the while he forced himself to concentrate on the task at hand rather than the powerful emotions roiling within. Could his daughter truly be so close?

The soldiers proved so cautious with the table that Carthalo stepped forward to assist, helping Publius bear the thing with the tender care employed by a wounded nobleman's servants. As was his inclination, Publius overexplained the steps, and how the straps had to attach to the specially constructed saddle in just this way to keep it steady.

One of the older soldiers, Nelius, spoke to Hanuvar as he placed the skull in his pouch.

His voice bore a hint of awe. "That's really the skull of Adruvar Cabera?"

"It is."

"Where did you get it?"

"I bought it from a Herrene, who said he had it from a tomb robber. It didn't take long for me to confirm it was genuine."

The platform holding Publius' sorcery was firmly affixed to the mage's saddle, between the horn and the horse's neck, but even so the mage could not ride at any great speed for fear of disrupting the spell, and Killian chafed at the plodding progress. As the afternoon wore on he rode up and down the line, twice demanding from Publius and Hanuvar if they had more to say. Hanuvar told him Adruvar was silent but brooding, and Publius simply said south, along the road, but that he thought the Cabera was close.

And so they traveled, on and on. So slow was their progress that they were passed by a wagon convoy bearing horse fodder and a whole pack of farmers and farm boys as well as two buxom young women in old-fashioned Turian farm dresses. They raised their heads and coolly ignored the whistles and invitations, as remote and removed from the soldiers as the stone doors built into the distant cliffs.

Just before evening they passed another low line of hills and looked down on a little town. Publius straightened in his high-backed saddle. "Here!" he cried. "The Cabera is up ahead. Very close! Probably in the village!"

"Keep your voice down." Killian rode closer. "What do you need to do to find her?"

"I just need to hold steady for a moment," Publius answered. "I'll adjust the spell a bit."

Killian was visibly irritated, then nodded tightly and pointed off the road. "Let's move over there. How long will this take?"

"Less than a quarter hour."

Killian waved everyone to where a brook ran along the road and the men dismounted and led their horses to drink while Publius hunched over his table and shifted powders around.

Hanuvar dismounted with the soldiers. He tucked the skull back into his satchel and let his own animal drink.

Killian frowned at him. "Adruvar's not saying anything?"

"I will have to pray again. And I will not waste my own spells until we're closer."

Mazentius lowered his waterskin. "Centurion, what was it like? To kill Adruvar Cabera?"

Clearly all of the soldiers had been wondering that, because all eight fell silent, listening keenly.

Killian's frown deepened, and Hanuvar felt certain he would tell them to mind their own business. But he held to the friendlier demeanor he'd settled on this morning. "He knew he was going to die," the centurion said finally. "We'd hit both flanks, and the center had crumbled, so it was only a matter of time."

This matched what Hanuvar had been told of the battle. Flaminian Marcius' scouts had intercepted a letter from Adruvar and he had marched his legion double-time through the night to link up with the legion that had been following Adruvar's army. When Adruvar woke he faced a force twice as large as the one he'd prepared to fight.

"Adruvar didn't want to be captured alive, or maybe he just wanted to take as many legionaries as he could with him when he went down. So he charged into a line of us. We cut his horse out from under him, but when he hit the ground he just kept coming." Killian mimed rolling his shoulders and standing upright. The men listened, spellbound, and Hanuvar realized he was doing the same. He wondered if the priest he pretended to be would look as fascinated, and he supposed he would.

"He was already bleeding and his helm was off, and in we came." Killian swung an imaginary sword. "Zip, zip. He cut them down. He was a big man, and he had one of those curved Volani swords heavy on the business end—falcata they call them. They can take a man's head off in a single blow if you've any strength. And Adruvar Cabera was strong. Seven men he brought down, and a couple of others he crippled. And then I was up in front of him. He'd just lopped off my optio's arm, and it was up to me."

Hanuvar could not have turned away now had he been told his daughter waited just behind him.

"Adruvar's left arm was hanging useless and his armor was rent and he bled from a dozen places. Probably those wounds would have finished him pretty soon anyway, but he was still up and killing and I had to stop him. So I did."

"How?" Mazentius asked, guileless and enraptured as a boy listening to a bedtime fable.

Killian shrugged, seeming embarrassed to add details. "I ducked his swing. It took off my crest and pushed the helmet up so the strap was over my chin. But you know what it's like in the middle of a battle. I didn't even feel that it had gouged my forehead."

Probably most of them didn't know what it was like in the middle of a battle, but they listened silently.

"I drove the sword up through a big tear in his armor and then I found his heart. I heard the breath leave him and he sagged. I kept hold of my sword and so when he dropped I fell with him, trying not to land on his blade or into a sharp gash in his armor." He looked at his audience as if measuring them. "You ever kill a man?"

None of them wanted to say that they hadn't, and Killian had the grace not to wait too long for them to admit it. "It's true, what they say about how a man's eyes glaze when they die. But first you see the strength of their life in their vision. How much they want to hold onto it." Killian's jaw had firmed. Hanuvar imagined the scene then, the centurion on the ground, suspended on one hand over Adruvar, eyes locked, close as lovers. Such a moment was always disturbingly intimate. If you stared too long, you saw too much.

"Their fear, you mean?" Mazentius asked. "Was he afraid of dying?"

Killian shook his head, his disappointment in the question manifest. "It wasn't like that."

This man had met Adruvar's gaze in his final moments and experienced the death lock prior to that glazed loss of focus. Some men reveled in it, or claimed they did. Killian, though, had clearly been affected by it. And it came to Hanuvar that his brother had fully planned to die, and that in a strange way his death by this centurion had been a mercy. Adruvar had fallen to a man who respected him.

Publius called from where he sat hunched in his saddle over the table. "I've got her! She's really close. I think I can find the way!"

With that news, Killian ordered them back into the saddle, riding at the mage's side as they headed down the brick road and into the little farm town.

Hanuvar knew the place. Melgar had fought a skirmish here against a Dervan scouting party, and Hanuvar had looked down on it from the south while listening to his brother's report.[14] Once, he had stood on that very ridge two miles beyond the other side of the

---

[14] Antires does not name the town, but from this description it must be Mertosa, close by where both the first and second battles of the same name were fought. —*Silenus*

town, standing not just with Melgar, but with their brother Harnil and the commander of cavalry, Maharaval.

That friend and all three of his brothers were dead, but the town still lived. It appeared much the same, with its wide fields spreading out across the hills to east and west, and the tidy square houses with their green tile roofs standing along winding streets, built to follow the roll of the land.

More than ever, it came to him that this was a mission of the dead. Why would Narisia shelter here, so close to where she had last been seen? Who was to say she had not already taken her final breath? Perhaps she'd been wounded during her escape and she and her friends had tried to nurse her to health in these hills.

Might it be that she had succumbed and had long since been buried along some lonely ridge? That would certainly explain why no one had been able to find her.

There was a fine line between anticipating outcomes and worry. Hanuvar had schooled himself toward the former, so that he might be ready for the vicissitudes of fortune. He knew that a man who had considered outcomes and determined reactions slept more soundly than a man who merely fretted. He wondered how well a man would sleep once he had stood before his daughter's grave.

V

Only the central street ran relatively straight through the village, and those who worked or purchased at the shops and tavern counters turned to stare at Killian and his troop as they passed through. They were keenly aware of Publius and the narrow wooden platform stretching from his saddle horn to his horse's mane. They pointed at the dried finger he dangled on its string and whispered among themselves.

Killian didn't care. For the first time since they'd begun this journey that old, keen sense of excitement burned in his blood. He was on a hunt, and his hounds had scented quarry. The men had felt it too, and paid no mind to taverns or women they passed. Even the priest seemed keyed up, though his mien remained grim.

They passed into the village's outskirts, where wider spans of ground separated tidy old villas set down shady lanes lined with ancient Turian stone pines. Publius seemed untroubled by their course, and focused ever more hungrily upon the terrible finger he held over his board with right hand while his left held the reins stretched beneath the platform. "The villa ahead, on the right. We're very close!"

A trio of children roamed the villa's grounds. The youngest, a little girl in a long, blue double tunic, jogged along its lane at the side of a large metal hoop, which she rolled with a stick. Another girl of ten or twelve brushed the mane of a bored gray pony while a teenaged boy bent low to cinch its saddle. Once it was clear that the troop of soldiers was riding toward their home, the boy called to the smallest, shouting her name, Drusilla, twice, before she ran to him. He pointed her to the house, handed the pony's reins to the elder girl and pointed her on as well, then stepped into the road.

Peeping constantly over their shoulders in curiosity, the girls walked for the white two-story villa four hundred feet further back, the pony clopping after.

Killian rode at the mage's side and did not miss the anticipation manifest on his face. The mummified finger continued to point straight ahead. "We're very close now," Publius said tensely. "Practically on top of her."

The boy waited in an ordinary tunic and sandals, but he carried himself like someone who expected obedience. Tall, slender, his arms and legs were gently muscled. He had a Turian's dark wavy hair, and a narrow, pleasant face with a nose slightly hooked. His eyes were dark, and alight with intelligence.

Killian drew to a stop before him. The boy's brow furrowed when he noticed the strange contraption affixed to the front of Publius' saddle, but he addressed Killian.

"Greetings," he said. "You are on the land of Senator Clemens Horatius Marcellus. Do you seek him?"

Marcellus was more than a senator. He had been a general in the Second Volani War, and one of the few to survive successive engagements against Hanuvar himself. Killian knew he'd been forced from active service after taking a wound that should have killed him. It had instead left Marcellus in recuperation for more than a year. By reputation he was a soldier's soldier. He held senatorial rank but was almost never to be found in Derva itself.

Killian eyed the boy, debating how exactly he should answer.

"It's him," Publius said in a low voice. Perhaps he thought it would not be heard by the boy, whose brow wrinkled further.

"What are you talking about?" Killian asked.

Publius had lowered the finger so that it was not visible over the rim of the platform. He raised it now and it pointed directly at the youth.

"It's him!"

The boy proved to be remarkably well possessed. "Gentlemen?" His voice was firm, but polite. "What brings you here?"

Killian bowed his head. "I am Killian Pullio Vicentius. We are on an errand for the state. Are you... the son of Marcellus?"

The youth answered without hesitation. "I am. Tiberius Paulus Marcellus, sir."

Far behind him, the front door of the villa opened and a white-haired patrician emerged, closely followed by a sturdy retainer. Both strode in haste. Drusilla had vanished, but the older girl looked anxiously back from beside the door, the pony at her side.

"How old are you?" Publius asked.

The boy's gaze drifted to the mage and a flicker of disgust briefly touched his features. He had noticed the mummified finger. "I am fifteen."

This wasn't going at all as Killian had expected. He searched for the priest, but didn't spot Brencis at first. The older man had dismounted to lead his horse up one side of the lane. He stared at the boy's face with such intensity Tiberius sensed it and returned the scrutiny.

A hoarse voice with the echo of the parade ground reached them. "What are you doing here on my land?"

Marcellus had shouted as he drew closer. He would arrive in only a few moments. Killian motioned Publius to move the finger, but the mage only stared blankly. "Break your charms," he snapped, then turned to the priest. "Well?" he said, then added, "Does your... advisor say anything? Is this boy one of them?"

"Adruvar does not know him," Brencis answered.

Killian cursed under his breath, reflecting then that the priest had earlier said only that the person they traced was not Hanuvar. It was Publius who had promised Narisia.

Marcellus halted before them, a dour, broad-shouldered manservant at his side. The senator was a hawk-nosed older man, vigorous, though his face was florid from his swift-paced walk, and he carried a layer of fat.

"Senator Marcellus," Killian said, then introduced himself. "You must pardon us. I was...hoping we might have the chance for...a conversation." He was stumbling, badly, but he wasn't entirely sure what he should say or do. He needed time to consider the best course of action. "Your son is a fine young man. Is he...yours by blood?"

The senator's brows had ticked up at mention of Killian's name, though he did not acknowledge recognizing it further, and his reply was coolly formal. "I adopted him when he was an infant, upon marrying his mother."

"Ah." Killian did not follow politics; he had little to no interest about the lives of the famous, and was aware of Marcellus only because he had met soldiers who spoke well of him. "Who is your wife?"

This was clearly the wrong question to ask, for Marcellus' heavy brows drew closer. His retainer stiffened. "What is this really about?" The old soldier practically growled, "Who sent you?"

Killian cleared his throat. "Perhaps...perhaps this might all be cleared away if we could speak privately."

"I am in the midst of other duties at this time." The old man's voice was steely.

"Your pardon. This evening, then?"

"If that is your wish." Marcellus' glance passed darkly over the rest of them. "Leave your entourage behind."

"Of course." Killian bowed his head.

The senator motioned his son to follow then about-faced. Tiberius glanced back at them, dubiously, and followed. The retainer stared warning for a moment, then fell in after.

Killian spoke quietly to Publius. "So it was him. Definitely him, the youth?"

"I'm certain of it."

Mazentius spoke to him from behind. "You saw Adruvar's face. Does this kid look like him? Maybe it's his son."

The soldier didn't have the years right. Killian shook his head. "He's too young. Adruvar's been dead eighteen years. And this doesn't help us at all anyway. The boy's too young to have been at war against Derva, and he's been raised by a Dervan senator." He licked his lips, and spoke to the priest. "What of you? Anything to report?"

Brencis' eyes were a peculiar gray as they caught the light, and the sad, determined expression was so similar to that upon Adruvar's face as he died that it was momentarily startling. Killian's impression of the priest's power had increased, but only now did he understand how truly magical the man must be. "Could that boy be Hanuvar's son?"

"He is no child of Hanuvar's," the priest answered. "But for answers I must speak with the spirits and coax more from them."

"Is there another possible Cabera around here?" Killian demanded.

"Only the skull and the boy," Publius said, looking as though he expected a dressing down.

Killian turned their column, moving through the others to lead them back into the village. He supposed they'd have to find room at one of the inns. What could he even say to Senator Marcellus? Was there a point left in talking with him?

VI

There was no mistaking the young man for anyone other than a child of Harnil Cabera. It wasn't just the shape of his face, it was the way he tilted his head to one side while questioning, and the burning intellect in his gaze, not to mention the incredible self-possession.

Another Cabera lived. Hanuvar had thought himself only an uncle once, to Edonia, wherever she might be, for Adruvar had sired no children and Harnil had never married. But this boy, no matter darker coloration, was unquestionably his brother's child. What he was doing here, in the family of a Dervan general driven from this very village by Melgar himself, was the least of the mysteries before him. The greatest of them was what he was to do with the knowledge. The young man had been raised as a Dervan. How might Hanuvar even approach him?

He wasn't the only one befuddled by their discovery. Apart from selecting an inn for them and delegating Carthalo to arrange for rooms, Killian had nothing to say, and headed off for his inn chamber with a bottle of wine and an order for a meal.

Hanuvar retreated to a room of his own. He opened the shutters and leaned out to face south, where it was just possible to see a tree on the edge of that distant property. An oak his nephew might have looked upon every day of his life. The tree and this village were more familiar to the young man than his own bloodline. What did he know of Volanus?

Someone rapped at his door.

"Who is it?"

"It's me," Carthalo answered.

"Enter."

Carthalo opened the door. He bore a wash basin and pitcher. He was followed by a plump Turian woman and her wiry son, both carrying platters they sat on a scarred table near the window. Carthalo thanked them and sent them away.

"Why are you here?" Hanuvar asked.

"Killian is sulking in his room and most of his men have wandered off." Carthalo poured water into the basin. "I thought you might want to freshen up."

"Harnil preferred the company of men," Hanuvar said, moving over.

"But not exclusively," Carthalo pointed out. He dipped his hands into the water and scrubbed his face. He stepped back and pointed to the basin, but Hanuvar demurred. The role Hanuvar played was uninterested in cleanliness.

"At least wash your hands."

He looked down at the foods—some dark bread with nuts and seeds baked in, some smoked trout and some particularly pungent garum, a Dervan fish sauce rendered more fragrant owing to the Turian preference for strong flavors. He dipped his hands into the basin, scrubbed the worst of the dirt from them, and then broke off some of the flesh from the fish. "You wish to speculate," Hanuvar said.

"Harnil sometimes served with Cordelia. She was sly, witty, and capable. Tall, and dark eyed. Turian."

Hanuvar had not known everyone in the intelligence network. "Go on."

"She was pregnant before the end of the war. After Harnil's death. She returned to my service, but gave the child over to a sister in Turia."

"A sister married to Marcellus?"

"Not that she mentioned." Carthalo broke off a slice of bread. "Cordelia didn't survive long after the war. So we can't ask her. What do you want to do?"

"I don't know." Hanuvar was seldom at a loss for a course of action, but so far he had not developed one, and the halting course of his speech betrayed his confusion. "I want to speak with the boy—find out what he knows. About his family, and his past."

"Cordelia was smart, so he probably knows nothing. For his own good. He seems happy here."

"Happy among people who killed his own." Hanuvar chewed the fish, though he was not hungry. He barely registered its taste, despite the spices.

"You don't sound like yourself."

He lifted his other hand, showing an empty palm.

"You know Dervans can be fine people. And Marcellus was one of the better commanders. Melgar thought him honorable."

Melgar had arranged a prisoner exchange with the general, and had even briefly spoken to him in person.

"I don't understand why Cordelia didn't pass her son along to you. To us."

"She probably intended to raise him as her own. I doubt she meant to die."

"No," Hanuvar agreed. He realized the fish he clutched was disintegrating in his fist. He relaxed his grip. He was reacting with the emotional equilibrium of a teenager in love. "No," he agreed, with a deep exhalation. He thought then of the young woman, leaving perhaps on some scouting foray or courier mission when the Dervans were overrunning the countryside, turning the care of her son to her sister and wondering if she would see him again. "I doubt she intended that."

They heard the unmistakable sound of hobnailed boots in the corridor. Someone delivered a hard rap against their door.

Hanuvar shot Carthalo a warning look but the spy shrugged, as if to ask what did it matter now if they were together?

"Who is it?" Hanuvar asked. He did not have to feign the priest's irritation this time.

"Killian. Is there anyone in there with you, priest?"

"I am," Carthalo answered.

The officer pushed open the door and stepped in, his expression somber.

"What's this about?" Carthalo asked.

"All the men have left. Even Publius."

That the reclusive scholar was involved told Hanuvar all he needed to know.

Carthalo swung his feet off the bench and reached for his weapon belt. "They're going after the boy, aren't they?"

"They think they're due some glory."

"What are you going to do?" Carthalo asked.

Killian breathed out in resignation. "Marcellus has pull. If these jackasses upset him, it could make trouble all the way to the emperor, and Legate Aquilius. And I don't want the revenant legate mad at me."

"Not if he's the one paying us." Carthalo buckled on his weapons belt.

"That too." Kilian's gaze shifted to Hanuvar. "I need every man I can get, Brencis. I could use the help."

And Hanuvar wanted to protect his nephew. He just wasn't sure how the character he played should act, and so he was a moment answering.

"I know you want a Cabera," Killian continued. "But the boy's as Dervan as me, raised by a senator and general."

The soldier had bluntly stated the same truths Hanuvar had been wrestling over. Killian misunderstood the furrowing of Hanuvar's brow. "You don't believe me?"

"I believe you," Hanuvar said finally. "What's in it for me?"

"I'll get you the pay due an officer for a month and a bonus to boot, same as these bastards were getting."

Hanuvar pretended he was weighing it over, although he was aware of the press of time. His brother's son might be facing eight angry soldiers and a mage this very moment. He drawled out his answer, as though reluctant. "All right."

Kilian must have sent word for the stableboys, and been hoping both men would help, for all three horses were saddled. The trio were soon mounted and moving out at a canter.

Evening was nearly come, and the light through the trees was muted. This time, no children were visible in the villa's yard. This time a string of horses cropped grass in front of the open villa door.

They left their mounts with the others. There was no question about which way they should go. Shouting echoed through the halls and led them to a wide courtyard with a central rectangular pool. Harnil's son stood with Marcellus and his man; they were all but ringed by legionaries, with the heavyset Mazentius at their center point. The young soldier pointed to Killian. "Are you here to help?"

Killian put a centurion's snap in his answer. "Our investigation's over. We were hunting fugitives. There are none here."

Mazentius shook his head. "We were hunting Cabera. And we found one."

Marcellus turned to Killian, hand thrust angrily to Mazentius. "This man has invaded my home and pawed over my private papers. He has no business here. Will you please remove him?"

"You want to remove me?" Mazentius' voice rose mockingly. "You're harboring a Cabera!" The soldier shook the scroll, then addressed Killian. "First thing I found in his document chest—adoption papers. Then this!"

"You have no right!" Marcellus roared.

"But I do!" Mazentius said, almost crowing. He smiled as he returned his attention to Killian. "When the senator's wife fell ill, she left this letter for her husband, to be opened on the boy's sixteenth birthday." He waved the scroll at the boy. "He is the son of Harnil Cabera, brother to Hanuvar!"

"None of that matters," Marcellus snapped. "He's my son now."

Mazentius laughed and his companions looked smug. "Cabera blood matters a great deal."

Hanuvar checked the boy for reaction, but Tiberius' grave expression had not changed.

"And it's a curious coincidence, isn't it, that Marcellus spoke out against the Third Volani War?" Mazentius asked. "Just like Ciprion. Makes you wonder what little secret Ciprion might be hiding, doesn't it?"

"Are you aiming for a job in the Revenant Corps?" Killian asked. "You don't want to make trouble for a senatorial war hero."

"He *is* a revenant," Publius spoke up. "Did you think they'd send one of their best mages out without a guard?"

Hanuvar put his hand to his hilt. Violence was imminent.

"This is enough!" Marcellus declared. "No one has authority in my villa but me!" He pointed at Mazentius' group. "I'll report your conduct to the emperor himself! Now give me back my property!" Marcellus strode forward, hand outstretched for the scroll. As Mazentius backstepped one of the others raised a palm as if to stop the old general, who swept it aside. The soldier grabbed his arm and the two tussled.

Marcellus still knew how to fight. He slammed his elbow into the legionary's nose. Blood sprayed. Marcellus' attendant shouldered in, to be immediately opposed by a pair of soldiers, drawing swords.

And then the senator stumbled back. The opposing soldier held a bloodied knife, and a crimson stain splattered the old man's side.

For the briefest of moments the only sound within the courtyard was the sigh of the breeze through the decorative trees. And then Marcellus gasped. The boy cried out, and the soldiers moved on him and his father both.

"Protect the boy," Hanuvar ordered Carthalo, and started in, one of his secreted blades in hand. Killian moved at the same time. One soldier came at him with bared blade but dropped after a savage hack drove through his jaw spattered a mass of teeth. Killian cut off the howl of pain by slashing deep through his opponent's forehead.

Tiberius bared a knife and shielded his adopted father. A slim legionary advanced on him, sword raised. Hanuvar's throwing knife embedded deep from such close range, and the soldier crumpled with the hilt protruding from his eye socket. The boy spun in surprise, staring briefly at Hanuvar before another man advanced on Marcellus' retainer and crossed blades with him.

In one hand Hanuvar carried the gladius he'd hidden in his robe, in the other he drew another knife. Carthalo advanced to protect Killian's flank. Hanuvar winged his second throwing knife for Publius, who chanted and sprinkled black powder. His spellwork stopped abruptly as the knife planted firmly just above his collarbone. He choked, flailed his arms spasmodically, and ripped the weapon out. He patted feebly at the spurting blood, tripped backward, and then Hanuvar could spare him no more attention, for Mazentius had left his last three soldiers to run interference against Carthalo.

The disguised revenant turned on Hanuvar, his bared sword streaming black goo. From previous encounters with the black order, Hanuvar knew poison had coated the blade the moment it was ripped from its sheath. Hanuvar ducked the high strike; poison droplets spattered the floor. Hanuvar parried the back swing and slashed down into Mazentius' sword arm. The younger man screamed in pain, freezing with head raised and mouth parted. Hanuvar had plenty of time to slice through his face, but then had to let go of the blade jammed into his adversary's skull to duck a swipe from the brown-haired soldier on his left.

He slid on blood slick pavement. Mazentius' body thumped to the ground beside him and Hanuvar snatched the still steaming sword from limp fingers. He swayed his head from the thrust of brown hair and felt the legionary's fist, clenched about the hilt, punch past his cheek. Hanuvar drove the smoking revenant sword up through his loins and the legionary stumbled past Harnil's son, teeth parted in a silent scream. He splashed into the pool.

Hanuvar scanned the area. A paling Marcellus had balled up his tunic to protect his side. The retainer warded the old man and his adopted son, but no other opponents advanced against them. Killian and Carthalo dueled a final pair. Hanuvar was readying to assist when the centurion dropped his man. Carthalo finished his own opponent with a jugular slice. The soldier put hands to the blood gushing from his neck, accidentally gashing his own face with his sword, then folded. Killian stepped back to watch, his blade dripping blood. He swayed, glassy eyed, and Carthalo reached out to steady him. He was too late—the veteran sagged, and Carthalo helped guide him to the ground.

"Brencis," he called weakly.

Hanuvar would rather have joined his nephew, watching with wide eyes. But he still hadn't decided what he would say to him. And so Hanuvar walked through the carnage to reach Killian, realizing when he saw the white face and the blood pooling on the stone beneath him that the soldier didn't have long. Carthalo's glance showed agreement.

"Cut by a revenant blade," the spy said. "There were three in all. The tall quiet soldier," he added.

The dying man's eyes held the sharpness of the healthy man suddenly facing death. His gaze seemed to probe deep, touching Hanuvar's soul. There was recognition there. Seemingly far away a voice called for bandages and aid, and a little girl cried out for her father.

Killian's mouth moved, and Hanuvar had to strain to make out his words. "I thought you were just a Volani hater. When we met the boy, I saw you were staring at him. Intensity." He paused to try for a breath he couldn't catch, then pushed on. "I get it now. Recognition. The way you moved..." Almost he laughed. "Just like Adruvar." He smiled weakly and let out a cough. "Clever. Looking for... daughter?"

Hanuvar nodded once.

"Your brother died bravely," Killian whispered.

"So have you," Hanuvar assured him.

Had someone ever told him he would speak kindly to the slayer of Adruvar, or grip his forearm as he passed, Hanuvar would never have believed it, but this he did, and when Killian stilled he closed the man's eyes himself. He then wiped clean the soldier's jeweled blade and passed it on to Carthalo.

Only then did he turn to see what had befallen Marcellus.

The old general sat on a bench, his tunic torn open along the left. A pair of slaves had arrived with a pungent cask of vinegar and bandages and must already have cleaned the wound, for the retainer was sewing up a short gash along the senator's sturdy side. Marcellus held his lips clamped shut while Tiberius looked on. A matronly older slave had hands about the shoulders of both of Marcellus' daughters, watching open mouthed from a doorway to the courtyard.

There was no scent of digestive fluids from Marcellus' wounds, so the slice had probably missed organs. The old soldier watched their approach from under drawn, heavy eyebrows, then nodded to Hanuvar and Carthalo, waiting to speak until the final stitch was pulled taut. A deep white scar puckered his abdomen a little lower down.

"I don't think this one will kill me if that one didn't," Marcellus said, having seen the direction of Hanuvar's gaze. "I am indebted to you men for your help. I can recognize a legion man when I see one.

You handled yourselves like seasoned skirmishers, not line men. Who did you serve under?"

"Ciprion," Hanuvar answered.

"And now you're a priest of Lutar," Marcellus said. "Well, I'll need no rites performed for me today. The revenants hire you?"

"The revenants hired Killian," Hanuvar explained. He could not help his eyes tracking to Tiberius. It was almost like looking on Harnil again. The boy returned his careful scrutiny without understanding it. There was gratitude there, and curiosity, and shock. He had seen brutal death this day, and his father wounded, and maybe feared he'd be hauled away by revenants.

"And he hired us," Carthalo finished. "But two of the 'normal soldiers' they sent with him were revenants."

"He should have seen that coming," Marcellus said. "I always hated those bastards."

The manservant finished tying the threads and turned, breathing heavily, to consider Hanuvar and Carthalo.

Marcellus' gaze grew hard. "What the revenants were saying about my son . . . Am I going to get trouble from you?"

Hanuvar had a hard time answering, but not for the reason the old man probably thought. Finally, he shook his head. "No, General."

"We're very good at keeping secrets," Carthalo promised.

"I've a question for your boy, though," Hanuvar said. "If you don't mind me asking."

"You risked your life to keep him free," Marcellus said. "I think you've the right. But it's up to Tiberius. What's your name?"

"Brencis," said Hanuvar. "This is Silvio."

"Well, the least we can do is host you this night, but I'll see you're both rewarded."

"We didn't help in hope for a reward," Carthalo said.

"Any man could see that," Marcellus replied gruffly. "You fought for the right of things, like we're told good Dervans do. Precious few of them. All right, priest, what's your question?"

Once again Hanuvar studied the slim young man before him, remembering Harnil at a similar age. Perhaps he'd been a little taller. His hair hadn't been quite as curly. But they were close enough in appearance it was like peering back through time. The boy's expression grew more and more perplexed, and Hanuvar realized he'd stared too long. "When the revenant told you your origin, you didn't act surprised at all. Did you already know?"

"I've known for years my blood father must have been a Volani officer. They occupied nearby lands during a lot of the war." Tiberius looked to the old general, watching closely. "Father told me one day I might learn I wasn't who I thought, but that I should be proud of my heritage. He said I came from a line of warriors."

"I was supposed to wait to read the letter," Marcellus explained. "But I didn't want any mysteries about my son to turn up and surprise me. If she'd lived, my wife would have told me. Three wives I've lost now," he added. "Each one young and vital. And look at me. I keep collecting scars and somehow I keep going. Life's just not fair sometimes."

"No," Hanuvar agreed. "But I suppose we have to thank the gods for the blessings we receive, and find a way forward when their reasons leave us in darkness."

"Just like a priest," Marcellus said, although not unkindly. "I'll have my people tend you. I should have a word with my daughters now. They've just witnessed things I never wanted them to see." He groaned as he pushed to his feet.

"We left much of our gear at the inn," Hanuvar said. "We'll best go gather that."

"Well, don't be too long about it. We'll pull down some fine wine and you can tell me about your campaigns." He took in the mass of bodies and he shook his head in disgust. "My poor slaves are going to have to clear all this up. And I'm going to have to report this. I don't even know what I'm going to say."

"Tell them an agent of the revenants foiled an assassination attempt," Carthalo suggested.

Marcellus' chuckle at his cleverness died as he felt his side and groaned. He then walked toward his daughters. "No, don't come in here, girls. No need to come any closer. Your father's fine. It's just my clothes that need to be thrown out, not me." His retainer walked with him, watching as if he expected the old man to faint.

Tiberius remained.

"Gather our weapons," Hanuvar suggested to Carthalo.

His friend absented himself.

Hanuvar knew he did not have long, so he spoke quickly, with quiet confidentiality. "I met your blood father. You resemble him strongly."

"Do I? What was he like?"

"He was a brilliant man, and a brave one, but what I remember most is what a fine laugh he had. He was one of the funniest men I ever met, and very charming. He was a natural storyteller. He loved plays." Probably he was saying too much, but the boy listened raptly. "Do you like plays?"

"I always have," he answered eagerly. "And books."

Hanuvar nodded. "He was always reading."

"Did you know him well?"

Hanuvar knew now that he had said too much, but he could not help himself. And he wanted the moment to last, for he knew there would likely never be another. But what more could he say? Should he ask the boy about his favorite books, the foods he liked, the places he'd been? What had his childhood been like, and when had he learned to ride? Was a marriage arranged for him already, and did he like the girl? What did he hope to accomplish?

How might he squeeze a life's worth of encounters and connections into the course of a single conversation?

Sadly, he knew it could not be done.

"In coming years," Hanuvar said, "this evening may be a blur, in which only a few terrible scenes stand starkly. Hold to the brighter ones. Recall how bravely your adopted father faced the men who wanted to take you away. Know that the dead man there killed your uncle Adruvar, but that he died defending you. He acted with honor in both instances. A man's life can take strange directions, but if he models himself after people of character, and acts accordingly, he can lift his head high even in the bleakest of circumstances."

The boy seemed to be listening, but who could ever really tell how much the young took from the old?

Carthalo drew up beside him, waiting at his shoulder. Marcellus, leaning now against the older daughter while the younger clung to his good side, was directing slaves into the room, apologizing to them for what was going to be a terrible effort, even as they affectionately chided him and told him he should get to a bed. He was apparently one of those like Ciprion who treated his slaves as valued employees, a Dervan ideal more exception than reality.

Hanuvar extended his hand to Tiberius, who took his arm a little questioningly.

"I'll remember your counsel, priest Brencis."

"Don't think of me as a priest of Lutar. I'm just a gray-eyed man who's lost a lot of the people he loved. I'm glad you didn't lose your father this day. May you live long and well."

"Thank you. I hope the same for you. Are you not coming back?"

"I don't think that will be possible. Some day I hope you'll understand."

The young man looked at him strangely, then bowed his head. "Thank you, again."

Because he had trouble letting go, Hanuvar held the clasp a moment longer than he should have, and then he and Carthalo walked past the rectangular pool with the floating body and its billowing blood and on out to the road where they collected their horses. Hanuvar delayed briefly to scatter Publius' powders and retrieve the small bag with his father's scalp.

Carthalo did not speak until they were in the saddle once more, riding side by side down the roadway. "You didn't tell him about yourself or our people."

"No." They had left no gear at the inn; it was time to start the long way back to Apicius.

"I heard a lot of what you said. He seems a smart lad. He'll probably figure out who you are, someday."

That had been Hanuvar's intent, although what he would really liked to have done was sweep Tiberius into his embrace—to take him with them to Apicius and raise him the rest of the way as a proud Volani. He could hear of his uncles and his aunts, and his ancestors. He could sit at Hanuvar's right hand and help to build New Volanus.

Maybe, in some better world, Hanuvar had ridden off with Harnil's son to shape the future. As long as he was dreaming, though, why not imagine a world where the child had grown up in Harnil's company, and where father and son might have joined Hanuvar at the table for dinner every week, where his cousin Narisia could have taken him riding along the shore, and when he might have grown up playing board games with little Edonia?

These seemed simple wishes, and he hoped, somewhere, that they were true.

"If I live long enough," Hanuvar said, just before they reached the end of the lane, "maybe I'll send him a letter and tell him more about his father."

"Maybe?"

A long moment passed before he found the strength to answer in a normal voice. "It might be best to leave him to this life. It could be he's ended up the luckiest Cabera of them all."

❊ ❊ ❊

Hanuvar had grown to be forthcoming about his experiences, but upon his return to Izivar's villa it was long days before he was willing to relay many details about what had happened. Even if Carthalo had been inclined to speak with me—and he usually wasn't—the spymaster stayed only long enough to write his daughter, in command at their complex of shops in Derva, before returning to the far south, a region too well travelled by Hanuvar for him to risk personal appearances.

Killian's sword he eventually arranged to be melted down, though not before the gem in its hilt was added to our stores.

Before that could be arranged, though, we were quite busy with other matters, for the emperor had sent word that he planned a visit. He and Izivar were regular correspondents. Although the young man had seemingly been convinced that there was no romantic future for him and Izivar, he still thought of her as a friend and of himself as her protector, for he had sworn to her brother that he would care for her. And thus they wrote several times a week. On one memorable occasion two letters sent the same day arrived for her via different ships.

Officially, Enarius was coming to assess an old property he had purchased overlooking the harbor, and while he did indeed mean to give the villa a onceover, he was really making a stop after personally travelling to the west to obtain scrolls of rare provenance.

According to legend, shortly after Derva's founding, a prophetess, Sidyl, had come to old King Tarqus with scrolls she'd written foretelling the city's future. For the nine fat scrolls she demanded an exorbitant price. He'd refused, and she'd burned them, one by one, still asking that same price each day for those that remained. The king finally relented when there were but three left, and from that day forward the three scrolls had been consulted by priests whenever dire events were in motion, so that the rulers of Derva might see a way clear.

Only the month before, Enarius had been contacted by a temple in

Greater Herrenia, in one of the colonies the Herrenes founded on Tyvol's western shore. The priests claimed that they had located copies of the lost six books.

Enarius hadn't wanted to dicker or in any way delay as that king had done, nor had he wished to entrust something so valuable to intermediaries. He'd retrieved them himself and was now on his way back. The public was not supposed to have known about the reason behind his journey, but there are few true secrets in a palace, so word had naturally gotten out about his destination, perhaps further than even he could have anticipated.

And of course he had said something about the matter to Izivar, which is what inspired our frenzy of activity. She agreed to host some architects Enarius had sent for, and she readied for a celebratory feast despite the emperor's stated desire for a simple repast. And, for the safety of the Volani people, we devised a means to get our own look at those scrolls.

—Sosilos, Book Fourteen

Chapter 7:
The Heart of the Matter

I

From the second floor windows of Izivar's harbor office, Hanuvar gazed out past the fishing boats and yachts anchored by the docks. The sunset threw coppery-red beams and little glittering highlights across the bay's dark waters.

Tiny praetorians strutted along the deck of the distant toy-sized bireme flying purple flags while anchored at the harbor's longest pier, near the small fortress. The white horsehair helmet crests of the emperor's finest stood out stiffly as they patrolled the deck to impress the townsfolk swinging by to ogle the ship.

Hanuvar wasn't interested in any of them as individuals, but he contemplated the power they represented. A dozen of their fellows had been posted along the outer walls of the Lenereva estate when he'd departed it earlier in the day. The emperor himself might still be making the requisite tour of the magistrate's villa and offices along the central square. Regardless, Izivar's home would remain under imperial watch, for those were to be Enarius' quarters during his brief visit.

Enarius had claimed not to wish to disrupt the normal pattern of Izivar's household, not realizing his arrival would always be an imposition, and unaware that Izivar's entire household had been bustling to ready for his visit since news of it came last week. Even though the meal was planned to be a relatively intimate one, it had to be prepared to the finest standards, and thus the cooks had been at work for the last two days.

While he'd left the harbor window open, Hanuvar had shuttered the ones overlooking the deck, so he could not be observed. As a result, he could not see who now climbed the wooden stairs. The tread was light, but certain. Probably a woman, then, and not a child. His visitor rapped the door with her sandaled foot.

"We're closed," he announced.

A familiar female voice addressed him with mock gravity. "But I'm a poor widow woman, in dire need of a good book. Old classics in verse are my favorites, truth be told."

Hanuvar winced. Aleria, not so subtly announcing that she was not only aware of the famous Sidyline scrolls Enarius had brought with him, but Hanuvar's own whereabouts. More complications. As if it wasn't difficult enough at the moment to hide a smuggling operation orchestrated by the empire's most hated enemy.

Hanuvar massaged his forehead, moved out from behind the desk, and opened the door.

Aleria waited just past the threshold, wisps of her brunette hair highlighted by the sinking sun. She was disguised as a patrician woman, though no slave accompanied her. With her fine features she could manage a variety of styles, one of them the coquettish beauty before him this evening. Her eyes brushed Hanuvar's as he looked back soberly. "What, no hello? We should have a book talk."

He stepped aside so that she could slide through the doorway and lower herself onto the visitors' red-cushioned couch. She pretended to adjust her dress. Hanuvar wasn't distracted by the flash of cleavage but he appreciated her effort.

"What can I do for you, Aleria?"

She placed a hand upon her bosom, presumably to further draw attention there. "My name is Cassandra. I'm a recent widow vacationing from Derva, making the rounds to homes of my class— as we women folk do to distract ourselves from the tedium of our lives." She affected patrician hauteur by flapping her eyelids.

"I'm sorry your life is dreary. Should I express condolences for the loss of your newest imaginary husband?"

"Speaking of imagination, imagine my surprise when I came

calling at the home of Izivar Lenereva yesterday and glimpsed her security adjutant crossing the garden."

Hanuvar groaned inwardly. He'd known Izivar was entertaining a house guest, but had been told the visitor was just another of the bored patrician women Aleria now feigned to be. It seemed he could never be too careful.

"You weren't visiting," Hanuvar said. "You were scouting."

"You impugn my motives, Helsa. Or should I say Decius. Did the Lady, at last, reveal your real name to me? You don't look like a Decius," she added.

"I do for now. If you were scouting well, then you know it's mad to try for something tonight. Not only are Izivar's people in place, the Praetorian Guards have the villa surrounded. And a whole lot of the emperor's staff are on the inside."

"You're more clever than that, Helsa." Aleria settled into the couch cushions as if she planned to stay awhile. "And besides, the Lady Izivar invited me to dinner this evening. I'm an interior-design expert, did you know? I gather the emperor needs help planning his villa remodel. And here I am, suddenly in the neighborhood." She eyed Hanuvar. "I bet you're a delight at parties. Do you juggle?"

He answered only with silence.

"I know you can be far more fun than this. You're quite sour this evening, and I assume it's because you're afraid I'm going to intrude in some kind of play you're making. It must be a long game, because I gather the arrival of the Sidyline books and the emperor was a surprise to Izivar. Were you surprised too?"

"I'm surprised."

"I can't tell by looking. If you're after something, we can work together. Or are you only here for the pretty Volani woman? She seems a bit staid for you, but she's wealthy and has nice taste. I think you could do better, of course."

"I'm touched by your concern."

She leaned forward, voice dropping conspiratorially. "You do know that the emperor is sweet on her, don't you? I'd imagine it would be risky to get in between the two of them. She's the one you freed those singers for, isn't she? Have you been running other sorts of errands for her?"

"You're enjoying yourself too much."

She smiled. "It's just fun to see you on your back foot, Helsa." She clucked in feigned disappointment. "Again so unprepared. Are you slipping?"

Her interference could jeopardize not only his carefully laid plans but a great number of lives, including his own. "Don't try for the books." He cast around in his mind for better ways to discourage rather than intrigue her.

"It's a once in a lifetime opportunity, you know. There will never be a better chance to lay hands on them. Those scrolls are worth a fortune. Once they're stored away in the temple of Jovren, it would be a lot harder to get at them, even if I know you're up to planning it. Why go to all that trouble?"

"They're probably not real," Hanuvar pointed out. "Sidyl burned the first six day by day while negotiating with King Tarqus. What are the chances these secret copies were really hidden in Greater Herrenia?"

"You're worried too much about the facts. People don't care about those. Not when they've already invested so much emotional energy. People want to think these books are real, so they'll pay through the nose for them. Any number of foreign kings could set me up pretty nicely for the promise of knowing Derva's future. Or..." Her deep brown eyes met his own. "They could pay *us*. You could walk right into that vault tonight and slide away with the books—real or not— and then we can sail away and live happily ever after. With lots of gold."

"I have a few years on you."

"Like that's ever bothered a man. You're not at all bad looking, and you're dependable, which is remarkably rare, as I'm sure you've noted. And you're not always on the prowl or trying to get me to take care of you or boring me with stories about how impressive you are. As a matter of fact, you're downright silent most of the time. A woman could get used to that. But we don't have to stay together after we split the gold."

"Aleria, it's not going to happen. And I am working on something else. There's a way I could use you for it. But it requires staying on the good side of the Lady Izivar, and not getting killed by praetorians or foreign potentates."

"What kind of something else?" Aleria was suddenly more focused than a hunting dog at point.

Hanuvar had long contemplated a return to the Volani Isles of the Dead. Between himself and Izivar they knew the locations of a number of additional tombs that could be looted. He had not planned upon Aleria's involvement, but her experience and cunning could certainly prove useful in distracting the current landholders, and it would be better to have her working with them than against. "It involves jewelry."

"Jewelry," she mused. "How much?"

"More than you're likely to imagine."

"I thought by now you'd know just how imaginative I can be. Would you care to share the details?"

"The details rest with the favor of Lady Izivar. Whose future may not be so bright if something goes wrong with the Sidyline books while they're in her care."

"You do like her."

"I like you, too. Don't chance it, Aleria. Those scrolls going missing would light a blaze to destroy more certain riches only a little further on, even if they don't manage to incinerate us all."

Her expression was meditative. "So . . . no details?"

"Only after the emperor leaves."

"Hmm. Well, you can't blame a woman for trying." She climbed to her feet. "Will I be seeing you at dinner?"

"No."

"No? Why not?"

He hoped to avoid a meeting with Metellus, Enarius, or any of the Praetorian Guards. Now that Metellus was working veteran centurions into their ranks, there was a chance one of them might have encountered Hanuvar in the field.

"I need to catch up on my reading," Hanuvar answered at last.

"I know you could lie better if you really wanted. Women like a man who puts in effort."

"I'll try to remember that." Hanuvar moved to indicate the door.

She smiled with her eyes. "A shame. I'm off then. It's not very often I get to rub shoulders with an emperor. Does he fancy brunettes?"

"You could wrap that young man around your finger."

She laughed. "I have a few years on him. But I gather he likes that. Or maybe it's just the exotic Volani thing."

"He likes the Lady Izivar because she's kind."

"I can be very kind, when properly motivated." Aleria put her hand to the latch. "I look forward to hearing all about these jewels." She started out, and paused on the threshold. "Oh, just so you know—the emperor's two architects turned up while I was passing just now. If they're renowned builders I'm a Ceori chiefess."

"What makes you say that?"

"They're two old confidence men. One of them's a half-assed sorcerer to boot. You might want to keep your eyes on them." She left, delicately shutting the door behind her. He heard her light steps on the stairs and then the sound of her departure was lost among the cry of seagulls and sounds of the harbor. He exhaled the breath he didn't know he'd been holding.

He needed to warn Izivar not just about Aleria, but the architects as well. He would have to hazard a trip back inside.

II

Serliva knew that her feelings for Metellus were faintly absurd. She was too mature to drown in romantic poetry, and she'd never been one to moon about the perfect household or all the children she'd fill it with. And yet in the year since she'd first met the praetorian, he was in her thoughts more regularly than was sensible.

It wasn't just that he had carried her to safety, holding himself together to get them past horrors until he collapsed from his terrible injuries, although that had certainly been heroic. It was his ongoing, stalwart defense of Enarius, of whom she herself was fond. She'd heard how Metellus had gotten himself even more grievously wounded fighting off another band of assassins attacking the nice man she still struggled to think of as the ruler of all the empire. And beyond his unquestioned bravery, Metellus somehow remained humble. The chroniclers of his life emphasized how difficult it had been to get Metellus talking about his most famous exploits. Perhaps it was his background. Serliva had learned that he was the third son of a provincial patrician and hadn't been expected to rise very far or very fast. He'd probably never anticipated the heights he'd achieve in his life.

Serliva understood completely. Her parents had planned on her taking over their tailoring shop and marrying someone to help. She'd never been particularly interested in either option. She'd been delighted when a first cousin stepped up as a proper apprentice to her parents, and soon after accepted a job as a lady's maid because it offered travel, discovering herself tolerably good in the profession. She hadn't planned to remain in it for so long, but then she'd been taken prisoner on a ship docked in Ostra at the outbreak of the war, and, like many of the first wave of captured Volani, treated reasonably well. She recalled the anxiety of those days with some chagrin because certainly her own trials had been nothing like those endured by the survivors of the sack of Volanus itself. Compared to the horror stories she'd heard from those recently freed, her own imprisonment had been nothing but a minor inconvenience, especially as she was purchased and liberated by the most powerful Volani woman left free inside the Dervan Empire.

Just like Metellus, she surmised, she wasn't sure what she was meant to do next, apart from continuing in service to the best employer and mentor she could possibly have been hired by. Sometimes she still imagined sailing off to see the Eight Wonders, and could not square that with the much more practical plan of joining Izivar in New Volanus. Though curious about the last gathering of true Volani, it would surely feel like an isolated frontier village for at least a generation or two, and that really didn't excite her.

Mostly she lived day to day, assisting Izivar with clothing and organization and occasional advice, whether requested or not. No matter that Izivar's activities and even location were different week to week, Serliva's duties were fairly similar each day, and when she'd learned Metellus would be visiting along with Enarius she had determined to finally have the proper meeting that their schedules had so far precluded.

Her best assets were too well hidden within a conservative Dervan stola, so she had donned her finest Volani garments. She wore a close-fit blue top with a low neckline and long, flounced skirt of red and blue and gold that swept to her calves. Wrists and ankles alike were graced by inexpensive but pretty jewelry ornamented with tiny bells. Ear pendants dangled nearly to her shoulders, and her dark hair hung in ringlets. Carefully drawn outlines of kohl enhanced her eyes. As a final touch she had skillfully applied diluted honey and lavender fragrances in the places experience had taught her were of greatest utility.

Then, like the most practiced of hunters, she entered the domain of her quarry and selected a vantage point from which to await his coming.

Serliva had asked the other serving girls to cover her absence and kept Izivar from her scheme. Normally she would have taken her mistress into her confidence, but Izivar seemed somehow immune to the gallant Metellus' attractions.

She supposed it might have helped if Izivar actually read the little scrolls about him sold by book vendors throughout Tyvol, but she couldn't bring herself to share her collection. While some of the tales seemed clearly exaggerated, if not downright fabricated, she herself could attest to the truth of the most popular account, for Metellus had certainly endured the three parallel wounds the evening he had rescued the emperor, and those scars had inspired his noble epithet: Bravescar. Not Clawface, as jealous praetorians were rumored to call him behind his back.

Serliva smiled indulgently at memory of finding herself mentioned within that particular scroll. Not by name, of course, but as the "chaste maid of peerless beauty, carried from jeopardy in tireless arms." The writer claimed to have conferred with Metellus on multiple instances so that his account could be relayed with the utmost veracity, and that meant Metellus himself must have described her loveliness, for the writer had certainly never talked with her. It was charming that he assumed her chaste.

Metellus had shown no open interest in her since that day, but then their encounters had by necessity been brief. Perhaps he was shy about matters of the heart. Upon his arrival at the villa today, well ahead of Enarius, Metellus had not taken the opportunity to interact with her and instead headed immediately for the kitchens. Her fellow servants had told her he seemed chiefly interested in food, by which she understood Metellus was probably concerned about the threat of poison to the Emperor.

Come evening he had advanced alone into the garden, announcing he meant to patrol the outer wall for potential weak points. And so she had followed, ensconcing herself in the arched grotto to Jovren that Izivar's father had erected to curry favor with

Dervan visitors. The concrete shrine suited her purposes perfectly, for it stood on a rise slightly above the rest of the garden and provided a fair vantage from which to watch comings and goings. Moreover, its dark interior was secluded. She herself sat just inside, the better to be caught by the waning sunbeams.

She rather wished he'd hurry up and walk past so he could see her, because she was running out of light.

The scrape of timber against tile was so startling Serliva nearly jumped. Izivar had showed her the hidden exit from the garden, but she'd been so preoccupied she'd forgotten it lay behind a panel in the cave-like shrine's rear wall. She stared into the darkness, realizing after only a moment that she should not have been surprised to see Hanuvar emerge from the gloom behind the frowning statue of the bearded sky god.

Hanuvar met her eyes, considered the villa opening onto the garden, then the sky. Evening blues were purpling on toward night and the shadows were long. In the gardens distant servants were finishing supper preparations, although they had been told to slow the process, for the emperor had wandered out on a goodwill tour and was late in returning. Crickets filled the air with their susurrations, accompanied by a chorus of frogs.

"You gave me a scare," Serliva said.

"I'm sorry. I'd hoped to see Izivar, but giving the message to you will be simpler. Do you have a moment?"

"Um. I . . . Yes." She didn't want to miss her opportunity so thought to get rid of him quickly by hastening his communication.

But he didn't seem as much in a hurry as she'd like. Hanuvar sat down upon the north facing wooden bench, glancing down as the old wood wobbled beneath him. He froze a moment to make sure it would remain steady. The ominous statue, one hand upraised in a fist and the other gripping a jagged lightning bolt, was just visible in the gloom behind him. He addressed her quietly. "How is Izivar?"

"She's hiding all of her worries. But she's nervous, I can tell. She's worried about you, and, well, everything. Why are you here? I thought you were staying away."

"I've learned three of her dinner guests will need especial monitoring."

"What kind of monitoring?" She hoped it wouldn't require her to seek Izivar's ear immediately. Surely Hanuvar would go back to his hiding spot as soon as whatever he wanted was relayed, and if the matter could wait until dinner she'd still have time to complete her own mission, or at least make a good start. Serliva grew conscious of a tickle along her leg and reached down to brush whatever it was away, only to touch fingertips to a moving creeper with too many legs. She let out a cry that rose into a shriek when she glanced down to find a huge black spider had plopped from her calf to the top of her sandal. She kicked it free as she shot upright so quickly that she swayed on her other leg, lost balance, and collapsed into Hanuvar.

He caught her, but the sudden introduction of her weight with his own was too much for the old bench. Their end sank beneath them and sent both sliding to the ground. The legs on the far end slammed back against the stone floor with a loud smack. The next thing she knew she was lying face down in front of Jovren's foot. Hanuvar sprawled beneath her, hidden by her dress, his head beneath her pelvis. His hands felt for her waist to lift her away.

"What's going on here?" The right voice at the wrong time demanded sternly behind them, and she felt her heart speed almost to bursting. Metellus.

A lantern played into the dark space, and she was conscious that most of her right leg was bare to the light as she swung off of Hanuvar.

She recognized Metellus' silhouette in the opening. Beside her, Hanuvar propped himself up on his elbow.

And Metellus burst into laughter. He lowered the lantern. "I thought some girl was under assault until I saw you underneath her!" Still chuckling, he shook his head. "You must be Decius. You look just like your sons."

By this Serliva knew Metellus believed the fiction that earlier encounters with Hanuvar when he was magically de-aged had been with sons of "Decius." Again Metellus laughed. "I halfway thought you'd be after the older Volani, but here you are at the maid. Nicely done."

Serliva's spirit fell. "It's not like that," she protested.

Metellus ignored her and addressed Hanuvar. "It's nice to see an older guy can still get some action." He laughed in a sort of smug comradeship.

"He's not my lover," Serliva insisted. "There was a spider on my leg, and I jumped and fell onto him."

Metellus snorted.

Hanuvar got his feet beneath him.

Serliva searched quickly for an explanation that sounded reasonable and that wouldn't put Hanuvar in danger. "He doesn't even like women."

"Don't be absurd." Metellus sneered.

"It's true," Serliva asserted, ignoring the questioning look from Hanuvar. "He was here to ask advice about a man he's interested in. I really did shriek when I saw a spider and he was so awkward in catching me when I jumped that we fell over."

"Is this true, Decius?"

"I can't argue."

Metellus wagged a finger at her. "He has children."

"He fulfilled his obligation to the family," Serliva said.

The praetorian grunted skeptically. "I still don't see why he was alone, in the dark. With you."

"He wanted to ask my advice about that handsome architect who turned up."

"The one who smiles too much?" Metellus surveyed Hanuvar. "Well, well. Are you a pitcher or a catcher, Decius?"

"Your pardon," Hanuvar said. "I think I'll excuse myself. I've other matters to tend to."

"Don't leave on my account," Metellus said with a grin, then laughed. Hanuvar headed through the twilight for the villa doors.

Serliva congratulated herself on her quick thinking. Her pulse thrummed as Metellus turned to admire her. She could just make out the bright, cheerful spark in his remaining eye. He was really quite striking, no matter his terrible scars.

"I've been wanting to talk to you for months," she said, tentatively touching his arm. "But this isn't how I'd hoped it would happen."

"What do you want to talk about?"

The question was so direct she wasn't entirely sure how to answer. She cleared her throat and brushed hair from her forehead. "To thank you. For your bravery. For saving me, and for doing so much for our emperor. I'm very fond of him myself."

"It's my duty to watch out for him," Metellus said carelessly.

She drew infinitesimally closer, and detected the strong scent of the oil he used to clean his weapons. "I've read some of your accounts. And I know that those have a lot of nonsense in them, but it's pretty clear where the truth lies."

"Is it?" He sounded almost wary.

"I understand how it is. You just want to have fun, but you get pushed into greater responsibilities and you do your best to make it work and the next thing you know you're involved in all kinds of things."

"Sure." Her words must have reassured him, for he sounded relaxed and casual. "Thanks for cluing me in about Decius. That bit of information's going to come in handy." He reached behind her and swatted her on the butt cheek so forcefully the sound startled the nearby insects into silence.

She let out a yelp and jumped.

He chuckled. "I usually like breasts so big I can hide my face in them, but if I get time later, I'll give you a tumble. Do you know how much longer it'll be until they serve supper?"

"I . . . I'm not sure," she stammered, but managed to pull herself together. "I think my Lady's determined to wait on the emperor."

"Everyone's always waiting on that boy for something," he said, sighing, then wandered off into the darkness without so much as a farewell.

She rubbed her backside and stared after him in astonishment mingled with rising anger.

III

Hanuvar asked one of Izivar's servants to retrieve her and waited in a back corridor. Through an arched opening he observed the cooks and assistants in the tented outside kitchen, overseeing preparations on grills and in brick ovens. The combined scents of cooking fowl and fish and boar and various sauces were distracting. Two be-ringed observers from the emperor's household monitored everything; one stared at Hanuvar for a time before apparently deciding he was too far from the food to be planning a poisoning.

Izivar reached him with fair speed. She didn't waste time asking why he had changed plans, and motioned him to follow her to her sitting room. Lanterns glowed dully in the outer hall but nothing gave light in her private retreat, apart from the distant scarlet of the cookfires visible through the slats overlooking the garden. She closed the door and then impulsively came into his arms, granting him the sort of passionate kiss usually reserved for men returned from war.

But Izivar often greeted him thus, and he had come to realize she feared for him deeply whenever they parted.

Finally she pulled away, though she remained very close. "What are you doing here?"

"I was just thinking about how unfortunate it is that I prefer the company of men."

"What?" She pulled further back from him, trying to see his face.

"I'm sorry I didn't mention it earlier. Serliva's spilled the story to Metellus when he thought her my lover."

"Why would he think that?"

"He found us in the dark." Hanuvar paused to select his next words with care. "In the shrine to Jovren. Serliva startled, leapt into me, and knocked both of us down. Metellus heard her shriek, discovered me underneath her, and assumed her noises had been amorous. She was desperate to clarify she was available to him."

Izivar had no concerns about Hanuvar's fidelity; her scoffing sound had everything to do with Serliva's taste in men. "Metellus? I can't believe she's still interested in him."

"She was so clearly embarrassed, and her pleas so heartfelt, her half-baked story sounded almost convincing."

"What did you say?"

"Not much. I didn't want to get him suspicious or accuse her of lying. And so here I am, although I can't imagine why any man would talk about Metellus while holding you."

"Perhaps you fancy him."

He heard the smile in her voice, and squeezed her tenderly. "How are things here?"

"There have been a lot of complications, of course, but everything's in place. Metellus himself inspected the vault and couldn't spot a thing wrong with it. He even complimented me on the fresh paint. He supervised the placement of the chest with the Sidyline books, and another chest he says will be famous very soon.

I thought he was wanting me to beg for details, so I played along, but he just became quiet and looked awfully pleased with himself."

"Antires can clear that up."

"I'm sure he heard everything. If I know him, that will be the first thing he accesses."

Hanuvar suspected she was right. "You mentioned complications."

"Minor issues, all dealt with. The architects are a trial. They kept trying to bribe me to look at the books, if you can imagine." She pecked him. "Did you really sneak in just to see me?"

"Alas, no. Enarius still isn't here?"

"He sent a messenger to say his meeting with the magistrates was running late and to start without him. Naturally we have not. I foresee nursing a great deal of soup in our near future. But you won't be joining, will you?"

"No. There are two situations I've learned about. First, the woman Cassandra isn't who you think she is."

"No?"

"Her real name's Aleria, and she's a very clever thief. I've worked with her a few times, but she doesn't know who I really am, or what our aims are. She was scouting your villa to decide whether or not she would make a try for the books."

"A thief?" Izivar laid a hand to her throat and drew back. On stage it might have appeared affected, but with her it seemed as though she clutched protectively toward something deep within. "She's just arrived. Should I have her thrown out?"

"No. I've convinced her we've another job I'd like her for."

Someone rapped on the door, and the voice of Izivar's chief steward announced: "The emperor's carriage just turned the corner, my Lady."

Izivar addressed the closed door. "Thank you, Destrin. I'll be along presently. Send word for the first course to be set out."

Destrin confirmed her orders and departed. Even in the dusk Hanuvar felt her eyes upon him. "You trust her?"

"Only to some extent. Time's short. Where are the architects?"

"In their quarters."

"What's your impression of them?"

"They like to talk about arches and floor plans, as you'd expect. The younger of the two is an absurd flirt."

"They may be fakes. Aleria says she's met them before. I think she's telling the truth, but she may simply be trying to cause trouble. Keep an eye on them. All of them."

From somewhere in the villa a trumpet sounded; the start of a fanfare, which then sputtered to a stop. An odd, repetitive noise followed on its heels, something like an impossibly high-pitched bark.

"I must go," Izivar said. "Stay out of sight." She squeezed his fingers affectionately, then collected herself and left the room. For a brief moment distant sounds of chatter and the clatter of plates filled the air, dulling the instant the door was pulled to. He was left alone in the dark with nothing to keep him company but the after scent of her perfume.

IV

Enarius knew that it was love. He hadn't stopped thinking about the moment he would reach Izivar's villa for the last two weeks and now that the carriage approached it in the twilight his heart fluttered like a dove. He was so nervous as the horses clomped to a stop that he wished he'd taken the edge off with Ludmilla on the yacht this morning, then remembered how annoying her nasally moan was.

One of the slaves hopped down to open the door for him, and then another appeared with the essential little white dog. It was a small flat-faced thing with fluffy straight fur and immense black eyes.

"I brushed it again just now, sire," the slave said reassuringly. "And gave him a new bow. He kept working the other one loose."

"Well he looks wonderful," Enarius said, admiring the silky red ribbon about the furry neck. "Nicely done."

"Thank you, sire. I'm sure the Lady will like him."

That was good to hear, even if the man couldn't possibly know, because he worried about that. "Do you really think so?"

"Oh, I'm certain, sire."

The pup yipped excitedly as if in agreement, then squirmed in his arms and licked his chin.

Metellus made a habit of appearing unexpectedly, almost as

though he were some spirit called forth out of the gloom. With his eye patch and scars he had certainly grown much more sinister looking over the last year. But he grinned at Enarius as the slave stepped aside. "Did your visit with the magistrate go well, sire?"

"Yes, yes." It had been tedious, and he'd been forced to smile through a whole onslaught of speeches and gifts and silly compliments and carefully couched requests for favors. "Are the architects here?"

"Oh yes, and eager to talk about your new seaside palace. The books are secure. The villa's secure. And here's the best part. I know you thought there might be a rival here. Decius' children look just like him, incidentally, especially the older one named after him. You can see the resemblance across a room. Anyway, there's no rival, and your field is clear—I got all the details from that skinny maid."

"Serliva?"

"That's the one. She couldn't keep her hands off of me. Decius probably wouldn't touch Izivar if he were paid to. He wants to score one of the architects."

"He does?" The dog scrabbled at his chest and ruffed at Metellus.

"Decius is one of those who did his duty for the family. Just goes to show you how you never can tell."

"No," Enarius said. "I suppose not. Hush, pup." The animal ceased its growling and squirmed, yipping at something in a nearby bush. Or possibly it found the bush itself suspicious. "I hope you weren't too intrusive about your inquiries."

"I was the soul of discretion, sire. No one seems to think Izivar's involved with anyone."

"Well. I like the sound of that."

"They've been holding supper for you. I hope you're ready. I'm starved."

"I ate at the magistrate's, and sent word here to start without me. I should have known no one would. The last thing I want to do is annoy Izivar." Enarius wanted her to be in a fine mood tonight. "I shall have to eat some of the food. I'd hate to disappoint her. But I do wish I could talk to her first."

"Of course. She'll be thrilled by that dog. Women love stupid little things like that. Do you have the poem?"

"In my pouch with the ring."

"Well, get to the courting, sire!" Metellus smiled and gestured for his emperor to precede him.

Enarius took a breath to calm his nerves, adjusted the shifting ball of fur in his arms, and started forward.

The two white-armored praetorians posted outside opened the door for him. His uniformed trumpeter in the atrium raised his instrument and sounded a fanfare that twined about the dog's yipping even as Enarius shouted at them to stop. The trumpeter did, but the dog continued, as though it had been affronted by the instrument.

Enarius jostled the dog in his arms, shushing it and petting its tiny head. It gave up yapping and shifted to growling when Izivar's servants bustled forth, including a steward who looked familiar, all smiles and welcome, and an attractive brown-haired woman in a fine red dress. Before she could advance, two men practically ran her down to present themselves with multiple bows. One was a tall distinguished fellow in his early forties, the other a fading charmer with a smile that suggested he was vain. Both wore a sort of bland white tunic with leaves on its edges, belted at the waist. They said their names and something about their important building projects but were so busy talking over one another, and the dog was so noisy, Enarius couldn't make out much. The tall one thrust out a hand holding an intricately filigreed ring.

"Ah," said Enarius. "Thank you." While many Dervan patricians wore rings on every finger, Enarius bore only two on each hand. He tried passing the dog off to Metellus, who happened to be looking the other way. He then gave it to the steward, who received the shifting bundle of white noise with the delight of someone presented a soiled loincloth. The pup barked throughout.

At least Enarius could finally hear the tall architect. But he wasn't saying anything about the floor plans Enarius had sent him. He was still going on about the ring. "You should wear it, sire. A good luck charm from one of our inspirational trips."

Enarius glanced down, seeing a pretty green stone in a rectangular setting framed by some of the little animal letters Hadirans imagined was a workable alphabet. The gold work was quite good. He was used to receiving gifts and smiled blandly as the tall one blathered on, but didn't hear a word of what he said, for

Izivar swept in, arresting in an elegant pink stola. He was disappointed that she'd not worn traditional Volani garb, which he had found most alluring, for he loved the way it flowed about her ankles. Her hair was enchanting this evening, though, its tight ringlets held high by a silvery circlet, then arranged so that they flowed down behind her ears to her shoulders. She welcomed him with a beautiful smile, ensuring him her home was his own.

The dog had not yet ceased its yipping.

"Sorry about all the commotion." Enarius returned her smile. He took the animal and thrust it toward her. "This is for you. Straight from lands beyond Ilodonea. It's very rare."

"Oh!" Izivar's smile looked forced. "What is it?"

"I think it's a sort of noisy pillow,"[15] the woman in the red dress said. She had somehow maneuvered to stand nearer to Izivar.

"It's actually a very sweet dog," Enarius assured her, and petted the creature's head. "I'm told they're prized for their affection and loyalty."

"Really? Where are its ears?"

"Under the fur. It does have them." Seeing that Izivar appeared uninclined to receive the animal, he bent and put it to the tiled floor. Its legs were so low to the ground that its carefully brushed fur concealed them completely. "Go to your new mistress now," he urged it encouragingly.

The creature darted left past the architects and shot into an adjoining chamber. Its barks echoed through the halls as it passed more and more swiftly into remote regions of the villa.

"It should be easy to keep track of," the woman in the red dress remarked.

In a low, menacing voice, Metellus dispatched the trumpeter to find the dog, and the musician tucked his instrument under his arm and hurried off.

Enarius tried a smile. "Well. I'm sorry to have kept everyone waiting for the food. I know it will be delicious. You always set a fine table." He then noticed someone missing. "Where's Julivar?"

---

[15] The dog is actually known as a catuli, and had been, indeed, beloved by the Ilodonean aristocracy for long centuries. They are found in a variety of shades, including a red-brown, black, white, and a light-gray color known as "blue" so highly prized that dogs of that color were kept only in the household of the Ilodonean emperor and his favorites. —*Silenus*

"She's staying with a friend this week,"[16] Izivar answered.

He had always been fond of Izivar's little sister, and was a little sorry he wouldn't be able to visit with her. "Is she still practicing her martial moves?"

"She is."

Metellus' answering chuckle was an irritant.

"Those who laughed at the idea of women warriors didn't laugh long after encountering Eltyr," Enarius reminded him.

The praetorian legate raised his hands in surrender. "I certainly did not mean to impugn the fighting mettle of the Eltyr. Praise Jovren they can trouble us no further. But given Julivar's size, this indulgence ... well, I mean no offense."

"Cubs will one day be lions," Enarius said. "Or lionesses, as the case may be. I'm told the female lions are more dangerous even than the males."

"I see that you've met the architects." Izivar took his elbow and steered him forward. "And Cassandra is a local designer of curtain and cushion patterns."

At mention of their profession, the two men bowed deeply, like westerners, who had been abasing themselves before god kings for generations. "Your excellency!" they said as one. The tall one said something again about the luck charm, but Enarius waved that away. He'd already tucked the ring into a belt pouch. He motioned them to rise.

Izivar suggested they sit down for supper, and gestured them toward the triclinium.

Enarius found his courage. "If you don't mind, my Lady, I was hoping to speak to you privately." His voice sounded absurdly loud to him.

Her smile was very sweet. "If you wish, Enarius. But I would hate to keep our guests waiting much longer."

"Oh, we'll just start in," Metellus said with a grin.

The praetorian was even more difficult when he was hungry. "That's quite right," Enarius said. "You people should have at. Izivar and I will be along shortly."

---

[16] While Julivar was in truth staying with friends, they were Volani youths, who she had decided to help settle into their new temporary quarters in Selanto, in her first official mission on behalf of her people. —*Sosilos*

"Thank you, sire," Metellus said with a head bow, then addressed the steward. "Show us the way then, will you?"

Izivar inclined her head ever so briefly to the steward, who led them off. Somewhere far away the dog still barked.

Enarius followed his one true love. From somewhere came the sound of chairs scraping and platters being set on tables as Izivar's course led to the nearby lovely exterior walled garden, just visible in the twilight. Some of his praetorians were on watch beyond, he knew, but it seemed an abandoned oasis. Only a few paper lanterns hung under the roofed walkway beside the villa. Izivar arrived at a door and pushed it open. A tidy office was revealed.

"Where is Decius?" he asked. "I had hoped to meet him."

"I'm not entirely sure. He's probably making the rounds."

"I've heard he's very vigilant."[17]

She opened the office door and turned up a lamp burning low on a hook. She herself gestured to the cushioned chair behind the desk but he shook his head and settled on one of the two stools facing it. She looked thoughtful for a moment. "Oh—I meant to give this to you. It's a key to the vault." So saying, she undid a clasp from around her slender neck and pulled a key from her bosom.

Her eyes were warm as she pressed the key to his palm and he gulped, as though he'd never been touched by a woman before.

"You're so well prepared." His voice was admiring.

"Well, I've been managing a household for a while," she said with a laugh. She always emphasized their difference in ages, even though fifteen years didn't make her seem that much older.

As she retreated to the desk chair he glanced about the white-walled space and the ordered cubbies with correspondence and scrolls. He complimented her on that as well, and then found the subject he was after incredibly hard to voice, fearing it would not go over well.

"I wonder... I had hoped... there's something important I'd like to speak to you about," he said.

She sat down. "Is everything all right?"

---

[17] Enarius had first heard of the assumed Decius identity through his adoptive father, whose life had once been saved by Hanuvar in the guise of one of Izivar's security personnel. Enarius had met the de-aged Hanuvar twice and been convinced he was seeing two brothers, one several years older than the first. —*Sosilos*

"Oh, yes. I think so." He wondered why he was sweating so much. "Izivar... the throne is heavy."

"I hope you haven't been trying to lift it on your own," she said with a playful smile.

"Uh, no." He'd meant to say his rule was a heavy burden. His throat tightened, and he felt as though he could scarcely breathe. Before he had even given it further consideration, he blurted out: "You should marry me."

She blinked in consternation.

That hadn't been at all how he meant to bring that up, either, but he decided to simply forge ahead. He fumbled with the pouch at his waist and put fingers around the ring he meant to give her, though he did not bring it out. "Father's dead. His opinion doesn't matter anymore. And... I'm surrounded by things I barely understand and people I barely know. I don't trust them. I keep getting thrust into daughters and granddaughters—I mean—they keep getting pushed into me. Ah." His face reddened. "What I mean is that rich men want me to marry into their families. Some of them are very pretty—the women I mean, heh, but they're young and vapid and... And you're wonderful, and I want to be with you."

"Oh, Enarius." The sad tone in her voice did not inspire a great deal of hope.

He pulled the ring out, set it on the desk, and pushed it toward her. "It's not just for me," he said. "It's for the empire. The marriage, I mean, not the ring." His words sounded stupid now, even though they hadn't sounded stupid when he'd rehearsed them. "You would be one of my most trusted advisors. With you at my side, the entire empire would benefit."

"Enarius..." Her hand, with its silver bracelet, went involuntarily to the black mourning band almost hidden in her dark curls, and he thought to hear her demur by mentioning the deaths of her brother and father. "You know that I love you," she said finally. "But as a brother."

"The Hadiran kings sleep with their sisters," Enarius said. "I mean, they marry them. Um." Everyone in the world thought that was a terrible idea, apart from the Hadirans, and certainly including him. He had no idea how that had popped out of his mouth. It was as though his tongue was trying to make him sound as ridiculous as possible.

"It is a lovely ring," Izivar said, blessedly changing topic to something less idiotic.

"You should try it on. It would look lovelier on you."

She considered it. "It's Hadiran," she said. "Is that a message?"

Hadiran? He'd picked out a brilliant sapphire said to come from south of Nuvara. But somehow the ring the architects had given him had ended up in his hand.

"It matches my favorite hair band."

"Ah. Yes. I didn't mean it to say anything about. Um. Incest."

"You don't need to be so nervous. We're friends, aren't we?"

"Of course! And I swore to your brother to protect you, Izivar. I could protect you so much better if you were with me." This was going horribly. Suddenly he remembered Metellus' counsel, and dug around in his pouch. He touched on the face of the real ring, debated giving it as another gift, then came to the paper he'd folded up and pulled it free. "I've set down my thoughts in a poem I've written. Bear with me."

He had not recalled putting quite so many folds in the papyrus, and cleared his throat as she waited patiently. Finally, it was there in his hands, and he was reading out loud. "Sturdy were his marble thews and mighty was his blade"—that wasn't right, but in his nervousness he persevered, his brain trying to puzzle out what had gone wrong—"and stinking was the pool of blood his fallen foes had made—oh, Izivar, this is the wrong poem." He put down the paper and hiked up one hip to better access the bottom of his belt pouch.

In the silence, somewhere out there in the garden, the dog's almost rhythmic yapping drew closer and then swiftly dwindled, followed some moments later by the plod of feet and the panting of an exhausted man.

Finally Enarius gave up the poetry search. "That's a poem Metellus has been working on," he explained, "and we must have gotten our pages confused. I didn't mean to talk about people's thighs. But about empresses. I would make you an empress. I could quite literally give you the finest things in the whole of the world."

"I'm probably too old to give you children."

"Many women as old as you get pregnant," he said. "Not that you're old," he added quickly. "You're stunning, and look half your age—"

"I'm not sure that I want children, now."

He'd anticipated that argument as well. "Who needs them? We could adopt, like my um... like my father." He had never truly gotten used to referring to Uncle Gaius as his father, even after the official adoption.

"Enarius, in ten years I shall be old, and you will still be in the prime of life."

"That's in the far future. We should be happy, now."

"A good ruler must watch for what is to come. Both for himself, and his people."

He cut her off before she arrived at whatever point she was trying to reach. "Is there someone else?"

"What if there was?" she asked. "You would want me to be happy, wouldn't you?"

"Your happiness is the most important thing in the world," he said, though inside his heart ached.

"I want you to be happy, too. And to succeed. But I'm not right for you. Deep in your heart you know this, or you wouldn't be so nervous."

"Men are always nervous around the women they love." He leaned forward and gently took her hand. She eyed him doubtfully. "Just try it on, and think about it." She flinched as he slid the lovely band onto her finger.

"Don't say anything," he said. "Just... wear it tonight, and think about what it would be like to wear it always. To be with me, always."

She said nothing. Her expression, in fact, was rather blank, and suddenly he felt incredibly foolish. She didn't want him, or the ring, but he was too embarrassed to take it back. Probably she was shocked that he had been so insistent. "All right," he said softly. Still she said nothing. "I'll just wander out into the garden and gather my thoughts. I'll be in to join you for dinner in a little while. You can... you can take the ring off if you'd like."

Her gaze was stony with disapproval.

He took the lamp because it was fully dark outside now and wandered slump shouldered into the garden. He hoped she'd call him back, but she said nothing, and soon he could not have heard her, for the frogs were out in force, their chirrup a pulse beat of the wild.

Enarius passed a drizzling fountain with one of those stupid smiling cupids from Herrenia everyone seemed to have—except possibly for the Herrenians, from whom they'd all been looted—and then passed a pair of young lovers in stone, holding hands and looking toward the east. He envied the statues their apparent happiness. He was about to ask them why he, the most powerful man in the world, couldn't find happiness, but he heard sniffling.

He turned with the light, bypassed a piney hedge, and spotted a slim figure huddled up in the corner of a wooden bench near another decorative pond. Serliva shaded her eyes against the light beam, then wiped tears from them.

"Serliva," he said. "What's happened? Why are you crying?" He set down the lamp and drew up beside her, his own unhappiness forgotten. Izivar's maid hadn't been a central part of the household for long, but he'd come to like her and the protective way that she watched out for her mistress. She'd even called him out on occasional points of etiquette in Izivar's presence, something most servants wouldn't have dared, and he approved.

He slid in beside her. He could not help appreciating the colorful, layered Volani skirt she wore, or a slender ankle with glittering baubles upon it.

"It's nothing, En.... sire."

"Enarius will do. There's no court here."

She sniffled.

"You can tell me. I daresay the emperor can probably help straighten it out." He said the last with bravado even though he felt more powerless than usual tonight.

"Can you make men be less terrible?" she asked, and sniffed again.

"Has someone hurt you?"

"I can't believe how I'm reacting." She hesitated a moment, then demanded of him: "Do you think I'm too skinny?"

She was certainly on the lean side, but he'd always thought her rather fetching in a long-limbed, long-chinned way, and tonight, well. Tonight she was practically radiant, apart from those tear-streaked eyes and a bit of black makeup that had run along one cheek. For whatever reason, a woman in Volani garb was especially appealing.

"The gods made all different kinds of beauty. Dark and pale and thick and thin and tall and short..." Her eyes were on him questioningly and he understood he'd best get to the point. "You're beautiful, and any man who can't see it is a dullard. Who told you that? You want me to exile him?"

"I wouldn't mind. It's Metellus."

"Metellus?" He repeated the name in stunned horror. "You were having an affair with Metellus?"

"No!" Her voice rose in abject horror. "I was simply trying to get him talking and he pretty much told me I was too flat chested to bother with!"

He couldn't help laughing, although seeing the stricken look on her face he quickly quieted, and extended his arms. The next thing he knew, he was enfolding her and stroking the back of her head. He was aware of the press of her breasts, and a scent of lavender and honey that was almost intoxicating. "Oh, Serliva. You're far too sweet for him."

"I thought he would be kind and thoughtful but he's so... mean."

"Well... he's a soldier. He's seen some awful things."

"You've seen awful things, but you're not mean." She looked up at him through long lashes and pushed hair back from her forehead. "You're always kind. To everyone. Even servants."

"Well..." Something in the way she regarded him made him even more conscious of her proximity, and the soft parts of her body that were pressed close to his own. "If we can't be kind to the people who're working hardest for us, uh, then we're not really um." More and more he was aware of the beat of his heart.

"That's why you're an exceptional emperor," she said bracingly. "Everyone knows that you actually care."

"I care," he said. "But me being emperor is just happenstance. Look at me." He raised the hand that wasn't still wrapped about her back—her warm back—and let it flop back to his side. "Three years ago I'd decided my big goal was to tour the empire and visit all of its greatest boxing rings. I mean, that's still something I want to do, but... I guess what I mean is..." He had never noticed how pretty her eyes were. "I don't really know what I'm doing," he confessed. "I want to be a good emperor. But I'm surrounded by people who are after something all the time. It feels like everyone's running some kind of racket. Do you know I'm going to have to pass a law to make it illegal to drop waste into streams that feed into Derva's aqueducts?"

"There isn't a law against that already?"

"No." He shook his head in disgust, though he did not fully take his gaze from those enticing eyes. "And why should there be? Even the dumbest barbarian knows you don't crap upstream from your village. But there were some silver miners dumping things into a river and it was making people sick in Derva. And they didn't care! The mine owners, I mean. It would have inconvenienced them to move their trash further." His mouth twisted in contempt.

"You could just decree it."

"I want the laws to outlive me. We should be a people of laws, a just people. You wouldn't believe the stupid excuses they made for dumping into the stream. No one would give me a straight answer, or tell me the truth."

"People should be honest with each other," she said.

"Yes."

"I remember when you'd come in with poor Indar trying to court Izivar and I'd see how hurt you were that she wouldn't take you seriously. You'd turn away, and your brow would be creased." Her fingers against his forehead were cool, which was nice, because he himself felt increasingly warm. "And I'd wish I could make you feel better. I'd wish I could tell you how sweet you were."

"You can tell me now," he suggested.

"You're the kindest man I've ever met," she said breathlessly.

It was the most natural thing then that they should lean forward into one another. He thought it the sweetest kiss he'd ever felt. Her lips were smooth and yielding and it seemed a freely given offering rather than an obligation or a performance. His heart hammered as they pulled apart. She smiled shyly at him, and they leaned into one another for a longer meeting of lips, she bringing her trim body against his own.

ν

Plautus completed another circuit through the little blue-walled guest room, turned at the hall door, and headed straight past the closed exit to the garden and for the table between their beds where the candle stood. His classically handsome features were twisted in worry.

Terrence, sitting against the headboard, scratched his beard. He'd grown it for this role and regretted it by the third day. He watched Plautus reach the door, turn, and pace back between the beds. "You need to relax," he said.

Plautus threw up his arms. "How can I relax? He's not wearing the ring! It's not going to work if he's not wearing the ring!"

His old friend tended toward the histrionic, but he was right, and Terrence wasn't sure what to do, which is why he'd suggested they retreat to their guest room to think after making professional-sounding excuses to leave with a few plates of food.

Probably the scarred praetorian and the pretty female guest were wondering why they'd both withdrawn, and the steward seemed disgruntled, but Terrence didn't care about that.

"If you can't figure out what to do, we're going to have to run for it," Plautus continued.

"Aminius is going to have our hides if we lose his ring *and* the scrolls."

Plautus' face screwed up in dismay and he stepped close, his voice an angry whisper.

"He told us not to say his name!"

Terrence rolled his eyes and spoke in a conversational tone. "Aminius. Aminius, Aminius, Aminius. He's not here to disapprove. And no one's listening in."

"You don't know that!"

"If they're listening in, we're already done for." Terrence rapped the headboard behind him. "Hey, anyone listening in, we're frauds. Senator Aminius sent us here and is paying us a lot of money to use a magic artifact on Enarius."

Plautus gaped. "I can't believe you did that."

Terrence shook his head in disgust. "No one's coming. The entire household is catering to the emperor now."

"Who's got the ring in his belt pouch," Plautus all but jeered. "How can you possibly get it to work if it's not on his finger?"

"I'm thinking," Terrence said. "Silence."

Plautus seemed to believe his eye roll and his mocking repetition of "I'm thinking" went unnoticed.

Terrence looked to the table beside him where the brassy old crown sat. He supposed it wouldn't hurt to try. He picked it up and stepped to the shuttered window. For all that he'd chided Plautus for worrying about someone overhearing, he wanted to ensure no one was in earshot before he dared magic. Nothing lay close by apart from the window flowerbed, recently stuffed with blooming daisies, and one of those new wheelbarrow things beside it, left by some slave after transporting the flowers.

"The ring's not going to work if he's not wearing it," Plautus reminded him.

"We won't know for sure unless we try." He slipped the crown over his head. It was tight. From memory he whispered the Hadiran words, so ancient that the sounds he intoned would not have been understood by men and women walking the sun blasted streets of the river kingdom today.

Somewhere far away, his senses stretched to perceive an environment of darkness, but could neither see nor hear. He supposed he was detecting the stupid emperor's stupid belt pouch.

Plautus was going on about the danger they were in, for Aminius was famously vicious when men failed him. Not for the first time Terrence wondered just how much they could get if they simply sold off the crown and the ring, and remembered again the dire threat Aminius had made—if they did not return the Hadiran artifact he would spare no expense to see them perish as painfully as possible.

Aminius had also warned that the magic could only work for a short period of time. Less than an hour, he had said. Further rituals required to make it work longer were apparently cumbersome and expensive.

He had just about decided it wasn't going to work when it felt as though someone had slapped a skewer into his temple.

He sucked in a breath and stiffened, stars showing in his vision at the same time as he perceived something else—a ghostly overlay of a room and a seated man with a hangdog expression. The emperor! Somehow he was looking at the emperor! Then who was wearing the ring?

He could also make out some words, although it was hard to hear over Plautus demanding to know what was wrong.

Terrence held up a hand to him and closed his eyes.

Now the ghostly overlay resolved into an image. He was actually watching through someone else's eyes! And hearing with someone else's ears! It was remarkable, and impressive, even if the view was very dull and washed out, as if seen through fog. The hearing, too, was muffled.

"What's happening?" Terrence demanded.

"It's the woman," Plautus said in wonder. "The Lenereva woman is wearing the ring!"

"Why?"

"Obviously I don't know! Shut up so I can hear what the emperor's telling her!"

It didn't take long for him to understand the emperor was a lovesick young fool pleading for the woman's hand. Plautus was still babbling, saying that the woman could get the scrolls, which was absolutely true, but Terrence told him to shut up.

"Can you take control of her?" Plautus demanded.

"I already am! She's frozen stiff and the emperor hasn't noticed. He's leaving—"

"Amin . . . our benefactor said it has limited magic," he warned. "You should—"

"Gods, the emperor is a sad sack," Terrence gloated. "He's going off to sulk."

"Take control of her!"

Plautus' voice betrayed the dual pulls of terror and eagerness. Seeing that the emperor had disappeared with his lantern into the garden, Terrence put his hand to the square gem housed in the crown at his temple, grasped its beveled edge, and turned.

This time it was not him alone who felt the pain, but the woman, who doubled over. When the pain faded and he stood upright, she straightened with him.

"Did it work?" Plautus asked.

"Yes," said Terrence, and startled himself, for the woman spoke as well. He then addressed Plautus in a whisper, and heard her speak with him. "I have her," he said. "But she's saying everything I say."

"That's amazing!"

And the first hint of the challenge of controlling her, as it turned out. He couldn't feel much of what she felt. And the emperor had left her in the dark, so there was only a slim strand of lighter darkness from the courtyard to see by, owing to the partly open door. Walking proved laborious, because he had to mime walking forward to get her moving, then suspend control for a half heartbeat to turn and keep walking in the same direction, or she would turn with him. Anyone who saw her moving was going to immediately be suspicious. Izivar Lenereva was a woman of refinement but he suspected he maneuvered her like a drunken arthritic. He halted, puzzled for a moment about how to push the door open, then reached out and sensed her fingers touch it even as his own brushed air. The door swung wide, and he got her heading along the courtyard walk.

He had to stop once more when he neared the hallway into the courtyard.

"What's wrong?"

"It's hard to turn without being right next to the wall," Terrence whispered.

"I don't see why this hasn't been used to get assassins to kill people, and all kinds of things," Plautus said, a gleam in his eye.

He was an idiot. It was just possible you could kill someone by puppeting their assassin with this magic, but they'd see their killer coming from a long ways off. The victim would have to be insensate or asleep. And maybe you could take possession of someone and walk them off a ledge or into a river, but then you'd lose the ring, and aside from that, Aminius had said life-threatening shocks might let the real person wrest control back. "And using it to seduce women is a tremendous disappointment," the senator had added, his thick lips twisting, "unless you've a friend to run her, and you fancy making love to statues who turn into shrieking harpies when they're half disrobed."

Terrence would never have guessed a man as wealthy as senator Aminius needed magic to get women to bed, but had kept his surprise to himself. He walked slowly, trying to add a little bit of a sway, the way a woman might, and Izivar headed down the hall. If she was conscious and aware of his actions, he couldn't feel it.

A few dull lights burned ahead, and he faintly heard the sound of the banquet. He didn't want to interact with that, at all, but fortunately some other rooms opened up to him, and he turned through them. They were dark, and he almost walked into a table, but he made it past, and beyond another doorway. Other hall lanterns showed him the way forward, and soon he would be closing on the meeting room where the woman had told them the vault lay.

Before he reached it, though, a tall stranger interposed himself, a well-built fellow with gray-streaked hair.

"Izivar?" he asked questioningly. "Is there something wrong?"

This must be the head of her security they'd heard about. Terrence put a stern note in her voice. "It is none of your business," he said, and heard Izivar mouth the same lines. "Return to your duties."

"I see," the man said. "Very well." He stepped aside, and Terrence maneuvered Izivar onward down the hall. "Starting to get the hang of this," he whispered, pleased with himself, not minding that Izivar softly said the same thing. Then he thought of something else. "Damn. I'm probably going to have to find her a lantern."

VI

Aleria didn't think the two architects had recognized her. But then they'd both been so nervous they hadn't seemed to notice much of anything. They departed without even once sitting down, announcing with comic ineptness that they had undefined work to be done and added that they were experiencing stomach pains.

It must have been clear to Metellus that there was something odd about them, but he gave them only a baleful warning look before he took a seat, complaining to Aleria about having to sit upright like commoners, for the meal was to be served Volani style.

The first course came, and the praetorian tore into the duck with gusto.

Aleria thought about making conversation with him, but his manner repulsed her. She listened for the approach of either Enarius or Izivar. Hearing neither, and deciding against pursuing engagement with her lone companion, she excused herself for a wash area, assured a servant she could find her own way, and proceeded into the darkness.

The halls seemed empty until another serving girl appeared to ask if she needed directions. Aleria told her that she did not, but then had to actually walk with the servant to the very threshold of the wash room before she was rid of her. Once Aleria emerged, only moments after she had heard the girl's receding footsteps, she headed once more toward her goal, only to encounter, as if by chance, a second serving girl. When this one asked what she desired Aleria feigned interest in an elaborate baked dessert she had once seen at a senator's party, ticked off the ingredients she supposed it contained, and with her best pampered patrician manner insisted the young lady scurry off to request the cook look into making it, or something like it.

Only then did she turn toward the rooms that led to the vault. Aleria had no interest in interacting with the guard outside it. Instead, she hurried into a side hall, halting before a door she'd noted during her tour of the villa. From her calculations it lay directly beside the room with the vault. It was locked, naturally, but even a stiff lock like this was little challenge to someone with her skills, and she was through it soon and into the black little room beyond.

It seemed nothing more than a storage area cluttered with some old couches, piled one upon another so that the topmost furniture had its legs pointing upward. There was also a cabinet with a sagging hinge, two small storage shelves, and a row of tall amphora. Just beyond the shelves, against the wall opposite the door, she spied a third empty shelf unit. Unless she missed her guess, the wall it stood against would offer direct entry into the vault.

She hadn't failed to notice that many of the internal walls were plastered over wattle. All an enterprising woman would need to make her own door was a good blade, one of which she just happened to have strapped to her thigh.

Aleria climbed carefully over the broken furniture, finding it fortunate that there was such a wide space between the clutter toward the room's front and this back wall. Moving the empty cupboard aside would be ever so simple.

She put her hands to the furniture, readying to tilt the shelf unit out so that she could carefully drag it to one side. When it came forward, for a brief moment she thought it was falling, and took in an anxious breath. Less than a heartbeat later she perceived the furniture was actually swinging. It apparently was fixed to the wall on a hidden hinge, and as it came open she perceived some clever person had already cut an aperture in the wall behind it, through which light dully shown.

"Who's there?" A startled male voice whispered. And a moment later a bearded Herrene was crouching beneath the low door lintel and staring at her. It was the same man she'd seen in Helsa's company before. Behind him was what was almost certainly the real side wall of the vault, upon which a handle was affixed. He himself was hidden in a narrow space with a small desk, lamps, and oil.

Upon the desk was a scroll that the Herrene had been writing, and another propped open on upright wooden dowels in front of it. On the instant she understood everything: Helsa hadn't planned to steal the Sidyline books, but to copy them. This hidey hole allowed access both to the vault and the room beside it. That meant Izivar had to be in on the entire plan. Probably Aleria should have been irritated this rendered her own work fruitless, but she couldn't help laughing at the enterprise's audacity.

"What are you doing here?" the Herrene whispered.

She replied in the same quiet tone. "I *was* going to liberate the scrolls. Now I think I'm going to ask how much you'd charge for a copy."

"How did you get that door open?" he asked softly. "We put in a rusty lock that takes a lot of effort to open."

"I'm good with my hands. How are the scrolls? You learning secrets about the future?"

He snorted. "They're ridiculous."

"Are they?"

"Worthless. Obscure, and badly rhymed. These have to be fakes."

There was no mistaking the sound of plodding footsteps nearby. The Herrene's eyes widened in panic and he turned toward the far wall of his hideaway. Aleria slid through into the space after him, closing the chamber with a handle she discovered on the lower back of the book case.

The Herrene gave her a suspicious glance, then doused the light and adjusted something along the wall. A moment later she realized he'd opened a tiny aperture along the side, for lantern light shown through from the vault beyond. He stared, then drew his head back in obvious astonishment. He eyed her then with a kind of "why not" look, motioned her forward, then slid to one side.

The lantern showed her a well-ordered room little larger than a servant's chamber and smelling of fresh paint. It contained a number of shelves with chests of varied sizes, some filigreed and some not. An old chest with black markings sat upon a pedestal in the room's center, with a smaller chest boasting gold filigree atop it.

Izivar Cabera set the lantern on a shelf and considered two chests, studying them as if she had never seen them before. Her manner was uncharacteristically stiff, so that when the Herrene started to put his hand on the latch that would open the wall, Aleria restrained him.

The woman reached out with a peculiar, jerky movement, clasped the smaller chest to her breast, then turned awkwardly. She left the lantern behind her and moved on, her gait labored, her butt swaying ludicrously every second step, as though she were a prostitute on a field march. Finally, she pushed the door closed behind her.

Antires shut the peephole and turned up the lantern. The handsome Herrene's brows were drawn in confusion.

"Why did she take the scrolls while you're copying them?" she asked.

"She didn't take the scrolls I was working on. She took Metellus' lousy poem."

"Poem?"

"A heroic epic about the chief praetorian, Metellus. When I read the first page I laughed so hard I was afraid someone would hear me. This doesn't make any sense. She's acting strange."

"Maybe I should follow her." Aleria put her hand to the bookshelf latch.

"I'm not sure I like that."

"It's a little late to worry about trusting me now, isn't it?"

"You could run and tell someone."

"I want a copy of this, remember? Your secret's safe with me. You stay here and keep working and I'll look into things."

Before he could dither she was out the fake door and shutting it behind her.

VII

Hanuvar ignored his first instinct, which was to pull the ring from Izivar's finger, for it seemed obvious the radiant jewelry had her ensorcelled. Experience had taught him an interrupted spell could have terrible consequences for those involved, and so he pretended to obey her orders to let her be, following at a distance as she advanced through the halls of her home to retrieve a lantern, sometimes shuffling and sometimes twitching her rear. Her movements would have been laughable if he weren't afraid for her.

The guard stepped aside and then she entered the vault room. The Dervan legionary glanced suspiciously down the hall toward him, but Hanuvar raised a hand in acknowledgment and the soldier nodded after a moment.

He waited in the shadows, certain now someone had suborned Izivar's will to hunt for treasures, almost surely the Sidyline books. He forced his hands out of their clench, suppressing a surge of rage.

It seemed a lifetime before she emerged cradling a small, sturdy chest. The guard had been told only the Lady Izivar or the emperor himself were permitted access to the treasure vault, but still stopped her to politely, softly, inquire what she did. Hanuvar didn't hear the entirety of his question, although her reply, nearly shouted, could not be missed.

"I am retrieving this for the emperor! Keep up the good work!"

The soldier watched, befuddled, as she performed a wobbly turn and headed out through the back rooms, ignoring a confused glance from a servant hurrying by with a lantern and a basket of flowers.

Izivar took the long way on toward the guest quarters, and passed a stout male servant standing at a side table folding napkins. It was an odd place for the work and Hanuvar guessed that Izivar or her steward had given word to unobtrusively keep track of the guests.

Ignoring the napkin folder's greeting, Izivar staggered through a door that opened before her. The door was shut before Hanuvar was close enough to see who lay beyond.

He was upon it in moments, ear pressed to the surface. The servant watched him in surprise.

"We've got it!" a male voice rejoiced. "We've actually got it! Now what?"

Another deeper voice answered. "I can't just leave this expensive ring around her finger, can I? Aminius wants it back. But she'll come around the instant I take it off her."

"I thought you were the master planner," the first voice responded acidly. "What were you going to do about the emperor wearing it?"

There was no answer.

"We'll tie her up," the deep voice said after a moment.

"With what?"

Hanuvar had heard enough. Satisfied that Izivar would be unharmed if the spell were interrupted, he was readying to push through when someone came up behind him.

Hanuvar discovered Metellus at his rear.

The praetorian's voice was a mocking whisper. "Listening at doors, Decius?"

He neither liked nor trusted the praetorian, but might need assistance, and suspected Metellus would happily join in any head bashing. He rapped loudly on the door.

"Open up!" he called. "Release the woman!"

A male gasp of fear and a curse came from within, followed by the shout of someone saying "They're onto us!" and then there was a clattering noise, a thump, cursing in pain, and the sound of an opening door and retreating footsteps. The two men had gone out through the garden door.

Hanuvar put shoulder to the door once, then put his foot to it. It sprang open with the second kick and swung violently inward. Izivar was nowhere in sight. A single candle burned on the side table between the two beds. The courtyard door hung open, and two figures could be seen running into the gloom, the tall one pushing a wheelbarrow with a limp figure slumped inside.

"They've got Izivar and the scrolls!" Hanuvar said, and followed on their heels. Metellus swore, and likely motivated by concern over the second part of the declamation, ran after Hanuvar into the courtyard.

The occasional lantern burning in the garden wasn't enough to clearly see his quarry. The scholars were visible mostly as a deeper blackness in motion before the surroundings. They cut suddenly to the right; Metellus sprinted straight ahead past Hanuvar, perhaps thinking to cut them off, shouting for the guards. And then, quite suddenly, two figures near one of the few lights reared up from the grass at the same moment a small bundle broke into a growling yip and charged Metellus' legs. He staggered and promptly fell sideways to land in an ornamental pond, striking with a resounding splash that sprayed water widely.

Hanuvar discerned Enarius himself climbing hastily to his feet, adjusting his tunic. His hair was mussed, his expression confused.

Serliva pushed up from the grass, her skirt hiked up, her blouse pushed down. She hastily adjusted her hair while trying to cover up. A small dog dashed along the edge of the pond, yelping furiously at Metellus' every splash.

Hanuvar dashed right, gaining quickly on the two phony architects, who had apparently noticed the pool that the one-eyed praetorian hadn't. As they pushed on for the back wall, Hanuvar heard someone else on his heel; a lighter tread than Metellus'. In a moment Aleria was at his side.

"What are you doing here?"

"Long story," she said.

The tall kidnapper looked over his shoulder as his companion reached the ivy-covered wall and leapt for its height. He let go the wheelbarrow then hurried after his companion.

Hanuvar halted to check upon Izivar.

She sprawled in the cart's base, legs drooped overside, and was still and quiet, though she blinked, and the jade ring glowed dully from within. He lifted her hand, put thumb and finger to the ring, then carefully pulled it free, dropping it on the ground beside him. He smashed the stone with his heel, driving it into the ground. The tall architect reached the top of the wall, huffing, and dropped over the other side.

Izivar put a hand to her head. "What happened? Where am I?"

"I'll explain soon. You're all right?"

"I think so..."

Hanuvar rose and started for the wall.

Aleria cleared her throat. "If you're worried about the scrolls, they didn't get any. They're still safe." A ghost of a smile touched her lips. "The morons stole some poem Metellus' wrote. By accident, one assumes."

Hanuvar returned and looked down at Izivar. "They didn't hurt you?"

"No. I'm just a little dizzy." She sat up, and he helped her climb from the little cart. "I'm a bit vague on how I got here—"

"The architects rolled you here in a handcart."

"What I don't understand is why I don't hear the praetorians chasing them—" Aleria asked, then fell silent at a sudden onrush of armed figures.

"Where are the thieves?" one of them shouted at the three of them, his manner menacing. Hanuvar and Aleria pointed at the wall.

"We were chasing them!" Aleria added. "They'd kidnapped Izivar Lenereva, but we just got her back!"

The lead soldier seemed to recognize Izivar as Hanuvar steadied her rise. "It's true," she said.

The soldier pointed others deeper into the garden, presumably just in case these civilians had the details wrong, then led the rest over the wall in pursuit. The two sets of running feet receded in opposite directions.

Izivar let out a sigh and faced Aleria. "What's your place in all this?"

"I couldn't resist a look at what you were doing," she said. "Very clever. I expect you to sell me a copy. Your man says it's worthless, but, well, simpletons pay a lot for ridiculous things, don't they?"

"They do," Izivar mused.

Aleria shifted her attention to Hanuvar. "Next time I'll wait for you." Then she smiled slyly. "If you ever get tired of her, look me up. She's charming, but I'd wager you and I would have more fun."

She left them then, jogging into the darkness of the garden.

"How well do you know her?" Izivar asked, a hint of sharpness in her voice.

"Not at all in the way you're thinking," he replied. "You sure you're all right?"

"I think so. The dizziness has passed."

From deeper in the garden came a shout from Metellus, calling for the guards. Hanuvar frowned. "You're going to tell Metellus where the architects went. I'd like to stay clear of Enarius and any interrogating officials. You can tell him I'm off searching beyond the grounds."

"Will you be?"

"No. Let the praetorians handle it. The less I'm seen, the better." He pointed to the ruined ring. "Show him that." He traded a light kiss with her, then headed for the shrine to Jovren.

VIII

Enarius thought it prudent to leave before breakfast the next morning. Accomplished hostess that she was, however, Izivar presented herself outside his quarters while the slaves were still arranging his belongings.

He managed a shy smile and watched her face, wondering if he'd see disgust there, or even disappointment, but she held herself completely normally, as though he hadn't declared his love for her only to lie down with another, her own maid no less, in the next hour, as though he hadn't sent for impostors who had broken into her house after state secrets and used a spell to take control of her body. She was dressed demurely as usual in an ankle-length green stola. She didn't even appear especially tired.

He returned her wish of good morning, told her she looked well rested, then quickly adopted a new line of conversation. "I wonder what's happened to the real architects. I shall have to send word."

"I hope they're all right."

"Yes. Um. I don't want you to think that my ... feelings for you were feigned in any way. I ..."

"I know that your feelings for me are real. But you know I'm not the right woman for you. You need someone your own age. Someone you can trust."

She always managed to get right to the heart of a matter. "Those are few and far between."

"Perhaps. But Serliva has been fond of you since she first met you, because you are kind and charming and handsome. She used those terms to try to persuade me about you many times, and she used them last night when she tearfully relayed all that happened. Not that household gossip hadn't already gotten to me."

He grimaced.

"I'm not saying that a single night's tryst is the basis for everlasting love, but there's surely more than desperation involved for both of you."

He did like Serliva, very much. "But if I were to take a ... maid to be my ... lover ... or wife ..."

"So you're willing to risk the gossip about marrying an older woman of the wrong people, but not for a younger one who could give you heirs?"

She'd discovered an interesting flaw in his reasoning. He blinked at thought of it. Then he sought to correct one of her implied points. "You're not beyond childbearing age. And you're of higher social status."

She made a scoffing noise. "I'm not trying to push her on you, I'm just saying that you shouldn't allow others to make this decision for you. Even though you need to look ahead to anticipate problems, you also have to take care of your own needs. And you need somebody who likes you for you are, not what you are. Aren't you the one who used to tell me I should learn to please myself and let others envy my happiness?"

"You are always so smart," he said, because she was.

"It's called wisdom, and it's taken years to acquire."

"Well, I'm just glad that the books are safe. I hope that they shall guide me."

"Let your heart and mind and councilors guide you, not some dusty old couplets any soothsayer could twist to mean they need more coins thrown their way."

He didn't understand why she was being so skeptical about the scrolls, although they were rather hard to make any sense from. "You don't know that's what they are."

"I just surmise, knowing how convenient it is that these were found just now, when a young ruler might be searching for guidance."

"You're right again." Her insight never failed to impress him. "I wonder... would it be... would you mind if I spoke with Serliva? Perhaps... do you think you might spare her?"

"If she wishes to go, I will miss her terribly. But I think she is fond of you and would like to see more of the world than I am likely to show her. At the very least you two should talk before you depart."

She was right. That would be proper. It wasn't just that they had been lonely; there really was a connection there. And Serliva did like him for who he really was, not for his title. She had known him before that. "I think I will."

Izivar bowed her head. "I'll guide you to her room."

He fell in step beside her. How different the hallways were by light of day.

"I'm sorry that Metellus lost his poem," she said.

"Yes, I don't know how those fellows managed to escape the Praetorian Guard. Metellus is furious. He told me he'd planned on hiring someone to pretty it up a bit once he had the basics down and now he'll have to start over."

Izivar stopped shy of a door. On its other side came a series of yips, and a woman's baby-voiced plea to quiet down.

"You must tell me," he said. "Be honest. Is there something between you and Decius? Metellus said he thought he was only interested in men, but—"

"Should it bother you if there was?" There was a challenging note in her voice. "If you love me, wouldn't you want my happiness?"

His chest felt tight. "Yes, yes, I do. And you have suffered so much, you and your family. He is a man of nearly your age, from what I hear. And a good father, judging by his children. So are you? In love with him?"

"My next husband will be of my own choice, no matter who he is."

"Quite right." He sought her eyes. Here in the daylight he noted the little signs of age upon her. They still didn't matter. But he made careful note of her resolve, and thought of her words. He bowed his head to her.

"If I can ever be of service to you, in any way, I am ready to help."

"I know." She indicated the doors. "Serliva was breakfasting in there. I'll warn you, she's tearful and confused and probably not at her best because she was embarrassed about last night."

Enarius himself had been embarrassed, and more so now, realizing that of course Serliva had been. She must have felt terrible to have been caught in the middle of all this, and lonely as well, for she'd probably expected she would be abandoned. He straightened and rapped his foot against the door. At Serliva's hushed inquiry about who it was, he said "It's me," and opened the door.

Serliva waited on a low bed, her head pressed to the furred body of the little white flat-faced dog. It yipped and wagged its stubby tail enthusiastically.

"You're leaving, aren't you," she said, her lips quivering. "And you've come for little Fluffers, haven't you? Does he have a name?" She rubbed his head, her voice dropping to baby talk. "I named him Fluffers because heesh sho fluffy."

"It's a perfect name."

"I will miss him," she said.

"Why, are you leaving him here?"

She sniffed, wiped one eye and gazed blankly at him.

"How would you like to come with me?" he asked.

Her slowly spreading smile looked as though it might light the world.

※ ※ ※

So began the romance between Enarius and a former maid that was the summer scandal. Dervan matrons lifted noses and chins in disdain and sternly proclaimed they would have no stepped-up foreign slaves on their guest list, and then found themselves removed from any palace invitations. Gossips painted Serliva as a scheming harpy who'd enslaved the emperor with decadent Volani bedroom secrets. The truth seemed to be that they were two sweet young people of about the same age and intellect, lonely for company and fond of one another.

For all his affability, Enarius proved intractable once he had made up his mind about a subject, especially when he was opposed, which might have been part of the reason he stuck by Serliva.

You probably wonder about the Sidyline books. Hanuvar had expected them to be folly, but had not passed up the opportunity to examine them for any hints as to future challenges to his own goals. Most were devoted to events from ancient Dervan history that had already happened, written by someone who obviously knew what the outcome would be. Another was vaguely worded nonsense about the future of the Cornelian dynasty and the many sons who would follow from Enarius, which, of course, is not how things fell out at all. Occasionally the phrasing had a little grandeur, but, speaking from experience, the writing had been a rush job, not divinely inspired prophecy.

As for that poem featuring Metellus, you've probably heard what happened there. I can't speak as to Aminius' state of mind, but his lackeys must have made it all the way back to him without his rare ring, perhaps thinking the controlling crown part plus the chest they'd liberated would appease him. They were never seen again. Still harboring a long held dislike of Metellus, the senator turned the praetorian's hagiographic poem into a comic gold mine. He altered the name of the hero from Metellus to Scarellus, changed a few key words here and there, and then just left the rest of it alone, because the rough draft was hilariously bad.

Rather than a popular book amongst the masses to raise Metellus' standing, it was a thinly veiled satire whose subject was blatantly obvious. It bolstered the praetorian's fame, but not as he would have liked, and made booksellers a tidy sum. Probably Aminius himself could have cashed in on the success, but he sponsored the whole thing anonymously, which was fortunate, for Metellus went into a rage when a copy fell into his hands. He set the Praetorian Guard to hunt down the men behind its publication until overruled by Enarius, who said no one would trust a government without a sense of humor. The young emperor had quaint ideas about how governments normally ran.

Metellus eventually learned about Aminius' role, of course, and it remained just one more point of contention between the two.

At this remove I recall very little of the text, apart from the opening lines:

> Whenever evil threatens
> the sacred Dervan throne;
> whenever men have got their backs
> against the walls of stone;
> whenever witches scheme and spell
> and plot for our defeat,
> up strides brave Scarellus
> on his big heroic feet.
>
> —Sosilos, Book Fifteen

Chapter 8:
The Wonder Garden

I

Danisal arrived at the private Hadiran section at the same moment the glassy-eyed visitors passed up the stairs from the misty underground. Though they looked toward him, none saw him, either as a Wonder Gardens employee or more broadly as a slave; those who'd gone below to breathe the vapors emerged with their thoughts upon the other world. If they had seen him, they would probably have paid him little heed, for at first glance he was not so remarkable, small and slim and plainly dressed. Closer consideration would have revealed a shrewd cast to his features, a natural charm with which he veiled a newly flowered tartness.

Slowing his progress, Danisal watched the Dervans emerge. Each turned immediately to the towering images of Hadiran gods arranged about the clearing, their shadows lengthened by the evening sun. A thin woman in an austere yellow stola preened before the deep-bosomed cat-headed statue.

"Who are you?" Philipa called. Her voice boomed from a speaking trumpet. She herself was hidden behind a thick stone.

"I am a powerful, sensual woman," the patrician said, stroking her hair and then striking the air with her free hand as though it were tipped with claws. "With the blood of a lioness!"

Danisal let out something that might have been a laugh, although his joy this evening was muted.

A mincing high-shouldered man stopped before one of the other statues, and he cried out, in a quavering voice, that he was a cunning fox, just as an older knock-kneed fellow declared he was an eagle, sharp-eyed ruler of the heavens.

Their choices were usually simple to predict, for over the course of a day's fasting and prayer most had already shown an inclination toward certain animal imbued deities. The best odds were never on the selection but on the expression their erring adoration would take.

Absurdity could be glimpsed in many regions of the Gardens, particularly in the areas segregated for adults, but none of the other special ceremonies were as dependably ludicrous. Danisal never tired of watching pampered Dervans make fools of themselves.

But he quickened his pace. The messenger had told him Paulus was deeply flustered by some new calamity, and the man could act rashly when excited. Danisal needed to calm things down.

A trio of stakeholders had put up the opening capital for the Gardens, but the initial idea had come from Paulus, and it was he who devoted the most energy to seeing it prosper. He lived on the grounds and involved himself so actively in the Wonder Gardens' day-to-day affairs that he often spoke through the trumpet Philipa now used at the end of the Ancestry Ceremony.

Today, Paulus waited just beyond the gaudy red marble stairs that led to the stony fissures from which the vapors flowed, in a side cave that had been set up as an office, complete with rug and wall hangings. Sconces with expensive colored glass had been driven into the dark stone walls, and flames writhing within threw amber light across the desk and the chairs and the couch and the spindly old man lying motionless on the floor.

Paulus stood behind the desk pouring through a stack of papers. Two of the pretty, muscular guards waited nearby, and both visibly relaxed at Danisal's arrival.

"He's here, Master," one of them said.

Paulus looked up. "Danisal! Just who I needed!" He was pretending calm, but his voice betrayed a manic edge. Shadowed, liquid eyes, refined nose, cleft chin, wavy dark hair—he would have resembled a heroic bronze come to life if his belly didn't sag. Danisal knew he was on a strict diet, and how frustrated he was to be growing thicker.

"What's happened!?" Danisal asked. Unlike the rest of the park slaves, he no longer referred to his master by any title. He paused over the body, which lay face down. "This is Senator Terentius, isn't it?"

"It is!" Paulus said. "He slipped in the mist and hit his head. I thought I'd have his body thrown into one of the ponds. All the other believers will think he drowned."

Danisal thought quickly and spoke delicately. "That might not work. The senator's family and doctors will carefully examine his body. They might be able to see he didn't drown." He hoped Paulus was relaying truth about the aged senator's accidental demise. Though impulsive, Paulus was not prone to violence and this senator was a special guest he'd been hoping would sponsor expansion plans.

"They can tell?"

Danisal said gravely: "Skilled doctors are said to be able to determine if people actually took in water as they died."

Paulus' be-ringed hand fluttered petulantly. "What am I going to do? This is terrible timing. Terentius was just telling all the rest of the believers about how he was going to donate a pile of money to improve the Hadiran temples! And then he up and died!" Paulus slammed his palm on the desk, then lifted a hand holding a sheaf of the papyrus. "Here's all the letters he's sent me about how much he longed to return for another ceremony!"

Danisal could sense where this was going, but knew he'd have to wait for the proper opening before guiding Paulus forward.

"I have all the proof of his intentions, but I won't be able to get the money. Not now. Unless..." He looked imploringly toward Danisal.

"Unless Mikas forges a letter," Danisal suggested. Mikas had smoothed an occasional challenge over with some carefully duplicated signatures. "But if anyone saw Senator Terentius die—"

"No one did," Paulus assured him. "All the believers were getting drunk on the vapors. And they probably won't notice he didn't come out with them until they recover. But if they find out he died in the chamber, then they'll know he didn't have time to write the letter. And they must know he went in with them. They saw him heading down."

"So he just fell, then, in the last little while?"

One of the two guards spoke. "I saw him go down. He was taking his time, and lingering at the back."

A lot of repeat believers did that, having learned that the longer they spent in the vapors the more profound were the visions they experienced.

"I held my breath and dashed in to check on him, but I think he was already dead. He hit his head on a rock. There's a bump on his head," the guard added helpfully.

Danisal had reasoned out an answer that felt satisfactory. "All right. Here's what we do. He's old. We'll say he complained about stomach pains and came back up, wrote his legal document for you, then tripped on the stairs. Blood would be better than a bruise, and if he hasn't been dead long it will look right when it flows."

"You're saying we should... make sure he looks worse?" the other guard asked. For a big, powerful man his face screwed easily into a boyish grimace.

"Brilliant!" Paulus clasped hands tightly. "I knew you'd come up with something. But do you think Mikas can fake the letter? It's really distinctive handwriting."

"If you have the letters he can copy from, Mikas can do it. He should keep it short, especially if we're to pass along that the senator had a stomachache."

Paulus nodded his head in admiration. "Absolutely right. What would I do without you?"

From another area of the compound a deep bell tolled. The seventh hour of the evening had arrived, which meant Danisal was not where he'd said he'd be. Paulus saw his troubled expression.

"Is something wrong?"

"I'm going to be late for a meeting," Danisal answered.

"A meeting?" Paulus asked. "With whom?"

"Some outsiders. There may be a lot of money involved, or it may just be a lure. I wasn't going to bother you with the details until I found out for sure."

"Well, get moving then," Paulus said with a nervous laugh. "The boys and I can take it from here. May the gods grant you luck!"

"I make my own luck," Danisal said, knowing it would make Paulus smile.

Paulus was in such a fine mood now that he chuckled.

Danisal bade his master farewell, glanced down at the little dead man on the floor who'd thought his bloodline one with the absurd crocodile-headed god of ancient Hadira, then hurried up the stairs and into the sunlight.

What to say to Paulus if this meeting proved legitimate? He could not imagine, but he would just have to trust to his ingenuity. He wasn't entirely sure what he'd do with freedom anyway, especially since Paulus had told him he'd be manumitting him in another year or so. But the Herrene who'd reached out to him was offering freedom to all the Gardens' Volani, and hinted that there'd be a lot of money in the offer. Paulus would at least want to hear about the numbers.

II

Antires continued his low-voiced complaints as they advanced along the cobbled street, heavily strewn with rushes. "What fool would place a Ceori region right next to the Herrenic one? Their lands are across the ocean from each other."

"A fool making a lot of money," Hanuvar offered.

Though they walked warm Oscanus lands under a late summer sun, they passed round Ceori huts common to the high mountains where a pretty, freckled blonde waited by an entrance in something approximating a Ceori dress, but with a lower neckline and much higher hemline, smiling as she beckoned all who passed to enter. A heavyset man shepherding a gaggle of children took her invitation. Within the structure they'd supposedly see the sorts of beds where Ceori slept, the kind of tools they used, and even some of the games their children played. So Antires discerned from the woman's patter.

He and Hanuvar had already passed a row of huts selling Ceori-approximated leather goods and foods, even the terrible Ceori beer, the smell of which had soaked into the trestle tables where men sat drinking and eating greasy sausages. Up ahead, beyond a wall of rounded timbers that looked more like a legion wall than an actual Ceori fence, a wooden gateway carved with images of long-legged hounds and foxes and ducks opened into an entirely different space, one of dark stone.

How could he have forgotten? "Nuvara," Antires said in disgust. "That's even worse." He had a hard time believing even Dervans would place two representational regions beside one another that were separated by a sea, a desert, and at least two large mountain ranges, let alone a vast gulf of culture.

"For someone fascinated with stagecraft you're awfully critical of its practice," Hanuvar said.

"But the Wonder Gardens are being advertised as the next best thing to travelling to these different lands," Antires protested. "They could at least try a little harder to get it right."

"They're trying just hard enough to make money."

"And these people don't know the difference," Antires groused. "This place is terrible."

In the lands of Nuvara they passed a pair of men garbed like warriors of ancient Derva, complete with old-fashioned feathered conical helms and square-sided breastplates shaped like muscular chests. They were part of the security troops patrolling the park, fit young men alert for troublemakers but lacking the hard eyes of the legion veterans.

Antires noted Hanuvar looking with some interest upon a square stone temple and its trapezoidal entrance; the painted blues and yellow diagonals along the sides of the building labeled it as a palace. Like his friend, Antires had heard Nuvaran lands described, but never walked them. He had seen their garb, however, and the handsome young men and pretty young women working shop fronts and gesturing visitors to enter faux dwellings wore the loose, bright clothing of that culture without the alteration given the Ceori woman's dress, perhaps because the warmth of their lands already ensured their garb was mostly ornamental. Men wore only short kilts and the breasts of the women were bared.

"The first time I passed through," Antires said, "most of the 'Nuvarans' were really Herrenes. Some of these are Ruminians. I expect a lot of Dervans can't tell the difference. So long as they're brown."

"Surely you're not suggesting the Dervans need to conquer another people to improve the Wonder Gardens?" Hanuvar asked.

"I'm just saying that they don't do these places any justice," Antires objected. He was about to explain further, but Hanuvar stilled him with a hand to his arm. Antires followed the direction of his friend's gaze.

They had entered a square where outdoor seating composed of curved benches of dark wood were arranged about oval tables. All were shielded from the sun by sagging fabric of bright colors. Dozens of men, women, and children sat about the tables eating from platters of steaming Nuvaran food—primarily bowls with a dark stew, or a large, spongey beige meal cake.

Antires would have been curious to try their fare, for there was a pleasant smoky scent with an unfamiliar spice in the air mixed in with what smelled a little like roast boar. But he followed the direction of Hanuvar's gaze to a trio of women sitting with a pair of children. Two of the women were younger, probably slaves from their simple dress. The children, though, he would have recognized anywhere, for they were the granddaughter and grandson of Ciprion. Sober nine-year-old Calvia munched on a deep brown pastry, intently eying a pair of tall, fierce-faced wooden statues of spear-bearing warriors beside their table. Young Marcus was talking with abandon to one of the slave girls, oblivious to brown sauce smeared across his chin.

The woman across from them sat with her back to Hanuvar, but Antires knew on the instant from the set of her shoulders and the dark hair arranged with unadorned clips that he looked upon Amelia, Ciprion's wife.

It wouldn't do to blunder into a reunion in the midst of a mission.

Hanuvar put his hand to his face and turned his head, striding quickly past a low fence where younger Dervan children were oohing and aahing over cages full of tiny gray rabbits and leopard kits.

Antires, scratching his beard to effectively shield his own features, followed. "I don't think she saw us," he said softly.

They took a shortcut through the large, central area where children were forbidden entry. Most of the visitors here were men, for most of the dwellings were themed brothels.

They hurried past a voluptuous woman in a short skirt and golden armor, holding a whip in the entryway to a round building painted starkly white. Antires only realized the building was supposed to be a Volani silver tower when she cracked the whip and called to them with an exaggerated Volani accent. "Are you two man enough to ride an Eltyr warrior?"

Hanuvar's jaw clenched and he looked away. He nearly walked

over a small dark woman, scarcely more than a child, who called out for men who dared to test their endurance with the Hadiran special.

"It's just make-believe," Antires assured him. "She didn't really sound Volani."

"I know," Hanuvar said. But he did not speak again until they left the adult section and moved on toward the Hadiran reserve, one of the largest areas in the park. "I've made up my mind," he said numbly. "You are right about this place."

III

Beyond some imported Hadiran plants, native Oscani trees and bushes grew in profusion, a narrow band of woods serving as one of the park's impediments to clear sight lines, the better for each distinctive area to feel like a remote region. Danisal slowed from his jog so that he wouldn't be out of breath when he reached the arranged meeting place.

He wasn't entirely sure what scheme his visitor was trying to run. He'd been mulling it over since the week the Herrene, Arjax, had reached out to him. Today the man was supposed to return with an actual Volani to explain matters, at which point Danisal imagined the con would become obvious.

He was half certain the Herrene wouldn't show, but he found the handsome bearded man waiting in the tiny employee eating area within the woodland. There with him was a Dervan of middle-age, his well-trimmed hair starting to gray. Danisal knew then there'd be no pretense about an actual Volani conversation, and was surprised to discover how disappointed he was.

"So," Danisal said. "You're back."

"I'm back," Arjax agreed, "and I've brought a colleague."

"Who's going to offer me a once in a lifetime opportunity, I suppose?" Danisal asked. "Do you expect to convince me because he's good-looking too? What's your game?"

"We're not here to play games with you," the stranger said. His Volani was flawless. "I've come to acquire the freedom of the Volani held by this enterprise, and I'm told you lead them. But I don't want to waste my time, or yours."

That was an exciting development. Danisal reminded himself not to get all swept up in the possibilities. It was a trick, just one he didn't yet understand. He kept his voice level, skeptical. His eyes were hooded. "Who are you?"

"You may call me Gisco. What part of Volanus are you from?"

Danisal studied the man's features, recognizing something familiar in them, and it came to him that someone from Volanus might well pass for Dervan if they cut their hair just so, and presented themselves with the right Dervan arrogance.

"I am from Sodanus," Danisal said slowly. To say that name was to give the town life in his memory, and he smelled the burning wood of the home he had shared with his husband and his sisters, and heard the terrible sound of his nephew's face being ground in by the Dervan shield.

"I knew Sodanus," Gisco said. "Some of the finest horses were sold there."

This was true, but he was distracted by the remembered odors of his family's blood, the anguished scream of his sister as she reached for her dying child, and the laughter of a Dervan soldier.

"How do I know you're not running some complicated con?" Danisal asked.

"He isn't," Arjax insisted.

Danisal snorted. "Some of the Gardens' best money is earned by people in elaborate pretense. Whether they want a whipping from a woman dressed as an Eltyr or to reenact Iskander leading a chain of Cerdian boys to bed, Dervan fantasies are all about game playing, with people as pieces. Maybe your fantasy's to see slaves crucified for rebellion."

"I offer freedom, not exploitation."

These seemed like words only a fool would believe. "We are as free as Volani can be in these times," Danisal said. "We eat well. We do as we like when we're off duty."

"Do you want to stay here, then, performing for the Dervans who can afford the price of admission?" Gisco asked. "Is that what you feel called to do?"

"What choice do we have? We put on some theatre and we get to see Dervans make fools of themselves. It's not a bad life."

"For a slave," Arjax said irritably. "I don't know why we're having to work so hard to offer you freedom. You said you wanted proof that real Volani were in charge. Here's one."

"Why does he want to help us? Out of the goodness of his heart? Please."

Arjax turned to the other. "I told you he was going to be like this."

"He has every right to be suspicious. He has more to lose than many." Gisco continued to speak to the Herrene though his gaze met Danisal's own. "He's relatively well off here. It's not as though he's chained to an oar. Or working to an early death in a silver mine. Or locked in a revenant dungeon. Or being raped every other day."

A chill touched Danisal's spine as each of these fates was offered, and such was the sound of Gisco's phrasing and the look in his eyes Danisal was almost convinced he himself had encountered people who'd experienced those traumas.

Gisco addressed him with slow gravity. "For everyone's safety there's little more we can tell you until you're away from here. We offer you transport to a place of security where you'll find other Volani, living free."

"Can you afford to free us?" Danisal asked. Against every inclination he was beginning to believe this offer might be real. "Paulus won't let us go cheaply."

"For the others, half again what Paulus paid, because your training's made them valuable to him. For you, three times that. I know how essential you are here."

"You've been poking around, then."

"Of course," Arjax interjected.

Danisal decided to maintain a hard front. He knew never to let them sense you wavering. "So you expect me to trust you," he continued. "What's to keep you from buying us, then taking us away to some awful fate?"

Gisco slowly shook his head. "I will sign the paperwork declaring you free the moment I pay. If you think Paulus can be convinced to sell."

"What paperwork?"

The Herrene dug around in his shoulder satchel. Danisal readied to run, but was soon confronted with nothing more than a sheaf of papers, which he accepted tentatively. "What's this?"

"Written letters of manumission for all seven of you. I will sign them before a witness, so that the moment I pay off your owner you will walk free."

Danisal found that difficult to believe, but he was no stranger to contracts, and scanning through the papers he quickly saw that they were absolutely in order, written with all of the appropriate legal phrasing.

What was more, the strangers had paperwork for each of the Volani here in the gardens, down to the name they had been sold under. Gisco and Arjax must have done some very careful digging to learn that particular information.

"What's to keep you from holding a counter stack of papers saying these are null and void?"

Arjax put his hand to his forehead and addressed his companion. "Will you believe this?" He then faced Danisal once more. "There isn't an endless supply of money, or time. You think you're the only people we're trying to free?"

He looked as though he meant to say more, but Gisco silenced him with a raised hand. "At some point you will simply have to trust us. I promise I will tell you much more once your freedom is won. Now, tell me. Will Paulus sell?"

"I... Maybe. He's always been pretty logical about business matters." Danisal felt almost as dazed as he had when he'd descended into the vapors to better understand what the believers experienced. His memory was alive with images of Sodanus, and his childhood, and the red rays shining along the stalks of ripe grain as the sun sank behind the great gray-black bulk of the Kalak mountain range.

His mind was at war. He wanted to trust in Paulus' affection and basic decency, and yet recognized that he couldn't thoroughly predict the man's reaction. Paulus was a showman, and he liked to project confidence, just as he liked to project magnanimity, for he believed good leaders possessed those traits. Danisal had encouraged all of those positive behaviors and he thought their growing prevalence in Paulus' conduct meant they had a strong foundation. Sometimes, though, he worried he was simply deluding himself, making the best of a situation that was in some ways a horror, especially when compared to his previous life.

He had twisted himself to improve what was left of life, not just for himself, but for his fellow slaves, and he would not hazard mentioning this offer to Paulus until he had consulted with them. "I'll talk with my friends," he said finally.

"How long will that take?" Arjax asked.

"It can be done this evening. If you... if you want to wait in the Gardens, we can find some place to meet all together. To sit and talk. Over in the Herrenic area," he added. "That's where the central offices are. Find a spot and I'll get word to you one way or another. And if I think Paulus is interested, I'll bring him with me."

Neither Gisco nor the Herrene seemed to like that very much. "We will wait in the Nuvaran area," Gisco said finally.

Arjax beckoned for the papers. Danisal found it difficult to relinquish them. Then he raised his hand in farewell, and watched as both men turned and melted into the woodland. After a brief moment he heard a brush rustle behind him.

Waiflike Arabeta slipped out of hiding, her eyes large and questioning.

"Well?" Danisal asked. "What did you think of them?"

"You won't believe me."

"What do you... of course I'll believe you. I asked you here because I trust your judgment."

She pointed the direction Gisco and the Herrene had gone. "That's Hanuvar."

Danisal snorted. "You're right. I don't believe you."

"No, that's him," Arabeta insisted, her eyes imploring. "I've heard him speak. He's shaved, and he's changed his haircut, but it's him. Not just the sound of his voice, but the way he uses his words. The way he moves. That's *him*. He's *alive*. And he's come for us." Arabeta's voice had grown more impassioned, though she still spoke quietly.

Danisal had a hard time taking that in. "Children's stories."

She shook her pretty head. "Sometimes stories are true. Sometimes good things happen, not just bad. You do know that when Hanuvar left Volanus, ships went with him?"

"Sure. People say that. People say lots of things. Everyone with sense says that Hanuvar drowned."

"And other people say he's been riding around Derva hunting down enemies and their children. I think that's him, and he's going to take us to New Volanus."

"You think that, or you want to think that? Why's he with a Herrene?"

"Why wouldn't he be? He sent the Herrene in to talk with you first; you wouldn't believe him, so he came himself."

"So you think it's real," Danisal mused.

"You're so used to pretending you've forgotten what real feels like." She offered a tentative smile. "I know you're just trying to watch out for us. But this time something wonderful is happening, Danisal."

He wanted to believe, too. But then everyone wanted to believe in something, as Paulus was fond of saying.

"I have to get back to the bakery stall," Arabeta said. "Sillela isn't going to be able to handle the crowds without me much longer."

"Hanuvar," Danisal repeated. He felt a sudden chill, but then shook his head. The man he'd spoken with hadn't been a spirit.

"The gods have sent him to us," Arabeta said reverently.

Danisal frowned. "There are only gods for deluded men and women who drink too deep. I'm going to talk to the others..."

"And talk to Paulus. He likes you. You can make this happen, and then we'll be free." She looked off into the distance. "For now, though, I've got to go."

She bade him farewell, and Danisal left a moment after. He was next scheduled to inspect the pulley system on the Herrenic ship swing. But that could wait. He had five Volani to share impossible news with.

IV

Hanuvar didn't expect an outright betrayal from Danisal, but he remained alert for the unexpected, and had sighted three separate egress routes from the Nuvaran section of the park should things turn.

He had no way of knowing which regions Amelia and her family had visited, but could reasonably assume that since they had passed through "Nuvara" their return was unlikely, which was the primary reason he'd selected the area as the rendezvous point, the secondary being to never let an adversary choose the ground. He couldn't be sure Danisal was an adversary, but he did not mean to permit any advantage.

He chose a table that lay in shadows of twin stern-faced Nuvaran statues. Any passersby would be much more interested in the statues than two ordinary-looking men nursing a meal. A further enticement was that he was curious to try the fragrant meat dish, which the cook told him was goat, seasoned with traditional Nuvaran spices. Antires admitted he'd been intrigued himself, and ordered the same meal. Soon both men were trading disappointed looks, for the first bite made clear the meat had been overcooked. It wasn't burned, just incredibly chewy.

Antires ate less than half of his portion, then wandered off to investigate the nearby shops while Hanuvar remained in the shadows, slowly sipping a watered wine. He tried to imagine how long it would take Danisal to consult with his people, starting with the one who'd been quietly observing them.

He liked that Danisal was cautious. One of Carthalo's agents had made discrete inquiries about his background prior to Antires' initial contact efforts, and the man seemed universally liked by his fellows. The youngest son of a family that owned a large stable, Danisal had grown up learning to manage both horses and people. Once in Dervan custody he had emphasized his managerial talents to the slave auctioneers, then skillfully advised his purchaser on additional personnel for the Wonder Gardens. He had protectively shepherded those same people ever since, lifting all under his aegis into positions of greater responsibility. In a little less than a year Danisal had risen to become one of the most valued slaves in the Gardens, owing not just to his organizational skills but to innovative ideas that had transformed the attraction from little more than a human zoo with tawdry elements into a lucrative endeavor attractive to a large swath of Dervan tourists.

From a terrible starting point Danisal had maneuvered himself and his people into a position of security and privilege. Hanuvar didn't just understand why Danisal was cautious of change, he respected the man and his accomplishments.

A graying Herrene stepped into the Nuvaran region, carrying a staff, no matter that he walked briskly. A boy of seven or eight was at his side, pointing in Hanuvar's general direction.

Neither seemed to have seen him, though. The boy stopped before the statues, sat down in the dirt, then took the drawing slate the man offered him and set to work with charcoal. The Herrene looked on thoughtfully.

Hanuvar knew them both, though he had not been introduced. The first was Silenus, tutor to the grandchildren of Ciprion and Amelia. The child, a little younger than Calvia, was almost surely the tutor's son Delmar, whom Ciprion had described as having artistic gifts.

Antires stepped out of a false Nuvaran temple and advanced to converse with the Herrene. He too had been in Ciprion's burning home, but had apparently failed to note the child or the tutor amidst the chaos, for neither seemed to recognize the other. Hanuvar overheard Antires questioning Silenus about his home city. Among many Herrenes the next point would be favorite playwrights or poets, and the conversation predictably turned there after only a few moments.

Hanuvar surreptitiously leaned further into the shadow. Perhaps only the tutor and the boy were here, and the rest of Amelia's entourage had seen enough of the area.

The boy's focus intrigued him, for he seriously applied himself to the drawing. Had Hanuvar not wished to remain hidden he would have risen and stepped around to observe his work.

Other visitors passed in and out through the Nuvaran region, and many stopped to purchase food or drink. Young ladies perused the jewelry and fabric and eyed the distinctive red-gold pottery. Some wandered over to the craft booth where a handful of actual mahogany skin-toned Nuvarans shaped clay. Young people of both sexes admired the beautiful people dressed in Nuvaran clothing. So heavy was the traffic that Hanuvar almost missed the significance of the girl who skipped in as part of one group.

He identified her as Calvia shortly before she stopped at the statues. She conferred with the young artist, said something to Silenus, then turned to take in her surroundings.

She was tall for her age, with light brown hair worn in tight braids, a small pointed chin, and honey-colored eyes that seemed to miss nothing at all. Most children could be counted upon to be lost in their own world, but Calvia was atypical. She spotted Hanuvar and made her way toward him in the same instant he moved to shield his face with his hand.

In moments she stood at Hanuvar's table. "Hello, sir," she said. "I do believe we've met. You are a friend to my grandfather."[18]

Her voice was soft but formal and precise. And her gaze was both guileless and full of tremendous curiosity.

"Yes," Hanuvar answered. "I am. Are you enjoying your visit here?"

"Yes. My tutor says some of the elements in each display are quite accurate, although many of the actors in this region are not actual Nuvarans."

"I believe that's true." Hanuvar had observed the arrival of one of the young women he'd assumed to be a slave brought to help mind the children, now searching the crowd nervously. A little ways behind her was the other slave girl, Ciprion's grandson, and Amelia herself. So much for avoiding that particular encounter. "Is Delmar interested in Nuvaran depictions?"

"Yes. He remarked that the exaggeration around the eyes conveyed personality despite the stiffness of the forms," Calvia said. "We are writing a book about trees and are quite close to completion, although we are thinking about adding a chapter devoted to interesting statues."

"Perhaps that should be a different book," Hanuvar suggested.

"That is certainly more conventional," Calvia agreed. She looked up with Hanuvar to observe Amelia's approach. "Hello, Grandmother. I was just chatting with Grandfather's friend about the book Delmar and I are writing."

Amelia's cheeks were colored from the sun. It would have been obvious to many that she had wealth, for she was a handsome, well-cared-for woman of middle years travelling with a small entourage of slaves, but any judging from her simple dress and hairstyle might have guessed her nothing more than a prosperous merchant's wife. This was deliberate, for Amelia did not care to be fussed over.

"It sounds quite an undertaking," Hanuvar said to Calvia. "I wish you success with it."

---

[18] Calvia was not at all aware of Hanuvar's true identity, but she had observed the uncommon regard with which her grandfather had spoken to him the previous year when her brother had been abducted, and deduced that he had been instrumental in her brother's safe recovery. More recently she had glimpsed him at her grandfather's side when the villa she was visiting caught fire. She reported that it seemed her grandfather's friend appeared only when her family most needed assistance, almost as though he were a guardian spirit, and thus she wished to speak with him and take his measure. —*Silenus*

"That's kind of you to say, sir."

Amelia spoke to her fondly. "Calvia, why don't you run along. I'm going to visit with your grandfather's friend now."

"Yes, Grandmother. I hope you enjoy the rest of your day, sir."

"Likewise."

"Thank you ever so much."

Amelia sat down not across from Hanuvar, but beside him, probably so that she might better watch the children and her servants.

Antires had noted her arrival and raised a hand in greeting, but remained in earnest conversation with the tutor. Calvia rejoined Delmar and turned to examine another Nuvaran statue.

Amelia fanned herself. Hanuvar poured from the small jug of wine into Antires' empty cup and passed it to her.

"Thank you. Do you know, not so long ago, I would have been horrified to learn you were anywhere near my granddaughter."

"I never made war on children."

"I don't suppose you did but it affected them nonetheless." Amelia sipped.

"That is sadly true. I'm glad that no one in your household was harmed in that fire."

She raised her hand to forestall further comment from him. "There's no need for apology. I know it's not something you wished, and we're grateful to you for your help fighting it." She turned to watch the children. "I'm not sure where Calvia gets all of her curiosity. Cornelia's always liked the outdoors, but with her it was horses and flowers. She certainly didn't sound like Calvia, and Calvia's father isn't much of a scholar either."

"I like her. She's a smart young lady."

"That she is. I have to confess I'm a little surprised to see you here. And in the Nuvara section, of all places." She scanned the nearby shops while she drank. "I just saw Hanuvar, you know. Every day about this time he 'escapes' and is pursued through the Volanus region by men in legionary costumes."

"What did he look like?"

Amelia lifted a hand over her head. "He was a tall hairy fellow with an eyepatch. He pretended to chase some children until the troopers turned up."

"It's nice to hear the Dervans remember Hanuvar so accurately."

Amelia smiled crookedly and finished another drink. "I was honestly worried they might have someone dressed as my husband come out and tackle him." She set the cup down. "The spice taste in this wine keeps building the more I drink."

Hanuvar nodded.

"You're here on one of your missions, aren't you?"

"Yes."

"I should go then, shouldn't I. Am I interfering?"

"I don't believe so. But there's always an element of risk to these things, and it's probably better for you if you're not involved."

She leaned toward him. "Now you have me intrigued, but I'll save my questions. Perhaps you can tell me later." She started to rise. "Is this a dangerous mission?"

"It will hopefully involve only an exchange of money. Which is honestly refreshing," Hanuvar admitted.

"Good luck with it."

"Thank you. Enjoy the rest of your evening."

She departed to where the little boy was observing a dancer whirl large wooden hoops around her neck and arms.

V

Paulus had listened expressionlessly to Danisal's account of his meeting with Arjax and the man who might be Hanuvar. Danisal hadn't mentioned Arabeta's supposition, only Gisco's large suggested price.

"That's a very generous offer," Paulus said. "But, I mean... what would I do without you? Would you... would you still want to work with me?"

"Of course!" Danisal said. The two sat alone, so he patted Paulus' hand reassuringly.

Paulus remained troubled. "The whole thing is strange. Why only Volani? Why give you your freedom? Do you think..." His eyes were suddenly hard. "Freedmen can testify. No one believes a slave in court."

Danisal almost asked why anyone would want to have him in

court, but stilled his tongue. To the left of where he sat a dead senator's body had recently been lying.

Paulus shook his head and rapped the surface of his desk. "It's a trick. I'm sure of it. Montius set this all up to try to ruin what I've built here."

"Oh, I really don't think—"

"Don't you? You're really smart, Danisal. Are you just not thinking about this because it's something you want? You know it's strange, don't you?"

"It is," Danisal admitted. Almost he said something about Hanuvar, but if this really were Hanuvar, might Paulus try to profit off that knowledge?

Paulus was thinking out loud. "Suppose you're Montius and you've heard about two or three of the accidents we've had here, and the donations left us. Like the one today."

Danisal hadn't needed that clarification, but did not interrupt to point that out. He was more troubled by Paulus' mention of accidents, plural, as though there had been more. Before he could think how to inquire, Paulus continued his speculative ranting.

"You want to maybe claw some of that money toward you, so you need proof. Who better than you, my most trusted slave? And your Volani are intimately involved in a lot of your management. They've seen things, like Mikas. It could even be some rival trying to buy you away from me and build something of their own to put me out of business!" Paulus could work himself up into great agitated furies. "Where did you say you were supposed to meet these people again?" he asked. "In the Nuvaran area?"

"Yes."

"I want to see them."

Paulus proved to be speaking literally, for the park owner felt so apprehensive he wished to observe from a distance. They relocated to look out from the second floor of the faux Nuvaran palace, in a cubicle in the upper floor designed as a spy hole for their security people. It had been Danisal's contention that folk must be safer here even than on public streets if the Wonder Gardens were to attract visitors, and that meant having guards both on patrol and watching unobtrusively.

Spotting the Herrene proved simple enough; he was talking

animatedly with a countryman. The man who might be Hanuvar, though, was almost invisible in the evening shadow, and Danisal had to point him out to Paulus.

"Him? Who's the woman beside him?"

"I didn't see her earlier," Danisal admitted.

Stanos, Paulus' sturdy chief of security, waited just behind them. "Who's she?" Paulus asked him. "Did those two come in with her?"

"My people didn't pay particular attention to those two when they paid their entrance fees." Stanos sounded pleased with himself, as though he was about to convey important details. "But one of my people recognized the woman. She came with a bevy of slaves and her grandchildren, but not the two men. She is Amelia, the wife of Ciprion."

"Ciprion?" Paulus repeated, so loudly that he glanced out the spyhole to make sure he hadn't been overheard. "*The* Ciprion?" he asked more softly.

"Yes."

Paulus scoffed and jabbed a finger at the wall while starting at Danisal. "And there your stranger is sitting next to her. Tell me why any Volani would be associating with the wife of the man who defeated them!"

Danisal's face flushed with embarrassment. "I don't know."

"They wouldn't," Paulus said waspishly, and paced off toward the other wall. "This is some kind of trick. Just like I said. I can see it now. Ciprion's gotten suspicious of what I'm doing and is going to use the Volani as witnesses. I bet he wants to buy up the Gardens! They've so much potential for making even more money!" He wrung his hands. "Was he asking questions about us, and what we're doing?"

"Not a one," Danisal said. "The discussion was entirely about buying our freedom."

Stanos stepped to the spyhole.

Paulus mulled over Danisal's information before deciding what it meant. "This man's sticking with his cover story to win you over. He won't start prying for details until you're free. And I use that term loosely. He'll find a way to keep you under his control. We're going to have to talk to them."

Stanos turned to address Paulus. "The woman's leaving, sir." A freeborn man, he did not have to address his employer as master.

Paulus cursed nervously. "I want to talk to her. Send someone to pick her up... but nothing, uh, alarming. Tell her she's been singled out for a special meal or prize or something and then I'll talk to her. Distract the kids and slaves with some treats. Bring her to me in the downstairs office."

Stanos assured him he would and hurried off.

"I think you should slow down," Danisal advised. "You don't want to antagonize the wife of a powerful senator." Ciprion was in a whole different league than Terentius—he was not only connected at the highest levels he was practically revered by some Dervans as a national treasure. Was Paulus blind to the danger here?

"I'm just going to politely chat with her."

Danisal worked to dissuade him but Paulus proved obstinate. He had just settled himself behind the desk in the little ground floor office when the door opened. Amelia was hustled in by a muscular Ruminian girl.

"The slaves and children are all delighted," Stanos reported as he closed the door. "The woman was too until we guided her further off."

Amelia advanced to stand before Paulus and addressed him with icy disdain. "You will release me at once."

"We're just having a friendly conversation," Paulus said. "A man has come to me claiming to wish to purchase the freedom of Volani. I know he's an agent of yours. What does Ciprion want with my people?"

"My husband has no interest in your people."

Paulus laughed. "How stupid do you think I am?"

"I don't even know who you are," Amelia said. "And I don't particularly care. But I can tell you that my husband won't like you taking this demanding tone with his wife."

"You have nothing to fear from me," Paulus assured her. "I'm just trying to get to the truth." Danisal thought his insincerity was manifest to all, and shook his head quickly, trying to warn him to change course. Paulus should have known that threatening Ciprion's wife even covertly was a terrible idea.

But Paulus ignored him. "You clearly know this man Gisco well. What were you talking about?"

Amelia frowned. "He is a family friend. He sometimes buys slaves as part of his business."

"For whom? Himself? There is something strange to your story, Lady Amelia."

"You are the only one acting strange. Things will not go well for you if you threaten me or that man. And if either of us is harmed," she added with chill certainty, "my husband will take this place apart, brick by brick, and throw you in a prison so deep you'll never see the sun, if you survive the process."

A wiser man would have understood the conviction in her voice. Paulus merely chuckled indulgently. "So he is important to Ciprion. He's one of his agents, isn't he?"

"My husband would find that funny. He is no employee of ours. I assure you."

Paulus sighed. He nodded to the guard. "Take her away. Give her some of the tea, show her the Gardens. I need to speak to the man alone."

"You will release me, at once," Amelia commanded.

"You'll be unharmed," Paulus said with an unctuous smile. "Take her away."

She held herself stiffly as the two guards led her off.

"Paulus," Danisal said. "I don't think—"

"Danisal, go get the man. Don't let him know anything's wrong. Tell him I want to speak with him. Oh, and bring the guards in here. Four of them," he added. "He doesn't look that big, but . . . I don't want any trouble."

Danisal bowed before Paulus could second-guess himself again. He found himself leaving almost against his will, as though he were a child's wheeled horse pushed into motion across the tiles and unable to stop of its own volition. No good would come from anything Paulus had just done. And the mention of the tea used to make the believers sluggish and suggestible was ominous.

And yet, the next thing he knew, he was stepping out of the faux palace and making his way through a small crowd. He needed time to stop and think, and he didn't have it.

The Nuvaran area was never as busy in the evening, when many of the visitors liked to eat more familiar food. The man who'd identified himself as Gisco somehow sensed his approach and looked up at him. He was sitting now with Arjax. When Danisal appeared before them, both started to rise. Knowing Paulus only wanted Gisco and not the Herrene, Danisal shook his head. "Only him. We'll be back in a few moments."

The man rose, waved off the Herrene as though he felt comfortable talking with Danisal alone, then moved with assurance to follow. Watching him, Danisal's anxiety grew even more pronounced. This fellow felt familiar. He had spoken so easily in Volani. But then he'd been sitting with Ciprion's wife, hadn't he? And Ciprion was purportedly a very clever man—wouldn't he find someone to put his opponents at ease, before he struck? Someone fluent in Volani?

Explaining that Paulus was interested in his offer and had cancelled an appointment to talk things over, he waved Gisco to his side as they entered a shop that led to the office.

"Did you talk to your people?" Gisco asked. He scanned the interior as they moved through and around a pair of teenaged boys studying a display of black Nuvaran spear points.

"I did." Danisal held open a door labeled in three languages with expressions meaning no entry. Gisco gestured for him to precede, and Danisal did so.

"And what did they say?"

Danisal didn't answer until the door had shut. He laughed a little. A lantern hung in the dark hall lit their way toward two separate stairwells and the door to the office. He pitched his voice low. "They were all for accepting."

He opened the door and gestured for Ciprion's agent to enter. Once again Gisco insisted Danisal precede him.

He saw two guards behind Paulus, smiling nervously from behind the desk. Not until the stranger was further in did the two additional guards trot down the stairs and enter, closing the door behind them.

Gisco saw then he was cornered and advanced to the center of the room, eyes on Paulus.

Danisal made his way around the edge of the room to stand at his employer's right hand.

"I don't want you nervous," Paulus said. "But there are things that just don't add up for me. And before we come to any kind of agreement there are questions that have to be asked."

"Ask them."

"Why were you sitting with the wife of Ciprion?"

"She is a friend."

"So you, who want to buy Volani, are friends with the man who defeated them? Who are you, and what do you really want?"

Gisco answered easily. "My employer likes what you're doing here. He wants to build something similar, but private, just focused on the Volani. He doesn't intend to compete with you, since his gardens won't be open to the public. He understandably wants genuine Volani to advise him. I know you've valued them, but you don't seem to specifically need them now yourself."

He sounded so reasonable that Danisal almost believed him himself.

Paulus looked uncertain for a long moment, then laughed. "I don't buy it. I truly abhor violence, but I am capable of it."

Gisco didn't look worried, merely disappointed, as though Paulus were a child who'd failed to understand an important lesson. "I don't think you realize the mistake you're making."

His statement gave Paulus honest pause. "Mistake?"

"This deal could make you quite rich." Gisco reached slowly for his belt pouch and, while the guards watched carefully, removed a flattened green gem that threw back torchlight.

Paulus motioned Danisal to take it. Danisal kept his gaze downcast until he was directly in front of Gisco, and then he searched his face. For a brief moment their eyes locked and Danisal saw the man's utter conviction, entirely at odds with the morass of confusion typical of Paulus.

Danisal looked down at the stone until he walked it to Paulus, who then held it up to the light.

Paulus' face shone with avarice. Visibly mastering himself, he slowly closed his hand over the stone. "There are more like these?"

"Yes. I can give you three, beyond the money I've already promised."

Paulus gulped. He didn't know what to do. His pleading eyes sought Danisal.

Unfortunately, Danisal wasn't sure what to do either, for he had begun to suspect Gisco had been telling the truth. He had presented a cover story to Paulus that sounded reasonable, but he had meant every word he'd said earlier and Arabeta might even be right about his real identity. It still didn't make sense that Hanuvar would know

Amelia, though, did it? But then weren't Amelia's husband and Hanuvar supposed to respect one another? Might they actually be friends?

Hanuvar, if that's who he truly was, looked boldly at Danisal, as if daring him to understand the truth.

"I need to think," Paulus said, and pointed at the guards. "Take him to the holding area." He addressed his prisoner. "I'll consider this and come talk to you."

"Don't think too long." The man who might be Hanuvar allowed the guards to approach, but made clear by his narrowed eyes that they'd best not touch him. They refrained, though they stepped close. He allowed himself to be marched away.

Then it was just Danisal and Paulus, eying the gemstone.

Danisal spoke with quiet respect. "I think you should take the deal, and forget whatever you think you're going to do about Ciprion's wife."

Paulus smiled indulgently. "You don't need to worry about any of that." His hand closed over the gem and he seemed to weigh it in his hand. "I'm going to take care of everything."

Danisal sucked in a breath. "You asked me to tell you when you're being too risky, remember? Tell me what you're planning to do with Ciprion's wife. Why are you giving her the tea you give the believers?"

"She's going to have a sad accident is all, over by the ponds."

He'd lost his mind. "You're going to drown her? You can't do that!"

"It will all make sense soon."

"I thought you didn't want attention! You don't think that will bring you some?"

"I can make it work. And you can help me."

"And what about that man?" Danisal still couldn't quite manage to say his name.

"I think he and I will come to an arrangement to get the rest of the gemstones." Paulus smiled and stood. "I can see you're confused. Someone's just trying to take advantage of you, again. To trick you, again. I'm looking out for you, and the money we'll get from this little venture will really help us build our future."

"What if they're telling the truth, and acting against those two will destroy everything we've built?"

Paulus lifted the emerald. "I'll think about it."

Danisal knew that his employer had fixed upon a terrible course. "Paulus, listen—remember when you insisted it would enhance the realism to let the crocodiles roam around the Hadiran area so long as we kept them well fed? You asked me to tell you if—"

"Shut it!" Paulus backhanded him across the face.

The blow caught him completely off guard. It sent Danisal stumbling into the wall. His cheek stung, but was still not as great an injury as his surprise.

"Look what you made me do!" Paulus cried. "I'm the master, you're the slave, and I am not going to sell you! Do you get that?"

"Yes."

"Yes what?"

"Yes. Master," Danisal said softly.

Paulus' mood cooled on the instant and his voice grew wheedling. "You have to be reminded who's in charge sometimes. We need this money, don't you see? We can keep expanding. We can add more areas. And I'll let you design them."

"Yes, Master."

His answer set Paulus into a whole new rage. "Just get out! I need to think!"

Danisal left, rubbing his cheek. Paulus was going to kill Amelia. He was probably going to kill Hanuvar, too, after he tried to get more money out of him. Danisal had scoffed so often at the believers and their desperate search for something more important than themselves he hadn't realized how he'd done the same thing himself.

The old hillside over which the Wonder Gardens were built was layered with caverns. One run of them was directly connected to the fissures from which the vapor wafted, but others had long since been used for storage, and so previous owners of the property had built steps into the caves and fitted them with sconces and even occasional doors. One had kept guard dogs. Over a narrow cul-de-sac, a door constructed from iron bars had been attached, to keep the long-vanished guard animals in, and Paulus had occasionally employed the place as a disciplinary tool, always saying how much he regretted its use.

When Danisal arrived at the cell after a few minutes of labored running, he expected to find at least one man on guard, and he expected to lie to him about some orders from Paulus. What he found instead was Hanuvar spinning to face him after locking the door in place.

The older man was alert and unblinking. He held no weapon, but the threat inherent in him was frightening.

Seeing that Danisal was alone and out of breath he relaxed only slightly.

"Where are the guards?" Danisal said.

Hanuvar pointed to the cell.

Danisal could just make out one motionless sandaled foot in the darkness.

"Are they dead?"

"No."

"What happened?"

"We disagreed about who belonged in the cell. Where's Paulus?"

"Still staring at your jewel, I'd bet," Danisal said, a little stunned by Hanuvar's simplified explanation. "I came to get you out."

Hanuvar shifted to Volani. "So you're with me? Or are you with him?"

"With you."

"Where's Lady Amelia?" Hanuvar asked impatiently.

"That's another reason I came," Danisal said. "Paulus means to kill her."

Hanuvar's answer was a growl. "Where?"

"He's giving her a sleeping draught, so he can drown her."

"Where?" he repeated with more emphasis.

"I can show you—"

"You'd best be ready to run again."

VI

Antires had noted Hanuvar's signal to remain vigilant. He already had been, although he wondered if he ever would be as sensitive to details as Hanuvar, even after taking careful note of his friend's actions for a year or more. By this time of the evening he was frequently writing down his thoughts, or organizing previous drafts of their adventures in the code he'd agreed to use, but instead he watched for suspicious activity, particularly groups of three or more who might be gathering to maneuver from behind. He could still see through the restaurant doorway to where Silenus and Amelia's slaves sat with the children, all enjoying honey cakes and mixed fruit juices. That they had been singled out for special treatment had not struck Antires as particularly concerning, for powerful patricians and their relatives were often given honors if they were recognized, in the hope that those bestowing gifts would be remembered when favors were needed.

But Hanuvar had not cared to see Amelia invited away, remarking that someone could have been watching the two of them talk.

"No one," Antires countered, "would antagonize the wife of Ciprion."

Hanuvar had allowed that no one with any sense would do that, then reminded Antires how many stupid people they'd encountered over the course of their travels.

Antires still mulled that over as he watched the feast underway. He guessed he'd be welcomed to join if he were to walk across the lane, but more and more he looked off toward where Hanuvar had gone. Perhaps being alert meant having a better understanding of what was happening, but right now he had none.

He'd observed Danisal leading Hanuvar into the two-storied "palace" housing the Nuvaran artifacts, and recalled seeing a closed door there beside a sign saying no one was permitted entry. Given that he'd seen no other exit from the building, he was certain Hanuvar had been led beyond it.

Though he had complete faith in Hanuvar to endure any number of challenges, he also knew his friend had been in tight spots before, and as time plodded on he began to grow concerned that this might be one of them.

He eased off the bench and headed into the faux palace. A trio of adolescents were talking to the pretty pair of girls behind the counter displaying Nuvaran charms. The young people had eyes only for one another. He headed for the door in the wall as though he had every right to open it, then did so and passed through into a hallway lit by lanterns. One direction dead-ended in a narrow stair going up with another going down. Antires went the opposite direction, which stopped at a door set in the gray stone. He listened, heard what sounded like someone chuckling, and opened it.

Before him was a small office, complete with desk and chair, a cupboard, and a big wax board that looked like a duty roster, judging by names stenciled in it. A single window looked out on an overgrown garden area he'd seen from outside, around a corner of the "palace."

Seated behind the desk was a handsome man growing jowly with easy living. Rings gleamed on every finger, and they were the gold ones that stepped-up merchants liked to wear in demonstration of their wealth, as though stylish haircuts and fine clothes weren't signifier enough.

The man stilled at the sight of Antires. One of his hands was outstretched toward the large candle in the holder on the desk. He held a small, flattened emerald between thumb and forefinger and had apparently been enjoying the play of light through the stone.

Antires supposed it could have been someone else's emerald, but he knew it for the kind that Hanuvar carried with him, one from a dwindling stock pried from the tomb of his ancestors.

He closed the door behind him and advanced, for he had learned that much from Hanuvar—seize the initiative.

The stranger pulled the gem toward himself protectively. "Who are you? Get out. You don't belong here."

"Where did you get that gem?" Antires didn't slow until he stood before the desk.

"I've had it for a long time. You're trespassing."

It was just possible that Hanuvar had worked out an arrangement, but Hanuvar had taught Antires to trust his instincts, and every one of his senses screamed that this man was not to be trusted; he was nervous, and a poor liar. "Where are Gisco and the Lady Amelia?" he asked.

"There's nothing wrong with them," the man said quickly. "They'll be fine, and be out in just a bit."

He hadn't asked if anything was wrong with them, just where they were. He'd heard enough. When he stepped around the desk the man stood, fumbling to unbutton a flap at his side that looped over a knife hilt. Antires surprised himself by how quickly he acted. A single punch to the fellow's soft gut doubled him over. He couldn't quite bring himself to slam the man's head against the desk, as he expected Hanuvar would have done, but he did push him back into the wax duty roster in its frame, rattling it, then, when the man was still off balance and opening his mouth, Antires drew his own knife and twisted one of the fellow's arms behind his back.

"The emerald's mine," the man said. "Gisco gave it to me."

"That's nice," Antires said. "But I have some other questions. And I expect you to answer quickly."

VII

The clouds glowed dully with the moon's light, as though a great lamp hung behind a veil in the sky. It seemed almost as though the moon were trebled in size.

Far beneath it, Danisal kept up with Hanuvar, though he was breathing heavily by the time they reached a walled-off garden beyond the Hadiran region. Set on the side of a gently sloping hill, it held a mix of flowering and fruit trees and well-shaped bushes, spread among ornamental ponds. Evening was darkening on toward night, but their objective was made simple by someone holding a lantern about halfway down the gentle slope. Hanuvar accelerated into a sprint toward a trio of figures who appeared to be dancing along the side of one of the pools.

It was not a dance, though. Two of the people struggled to push the third forward by the light of lantern borne by a fourth.

Hanuvar was only a few hundred feet out when the two succeeded in shoving the other into the water, where she landed with a splash and a feminine cry of surprise.

The lantern bearer turned at the sound of Hanuvar's approach.

Danisal still labored to catch up. The few remaining doubts he'd held about the identity of the man he followed vanished in the coming moments as Hanuvar rushed straight on for the guards.

He drove a knife through the lantern bearer's belly, pushing the man away as he crumpled. Hanuvar then sprang at the closer of the two at the pool side; so fast had he acted that the other, slim Stanos, still watched the progress of Amelia's drowning.

The guard slung a sap weighted with sand at Hanuvar's head. He ducked and drove his knife into the man's chest, then plunged it with terrible speed again and again.

Danisal neared at last, smelling blood and bile as he sucked air into his laboring lungs. He was acutely aware that the splashes out in the pool had grown feeble, to be expected from someone both drugged and knocked senseless. Time was scarce.

Stanos, alert at last, bore in with a professional sword thrust that Hanuvar slid back from.

Danisal didn't wait to see how the battle resolved. Still panting, he reached the stone lip framing the rectangular pool and kicked off his sandals. Bright though the moon was he saw no way to judge the depth, but he spotted a mass of rags floating about six feet out from the side and threw himself at it.

He hit the water and dropped, plunging until he touched bottom. He pushed up, gasping, discovering that when he stood at full height the water reached to his lips. He kicked forward through the water, arriving at the wet cloth and seeking quickly through it for something human until his fingers closed on an arm. He planted himself, discovered Amelia's head, and raised it above the level of the water.

That didn't seem to help anything. She didn't move.

Another splash sounded from behind him and he discovered Hanuvar in the pool. Together the two men guided Amelia to the side, supporting her head above the water. Hanuvar then vaulted up to the edge and Danisal helped lift her to safety.

She wasn't breathing.

VIII

Hanuvar crouched beside Amelia while Danisal struggled to pull himself from the pool, wheezing heavily.

While Hanuvar hadn't spent the long years at sea typical of his people, his culture had roved the waves since time immemorial and had long since learned how to help those who'd breathed in water. He turned Amelia over, pressed her back again and again, moving her arms over her head and back down, and was rewarded after the fifth press with a light cough. After more presses, Amelia moved feebly and water rolled from her mouth.

Finally she pushed up on her hands, her dark hair straggling down the sides of her face, and vomited.

"Praise be to Melquan,"[19] Danisal muttered.

Amelia gagged again and pushed away, her arms shaking. Hanuvar helped her to sit upright. Part of her vomit had dripped down the front of her wet dress. Her dark hair streamed down raggedly across her forehead and shoulders.

"I must look terrible." Her raspy voice was incredibly soft.

"No, you're radiant in the twilight," he said, and she laughed so hard that she launched into another coughing fit and expelled more water.

He put a hand to her shoulder. He feared she might overbalance and fall back in.

"Is this how things always work out?" she said, voice still soft. "Something goes awry and you have to rush in and fix it?"

"Often. But sometimes I can't get there in time." He didn't want to reflect on how close he'd come to failing. Or how much harm she'd come to simply because she sat next to him at a park. "If Danisal hadn't helped, I'm not sure you'd have made it. Come on. Let's get you away from the side. How's your balance? Did they hit you in the head?"

"Yes—" She reached up to feel the back of her skull and winced. She tottered as he helped her upright, and she coughed out more water. "Gods, but I feel awful."

"Is your vision clear?"

"I think so."

"How well can you walk?"

"Not well," she said. "My head still feels fuzzy, but that dip seems to have cleared things a bit." She only now seemed to become aware of Danisal, still breathing heavily to the side. "Who's this fellow? Wasn't he in the room with that odious man?"

"This is Danisal. He jumped in to save you," he explained, then added, "he's on our side." Hanuvar guided her by the elbow past the bodies. "You might not want to look there."

But she did, and sucked in a breath. "Sweet Jovren. Did you kill them all?"

"I did." He thought at first she objected, and then she made herself clear.

---

[19] The Volani lord of strength, stamina, and some say the protector of the innocent, but regardless, one who safeguards life. —*Silenus*

"By yourself?"

"You were drowning. There wasn't time to take prisoners."

"I'm not criticizing. I'm just impressed. And grateful. Have I thanked you yet?"

"You managed not to vomit on me, which I appreciate."

She patted his arm. "Thank you." And then her eyebrows shot up in alarm. "The children! By the gods... I can't believe I forgot the children!"

Footsteps raced toward them and a figure ran out of the gloom. A pair of men trailed after, calling for the interloper to stop.

Hanuvar guided Amelia further away.

Antires reached them, looking over his shoulder as two helmeted figures ran up, shouting that he had to clear out, and that this was a special guest area. So far the darkness had obscured that bodies lay behind them, and the guards must not have overheard the earlier commotion.

Danisal interposed himself. "These people have my permission to be here."

The two pursuers resolved themselves into two of the guards costumed in ancient Dervan armor. While they seemed deferential to Danisal, who held authority in the park despite his social status, they were curious about why he was sodden. Some explaining in a reassuring tone was undertaken.

Antires stopped before Hanuvar and Amelia, speaking as he recovered his breath. "Praise the gods you're all right."

"Thanks go to Decius," Amelia said.

"What are you doing here?" Hanuvar asked.

"I got to worrying about you." Antires shook his head in chagrin. "But you had things in hand, as usual."

"Barely. How did you find us?"

"I went into the Nuvaran palace, looking for you, and found a nervous man staring at one of your emeralds. First he claimed never to have seen you, then to have taken you for questioning." He continued with obvious pride, "I got the truth out of him. And your emerald."

Hanuvar laughed. "Nicely done."

Danisal rejoined them as the guards headed away.

"Where are my grandchildren and little Delmar?" Amelia's voice was tense with apprehension.

"The last I saw, they were still eating free desserts the park offered them," Antires answered. "Silenus and your family slaves were minding them."

Hanuvar felt Amelia let out a long breath in relief. "Where's Paulus?" he asked.

"I tied him up in a storage room. Some of that training you've shown me has paid off," Antires continued, still clearly excited. "He must have sent most of his guards with you." He tipped his head the direction his two pursuers had gone. "Because that pair didn't start chasing me until they saw me running past the Hadiran lodges."

Hanuvar nodded his approval, and Antires smiled.

Amelia squeezed his arm. "Well then, all has worked out. You're going to take me back to my family, and while you round up your people and get them out of the park, I'm going to send word to the local legionaries, and then I'm going to see that strange man arrested for trying to kill me."

"There are some freedmen working for him who can testify to other crimes, I'm sure," Danisal said. "The ones he thought you were going to uncover." He turned to Hanuvar. "You really are here just to liberate us, aren't you? And you're Hanuvar? Like one of my friends said?"

Hanuvar didn't want it to be said he had ever identified himself in front of Amelia. "We're here to set you free," he confirmed.

"It's like a play," Antires mused. "The park's owner brought his own end by calling attention to his fears."

"I don't recall plays making me so wet," Amelia said testily.

Hanuvar leaned toward her and spoke softly, as if unaware Antires could hear. "He thinks everything's like a play."

"'I could live long without the maunderings of poets, playwrights, and philosophers,'" Antires said, quoting Etipholes.

"It's not poets who are bothering me today," Amelia responded. "It's grasping madmen and their minions. But enough talk. You need to take me to somewhere less horrifying. Decius, the next time I see you out in public I'm going to look the other way."

"I wouldn't blame you for that at all," said Hanuvar.

※ ※ ※

You may be interested to know that Paulus' arrest and conviction actually drew more visitors to the Wonder Gardens, and that owing to

Danisal's innovations the place remained profitable for almost a decade, until nearly everyone who could afford them had attended a time or two. The year it finally folded, it was a sad ghost of itself, having fallen into disrepair. Perhaps if its new managers had understood that they needed to invent new attractions, or had at least practiced upkeep on the existing ones, it might have endured a little longer despite its flaws.

When Hanuvar and I returned with these Volani slaves we had achieved nearly all that we had set out to do in the Oscanus region. The last group of children arrived from Amelia's villa, and once we had arranged for the release of a few slaves housed in more pleasant circumstances, and Carthalo secured the freedom of the last individuals to the far south, we would be on our way to Selanto, and the north, and from there we would depart for more distant regions of the empire.

I am tempted to say that we had achieved these goals against all odds, but in truth it had more to do with exceedingly careful and clever planning carried out by extremely capable men and women. For all that, we knew we had been fortunate.

One major goal was left unrealized: Hanuvar had still heard nothing about his daughter.

—Sosilos, Book Fifteen

Chapter 9:
The People in the Stone

I

As one the boys and girls stepped, their mouths taut, their eyes alight. As one they thrust their "swords."

All nine held that pose as Hanuvar walked the line, gently tapping one ten-year-old in the leg with his stick as a reminder to lengthen her stance. He nodded approval when she adjusted, then ordered all of them back. They lowered wooden blades, turned, and retreated twelve paces to the side of the ornamental pond before facing forward once more, at loose attention in their short tunics and sandals. Eight looked different combinations of excited and nervous. The expression of the ninth was fixed and determined.

Julivar had thrown herself into training with unwavering commitment, just as Hanuvar had been told his own daughter had done. Was her manner, then, reminiscent of Narisia during the long years they were apart? Would he come to know the daughter of his old political enemy more than his own?

While he strove avoid such fruitless ruminations, the elusive nature of Narisia's fate had never stopped plaguing him. As the major operations in Tyvol drew to a close, Hanuvar had found himself with extra time to contemplate the mystery of her whereabouts. Carthalo had dispatched inquiries to the island of Surru long weeks before Bomilcar had sailed off to do the same. Presumably if there was word of her, it would already have been found and returned, for Surru was a week's sail at worst.

He retreated from his unprofitable thoughts and from long habit set his mind on the task before him. These nine children were mostly younger than those given official military training in Volanus, but he himself had practiced these drills at their age, and earlier. Ideally he would have instructed them on brick pavement, rather than garden grass with fountains, birdbaths, pools, and a two-story villa as a backdrop, but the ground was fairly level and these exercises weren't meant to hone deadly warriors so much as to provide a taste of martial discipline and instill some rudimentary self-defense skills. And, he admitted to himself, to grant him the pleasure of teaching them.

He would have liked to have presented these young people with the traditional weighted wooden swords carried by trainees, but those were either burned or hanging in the halls of Dervan aristocrats. Here, in Apicius, the children had to make due with simple wooden slats to which crossbars had been nailed. They were naturally impatient to hold real weapons. Young people always were.

Apart from Julivar, they had been living at the villa of Ciprion and Amelia until very recently. They were the last of the children transferred through Izivar's home to their new quarters in the north, and had arrived with their Volani instructors. Izivar had delayed her return trip to spend more leisure time with Hanuvar, and the youngsters, having seen Julivar at her training, had asked to join.

Hanuvar demonstrated an upper block, then advised them to watch their footing as they advanced and raised their sword arm in a parry twelve times. This was routine work for Julivar but she was no less dedicated, which he found heartening.

He had just called them back to the starting line when Izivar stepped out from the villa and onto the garden path, calling to him by his assumed name, the one all the children knew him by. "Decius? You have an important visitor."

Stressing that the visitor was important was for the benefit of his students. He knew Izivar would not have interrupted without a significant reason. He requested Julivar show them two more blocks and then run them through stretches. The young would hardly feel the need for them, but that, too, was a habit to ingrain. "After, collect and store their swords. They're to be stowed with the same care you'd handle actual weapons," he reminded her.

Julivar was often garrulous, but upon the practice field she seldom spoke at all, probably because she imagined Eltyr would not. Hanuvar had seen seasoned Eltyr at practice and overheard their ribald jests. They had been active, athletic women with keen eyes and sharp minds and tongues to match, but most of them were dead, and if Julivar wanted to imagine them as stern heroes he would not gainsay her, for they had been that, too.

Izivar lingered in the doorway to the breakfast nook, where refreshments waited. Traditionally, trainee warriors would have had water, but Izivar had adopted a honeyed melon juice recipe from Amelia and had a pitcher of it waiting. Her smile was distracted as she conducted Hanuvar inside. "They look like they're enjoying their training."

"They are. Especially your sister."

Izivar had not entirely warmed to Julivar's fascination with soldierly pursuits, but only a pursing of her lips betrayed her ambivalence. She shifted subjects. "Calenius has come."

Hanuvar could only have been less pleased if Metellus himself had appeared for a visit. "Did he say what he wants?"

"To speak with you." She led him deeper into the villa. "He was quite cordial. He gave me an amphora he said was of the finest wine, acquired from an estate in Herrenia."

Hanuvar frowned at that, but expected that if Calenius meant to cause trouble he would simply call the Dervans in upon them. The wine was likely a peace offering of sorts, but why? He followed Izivar through the empty dining room chamber, its best chairs arranged to look into the garden where Julivar led the other children through a down-block drill.

Calenius sat in the shade of an olive tree beside Antires, in the smaller inner courtyard, out of sight and sound of the children at practice. Izivar's caged song birds and the flow of the fountain into the oval pool at the courtyard's center were incidental music. The huge red-headed visitor spoke animatedly about someone's gift for expression, presumably a playwright, for Antires listened attentively. A jug of wine and two cups stood on a trestle table on his right.

The moment Calenius perceived Izivar's approach he climbed to his feet and inclined his head toward her. Today he looked a barbarian recently come to Dervan ways. He wore a lightweight green tunic with a keyhole pattern about its edges, and soft Dervan riding boots. His was an immense, muscular body, and while that did not necessarily identify him as a foreigner, the style of his flaming red hair did, for it was tied in a long queue behind his head. He retained a slight accent Hanuvar had never identified. "Decius. You look well."

"As do you."

"I was hoping we might talk."

"Of course." Hanuvar revealed neither caution nor suspicion. He gestured to the bench Calenius had vacated, then took a seat beside Antires.

"I had hoped we might talk alone," Calenius said.

"He'll hear about it all later. He's decided to chronicle my life."

Calenius smirked. "I wouldn't have suspected you for a self-aggrandizer."

Antires let out a bark of laughter. "Him? It took me weeks to get any details out of him at all. He still hates talking about himself. That's why he prefers to have me on hand."

Calenius chuckled. He looked to Izivar. "Will you be joining us too, then? I suspect he includes you in his counsel."

"I have other duties," Izivar said. "I'll leave you three to your talk." She raised a hand in farewell, then left them.

Calenius lifted his mug as if in salute to her turned back, though he did not drink. He turned his attention to Hanuvar. "This is a nice home."

Hanuvar could not help hearing an unvoiced threat, and wondered if Antires noticed. Calenius' look seemed to say: "It would be a shame if something happened to it."

The larger man inclined his head ever so slightly to Hanuvar and continued: "Your woman's well-spoken, and educated, and pretty."

This time there was almost a wistful quality to the wizard's comments, which was well for him, for Hanuvar would not have liked to have heard even the ghost of a threat about her.

"The home is hers," Hanuvar said. "And so is she, though you've rightly noted three of her remarkable qualities."

"I've put you on your defense." Calenius' brilliant blue eyes were searching. "I seek only amity. With an offer you're free to refuse. I play no double game here, and mean to imply no threats."

"Speak, then."

Antires shifted, watching but silent. Calenius glanced at him and then continued as though he were not there. "I've a problem that needs solving. I'm short on time and require someone capable to assist."

"Someone beyond your experts?"

"My lieutenants are busy with other matters. I could probably handle this on my own, but I like to stack odds in my favor. I need to retrieve something that's a few days away. And I think I could rely on you to help."

Hanuvar had never anticipated this particular kind of interaction with the man. He was uninclined to become further involved with him, but could not help being curious, especially because he worried about how Calenius' mysterious project might affect his own. "Interesting. What do you offer in return?"

"I may be able to aid your efforts," Calenius said. "I have money. Material resources. Even... other things." He did not say magic, not even in this private space. Hanuvar knew from his look what he meant.

"Money is always a necessity," Hanuvar agreed.

"I could help you find your people. I know that's what's most important to you."

Calenius couldn't know how far along their efforts had come. How specific could his assistance be?

Hanuvar decided to learn. There was one person above all others he wanted to find. And yet... Carthalo's agents and Bomilcar himself were seeking her. She was apparently able to take care of herself, given how well she had avoided capture. There were a few others, sold to some unknown land; one of his own blood was in that category. "I need to locate my niece."

"Your niece by blood?"

"Yes."

"Have you other nieces or nephews?"

"One."

"Have you any clue where your niece is?"

"Very little."

Calenius frowned. "And the other? Do you know where he or she is?"

"I do."

"We ought to be able to exclude that one from the search, then." He swigged some wine. "I can help with this. It would require preparatory time."

"How much?" Hanuvar asked. "And would you be able to lead me to her?"

"A few hours to a day, depending. I can't lead you to her, but if she's still alive I could show her to you."

"That's amazing," Antires whispered reverently.

Calenius did not joke. To Hanuvar's inquiring look he added: "You would be able to see her, with great clarity, as though you observed her through fine glass. I cannot manage an auditory component, however. Not without an active mage on the other end of the spell. I recommend seeking her during the day so details are more clear when you see where she is. It would do you little good to examine a darkened bed chamber. Be warned that you may not like what you see, or glimpse enough to know exactly where she is."

This was powerful magic indeed, but Hanuvar did not doubt the wizard's promises. He had witnessed the result of his sorcery before. "Will your spell hurt anyone?"

"Only you—and all I need is a lock of your hair."

"Not my blood?"

Calenius shook his head, dully amused. "Blood is flashy, messy, and overrated. It dries out too fast and is easy to contaminate. For this purpose I'd need just a little hair to burn in a ritual fire, so my magics can seek out the right match."

"My old advisors would have warned me against letting you have access to it."

"If I wanted you dead, I could have arranged that weeks ago, and you know it. I've nothing to gain by harming you at this juncture. Besides, we two are men of a kind."

Calenius meant this as compliment, although Hanuvar understood Calenius thought him a junior member of whatever brotherhood he proposed. To the wizard he was a promising up-and-comer. "What would you want in return?"

"You've seen the dangers of the under tunnels. I need something recovered that's almost surely guarded. And I want someone to watch my back as I work magic. Someone who's not just brave and skilled, but who can think for themselves. I've a number of competent followers, but those fitting that description are in short supply."

That explanation sounded reasonable enough, but Hanuvar couldn't help thinking there was more to it even than Calenius revealed. He pretended the answer satisfied him.

"How long would you need me for?"

"Eight to ten days. Our destination is inland to the south, in the mountains. We'll be travelling through some fairly remote regions beyond Turia."

That would leave him out of the final efforts during the theatrical festival, but Izivar and Antires were surely up to the task. It was Izivar who'd suggested an excellent backup plan, should normal means of liberation prove impossible. Still, he'd have to give this proposal serious thought. "How dangerous will the expedition be?"

"About as dangerous as the tunnel. Maybe a little more. I don't think we'll face the same kind of guardian."

"And what is it you're after?"

"An artifact of my people."

"And if I asked why?"

Calenius' smile was reflective, almost mocking of himself. "Let's call it sentiment."

"You're not beyond that, then?"

"It seems not."

"I'd like to consider this."

"I can give you today."

"Where shall I send word?"

"My quarters on the mountain. I have nothing half so comfortable as this, nor as charming a hostess. I'll have my men watching for you, or your messenger." He rose. "Oh, and I do not want your chronicler. I mean no offense, but I must insist that you come alone."

"Why is that?" Antires sounded almost sullen.

"Because I wish it," Calenius said shortly, like a king unused to challenge. He stood.

Hanuvar saw him to the door. Calenius paused on the threshold and looked back at the cool atrium, decorated with ivy. His gaze suggested he felt a warmth here, a comfort that he might, even briefly, have envied.

Hanuvar walked out with him and waited while his horse was saddled and brought around. "You'll have my answer in the morning."

"I'll look for it."

Hanuvar watched him go, then gathered Antires and Izivar in her office and sat down with them to work through his reactions. When Izivar asked him what Calenius had wanted, Hanuvar explained.

"Calenius wants me to help him with something dangerous. Like that thing in the tunnels. He says his lieutenants are busy with other matters. I can't help thinking he's nearing the end of his project and he needs a few final pieces."

"So his plan is nearly complete," Antires said. "Like ours."

"He said he can use sorcery to help me find Edonia."

Izivar's eyes widened. "You believe him?"

"I do."

"It might be a trick."

"It might," he said. "But I think he's speaking the truth, at least about this."

She let out a long sigh. "And you also want to learn what Calenius is up to."

Hanuvar thought this a clever deduction, and acknowledged it with a nod of the head. "I am uneasy about the voices Teonia said she sensed around him. The Volani voices."

"Voices of the living?" Izivar asked. "Or the dead? If it's the dead, how can you possibly help?" She studied him, and though he thought his expression neutral she divined his intention. "You've already determined to do it, haven't you."

"He's been worried about how he'll find Edonia for weeks," Antires said. "She could be in terrible danger."

Hanuvar thought himself fortunate to have two people who understood his thought process so well.

Izivar's look softened.

Antires continued. "We've known Calenius is plotting something, and he's very powerful. It may not intersect with what we're doing, at all. But what if it does? And what if it involves these voices the little girl heard?"

"If you had already decided to go, why ask our opinions?" There was a hint of ice in Izivar's question.

"I wanted to see if either of you could provide better counter-arguments than the ones I'd thought of."

Izivar spoke sorrowfully. "It makes sense. Your choices always make sense. That doesn't mean I like them. Do you need to take this risk? It won't be long before we're completely beyond Calenius' sphere. We may never need to worry about him again."

"I can't say what we're beyond, because I don't know what he's doing," Hanuvar said. "And this may be the only chance we'll get to see where Edonia and the two girls sold with her are."

Izivar sighed, then nodded with understanding.

"There's another issue. I'll be gone more than a week. Do you think the two of you can manage the final rescues during the festival?"

"Yes," Antires said readily. He'd obviously already been thinking about it, for there was no hesitation in his voice.

Izivar gave the matter more thought. "I'd like to review the details, but, yes, we should be able to handle things." She had once pointed out to him that she ran a shipping empire with vessels and goods in dozens of ports across the Inner Sea, whereupon he emphasized that he thought her perfectly capable of arranging complex operations.

Her acceptance brought the meeting to a close. Izivar did not speak of the trip with Hanuvar during supper that night, except obliquely as they reviewed details about the final slaves and discussed supplies he would need packed. She expressed caution that Antires was not to accompany him. Hanuvar didn't mind the last; if something were to go awry he depended upon his friend to assist her with all the rest of their plans.

After dinner Hanuvar retired to his bedroom to read a letter from Carthalo. Through his friend's stripped down report he discerned the outline of a complicated web of blackmail through which Carthalo had finally gained leverage to free twenty-five fullers, seventeen of them Volani, held in truly wretched circumstances. Much more elaborately Carthalo described the current Dervan political situation, as relayed by his daughter, still collecting information from the capital. New legions were being trained to replace those on their way to Cerdia, and the emperor had been irritated by the return of Senator Aminius from the Cerdian border. Ostensibly Aminius had arrived to personally plead for additional funding and reinforcements, but he seemed much more interested in whipping up sentiment against some of the emperor's proposed agrarian reforms, then had slipped away to let unsubtle firebrands take up his arguments.

Hanuvar never missed his own involvement in politics, and did not envy the young emperor's challenges. He hoped Enarius had the wisdom to find his way forward.

As important as it was to keep abreast of the Dervan government, Hanuvar wished Carthalo had described his own efforts in more exacting detail, and then thought wryly of Antires' frustration with Hanuvar's succinct descriptions of his own doings and how long it had taken the young man to persuade him to be more revealing. Maybe Carthalo needed a chronicler of his own. It was too bad that he and Antires seemed to irritate one another.

He had just finished watching the letter burn when he heard a key in the lock.

"It's me," Izivar's voice said, and she finished turning it and slid into the room, closing it behind her.

She sat down on the bed beside him and took his hand. She held it for a long moment before addressing him with a blunt confession. "I'm not ready for you to go. Every time you leave, I think it will be the last time I see you."

"I hope a time will come when I won't have to leave."

Her grip on his hand tightened. "We have lost so much. Must we lose you, too?"

"If Julivar were missing, you would do anything to find her, wouldn't you?"

"I would. It wouldn't be enough that other people were seeking her, either."

"Then you understand."

"Understanding and liking are two different things." She studied his face in sad silence for a long moment, the lone lantern casting her features in shadow as she leaned forward to kiss him. Soon she was in his arms, and before much time had passed they had helped one another from their clothes and slid into bed to salve their troubles in a moment they stretched out as long as possible.

After, she nestled against him, one leg thrown across his own. He idly toyed with her hair, enjoying her warmth and the press of her skin.

"Do you really think they will welcome me?" she asked softly.

She did not need to explain who *they* were; she meant the people of New Volanus.[20] The subject preyed upon her.

He brushed her shoulder. "By the time we arrive all will know how instrumental you've been in procuring their safety and freedom. And I will set anyone right who dares speak against you. Everyone should be beyond these kinds of disagreements now."

"Most people aren't as rational as you. That's probably your greatest failing. You see the best in people who don't deserve it."

"I expect them to give their best, and that's a different thing."

"I suppose it's selfish of me to ask you to stay," she said, softly, and pecked his chest with a kiss. "But I worry for you. We're so close now to finding them all and getting away. How can I live, without my home,[21] and without you?"

He loved that she was strong, and fierce, and deeply caring. This once, she sounded small and vulnerable. "You have become my center," she finished quietly.

He did not tell her that she had been centered long before him and that she would be centered again without him. He rubbed her back, wondering if it was sane still to drive further onward. Would he know when to end? Did he seek Edonia and Narisia and all the others because he felt guilt? Was he set on this course because when he rested for very long at all he could not help thinking about all that was lost, and all the horrors that had been done, and all the blood that had been spilled? Or had he succumbed to uneasiness about lingering with anyone because those closest to him tended to die?

He spoke to her of none of these things. He turned and kissed her lips, not with fiery ardor, but with tenderness. "I love you. So long as I live, I will return to you."

She snuggled closer, and dozed in his arms. He did not surrender to sleep until he had felt her relax.

Early the next morning he left for Calenius.

---

[20] New Volanus had been founded by adherents of the Cabera family, who held no love for the Lenereva, because Tannis Lenereva, her father, had masterminded the exile and betrayal that had driven Hanuvar from the city of the silver towers. —*Silenus*

[21] While Izivar's family had lived in several homes, that in Apicius was the one to which she had been most attached, for her father had preferred to spend time in Ostra. She had arranged it to her liking after the death of her husband, and it was with some difficulty that she prepared to leave it for New Volanus, never to return. —*Silenus*

II

Hanuvar reached the slope of Esuvia an hour after dawn, and was conducted to a large canvas tent set in the lee of one of the walls Calenius' men had excavated. Few of the wizard's slaves remained in the camp. Hanuvar spotted a number of them digging high along the mountainside, near a flattened outcrop below the final height of the cinder cone. Others labored further downslope, and it struck Hanuvar that they appeared to be readying entrenchments. But who would be besieging them upon the mountain?

Calenius had his tent flap open. He sat in a canvas-backed chair, studying a scroll, and looked up when the slave announced Hanuvar, then stood and offered his hand. They exchanged not the arm clasp common to the people of Tyvol, but the firm closure of palm that Calenius had given him once before.

"I thought you'd come," the big man said. "I'll need a lock of your hair."

Hanuvar patted a belt pouch. "Cut this morning."

"By the charming Izivar, I expect," Calenius speculated. "I made some initial preparations, but this will still take me a few hours to ready." He asked for location details about the nephew or niece Hanuvar had mentioned and then bade him wait in the tent. "Take your ease. I've some books that might interest you, and I'll have my men bring you a meal. I won't need your hair until the ceremony starts."

Calenius passed orders along and a servant brought Hanuvar food and drink, then shared it quietly with him, as if to demonstrate it safe for consumption.

Less than two hours later another slave called Hanuvar out from the tent, where he'd been reading the very play of a doomed king that Antires had told him Calenius had been talking about. The ruler's determination to launch a war to avenge his son's accidental death wasn't the overwrought work he had expected, but he wasn't sure he needed just now the catharsis that the tragedy was supposed to provide.

Calenius was washing his face. Sweat wetted his hair. He paused to pull a fresh shirt over his scarred, muscular chest, and while he finished freshening up Hanuvar inspected the large black bowl the wizard had erected under the tent's peak. Its rim was incised with hash marks and small pictograms. The earth beneath the bowl and its pedestal was scored in the shape of a hexagon, with other characters burned into the grass along its lines. An unlit gold candle stood at each of its points.

"When I motion you forward, you're to peer into the water while thinking of the relative you seek. Don't touch it. Understood?" Calenius asked.

"Yes."

Calenius stepped to the tray table and pulled the cloth from what proved another candle, this one stubby and black. He lit a taper by striking a spark from flint with what seemed a golden rod, used the taper to touch the candle's wick, then lifted it. He bent to use it in lighting each of the candles upon the hexagon points. When he had lit the final one, he motioned to Hanuvar, who passed over the hair.

Accepting it between finger and thumb, Calenius began to chant, walking widdershins around the hexagon. After long moments he stopped and lifted the hair far above the flame of the black candle, suspended over the bowl. He dropped the hair toward it.

It should have blown free, or drifted down into the water. Instead each dark strand fell as though weighted, bursting into golden motes of light the moment they neared the flame, then sprinkled down into the water.

With tired eyes, the wizard directed Hanuvar to the bowl.

He decided against crossing the hexagon. He kept Calenius in his sight and bent down across the shimmering liquid.

For a brief moment his own image looked back at him. Then the water rippled as if struck by a stone, and he perceived a sinuous winged serpent drawn upon a large wax tablet. Lines leading from elegant curled lettering pointed to portions of the asalda's body—the eye, the leg, the head, the wing.

A trio of young women sat cross-legged before the tablet while a stern-faced older woman in a long blue dress pointed at each section with a stiff reed. When she pointed, the young women moved their mouths.

The smaller of the three could only be Edonia. She had her mother's features, blossoming now toward true beauty, and they watched not the image, but the woman's pointer, with hawklike vigilance.

All three of the girls wore the same long blue garb, a formal short-sleeved, long-skirted dress. The lettering looked western but he could not fully identify it, although he feared it might be Ilodonean. Certainly the instructor's coppery-toned skin suggested Ilodonean ancestry, and the reclusive culture claimed that their emperors had mastered the will of asalda.

Hanuvar's nostrils flared. Ilodonea was incredibly far away, beyond even the desert west of the Cerdians.

The tidy square room itself was bare apart from the bench, a plain wooden door, and the upper half of the plastered wall, painted in a soft red. Sunlight flowed through an unshuttered window.

Just as he was sorting through the information before him the woman slapped the side of the head of the tallest of the girls with her reed, then pointed at her with the implement. The girl's face screwed up in pain, and then her mouth moved again; once more her head was smacked, and again she seemed to speak. Her pronunciation apparently was not as fine as that of Edonia and the other girl. The instructor pulled back for another smack then turned abruptly; the door had been pushed open behind her.

To Hanuvar's eyes the man who entered seemed Cerdian, from deep olive skin tone and aquiline nose and shade of hair to the style of sandal and even the flowery hatching about his wide, simple tunic. He expected Ilodoneans might own Cerdian slaves, but would they allow them to dress in their native clothing? The more he saw, the less Hanuvar understood what he perceived. The instructor clapped hands and pointed toward the male slave. The three girls hurried to their feet and formed in single file, the instructor coming after. They followed the man through the open doorway.

"Have you seen enough?" Calenius' voice was strained.

Hanuvar shook his head no. Where was Edonia being kept?

Now the three Volani girls followed the servant through a hall with polished wood floors. He glimpsed a flowering garden a floor below, and its decorative square roof cornices looked Cerdian too. They passed into a grander corridor, paved with blue marble, its walls painted with blue and gold diamond patterns beneath bounding lions. A symbol of Cerdian kings.

Two grand gold doors lay at the hallway's terminus, and a man in gleaming armor stood with a spear beside each. From their peaked, crestless golden helms and their curling beards he knew for certain they were Cerdians.

The servant gestured toward the doors but did not enter. The soldiers opened the doubled portal and the girls with their instructor swept into a wide, sunlit room full of a host of Cerdians and advisors from other nations. And there, standing to one side in banded brown armor, stood his daughter, Narisia. His breath caught to see her alive and well. Her hair was uncovered and tied in a tight bun. She was older and graver, and solemn as her sea-gray eyes took in the young women. She was not surprised by them—this, then, could not be the first time that she had seen them here.

A large cloth map lay upon the wide table at the room's center, and men in plain white slave's garb were placing markers upon it. A skillful hand had stitched mountains and coasts and deserts, as well as cities, and Hanuvar realized that the eagle markers along the border were legions.

A tall young man crowned with a golden circlet and garbed in purple stood at the table's head, although he appeared more interested in surveying his wine goblet than the tactical display. The trio of aristocrats beside him, in striped tunics bright as tropical bird plumage, studded with be-gemmed rings, looked more curious.

This, then, was almost certainly the Cerdian capital, and likely the palace.

Narisia advanced to the table to make some point with a finger jabbed at the map. In the years since Hanuvar had seen her last she had apparently grown no less outspoken. She pushed a brown marker from further south up toward the border, and brought another legion down from the north.

She was advising action the others appeared reluctant to take. How long had she been on the Cerdian staff, and how was it that no Dervan spies had caught wind of it?

Edonia and the other girls halted beside a tall man in his thirties, a fellow in the sweeping silks of an Ilodonean, his skin coppery, his slim nose high and proud, his eyebrows thin and arched. He said something that attracted the king's attention, and motioned the girls to speak. Whatever it was they said, it was in unison, and while they talked, he shifted another marker from the map edge to its center, a ribbony figurine with wings.

At the same moment Hanuvar recognized it for an asalda, the Ilodonean's eyes seemed to light with gold from within and Hanuvar could have sworn he looked right through the pool and out at them.

Calenius snuffed the candle and the water sloshed as if it had been bumped from below. An icy wind blew out each of the remaining candles. He let out a heavy breath. "I could hold it no longer. You saw your niece, though, didn't you?"

"I learned that she lives, and where. But I'm left with a host of questions."

"It's always the way. And I cannot answer any except to say the Ilodonean felt our magics. But then he appears to be the sorcerer to a king, and must have been chosen for his knowledge."

Hanuvar nodded slowly. His niece lived; moreover, her companions did, and his own daughter held a prominent position in the Cerdian court, and was surely working to aid the girls. He could wish that Narisia was not involved in the war with Derva, but he was thrilled simply to have seen her and Edonia both. In a word, the moment had been miraculous. He looked across the water at the man in front of him. "You have held to your part. I will hold to mine."

III

Hanuvar drafted a coded missive to Antires, writing that both daughter and niece were alive in Cerdia's capital, and asked him to convey that news, along with his love, to Izivar. One of Calenius' slaves trotted off to deliver it, and then Hanuvar and the big wizard were riding away, leading a single packhorse.

They skirted the edge of Apicius but did not stop, riding south along the main road toward Turia. The skies were clear, but the sun's warmth had begun to ease as summer waned. They passed carts laden with goods and passengers headed both north and south.

For the most part they rode in file. Calenius seemed disinterested in speech and Hanuvar contemplated the steps that lay ahead. The Cerdians, with Ilodonean help, apparently thought to deploy an asalda to fight the Dervans. How they hoped to command one with three Volani girls trained only to aid them was yet another puzzle he couldn't solve without more information.

His daughter advised the Cerdian king, or at least attempted to, about their brewing war with Derva. How much of her life had she invested in a conflict for a people not her own? How likely was he to convince her to leave for New Volanus? She had known of its existence. That she had not come seeking it suggested her heart was turned toward vengeance. But then she had lost not just her city and father and husband, but her Eltyr sisters, and her children. She might well feel she had no other recourse.

In the afternoon Calenius slowed at last and Hanuvar caught up to him. The sorcerer's black horse was a few hands higher than Hanuvar's, and the man gazed down from his saddle. His vivid blue eyes were bagged with fatigue. He had forged on despite spell work that had exhausted him.

"We'll stay the first night at an inn. After that we'll be in the wilderness."

Hanuvar nodded.

The reaction appeared to amuse Calenius. "I know you're curious, but you're not asking me anything."

"You could tell me what you did for the Dervans during the siege of Volanus."

Calenius looked almost disappointed. "What I was paid to do. I'm a mercenary. And my circumstances at the time required cooperation."

"That's vague."

"It was a war. I have nothing against your people, but my needs set me against them. You don't want details."

He did, but he didn't press. "What are your circumstances now?"

"Now I'm on my own, and beholden to no one. I don't think the revenant legate holds me in high regard. But you can't always choose your enemies."

"You don't seem troubled about it."

"I have more pressing concerns."

Hanuvar understood that level of focus, though not its target. "Are those concerns anything I should worry about?"

Calenius' sidelong look was appraising. What it was meant to communicate was uncertain. The sooner Hanuvar and his people were away from Calenius and this region, the better.

They stopped late that evening at a village lying at a crossroads. Calenius paid for two separate rooms, ordered food sent to his chamber, and went upstairs to eat it. Hanuvar saw to his own horse and watched for a time as the stableboys cared for the other two, then ate at one of the outside tables, away from the dining hall crowded by boisterous locals.

There amongst the eight outside tables were young lovers and travelers and older people like himself more interested in quiet. He finished the simple Dervan fare, then walked about the little settlement as though curious about his surroundings. In reality he was assessing the best points of attack upon the inn, the best routes for a swift departure, and any potential conflicts, more out of habit than any real need. Near the end of his circuit he passed the stone outbuilding where the cooking took place and spotted a dark furred shape sitting expectantly beside a shuttered window. It was a dog, its snout pointed toward the sill.

The animal turned to regard him and he approached slowly. It was a young male mastiff with expressive orange-brown eyes and calm demeanor. The animal sniffed at him, thumped its tail, then returned its attention to the window. Hanuvar now perceived that someone had placed a soup bone there. At shoulder height it was too far for the animal to reach. Had someone left it to cool?

Hanuvar didn't see anyone. He looked down at the dog. "Lie down."

The mastiff considered him only briefly before obeying the order. Impressed, Hanuvar tried a second command. "Sit."

Immediately the dog rose onto his haunches.

Hanuvar removed the browned soup bone, only a little warm to the touch, and handed it down. "Good dog."

The mastiff accepted the bone without snatching it, and Hanuvar scratched the animal's head. The dog wagged his tail, trotted a few feet to the right, and plopped down to gnaw on his treasure.

"That's my dog."

Hanuvar hadn't heard the gravelly voiced man come up behind him. He turned to find a slender figure a few paces to his side, mostly hidden by shadow. He smelled of dogs, and sweat and road dust.

"You have a well-mannered dog," Hanuvar said.

The stranger still seemed inclined to be critical. "You gave him a bone?"

"He asked politely."

That answer must have pleased the stranger better, for his next question was more neutral. "You like dogs?"

"Better than some people."

"They're more dependable," the stranger agreed. "You spoke to him like a man who's trained them."

"Never had the pleasure. I've trained horses."

The stranger stepped nearer. He was rangy, one of those whipcord-thin men seasoned and strengthened like old leather. His voice was low. "You're travelling with the big man?"

There was no question who he was referring to. "I am."

The houndman looked down at his animal, happily gnawing away, then back to Hanuvar. "That may prove bad for your health."

"What makes you think that?"

He shrugged high shoulders. "You might do better to find a different employer."

Whoever this man was, then, he didn't know anything about Hanuvar or his goals. "I'm honor bound, after he did me a favor," he explained.

"Honor bound." The houndman repeated the words as if unaccustomed to hearing them. He sounded almost disgruntled. "Well, enjoy your evening." He whistled once to the dog and it climbed to its feet, bone between its teeth. The dog fell in at his side and the two left together. It was only as they drew closer to the light of the lanterns at the outdoor tables that Hanuvar noted the gleam of an opal on the ring of the houndman's hand. He had taken a very similar ring from the severed hand of a revenant earlier that summer. He carried it still in one of his belt pouches.

If revenants were active in the area, they did not make themselves known that night, or in the morning, and soon he and Calenius were riding west along an old dirt road and then southwest along a rutted trail scarcely wide enough to accommodate a cart. They wound their way just east of the foothills of the spiny Vertigines range, whose pine-girt upper slopes rose above the morning mist.

After the first few hours Hanuvar occasionally noted a large sable mastiff trotting to their rear. Then, near noon, Calenius commented he had glimpsed one stepping out of some woodland ahead.

"This summer I met a revenant with a dog," Hanuvar said.

"I'm not worried about the revenants. They gave me leave to work my magics unmolested."

"That was before things went badly with the false Hanuvar, wasn't it?"

Calenius scoffed. "If the revenants wanted me, they'd come for me."

"In your base of operations, surrounded by your men?"

Hanuvar's observation gave Calenius pause. "I don't have time for this," he grumbled.

He scanned the ground ahead and to the side, and veered for a bushy knoll rising above the scrubby grassland. Hanuvar supposed it was a decent enough defensible position, but hardly ideal.

Calenius arrived at its base, dismounted, and continued to scan it as he led his horse up.

"What are we doing?" Hanuvar asked.

"Drawing them out."

Hanuvar didn't like that Calenius passed the reins of his own animal over to him when they reached the height.

The hilltop was just under a hundred paces in circumference, and heavy with scrubby brush and weed trees. The south and eastern slopes were steep drop-offs.

Calenius finished his brief survey then opened his saddlebag. "This will take a little while. Picket the horses in the center."

Hanuvar didn't care for the thought Calenius would be working more sorcery, nor did he like his companion's mysteries, and he had to admit to himself that he chafed at being treated as a lackey. Despite some playacting along those lines, he hadn't truly been a line soldier for decades now. He reminded himself that he had learned that both Edonia and Narisia were alive and healthy, and discovered their location. Surely that had been worth enduring the sorcerer's companionship for a few days.

He kept watch while Calenius drew in the dirt, measured out powders, notched candles, and quietly chanted.

Before very much longer Hanuvar saw dogs, half again the size of the young one to whom he'd given the bone. They were heavy and various shades of brown and watched from within the distant tree line. While he had not observed the color of the animal that had attacked him and Ciprion on the beach in the dark, these seemed a similar sort. Whatever the houndman intended in the end, now he seemed merely to be monitoring.

The blinding white sun sank slowly. After more than an hour, Calenius withdrew a flat blackened stone from a scarlet sackcloth. The size of a hand shield, its shining top had been painted with a scarlet hexagon. The mage traced its surface, muttering, then stood and stretched his back. He took a long swig from his wineskin.

Hanuvar's eyes were drawn to the stone even as they recoiled from it. The briefest glance chilled him in a way he'd felt only when in the presence of things from other realms, around creatures that had hungered for souls and lives and blood.

Calenius saw the direction of his gaze. "Stand ready. I'm going to call in the dogs. There's seven of them."

"What do you mean 'call them in'?"

"I'll bring them to me, even if they don't want to come. They won't like it. But whoever's behind it won't be able to follow us after."

The big sorcerer capped his wineskin and restored it to his belt. He laid out his bow and strung it, then planted arrows in the ground beside him. Finally, he pulled the stubby wand from his belt once more, drew in the air, and that sense of wrongness, of revulsion and discomfort, rippled out from him in a wave. Hanuvar bared his teeth but kept his place. He loosed his sword in its scabbard.

A thick brown dog shape broke cover from the right, only a few hundred feet out, and charged the hill. Another darted out of the woods further south and raced for their position.

A human whistled from somewhere out of sight even as a third dog broke cover to the west and hurried for them.

Loping toward the slope, the first bared teeth. Calenius' bow creaked as he pulled the string back and let fly. The shaft struck through the dog's head. The mastiff tumbled spastically over its front legs and crashed to a halt against a low bush.

Calenius had already nocked a second arrow and sent it flying. His shot found a dog's breast. It dropped on suddenly useless legs, whimpering fitfully for a time before falling still.

He drew a bead on the third dog but held fire as it closed. Hanuvar watched, wishing for the animal to veer away. Its eyes were wide and fearful and it whined; it did not want to be here, in the open, running against its will.

Might Calenius use this power on people? It was chilling enough to see its effects on dogs. Hanuvar fingered the ring in his pouch but did not slip it onto his hand, for he was not certain what it might do, or whether it would be of use.

A man cried out from under cover to the south, whistled, then called desperately. His voice was thick with anguish. Hanuvar bit back a plea for Calenius to stop. These were war dogs, and the houndsman had almost certainly been dispatched to hunt them.

The animal bayed once, a sound cut short as Calenius put an arrow through its gullet. Its momentum sent it tumbling end over end until it lay twitching.

"Bastard!" the houndsman shouted.

"Come after me again and I'll kill the rest!" Calenius cried.

There came no answer.

"He's leashed the others." Calenius spoke like he mouthed a curse. He slashed the air as if cutting an invisible line and some of the tension in the air faded, but normalcy was unrestored until he had bagged the black stone.

"Let's ride," Calenius said.

Hanuvar was happy to be gone from there. Some of his allies had worked with warhounds, and while he'd seen how effective they could be in combat, he hated to see them slain, in the same way he hated to see the death of elephants or horses. All the animals wanted was to follow their training and please their masters. They had no concept of the greater stakes and the alliances of the men who brought them to battle.

But then that could be said of many of the soldiers who filled out the world's armies.

Calenius led them deeper into the wilds. If the hounds still followed, Hanuvar did not see them.

He didn't speak with Calenius again until they stopped to rest their horses and stretch their legs.

"At the inn last night I met a man with a well-trained dog," Hanuvar said.

Calenius waited, sensing rightly Hanuvar wouldn't mention the information unless he had more to say.

"When he passed near the light, I noticed a ring he wore. It resembled one I'd seen on the hand of a revenant who'd sent a hound against me."

"You want me to know this is revenant work."

"I suspect them. Do you have other enemies?"

"I do."

"Your magic sensed the hounds. Was there anything unnatural about them?"

The question set Calenius thinking. "Was there something unnatural about the one you saw earlier?"

"Resiliency. Speed. A focus on purpose beyond ordinary."

"There was something lying quiescent in them all. An inactive power. It allowed me to sense them better. Why didn't you mention this sooner?"

"You're as used to shadows as I am. I didn't think you'd want to jump at them."

"I suppose not."

"Can that spell you controlled them with be used against people?"

"At some cost, and in limited numbers, yes. Does that trouble you? You don't strike me as the type that needs a fight to be fair."

"Not a fight that needs won," Hanuvar said.

"Exactly."

They walked their horses for a while, munching on dried rations, then rode them until nearly twilight. Calenius informed him they needed to eat dry rations again that evening, so anyone hunting them would see no campfire. "We'll cook breakfast," he added.

Calenius set out the black stone once more and noticed Hanuvar watching him. "Do you sense anything from this?"

"A feeling of disquiet. Either the stone itself or the magic attached to it doesn't belong here."

"I might have said the same thing, once. I wasn't always a sorcerer. I didn't like them, or trust them." He sneered. "I still don't."

"Why become one then?"

"You master the tools you need to achieve your goals."

Hanuvar understood that. Just as he understood that sorcery usually took years to master, like any difficult art. He already knew Calenius was older than he looked. "What is the stone?"

"Our safeguard, this night. If something closes on us, the powers within will alert us. Before our enemies get close." Calenius stood and an arrow plunged out of the night. Incredibly, he seemed to sense it and had begun to move, but could not completely avoid it. The shaft stood out from his right bicep.

Mastiffs then burst from the undergrowth and tore forward, their images blurred behind them as though their physical forms outsped their spirits.

Hanuvar rose and struck but the dog slid past his blade tip and circled for him, a blurred image in its wake. At the same time Calenius flicked a finger toward the black stone and a glowing, transparent man shape streamed up. It came straight at Hanuvar, its ghostly face strained and mournful. Hanuvar's skin chilled as the thing made eye contact. And while he did not recognize it, the specter seemed to register him, for its mouth parted in something like awe before veering past and springing upon the dog.

The animal shuddered to a halt, twisting and turning as the phantom wrestled with it and then drifted away, bearing a transparent dog shape into the sky and leaving behind an unmoving animal.

Another arrow launched as Calenius ducked, and a second mastiff leapt. Calenius caught it in two hands and broke its back across his knee.

Hanuvar dashed on toward the tree where he'd seen the archer take cover, only to encounter a final dog. He'd slipped the ring onto his finger. A phantom woman flowed past him, her expression shifting from pained horror to one of curiosity; he had the sense that in her recognition she deliberately kept further from him. And then she interposed herself between him and the final animal, tearing its living spirit free before fading into the night.

The houndsman lifted his bow at sight of Hanuvar, who threw himself forward, landed on his hands, and came up in a roll. He heard the twang of the string and felt the brush of air as the arrow passed over his shoulder. And then he was pushing off a crouch and burying his knife in the houndsman's breast.

The man fell back, whacking Hanuvar in the shoulder with the bow. A smaller dog growled but did not advance. Hanuvar recognized it for the younger one he'd befriended.

The houndsman staggered up with a knife slash that Hanuvar

leapt backward to avoid; he brought his sword down, hard, against the arm and cut halfway through it.

The dog came forward, growling, but Hanuvar's sideways sweep of his leg forced it away. The houndsman sank to his knees.

His eyes sought Hanuvar's own. They were half closed in pain, but their look was pleading. "Don't kill my dog," he gasped.

"Who sent you?" Hanuvar placed the sword to his throat.

The man was having trouble breathing. "My dog—you promise?"

"Yes."

"Aquilius."

Calenius came from the side, bent, and plunged his sword through his chest. The houndsman slumped in death.

The young dog bared its teeth and growled.

Calenius pivoted and struck down toward the animal.

Hanuvar caught the weapon on his own, a blow that all but numbed his arm.

The dog slunk away into the undergrowth, tail between its legs.

Calenius stood panting. Hanuvar smelled the blood trailing down his arm, heard the spatter of its drops on the grass. A feathered arrow shaft stood out from the big man's arm.

Swords still locked, they eyed one another.

After a long moment Calenius pulled his blade from Hanuvar's own. "You only promised YOU wouldn't kill the dog. You should be more flexible."

"The death was unnecessary." Hanuvar lowered his weapon.

Calenius examined his blade, judged it clean, and sheathed it. "You can take that man-of-your-word business too far."

"Do you?" Hanuvar asked.

"Sometimes I have."

Hanuvar wiped his blade clean on the dead man.

Calenius knelt over the body and searched it, seemingly uncaring about his wound. He discovered some coins, some hidden knives, and, lastly, the ring, which he raised to the moonlight and studied with care. Finally he tossed it toward Hanuvar, who only decided to catch it at the last moment. He had already removed his own.

"It's not poisonous. You like dogs. Take it."

"What is it?"

"It's ritually bonded to something alive. Probably that remaining dog. If it ever comes within range again."

Hanuvar slipped it into a belt pouch. "We should see to that wound."

Calenius glanced to the shaft sticking out from him. Hanuvar almost expected him to pull it free, like a hero from an epic. "All right," he said. The big man didn't add that he could have handled it himself. It could be challenging to treat your own injury though, and Calenius wasn't so determined to prove his self-sufficiency that he would turn down the offer of assistance.

He stoically endured having the shaft pulled free, and spoke while Hanuvar readied the wine to drip against the bleeding tear through his muscle. "This land was very different once. A long lake lay at the foot of these hills, and they were taller then. A great road, wider and flatter than those the Dervans make, wound through them to a fine little city full of pipers famed for their talent and lithe, pretty women who loved to dance."

Hanuvar poured the wine over the torn flesh and the big man winced.

"Your home city?" Hanuvar asked.

"What? No. One of the allied states. You don't question the truth of what I say?"

"I know when I'm hearing truth. How old are you?"

"Not as old as the hills. Not quite. Here's the place where you ask my secret. Or ask me to share it."

"The secret of your long life?"

"Yes."

"I don't care about that."

"You're an intriguing man, Hanuvar."

He had not called him by name since the day of their first meeting.

Calenius rose and fumbled at his own belt pouch. He withdrew a small glittering disk, the size of a coin, but unmarked. "These take months to fashion. Normally I'd just let the wound heal on its own but... we need to be on our toes soon." He pressed the disk to his arm and it sank against his skin. He sucked in a breath and held it. The gold patch sparked, then lit with azure flame. A moment later, it had vanished, leaving fresh pink tissue in its wake.

"Amazing," Hanuvar said.

"Like all magic, it has its cost."

"Where did you get the Volani spirits?" Hanuvar's casual tone belied the intensity in his expression.

Calenius lowered his arm. He did not ask how Hanuvar had been able to tell. The woman's spirit had been obvious, but it was possible Calenius had been too busy to see their garments.

"They are free to move on now," Calenius said.

"How many more do you hold?"

Calenius lowered his arm. "That's my business."

"They're my people."

The other man shook his head. "They're dead people. And if not for me, the revenants would have had them. You can probably guess what they wished them for. With me, they're free to move on once they've served their purpose."

Hanuvar kept his breath controlled, thinking of the trapped, lonely voices young Teonia had spoken of. "You haven't answered my question. How many do you have?"

Calenius' voice grew stern. "I've never counted them. Do you mean to break your word to me? I pledge that I will not harm them, and that come the next full moon I shall let them all go."

"Why?"

"It's enough that I speak the truth. You know me for a man of my word."

"I shall keep my word," Hanuvar said finally. "But I want the full truth from you."

"They were dead already, or going to be. It was war. I thought you could see far enough to understand that, but you're chained by sentiment."

"And you are not? You yourself said it had brought you to this point."

"So I did." Calenius flexed his arm a final time and then climbed to his feet. "Let's find a different camp site."

Both men were alert for other signs of pursuit, and before long they spotted a furred shape slinking in the distance after them. The surviving dog. Calenius gave Hanuvar a wry look.

He hadn't donned either ring. That, though, didn't seem to matter to the animal, who wandered in just beyond the campfire that night, downwind of the horses. It paced around a while and then hunkered onto the ground, its eyes just visible by reflected firelight.

The big man seemed entertained by its presence. When Hanuvar tossed it some of the rations he even chuckled and threw some himself.

The next day it followed closely enough that Calenius joked Hanuvar would have to name it, and the animal ranged even nearer to the campfire that evening.

In the succeeding nights Calenius had no more call to use the black stone, for they saw no other followers. They sat at a fire with the dog near Hanuvar, watching quietly, and Calenius spoke of the land as it had been, and olden times, with a strange vulnerability that reminded Hanuvar of the way Volani survivors spoke of their city.

"What happened to it?" Hanuvar asked.

Calenius was a moment answering. "Men happened to it. Men swollen with pride and men hungry for things they thought they needed. War came and famine followed."

"And you were there."

"Aye, and I fought against the end of things, and sometimes I brought it, and eventually I soured of it all and wandered. I have lived many lifetimes and learned many things."

"You have become a sorcerer. And a scholar."

"By necessity and accident. It's easy to know history if you've lived it, easy to know languages if you have spoken them. Look at you and the languages you speak, and the skills you've mastered to further your goals. Think how many more you would know if you were like me."

It sounded as though Calenius had familiarized himself with Hanuvar's activities, at least in part. He did not comment upon that. "So you're immortal."

"I don't age, which is a different thing. I am merely hard to kill." He fell silent, and the campfire drew flickering shadows across his heavy features. His eerie blue eyes fixed upon Hanuvar. "Most men, knowing this, would ask me how this has been achieved. You never do. Why is that?"

He could have told him he had been given an inkling of how that might be done last fall, and how unclean the experience had been. Instead, he shrugged. "What is a man without his people?"

"You would have endless days to see the new wonders men wrought, to glimpse new vistas. To chance new things."

"You sound like you're proposing a sale."

"What if I was?" Calenius' look was piercing, though he affected a breezy manner. "I could not offer it to you in the way I have it, but there are methods."

"You are lonely."

"I have company whenever I want. What I don't have is a peer."

Even with a companion Calenius would think himself peerless, but Hanuvar did not say that. "Give immortality to a philosopher, or a poet, or an inventor. Someone who can help to build a land where swords are needed less, and the children prosper."

"You think I haven't tried that? The playwright drowned himself after 150 years. Heartbroken after his village was wiped away by plague. A zealot killed the scientist. None of them could endure."

"And you think I could."

"You and I are of a kind. Oh, you're soft still. I see some of the mistakes in your thinking I used to make, but the potential's there. In a century or so, when the world's changed and any surviving descendants are remote, you'll grow beyond worries about a dog, or damaging the little lives you cross. Most of them matter no more than ants. If you step on one, others will come and it makes no difference in the larger scheme."

"You sound no different than a man born to great wealth. And yet I know you've suffered and struggled in a way those men rarely do."

Calenius looked mildly affronted. "There's a world of difference. I've tried to lift them up. But each generation they make the same mistakes. They stumble into the same hatreds and the same tragedies."

Hanuvar's thoughts turned fleetingly to the thirst for revenge he'd seen in the eyes of Bomilcar and his crew, and the same yearning he guessed present in his daughter. Was Calenius right? Were men and women doomed always to repeat the same kind of errors? "So what is it that you're working for, with all this searching, and this trip into the wilds? Something for yourself?"

"Perhaps. Or perhaps I'm not as far removed as I thought I was."

"Riddles. You hint you wish me to join you, but won't share your vision."

"I don't think your perspective is mature enough to understand it."

"You could explain."

"Perhaps." Calenius eyed him. "I will consider it."

Hanuvar did not crave immortality. The strength to carry on in health to see his goals won, certainly. But to achieve so much remove that he could view his fellow men as insects struck him as monstrous. He decided to probe further. "You try to sound calculating and unfeeling. But love for something drives you on. I think you may be a better man than you've convinced yourself you are."

"You don't know me."

"I've known the kind of men you pretend to be. They lack insight into the feelings of others. Their whole lives revolve around their own needs, and if they feel any kind of love it's mostly a sense of ownership. You're too perceptive to be one of them. Are you trying to fool yourself, so that your existence is less painful? Or have you fallen for your own deception?"

Calenius' gaze was long and searching. There was challenge there, and surprise. He looked as though he wished to say something, and went so far as to open his mouth. It was still a long moment before he spoke. "What do you mean to do, Hanuvar? Where are you taking them?"

"You don't know? You worked for the revenants."

"There are rumors of a colony, somewhere far away. But even the legate doubts it." Calenius' gaze was certain. "He underestimates you, doesn't he. He makes the mistake of believing you think like him. That you are centered around Derva and its doings so are envious and vengeful. You don't actually care about that background, do you? What's the place like?"

"You saw the beauty of Volanus," Hanuvar said wearily. "It is nothing so grand, except that it, too, sits by the sea, and my surviving people dwell there."

"And you mean to find them all. To take them there." The expression on Calenius' face shifted between admiration and ridicule, as if he were pulled back and forth between contrary emotions.

"While I still breathe, I will not abandon them."

"Most will not deserve that measure of loyalty."

"Am I being too sentimental? What is it you're really doing, Calenius?"

The big man looked almost as though he were ready to say. And then his mouth snapped shut.

"Will your plan harm my people?"

Calenius was a long time answering. There was only the sound of the fire crackling. The dog snuffled in its sleep. "Nothing I'm doing will bring direct harm to your people," he said finally.

Hanuvar recognized that as a reply carefully structured to speak truth while leaving damning details untold. "And indirectly?"

"I'll be working with powerful forces. But most of your people are far away, aren't they?"

"Yes. And the rest should be soon."

"I'll begin the spell on Esuvia the evening of the full moon."

"You're saying they should be gone by then. That doesn't leave us much time. What about the Dervans?"

"You can't honestly tell me you care about the fate of the Dervans."

"The majority had nothing to do with what happened to my people."

The sorcerer shook his head. "You had me thinking just now that we were even more alike than I thought. And then you go and say something like that. I've told you more than enough. You gave your word. Will you hold it?"

"I am a man of my word."

Calenius climbed to his feet. "Enough. We should sleep. Tomorrow we'll reach the mountain, and the guardian."

"What will this guardian be protecting?"

"An ancient tool."

"Is this what you sought in the tunnels?"

"No. I've found that. This is something else."

He stopped asking for details. If Calenius wished to say more about it, he would have. Apparently he'd had more candor than he could stand this evening.

IV

The next day they woke to gray skies. As they reached the forested slope of a spindly mountain the clouds opened up and soaked them for almost an hour. After, the sky remained overcast in dirty gray clouds, layering the remote countryside in shadows. Tyvol had been settled for long centuries, but in this rough hinterland they had gone two days without seeing so much as another cookfire. Untamed wilderness stretched to the horizon.

Once the rain abated they picketed their horses and worked their way up the mountain side. So used was Hanuvar to protecting against his old knee injury that he mentally readied for it to start bothering him on the long uphill climb. Just as swiftly he remembered he'd been untroubled by it since his magical accident late last year.

The view proved splendid. Rolling foothills, their greenery brightened by the rain, stretched into the distance, and once they were upon the mountain's forested shoulder Hanuvar discovered a river flowing just on its other side, swollen from the recent rain. Here at last were signs of civilization, for distant smoke rose against the southern sky.

Nearer at hand were signs of a far more ancient settlement. Walls of shining black stone peeked out from behind vines and bushes. Calenius examined them without comment and strode further uphill, from time to time pausing to collect his bearings.

His path took them further and further west, up to a wide, rocky ledge before a cliff rising toward the mountain's final height. Calenius chopped through some low-lying brush, revealing a cliff wall decorated with small letters and images.

A few months before Hanuvar had stood before images carved into the ruins that Calenius excavated upon Mount Esuvia. These were similar, precise marks with either perfect curves or perfectly straight lines carved deeply into stone, sided by depictions of the same huge bull-serpent hybrids. The recent rain darkened the etchings with peculiar clarity.

Calenius walked left to right along the rock face, studying them.

Hanuvar watched, his attention shifting sometimes to the stark peak rising above, or to their surroundings. Vegetation-wrapped stone pylons lay like the carcass of a monstrous beast, extending forty feet into empty space above the river gorge, perhaps the remnant of some ancient bridge that would have crossed to the mountain opposite.

The young mastiff inspected the grounds cautiously, sniffing, then moved to Hanuvar's side.

Calenius traced a span of the wall symbols with his fingers as he walked, then stopped and swept hands along twin sets of long, sharp characters.

The wall before them shuddered. Dirt and grime exploded in a cloud of dust; an arched stone door swung wide, revealing a dark cavern.

Calenius stood in contemplation, his red-maned head tilted to one side. He put one hand to his sword while the other was spread before him.

The dog growled.

After a long moment Calenius dropped his hand to the side. He spoke softly. "Ready a torch."

Both carried shoulder packs stuffed with equipment and supplies; Hanuvar slipped his off and took out one of the pre-prepared sturdy bundles of stiff plant fibers. One end had been dipped in wax. He chose a flat spot to lay out dry tinder. The dog watched closely, probably thinking they'd be cooking food.

Hanuvar's practiced hands soon raised a spark, and before long he rose with the light and stepped up beside Calenius.

"Here's where it gets interesting," the big man said.

Hanuvar would have preferred someone else hold the flame, but understood his role as assistant was the price for the information he had gained.

Calenius stepped forward into the cavern, Hanuvar just behind him. The torchlight revealed a rectangular hall carved into the mountainside, and threw back the glitter of gold, for the ancients had inlaid enough precious metal into the images on these black walls to set the emperor's accountants salivating.

The dust of long centuries coated the floor. The interior lay empty save for a rectangular stone plinth at its one end, crowded with figures and images in those flawless lines and curves. Behind it stood a peculiar elephant-sized sculpture resembling the inner workings of a complex pulley system, for it contained gears fashioned from some hard black metal. With its long black rods and elongated frame, the object looked a little as though a mad artist had begun fashioning a giant cricket from scraps found in a shipping warehouse and stopped before completion.

Calenius motioned for the torch and Hanuvar passed it over. The wizard walked to the shrine, the torchlight mirroring off the sculpture's shining black gears. To Hanuvar they alarmingly resembled the joints on a crab.

The tail of the big man's long red hair swayed as he lifted the torch high overhead. On the wall above the sculpture, man-shaped images pressed hands to round objects from which straight rays emerged, as though gods lay hands to the sun. One figure pushed a sun to the left, one to the right, and one in the middle lifted it over his head.

The figures themselves were depicted with the bare minimum of details—only flat lines suggested hands and feet, and the oval head had no features whatsoever.

"To what god does this temple belong?" Hanuvar asked.

"The Dervans have no real name for him, but in my tongue he is the lonely one, the lord of days."

Hanuvar then understood the god to represent the entity the Herrenes dubbed Tondros, the lord of time. He did not say it, but Calenius' look sharpened, as though he had recognized realization in Hanuvar's expression.

Calenius passed the torch back to Hanuvar, who took it, keeping his eyes from its bright heart.

The big man knelt before the dark stone and began to hum, his fingers slowly tracing over curving symbols.

The melody was striking and strange. Though highly repetitive, each pass through its darkly lyrical progression added an additional note so that it grew in complexity.

Calenius shifted along the altar upon his knees, tracing the figures more and more quickly, though the speed of his humming did not change.

Finally he arrived at the far end of the characters. His melody stopped abruptly, without resolution. He held his position, fingers splayed over the final symbols. His eyes lifted to the image on the back wall. Hanuvar's own gaze was pulled to that peculiar sculpture. After a long moment, some of its gears turned, despite the absence of visible rope or pulley. At the same time, high in the wall, a small rectangular door swung wide, revealing a cavity in which a curved white ram's horn rested upon a marble stand. Decorative metal reinforced the instrument's rim and formed a trumpet mouth piece, the torchlight setting it gleaming redly beneath webbing and dust.

Hanuvar returned his gaze to the sculpture. Its wheels had stopped their movement.

Calenius climbed to his feet. "It appears the measures I took countermanded the guardian."

As though it were a machine powered by hubris, the sculpture rose, poised on lean legs of black metal. It lifted a spinning circular gear at the end of a long black neck like a terrible head. It was not a cricket, but a wide centaur of metal with curved black arms like scythes. Its long metal legs sent vibrations through the floor as it stamped toward them.

Calenius darted in with his great sword and swung, only to have his blow parried by one of the curved black arms. Behind them the dog barked warnings, frantic with distress.

The metal thing scurried forward with a sudden burst of speed, and as Hanuvar backstepped he studied the joints and the spinning gears, seeing them as weak points if he carried the proper weapon. But he was unwilling to relinquish his sword to jam a gear. Calenius retreated with him, his brows drawn in concentration.

"It may not have power beyond the chamber," he said.

They passed beyond the threshold and the metallic thing clattered after, somehow all the more horrific in juxtaposition to the green mountainside, for there was nothing of the natural world about it. It paused briefly, its spinning head rising as if it sniffed its surroundings.

"Now what?" Hanuvar asked.

"Draw it left!"

Hanuvar waved his hands above his head and stepped away. The thing stamped after him, not swift, but certain, relentless, its pointed legs scoring the dirt and stone. Hanuvar backed toward the bridge remnant. The dog rushed the thing's side, barking, then crouched beneath a scythe-like blade that just missed taking off his ear tips.

Calenius raced from behind carrying a gleaming silver circlet the size of a dessert plate. He tossed it at the thing's back legs and the circle fastened about one of the metal limbs, at the same time lashing out with a snaky tendril for a second. The pressure pulled the legs toward one another. Though slowed, the thing limped still for Hanuvar, using the linked legs like a single one. It stretched its long cylindrical neck toward him, the headlike gear at its end spinning like a sling.

Hanuvar threw himself back as the gear shot his direction. He landed flat, the metal spinning over him and out beyond the cliff. He slapped the ground with his hands to absorb the impact, but unintentionally struck a rock with the back of his head. Stars flamed across his field of vision as he forced himself upright. Pained and dizzied by the impact, his footing was off, and he could only retreat toward the bridge as the metal monster limped on, swinging its blade arms for him again and again.

Calenius tossed a second of the silver circles, but the thing seemed to sense the attack coming, for it sidestepped. The circle rolled ineffectively to the right.

"Keep it distracted," Calenius shouted.

Hanuvar was too busy dodging to dignify the instructions with a response. He was being herded perilously close to the cliff's edge and the bridge remnant, and as Calenius dashed off he wondered if the wizard were simply hurrying away to grab the horn.

Only about eight feet to the left Calenius' second circle of metal lay glistening against the rocky soil, a plate-sized disc that might be of aid. The trick was reaching it without being sliced in half. Hanuvar gauged the timing of those swinging arms, readied his sword, and ducked beneath a scythe. He jammed his blade into a spinning gear at the base of the right blade arm.

The arm stopped its sideways movement but the thing turned and swung its neck at him. It wasn't a blade, but a metal club swung with such force could maim or kill. Hanuvar rolled sideways, wobbling when he came upright. His balance was still challenged from his head blow.

But he had arrived at the silver disc. He closed his hand on it, wondering how to activate the device, for there was no obvious trigger. Magic. He scowled, shoving the disc into his tunic before unlimbering his knife. The monster ignored the barking dog and limped on for him.

He supposed the best option left was to time a rush under that damaged limb, but he didn't fully trust his reaction speed. The remaining arm scythed back and forth as if it were eager to get into slicing range.

Calenius ran up on the opposite side of the metal monster with a sturdy tree limb twice the length of a spear. Immense muscles stood out on the wizard's heavy arms, and his teeth were clenched with effort.

Just before he made contact the bizarre machine pivoted, somehow sensing Calenius' approach. The log struck amongst its tethered legs and wedged in the pipes forming its greater body mass.

It flailed with legs and arms, either to seek purchase or to finish Hanuvar—without an obvious head it was hard to tell, but it was clearly being pushed into the only space left to him. He leapt out from the cliff and away. For a brief moment he was suspended in space and then he had landed athwart one of the pylon beams jutting above the turbulent river running swift and deep far below. He struggled to regain his breath. The black stone of the old bridge itself was slick, but the ivy coating was his salvation. He gripped the thick roots, twisting to watch the final moment of the battle. The thing had pressed all of its limbs to the earth, even its neck, seeking traction. The rocky soil it touched sparked and shrieked in protest as Calenius pushed it on for the cliff edge.

With a final savage shout Calenius shoved it over the side. The metal monster plunged into a stony projection fifty feet below, hitting with a loud metallic clang. Limbs and shards shot out in different directions, and then the greater mass tumbled into the foaming water.

The cliff's edge and safety lay only a few feet to Hanuvar's right, but he waited to catch his breath before he dared sidling along the bridge beam.

Calenius crunched up to the precipice and looked out at him, chest heaving.

"What was that?" Hanuvar asked.

"A guardian of the old ones," Calenius said. "I must have forgotten some of the ceremony."

"Pity."

"I couldn't have done this without you," the sorcerer said slowly, and the regret in his voice immediately alerted Hanuvar. "Which means I owe you my eternal thanks. My people, too, will thank you."

"Thank me by helping me to safety."

Calenius didn't move. The dog had trotted near him but eyed him with continued distrust, his gaze shifting back and forth between Hanuvar and the big man's leg. He let out an alert bark.

"I didn't plan this part," Calenius admitted. "I meant to take your measure, and I have. I'd have liked to have brought you with me. But I think you've figured it out, and I know now you'd try to stop me."

Hanuvar hadn't entirely deduced the man's plan, and watched him, one hand shifting first toward his throwing knife.

"I regret this," Calenius continued. From his belt he lifted a hatchet.

The dog had apparently seen enough. It launched at the wizard's leg.

Calenius pivoted, lashing out with one foot, and struck the mastiff's chest. The dog yiped and scrambled backward, then lost his footing on the cliff's edge. His back legs tried to dig into the cliff wall as his front paws struggled for purchase.

Hanuvar sidled right, hoping to reach firmer ground while Calenius was distracted, but the vines proved poorer purchase than imagined and his timing was off. Down he went, the dog plummeting after.

The moments stretched on, lengthened by his stress. The river implacably coursed below, and it seemed he had an eternity to consider the rising volume of the water and his oncoming doom. He recalled a Ruminian bragging about the way to survive cliff drops into the ocean, a game their young men sometimes played. He had quizzed the fellow at length, and his companions had chimed in. Strike feet first, they had said, with your arms folded across your chest, expel your air when you hit and kick for the surface.

How high was he? Somewhere he had heard no one survived a plunge from further than seventy-five feet and he felt certain he was higher than that.

He smelled the water as he neared, heard the smack of it as his feet took the surface. It smarted and his left ankle felt as though he'd been stabbed. He didn't cry out, though, for he was already under the cool water. The sound of the dog hitting nearby was a rush in his ears.

He expelled his breath, kicked to the surface. Something was wrong with his foot but he moved through the sharp pain around his ankle, and somehow his head broke water and he drifted, disoriented, the current sweeping him onward.

The dog paddled weakly nearby, spinning in circles. Everything had a dreamy, unreal quality. The river rolled him on past steep-sided mountain glades, beautiful and wild. Hanuvar wondered if he was going to die not from the terrible drop but because there was no way out of the current.

They were carried past rounded rocks and beyond a bend and down past another craggy mountain. Hanuvar, weakening, his arms heavy, his left leg numb from pain, his sandals clumsy weights, at last spotted a weed-choked gap along the rocky shoreline. He tapped his final reserves, fueled more by desperation than strength, and fought stroke by stroke against the water's pull until he'd reached calmer water. He pushed on into the shallows and got his feet under him, although his left would barely hold him. He stopped to take stock of himself and spotted the dog fifty feet behind, still paddling.

He paused his panting to whistle.

The animal saw him and made efforts in his direction. But the mastiff must have been nearly spent, for he advanced little.

Hanuvar moved out until he was almost shoulder deep, his arms extended. He called again, and the white-eyed dog struggled for him.

He came within a few feet, his ears up, his eyes wide, but didn't quite have the strength to make that final push to safety. Hanuvar leaned out, grabbed the mastiff's left front paw, and was spun himself into the current. Still holding to the dog, kicking through his pain, he fought again into the calmer water, swallowing a mouthful for his trouble.

But he got his good foot under him and released the dog, who struggled on to the shore. Hanuvar forced himself after. The mastiff staggered out of the water, head low, and trembling. He then plopped down on his side without even shaking off the water that streamed from his sodden fur, and lay panting.

Hanuvar scanned the environment as he limped dripping onto the sandy beach. He only just then registered how cold he was. A low hill lay before him, and piney mountains rose on either side. He saw no sign of human habitation, and they'd been carried far enough that both Calenius and his mountain had vanished from sight.

Hanuvar sank down beside the animal, whose tail wearily slapped the muddy bank. He reached out and ruffled his head. "Good dog."

He bent forward to feel his lower calf and ankle. Grimace-inducing pain followed his exploration. Gazing back the way they'd come, he imagined the mountain that lay beyond his sight and wondered if Calenius had seen his survival. He might be looking southward even now.

He hadn't entirely deduced what Calenius thought he'd want to stop, but knew with certainty he must. Unfortunately, he was on the wrong side of a river bank, deep in the remote Turian countryside, injured, and with almost no resources of his own, many days away from Calenius' home base, where he surely meant to work some great magic. The wizard intended to launch his ceremony on the full moon. That gave Hanuvar just over seven days to work his way back, on foot, and find a way to counter a man of vast resources who was stronger, faster, more experienced, and quite possibly smarter as well, not to mention a wizard of frightening potency, likely to have shielded his operations with any number of unseen protections. He'd certainly been fortifying it with visible ones.

The confrontation was not a pleasant prospect, but he forced himself upright. Though weary, dizzied, and in pain, there was no time to waste.

※ ※ ※

Long days were to pass before any of us back in Apicius grew concerned with Hanuvar's absence. After all, so far he had not been gone longer than expected.

Izivar kept herself occupied by managing her business. She had begun to divest herself of its more far-flung holdings, and, with some regrets, oversaw the packing and removal of many of the family treasures from the Apicius villa, which had long been her favorite of all the Lenereva properties.

We were soon to be swept up in matters beyond our control. First, a series of small quakes rocked the entire region, and Esuvia regularly sprouted smoke. Rumors spread that the wizard on the mountain had angered the local gods, and some even claimed that his people were digging strange trenches up and down the mountainside. This was something of an exaggeration, although eventually we were to learn the truth that had led to it.

Though the ground rumbled and Esuvia smoked, visitors flooded Apicius, for the Festival of Athelius was shortly to begin. And while Izivar and I naturally wondered how Hanuvar fared, we had other problems, namely the liberation of some that the festival had brought conveniently close.

—Sosilos, Book Sixteen

Chapter 10:
The Cup of Fate

I

A horde had descended upon the city and Antires strolled among its tents that morning. Men and women of all ages bustled in bright robes and tunics beneath the clear skies of the late Oscani summer. One older gentleman stood apart sonorously pronouncing his syllables in an ages old elocution exercise. Two women applied paint brushes to an elaborate wooden backdrop of an ocean scene to carefully add wave peaks.

Some two dozen separate acting troupes had arrived for the Festival of Athelius, and their temporary settlement spread beyond the city's outskirts near the outdoor stage built into a hill above the harbor, where the blazing orange sun now hung only a few handspans above the sea. Normally the actors would have found lodging in the resort town's many inns, but those already overflowed with out-of-town guests, some here for the holiday season but some specifically for the festival, which Izivar had said grew larger every year.

Long months had passed since Antires had walked among stage actors. It had been years since he'd seen so many, and his chest swelled with pleasure at the sights, and sounds, even the particular scent of wet scenery paint. He missed this life, challenging though it was. Had he wished, he was certain he might have tracked down some acquaintances. That probably wasn't a wise idea, though. Much as he would have loved to sit down with some fellow professionals and talk craft, he searched for a particular manager.

Many managers were actors, especially in the travelling troupes, but not all who fell in love with the stage could act, or write, or manufacture. Some were there owing to a talent to inspire and organize. And some were there because they had the money to fill a yearning for fame. Antires knew that was said about the man he sought today.

The tents of Antony Camillus were arrayed along semicircles in distinct units an eighth of a mile apart from the rest of the groups, for Camillus had actually purchased the closest land he could find to the festival, and even erected a small wooden stage of his own for practice purposes. His people adjusted backdrops upon it and rehearsed in little groups. A woman shouted that they were out of gold thread and the messenger boy better get back with it quick.

As he searched for someone in authority, a small plump woman passed before him and came to a sudden halt. She then turned her head to consider Antires with an intensity that grew disquieting.

She was about his own age, nearing her late twenties, and wore a simple brown tunic over a lush body. A necklace of small, dried flowers pointed toward deep cleavage. She was not at all the type to whom Antires was normally drawn, for he preferred his lovers lean. But he could not stop staring. Perhaps it was the directness of her gaze, or the outright beauty of her face. She was full-lipped, with the clear, dark olive skin of a westerner, and she possessed great dark, long-lashed eyes, but it was her unique sense of style which struck him the most. Her garb was very simple and spoke of a person possessing few resources. And yet she had done more with what she had than many a wealthy person commanding a phalanx of slaves. Her wavy hair was well kept, and decorated just so with a white bud, off center among a crown of dried wildflowers that matched her necklace. A tiny arrow of brown paint with a spiraling shaft decorated her left cheek, directly beneath her eye. Her short brown stola suited her so finely that despite its humble appearance it seemed the work of a master tailor.

"What do you seek?" she asked. Though accented, her pleasant alto was clear enough. He didn't quite place her home language. Possibly Cerdian.

If he'd been able to think more clearly, he might have tried a clever line about having come with another purpose and now being devoted to learning her name. "I'm looking for Antonius Camillus."

Her face fell. "I will take you to him. Come." She beckoned him to follow and started away without waiting to see if he would.

He jogged to reach her side, enjoying the scent of wildflowers wafting after her. She was silent as they moved past a pair of men holding up costume shirts to the sunlight. One groused that they were looking old.

Antires could not help wondering about the strange regard with which she had first eyed him. "Do you recognize something about me?"

"We have never met."

That was not what he had asked. He decided on a different course of action. "What is your name?"

"Ishana."

A Cerdian name, he thought, and since she did not give her family name, she was almost certainly a slave. "I am Stirses Arbasis."

"It is a pleasure." Her glance was brief but he felt as though she had brushed him with cool fingers. He wondered as to the strength of his reaction and almost convinced himself that it was due to him not having lain with anyone for long weeks.

She conducted him to an open-walled tent near the stage. A bald actor with handsome angular features stood at one corner, gesturing broadly as he spoke. Antires guessed him Hadiran by the light brown skin and blackness of his almond-shaped eyes. A young man in a fine white tunic with green edging listened, fiddling with his glittering rings before reaching for the stem of a goblet on a pedestal table. His was a large Dervan nose; his small brown eyes were intent, focused, impatient, as though the world's fate rested upon the actor's lines.

Antires and Ishana waited in the sun while the actor finished a stiff recitation. It sounded like someone had poorly translated the tale of Radanthes' heroic search for the cup of fate. The actor was describing his emotional state in great detail and contrasting it with the deep foliage through which he moved. Antires had seldom heard so clumsy a revelation of a character's feelings, but the Dervan nodded along, his eyes fixed and dreamy, as if he thought these words the height of eloquence. Antires looked to Ishana, who tipped her pretty locks toward the Dervan. This, then, was the man he sought.

Finally the actor halted, and Camillus started. His voice was cutting. "What? Go on, go on!"

The actor swiped his hand at the single parchment he held. He was skilled enough that he had barely glanced at it once. "I just keep talking about how brave and clever I am. Shouldn't I be doing something that's brave or clever?"

"How else are we going to hear about all the other things Radanthes has done?" Camillus' thin smile was triumphant, as though he'd won a victory. He took notice of Ishana. "What's this?" His attention swung to Antires. "Who's this?"

She bowed her head to him. "Master, this man seeks you. He is Stirses Arbasis."

"Excellent!" Camillus set down his goblet on a side table. "The new writer's here! Come on, man, you're late. So, you're a playwright?"

Antires had no prior appointment with Antony Camillus, nor did he have a reputation as a writer, for he'd never published anything under his assumed Stirses identity. But Antires answered as he moved in under the shade. "I am."

Camillus pointed loosely at the Hadiran, still waiting in the corner. "So what did you think of the script? I made changes based on feedback from Hypatia herself."

The famed literary critic Hypatia was one of the festival's sponsors, and Antires was momentarily impressed that she had given Antony any kind of time at all before remembering just how many doors money opened. He decided it would be wise to make clear he was not whom Camillus thought. "I think you have me confused with someone else."

Antony drew himself up as if insulted. "I am never confused."

For a brief moment Antires thought the Dervan joked, then saw no self-satisfied gleam in the other man's eyes. Antires cleared his throat to hide a smile. "You've confused me for some other writer. I'm not here about writing for you."

"But you are a writer, yes? Well, the one I sent for is late, and I need some help with a script. I'll pay you for your time."

Spoken, Antires thought, like a merchant, who, when unable to obtain one product, switches to selling another. He wanted to tell him that writers were not interchangeable, but he couldn't resist asking for more detail. "What sort of script?"

"It's about the hero Radanthes and his search for the cup of fate. The part you just heard is going to take place while Radanthes is creeping through the forest toward his rendezvous with the witch, and the serpent at the river crossing."

Everyone knew that Radanthes didn't meet the witch until long after he crossed the river. Antires chose to say nothing, understanding Camillus was one of those who loved his own voice above others.

Camillus repeated mention of the celebrated theater expert: "I'm in personal contact with Hypatia, who's quite fond of me. She's been giving me lots of excellent pointers. She wants my scripts to provide more insight into character."

"That sounds like good advice." Antires tried to ignore the watchful gaze of both the actor, whose mouth twisted scornfully, and the haunting Ishana.

Before Antires could speak further, Camillus continued. "A lot of people are saying I have a good chance to take home the wreath this year."

Almost, Antires asked for clarity, for so far as he knew there was no wreath for managing plays, only for writing them or being the finest actor or company. But he refrained and finally changed the subject when Camillus paused for breath.

"I'm here to offer money for some of your slaves."

"None of my slaves are for sale," Camillus declared flatly.

Antires tried his warmest smile. "Everything's for sale if the price is right."

Camillus' eyes narrowed. "Who do you work for?"

"My client wishes to remain anonymous."

Camillus clucked his tongue. "It's Atticus, isn't it."

Antires had no idea who that was. "I'm not at liberty to say."

"Be mysterious then. I shall ferret it out." His chin rose in defiance. "None of my actors are for sale."

This statement so surprised Antires he couldn't help blurting out a question. "Your actors are slaves?"

"Some of them. My Hadirans. The Cerdians."

"Now he'll tell you Hadirans can't act, and that only Herrenes are worth casting," the actor said with a malicious look.

Antires addressed him directly. "As point of fact, I've encountered fine actors from many lands." He probably should have stopped there, but could not resist adding: "Although Hadirans are trained in more representational drama and ritual. Their performances tend to be somewhat wooden."

"There it is," the actor said, softly triumphant.

Antires opened his mouth to clarify, then decided against pursuing the tangent any further, much less declaring that actors must be free to practice their art. He turned to Camillus. "I'm interested in your scenery and costume workers."

"Out of the question. They are essential to my performance."

"I'm not talking about now. I've no interest in hurting your performance. I mean afterward. You ought to be able to buy or hire different ones after the festival."

"They're Volani," Camillus sneered, as though they were late-season fruit. "Why do you want them in particular?"

He'd long since devised an explanation. "My client wants to reconstruct Volani plays. Most of the copies went up in flames and so did most of the actors. A lot of great works were lost. But people who worked in Volani theatre can help recall the lines."

Camillus waved his hand dismissively. "That's the old. Anything older than ten years back is worthless."

Antires doubted Camillus had come to such a profoundly idiotic idea on his own and wondered which fool's opinions he was parroting. And he didn't realize his mouth was open until he heard the actor jeer. "Look at him. He's gasping like a fish on the dock!"

Camillus lapped up the attention and continued. "These are modern times, not antiquity. Certainly, we can stand on the bones of the ancients, but we need to cast our eyes up, not down. Drama needs to address today's truths, even if it's using the old stories."

While he might have a fair point, it was so intertwined with others of arrogance and ignorance Antires saw reaching accord with Camillus on the subject of writing would be an exercise in frustration. "About those slaves?"

"I'm not interested in that. But I need a writer." He watched Antires speculatively.

"I thought you wanted a modern writer."

"You're living in modern times, aren't you? You can be modern."

"I really just want to negotiate for the slaves."

"I'll cut you a deal if you can do some writing for me."

Antires wondered what kind of fool would hire a writer without knowing anything about his skill. Still, at least Camillus was willing to consider selling. "What kind of deal?"

"Two thousand."

He wanted to make sure he understood. "Two thousand all together?"

"Each."

That was a high price for a male slave unless he was highly skilled in his craft. "I'll tell you what. You want Radanthes to be heroic? I happen to be an expert on heroes. I've been collecting tales of... military men and their exploits. Bravery. Monsters. Daring plans."

"Perfect!" Camillus cried.

"I'll act as your script advisor if you sell them for five hundred a piece."

Camillus' enthusiasm ebbed. "You think highly of yourself. Such rare workers are a bargain for one thousand each. And one of them is a woman."

"I'm interested in her for her knowledge, not her feminine attributes. Seven hundred fifty."

"Done."

Antires heard Ishana suck in a breath through her teeth, and, turning, detected a warning look in her eyes, but it swiftly vanished as Camillus noted her. "What are you still doing here? Get back to work."

"Yes, Master." Ishana left with a final backward glance to Antires. He wished he could understand what she was trying to communicate beyond caution. He was already wary around Camillus, whom he neither liked nor trusted.

She inspired Antires to suggest a condition. "I should like to consult with the Volani first to ensure they're who I need."

"I want to see what you can do before that." Camillus pointed to the actor. "Go see if the costume changes are complete. I'll have some new lines for you soon."

The actor bowed to him, fixed a prim, skeptical look upon Antires, and departed.

Camillus stepped to the side table at the back of the tent and removed a thick box from beneath a cloth. He walked toward Antires and opened what first seemed a hinged box lid. Antires then saw it was a wooden cover over a sheaf of paper that had been bound together along one side.

"This is a new way to keep books and plays organized," Camillus said proudly. "I want you to sit down at this table. I'll bring the stool over. Write down neat things heroes can do. On these pages."

Antires wanted to make sure he understood his instructions. "You want me to write... anecdotes?"

"Write some great scenes. With action! Prove to me that you're worth working with."

Soon Antires was seated at the table in front of the blank page. Camillus pushed the ink well and stylus toward him. He could reproduce any number of moments he had witnessed at Hanuvar's side—suitably changed to disguise Hanuvar's identity, of course—but he wanted to make sure he'd be giving the manager what he wanted. "I don't write like... that speech I just heard. I try to replicate how real people sound. At their best, though."

Camillus shrugged that off with disinterest. "All right."

Antires might have pointed out that he would probably be writing like those unworthy older writers, but decided against it.

He sat with stylus in hand, contemplating his options, then dipped its end into the ink, set it to the paper, and began the strangest writing assignment of his life. He immediately sketched out a moment similar to the one he'd faced with Hanuvar in the mountains when the lovely ones attacked, adding in the bird spirit Hanuvar had met earlier. Camillus stood at his shoulder, watching.

Antires glanced up at him. "How much do you want me to do?"

"Five or ten pages. Ten. Stay at it. I'll get you some wine."

Camillus didn't actually fetch it himself. He clapped, called for a slave boy, then sent the youth running.

Antires found that there was so much to say about the conduct of heroes that ten pages filled with incredible speed. He'd only downed a little bit of the wine by the time he concluded, continuing on to page eleven just a little so he could finish his thought. He lay down the stylus, flexed the fingers of his right hand, and took another sip of the sweet red.

Camillus swept up the papers and flipped through them. "This seems promising. I'll look it over and get back to you. You can go." He closed the cover flap and waved someone forward by wiggling the gold be-ringed fingers on his right hand.

Antires hadn't noticed the bull-necked fellow until he trod into view. With his size, his broken nose, and his unfriendly expression, his job title of bodyguard might as well have been stenciled on his forehead.

"What about our arrangement?" Antires asked. He climbed to his feet as the big man halted nearby.

"I'll get back to you on that." Camillus stepped to the front of the tent. The enforcer paused only an arm's length out from Antires, watching his employer for further command.

Though he didn't like the look of those hands, or the thought of one reaching for him, Antires was angered enough that he dared objecting. "You don't know where to find me."

"Leave word with my servant," Camillus said with marked disinterest.

Antires' voice rose in protest. "We agreed that you would trade slaves for my writing!"

Camillus smirked. "That's not the way I remember it. Did you get anything in writing from me?" He nodded to his bodyguard.

The big man cracked his knuckles, made a fist with one hand and lifted it, then indicated it with his free hand. He then suggested an alternative to the fist by using that same free hand to point away from the tent. Though furious at Camillus and irritated with himself for not being more canny, Antires couldn't help appreciating the simple eloquence of the enforcer's wordless options, reinforced by his flat-eyed expression.

Antires stalked away, his anger with himself quickly outpacing his fury with Camillus. This was probably the worst he'd ever bungled an assignment for Hanuvar, and it was one he'd thought himself ideally suited for. His failure was rooted in his own pride. He hadn't been able to resist the temptation to show off, then had gotten so absorbed in story creation he had lost sight of the real world, and the real people whose freedoms were at stake.

All he could do now was retreat, contemplate the weaknesses of his opponent, and devise a different approach. That, at least, is what he knew Hanuvar would do. It was the how, not the what, that stumped him.

II

Camillus nodded to himself as he considered the text again. The blathering Herrene had some decent stuff. Maybe even a little better than the last few fellows. There was definitely a lot of action in the two scenes, as well as a little detail about inner emotional states, and he knew Hypatia would love that.

He called for Ishana, whom he waved toward to the lacquer chest at the back of the tent before pouring himself another goblet of wine. Even mornings in Oscanus were hot, no matter that famed sea breeze.

He didn't like the way Ishana used her eyes, like she did now, as she rose from the chest and walked toward him. She held the little brown box in one little brown hand.

He handed her the book the Herrene had been writing in. "Use both the comedy and the tragedy," he instructed.

Ishana's double chins creased as she frowned. "Master, the priestess said not to use more than a single tress at once."

He hated uppity slaves. His life overflowed with them. "You think you remember better than me?"

She bowed her head but pressed on. "You bought me for my gift of insight."

"I bought you because you were supposed to see the future."

"My previous master exaggerated my ability. But I do sense the currents of fortune, Master, and that man who left is at or near the center of some."

That was so surprising he peered at her to see if she lied. Lies were easy to detect with most slaves, but he had never caught her in one; her previous master had also claimed she was sworn to speak truth. He still had trouble believing what she'd told him. "That chatty Herrene's important? He's a nobody. Just a writer."

"I see what I see."

"You're saying that man is as important as me?" Camillus tapped his chest.

"I'm saying he's where events are being shaped."

"You said the festival was that place, which makes sense because my play is going to be staged here soon." He pushed the manuscript at her, but she still did not take it.

Ishana's voice took on a plaintive quality. "I think we're at something rare, Master. A nexus. Think about it. Many have gathered here. Maybe many of importance, drawn by the festival. Many whose actions shape the course of events."

"And the Herrene is one?"

"I didn't say he was a shaper, merely that I sense his proximity to important currents. It may be dangerous to work with his words."

After a moment's consideration Camillus understood what she was seeing. Limited as slaves were, she observed without being able to draw an intelligent conclusion. "Maybe he's important to bring my ideas to life. His words are better than the last three. And he sounds more like Hypatia. Which is why I've got to use this to improve my play." He crossed his arms in satisfaction.

Her lips pursed. "Then choose comedy or tragedy, Master. Not both."

"Both," he said. He thrust the sheaf of papers toward her.

She could not hide her disappointment when she accepted it. "As you wish."

He watched while she carefully undid the cover and all but a single strand of the current binding from the pages. Then she lifted the long, ribbon like tresses of brunette and black hair by passing them through the loops carefully punched through the paper sides. "They're so lovely," she said. She always ended up commenting in admiration over the hairs. "They never fray."

"Of course they don't," he snapped. Why would they? But then she was a slave, and given to stating obvious things.

He thought over what she'd said earlier as she tied the cover into place. "Maybe we should learn who this man is working for. Did he tell you his name?"

"I told you his name, Master."

"That's not what I asked. He was a nobody, and I wasn't paying attention. Do you recall it?"

"I do."

"I want you to find him. Learn who he works for."

"He may not wish to talk, Master. Are there moneys to bribe him with?"

"Oh, bribe him with your body. You're appealing enough. And stop looking at me like that."

"Yes, Master. The book is ready."

"Get moving, then." He took it from her, and she was a moment late in releasing it. He elected to ignore her impertinence. "Find out who sent him, and why he's important."

"Yes, Master." She departed without a backward glance, or further argument.

Camillus ran his hands along the hairs now helping bind the book. Ishana was right—they really were incredibly smooth.

Retreating to the chair, he cleared his mind of anything but the glory of drama—his drama—and thought about the theatre, and the crowd standing and applauding him as he was crowned with the laurel leaves for the great work he'd done. He imagined the beautiful Hypatia's beaming smile being directed solely at him, and the envy of those when they learned that she was his, then flipped open the page after the one the Herrene had been writing on. He had copied the phrasing enough times now that he had it memorized.

He dipped the stylus in the ink well and began to write. "Muses I praise thee," he began. He continued: "I want to write a play in the style of the man who wrote these scenes. A heroic play about Radanthes and his search for the cup of fate, full of action without any boring parts, and also with good dialogue that Hypatia will love."

And then he gingerly closed the book, solemnly placed his hands upon it, and carefully repeated the old Herrenic words that drunken prune of a priestess had shown him.

The first few times he'd used the method he had felt a surge before the gods blessed him. This time he experienced a sudden warmth, as though the sun were briefly illuminating him and him alone. Sweat stood out on his brow and he wondered a moment if he had erred.

Then the moment was gone, and all was ordinary once more. He took his trembling hand from the book and opened it. The pages were dense with ink. He quickly rifled through the eleven pages at the front, and then, there it was, in his handwriting, his newest masterwork. Ordinary writers had to slave for long hours to channel the muses, but with his shortcut all he needed were their hairs and a special prayer.

He looked down at the words on the next page, written in his own hand: *The Cup of Fate*, Scene 1.

He laughed with pleasure. Too bad he'd sent Ishana away. He would have to unthread the binding himself—he trusted no others—then get his slaves to copying the manuscript for the actors.

III

Antires and Izivar were conducted through rooms cluttered with Herrenic sculpture and walls enlivened by murals of swans and heroes and horses and ships, and out to a high-walled garden thick with the scent of flowers. The smiling slave stopped to gesture to a narrow-columned cupola where Hypatia lazed upon a couch in the shade, sipping wine and pouring over a sheaf of papers. She could not have been much older than Antires, a slim Herrene with warm eyes, a small nose with an upturned tip and a smattering of dark freckles on her light brown cheeks.

A Dervan woman would have greeted an acquaintance more formally, but Herrenic women were much less staid, and thus Hypatia remained seated, smiled widely, gave them a friendly wave, and beckoned them forward. Nor did she set her manuscript aside, as almost any Dervan patrician might have done, for among Herrenes it was not considered rude to entertain with work in one's lap.[22]

Hypatia's history and analysis of great tragic works had caused a sensation amongst the intellectuals of the inner sea, one that had spread more widely once her gender was disclosed, and the fact that her beauty was said to rival that of the gods. That was hyperbole, although Antires found Hypatia comely.

Having met her at the festival two years previous, Izivar had requested a visit and been invited for a light lunch at the villa that the famous scholar rented each year at this time. Antires couldn't help wondering what the critic had made of her home's sculptures, looted from the cities of their people. From the elaborate cornices he knew the origin point of two pedestal bases for Orinth, a city the Dervans

---

[22] That a freeborn Herrene held a position of wealth and authority in Dervan society was not uncommon even in the days of empire, for the Dervans admired the older culture and its arts even as they conquered it. Herrenic scholars in particular were prized and were often bestowed with lavish gifts that might include slaves, property, and even citizenship, though Hypatia, as a woman, would not have been granted the latter. —*Sosilos*

had crushed almost as thoroughly as Volanus. Did Hypatia prominently display the art as a statement most Dervans would be too unsophisticated to understand, or had she simply ignored the graceless decorations placed by the villa's owners? If she proved open enough, he resolved to ask.

Izivar, as elegant and self-possessed as ever, introduced Antires as a writer friend, then, when invited, took the couch beside the critic. Antires sat beside Izivar, nearest the side table that supported a covered platter. An aged Ceori slave woman served Izivar chilled wine before turning to Antires to offer the same. In the meantime, Izivar and Hypatia inquired about one another's health at some length. Neither so much as glanced at the platter. Apparently neither of them were actually hungry.

As if to challenge Antires' appetite further, Izivar turned the topic to feasts associated with the festival, and segued into a mention of Hypatia's Volani cooks, and whether Hypatia was truly attached to them.

"Do you know, this is the second inquiry I've had about my cooks." Hypatia's Dervan was perfectly understandable, but her accent remained strong. She had been contacted by Carthalo's agents, and refused their offers. "They are quite marvelous," Hypatia continued. "And I could not imagine parting with them."

Izivar knew how to answer that. "If I can't persuade you to sell, I'd hoped to arrange meetings between them and Stirses. I'm certain that they're a storehouse of recipes from my people. I would like to record them."

Hypatia's expression cleared. "Of course!" Their young guide had long since departed, but the older Ceori remained. Hypatia turned to her, pointing to Antires as she did so. "Please take this gentleman to the kitchen."

The slave conducted Antires away. He heard Izivar thanking Hypatia and asking what she'd been reading and clenched his teeth when Hypatia revealed Antony Camillus had sent the papers she held round to her this morning. Before he could hear more he was led to a back building separated from the house by a stretch of tile.

There a young man and a middle-aged woman shaped bread dough. The bored Ceori introduced Antires as a servant of Izivar Lenereva and conveyed how their mistress had instructed them to share recipes with him. She then departed, stiff-backed, and the two slaves paused in their work to eye Antires. The woman did so with considerable skepticism.

The boy was no more than seventeen, spare and a little hollow eyed, as though he had witnessed horrors he still watched. The broad-faced woman was likely in her early forties and revealed nothing of her inner world in the colorless stare she gave Antires.

"Recipes?" she asked. Her Volani accent was thick. "For the Lady Lenereva?"

Antires addressed her then in Volani. His own skill with it had improved markedly in the last months, since it was the primary language spoken amongst his companions. "Does anyone else on the premises speak Volani?"

"No," the woman answered, her look warmed to careful interest.

"Then let us speak it, and quickly, before we come to discussing recipes."

"We need to talk while we knead. Step closer, Herrene, and tell me your name."

"You may call me Stirses."

He drew up beside them and they resumed their vigorous dough working on the wooden table.

"I'll get to the point so I've time to write some recipes. The Lady Lenereva would have you free and living among your own people, but your current owner refuses to sell."

The boy froze, gaping in astonishment. The woman's eyes widened, and she faltered before resuming, the white dough rising and following under her ministrations. "Our owner treats us well. Back to work, son."

"You are freeborn Volani. If you would be free again, I'd help you arrange it."

"Your Lady was traitor to our people."

That was hardly fair or accurate to Izivar, although he recognized that there was an element of truth to her assertion. Izivar's family had publicly sided with Derva, breaking with Volanus in the months before the war. A defense of Izivar now, though, would only complicate the interaction.

"She works in service for another, whose name I dare not say. You were employed by his cousin's family, and he once pulled you aside to praise you for the excellence of your braised fish stew, the one you served with the seared flat bread and oysters at the occasion of their daughter's promotion. He commended you to me, and told me your full name was Coriandra Anitasis, and that your employer declared you a treasure without price."

Coriandra eyed him more somberly. "Why do you lie to me? That man is dead, as is his cousin and his wife, both of whom I loved."

"I do not lie."

The boy asked quietly: "Who is he talking about, Mother?"

"The rumors that he lives are true," Antires continued. "He's won the Lady to his cause and works to free the Volani. Through her, through me, through others."

"And where would we live?" she asked softly.

"You served the man's family. Surely you can guess."

He saw from her eyes that she could, but she said so anyway. Her voice was almost breathless. "The colony. But where is it? And how many live there? And how did he survive? They said he fell from the sky, hundreds of feet—"

"There will be time to speak of that later. Know that he recalls you well, and that he would have freed you sooner except that there were others in far more terrible conditions. They had to be cared for first."

Coriandra raised a meaty forearm to her face to wipe at a cheek, wetting now with tears. "What would he have us do?"

Antires would have liked to have told her this particular arrangement was Izivar's plan, but he decided that could be explained later. It was she who had suggested taking advantage of the parade of costumed figures that closed the festival in five more days. The chaotic after party would provide the ideal screen for the removal of no less than two sets of slaves they'd been unable to obtain through Dervan legal means, if he could find a way to connect with the theatre people on the staff of Antony Camillus. Likely it would suit the recovery of an additional single slave as well.

For now, he concentrated on the specifics these two would need to know. They would be the simplest to remove of all the groups, for Coriandra was the master chef overseeing a party her mistress was throwing stageside on the heels of the final performance. She and her son would therefore be in close proximity to the inebriated crowd, and easily able to disappear within it.

Antires went over the schedule with them no less than four times, until he was certain they remembered the timeline and the locations and the details, and then he transcribed four recipes before returning to Izivar. He'd already written down eight other Volani ones ahead of time in case he'd be asked to show his work.

IV

When Camillus returned to Hypatia's villa that afternoon, he sent flowers before him. After an untimely delay he was conducted to the rear of the villa and the same courtyard where she had entertained him previously. He was a little surprised to discover that she had company, a pretty woman with dark curling hair, and the same Herrene who'd helped him write his masterpiece that morning.

Hypatia sat with the script—his script—in her hands, and open.

The Herrene stared at him with open loathing. Camillus didn't care about that, for the opinion of lackeys counted for nothing, but he knew a sudden chill. What if the man worked for Hypatia? Why else would he be here? He had not seen Ishana since this morning and swore under his breath at her for not getting back to him sooner.

"Welcome, Antony," Hypatia said. He thrilled to the sound of her accent. Her manner was always so much warmer than that of Dervan women, but not in a slatternly way.

She continued: "What brings you here?"

He bowed to her. "You, of course! Ah, you are as radiant as ever! And I see that you have received my script as well as my flowers!" He had seen those displayed in a vase inside.

"And your generous donation," she said. "It is appreciated and will go toward the support and upkeep of the festival."

He supposed she said that for the benefit of her companions.

She introduced him with one well-manicured hand. "This is Antonius Camillus, author of the text I've been reading you excerpts from. Antony, this is the Lady Izivar Lenereva, and her friend Stirses Arbasis."

"Charmed, I'm sure." He was pleased to hear the Herrene man was no close associate of Hypatia's. "So you've read my play then? What do you think?"

She did not answer immediately, and, disconcertingly, answered with a question of her own. "Why do you want to write plays, Antony?"

Why did anyone? "To be famous, of course."

The Lenereva woman's mouth downturned. Stirses shook his head. But their opinion didn't matter. Hypatia still smiled.

"What did you think?" Camillus prompted.

She ran her hand along the page edge and spoke haltingly. "There are fine lines throughout—although they are reminiscent of lines other poets have written."

"Like me," Stirses grumbled.

"And there's no depth of character here," Hypatia added. "These are just people doing things. And other people talking about them doing those same things. They all sound exactly alike."

"... but I told the paper—I deliberately structured it so that the characters' internal lives are brought forward."

"And you use deus ex machina in four separate scenes."

The chiding tone in her voice astonished him. "People love those! People still talk about Etiocles and the bit when Thereon was lowered on the stage by the hand of the god to set things right!"

Hypatia's expression grew pained. "Etiocles used the deus ex machina as commentary on the artificiality of a happy ending forced upon a situation brought about by men, one that could not end well without the intrusion of the gods."

What was that supposed to mean? "People love it when the gods appear on stage!"

She folded her hands over the pages and leaned toward him, her brows lifted sympathetically. "Antony, my oldest brother always wanted to be a great runner and to participate in the Herrenic games. He practiced and practiced. But he just wasn't very quick. He got faster, but not fast enough. Some people can't sing, no matter how much they love music. It might be that you don't have an ear for the way people talk... or behave."

He didn't appreciate her condescending tone. "I hear people talk all the time."

"I'm just saying that there's no shame in not being good at something. Find something you are good at, and—"

Her words stung deeply. How dare she? "My work is blessed by the muses of tragedy and comedy! How could you not like it? I spent a lot of money on that!" Almost he confessed how much he had paid for the muse hairs.

"It's not about money, it's about art."

"It ought to be a little about money," Stirses said. "He didn't give me any."

Who needed to hear from him? "Oh, hush," Camillus snapped. "You just wrote down a few ideas. I did the rest."

Hypatia's smile faded. "I'm sorry. I can't advise that you stage this." She leaned forward and extended the pages to him.

"You don't think anything in here is good?" He did not ask if she were blind, though he was tempted.

"There are some fine lines," she offered. "But are they yours?"

"Of course they're mine! I'm going to take this back and make it even better! You'll see! You want deeper characters, I'll give them to you!"

He heard her calling to him as he departed but he didn't take pity on her. He would show her yet.

V

Hypatia did not speak until the angry manager had stalked from the garden. "He's no worse than a lot of successful men," she said, as if in apology.

Antires thought Hypatia was being far too charitable. "He's a thief. He took my words, and the words of greater playwrights, chopped them up, and served them warmed over."

"Did you not do the same when you first began to write?" Her gaze was shrewd. "Poets often learn by imitation first."

He bowed his head in acknowledgment. She understood how the craft worked. "You're not condoning plagiarism?"

"No, I'm merely saying that in some form or another it is understandable when a poet is new to the work."

"The difference being that this man has the money and influence to peddle this work as his own, before he has improved. If he's capable of improving."

Izivar gave him a warning glance.

"I'm afraid we're boring our companion," Hypatia said.

"Not at all." Izivar turned to Antires. "Great work stands the test of time. Even if Camillus has this work staged, it will not endure. I'm sure it hurts to see poor productions succeed when you know other writers deserve better acclaim, but... there are many tragedies in the world."

Hypatia laughed lightly at her word play. A practiced hostess, she changed the topic of conversation rather than dwelling on the unpleasant. She eyed Antires. "So those lines I liked about regret—those were yours? Have you considered writing a play?"

He had, of course, and he'd written a few when he was younger, but he had no intention of showing her that early work, not just because it was raw, but because he lived under a pseudonym.

Izivar came to his rescue. "He's working on one right now, but he's such a perfectionist it isn't ready yet."

"Oh?" Hypatia asked. "What's the subject?"

"The fall of Volanus."

"Oh." Hypatia smiled uncomfortably. "That's a fine subject but... a little too contemporary. Dervans won't want to hear anything critical of their own recent history."

That was certainly true, and Antires nodded.

"You could set it at some other time so people could see the parallels. And if you're clever enough with it, maybe the ones inclined to be put off would just see it as a tragedy."

"I'm still in the research phase," Antires said. It was true, in a way. He was certainly recording details of the Volani rescue effort as it happened. "But I will consider your words when it's time to lay out the events."

Izivar came to his rescue again, turning the tide of conversation. "Hypatia, I hear rumors that you're working on a new book. One about the great comedies, and the art of humor?"

"It's true," Hypatia said with a laugh. "I can tell you a little about it while we eat."

Both subjects sounded of immense interest, but the return of the female Ceori slave at Hypatia's elbow diverted Hypatia's attention. "What is it?"

"Your pardon, mistress. A visitor has come to the servant's entrance, asking for one of your guests." The Ceori looked toward

Antires. He had no idea who this person would be. Certainly he hadn't told anyone he would be here. Nor, so far as he knew, was he waiting on word from anyone. Might Hanuvar have found some way to contact him?

Hypatia regarded him with a slightly strained politeness, for it was gauche to be called upon while visiting the home of a social superior.

"My apologies, Lady," Antires said quickly. "I left word with no one to seek me here."

Hypatia turned to the house slave. "Did this person identify himself?"

"*She* is a Cerdian slave woman," the Ceori explained. "A pretty one." She did not verbally suggest that the visitor was a prostitute, but her prim, disapproving look certainly suggested it.

"That sounds like the servant of Camillus, whom I met earlier," Antires said, more puzzled than ever. "I've no idea what she wants. Camillus certainly had no use for me."

"Should I have her sent away?" Hypatia asked.

He would have preferred to finally sample Hypatia's food and gladly have heard about her new book, but it might just be that Ishana could connect him to Camillus' Volani slaves. "Ah. No. I'll look into it."

Seeing Hypatia's look and the smug exchange the Ceori had with her he knew he'd just sunk lower in the famed critic's estimation. First, he'd seemed a mere "want-to-be" writer, and now he appeared low class, even a liar. "Excuse me," he said, hoping his face was not flushing too obviously, and turned to the slave. "Would you show me the way?"

Izivar gave him a searching stare and he lifted an empty hand to illustrate his true mystification, then followed the slave through the villa's luxuries and out to a walled back courtyard. Again he passed the cooks, now working on some elaborate confection that smelled wonderfully of honey. He nodded in greeting and waited as the Ceori slave opened a gate in the wall.

While he had remembered Ishana's eyes were striking, memory paled to experience. Already he had misremembered her body type as being thinner than it was in truth, but the roundness was pleasing.

"I am sorry to intrude, sir," she said. "I wondered if you might have a moment to speak alone."

Hypatia's slave waited with a look much more openly sanctimonious than it had been in the garden.

Antires frowned at her. "I will leave."

"Of course, sir." The last word was emphasized with a hint of irony.

He stepped out into a side street, the wall of a smaller home across from him. The gate closed and then the slave seemed to lower the cross bar on the other side with a conclusive thunk demonstrative of her contempt.

"I hope that I did not take you from something important," Ishana said.

He shook his head. "How did you find me?"

She started slowly down the alleyway and he walked with her.

"You presented a challenge, for it happens there are many handsome Herrenes in Apicius during the festival. However, I asked locals about your name and some eventually pointed me to the home of Izivar Lenereva, and workers there directed me here."

Her compliment flattered him, no matter its directness. "And why did you seek me?"

"I told my master you were important. He told me to find you, and who you worked for. And so I have."

"You could have stopped the moment you learned I worked with Izivar Lenereva."

"With, and not for?"

Ishana was perceptive. "Camillus just came to the villa only a short while ago. He surely knows who I work for now."

They turned onto a side street. In midday, the residential avenue was mostly deserted, and they walked side by side upon the raised sidewalk. A single horse-drawn cart passed them, the driver arguing with his companion over which chariot driver was the best. The chickens penned in the little cages in the cart behind them clucked and fussed.

"He may, or he may not," Ishana said. "He never examines anything deeply. It pleases me to know more, because I am thorough, especially when it comes to finding ways to stay clear of my master. Is it true, what you told him about why you want these Volani?"

Most Volani plays had been lost in the great city's destruction, and the stage workers were likely to remember sections of them, but that was not the primary reason he sought their recovery. Still, he had spoken truth. "Yes."

"Is there more to it than this?"

Her perception unnerved him, especially since he thought himself a practiced actor.

"Do you mean to tell him all I say?"

"Him? No." She laughed. "I ask now for me."

"And why should you care? And why did you say I was important?"

She paused at a corner, then with a hand suggested they turn up a narrow street veering uphill, rather than downhill toward a busy market. "I am a Faedahni spirit talker. Do you know what that means?"

"I know you should not say it very loudly in Dervan lands."

"Indeed. And because the Dervans maneuver the Faedahni city-states almost like puppets my training is not what it might have been a generation ago. But I sense the currents of fate." She studied him, as if watching to see whether he would mock her. When he did not, she continued. "I know that there is something underway, in this region. Something important that has nothing to do with my master or his play, at least in no lasting way. Something of consequence to me. There are many currents readying to collide at this time, and you are close to one of their centers. I feel it upon you, just as I feel in your gaze that you would be a kinder master."

She used those eyes against him once more, and as she stopped and peered up at him he was distinctly aware of her curves as she drew within a finger span of touching him.

He cleared his throat.

Her laugh was musical as she stepped back. "I have made you blush!" She took his hand, and his heart thrummed. "I thought you might be one of those Herrenes who loves boys."

"I have loved men and women," he said. "Though none of them wisely. Or perhaps very well," he added.

"Have I found an honest poet?" she asked. "I have met many writers, and they were boasters or mopers or a mix of those things."

"All writers are liars," Antires admitted.

"That seems overstated."

"I suppose some try to use their lies to shape great truths."

"Is that what you do? Who do you write your truth for?"

"I'd like to think the stories I tell would ennoble the hearts of all who read them. But maybe I'm as deluded as your master and all I really crave is fame, and approval, and the look I've glimpsed in your eyes. You tried to warn me about Camillus stealing from me, didn't you?"

"I wish I could have said more. He is too worried about the upcoming performance to consider parting with any of his slaves now. The master might yet sell the craftspeople after the festival, as you suggested, but I gather you do not wish to wait until then to see if that can happen."

"I don't. I can't..." He sighed. Hanuvar always made this seem easy. Much as he prided himself on working with words, he had trouble articulating to her what he hoped to accomplish without giving away too much. Because he could not buy the slaves at the outset, he hoped to sneak them out at the same time he helped the cooks to escape, but that would require consultation with them. He wished he could fully trust her to assist in doing that, for he dearly wanted to. She was fascinating. Not just because of her physical effect upon him, although that surely played a part, but because of her agile insight. He'd never spoken with anyone quite like her. He decided to test her with a question on a subject that had been puzzling him. "How did your master draft a script so fast?"

She lowered her voice and stopped once more in front of a wall scrawled with a rude limerick. "I shall tell you," she said softly. "This is his greatest secret. He has no stories of his own worth sharing, for he has a heart of stone and can no better understand another's needs than an insect can guess human thought. He can see no further than himself. He has fallen in love with the idea of people cheering for him and speaking of him as they do the great tale tellers."

"And he did something," Antires suggested. "Something with that bound sheaf of papers."

"Yes, the book. Again and again he paid court to the temple of muses in Arbos.[23] He donated generously to one priestess in particular and was given a special gift. Once, long ago, the muses visited the temple and presented the priestesses there with strands

---

[23] The temple to the muses lies not upon the acropolis of Arbos, but in the nearby countryside, in a small ancillary village, built into the side of a hill. —*Sosilos*

of their hair. From of old, when those strands were incorporated into bindings while a work was under way, the poets who employed them wrote greater works. They did not trouble over lines that did not match meter, or rhymes, or lack for ideas."

"I've never heard of this or seen that method of binding paper. Camillus said it was new."

"It is ancient, like the temple secrets. The hairs were stolen or dispersed to favored poets, and the final few have been hidden, used only by the priestesses in sacred rites and poems written to extol the virtues of the muses."

Antires found that surprising, but not as startling as another thought. "If Camillus' writing comes from the muses, why is it so bad?"

"Because he puts no soul into it, and little understanding. He but says what he desires based upon the words of others and then the magic fills in the rest, with no guidance or skill. The priestess showed him the technique, warning him to use it only for inspiration. She instructed him never to use more than one kind of strand, but he used two this morning."

"Two kinds?"

"He has locks from the muses of tragedy, comedy, and history."

Antires wondered what his own writing would sound like if it were paired with inspiration from the gods. Then he shook his head at himself. This was all quite interesting, but it wasn't germane to where his real focus ought to lie. "Do you think you could arrange a meeting between me and the Volani slaves?"

"Are you going to encourage them to run? Can you shelter them? You know that the master would be suspicious of your employer and seek there first, don't you? Can you keep them safe? They would be tortured to death if caught."

He did not answer any of her questions, but she replied to his silence.

"You've already thought through the dangers once they're free, haven't you?" She sounded impressed with him, and her look was warm.

Because little of the planning was his own, it seemed disingenuous to accept credit for having thought anything out himself. "You're using your magics to read me?"

"I'm just reading your body language. You, or those you work with, have anticipated much. Is Stirses your real name?"

Her insight was remarkable. He took her other hand. "Can you arrange a meeting with them?"

"I may be able to do so. But if you plan what I think, you must promise to take me with them."

"It shall be my pleasure."

"You must pledge to keep me safe."

"With all my heart."

He met those eyes and he saw her invitation in them. Her lips were soft and full. When they parted he was hungry for many more of those kisses, and his heart was a thundering drum. Her hands were warm and wrapped about his own. He could not tear his gaze from her.

"The master's performance is first after the ceremony introducing the first day," she said. "He will be celebrating afterward. I can think of no better time to speak with the slaves you want. Where will you be?"

"I can be at the stage then," he said.

"I will find you and lead you to them. What is it you mean to do now? Are you off to work this miracle for others?"

Once again her keen perception astonished him. "You see too much," he said. "I think you're dangerous."

"I will never be dangerous for you," she pledged.

"Maybe I like a little danger."

She tapped his nose with her finger. "We shall have to see what you like, later. I must return to my terrible master."

He kissed the back of her hand, astonished that he did so. "I look forward to seeing you," he said. "Shall I walk you—"

"Carry on with your own doings, and we will meet again soon."

He bowed his head to her. He would have liked to take her for a proper meal and then to some dark corner where he might gaze into her eyes and drink more kisses and perhaps advance his lips into other regions, but his time was not his own. He watched until she had turned the corner, then continued on for his next appointment.

The final slave he meant to free worked as a tailor for a famous Dervan actor. Ahuum had been low on the priority list almost from the beginning, for the actor himself had talked publicly about the excellence of Ahuum's work and how he treated him like the treasure he was. Now, with the main rescue efforts winding down in Tyvol, it was time to address the better off cases, and the festival had brought Ahuum's master, along with the tailor himself.

It turned out that the Volani man yearned for freedom as much as any and proved even less skeptical of Antires than the cooks.

Reaching him for conversation had required some complex maneuvering, and several more hours passed before Antires returned to Izivar's villa. Reshef, Izivar's reliable doorman, let him know the mistress had guests, a warning look in his eyes. "She was in the bath when they arrived and will be receiving them soon. I imagine that your company would be appreciated."

"Guests? What guests?"

Reshef lowered his voice, his homely face somber. "Captain Bomilcar and a young woman."

Antires could scarce believe it. "Did he return with"—he cut himself off before saying the name he wasn't supposed to speak—"Decius' daughter?"

"I don't know."

"May the gods show favor. Where's Izivar now?"

"The new girl was helping her get ready."

Antires found Izivar emerging from her chambers. Her hair was still damp but had been carefully brushed, and the teenaged volunteer brought from Amelia's villa was still adjusting the way it lay as they started into the hall. Izivar had confided that Serliva's replacement was woefully underprepared either for helping with garment choices or the arrangement of hair, but she was eager to learn and practiced on anyone who let her. Izivar thanked the girl, fussed with the collar of her light red stola, then took in Antires. "I'm glad you're here."

"Is Narisia with him?"

"I don't know. Let's go find out."

A young man and woman sat at one end of the long dining room table over some leftover bread, goat cheese, and wine. Both turned at Izivar's entrance. Antires walked at her elbow, watching them. Even after the brunette raised her hand in greeting it took a moment for him to recognize her as Elistala, for she looked very different from the determined, wounded warrior he had first glimpsed in the company of Hanuvar and Ciprion. In her simple Dervan dress she might have passed for one of the sturdy, sweet-faced farm girls common in the Tyvolian countryside.

She climbed to her feet a moment behind the man. Antires recognized him as Bomilcar primarily from his powerful chin, because all of their interactions had transpired by moonlight. He wore an ordinary blue tunic, salt and sun stained, and his light brown eyes shone brightly in his tanned face. He carried with him that scent of the sea somehow borne by sailors even after they left the bathhouse. And these two had clearly not visited a bathhouse prior to their visit.

Both visitors gave Izivar a formal bow and the captain addressed her in Volani. "Thank you for receiving us."

"You are Captain Bomilcar?" Izivar asked, to be certain.

He bowed his head once more. "I am, my Lady. Allow me to present Elistala of the Eltyr."

Elistala's sleeved dress was in significantly better condition than her captain's tunic. Almost certainly it had been pulled from storage chests, for he doubted the Eltyr wore Dervan dresses on ship.

Izivar spread her arms and offered the traditional Volani phrase of welcome. "My home is open to you. May its comforts fill your needs. I am Izivar Lenereva and this is Stirses Abasis."

"Stirses?" Elistala asked doubtfully.

"They know my real name," Antires explained to Izivar.

"Of course," she said. "I'd forgotten that you'd met them both."

"Where is General Hanuvar?" Elistala asked.

"We call him Decius," Izivar said smoothly. "He is travelling."

"Decius?" The Eltyr sounded scandalized. "Why do you call him Decius?"

At the same time Bomilcar asked: "When will he return?" His tone was brusque.

Izivar took the chair out at the head of the table and gestured to her guests to resume their seats.

Antires sat down beside Elistala. He reached for the wine pitcher and poured himself a cup the steward had set out. Out in the kitchens some servant dropped a plate. Its smash against the tiles rang through the house, along with an oath. Antires detected the scent of roasting lamb.

Izivar answered the first question. "We call him Decius so we're not in habit of using the other one and forget when we're in public. As for when Decius will come back," Izivar said, turning to Bomilcar, "he is likely a few days away, still. He's looking for information about his niece."

Bomilcar frowned. "We have news we know he'll want to hear. His daughter is well. And so is his niece, for that matter."

Their last communication from Hanuvar had conveyed that he had magically observed both Narisia and Edonia in Cerdia, but it was still fine to hear confirmation, and Izivar smiled with Antires.

"Why didn't they come back with you?" Antires asked.

Elistala explained. "Narisia's in Cerdia, readying them for the war against Derva." Her features twisted into a frown as she took note of Izivar's troubled look. "You don't approve?" While she did not state outright that a traitorous Lenereva would naturally side with Derva, her sentiment was obvious.

"The Lady Izivar wants to see Decius reunited with his daughter," Antires said. "That's all."

Bomilcar traded a significant look with Elistala, who fell silent but appeared doubtful.

The captain placed something on the table with a light thunk. When he lifted his hand Antires saw that he had left behind a short, thin wooden scroll tube. "The gen... Decius' daughter wrote that for him."

A letter from Narisia. Antires could scarce believe it. If only Hanuvar were here! "What does it say?"

"I don't know."

As Izivar studied the scroll's tube, Antires saw from her wistful expression how much she wanted him here. "I will keep it safe for him," she promised.

"See that you do." Bomilcar bowed his head formally, and then climbed to his feet. Belatedly, Elistala did the same. "We will return tomorrow."

Izivar stood too, in mild confusion. "You are welcome to stay. My cooks will have something ready for you shortly."

The captain again bowed his head. "You are very gracious," he said with hard eyes. "But we must return to the ship."

Elistala's uncertain glance at her commander put the lie to his statement, but Izivar pretended not to notice, and walked both to the door, where she bade them safe travels.

A quiet Izivar retreated to her office, and Antires followed. Only when she sat down in her chair behind her desk did she let out a sigh and reveal her long-held tension by rubbing her forehead.

He closed the door and sat down on the wall bench across from her. "That was challenging, but you handled yourself with poise."

"You're very kind." She stilled for a long moment before continuing. "It seems they cannot tolerate my company."

"Maybe they really did have pressing duties."

"Do you think these are the first of my people skeptical of my family during this enterprise?"

"These were Cabera adherents," he said. "Or they would not have left Volanus with . . . Decius. They'll be harder to win over."

"Most of those who settled New Volanus were Cabera adherents," she reminded him. "My father nearly handed Hanuvar to the Dervans. How do you think they're going to feel about me?"

"Decius will—"

"Yes, yes. He will tell them and they will at least pretend to do as he wants." She sighed again. "But they'll be looking for any reason to confirm their previous impressions. And how will they treat Julivar? Or the rest who left with us before the war? Will they too be blamed because they came to Tyvol with my family?"

"Some folk might have to be reminded of courtesy. But they will come around. Decius always works his miracles."

"He always does, doesn't he?" She sounded strangely bitter. "I was taught to hate him. He was a rabble-rouser. Listen to the way the people chant for him, my father would say." She changed the way she held her head and spoke more formally, dropping her voice as if in imitation of someone. Probably her father, although Antires, having never heard Tannis Lenereva, couldn't evaluate her rendition. "You can't trust a man who stirs others that way. He will carelessly lead them on to death. He's in love with the sound of his voice."

"You know that's not true."

She answered in her normal voice. "I know it's not true now."

"You think he was ever one of those?"

Her dark eyes were sad and knowing. "I think he has always loved certain ideals deeply. That he chased those ideals the way the devout throw themselves before their statues. His war cause meant more to him than anything else. The lives of his followers. The lives of his brothers."

"His own life."

Her answer was level. "Yes."

"It wasn't the war itself he wanted," he reminded her. "He hoped to make the world safer, ultimately—make it the kind of place his people could thrive in."

Her look was inward, her voice slow and reflective. "He is a brilliant man. Maybe the smartest that I've ever met. Imagine what he could have done in a softer world. He could have been an architect or a scientist or a philosopher. Maybe even a playwright."

"Maybe." Hanuvar didn't strike Antires as the play-writing sort.

"But he came to a father who raised him in an armed camp. And so he was taught from a young age how to master war, and the minds of others."

"He's no tyrant. You know that. Tyrants are only out for their own needs."

She smiled sadly. "He bends people to his will. Look at us." She lay Narisia's letter on the desk. "He has me desperately hoping for the welfare of a woman I've never met. Leaving a safe home for an uncertain one. Risking all for people who will most likely never welcome me."

"You care because you agree with him."

"Yes, but also because I care about him. Who he was, and why he acted as he did, was more complicated than I knew. Except... what if I'm fooling myself and I've simply fallen under his spell, the way father always claimed people did? You must admit that neither of us would be a knife's edge from disaster if he hadn't come along. Hanuvar's war... it didn't work. You'll tell me it could have, with a little more luck, but—"

"You're saying your father was right?"

"For betraying him to Derva?" She shook her head. "No. But was my father wrong to advocate for a different course than war?"

She knew the real answer, but he told her anyway. "The Dervans would have had Volanus all the sooner, as they have the cities of my people."

"Better than its destruction."

"So you question him?"

"I question myself." She put her head in her hands, then spoke quietly. "I love him. I cannot help but love him. He is... the finest man I have ever known. But what if he has fooled all of us? You, me, all of them. Even himself."

"And what does he fool himself over?" Antires asked.

"That he will win through in the end. That we can make a home from the troubles of our past. That he will come home to us alive." She sank back against her chair, one hand drifting down to rest upon her belly while the other covered her heart. "Now I sound selfish."

"It's not selfish to want him to survive."

"Do you think he wants that?"

"Of course he does."

"You're sure? He told me once he did not expect to get so far. Does he keep pressing on because he's not been killed yet? Is that a dark secret he keeps even from himself?"

"He presses on because there is no one who can do it better."

Her voice became hollow, and empty. "He will go too far one day. Maybe he does so now."

"I'm worried about him too."

She stretched out her hand to him and he took it and gave her a reassuring squeeze. She released it and straightened in her chair. "How did things go with the cooks, and the tailor? And who was that visitor at Hypatia's villa?"

He reported the results of his day's efforts and she listened in a way that reminded him of Hanuvar. He didn't mention that the cooks had been wary of her, only that they and the tailor had agreed to Izivar's plan.

"You trust Camillus' slave?" she asked.

"I don't fully understand her, but yes, I think I do. Hopefully tomorrow after the performance she can get me in to talk to them."

"There are a lot of these slaves who can be traced back to you, or me," she said. "Do you think we've arranged enough additional distractions?"

It was Carthalo who'd pointed out that slaves disappeared with every festival, but they had taken steps to arrange for the liberation of non-Volani as well, to divert suspicions. A band of Cerdian dockworkers housed in terrible conditions were set to be released, and another mixed group of sewage workers would be spirited away at about the same time. "Yes, and none of them can be linked to us." He then lifted an open hand, as if weighing a counterpoint. "There are a lot of moving pieces."

"But so long as they can reach the rendezvous point it's actually fairly simple," she reminded him. "Not that I don't wish he was here to deal with complications that may arise."

Antires smiled at Hanuvar's favorite word for the would-be-catastrophes that popped up from time to time. "It's a fine plan. He approved of it. And he'd have liked our modifications."

"I hope so. He's not here to offer improvements."

Over dinner Julivar expressed disappointment that an actual Eltyr had been in the villa and no one had sent for her. Izivar refrained from mentioning the troubling social overtones of the visit, then invited Antires to share some of the exploits he'd had with Hanuvar. He happily did so, though he kept his narration to lighter moments. In talking of his friend it almost felt as though he were there with them, so that when the tales were done his absence was more profound.

Antires turned in early so he would be well rested for the long day tomorrow. As he closed his eyes, his mind turned not to his friend, but toward intriguing little Ishana, and wondered again why she had such a strong effect upon him. The mystery of love, he thought, though he meant that in the broadest sense. For surely he could not have fallen in love with her already. He wasn't even properly infatuated, merely interested. So he told himself, and thus he passed into dreaming.

VI

With the slave woman gone that afternoon, Camillus had to prepare the pages himself. It was an irritant, but he was happy in a way, because at least she wouldn't be there to complain that he shouldn't use all three tresses.

He lashed in the earlier version of the script as the entire example and then added in the Herrene's notes as well as the necessary blank pages, and requested truly deep characters. When he performed the ritual this time, the experience was even more striking. For a brief moment he felt not just warmth, but a deep heat, as though the sun were burning through to his center, and a great god had found him wanting.

Then the moment was passed, the pages were full, and he saw to his delight that they were heavy with wonders. He'd never felt so ebullient. He hadn't been entirely sure what that word meant until today, and he repeated it again and again in his mind. This script, he was certain, would elevate him to greatness. There was still enough time for his actors to memorize some new scenes. They'd have to if they knew what was good for them!

He climbed out of his chair and shouted for the copy boys.

VII

The only talk about the new play of Antony Camillus that morning was how terrible it was likely to be. Traditionally the early slots were given over to the experimental, the untried, or the less skilled, so the timing of his debut was expected. Antires would have avoided it if he'd not hoped to be introduced to the Volani following the conclusion and if the public were permitted admittance during performances. He'd have to be on hand while Camillus was speaking to the judges and before the crew was shuffled off to make room for the next production.

The benches were sparsely occupied by diehards and the festival organizers and the bored early risers who'd shown up for the opening ceremony. The festival's formal start with its sacrifice had been conducted first thing in the morning, but there were still some dry speeches to sit through prior to the first play.

By afternoon, several thousand people would be crammed into the half circle of the Herrenic-style seating built into the hillside, but for now Antires had no difficulty taking a seat in the center, a wide-brimmed sunhat topping him and a cushion beneath him.

He spotted Hypatia, one of the principal sponsors, seated near the middle front row. Her servants had brought pillows too, and sun umbrellas.

Several gray beards moved on stage in succession to thank one another and various names behind the scenes for helping organize what the audience was about to see. Hypatia looked up from the papers she had been studying when she herself was mentioned as a prominent donor and acknowledged the smattering of applause from the meager crowd with a lifted hand.

Just as Antires was deciding even a bad play would be more entertaining than opening ceremonies, he felt a light touch on his shoulder. He turned and with a pleasant start found Ishana beside him. Today she wore a red dress with a black belt and bore with her that pleasant floral scent. Her dark hair had been fluffed and held back in place with a ribbon that almost matched the stola. Today in place of the small arrow a tiny hand had been drawn upon her cheek. Though she had obviously taken care with her appearance, her expression was markedly alarmed.

"There may be danger," she said softly.

"Danger?" Antires asked.

"He has used all three threads. The actors... there was something odd in the way they rehearsed yesterday, and into the night. They were tireless. I didn't think the nexus really was forming about the play before, but it is now. I don't think it's safe here."

"What's this about a nexus?" Antires asked.

"A storm is building and it if releases, many people will die."

"That sounds bad," Antires said, feeling foolish the moment he said so. He cleared his throat and tried to imagine what Hanuvar would say. "How can we stop it?"

"We must seize control of the book. But neither the master nor his people would let me near it."

Hanuvar would do something. Something bold. How much he planned things out ahead of time and how much he improvised Antires was never entirely certain. He didn't have any plan right now, and didn't see how he could, apart from the obvious. "Can you get us back to where the book is?"

"Follow me," she said doubtfully.

VIII

Camillus could scarcely contain his excitement. He had paced so many times to the archway to learn if the droning introduction was over, it astounded him when it finally concluded. He pushed at his actor to get moving as the stagehands wheeled the backdrops onto the stage.

At first the old Hadiran seemed to wear a simple white robe and a thick mask, but as he walked, the magic of the theatre transformed him into a handsome and eloquent master of ceremonies. The stage itself seemed to bend and twist. The decorative pillars built about the archways took on a different character, transforming into stately trees deep in the forest. As the Hadiran described the scenery it seemed as though the morning shadows were vanished. Somehow a nighted wood had come to life behind him. An actual mist flowed along the ground. The crowd gasped.

Then the chorus of citizens stepped onto stage right, robed and masked, and spoke of Radanthes and his quest to find the secret that would restore his mother's sanity and stop his half-brother's scheming for the throne.

Camillus thought it absolutely beautiful, and perfect, and couldn't believe that Hypatia wasn't watching. She was bent over some papers, immune to the magic already holding the rest of the crowd rapt. He would have liked for more people to be in attendance, but then that was the fault of the organizers, who had refused him a later slot.

He slipped away from backstage by a side exit and crept on toward Hypatia as the story unfolded. The audience watched with uncommon attentiveness. So great was the play's power that the atmosphere seemed even to have reached into the crowd, who sat no longer in the sun, but under the veil of stars. The sounds of owls calling in the woods rang about them.

Hypatia looked up a time or two, her expression perplexed. He stopped in front of her and the woman at her side frowned and leaned away to see over him as he crouched at her side.

"I'd hope you'd turn your lovely eyes to me," he said. "Or should I say the play's the thing to see?"

Hypatia noticed him. "Oh. Antony. How are you?"

"I think your lips are kinder than your eyes."

She shook her head, as if trying to clear sleep-fogged vision. "This confuses me."

"Look what I have wrought," he said. "Behold the tale that I have spun for you. Wonders abound—the words are sweet and true."

"The stage craft is astounding... Antony, money doesn't make a story. And you cannot write for me alone. Why does my opinion matter so much to you? You can't win my hand."

"What?"

"Turn your hunger to some other table." She looked momentarily surprised, as though she had said something unexpected, or in a way that she had not intended. "This one suits you ill. You've no gift for words, at least not those that come from other mouths. Your thoughts turn solely on the things you crave."

Her words sliced deep, and he bared his teeth as she continued:

*"You'd order all within your sight, make slaves
of us to stand or walk or crawl or kiss,
or whistle, clap, or shout out words of praise—"*

She shook her head as if trying to clear her thoughts, but continued, "You think you're owed all this by dint of birth. Not skill or practice or nights of labor... Why am I talking like this? I'm sorry. I've said more than I—"

He cut her off with a snarl.

*"I thank you for your words. At last the mist
is lifted from my sight. I would have kissed
those lips and pressed that heart to mine. Instead
I raise this knife—you look on me with dread?
You've naught to fear, for you'll survive to die
a thousand times beneath the open sky.
For folk crave witches for their men to slay."*

Thrice he stabbed her. Hypatia fell with scarlet breast; slaves and companions watched with whitened eyes then spoke with the chorus, in unison.

*"So struck the king and laughed. He did not think
Radanthes came to bring a blow to him."*

She blinked in astonishment, then her eyes fell open as her head fell limp and her expression blanked in death. For a brief moment he knew a twinge of regret—he hadn't wanted this, had he? He'd hoped to impress her... but no, she but played the part of the witch, in the play, and he was King Ildion, Radanthes' half-brother, raised by sorcerers and talented in magic. Camillus knew it now. In the tales Radanthes slew him, but he knew he would not be stopped, for this play was his. He had killed the witch before his brother could seek her advice!

He walked then for the serpent's cave, determined to find the cup before his half-brother. Camillus did not reflect upon how strange it was that the stone steps to the stage had become a hill or that a moon rode a black sky in the morning. All was as the story would have it be. His play, which was perfect, as he had ordered of the gods.

IX

Among Antires' people there was a phrase that meant captured by story. Antires had thought he had known its meaning when he was so consumed by a work that he could barely slow, and the words came fast, and time became irrelevant.

But this sense was different. It was both words that lay ready to pour forth and that heady mix of fear and love when you waited just off stage and knew your cue was coming and you would vanish into your part to walk out as the character you played.

He'd learned that stage hands had carried the book onto the set, and so he and Ishana now looked out from stage right, seeking the scenery element where they'd been told the book lay. Camillus' mania had directed that the book be within the "cave" where the cup of fate was supposed to lie. They saw no wood or curtain but an actual rocky grotto, and the stage itself had been replaced by a dense forest where the cries of bats and owls filled the air.

Antires could still perceive the sun, but distantly, as through a deep mantle painted with stars.

Ishana pointed onto the stage, and she seemed to be saying that the book was behind an archway, but she seemed also to say that the cup of fate was hidden in the serpent's cave.

And then she clasped his shoulder and he better saw the stage, though the forested illusion lay thick upon it.

The play continued. Part of the audience now spoke with the chorus, describing Radanthes' exploration from the river. The Hadiran actor had emerged from stage left and could be glimpsed passing among the tree boles, searching alertly as he neared center stage.

"Hold to me," Ishana said, guiding his hands to her round shoulder, then opened a small belt pouch. From within she carefully lifted unseen things, then passed one to Antires, holding it gingerly between thumb and forefinger. Only when he received it did Antires understood he'd been gifted with a tiny strand of dark brown hair.

"What is this?" he asked.

"I took a small bit from each of the locks of the muses, to protect me should something go awry."

"You foresaw this?"

"I knew something would go wrong. This should shield us as we move toward the book." She started toward the cave to stage rear. Antires followed. By concentrating he could just make out the actual floor.

Camillus ascended to the stage front, transformed into a pale robed man crowned with a dark metal circlet.

The audience spoke as one, describing the moment:

"Radanthes cannot see what lies in wait
The serpent lurks upon the riverside.
His hands shall never clasp the cup of fate
for up the serpent rears, its mouth stretched wide."

Upon the stage a great green form stirred the jungle fronds. Radanthes, though still searching, did not detect its approach.

Antires knew this wasn't how the story went: something had gone awry indeed. He wondered if he might affect a change. He lifted the hair of the muse, pinched carefully between finger and thumb, then called out across the stage.

"Radanthes, be alert, a serpent crawls to end your life and send you down to dust!"

The actor turned. "Who calls to me?"

Antires replied:

"Your cousin Thereon has bought you aid.
From deserts spare I raced to you and I
still wear the ring that wards the serpent's fang."

He hadn't meant to say that, or to lift his hand, where a bright sword now flashed.

Thereon was said to have ventured sometimes with his cousin Radanthes, but in no version of the tale had Thereon ever accompanied him in quest for the cup of fate. And yet the play changed to meet this new development. The chorus and the crowd itself commented with one voice.

> "The flowers on their stalks then swayed and flared
> and spat like snakes and cast a lethal snare.
> Caught unawares Radanthes took a breath
> and found his way below to lands of death."

Apparently the play was determined to kill the Hadiran actor, who sank to one knee and dropped flat when bright red blossoms turned upon their stalks. In no tradition had Radanthes been laid low by mystical flowers; that had been island hopping Lyessius in an entirely different story.

Camillus, the king, laughed and pointed to Antires.

> "It needs no teeth, its coils shall crush you flat.
> One gulp and you'll be expelled with its scat!"

Antires lifted his sword, which seemed fashioned of moonlight, and cast a rejoinder: "Your verse is bad, I'd slay for that alone!"

Laughter rolled through the crowd. Camillus gnashed his teeth and shook his arms.

The serpent slid through the boles, a monster of dark green scales that had slithered through the nightmares of men and women since time immemorial. Wide around as a barrel, it stopped a horse length from Antires, its eyes white and glimmering. Its head raised up, towering over Antires, and the audience gasped as one.

Antires—or was he Thereon?—leapt sideways, striking as the serpent lunged. He knew he held nothing, and struck nothing, and yet he felt the blade he didn't grip bite deep and his arm shook with the sword's impact.

The serpent hit the stage with a forest-rattling thump, and the ghostly trees swayed. But the monster had not been slain, no matter the deep gash that showed upon its length. It began to turn its vast bulk. Antires backed away, scanning his environment. Ishana had arrived at a dark opening in the earth, a wooden arch bearing a black curtain to stage rear.

Though she was obscured by trees, he feared sooner or later Camillus would note her. But the snake had finished its turn and once more the head neared him. He needed help. And so he spoke to change the play's course once more. "The king was wrong. Radanthes had not died. He'd feigned his death to lure him near his side!"

Camillus swung suddenly right and the Hadiran Radanthes staggered upright.

"With spell I'll slay thee!" Camillus shrieked.

But Radanthes raised his blade. "With sword I'll rend thee!"

Antires was momentarily pleased, but the snake reached him and reared high, a scaled tower of death with a flickering black tongue. The sword seemed puny and useless against such strength.

The crowd described the moment for him.

"Thereon's end was nigh; what good was man
when nature's wrath stood tall, for he is low—"

Antires gritted his teeth and warred against what the play would have him do. *"He shook his fears and struck a deathly blow!"*

When the snake lashed down he took its head in a great shining slash. The fanged maw sailed to stage rear; the body struck with such force it threw him from his feet. The crowd roared their approval.

The play, though, seemed finally to have taken note of Ishana, and assigned her a role.

"None saw what wily Thereon had done.
While eyes were turned away he sent his son
into the cave to fetch the sacred cup."

"Be warned," Antires cried, "break fast its hold!"

"You mewling pup!" Camillus shouted. "Radanthes, take your sleep!"

Radanthes slipped down again and the crowd spoke of the king's magic. Camillus turned toward Ishana at stage rear, shouting indignantly. "This is my tale, and yours is tragedy!"

But Ishana was lifting a great cup Antires saw superimposed over a sheaf of paper with shining bindings. She worked to undo them.

Camillus bent and rose with the sword of Radanthes, then stalked toward her.

The stage favored Camillus because it was his story, however wrong it was. And as Antires climbed dazedly to his feet he knew a greater thrum of fear, for he intuited the sense of Camillus' statement: Ishana wore the blessing of the muse of tragedy. Even if her will was slightly shielded from the play, her role was not likely to end well. Whose hair, then, protected him?

As he forced his way through the thick forest trunks, he knew. Cleila, muse of history.

Ishana raised her voice and lifted the cup toward the audience, and the oncoming king. "There's but one draught within the cup of fate. I'll drink it down and you'll not work your spells!"

"I'll slay you 'ere the nectar cross your lips!" Camillus loomed close, sword raised high.

The play had directed so many trees in his path, Antires could not advance, and Ishana's end was practically foredoomed. He needed a deus ex machina.

He bared his teeth in a fierce grin. Why not? He quoted Eledicles, at the end of *The Women of the Isles*, when the besiegers had breached the walls and the final spears had been flung: "When all seemed lost and hope was finally passed, the sun shone through and gods arrived at last."

Camillus turned in surprise and a brilliant scarlet light split the darkness. A single figure caught in that sunbeam descended from on high, unsupported by crane, a woman in a Herrenic gown.

All else faded. Suddenly Camillus was no longer a king, but a small man in a blood-spattered tunic, holding not a mighty sword but a dripping knife. The Hadiran groaned and sat up, adjusting his mask.

Ishana stood with the sheaf of papers, the hairs that bound it half undone along one side.

The goddess alighted upon the stage. She was the Herrenic ideal, with wide hips, small waist, high full breasts, creamy brown skin, and tightly coiled dark brown hair. Her beauty was beyond human, so great it was painful to look upon. Her eyes, ancient and wise, touched those of Antires and to endure that gaze was to be left breathless.

She said nothing, but he understood that she knew he had brought her here, and she had not decided whether she approved.

She beckoned Ishana closer, and the woman walked toward her with lowered head, book extended like an offering.

"That is my play," Camillus cried.

"You've wrought nothing of your own," the goddess said, her voice echoing, honey sweet even as it was implacably strong. The moment her flawless hand touched the papers they flaked away like fine embers that wafted into the sky. Camillus cried out as if in physical pain.

The flowing tresses faded too, and the strands Ishana had removed drifted toward the deity, vanishing as they touched her palm. Then, she turned toward him and Antires knew, with absolute certainty, that he looked upon the muse of history. Cleila walked across the stage to him and with impossible grace extended an arm.

Antires bowed his head and offered the final strand of hair.

Her fingers brushed his own, gently, as he returned it. "I but used this to stop a great wrong," he said. "I would earn your blessing through my writing."

"Work well then," she said. A smile touched her lips, and Antires felt it through to the core of his being, and the sight would haunt him until the end of his days. He suspected that she had shown him favor, but only if he labored. But then he had intended to do that from the start.

Again, he bowed his head.

She advanced upon Camillus, who stood frozen upon the stage. The muse's lovely brows clouded with wrath.

"I made a play," Camillus stammered, "to honor you and your sisters—"

"You brought honor to none, and craved only fame, and it is that I shall grant you." Her voice was level and cold. She did not bother lifting a hand to work her doom.

Camillus' skin sparkled with a glistening patina. He lifted the palms of his hands to better examine them, but his movements slowed then ceased altogether. His skin had taken on the character of brass. His features ran like melting metal until his face was monstrously twisted, a craggy ruin barely recognizable for once having been human.

The muse addressed the crowd, her voice sonorous and grim.

"Any who see will know his fate, but none shall know his likeness. Look well on his end, mortals, and remember how he earned it."

Cleila lifted her hands to the sky, as if in exaltation, then she glowed warmly, and disappeared in light.

The cries and screams of terror began immediately after she vanished, and seemed all the more frantic, probably because they had been held in place.

Antires hurried backstage with Ishana. Beyond, the bewildered stage workers were still shaking off their ensorcellment. Ishana coaxed the Volani husband and wife with her and she and Antires guided them off through the tents of the many theatrical groups.

Some of the crowd fled through the stage exits, crying out that a goddess had come, that Hypatia had been killed, and that a giant snake rampaged, among other things. Though Antires lamented the death of the brilliant woman, he took advantage of the chaos. As men and women dashed hither and yon through the neighboring camps it was easy to reach Hypatia's cooks, working under a striped tent for a midday meal for select guests. Antires then recovered the tailor from the rented rooms of his absent master, and disappeared with all his charges into the milling crowd.

※ ※ ※

All but a few in the audience claimed to remember the event only as scattered moments, as if through a drunken stupor. Many recalled seeing Camillus kill Hypatia in what they had first assumed was an aspect of the performance, reporting that after that they were so swept up into the stage magic that they had lost themselves.

I shaved the beard I had grown to confuse my identity, just in case anyone recalled the involvement of a bearded Herrene. I had adopted it to obscure any descriptions of Antires Sosilos, of course, but the time for worrying about that seemed ended.

Without Ishana I could not have won through, although she claimed it was me who had done the saving. We agreed that we had both done admirably then took one another to bed, like proper heroes from verse. Izivar, seemingly amused with me, had forged records of manumission created for Ishana, though she advised that my Faedahni lover would not be truly safe unless she sailed north with the other liberated slaves. Ishana elected to stay with me, saying she would keep to the villa until I should be ready to sail myself, which pleased me well.

After much debate by the organizers, the festival was resumed upon the following morning, and it was decreed that Hypatia was to have a funeral during the concluding ceremonies. Antonius Camillus, or rather, the statue left of him, was relocated to the city shopping square, a stark contrast among other monuments to famed warriors and politicians.

As it happens, the play festival that year was destined to fail. A flood of refugees arrived in Apicius with word that the countryside was in flames: once again marauding gladiators were running loose. Word had it that a Nuvaran named Tafari led a mighty band that had grown in number as he leveled the region's gladiatorial schools and raided industries.

As rumors spread of a rebellion more and more attendees and performers departed early, Bomilcar urged Izivar to leave as well, but she would not be moved until Hanuvar himself returned.

—Sosilos, Book Sixteen

Chapter 11:
Hillside Figures

Hanuvar leaned into the staff as he walked, the ache in his ankle a steady throb. He had hoped himself used enough to the pain that he did not need assistance, but ten steps had proven him wrong. For now, the shorn tree branch was a necessity.

His forehead was warm and each of his joints sore. He needed to hole up somewhere for a few days and heal. But there was no time for that luxury. And so he pushed himself forward along the old one-lane road through the rolling countryside, the mountains and hills of Turia on either hand. The sky was blue and dotted with fluffy clouds, the late summer sun's heat abetted by gentle breezes. Wildflowers bloomed in profusion near the roadside. He noted the beauty only as markers to be passed as he plodded on.

He did not advance alone, for the young brindle-brown dog trotted nearby. Hanuvar moved too slowly for the creature's patience, and so it ranged near and far, with him as an advancing center point of its circumambulatory investigations into weeds and rocks and occasional chases after birds or chipmunks. It had yet to latch hold of one.

He seemed an ordinary mastiff, and Hanuvar wondered whether the powers other members of the hound master's pack had possessed would manifest on their own, or if some terrible ritual had not yet been enacted upon it. If the powers did appear, would he need one of the rings he bore to control the creature? He had yet to replace one on his finger.

He lacked enough information to reach a conclusion. For now the dog seemed to have adopted him, and conducted itself in a trustworthy manner. Injured, fevered, bereft of money, and weaponless apart from one throwing knife and a belt knife, and incidentally long days from where he needed to be, Hanuvar meant to seize every advantage placed before him, even a juvenile dog.

The animal alerted to the approach of the mule cart long before he did but he didn't pay it appropriate heed. He knew his perceptions were sluggish, but knew also that he'd begun to discount the dog's curiosity, for everything seemed of equal interest to the creature. Hanuvar was lucky, though, for as the wagon gained on him he discerned no threat. A lone driver hunched upon the bench, hands on the reins leading to a tired gray mule. A collection of wooden crates filled the wagon bed. If the road wasn't so hilly and he had been more himself, he would surely have noted the cloud of dust rolling after its wheels before now.

The dog came to stand beside him along the road side as the vehicle neared. Hanuvar was at pains to look as nonthreatening as possible. A cart ride would be much better for his ankle and his progress. But lacking both a hand mirror and a whetstone, he had been unable to shave for two days running. He was well on his way toward a beard, and more and more resembled the man he had been when he had ridden nearby lands as an occupier. While the cart driver was unlikely to recognize him for Hanuvar, she would probably see him as unkempt and disreputable owing to his untrimmed facial hair, stained garment, and lack of belongings.

A sun-spotted wide-brimmed straw hat shaded the woman's blocky face. She wore a simple peasant woman's dress and short boots. Her bared arms were heavy.

In a strident, no-nonsense voice she ordered the mule to stop and pulled up a wagon's length before reaching Hanuvar, her hand on her riding whip. Her frowning face studied his own. Hanuvar saw a burly woman of sour disposition in late middle years, older even than his true age.

"Where are you heading?" Her delivery was thick with suspicion, as though she were long used to disappointments.

"Far north," Hanuvar said. "Likely farther than you're going."

She considered him with displeasure. "If you have money, I can help you get there."

"My coin purse was washed away with the rest of my belongings, including my hand mirror. But my dog and I can help you keep watch."

"Watch for what? Thieves? Beggars on the road?" She looked as though she were only a few words away from setting her cart in motion.

"I had a bad turn two days ago and slipped into a stream. I was lucky to get out with just a bad ankle, but my belongings were washed away. I can make it on my own," he said, inserting what he thought to be just the right note of stubborn pride, "but a little time off my foot would be nice."

Her frown deepened. "I suppose you're out of food, too."

He was nearly, but always kept a little jerky in one of his belt pouches. "I'll get by," he said.

Her jaw moved back and forth, as though she were chewing cud while she weighed her response. "Well," she said at last, "it may be I could give you a ride for a little ways. But if you cause trouble, I know how to use this whip."

"You look like a woman who can handle herself," he said. "I'd certainly be obliged for the transport."

"You don't seem a drunk. And you're rough around the edges, but otherwise well kept. You a legion man?"

"I've worked in their company."

"That's a strange way to put it. Don't you want to bray about your glorious comrades or your campaigns?"

"Not these days."

She grunted. "If I take you, this isn't charity. Your dog alone could intimidate, and you're a fair-sized man. I expect you to look mean if anyone gets in our way."

"Are you expecting someone to get in our way?" Hanuvar limped closer.

"You never can tell what you'll find along these roads."

"Life's full of unanticipated turns," Hanuvar agreed.

She grunted. That seemed to be the official invitation, so he leveraged himself up with his arms, hopped off his good leg, and maneuvered himself into the seat, aware of the woman's circumspect assessment as he did so. He straightened his injured leg and rested the staff between her and himself. He then clapped the seat beside him to see if the dog wanted to hop in, but he just looked back.

"He's young," Hanuvar said. "He likes to range."

The woman didn't acknowledge the information. She called to the mule and vigorously shook the reins.

The mule announced his displeasure with the work ahead by giving something between a wheeze and a sigh, and then got the conveyance in motion.

The dog trotted alongside and, after inspecting the mule's legs and the turning wheels, used the wagon as the new center point of his perambulations.

The cart held a rich odor of animal sweat and dung and the cabbage-like scent of turnips, stowed in crates in its bed. Craning backward Hanuvar spotted additional produce as well, including cabbages and radishes, but three quarters of the woman's produce was turnips, fresh enough that their green ends were still springy. Some even appeared to have been pulled early, likely to accommodate different cooking uses.

The woman didn't seem the talkative sort, which suited Hanuvar, so he concentrated on ignoring the throb of his ankle, and appreciated the pleasure of moving without greater pain. She gave him another once over as they reached a straightaway.

"You've got a nice haircut," she said, almost as though it were a mark against him. "I thought maybe you were a soldier, but I don't see any real scars on you. Maybe a centurion in some cushy posting?"

If she'd seen him last year she would have had an entirely different impression. "I've healed well."

"What are you doing in the middle of nowhere?"

"You don't look like the kind who wants a sob story."

"I don't."

"Passing through. I was attacked and left for dead."

"Bandits?"

"Someone I thought was an ally." He'd never believed Calenius a friend.

"There are bandits on this road sometimes."

Apparently the subject of bandits was more interesting to her than the attack upon Hanuvar. That suited him, too. He'd never liked talking about himself, and under an assumed identity he actively worked to avoid it. "Then why are you travelling it alone?"

"Because my people couldn't wait for an old woman to get her axle fixed and left earlier. And because I can't spare my boys from the farm."

"Who are your people?"

She answered with further complaints. "Market days, we usually travel together. But they couldn't wait." Her frown deepened.

"How many boys do you have?" It seemed polite to ask.

"I meant my second husband and his boy. He's simple," she added, and he inferred she meant the son, though he wasn't completely certain. "But he works hard," she added with the faintest hint of pride. Her eyes swept forward and they narrowed. She spoke with low venom. "That bastard Hanuvar killed my sons. And my brothers. And my first husband," she added, although that sting didn't sound as heartfelt. The depth of her anger presented the other bereavements as though they were recent wounds, no matter that they must have been dealt at least twenty years prior.

She had to mean that they had died in the war he had brought to this land, not that Hanuvar had personally set out to murder her family. That wasn't the way he had waged war, although that certainly hadn't made any difference to this woman or countless others. He had invaded these lands to smash Dervan power, and Dervan soldiers had died by the tens of thousands. Many had ample reason to hate him.

"Did you serve against him?" the woman asked, probably meaning Hanuvar. "You look the age."

"I faced a lot of Volani." He thought that would be the end of the discussion, because she fell silent.

Then she spoke at length. She was one of those who had a story that had to be shared to completion with anyone who spent time with her, regardless of their interest. Hers was a long litany of the evils visited upon her countryside and family but primarily upon herself by the blackhearted Hanuvar.

It didn't seem especially important to her that he comment, for her monologue left no room for it. He nodded lightly from time to time when she looked to him for shared sentiment While she spoke he reflected again upon the so-called Second Volani War, and how it had been a chain of events that he had helped set in motion. To his mind the Dervans had precipitated everything; they were already coming for the Volani colonies and he'd thought to break their power by taking the war to their own land.

In the end that had only slowed them, no matter how many farm boys and senators' sons had died on the battlefield. He'd had justified reasons for bringing war here, but he'd long since recognized the essential truth behind the woman's asseverations as she described the armies marching back and forth across the land and men dying and the crops not being tended and both armies taking food, and women. He could have objected that soldiers in his army had been severely disciplined for thievery and rape, not just because he and his people found both practices abhorrent but because he had hoped to win the countryside to him. That didn't change that thievery and rape had transpired when he delivered an armed horde into Tyvol. War was a scourge, and his had been the hand upon it.

He had reconciled himself to the wielding of war and death because they were the tools he had to defend his people, and he had once held a measure of pride in his craft, for he knew himself among the finest masters of war who had ever lived. Pride, though, could not shield his city, nor even himself when the clouds opened with rain. It was of less use than a threadbare cloak, and he had since cast it aside.

His father had declared war a hungry beast, saying that sometimes it was a thrill to hunt at its side, but that it would devour your soul if you let it. Himli Cabera had said much more on the subject of rage and nuances about the differences between individuals and groups and governments that Hanuvar had innately understood. As a child, he had listened and absorbed these and other lessons taught by both him and Himli's clever young advisor Andalaval, husband to Hanuvar's sister.

Now, though, when he thought of his father, he more often recalled the summer they'd been in the same fortress long enough to see the herbs Himli planted grow. His father had smiled to gather the leaves for seasoning their meals himself.

The clop of the hooves and the steady rumble of the cart and the recitation of the woman's misfortunes, stretching past the war and on into the scheming of neighbors who plotted for access to her well, lulled him into sleep.

When he woke it was because water was dripping onto his face. He came instantly awake, and as he automatically readied for action he jarred his leg and pain lanced through his ankle. The sky had grayed and rumbled at them but only released a few drops at a time. The woman still drove the cart, on toward rocky hills. The dog followed along by the right rear wheel.

"I'm sorry I fell asleep," he said.

She passed him a wineskin.

"Felt your forehead a while back," she said. "Your ankle's got you sicker than you let on. You need rest."

It was simple water, not wine, that greeted his lips when he drank. He found himself terribly thirsty but had only two sips. His stomach growled then, and at this she actually chuckled and told him he could help himself to some of her bread, which she had in a lidded wicker basket at her feet.

He thanked her and ate sparingly of a hearty dark loaf, enjoying the taste of it and the feel of dense, seedy texture mashing between his teeth. Probably the dog was hungry; he supposed it knew how to hunt, but he hadn't seen it eat anything but the bits of jerky he'd shared yesterday.

"I'll wager you saw a lot of men die, if you were fighting the Volani," she said to him.

"Too many," he agreed.

"They were sneaky bastards. I'm glad we finally got them. Doesn't bring my boys back, though."

They passed a gentle sloped hillside covered with flat white stones arranged in a huge picture, a somber figure in a robe, with long hair, likely a Turian queen, for the Turian influence had waxed and waned through the region before the coming of Derva.

After Hanuvar chewed on the bread for a while he forced himself to stop, feeling more feverish than before. They passed other large images, more ancient and yet more lively and fluid, full of simple energy, all fashioned of white stone upon the hillsides. He thought the best was a howling wolf[24] until he spotted a running horse in the distance, its legs and hooves spread out in what should have looked

---

[24] Although the white stone pictures dot the Turian hillsides for many miles of the region's remote hinterlands, most do not appear to be of Turian origin, and apparently predate even their arrival in the area. —*Silenus*

absurd but somehow perfectly caught an animal in motion, its head lowered for a flat-out gallop, its mane suggested by long white lines stretched behind its head. His thoughts turned toward his bay roan, left in the possession of Calenius. Would the wizard have cared for the mount, or would he simply let it wander free, or sell it? Hanuvar had grown fond of the animal and again wondered whether he should have named it. He'd had so many killed from beneath him he'd gotten out of the habit.

As they rounded a bend they neared another hillside, on which there was the outline of a gargantuan man bearing what must be a club. A pair of people walked along the man's edges, removing debris and washing grayer stones into whiter ones.

"I've never seen anyone caring for any of these pictures," the woman said, as though scandalized by the idea. Their presence must have been old news to her, because she hadn't commented upon any of the ones they'd passed.

The sky rumbled.

At the hill's base a small band sat at a cookfire beneath a rocky overhang, and they waved to the cart as it rolled toward them.

A skinny man with a kindly face raised a hand and stepped toward the road. "Come," he said. "Take shelter. We'll share our food."

The woman slowed the carriage and eyed him doubtfully. Hanuvar saw a mixed group of men and women tending the cookpot. The two upon the hill were starting down. All were dressed in the simple white tunic of the man speaking with them.

"What are you doing with the pictures?" the old woman asked.

"We're just tidying them up. They're long overdue for it, don't you think?"

The woman didn't answer. The sky grumbled once more and then opened up, a steady patter of rain.

The man laughed and offered his hand. "Come in out of the rain!"

They did not look an obvious threat, and Hanuvar and the woman needed cover from the rain, and he was tired. But he was wary. As he joined their ranks Hanuvar couldn't decide if their attentions were the solicitous preparations of the religious zealot readying visitors for the conversion pitch, or something more sinister. He had met many kind people in the world, and some had been inspired by their religious teachings. But then he had also met those who used beliefs as a means to exploit others.

Here, in the middle of nowhere with a fever running through him, with nothing to back him but some knives and a dog he hadn't trained, he found himself more suspicious than grateful.

When they joined the strangers under the rock outcropping he was presented a bowl of the same porridge they themselves were sharing, along with a platter of figs and what proved to be watered wine. The woman shared some of her bread, which was received with great acclaim, for they had none of their own.

One of the pair who'd come down from the mountain unhitched the mule and helped set the beast up with a feed bucket the woman fussed with.

The dog sniffed around in curiosity, ears up, and gobbled down some hardboiled eggs one of the men said were a little old. He gamboled around an old goat chained to a peg outside, who ignored him and contentedly munched wet grass.

Then they sat and talked among themselves about the prayer they'd hold when the rain broke. A few tried having a go at the woman to talk, but when asked directly about where she was going or why, she proved nearly monosyllabic. He did learn the woman's name at last, for she had been asked it by the leader, who'd given his own as Corvus. Her name was Leta. Hanuvar had always associated that name with girls, and so thought her unsuited for it, then chided himself, because of course girls who lived grew to be older women.

Tired though he was, Hanuvar pushed past the muddled slurry of his thoughts and pressed their hosts for information. "I'm new to the area. What are all these stone pictures you're tending?"

"They are shrines," Corvus said.

Hanuvar returned his scrutiny but not his idle smile. "Why are they being cared for now?" he asked. "They look as though they've been abandoned for some time."

One of the women, a slight thing with narrow shoulders and a receding chin, answered as though imparting great truths. "Rosigus has been asleep for centuries, and he must be wakened before the mountains do."

Most of the others nodded at this. Outside their overhang the downfall accelerated to a torrent. It was not a cold rain, but a summer shower, and he could smell it and the pleasant scent of the earth it made moist.

"The mountains are waking up?" Hanuvar asked.

This time Corvus answered him. "Indeed they are. Don't you feel it? The gods are stirring. Some who have turned away are paying attention once more. Rosigus called to me, and I assembled a flock from the villages to tend him."

This wasn't the first time Hanuvar had been told inattentive gods might be looking over the affairs of mortals again. At his apparently skeptical expression the man continued. "It's absolutely true. Calamitous times are near." Corvus' mouth thinned with conviction. "Maybe even the world's end. And Rosigus will help stave it off. At least for the faithful."

Hanuvar bowed his head. "Forgive me, but what is Rosigus the god of?"

"He is lord of the hilltops and the wild, lonely places," Corvus answered. "If the mountains are blown apart and the earth shifts, he will be most displeased."

Hanuvar expected the people near the mountains would be more displeased than the god, and thought perhaps Rosigus shouldn't have gone to sleep if he didn't want to be disappointed by change.

"But we're to hold a prayer today, on the mountainside, just as soon as the storm ends. He'll bless our work with his holy light. You should join us. The more voices Rosigus hears lifted in praise, the sooner he will wake."

Hanuvar nodded noncommittally. Weariness had leached through him. All his joints ached.

The woman, Leta, had finally opened up about her favorite topic. With nearly the same phrasing she described the woes inflicted upon her family by the treacherous Hanuvar and the covetous Volani. These listeners interrupted with questions, though it barely halted the flow of her diatribe.

Between the patter of the rain and the steady monotony of her hatred he had a hard time keeping his eyes open, and flexed his ankle so a wave of pain rocked through him. He'd thought that kept him alert until he woke to find the dog whining beyond his sandaled feet.

One of the younger followers of Rosigus hissed at it and swiped at the mastiff with a stick. Hanuvar didn't like that. He didn't like the sticky stuff on his skin—someone had cut open his tunic and smeared what felt like sap over his wiry chest hair.

"Stop that," he said, thinking to rise. But his voice was weak.

A young man was spreading the material on him, a wavy haired fellow with a simpering smile he flashed down at Hanuvar. "Shh. There's nothing to trouble yourself about. Go back to sleep."

Hanuvar sat up and snatched him by the tunic front. The man yelped, grabbed a heavy stick beside him, and lifted it above Hanuvar's head.

He'd had little doubt about the man's intentions a moment before, but the weapon raising settled the matter. He lacked the strength or stamina to subdue him. Though a little dizzy, there was no missing the man's chin, under which Hanuvar drove his knife blade, straight up through the floor of his mouth and into his brain.

Someone nearby let out a yelp as they caught sight of the man spasming in his death throes, and then Hanuvar forced himself upright. They hadn't bothered to move his crutch, so he snatched that in one hand. The hound growled at the man trying to keep him clear with frantic swipes of his cook knife.

The same slight woman who'd answered earlier at the fireside rushed Hanuvar with a long staff of her own.

Pain shot through his injured leg as he put weight on it. He punched the end of his crutch toward the woman's throat. She stumbled as she fought to avoid it, then he reversed his hold on the crutch and slammed her legs. Down she went with a splat into the mud beyond the overhang. He had only just noticed that the rain had stopped.

The dog clamped hard onto the other man's leg, and he cried out and flailed at the animal's hindquarters with his knife.

Hanuvar managed a limping lunge and slammed the man's temple with his own cudgel. The fellow crumpled.

The woman was up and crawling.

Hanuvar bent, grabbed her by the ankle, and dragged her back. Behind he heard the sound of a growl, tearing flesh, and a death rattle. Apparently the dog took threats to himself and his human very seriously. The woman's eyes widened as she looked past Hanuvar at the mastiff's deed.

"Where's Leta?" he demanded.

Her voice was weak. "The hill. For Rosigus."

"Is she still alive?"

"Maybe. Probably," she added, likely in hope that would prolong her life.

He was too weak to leave any potential enemy at his back, though for her sake he slew her with a quick knife thrust rather than siccing the dog on her.

The hound came up to him, its maw stained with the blood of the man whose throat he'd torn out. Its eyes were keen, its ears up.

"Good dog," Hanuvar growled. "You hurt?"

It wagged its tail.

"I didn't think so. These people are pretty weak. Were you and I in our prime, this wouldn't be a challenge at all."

He knew then he was still feverish, or he wouldn't have wasted effort talking to a dog. He left the overhang to save the woman who hated him.

The veiled sun shone in the gray sky, red as molten metal. The goat still munched at the end of its metal chain. Corvus and another woman were up near the top of the image of their god, arms lifted over a prostrate figure surrounded by raised stones, curved like fangs. A little pyramid of black stones had been piled directly behind her.

Hanuvar touched the dog's head. "Go. Attack."

Powerful muscles sent the dog springing up the hillside.

Hobbled by his ankle, the best speed Hanuvar could manage was a slow jog, aided by the staff. The wet grass was treacherous, so he struck the ground hard with the ball of his right foot with each stride to better plant himself and position the next movement.

He could only watch as the dog raced ahead. Corvus and his acolyte were too intent on their low chants to pay much heed until the dog was nearly on them. The woman was half turned when it leapt. Hanuvar heard her scream as she went down.

Corvus drew a sickle and seemed to hesitate over approaching the dog or gutting Leta. But his ally was screaming for help and beating the dog's sides in an attempt to keep it from her face and throat. She screamed once more as the animal latched hard onto her wrist.

That decided the priest, who went after the dog.

Hanuvar had discovered new muscle cramps as he forced himself uphill with the staff. His knee ached in a way it hadn't since his old wound, and one calf was seizing up. But he gritted his teeth and forced himself faster. He drew the only throwing knife left him.

The dog released the hand and sprang for the woman's throat. Corvus loomed over, sickle raised.

Hanuvar halted. He was at near maximum range and his chest heaved, so he took a moment to aim, assessing the ground's rise and the best trajectory. Then he threw.

His cast was too long for deadly accuracy, but his blade struck the priest in the shoulder and fell away. Corvus cried out in surprise and pulled back. The dog looked up from the woman writhing beneath him, blood dripping from his maw, showing his teeth in another snarl.

Were Corvus a warrior, he would have struck then. But a warrior would have shrugged off the knife blow and simply plunged his blade through the dog's back. Corvus turned and bolted. The dog was swift on his heels and quick to leap.

By the time Hanuvar arrived both the leader and his final follower were dead, and the dog came trotting up as happy and playful as if he'd just chased a squirrel. Hanuvar knelt and patted his head and praised him, and tossed down the rest of his dried jerky, which the dog consumed.

He then bent to check Leta's pulse. It beat, slowly but steadily. He crouched, catching his breath and leaning heavily on his good leg. His ankle was in agony. His eyes strayed to the chest high pyramid of stone, a shoddy work that would have embarrassed any professional mason. The left leaned noticeably, for the stones used to craft it were slimmer on one side than the other.

Hanuvar forced Leta to her feet. Her tunic gaped; a smaller version of Rosigus' hillside image had been drawn in sap beneath her sagging breasts.

As he got her moving she groaned and murmured something he didn't understand about the dog. He would have preferred to recover for a much longer moment, or simply to lie down, but the circle of raised stones reminded him too much of those he had seen sorcerers draw, and so he led her from them and set her down just past its edge, more roughly than he'd planned, for she hit the ground with a groan. There was no help for that.

He returned to recover his knife and search the bodies of the dead and sat beside the woman as the sun set, watching her struggle to fully wake as he got his breath back.

Eventually, when the sun was beyond the hills but the light was not yet gone, she was conscious enough to walk down. Though it was hard going, he went with her, and even managed to hitch the mule. Leta by then was sitting wearily against the back of her bench. Hanuvar rested briefly against the wagon side, then finished his search of the remaining dead.

He didn't trust their wine or their porridge, but some of the greens and dried meats and fruits seemed safe. They had hand mirrors and whetstones, several passable knives, and a single sword, pitted but better than nothing, all of which he took, along with the sword's battered sheath. They had spare garments, so he grabbed a tunic for himself and another that looked like it might fit Leta. And they had money, more than he expected. He kept that to himself, then walked over to release the goat. His first inclination had been to take him along for food, but the animal would be old and tough, and besides, had probably been planned as the sacrificial victim until handy strangers wandered up. It seemed hardly fair to kill him when they were going free.

The goat was unfazed by anything that had transpired around him, including the granting of freedom, but did wander further off as Hanuvar whistled to the dog and patted the bench. This time the mastiff hopped up, thumping his tail as Hanuvar patted his head. The animal had been drinking out of a stream and had managed to wash the blood from his mouth.

Hanuvar climbed up beside the dog, took the reins, and got them underway.

He felt Leta's eyes on him. Her voice was soft, little more than a mumble. "Those people were going to stab me, weren't they. If not for the dog."

"Yes."

She fell silent. For a long while Hanuvar thought she slept. But then, over the buzz of the night insects, he heard her voice.

"He's the right dog for that job." She stroked his head. "What's his name?"

"I haven't given him one."

"He's a killer," she said. "Call him Hanuvar."

That struck him as very funny, and he would have laughed harder if he weren't so tired. "I'll think about it."

The dog's tongue protruded as she gently scratched his head. "Good Hanuvar," she said.

※ ※ ※

The followers of Rosigus were not the only ones sensitive to a change in the region's natural energies. Reports of strange events multiplied throughout southeastern Tyvol. A flock of geese was seen to be flying backward, and rumors spread of a two-headed calf born to a farmer in the highlands. It was even said that a kind old wise woman went mad and slew every one of her chickens before throwing herself into the sea.

We were skeptical of these stories, although Ishana told me that the currents of fate were swirling fast, that energy was being gathered toward Esuvia, and that all kinds of weird effects were likely in the surrounding regions as it flowed. A series of small quakes rocked the countryside, and smoke regularly billowed from Esuvia. Not knowing what part the wizard may be playing in the growing dread we all were feeling, I reached out to Calenius' camp, but his people claimed he had not returned and refused to provide me with any details of his whereabouts.

Many left Apicius, including most of the aristocracy. Naturally we remained, having no intention of departing the area without Hanuvar. Ironically, we put our faith in the legionaries manning the small port garrison. They were mostly there to police shipping and secure the harbor, but their commanding officer increased the frequency and size of patrols. We expected they'd alert us if the gladiators decided to march on Apicius, but didn't learn until too late that the rebellion was already very close.

—Sosilos, Book Seventeen

Chapter 12: Death Grip

I

Leta had just told him the little market town lay only a little ways ahead when the boy rode over the ridge. He was mounted on a charcoal gray mare, and guided an old black gelding, saddled, by a long lead line.

Hanuvar hoped to obtain a horse as soon as he reached a settlement, and here was one directly in his path. He brought the wagon to a halt and called out to the boy. "Come here! I've a question for you!"

The child slowed and looked Hanuvar's way, his expression still focused inward, as though the words he'd heard intruded upon a more pressing reality. Probably he'd lived no more than thirteen years. He had a long face with a knobby chin. He wore his hair short, and it was straight and dark brown, red tinted from long exposure to the sun. His saddlebags bulged with sage, poking out from under the clasps, and the scent was stronger than that of horseflesh. The boy himself wore a necklace from which a long line of small bent nails dangled. This, then, was someone cautious of the dead.

The boy's gaze took in the grim-faced older woman on Hanuvar's right, studied him and the sheathed weapon on the bench beside him with growing interest, then examined the young brindle-brown mastiff standing with erect ears along the driver's side of the cart.

"What do you want with him?" Leta asked.

Hanuvar didn't answer, for the boy was riding close. A sheathed gladius in weathered wraps hung at the child's side. By the time he stopped, the boy's dark eyes were calculating.

Hanuvar had planned to open a conversation about renting the animal, for he did not carry nearly enough to purchase even an aging work horse like the one trailing the boy, and Leta meant to go no further than the nearby settlement. But the boy spoke first, his delivery pressured. "I see you've got a sword. Do you know how to use it?"

"Yes."

The boy could scarcely wait to reply. "Can your dog fight?"

"He's a killer," Leta asserted helpfully. "What's a boy like you need that for?"

"I need help getting my brother."

"I'm hoping to rent a horse," Hanuvar said. "I wonder—"

The boy cut him off. "My brother handles that kind of thing. Help me find him and we can loan it to you."

"Is your brother lost?" Hanuvar asked.

The boy hesitated, then explained, watching Hanuvar for reaction. "He and his friends went to stop the ghost in the cave. And they didn't come back last night. No one else will help me, so I'm going to do it."

He was young enough still to play pretend, but his tense manner did not suggest that he did so now. "How far away is this cave?" Hanuvar asked.

"I think it's less than a half hour from here. I've got a pretty good idea of where it is," the boy added, more as if to reassure himself than Hanuvar.

"Swords aren't going to help much against a ghost," Leta remarked dourly.

"That's what the magistrate said. The decurion couldn't even be bothered. Everyone's afraid. I've got wards against ghosts and a sword an old wise woman blessed. But if you don't want to come, say so, because I want to get there before dark."

Hanuvar had no interest in hunting a "ghost," but he needed a horse and he wasn't likely to get a better deal. He faced Leta. "You're almost at your destination so I'll leave you here. Good luck at the market."

"You take care of that dog." Leta had shared her food, but she'd never displayed much warmth apart from that she gruffly gave the mastiff. She nodded to Hanuvar after he climbed down and then she shook the reins and the cart lurched into motion.

After two days on the road Hanuvar thought himself well enough healed to ride, though he still had to favor the leg if he was afoot. He managed to walk almost normally to the horse, wearing the battered sword he'd taken from his would-be murderers. The animal appeared healthy despite a back bowing with age and graying muzzle. He stood just over fifteen hands high, and his dark coat was well brushed, his legs sturdy and hooves well trimmed. He radiated placid calm, which Hanuvar preferred to coltish nonsense.

"You're sure your brother's in this cave?" Hanuvar asked.

"First I want to check the shack in the woods where he and his friends go. There's a chance they're there. It's on the way." The boy then added detail: "People have been disappearing. Ever since they found that jewelry."

In an eyeblink Hanuvar had clarity. These were Turian lands, and the Turians had been a people who liked to inter their dead with distinctive grave goods. Enterprising descendants still sought out unopened tombs secreted in the hilly countryside. "In a Turian crypt?" Hanuvar suggested.

The boy seemed shocked that Hanuvar had deduced the truth so easily. "Maybe," he said, then decided upon confirmation. "They were bragging about it. Everyone knows, because they have big mouths for people who want to keep a secret. Justus told me he and his buddies had found a big cache, but his friends and their treasures started to disappear, and those left were going to get together yesterday and talk. Maybe even lock the tomb back up. Then he didn't come home."

"You have no parents?" Hanuvar guessed not, but he meant to confirm.

The boy shook his head no.

"Aunts, uncles?"

"My uncle runs the tavern we work at, but he's gone. We think the ghost got him."

Hanuvar climbed into the saddle. "Let's see this shack."

II

They headed away from the road and into the green, hilly Turian wilderness. The wind brought the mixed scent of lavender and myrtle, the white blossoms of which flowered along the forest edge.

Beneath overcast skies the land felt ageless and unwelcoming. Even the little farmsteads looked just this side of overgrown, as though despite centuries of occupation men and women had made no true impact upon the wilderness, which remained positioned to regain the upper hand the moment vigilance faltered.

The boy stayed silent until they were well into the hills, along a secondary path little better than a deer track. They had just passed a crumbling brown wall heavy with ivy when he turned his horse into a wide clearing. A wall of forest lay only a half mile ahead. Hanuvar drew up beside him. He had noted then that one of the boy's booted feet was larger than the other. A club foot.

The boy saw the direction of his gaze. "I can get around just fine," he said assertively.

"What's your name?" Hanuvar asked.

"Kliment."

"I'm Flavius."

The boy was more interested in the dog trotting with them. "What's your dog's name?"

"Kalak." When Leta had suggested calling the dog "Hanuvar," he'd eventually explained that he didn't want to be shouting that out in public and offered an alternative. The mountain range he'd named the animal after lay near Volanus and had been described in a famous Dervan poem as possessing a savage beauty. Leta didn't seem much of a scholar, but even she could cite a few lines from Ellius and had approved his choice.

The mastiff had romped curiously for the last mile or two, acting like the half-grown pup he was. Now, approaching the woods, something had him on the alert. He kept close, ears pricked, and eyes scanning the dark areas between the trees. The horses, too, seemed tense as if they knew the primeval power of the countryside rendered humans and their allies unwanted.

They picketed their mounts a little beyond the forest edge, then the limping boy slung the greenery-laden saddlebags over one shoulder and led Hanuvar down a trail. The shack sat in a small upland clearing only a few hundred feet from the wood's edge, a small stone structure with sagging, moss-studded roof tiles. The battered wooden door hung shattered in its frame.

The boy raised his voice as they drew close. "Justus? Are you in there? It's Kliment."

It didn't seem a place where anyone would linger. Kalak trotted forward expectantly and sniffed at the door.

"Back," Hanuvar ordered, not trusting the animal's sense about when to act with lethal force if there was someone hiding within. The dog obliged with seeming reluctance.

"Someone's kicked in the door." Kliment swallowed, then called out his brother's name again. "Justus?" The broken door creaked as he pushed it open. Dull sunlight stretched before him, illuminating the toppled table, a broken stool, and a red and stinking smear, as of a bloody body dragged across the dirt floor. Flies, agitated by their appearance, spiraled up from the mess.

Hanuvar lingered in the threshold, scanning the dark corners. He spotted a set of muddy footprints. Untidy wreaths of sage and asphodel hung on each wall. There were no closets, wardrobes, or doorways, no rug under which a pit might lie hidden. Returning outside, he saw no further drag marks, as though the corpse had been transported by that point. "Are there bandits in this area?" he asked Kliment.

"It's not bandits. It's a spirit. This is like what we found when it got my uncle. We've got to go to the tomb. Justus said he was going to go to the tomb." Kliment started past him, but Hanuvar stopped him with a hand to his arm.

"I think you'd best make a few things clear before we go any further."

The boy paused, his eye wide, his expression blank.

Hanuvar had seen that look in survivors of ambushes. He withdrew his hand and spoke calmly and slowly. "You need to tell me what's been happening. How many people have died, how did they die, and how long has it been going on?"

"I don't know how they died. People started to go missing the same night my brother and his friends found the old crypt." He blinked, and seemed to see Hanuvar, for he met his eyes again. His voice resumed a more even cadence. "There'd been another tremor, and sometimes that exposes doors on the hillsides, so they headed for a place where some others have been found, and there it was. They said the crypt was full of great old stuff, but it was really creepy, and they just grabbed a few pieces and got out fast. They took seven things. Lucky seven. They thought if nothing happened, maybe they'd come back for more." He gulped. "But things started happening. Gratian, the boy who found the tomb door, disappeared. Then our uncle went missing the next night. They gave him a bracelet because he thought he could probably find a market for it and some of the necklaces. Then Marcus vanished. Along with the jewelry they had. Well, Marcus had a cup."

"Is that everyone?"

"Yes. Until today, I guess." His eyes tracked to the doorway and the smear just visible through it. Possibly left by his brother's body. "Justus figured a haunt was coming after the things they took, so he convinced the other two to give everything back, and seal up the tomb. Extra tight. They wanted to go at Noon when we figured the ghost would be most weak. But that was yesterday."

"This one seems to be quite strong. Something broke through this door while it was barricaded. Did you see the that the door bar had been cracked in half?"

The boy blinked at him. "No. I don't understand why someone was here," he added.

Hanuvar could guess, and he hesitated telling the boy. But it was important he understand the implications. "You said the tomb was close. Do you think someone ran back here, from the tomb? Maybe because there were wreaths on the walls, to keep out spirits? But it didn't help."

"I think I know where it is. We have to check." Kliment fingered the necklace with its bent nails, as if in hope it would keep him safe more than the sage and asphodel wreaths. He looked around as if lost. "Look, I can give you Altus. He's my horse. I was riding my brother's. But you can have the one you were riding. You don't even have to rent him. But I don't want to do this alone." He sounded even smaller than before but, Hanuvar concluded, determined to go regardless.

Hanuvar closed his eyes for a moment to wrestle competing impulses. "Very well. Lead on."

Still carrying the sage-filled saddlebags over his shoulder, Kliment headed out. They didn't advance more than a few hundred yards before they came to a line of low hills. After another half mile they came to not so much a clearing as a thinning of the nearby trees, enough that wide shafts of sunlight sporadically broke through the canopy of oak and ash, which served less to illuminate and more to somehow emphasize the depth of the shadows.

After that point the boy appeared briefly unsure until he spied a huge oak and veered to the right, coming upon another line of hills. Again Kliment looked uncertain, scanning the terrain and walking slowly until he arrived before a rocky crevice. From straight on it seemed a narrow slit, but the boy limped ahead and through and they found themselves in a wider passage that stopped before a closed stone door set below a lintel built into the hillside. The dirt that had coated it before the tremor lay in a mound at its feet, indented with sandal prints and drag marks toward the door.

Kalak sniffed the area and growled, his ruff up.

The boy's gaze fell—he had observed the drag lines in the dirt. Hanuvar wondered if he too questioned who had closed the door. Certainly no one fleeing from the crypt would have politely shut it behind them.

Kliment addressed him quietly. "Justus said the door was on a pivot. That it just opened right up. I brought torches," he added, though Hanuvar had already noted them poking out of the left saddlebag.

Hanuvar borrowed the boy's flint to light one, expecting he would be faster at the task, then handed it to Kliment. He grasped the stone door at a carved ridge and pulled. The slab was a good seven feet tall, but swung open with astonishing ease.

No spectral monster waited just beyond. He saw only a man-high corridor through the dirt leading into darkness. The boy produced small, shoddy wreaths of sage from his pack, pressed one into Hanuvar's hands and put another around his neck, over the circlet of bent nails.

Hanuvar thought it too small to fit over his head, so wrapped it around his left arm and started in. Kliment followed, flickering torch held aloft. Hanuvar's good ankle had grown sore from favoring the other, and his injury had certainly not benefitted from the afternoon's walk. He limped inside, scanning the environment, conscious that the boy limped with him. The dog padded at his side.

Six feet beyond the entrance the tunnel opened into a stone hall lined with stiff carved Turian figures bearing chin beards and wide staring eyes and square fingers. Four of them glared solemnly down at the stone slabbed floor. The hall continued on, but Hanuvar stopped to contemplate a sticky black mass upon the slabs, and streaks trailing into the greater darkness.

Blood, recently spilled. A fair amount of it. Something had dragged the body that had housed that blood backward into the gloom.

The boy watched him, his expression fixed and cautious.

"You should stay here," Hanuvar said.

"I am going with you."

Apparently Kliment feared the darkness of the tomb less than being on his own, and so Hanuvar gave him only one other instruction. "If I give the word, run."

Kliment answered with a tight nod of the head.

There was a difference between battlefield fear and the hair-stiffening atmosphere of the supernatural. Hanuvar felt the heightened awareness, even the apprehension, but so far today he had not yet experienced the innate feeling of wrongness that came from the intrusion into the mortal sphere of things from elsewhere. Kalak stayed close, head shifting to right and left. The old tales always had it that animals were more sensitive than men to the supernatural, and he expected this dog might be especially so. Right now the dog still acted only cautious, not frightened, which reassured him. Even so he advanced with bared blade.

The boy's torchlight spilled ruddily onto a stone dais built into the central wall. To either side dark niches were laddered into the corridor, four high, each brimming with goods. Light flickered on a row of golden rings carefully arranged with identical distance between them. Small statues of gods or heroes stood in a line like the toys of a rich man's child. There was a long series of necklaces as well, and Kliment, attracted by the sheen on the nearest, stretched out a hand.

"Don't touch it," Hanuvar cautioned, and the boy quickly pulled his hand back.

"I wasn't going to take it." Kliment looked chagrinned but moved well away from the niches.

Hanuvar had caught a whiff of rotting flesh, the putrid sickly-sweet stink he knew too well from battlefields. Kliment, too, had noticed it, and put his hand tentatively on the handle of another sealed door. He looked grimly to Hanuvar, took a deep breath, and pulled it wide.

He gasped when it opened, not just because of the terrible smell, but because of the horror before him. Someone, or some thing, had sat six bodies against the wall just beneath a wide, empty wall niche. The three on the right were younger and fresher, but all were dead, their eyes vacant, their jaws gaping.

The boy advanced toward the corpses on the right and knelt before one with a sob.

Breath held, Hanuvar scanned them for signs of wounds, noting the scratches and purpling about their necks. Blood soaked their clothing.

Scanning the corridor of treasures, Hanuvar noticed a relief above a central niche, and recognized the Turian lord of the dead, he of the sad eyes and sympathetic brows. Someone had recently driven a nail into wall just beneath the god's extended hand and draped a wreath of sage there so that he seemed almost to be holding it.

The hairs on Hanuvar's neck stood upright and it was easy to imagine something gliding up behind him. He turned, seeing only the dog, and the chamber of goods, dark but empty of enemies. The long rectangle held few of the traditional accoutrements of the dead. There were not pairs of goblets, but multiple rows of them, each vessel slightly different in design. There was not a single plate, so that the spirit might imagine itself a meal, but ranks of them, each decorated with a unique pattern—one with tree leaves, another with ivy, another with winter branches. The finer details were hard to make out through the dust.

Hanuvar could not help reflecting upon his own family tomb, even briefly. Laid down by distant forebearers, its outer chamber had been impossibly, almost ludicrously, opulent, so that all who came to inter new bodies in the crypts beyond would be impressed that the Cabera family could afford such skilled artistry. But for all its grandeur the antechamber had celebrated the family as a whole, not individuals, who were interred beyond with nothing but their best clothing, armament, or a fine urn if they had been cremated.

This was different. Personal and strange. For all that, he had a more pressing question.

"Kliment," Hanuvar called, "is this all of the missing people?"

The answer was so low it barely could be heard over the whisper of flame. "Yes." Kliment choked back a sob.

"Tell me about these goods." Hanuvar pointed to a row of rings and necklaces. "Are any of these the things they took from the tomb?"

It took a moment, but eventually Kliment left the room of bodies. The boy turned his head from right to left but did not near the niches. "That looks like one of the necklaces. And that's the bracelet Uncle had."

Kliment's torchlight caught on the yellow in the painted mural above the shelves of goods, and the beaming image of the bearded man standing with spread arms, as if demanding viewers admire the valuables spread beneath him. The pride manifest in the man's expression suggested their acquisition equivalent to the defeat of monsters, the founding of cities, or the writing of epics.

"Is anything missing?" Hanuvar asked.

"I don't know."

"It's important that you do know," Hanuvar said. "You said there were seven items taken and there's an empty spot right here, between these two rings."

The boy was silent with thought for a long moment, then blurted a single name. "Callista." He faced Hanuvar. "Justus gave a ring to Callista, a girl he likes."

"She may be in terrible danger."

"You think the thing has gone after her?"

"It may when darkness falls," Hanuvar pointed out.

Kliment's voice took on a younger, whining quality. "Why does it care so much? The jewelry was just lying there, not doing any good to anyone! The dead don't need jewelry! They can't drink or eat! Why does it need goblets?" The sentiment, fueled by anguish, sounded sincere, but Hanuvar wondered if it was what the boy himself believed, or if it was something his brother and friends had said in front of him.

"Maybe it reminds them of the life they lost. Or the living thought it would make them happy."

"But even a living man doesn't need so many cups, and so many statues—"

"He was a collector. We need to go."

"But Justus... We have to take him out of here."

"I don't think anyone should linger here. And this girl is in danger."

The boy retreated only reluctantly, and before long they passed through the portal. Outside, a false twilight had come in advance of the real one, for dark clouds cloaked the sky. Kalak wagged his tail as he lifted his nose to the fresh air.

Hanuvar wasn't sure he wanted to engage with this issue any further. He'd held to his word and helped the boy find his brother. This fight wasn't his, and he could not afford to linger. And yet he still didn't want to leave Kliment to fight a battle on his own, or to doom a young woman.

Hanuvar's bad ankle was quite sore by the time they left the forest and reached their horses. Neither animal was particularly pleased to have been picketed near the woods, let alone when a storm threatened, and a few moments were required to calm them.

He held the boy's animal while he mounted up. "Guide us to the girl."

"Justus really wanted to impress her." Kliment threw himself over the mare and righted himself in the saddle. "Callista's family's rich. And her mother doesn't... didn't like Justus. But he wanted to show he could provide for her, you know?"

A wiser person would have known that giving expensive jewelry to a girl was no guarantor of impressing parents, especially if they were of higher social status, but there was no reason to point that out to Kliment.

"Thank you," the boy said suddenly. "For all this."

"I like to see a job through." Hanuvar climbed into his own saddle. "And you're not the only one to lose a brother in an unpleasant way. Let's go."

They skirted the corner of a strangely quiet Turian settlement and rode on toward a modest villa along its eastern edge. The boy's idea of wealth was relative. The home was well made but its exterior was sparsely decorated. It included a small separate stables, a half acre of olive orchard, and some fields, but it was nothing like the vast estates to the north and east.

By the time they dismounted the skies were dark. A chill wind blew. Their horses were restive and Kalak trotted close upon Hanuvar's left.

Kliment had led them to the servant's entrance, built into a courtyard wall. From its far side they heard the chatter of activity and the sizzle of food. The scent of fish and baking bread wafted through the air.

The two slid down from their horses and then the boy rapped the door with his lame foot.

It was opened by a thin man who glanced suspiciously at Hanuvar but seemed to recognize the boy.

"We don't want any eels, Kliment," the man said in a lugubrious tenor. "We already bought some at market today."

"I'm not selling eels. Is Callista here?"

The slave dropped his voice and leaned out. "You know I can't pass messages on to the mistress from your brother—"

"Justus is dead. I need to see her."

The slave's eyes widened in sorrow. "Oh, Kliment. I'm so—"

He looked to his left, surprised, then moved nervously aside. The door was pushed further open by a tall, older woman in a formal blue stola. Her eyes were a pretty blue, though there was no warmth to them.

"Kliment," she said sternly. "You're to tell Justus he's not welcome here."

"Justus is dead," Kliment repeated.

"Dead?" The woman did not look unmoved but appeared uncertain as to how she should react, and turned her gaze to Hanuvar, clearly seeking explanation. "Who are you?"

Kliment brushed at his eyes as he answered. "His name is Flavius, and he came to help me find my brother." He choked on a sob.

The woman's hands fluttered at her side. She raised them and started to reach out, then restrained herself against a natural instinct to comfort the boy.

The horses neighed as the wind picked up. The leaves susurrated in the wind.

Hanuvar thought it time to explain. "Justus and his friends took things from a Turian tomb. They've all been killed. We found them inside."

The woman looked back and forth between Hanuvar and Kliment as though she searched for some safe place to rest her eyes where they would not find anything unsettling.

"Justus gave Callista a ring," Kliment managed, wiping his nose on the back of his hand.

"He what?" The woman didn't wait for an answer. "Callista would never take a ring from a boy," she asserted, but her voice trailed off, because she clearly wondered if that was true even as she said it. She turned on her heel and shouted. "Callista! Come here immediately! Immediately, do you hear?"

The girl must have been lingering close by, for the woman, with back turned to them, began speaking to her while she was out of sight. "Is it true, Callista? Did you accept a ring from that stable boy?"

A young woman's voice was thick with feigned confusion. "A ring?"

"Oh shining Arepon. You did, didn't you? Your friend's mother didn't give that to you at all, did she? It was from that boy."

"The dead boy," Hanuvar reminded her. "Does she still have the ring?"

The woman had briefly been outraged by the shame of her daughter being courted by a social inferior, but the reminder of Justus' death centered her once more. She snapped at her daughter. "Go and fetch the ring. Let me see it."

"I've got it right here."

Finally Hanuvar saw a clear-skinned, auburn-haired girl, fifteen at the oldest. She wrestled with something upon her hand.

Behind Hanuvar, the dog growled. "What's this all about?" Callista was saying.

The wind rose, and something black and shifting drifted out of the night, a darkness given human shape. It floated in a straight line for the villa.

Hanuvar pushed open the door. The woman frowned at him and backed away while he noted the back courtyard wall and the twin ovens, the grill beneath an awning, some river fish roasting over the flames, and a bucket beside them. The skinny slave who'd opened the door waited apprehensively to one side. Another slave monitored the spitted fish while a second paused from chopping fresh greens on a wooden block and gaped at Hanuvar and Kliment and the dog as they barged into the space.

The woman objected to his entrance but Hanuvar didn't stop. Behind him the slave stammered in fright and pointed out the door.

The girl screamed at whatever followed. He spun to see it but did not unsheathe a weapon.

The haunt glided in, the wind its company. It couldn't quite hold a human shape. It was a curtain of darkness with burning eyes under which the memory of bones could be glimpsed, as through a shifting murky depth. It swept past the mother and the barking dog, ghastly hands stretched toward the stammering girl. From it wafted not just the cold of the world's high places, but an atmosphere of ineffable wrongness so disquieting Hanuvar himself backstepped. The boy gasped and slid behind him. Callista's mother moved to shield her daughter, face pale in horror. One cook fled screaming; the doorman shouted for the mistress to get to safety and pulled ineffectually on her arm. The second cook froze in place, staring with enormous eyes.

Hanuvar didn't possess a vast knowledge of old Turian, but he understood the icy words that rolled from somewhere within that phantasm, no matter their odd accent. "Mine! Mine! Blood for mine!"

The shrieking girl had finally worked the ring free and Hanuvar grabbed it from her. He took a tentative step away, testing his theory, and the thing shifted toward him.

"Callista," her mother cried, "run!"

But the girl was rooted to the spot. The haunt followed Hanuvar, vaporous hands outstretched. The dog menaced it but made no contact, barking with a mix of frightened whines.

"What are you doing?" Kliment cried.

Taking a risk, Hanuvar thought. It really depended on how long those eels had been sitting in the bucket near the grill.

By the light of the cherry red coals and a lantern dangling from the roof overhang, he saw the cluster of animals shifting in the bucket. They were still alive. He plunged a hand in, unsurprised to encounter the gritty salt that seasons and removes slime while slowly killing eels.

The spirit flowed on for him and Hanuvar fought down the instinct to take to his heels. Heart slamming, he fumbled for grip on one of the creatures, lifting the writhing eel and pressing its jaw open with his thumb.

The spirit reached for Hanuvar. No matter fire or grill, proximity to the chill leached through his clothes and numbed his skin.

Hanuvar thrust the ring down the eel's throat, brushing his fingers against the ridged teeth of its jaw, then dropped it into the bucket and threw himself to the right in a roll. He scarcely noted the twinge in his ankle as he came to his feet, heart hammering.

The spirit had risen with one skeletal hand holding the eel, which twisted only briefly before going limp.

The long fish still clasped in its hand, the haunt floated swiftly from the outdoor kitchen, out the door in the wall, and vanished into the night. The dog barked at the doorway but did not follow.

Hanuvar stood staring after it for a long time, catching his breath, willing his pulse to settle. He shuddered like a man exposed in a winter wind. Vaguely he heard the woman asking if he was all right.

He turned to find Callista's mother at his side, and he nodded slowly. "It needed to take a life in vengeance for the theft. Fortunately for us, the kind of life didn't matter."

"How did you know? Are you a mage?"

He laughed without humor. "No. Just observant. The spirit still needs to be dealt with. Maybe some priests of Lutar can send it on, but its tomb should be sealed, and soon."

"And Kliment knows where it lairs?"

"He does." Hanuvar nodded to the boy, talking softly with the drawn-looking Callista. "I don't think he has any family left. If he hadn't led me here, your daughter would be dead."

The woman considered Kliment for a long moment, then seemed to come to some final decision. "He will have us, then. His mother was a good woman," she added, then, after a moment, said, "and Justus was a nice boy, really."[25] The woman returned her attention to him. "But what of you? Is there nothing I can do for you?"

Her gratitude was honest and unrestrained. Hanuvar was touched

---

[25] When I tracked down this settlement I discovered that the Ranelian family had been true to their word. Kliment had been welcomed as their son and now cared for his ailing adopted mother as well as a growing family of his own. The girl, Callista, had married a neighbor boy. Kliment and his mother were able to corroborate everything from Antires' version of the account (again and again I found Antires' account to be accurate, enough so that in those instances where I could find no living witnesses I feel reasonably confident he relayed the truth). —*Silenus*

by it. There was little, though, that she could do to help him. "I must travel. If you can spare a little food, I will be quite content."

She offered him the guest bedroom that night, and he slept deep, though he was awake before the dawn. Kliment woke to see him off, and assured him he could keep the horse. The mistress of the house saw to it that he would not need to halt for food or drink for long days. Both must have had further time to reflect on what he had done for them, for their thanks were heartfelt, even if their words were simple.

He raised his hand in farewell, climbed into the saddle, and headed into the morning with the dog trotting after.

❦ ❦ ❦

Hanuvar pressed on through the Turian wilds as fast as his tall old gelding would take him.

By that evening, Tafari had arrived with his army of gladiators, occupying Apicius in numbers so great the legionaries retreated to their fortress. The citizen soldiers commanded the harbor and access to every one of the vessels berthed there, making this absolutely clear when a band of gladiators sneaked out in the early morning to commandeer one of the ships and the Dervans smashed it to pieces—along with all but two of the gladiators—by means of a few well-placed catapult stones.

Although Tafari kept his people under tight rein, the presence of so many armed, lawless men taking what they wished of the town's supplies was a cause for panic, and all those remaining who were able fled. Izivar welcomed into her home many who could not, mostly women with dependents, and through a fortunate quirk of events was able to act with a surprisingly free hand. Eshmun, the Volani soldier turned gladiator, was one of Tafari's trusted lieutenants. Discovering a small cadre of free Volani living upon the coast, his initial assumption that they were traitors changed when he learned that Izivar had purchased and freed many of her staff, and, perhaps surprisingly, Captain Bomilcar and Elistala relayed that Izivar and I were considered allies by Hanuvar. The captain in particular seemed to retain his own doubts, but did not pass them along to Eshmun, who was quite friendly from that day forward.

Izivar sought to shield the Lady Amelia as well, to no avail. Ciprion's wife had been apprehended and imprisoned following stiff resistance from some of her staff; fortunately, the grandchildren and other relatives were no longer in town. While Izivar could not arrange for Amelia's release, she saw to it that she was housed in comfort and treated with respect.

Then it seemed everyone still in the town settled into a stalemate. The legionaries had sent out a ship for reinforcements. The gladiators sought a way to pry out the warriors guarding the ships, for they meant to sail free and no other nearby harbors held anything approaching the quality and size of the vessels berthed in Apicius. Izivar and I waited for Hanuvar. And unbeknownst to us, Calenius had returned to Esuvia, where he continued to ready for the spell that would doom us all.

—Sosilos, Book Seventeen

Chapter 13:
Queen of a Nighted Realm

The two men laughed as they chased the screaming woman into the dark.

Hanuvar crept closer to the wagon and watched the lone bandit bent near its right axle searching the belt pouch of a dead man. The scream held the bandit's attention. He hurried his plunder and called out for them to save some for him. It was the last thing he said. Hanuvar clasped the bandit's mouth from behind as he cut his throat, then held his lips closed to muffle him while he bled out. The dog, Kalak, watched silently.

Hanuvar eased the body to the ground beside its fellow. The wagon sideboards were high, but he knew two more bandits looted the bodies at the camp beyond. He donned the dead brigand's cap as he started around the wagon, the dog at his side, but needn't have bothered with the thin disguise. One man guzzled from a wineskin and the other sorted rudely through the bags they'd already tossed off the wagon bed, complaining the merchants weren't carrying anything but cloth. The man with the wineskin glanced at Hanuvar just as he drew close enough to drive his knife point through his chest.

The cloth sorter alerted to the choking noise and started to draw as he turned, but Hanuvar leapt forward and struck in a single motion. His target tried to side-step, but moved only fast enough so that the belly blow took him in the thigh instead. He went down, and

Hanuvar dropped him with a knee to the man's abdomen and his knife to his throat. The only tricky part was catching the dying man's wrist as he tried to plunge his own blade into Hanuvar's chest.

The dying can manage desperate strength, but Hanuvar outlasted him and rose, weapon to hand, flexing his ankle, sore from the strenuous activity. He was impressed with the strength of the dog's training. He had ordered him to hold back, and the canine had kept clear and quiet. That was all for the best, for he'd not wanted the rest of the bandits summoned by Kalak's barking or the shouts of his victims.

Now, though, the mastiff growled, hackles rising as though it faced some terrible foe. Hanuvar hadn't seen where the woman had been hiding, only the sound of her discovery, and it had spurred him to act. He had no idea how she'd escaped her pursuers.

She now stood on the edge of the dying fire, small and slim in a dark dress. Precious stones glittered on her fingers and upon the filigree above her high brow. Her face was round and clear and beautifully formed, with full lips and wide eyes that seemed not to blink. She appeared to have been staring at Hanuvar for a while.

"Where are the men who chased you?" he asked.

"They walk the last road," she said, in a peculiar lilting accent. "From whence did you come?"

She spoke Dervan like a native Turian, though her pronunciation carried an unfamiliar, formal cadence. "Nearby," he said. He did not add that only the foolish light fires in the Turian wilds at night. He himself had bedded down before sunset, planning to finish the rest of his travel after moonfall. Robbers were not the only dangerous things said to walk these hills.

"Where were you hiding?"

"I was not hiding," she said, and took a further step. She stared down at the bodies. He expected she might fall to weeping, or kneel beside one of the fellows he supposed to be her husband, or father, or brother. But her attention was cursory at best and finally she stopped only a few paces out from Hanuvar, who had finished wiping his weapons on a dead man. The dog growled further, and she smiled indulgently, as though she found the beast amusing.

"You are efficient," she said.

"There may be more," he told her. "We should retreat."

Only then did she turn her smile on him. "As you wish."

There was something strange in her manner, and though he had killed these men only to save her, he had no desire to put his back to her. He gestured for her to precede him.

"Do you not wish to stop for their silver?" she asked.

Their, he thought. *Not our.* And she showed no interest in retrieving her belongings.

"No. I have what I need at the moment," he answered.

Her gaze raked him and then she turned and walked with graceful quiet into the darkness. He gave her directions and followed, Kalak close to his side. Soon they were over a hill and into the little shelter of trees where he had picketed his horse and laid his blanket down.

The black gelding shied from her as she walked close, laying back his ears, and then she strode about the little camp, seeing where he had made a smokeless charcoal cookfire in the evening.

She pushed hair back from her forehead. Her eyes did not leave him. "So you come alone, to Turia, and hide in the woods. Whom do you flee?" she asked.

"I flee no one."

"Then you seek someone."

"Something like that."

"Perhaps you seek me."

"Only to help you," he said.

She laughed at that.

"What are you doing here, in the wilds?" he asked.

"I'm trying to find my people."

That wasn't the answer he expected. "You weren't travelling with them?"

"Them? No. I happened upon the scene, like you."

He understood now that she had misled him, just as she had the bandits, and her scream had been for show. Now it was imperative he understand her game, and her nature. "Who are your people?"

She smiled, and was lovely. "You would not believe me."

"You might be surprised."

Once more she stared at him. "I think you are a hunter, like me."

"That may be," he said.

She walked to his left, quietly. He had seen leopards pace thus. Kalak growled again.

"There is a thirst in you," she said. "I see it now. You want revenge."

"A part of me does. But vengeance is time consuming, and I am short on time." He wondered now if his time was shorter even than he had thought. He had decided, at last, what was so strange in her movements. Her nostrils never flared; her chest never rose and fell. Whatever she was, she did not breathe. "Who are you?"

She smiled more widely, and while she was beautiful there was that of a predator in her look. "I think you know, now, Dervan, that I am not mortal. And it is your people who brought me to this." She snarled at him, and he sensed the strength in her and thought she was nearly done with her playing.

And so he spoke the truth. "I am no Dervan."

She tilted her head and regarded him, her fine eyes narrowing. "You do not lie," she said slowly. "While I sense your fear, I see it gives you strength. You intrigue me."

"Who are you?" he repeated.

She did not answer for a time, then flicked her fingers in a dismissive gesture, as if her deciding to grant his request was a minor thing. "I am the queen of a fallen people, crushed by the Dervans. My name is not important, for what is a queen without her people?"

He sympathized with that sentiment, one too often misunderstood by rulers. "You said you seek them. Where are they?"

"Dead. And I do not mean my waking death. The Dervans came for my lands. And I fought them. They were too many. One by one all fell, until there was nothing left but a small force, living in the hills."

Hanuvar now knew with whom he spoke. "You are Queen Philenia. The folk of Turia speak of you still, and how you died with sword in hand. How your body was spotted on the battlefield, but never seen after."

Her head tilted minutely and her eyes searched his. "Why do you not run, mortal man?"

Because he knew it would not help him. He sought to escape her through a different course. "The Dervans slew my people. I would have died with them, but for the aid of a friend."

Her eyes lit.

"You said you seek them," he pressed. "How?"

She touched the necklace and pulled free the palm of her hand.

Shining in her white palm were dozens of pale blue forms. "These are those I've gathered in the last little while."

"Your people?"

"The souls of those who walk my lands at night. Almost I have enough. And when their numbers match those I lost, I will trade them to Lady Death, and she will give my people back!"

She was mad, and very dangerous, and he knew that she was likely still to attack, but he could not help but respect her dedication. And he told her so. "You are brave and determined and cunning." And he added, because he sensed it remained important to her, and because it was true: "And you are very beautiful."

She lifted her head in approval.

"But what if your people do not want to come?"

Her fair brow creased. "What? They will come to me."

"I have spoken with Lady Death," he said.

Her eyebrows raised.

"It must be very pleasant there, with her, because no one returns, even when openings present." He thought of his brothers who had clasped his arms in farewell before returning to a realm beyond mist. "You never went to her, did you?"

"I resisted. What hold can she have on their allegiance? I was their queen!"

"I suppose that she is an end to strife," Hanuvar sad. "She is solace. She is . . . oblivion."

She bared her teeth. "You speak of her with love."

He shook his head. "I love my people. She has almost all of them." He could not help but speak with a hint of ferocity, and she heard it in her voice.

"You understand!"

"I do," he said.

She was but a step away, and the scent of her reached him. Kalak let out a bark, but Hanuvar motioned him still. The dog fell to growling.

The queen smelled of old soil, and new blood, and the wild places, but not of rot. Her eyes were shining, but she no longer played, and he did not think he saw thirst there. "I have nearly all I need," she said quietly. "And then I will make my trade. And I will see. If you want, I can show you how it is done. It may be that if we approach her together, with a great trade, we will have a better bargain for her. She will want these souls. She is always greedy for more."

"She is," Hanuvar agreed. "But she only takes. She never gives. Her patience is measureless. She will outlast us all."

Her teeth flashed as she snarled. "You think me a fool? You think I have wasted all this effort?"

"I think you are clever, and I think you are angry, and I think you love your people. But I think you should pick your battles better."

"What other battles are there for me?"

"I have need of friends," he said. "Your people are passed. But some of mine still live. You could help them."

Her face clouded. "You think I would help any of the living?"

"Not any," he said. "The last of my people." He saw her frown beginning, and spoke passionately: "To give them the aid you wish someone would have given you."

She stared at him for a long while, then addressed him in a passionless voice. "Leave me."

He extended his hand. "Come with me. You deserve a better end than this."

She considered him in bewilderment. For a moment, he thought she meant to say yes. "I feel the blood pulsing through you, and I feel the truth of your advice. I thirst for the one and rage against the other and yet I do not mean to kill you. Both rise to war with my reason. You have touched me in a way I have not known in long years. Would that I could wander away with you. But it is my... nature that I am tied to his land."

"If you cannot go, what will you do?"

She laughed too long, then shook her head. "New experiences are as formless as mist to me, compared to what was. But I will try to hold to what you've said. And work some other plan."

"Remember that you have at least one friend left."

"A friend," she repeated. "How curious. What is your name, friend?"

"I am Hanuvar."

She regarded him with head held high and dismissed him with the slow, regal wave of a hand. "Go now, Hanuvar. With a queen's blessing, whatever good it does you. I may forget much when next I wake. But I think I shall remember you."

"I shall never forget you, oh Queen." He bowed his head to her.

While he gathered up the bags and took up the reins, she vanished as if she had never been. He half expected to find her at his back, especially since Kalak continually looked behind them, but he rode the rest of the night and reached the hills at Turia's edge just before dawn without sight of her. In the dim light behind him he thought he glimpsed a lone figure along the road side, but it might have been a trick of the light, for when he peered more closely there was nothing there apart from a lone tree, swaying in the morning wind.

※ ※ ※

In Apicius we remained in a terrible kind of stasis. The gladiators had no luck uprooting the garrison, although they too constructed some catapults and traded occasional stones with the soldiers. Late one night a swift military ship reached the protected berth under the fortress walls and the gladiator's sharp-eyed sentries saw a few dozen reinforcements join the garrison. The next morning word went forth that Ciprion was among the new arrivals, in advance of a legion marching from the north. He proved uninterested in discussing terms, even with his own wife held as their prisoner, for Dervans were highly resistant to negotiating with rebellious slaves. When a society is built on the back of slave labor, any suggestion that those in bondage could improve their lot by violence is to be stringently avoided.

What Ciprion thought in private I do not know. At this point, enough days had passed that Izivar and I worried as to Hanuvar's whereabouts. Izivar conferred with the Volani gladiator, Eshmun, anxious that Hanuvar might be mistaken for a Dervan military man and slain by their forces.

Eshmun promised that he would keep alert for him. Learning that Hanuvar was somewhere nearby, the leader of the gladiators, Tafari, set his men to patrol for him, thinking the great general might be the answer to all his problems. You may recall that Hanuvar and I had met this Tafari, and that he was one of the few who had elected to remain with Gnaeus, the false Hanuvar, and then had not turned up at a later rendezvous. Tafari was a capable leader, and Izivar guessed what he must be thinking. Who better to get past a Dervan garrison than the greatest general in the world?

Out on his mountain, Calenius continued to work his magic beneath dark clouds.

—Sosilos, Book Seventeen

Chapter 14:
A Time of Reckoning

I

Hanuvar rode his way upstream through the knots of frightened, disheveled men, women, and children. Some families fled on wagons piled high with belongings, others sat horses or donkeys, but most walked, bearing only a few sacks of belongings.

Household slaves were common sights amongst those along the thoroughfare. Probably fear and familiarity kept them united with the greater majority of their owners, though Hanuvar supposed misplaced loyalty and even genuine affection might play some role.

Field and estate slaves were almost entirely absent. Hanuvar overheard that most had sided with a new gladiator-led revolt rampaging through the countryside. Given the brutal working conditions at many of the large farms, owned by patricians far from the property and overseen by miserly managers, the impetus of those slaves to risk rebellion was fully understandable.

The Dervan legions would violently crush this revolt, like those before it. But there were always those bowed by circumstances so desperate that even a few moments of freedom before death were better than servitude.

While Hanuvar sympathized, the rebellion's timing slowed his progress, and the lives of everyone, slave or free, depended upon him stopping Calenius before night fall. As he fought his way closer—the only one travelling toward rather than away from Apicius—he heard a mix of news that was alternately absurdly optimistic or improbably doom laden. Some said five legions were already on their way south, which was unlikely unless they'd been recalled from the frontiers weeks before the revolt began. Others claimed an army of gladiators thousands strong was readying to march on Derva itself.

Most of the refugees agreed that Apicius, or parts of it, had been occupied, and Hanuvar's fears for Izivar, Antires, and all his allies were only minimally allayed by reports that the Nuvaran in charge had kept his men under strict control. There were no stories of wholesale murders, rapes, or looting common to armed conflict, nor injuries visible in those leaving. Apparently Tafari had allowed people to depart the settlement relatively unmolested. What his real aims were, no one in the crowds could guess.

Drawing closer to the little seaside town, Hanuvar heard a further rumor that Ciprion himself was barricaded within the fort overlooking the harbor. That sounded almost as unlikely as some of the wilder contentions, but gave Hanuvar a small modicum of hope. Moving against Calenius would require an armed force, and he didn't especially care how he got one. It would certainly be easier to convince Ciprion of the danger than a gladiator he barely knew, but then if his friend had taken up post in the fort, Hanuvar would have to contend with the rebels to reach him.

He found a blockade of overturned carts along the road just south of the unwalled town outskirts. It was manned by warriors in a mix of gladiatorial and legionary armor and weapons. Beyond them the buildings along the brick streets looked intact. He saw no fires or burned out homes, nor did he glimpse bodies lying in the streets. He could hope then that Tafari truly had constrained his men, but was aware that he might simply have imposed tidiness upon them.

Hanuvar dismounted twenty yards from the road block and led his old farm horse forward. The half-grown brindle mastiff, Kalak, trotted at his side. Two men in front of the barricade watched him alertly as he drew up and one of them, tall with a bull neck, raised a restraining hand.

"The city's not taking visitors at this time."

That was a far more measured response than he had expected.

"I'm a messenger, sent to speak with Tafari."

The lead sentry eyed him more shrewdly. Over the last days Hanuvar had shaved regularly, with supplies purchased or gifted along the way, but he and his clothes alike were stained from travel. That could well be expected of a messenger, but such men were usually younger, and riding better horses.

"Who sent you?" the sentry inquired skeptically.

"Tell Tafari I have a message from Fabius, whom he met earlier in the year."

"General Tafari's busy."

"If Eshmun serves with you, he will vouch for me. The news I carry is quite important."

From the way the sentry's brows furrowed Hanuvar saw that he recognized the name of the Volani gladiator. Hanuvar understood the man's dilemma. The sentry weighed whether to risk a superior's condemnation at the word of a road-weary, name dropping, older man armed with a sword in a crusty scabbard.

After studying Hanuvar for another long moment the sentry ordered one of his companions to retrieve "Centurion" Eshmun. He then instructed Hanuvar to remove his sword belt, which he did, and motioned other sentries closer. He didn't warn that any suspicious behavior was liable to get Hanuvar beaten or speared; it wasn't necessary.

The gladiators didn't invite small talk and Hanuvar didn't attempt any. He studied the town beyond. Only a few men and women moved amongst the buildings, a shadow of the usual morning bustle. The harbor lay half empty, but a bireme sat at the long quay nearest the fortress, and the helmeted heads of many soldiers could be glimpsed above the ramparts. Hanuvar had hoped to see Izivar's ship departed, but could have anticipated that she would not leave without him. It floated among a handful of others.

After what seemed an interminable time, the messenger sentry returned at a fair clip with a tall, sun-bronzed younger man jogging at his side. This was Eshmun, who slowed just before reaching the barricade. He drew up beside the bull-necked sentry with a nod, listening politely as Hanuvar's claim was repeated. His eyes shifted to Hanuvar and then he grinned.

"You did right to send for me," Eshmun said to the guard, and walked for Hanuvar, hand outstretched. "It's a pleasure to see you—"

"Decius Antoninus," Hanuvar said quickly, lest Eshmun call him by name, or even title. He suspected the younger man had been about to address him as *general*, or *shofet*. "You recall meeting me earlier this year, I'm sure."

Though momentarily confused, Eshmun recovered swiftly. "Of course. Come with me."

"These men took my sword." It wasn't an especially good sword, but it was the only one Hanuvar had.

Eshmun ordered the lead sentry to give it back, and Hanuvar belted it on as he led his horse through the blockade. Kalak alertly scanned their surroundings from his side as the Volani walked them into the town. The inns appeared empty; upstairs shutters were sealed.

The young gladiator switched to Volani. "I'm very glad to see you."

"It's good to see a friendly face. Is Izivar Lenereva here, and is she unharmed?"

"Yes, and yes. I was called in as soon as it was clear one of the households was Volani and she's been under my protection. She's offered shelter to all the local women, though Tafari has assured her it's not necessary."

"What of Amelia, wife of Ciprion?"

"She's in our custody."

That alarmed him. "She's well?"

"Of course. She's too useful. Especially with Ciprion in the fortress."

So that news hadn't been nonsense after all. "What's Ciprion doing here?"

"Word has it he came in advance of his troops, who should arrive in the next few days, and to reinforce the garrison. The only thing that's holding us back from the harbor and its ships is the fortress. They'll sink us if we try to leave. But we've got our own catapults lined up now. They can't leave either. We need help. You couldn't have arrived at a better time. Tafari's going to be glad to speak with you."

The gladiators had taken over the municipal capital, a two-story brick building fronted with square pillars. Hanuvar was led through its main entrance, up interior stairs, and into a council room on the second floor with a long rectangular table plattered with food.

Windows overlooked the light blue waters and the dark sand of the town's best beach, empty of crowds, umbrellas, and merchant carts.

At the table's head sat the handsome Nuvaran, his kinked hair even more closely trimmed than Hanuvar remembered. With him were a half dozen advisors, among them a familiar man and woman. Both stood at Hanuvar's entrance.

Eshmun shut the door behind them, and Tafari raised a hand in recognition and rose. Hanuvar, though, had shifted his attention to Bomilcar, plain and bluff, happily striding toward him with Elistala, who smiled broadly. She wore a man's tunic and a long, thick leather skirt, and while she did not wear a chest piece or helmet, her hair was tightly braided, suggesting she was ready to don her warrior's kit at a moment's notice.

The enthusiastic Volani interrupted Tafari's line of approach. Hanuvar grasped the arms of both in turn. Sensing the excitement, Kalak thumped his tail vigorously, uncaring that it drummed a table leg.

"Bomilcar and Elistala," Hanuvar said in Volani. "It does me good to see you both."

"And me you, General," Elistala answered, smiling with savage pleasure.

Bomilcar beamed. "We found her, General. Narisia's alive and well."

He nodded in appreciation, and would have said more, but Tafari had grown impatient and came around the table to stress his presence. Eshmun and Bomilcar made room for him.

Tafari glanced down at the dog, then spoke in his cultured Nuvaran accent. "I bid you welcome as well, great General. And I hate to interrupt this reunion, but we've pressing matters."

"More than you know." Hanuvar had dozens of questions he would have asked Elistala and Bomilcar, but they would have to wait.

Tafari passed over any implication in Hanuvar's statement and continued: "Our soothsayer declared this a crucial time for action, while the moon is full and the planet of war rides above the constellation of the spear, so we have momentous planning and preparation underway. You've come just when needed most. Your mortal enemy Ciprion and a garrison are sealed up in the city fortress, and I need to get them out."

Hanuvar saw that he'd have to hear the man's wishes before he could change his course. Best, then, to let him say what troubled him before he asserted control. "What's your objective?"

"To sail away, just as you would have advised. But the Dervans command the harbor."

That was a far more reasonable goal than razing the countryside in rebellion or exacting vengeance on wealthy patricians. "How many men do you have?"

Tafari hesitated only a moment, then must have decided Hanuvar would have to be trusted if he were to be any use. "Eighty gladiators. Three hundred auxiliary, drawn from the men and women we've freed. We've been teaching them to fight."

"And how many soldiers are in the garrison?"

"We can't be entirely certain. But we believe there to be close to a hundred."

"And where is Calenius?"

Tafari's expression clouded. "Calenius?"

"The big red-haired man," Hanuvar explained. "He controls a dig site on the slope of Esuvia."

"He's on that mountain. Why is that important? He has a small force entrenched there, but they've shown no interest in coming after us."

"He's more dangerous than Ciprion and the legions. How many followers does he retain?"

Tafari shook his head. "I don't know for certain. Our scouts estimated around a hundred. But we are not concerned with him. Ciprion"—he emphasized the name as if Hanuvar hadn't heard him properly the first time—"is in the fortress. If we try for the harbor he'll either sink the ships or set them on fire. His entire legion is marching down from Derva and should be here in two days, so we're short on time."

"Calenius has to be stopped this evening."

Though all in the room had been listening, Hanuvar's declaration stilled them completely. Their scrutiny intensified.

Tafari looked especially puzzled. "Stopped from what?"

"He's been readying a spell that's going to destroy the region. Tonight. Friend, foe, and everyone in between will be lost."

"Spells," the Nuvaran muttered. "This is no time to worry over some charlatan's show."

"He's the sorcerer who fashioned the false Hanuvar. And he did that in his spare time. He's been preparing for this night for a very long time."

Tafari's brow furrowed and he shook his head impatiently. "We must get my people out of here before the legion comes." His hand tightened into a fist that he raised, his dark eyes lighting. "Now's your chance to fight Ciprion and gain your vengeance."

"You're not listening."

The Nuvaran's smile shifted into a frown with the speed of a rejected lover. He slammed a palm against the wall.

Kalak growled warning, and Hanuvar shushed him.

Tafari shouted. "You're not listening! I want a war leader, not an old woman. My people are in danger, and I need to get them out. The man who beat you is down in the fortress!"

"All of us will die unless we fight Calenius."

Tafari studied him in disbelief, then addressed him with quiet contempt. "You're frightened of Ciprion."

"On the contrary. I intend to meet with him today."

"What?" If Tafari had looked surprised before, his expression now betrayed utter confusion.

Bomilcar, Eshmun, and Elistala talked at him in Volani at the same time, questioning his judgment with varied degrees of politeness. Elistala offered that the general she'd met might be an honorable man, but that some struggles could not be avoided.

She and the others fell silent as Hanuvar held up a hand and addressed Tafari. "Yes. Ciprion will hear me. And we can come to an accord when I explain the situation."

The floor trembled; a rumble of thunder sounded. The legs of the table rattled against the stone floor and plaster dust rained from the ceiling. Just as Hanuvar's gaze swayed up, wondering if the building was going to collapse around them, the tremor stopped.

While the others exclaimed and nervously compared observations, Hanuvar strode to a side window and flung open the shutters, leaning out to better take in the horizon. People in the street below were gabbling among themselves and some pointed toward the cone of Esuvia, whose forested slopes lay down a dark line of road. Black smoke pillowed from its height.

Hanuvar pointed to it. "Calenius is on the slope of Esuvia right now, working his magic."

"Does he mean to destroy himself as well as all others?" Tafari asked caustically.

"His aims do not include suicide, just the erasure of everyone else. I need to speak to Ciprion about them."

Tafari contemplated the volcano. "Fine. Go talk to Ciprion. If he gives us ships, none of his people die. If he doesn't, I start with his wife."

This man might be a capable leader, but he had much to learn about the nature of his opponent. "If you hurt his wife, you will succeed only in making Ciprion very angry."

"And I should care about making him angry?" Tafari's astonishment made it seem as though he thought Hanuvar crazy.

"You should care about making him reasonable," Hanuvar countered. "I'll take Amelia with me to demonstrate we're serious."

Tafari laughed in disbelief. "You want to give both yourself and his woman to him? Right now we have the superior position—"

Hanuvar sliced the air with a hand. "I know him, which is far more important than any abstract study of warfare. Conflict isn't a set of patterns you memorize then execute without examination. You must constantly evaluate not just the ground, but the leaders who hold it."

Tafari frowned, uncertain and dismayed.

"The Dervans will kill you, General," Eshmun objected.

Hanuvar shook his head. "I have something else in mind."

The room fell silent while Tafari considered his choices. Bomilcar and Elistala exchanged troubled glances.

The rumbling resumed. Hanuvar turned again to the window. The mountain continued to smoke, though the vapors were whiter than before, more like storm clouds.

"Very well," Tafari snapped. "Take the woman. You're either more clever than I understand or a damned fool, and I've no love for torturing a woman in any case. If they kill you, I'm hardly worse off than I was this morning."

The Volani seemed about to protest before Hanuvar silenced them with a flinty look. That was about the best he could have expected. Hanuvar stepped to the table and helped himself to a hunk of bread and some of the peeled hardboiled eggs that had been laid out, wolfing them down. Bomilcar hurried to assist him but Hanuvar was already pouring himself a goblet of wine as he chewed.

He swallowed and paused with the wine halfway to his mouth. "I need a black eyepatch," he said. "And some armor. If the Dervans are receiving Hanuvar, let's give them the man they expect to see."

II

To Hanuvar's knock Amelia said: "You're going to come in anyway, so you might as well not pretend at civility."

She glowered from where she sat under a small lattice window, a scroll in her lap, then gaped at sight of Hanuvar, now wearing a centurion's breastplate. He did not carry the concave shield of a legionary but a smaller oval one handed him by a gladiator. His helm, too, wasn't standard issue, but a modern version of an old Herrenic model, with cheek pieces that nearly covered the whole of his face apart from slots for his eyes and mouth. He had already donned his eye patch.

He wasn't entirely sure that she recognized him until he said: "Are you ready to get out of here?"

"By glorious Jovren," she said softly, and continued to stare.

She wore a fine blue stola and appeared reasonably comfortable. But then she'd been housed in a downstairs office complete with small, barred window, a shelf with books, a chair, and a table. Someone had even dragged in a worn old bedframe, narrow and dark and clashing with the fine lines of the office furniture.

When Amelia seemed uncertain how to reply, Hanuvar spoke again. "If you're happy where you are, I can just meet Ciprion without you."

She let out a single, soft bark of laughter and set her sandaled feet on the floor.

Amelia was rarely one for extravagant beauty steps. In captivity she had no maid to help her with her hair, but she looked little different, a handsome woman of middle years trending toward stoutness. "Have you been injured?" she asked. "Or are you in some sort of costume?"

"In point of fact, I have been injured. But my vision's fine. And this *is* a costume. I'm the terrible Hanuvar. Don't you recognize me? I'm here to transport you to safety."

She adjusted her stola. "You are full of surprises. I didn't hear any swordplay, or battle cries."

"Those are overrated," he said, and she chuckled.

"Why is it that it's always evil barbarians rescuing me? That never happens in the stories."

"Maybe you're reading the wrong stories." He grew more serious. "I'm told you were treated well. Is it true?"

"There were no . . . indignities forced."

"Good. Come. Time wastes."

She felt her hair, patted it, then he stepped aside and she came with him into the hallway.

Tafari and one of his attendants escorted them to the outer door, followed by Bomilcar, Eshmun, and Elistala. Before them Amelia's pleasant countenance retreated into cold hauteur. She noted the dog but did not comment. Indeed, she said nothing, and Tafari did not address her.

"I hope you know what you're doing," the Nuvaran said in parting.

That went without saying, and Hanuvar saw no real point in reply. He had penned a brief note to Izivar, who would surely share the information with Antires, and requested Elistala and Bomilcar deliver it to her. Then he and Amelia and the dog started down the road and on toward the hill above the docks where the fort sat. Eshmun walked along their right, a torn white cloth drooping from a spear shaft that he leaned against his shoulder.[26]

Amelia was quiet for long strides. All watched the shining helmets upon the distant battlement as their approach brought them gradually better into focus. The streets were mostly deserted; carts were overturned as incremental barricades, behind which gladiators were positioned, and they stared as the trio and the dog passed them.

"You have acquired a dog," Amelia said at last.

"More precisely, he acquired me."

"What are you planning to do?" she asked quietly. "How did you arrange my freedom?"

"I convinced Tafari that the only way to confer with your husband was to take you along, unharmed, as sign of our good faith."

---

[26] Though the Dervans indicated the desire for parley with a raised shield, the Volani deployed white cloths, and Hanuvar expected Ciprion and his officers to be familiar with the symbol. —*Silenus*

"That was very kind of you. But what are you going to do then?" Her aristocratic façade had vanished, and she spoke to him now as if they were old confederates.

"Calenius is planning something that may kill us all."

Her eyebrows arched in consternation.

"So naturally I'm planning something mad."

"How mad?"

"I'm going to propose an alliance between escaped slaves and the forces of Derva."

"That is mad," she said after little reflection. "There is no bargaining with rebellious slaves, ever."

"Very true. Nor can there be peace between the noble Ciprion and the treacherous Hanuvar."

She snorted.

"But we have little choice," he finished.

"She's right, sir," Eshmun said cautiously, and Amelia finally acknowledged the gladiator by meeting his eyes. "The Dervans have never truly negotiated with slaves, and they have never granted any of their demands."

"When the storm winds rise, adversaries must take the oar bench," Hanuvar said in Volani. To Amelia's questioning look he said in Dervan: "In desperate times, men must align or drown."

"What is it, exactly, that Calenius is doing, and why?" she asked.

"You wouldn't believe me."

She scoffed. "I can believe quite a lot at this point."

They passed the final barricade. They were now well within range of the fort's ballistae. Helmeted heads upon the battlements shifted as officers were made way for. At this distance Hanuvar could not discern whether Ciprion was among them, but someone up there was a revenant, judging by the black helm with black crest. He was also on the smaller side, and Hanuvar wondered if this might be Legate Aquilius himself. There was also another figure in white armor, helmetless, with an eye patch of his own. Metellus.

"Any idea why the revenant legate would be here?" Hanuvar asked.

"None. But then my husband arrived via ship after the slave revolt. I have not had the pleasure of his company."

"I think you're about to, Lady Amelia," Eshmun said with tight politeness. "Unless I miss my guess."

The helmeted heads at the battlement made way for another who planted hands between the merlons and stared down at them. He raised his hand and spoke to the men at his shoulder.

Hanuvar called his companions to halt a few dozen feet beyond the sealed, brass-studded wooden gate of the fort. He saw the stern look upon his friend's face. If Ciprion felt relieved by the presence of his wife, he did not show it. Amelia's own expression had shifted into a tranquil mask, for it would be unseemly to betray emotions construable as weakness in public.

Eshmun waved the flag the legionaries had surely noticed long before, and Hanuvar made a speaking trumpet of his hands. It wasn't until he began to talk that Ciprion recognized him, for he straightened in surprise.

"Legate Ciprion! I come in peace, and have arranged for your wife's freedom as sign of my good intention. You and I need to meet in conference, but you must pledge that I can go free after." He said that not because he believed Ciprion would imprison him, but so that others understood his intention from the outset, and would hear the general's pledge.

Black helmed Aquilius stepped to Ciprion's side and others consulted with him. Hanuvar heard none of their exchange.

Before very long Ciprion stepped away and called down to him. "I will meet with you. I pledge, by my honor, that you may depart unharmed at the conclusion of our talks."

Eshmun frowned.

"He will be fine," Amelia assured him, with more confidence than Hanuvar himself felt.

"Retreat," Hanuvar instructed the young gladiator.

"What should we do if they won't hear you out?" Eshmun asked.

"He will."

"It doesn't seem likely," Eshmun said. "But if there's one man who can achieve the impossible, it is you, sir."

A sally door built into the left gate panel opened. Hanuvar gestured Amelia to precede him, and she started ahead. Hanuvar bade Kalak to stay and he did, though he whined. He'd commanded plenty of soldiers less obedient.

An entire phalanx of Dervan legionaries waited just beyond the open portal, their expressions grim. Their spears weren't pointed at

Hanuvar, but they looked ready to use them at the first sign of provocation.

A centurion, his rank obvious not just from his campaign medals but the transverse horsehair crest on his helmet, ordered the door shut behind him. "Turn over your weapon," he snapped at Hanuvar.

"Leave him be," Ciprion called down from the stairs he descended into the courtyard. The centurion, frowning, stepped back.

Amelia remained beside Hanuvar, almost protectively, until Ciprion and a small cadre of officers had climbed down the stairs built into the wall. Her husband walked in front, and Metellus and Aquilius flanked him, though keeping well clear of one another.

Ciprion's eyes caught his own; there were questions in his gaze, but he did not speak them.

"Who is this man?" Aquilius demanded. "The empire does not negotiate with slaves!"

"This is no slave," Ciprion said simply. He stopped before Hanuvar, and his eyes shifted to Amelia. Neither hugged the other but their eyes were alive with pleasure.

"You look well, my wife," he said.

"Husband. I've merely been inconvenienced."

Metellus had only one eye, but it was sharper than that of Aquilius. He actually chuckled. "Decius! What are you doing in the middle of this?"

Amelia answered him. "He convinced the leader of the gladiators to release me."

Ciprion bowed his head to Hanuvar. "I thank you."

"Decius?" Aquilius repeated. "Who is Decius? The one working for the Lenereva woman?"

Metellus smirked. Aquilius' dark brows furrowed and he peered suspiciously at Hanuvar's face.

Ciprion waved one of his men forward. His voice was kind, and softer, as he spoke to Amelia. "My aide Cantor will see to your needs. We will talk later."

"I look forward to it."

The warmth in her gaze spoke more volumes than their sober words. Ciprion ordered the young man to see that his wife was given food, drink, and anything else she required, then motioned Hanuvar after him. The others fell in step behind as Ciprion headed for the door of the stone building built into the far wall. A white-armored soldier stood on either side of it, which clued Hanuvar as to who was likely to lie beyond.

As soon as the door was opened, Hanuvar saw his guess had been accurate. Standing just inside the mess hall was a familiar young man with handsome, affable features and unruly brown hair. Enarius, the emperor, who cut a dashing figure in the legion armor someone had loaned him. He wore neither helmet nor greaves, but a sword belt with sheathed gladius hung at his waist.

"So your wife is well?" Enarius asked Ciprion. "And who's this?"

Metellus answered before anyone else could. "It's Decius," he said, "Izivar's security man. Disguised as Hanuvar," he added with a grin.

That explanation suited Hanuvar just fine, and so he removed his helmet even as Aquilius could be heard to wonder gruffly why he was disguised. "The real Hanuvar doesn't have an eye patch," he finished.

Enarius stared, his mouth opening ever so slightly, in recognition that grew more pronounced as Hanuvar removed the eyepatch. He laughed.

"Sire," Hanuvar said with a head bow. "My sons have spoken well of you."

"By the Gods!" Enarius said. "The resemblance *is* uncanny!"

"I told you," Metellus said good-humoredly.

"But what are you doing here, dressed like this? Is Izivar all right?"

"I haven't seen her in weeks, but I'm told she's unharmed."

Enarius let out a relieved sigh.

Aquilius had finally recognized Hanuvar from their encounter earlier in the summer. The little man's heavy chin dropped. "Decius?" He pointed at Hanuvar and addressed the emperor. "I met this man and he gave me an entirely different name."

"I was in the field, in disguise," Hanuvar explained. "I apologize for the deception."

Aquilius frowned at that. Hanuvar hadn't said it for his benefit, but for Metellus.

"Who exactly do you work for, then?" Aquilius demanded. "The praetorians?"

Ciprion cut him off. "That's not important right now."

Hanuvar had an answer in mind, but was grateful for the change in subject.

"Can you give me a disposition on the enemy troops?" Ciprion asked.

"Why don't we sit, like civilized men, with some wine," Enarius suggested. "Let's talk at the conference table."

Through a door in the mess hall lay a small meeting room with an oaken table, benches, and a door into what was almost surely the commanding centurion's office. Two slaves bustled inside, quickly pouring goblets, although only Enarius and Hanuvar himself seemed interested in taking one. After the tense walk here, in the sun in a helmet, Hanuvar's throat was dry, and he reasoned the emperor's wine would be worth drinking.

The slaves left them, and then Enarius gestured for everyone to take the benches after he occupied the chair at the table's head. Ciprion sat on the emperor's right hand, Metellus on his left. Hanuvar ended up beside Ciprion, across from Aquilius, who continued to frown at him. He stretched out his leg beneath the table and flexed his sore ankle, then placed his helmet on the bench. Metellus did the same, then raked his hair into shape.

"So tell us about the gladiator army, and what you're planning," Ciprion said.

Hanuvar took a long gulp of the wine. He was right, it was excellent. He set the goblet down and eyed his friend, and then the emperor. "Defeating the gladiators can't be our focus right now."

"Why not?" Aquilius demanded.

"Because Calenius will release a spell tonight that's going to kill all of us. Everyone. No matter their allegiance."

Aquilius' lips shaped a horrified circle of surprise. Ciprion blinked. Enarius and Metellus appeared confused and doubtful, respectfully.

"Who is Calenius?" the emperor demanded. "And why would he do that?"

"He's a powerful mage," Ciprion explained. "The revenants used him in the siege of Volanus, and he's been up to something secret around the volcano, on his own." He turned to Decius. "What's he doing?"

Because what he said would challenge belief, Hanuvar explained it bluntly, and as simply as he could. "He's going to summon the lord of time and trade the souls of the Volani killed when their city fell to bring back an epoch he craves, effectively erasing all of us."

Silence reigned for a long moment. Metellus openly laughed.

Enarius, though, was both serious and curious. "What do you mean, erase us?"

"He means to change the past so his ancestor's [27] lands never fell. And that will mean all of us cease to exist. If their cities had stayed in power, Derva would never have risen, and none of us would be here."

Metellus scoffed. "That's preposterous! Why are you wasting our time with this? We should just stick with our plan for the raid tonight."

"Tonight will be too late," Hanuvar said.

"Decius would never waste our time," Ciprion said coolly.

Enarius trusted Ciprion, clearly, for he absorbed this input before shifting his attention to Aquilius. The revenant legate had removed his own helm to expose his pale, blocky features. For a man heading up one of the most secretive organizations in the world, his own expression was extraordinarily transparent. His dark-brown eyes were furtive.

The emperor had noted Aquilius' alarm at mention of Calenius. "This man has worked with the revenants?" he asked. "You look concerned, Aquilius. How powerful is he?"

"He has...some talent. Although I myself have been underwhelmed by him."

"He's the one who fashioned that fake Hanuvar for you, isn't he?" Metellus crowed.

Ciprion's gaze was calculating. Aquilius actually gaped for a moment before slamming his mouth shut.

"Fake Hanuvar?" Enarius prompted.

"Those Hanuvar sightings?" Metellus said. "Earlier in the year? That was some half-assed plan Aquilius cooked up with a sorcerer to try and draw out Hanuvar's daughter or something." Metellus smirked and then fell silent, watching. Hanuvar wondered how long the praetorian's own sources had known about Aquilius' bungled efforts and how long he had been waiting for just the right moment to reveal them to the emperor.

---

[27] Hanuvar well knew that Calenius meant to return to his early days or bring that past to him here, but told Antires this is how he presented the information, because he didn't want to have to complicate the situation with additional details. —*Sosilos*

"Is this true, Aquilius?" Enarius demanded.

Almost Hanuvar interceded, because all of this delayed action. But he recognized that the drama needed to be played out, and kept silent.

"I involved Calenius not to draw out Hanuvar's daughter, but to find the man himself."

"By creating a lookalike?" Metellus asked, smirking.

"By fashioning a man who thought like him!"

"And he escaped," Metellus said, gloating.

Aquilius glared daggers at Metellus.

"That man almost had the whole south in an uproar," the emperor said. "That doesn't strike me as very wise, Aquilius. Why was I not consulted?"

"The leader of these gladiators is one of those released and inspired by the false Hanuvar," Hanuvar said.

Aquilius turned his ire on him. "This man looks much more like Hanuvar than the one I conjured ever did. He was even travelling with a young Herrene the time I saw him, just like Hanuvar was reported to do!"

"Is travelling with a Herrene a crime?" Ciprion asked.

Metellus relished the revenant's discomfiture.

But Aquilius' nostrils flared in anger. "If this is the Decius Antoninus who's assisting the Lenereva woman, I've run security checks on him. Do you know that there's no known information on the origin of either him or his children?"

The troubled gaze Enarius fastened upon the legate suggested he listened to a desperate man.

Aquilius sputtered. "You do realize that most of the Volani have gone missing, don't you? That they've all been bought up or escaped or simply disappeared? Who do you think is behind this? I have conclusive proof that Volani all up and down Tyvol have been systematically removed!"

"How is this germane to the matters at hand?" Ciprion asked calmly.

"Izivar Lenereva is behind it, and I submit that this man beside you is her agent! He may even be Hanuvar himself! When my men found him he was on the road with slaves I'd bet were Volani, and a Herrene! Just like Hanuvar!"

"And you didn't think to arrest him at the time?" Metellus asked, still smirking.

"I had other things on my mind!" Aquilius snapped.

"You're saying this is Hanuvar." Enarius' voice was cool and level.

"Yes! Or someone in his service."

Enarius' voice hardened. "This man, whose children saved my life, twice. This man, who saved my father, the emperor, from assassins, in the home of Izivar Lenereva. You're telling me he's Hanuvar."

Aquilius saw his arguments were failing, and grew more passionate. "Don't you see? It could all have been arranged to blind you to the Volani plans! To win your trust! To slide that young Volani woman into your bed!"

Only after he said the last did the revenant legate understand he had gone too far. For the first time Hanuvar had ever seen, Enarius actually looked angry. His jaw firmed, and his mouth was one straight line. His brows were drawn.

Metellus grinned in triumph but put a hand to his mouth rather than bursting into outright laughter.

"I apologize, sire," Aquilius said quickly. "I did not mean to imply that your mistress—"

"Leave," Enarius said, his voice icy. "Now."

"Sire?"

"You are dismissed from my service. You are dismissed from the revenants. Do not speak again, or I shall not bother with a stipend."

Aquilius gulped and stood. He opened his mouth, staring helplessly at the emperor, his gaze swinging to Metellus.

The praetorian couldn't help a final dig. "Idiot. Ciprion's met Hanuvar. Don't you think he'd recognize him?"

Aquilius couldn't hold himself back from that. "He's in on it!" He thrust a finger, shaking with rage, at Ciprion. "He bought Volani children and sold them to Izivar Lenereva! Don't you see the connection?"

"You're through!" the emperor shouted.

"It's Metellus you should dismiss!" Aquilius shouted back. "I've tracked all of his schemes for the last year. It's all there—every denarius he siphoned from the praetorian funds! Witnesses, payments, everything! I can prove it!"

Metellus' expression closed and cooled. Enarius did not look at him. He stood and pointed to the exit.

Aquilius strode for it, opened it, exited, and slammed it behind him.

Metellus cleared his throat. "I hope, sire, that you don't give those accusations any more credence than—"

"I don't care about any of that right now," Enarius said, a growl in his voice. "I want to hear about the wizard Calenius and what he's doing. Decius? You're sure about this? How do you know?"

"I've seen his preparations. I travelled with him, in his confidence, when he sought one of the tools to work his magic."

"How are the gladiators involved?" Enarius asked.

"They're not with Calenius. Their leader doesn't believe a word of what I'm telling you."

The emperor stroked his chin. "What's your connection with them?"

Hanuvar smiled ruefully. "They think I'm Hanuvar."

The emperor let out a bark of laughter. Even Metellus, obviously troubled, appeared faintly amused.

"How did you convince them of that?" the emperor asked. "Why would you?"

"I have to improvise to get the job done."

"And what's your job?"

"Right now, it's keeping the empire safe."

"And before now?"

"Among other things, it was keeping you safe."

Enarius considered this. "Who do you work for? Ciprion?"

Hanuvar had an answer ready so that he would not involve his friend in a further lie. "Lucius tasked my family to watch you at key junctures."

"Lucius, the priest? But he said he couldn't entice your sons to work for me." Suddenly the emperor's expression cleared. "Gods— that's because he wanted them free to move about, wasn't it?"

Ciprion wisely chose to shift the topic of conversation. "So what do you propose we do about Calenius and the gladiators?"

Hanuvar was glad his friend was at hand to cleverly divert problematic avenues of inquiry. "Calenius has to be stopped. Today. You have two options. One, agree to let the gladiators leave on the ships while we deal with Calenius."

"Out of the question," Ciprion said.

"It's unthinkable," Enarius agreed. "What's the other option?"

"You're not going to like it," Ciprion said, for he had already deduced what it was.

"He's right," Hanuvar agreed. "You won't."

"I won't?" Enarius looked back and forth between them. "What is it?"

Hanuvar explained. "You agree to pardon the gladiators if they help you fight Calenius."

Enarius had been reaching for his goblet. His hand froze and his eyes bulged. "Impossible! These are escaped slaves! If we show clemency to even one—"

Hanuvar cut him off. "Calenius is going to wipe all of us out. All. Men, women, children. Nobles and slaves, soldiers and fish mongers, emperors and revenants. And we don't have time to hesitate. He's almost a half day's march away and it's closing on eleven bells."

"What do you get out of this?" Metellus asked. "Lucius is long dead." He shifted his attention to the emperor. "I know this man's family has done you good turns but this entire magic time story is preposterous. How do we know he doesn't just have some longstanding grievance against Calenius?"

"Decius has my complete trust," Ciprion declared. And apparently that meant much to Enarius, who eyed him soberly.

"And it seems he should have mine as well," Enarius said. "His previous actions have surely earned it."

Ciprion turned to Hanuvar. "What about Calenius' forces?"

"Information is limited. It is thought he has a small private army of approximately a hundred men." Hanuvar reasoned that many were recently employed mercenaries but didn't elaborate. "The gladiators report that his men have fortified Calenius' position. About two weeks ago I saw them readying some entrenchments on the side of Esuvia. There are certain to be some sorcerous safeguards as well, but I can't estimate their strength. Calenius is a dangerous adversary because we cannot know the extent of his power or his preparations and we don't have the luxury of scouting this out. He must be stopped today."

Enarius listened, sipping slowly. Metellus watched, a troubled man failing to hide his unease. He wanted to demonstrate his worth to the emperor but had yet to see a way to distinguish himself in these unfamiliar conditions.

Ciprion tapped the tabletop. "He would never expect us to join up with the gladiators."

"Exactly," Hanuvar agreed. He halfway expected Calenius' machinations had somehow helped bring this revolt to life, the better to sow confusion and improve his chances for success, as his military preparations on the mountain could not have gone unnoticed indefinitely by a state paranoid about any challenge to their power.

"How disciplined are the gladiators?" Ciprion asked.

"The ones I saw were well regulated. I'm told they've trained a further three hundred."

"They won't be veterans," Enarius cautioned.

"We can still find use for them," Ciprion said. "Just seeing the approach of that large a force might get Calenius' men to change their positioning."

Metellus shook his head. "You can't honestly be considering allying with escaped slaves."

"I'm considering how to win a battle for the empire's safety," Ciprion said.

"Metellus is right," Enarius said. "If I work with these men, I'm setting a terrible precedent."

Hanuvar had known that he would hear that objection, and had a counterargument ready. "It's a unique circumstance, one that they and others must be told won't ever come again. They have to earn their pardon. You're elevating them in the state's hour of need to fight under your banner and providing them with a chance to be freedmen if they gain their emperor's favor. Same as happens in the arena. Offer them this choice, and be a leader that can grant the honor and recognition they crave."

Enarius grasped the goblet's stem and thought it through. "You think the gladiators will accept this offer? Will they believe you?"

"I think they will believe *you*. I can prepare the way, and then you will address them. So far they don't know you're here, and I think that surprise will help."

"We can have them pledge their loyalty to you," Ciprion suggested. "If they agree to fight, they will have their freedom. I'll write up an oath."

Metellus sullenly watched the young emperor swirl wine in his goblet. Probably he struggled now to develop a different gambit to prove useful in the course of the conversation. Hanuvar didn't like or trust him enough to invite his input as he brooded silently, a dark look cast upon Hanuvar and Ciprion.

"Very well," Enarius said finally. "I have placed a great deal of trust in you, Decius. If not for the aid your family has already given me, and the word of Ciprion, I would be more hesitant. I'm also frankly inspired by your dedication to the empire, as well as your bravery. What you've done already must have been accomplished at considerable risk."

"I do what I can," Hanuvar said. "Once I leave, give me a half hour to address the gladiators, and then ride out with an honor guard."

"Very well. Ciprion, I think I should like to write this oath myself. Metellus, get us some paper and ink."

His expression that of a man sucking lemons, Metellus pushed out from the table and stalked for the door.

Ciprion rose. "I'd like a few moments to confer with Decius about additional military concerns," he said.

Outside in the hallway, Metellus could be heard snarling for a slave.

"Of course." The emperor stood. "Good luck to you, Decius. If this succeeds, I will honor you above all other men."

"I don't think you ought to do that," Hanuvar said, "but that's a topic for another day. Convincing the gladiators to side with us is just the first step. Winning against Calenius is a whole other challenge."

"One the empire can face."

"I hope so." Hanuvar saluted the young man, Dervan style. Ciprion did the same, and the two excused themselves. Metellus scowled at them as he reentered, followed by a nervous slave supporting an arm full of paper, an ink jar, and a clutch of reed pens.

Ciprion led them halfway across the empty hall and then stopped in its midst after Metellus had shut the door to the briefing area.

"Did you ever think to hear a promise of a triumph from the emperor?" Ciprion asked quietly.

"I had something of a nightmare about it once."

Ciprion offered his arm, and Hanuvar clasped it. The Dervan

general's gaze and grip were firm. "Thank you for bringing my Amelia."

Hanuvar inclined his head. "She was kept in a room with a bed, and books. As prisons went, it wasn't a terrible one, and she told me she was not mistreated."

They released arms. "You think you can reason with the gladiators?"

"Most of the gladiators, yes. I may have trouble with their leader."

"How dangerous is Calenius?"

"He is ages old, a skilled warrior, and a powerful mage. I don't think they come more dangerous. The revenants may be able to tell you more, though I don't know how you can trust what they say. We'll be going into battle with very little understanding of the weapons at his disposal. It's liable to be costly."

Ciprion nodded, once.

"I've seen him send spirits out to rip the souls from his opponents. But he may be disinclined to use them, because these spirits are his currency. He has tools that cut deeper, or bind. And he can quickly heal himself. He's fast and strong and liable to have other sorcerous defenses I can't anticipate."

"We'll have to be adaptable, then. There are surveyor's maps of Esuvia in the archives here. We'll scour them while you arrange this alliance." Ciprion paused to consider his friend. "How can you possibly play all of these roles? A real Hanuvar for the gladiators, a man the Dervans think is pretending to be Hanuvar, and...others. It can't hold up for long."

"It just needs to hold up until the battle's over. Then I intend to vanish. My work in Tyvol is nearly done." Hanuvar lifted his chin toward where the praetorian legate was closeted with the emperor. "What was this raid you were planning?"

"We've made some swim bladders. I was going to lead a crack group out across the harbor late tonight and take out their catapults. Then we could at least get the emperor out. He insisted on accompanying me here."

"I thought as much. Had you just come to reinforce the garrison, or did you have some other plan in mind?"

"The garrison had only a few dozen men—I was afraid the gladiators could overwhelm them. And...I wished to see the conditions of the town and attempt a parlay with Tafari. But that hasn't gotten us anywhere, because there are few terms I can offer. He kept hinting about Amelia, and I was certain he was going to do something terrible."

"For a warrior, he's pretty considerate. He reminds me of that Ermanian mercenary you told me about."

Ciprion laughed. "Hortlekt! His brothers mocked him when he refused to let them kill those captured horses for meat. And it wasn't about the value or practicality, he told me it was about the look in their eyes." He sighed wistfully. "We never have managed that proper dinner so we can trade more war stories."

"If all goes well, in an hour we can share some rations while staring over a map of terrain."

The Dervan general was silent for a moment, then smiled slowly. "We shall finally wage a battle on the same side."

"Let's hope that's enough to win us a victory."

III

Hanuvar found Eshmun waiting beyond the wall of carts outside the fortress, his face bright with expectation. The dog had remained nearby and leapt with pleasure, wagging his tail. Hanuvar patted Kalak and praised him as the gladiators standing watch declared they hadn't thought to see him return alive.

"Don't be alarmed when the gate opens," Hanuvar said. "A procession will emerge soon, under truce. The emperor himself will be riding forth to speak with you."

The gladiators repeated this news with disbelief.

"But what's he going to say?" Eshmun asked.

"He's going to offer freedom to those gladiators and their allies who join forces with him to fight the wizard on mount Esuvia. Eshmun, I need you to gather everyone who's not standing guard at the roads. Tell them to meet on the steps of the town hall. Tell them Hanuvar will lead them."

Eshmun looked as though he wished to ask more. "Go, man!" Hanuvar urged. "Time wastes!"

The young gladiator dashed away. Hanuvar looked back at the

fortress and the silent, helmeted soldiers watching from the battlement, and strode the rest of the way up the street, on past the silent shops. The dog trod the bricks at his side.

It did not take long for word to spread, and by the time Hanuvar arrived at the town square gladiators and the former slaves Tafari's men had trained as soldiers were filtering in, talking among themselves about Hanuvar and the emperor's plan to grant them freedom.

As Hanuvar climbed the stairs to the capital building's portico, dozens already waited expectantly in the street. Eshmun must have told other men to aid him, for shouts rang through the town that Hanuvar himself had forged a deal with the emperor and had come to lead them in a battle for liberty. Who would not have gathered to hear about that? Shutters in the apartments above closed shops were thrown open and people looked down. Before very long at all, hundreds had formed up: men, a few women, and even some children.

Some of the townsfolk huddled in groups apart from their occupiers. And there, at the crowd's edge, he spotted Izivar and a retinue of her retainers. Antires was pushing his way toward Hanuvar, his hand raised in greeting. Hanuvar returned it, although his eyes found his lover, whose expression was clearly troubled, and perhaps a little angry, probably because he had publicly identified himself.

"What have you done?" an irate male voice demanded behind him.

Tafari had emerged from the government hall, his mouth twisted in fury. His voice was low as he crowded up to Hanuvar. "You called these men here? Without consulting me?"

Hanuvar removed his helmet but kept the eyepatch in place. His own reply was soft. "You either need to join me, or get out of the way."

"You dare?" Tafari was the larger man, and leaned close, one hand upon his sword pommel.

Hanuvar did not back down, though he stilled Kalak's growl by putting his hand out. "I have forged an alliance, and a path to your freedom."

"My freedom?"

"The freedom of all your people. But they must fight."

"They are prepared to fight," Tafari said through gritted teeth. "At my command."

"At the emperor's command," Hanuvar countered.

Eshmun had joined him, and Bomilcar and Antires had reached his side with Elistala, ranged behind him in a protective cordon to match the one about Tafari. The gladiator fumed but said nothing more as Hanuvar turned to the crowd with hands raised.

They silenced their chattering as he began to speak, his voice pitched to carry through the streets. "You know me. I brought the Dervans to their knees! Go ask them who ambushed their legions at Lake Tralesis, and who destroyed eight legions in a single day at Acanar!"

He had them then; he had not felt so much attention from so many upturned faces since he had addressed the people of New Volanus on the third anniversary of the colony's founding. "I have no love for Dervans! Like you, I fought for the freedom of my people! But I am not here today to bring war to them. I have returned from consult with general Ciprion, and we spoke to the emperor himself. Both are men of honor, and they have given their pledges to me. And they mean to give that pledge to you! A great battle looms on the mountain, where evil forces even now shake the earth. If we take their side to defeat it, you will have your freedom!"

Gasps spread through the crowd, which then broke into excited murmuring. Their exchanges trailed into silence as Hanuvar resumed. He pointed toward the cone of Esuvia. "On that mountain, an enemy plots to destroy us all. By midnight tonight, his magics will have killed every man, woman, and child within a hundred miles!" He would exterminate many more than that, but Hanuvar didn't want to complicate his message any further than necessary. "His sorcery cannot be outrun, but it can be outfought! If we work together, we can take battle to the wizard. Legionary and gladiator, warriors all and slaves no longer, striking a blow as one!"

A gruff male voice cried out that the Dervans couldn't be trusted and others called their agreement even as others shouted them to silence.

"All that I've said is true," Hanuvar declared. "The emperor himself is coming to warrant my words!"

The gathered men and women talked loudly among themselves. Someone cried to Tafari for confirmation, and Hanuvar turned to him.

Tafari stalked close, fire in his eyes. Bomilcar stepped to intervene, but Hanuvar motioned him back and allowed the leader forward.

"You're stealing my army," Tafari said with a snarl.

"I'm giving them what you wanted for them. Freedom."

Tafari's nostrils flared in frustration.

Hanuvar knew he had only a brief moment to win him over. "I need you as much as you need me. You know your men and their qualities. I don't have days to learn them. I have delivered promise of their freedom, but they are *your* warriors. Loyal first to the man who's led them so far."

Tafari weighed his words and some of his anger ebbed. "And what about when this is over?"

"Assuming we live," Hanuvar said, "I will not need your army. My plans will carry me far away from here as soon as possible."

"And you trust the emperor? Why should I believe him? Or you?"

"You think I would league with the emperor of Derva if there were any other option?"

Tafari was silent for a long moment, then shook his head no. "You think he will keep his word?"

"Against all odds, the youngster on the throne is a man of principal. And Ciprion, his general, is a man of integrity no matter our prior conflict. I would trust him with my life. So yes. I think their oaths will be honored and I think this is the best opportunity you will have. Are you wise enough to seize it?"

Shouting erupted from outside their field of view, and the words, indecipherable at first, spread through the throng: the emperor was riding to the town square.

A tall man with a bushy beard cried out that now was their chance—they could take the emperor and bargain for anything they wanted.

Hanuvar stepped to the edge of the stairs. "Hear me!"

He had to shout twice more before they had quieted enough for his voice to reach them. "Don't be fools! Would you live free for a half day, or would you win freedom for the rest of your lives?"

His words set a fresh round of arguments in motion, though none were directed at Hanuvar. Tafari listened to the factions calling to one another and stepped up beside Hanuvar. "The emperor says he will offer us freedom! Let us hear him out!"

That caused a lull in the commotion, over which the steady clatter of multiple hooves grew audible. Those in the crowd settled then and looked expectantly east.

A pair of praetorians, fully armored, their white horsehair crests bobbing, rode in the vanguard. Their advance forced the crowd back without threat.

A slim figure in ordinary legionary armor sat saddle on a spirited ebon mount at the center of the small procession, beside the helmetless Ciprion. A centurion amongst the horsemen called a halt, and then all was so silent that one of the horses snorting sounded like thunder.

The slim figure beside Ciprion removed his helmet, revealing the handsome countenance of Enarius, his dark hair even wilder than usual. He coaxed his gelding ahead, and it clopped through the praetorians until he sat saddle only a few spear lengths out from hundreds of escaped slaves. Ciprion followed on a white horse.

Enarius' curious gaze raked over the men and women before them, and strayed to a handful of children. He took in Izivar, on the far edge beside a shorter, rounder woman, and lingered there for a long moment before his eyes brushed across Hanuvar's. Finally he lifted his head and addressed the throng. "I had planned to bring retribution to enemies. But I do not see enemies. Today, I need brave warriors to join me in the fight. I don't care what you've done in the past, only what you will do for me now. A madman means to kill us all with his magics. Working together, we can stop him. Working together, we can win. And I pledge you this—fight under my banner, and you will have your freedom!"

Stunned silence followed the young man's declamation. A few murmured among themselves. Hanuvar saw that Enarius appeared confused, even disappointed by the reaction. The crowd wasn't sure how to respond.

Hanuvar raised his fist and shouted. "Hail the emperor!"

The call was taken up by another man out in the crowd, and then Hanuvar shouted once more: "Hail the emperor!"

His cry grew into a chant that crackled through the square. Enarius smiled and lifted his hand. Ciprion, still eying the throngs, rode up to the ruler's side.

As the chants faded, the same tall, bushy-haired man who'd cried to take the emperor hostage called out: "What kind of magic will they be using against us?"

Ciprion raised his palm for silence as others demanded similar details, and the throngs stilled to hear him.

"I can't say what kind of sorceries we'll see," he said. "But I ask you this. How could a wizard prevail against a band of warriors such as yourselves, allied with the legion's finest? With a force led by none other than Ciprion and Hanuvar?" His voice rose. "Who can stand against us? No one!"

Cheering erupted then, followed by another chant for the emperor, and then one for Hanuvar.

As that died down Tafari ordered his men to gather with equipment and a day's worth of supplies. Ciprion sent two of his soldiers back to order his men out of the fortress, then advanced with the emperor and the rest of the honor guard to discuss strategy. Metellus, Hanuvar noted, was distinctly absent.

While many dispersed, many more remained to stare at the unbelievable sight of the Dervan emperor dismounting to clasp the hand of Hanuvar. Quietly, Hanuvar praised the young man. "Nicely done, sire. What about the oath?"

"I'll have them swear it when they come back in armor." Enarius grinned. "That way they can raise their swords to me."

Hanuvar approved. He introduced Ciprion and Enarius to Tafari, who bowed his head formally, his discomfort with the situation apparent only in the stiffness of his expression.

"We've plans to make," Hanuvar said. "But I hope you will give me a moment." He bent toward Enarius and spoke quietly. "The Lady Izivar is here, and I'd best explain about my assumed identity so she doesn't say something to set things awry."

Enarius' expression cleared. "Of course," he said.

"We'll need to consult the maps," Ciprion said to Tafari as the man ushered them forward.

"Naturally."

The others headed in, followed by a small train of centurions, praetorians, and officers of the gladiator army, each group skeptically eying the other. Hanuvar remained outside with Bomilcar and Antires and Elistala. Izivar, accompanied by her muscular doorman, Reshef, and the unfamiliar younger woman, made her way through the thinning crowd and started up the stairs, her expression cloudy.

He wished dearly to embrace her and he saw that same impulse in her own eyes. She wore her green this day, a Dervan stola, though her arms were graced with Volani bracelets, and glass beads of Volani make dangled from her ears.

Hanuvar glanced at her companions. "Give us a moment."

"But I've got a lot of questions," Antires objected. He was clean-shaven and better groomed than when they'd last spoken. The unfamiliar woman lingered close beside him, and her striking brown eyes studied Hanuvar in that uncomfortable way mages had, almost as though he were more specimen than man.

"Question later," he told them both.

The playwright sighed and stepped apart with the others, the woman taking his hand. Izivar searched Hanuvar's face, as if to sort her own warring emotions. Her eyes had fastened worriedly on the eyepatch and he shook his head to reassure her. "Nothing's wrong," he said quietly. He thought that he really ought to kiss her, since their proximity made their relationship blatantly obvious to anyone, but they quietly drank each other in for a moment.

Her eyes swept down to the dog, standing protectively beside his master, then she spoke softly to him, in irritation and disbelief. "You've told Enarius?"

"He knows that I am Decius, pretending to be Hanuvar."

She blinked in astonishment. "How long do you expect that to last?"

"It needs to last no longer than today. After that, we can be on our way. Is the household prepared for departure?"

"It is. I sent—" She broke off in midsentence before resuming. "I sent our mutual friend north with the rest of what we recovered, and much of the baggage and all but a few servants." She meant Carthalo, a name she did not wish to repeat in front of others. "His work to the south is finished. You were gone too long," she said in a rush. "We'd had no word. Bomilcar turned up but then the gladiators swept in—"

"But you're all right?" he asked.

She sighed, clearly restraining any number of passions. "I am now. What happened? Do you really have to go off to war?"

"We do. Calenius has been planning this moment for a long time. He tried to kill me once he thought I understood what he was doing, but it took me a few more days to work it out."

"What is he doing?"

"He either engineered or capitalized on the deaths at Volanus to capture souls."

Her expression changed to one of horror as Hanuvar continued. "He means to trade them with an entity he'll summon this evening to either turn back time, or transport himself into the far past. Either way, everything we know will vanish. If his people never fall, ours will never rise. Entire civilizations will cease to be."

She appeared to be having trouble taking in the idea, so he explained further. "If even one of our ancestors is removed from the chain that leads to us, then we never come to exist. Or at least, not the we that we are."

"I guess I understand." She frowned. Her eyes bored deeply into his own. "Why does there always have to be a battle? We're ready to shift focus to the provinces and the lands beyond. It shouldn't take much longer. But you... you're marching off to fight a dark wizard." She lifted a scroll tube. "And there's this. Your daughter has sent it for you. Can't you leave this fight to Ciprion and the gladiators?"

He took the paper, glancing at the thing in his hand he had wanted for so long, then met her pleading eyes. "I have to do this," he said finally. "I have faced Calenius. I know his strengths and his weaknesses better than anyone else."

"Ciprion's very clever," she insisted. "You've said so yourself."

"But he has not faced Calenius."

"You want to do this," she said curtly.

"Not really. But it's too important to trust to other hands. If we lose, there's no second chance. We'll all be swept away." He weighed the letter in his hands. "What does she say?"

"I do not know," Izivar answered wearily. "I have been awaiting you to open it."

He push the scroll back toward her, and she accepted it reluctantly. "I will read it at my leisure. At your side. Now, I must plan our steps. We haven't long."

"And I will be waiting." There was no missing a note of bitterness in her voice, or the sorrow in her eyes. He wished to kiss the pain away, but he merely nodded, and stepped apart. Antires, Bomilcar, and Eshmun fell into step behind him.

"I feel like I've missed much," Antires confided to him as they passed under the archway.

"True. But I gather the same. Who's that woman who was with you?"

Antires cleared his throat awkwardly. "That's Ishana."

"So she's a new advisor? Your barber, perhaps?" Hanuvar couldn't help smiling.

Antires' cheeks colored and he chuckled. He offered empty hands and then sighed with pleasure. "I like her. A lot."

IV

Hanuvar had seldom spent less time learning the ground over which he fought. His father's old maxim was to know the enemy as well as a lover and the battlefield even better, and to avoid any fight when you were going in blind.

The eyepatch he wore among the Dervans—who thought him pretending to be Hanuvar so as to fool the gladiators, who actually knew the truth—limited his sight, but it did not limit his insight that careful review of the maps would not reveal all the secrets that lay before them. He and Ciprion knew Calenius would take better advantage of terrain, thoroughly explored; knew that he would have counterattacks ready for them; knew that he would see their approach for long hours.

But they could not delay, even to advance under cover of darkness. And thus they headed forth, some of Tafari's spearmen and scouts under Ciprion's command, to better even out their numbers. Once separated into their twin companies and on the march, Hanuvar removed his eye patch. The time for play acting had passed.

He had left the old farm horse with a stable for safe keeping, thinking he would have the gelding returned to Kliment if they managed to survive. Hanuvar now rode a dark gray that Ciprion had found for him, a reliable and responsive animal with a good gait. He often preferred to walk with his soldiers, but he needed to rest his leg, which was still weaker than he would have liked.

With Hanuvar came Antires, outfitted with armor the gladiators had given him. He looked a Herrenic hero of old. Bomilcar, Elistala, and Eshmun helped fill out Hanuvar's personal protective squad, along with Kalak.

Over the afternoon march toward the smoking mountain Bomilcar told him what he'd learned from Narisia—of her desperate escape with her companions, and how one of their number, badly wounded, sacrificed herself to lead pursuers astray. Narisia and the survivors had remained hidden in Turia for long weeks while she recovered from a festering leg wound, then stole a fishing boat, narrowly missing a Dervan trireme on patrol. They had stopped in some Herrenic colonies, landed at Surru, and were then blown off course when they headed further west, eventually finding their way into the confidence of a Faedahni prince, who wanted to join with Cerdia in a fight against Derva.

"They mean to build a league to oppose the empire," Bomilcar said. "An army of gladiators would be welcome aid."

To Hanuvar's mind, a small force of gladiators would fare no better against the Dervan war machine than his well-trained levees, much less those commanded by Cerdian aristocrats, but he said nothing.

Antires did, though. "The time for an alliance was a generation back. Where was Cerdia when three of the Herrenic cities rebelled? When some of the Faedahni cities declared for Volanus?"

"We can't do anything about that," Bomilcar said impatiently. "But the Cerdians have reached out again to the Herrenes, and the Ilodoneans, and other lands."

The misplaced optimism was tiresome. What city-state was left among the Herrenes to oppose Derva? Their great leaders were dead or in exile, and the cities determined upon freedom were crushed. The most rebellious of them had been razed like Volanus, as an object lesson to the rest. Only fools could expect much help from Herrenia now. Most of the Faedahni cities were Dervan satellites, and the Ilodoneans could be trusted only to use other states to run interference for them.

"My niece was purchased by Ilodoneans and I've learned she's now in Cerdia, correct?" Hanuvar wanted to confirm that Narisia was able to protect Edonia.

Elistala looked honestly surprised. "How did you know?"

"A long story. What's she doing with them?"

"The Ilodonean prince has promised to free her and the others after they perform some sort of mystical spell to call an asalda," Elistala answered. "Edonia's been permitted regular contact with Narisia, and is being well cared for."

To Hanuvar's questioning look, she added: "Narisia doesn't like it, but they're in a foreign land, and the Cerdian customs are different." She swiftly shifted topics to Narisia's goals. "The king and his advisors can't agree on their tactics. They don't have any true generals."

Bomilcar's eyes shone with anticipated pleasure. "You would arrive like a thunderbolt. Think how the Dervans would feel to see you at the head of a Cerdian army."

"They'd be nearly as surprised as me," Hanuvar said. "One battle at a time. Narisia is well?"

"She is," Bomilcar confirmed.

"She cried with joy when she heard your survival was no rumor," Elistala added. "She knows you could whip the Cerdian army into shape. And they might listen better to your advice. Even though she's your daughter, and an Eltyr, they still discount her because she's a woman." Elistala shook her head in disgust.

Antires shot him a questioning look. Hanuvar guessed the younger man knew his thoughts. Unbidden, a memory of Calenius' words came to him: that men and women made the same mistakes each generation. He looked off toward that green-girt mountain beyond the helmets of the troops marching before him, thinking that the big man was right.

It was easy for the inexperienced to dismiss wise counsel. When very young himself he'd thought he'd never grow weary of the fight, as had his brother-in-law Andalaval, worn down by the stress of holding their forces together in Biranus. He had not then appreciated all the political headaches Andalaval had borne after the death of Himli Cabera. His brother-in-law had led the Volani forces in the colony until his own assassination.

Hanuvar had never used rash words against Andalaval, but the man had surely known Hanuvar's impatience, sometimes bordering on contempt. He had seen further than Andalaval, but he understood now that, bright though he had been, there were things he did not appreciate simply because he lacked the perspective of long years in command. How much further might he see from where Calenius stood? With centuries, possibly eons between him and others, might he sound much the same as the wizard? With the requisite power, might he follow a similar course?

He would like to think not, and wondered if that was arrogance. For Hanuvar already felt a distance from these people twenty-five years his junior, and did not know how to explain to Elistala and Bomilcar and his own daughter the futility of their aspirations for vengeance. He'd spoken to Bomilcar about it before he'd left, but the captain seemed not to have taken the message to heart. Hanuvar had hazarded every bit of his being uncounted times to save his people and yet with sudden clarity understood that any gratitude they felt did not necessarily bend their thinking to his own. Wisdom was hard to come by. Anger was far easier to grasp, and less ephemeral, the blanket on a chill night rather than the faded lettering on an old scroll read by guttering candlelight.

For all that, he would find a way to reach them. He must. But that too was a problem for another time.

They travelled through the afternoon, splitting their forces further when they arrived at the mountains' base. The gladiators and their allied spear and bowmen accompanied Tafari and Hanuvar to the east slope, swinging past Calenius' abandoned excavations, the black stones from his bygone youth thrust up like the bones of giants. Ciprion's force headed for the south.

Esuvia's clouds rose, blending with a gathering thunderhead.

Hanuvar dismounted and sent his people up the slope. For the first hundred feet it felt as though they would rise unopposed. But the archers of Calenius had merely waited for better range.

The scouts fared worst. It was easy to pick them off during the ascent, for tree cover was sparse and Calenius had positioned his marksman on bluffs. A dozen gladiators were down before Hanuvar's spearmen were in position, and six more fell getting close enough to pin down the archers. Had he Melgar's slingers it would have been a simple matter, for their accuracy had been astounding.

The gladiators charged, cleared out the archery nest, and were all for racing further up slope, but Hanuvar shouted for them to fall back, and it was only Tafari's repeated order that halted them.

It was well for them they heeded his command, for the surviving archers had meant to lead them into an ambush against some thirty of Calenius' spearmen, discovered by one sharp-eyed scout who shouted their location. The spear one of the ambushers tossed only grazed him, but the poor fellow slipped on a steep bluff and plummeted into the scrub below.

The death of their comrades enraged gladiators and former farm slaves alike, and they charged upward. Fury more than skill took them close, despite heavy losses. A well-trained force would have handled it better.

The next few hundred feet passed without challenge. Hanuvar heard the sound of trumpets and the shouts of men, and screams, and the clash of arms. Around the mountain's side Ciprion's forces must have come to grips with another band Calenius had set.

"Do you think we've seen the end of it?" Antires asked. There was that in his voice that suggested he knew the answer. Hanuvar's return look confirmed it. Calenius possessed more armed men than they had known.

Above them loomed a sixty-foot rise over bushes and scraggly pines. Beyond that lay a wide shelf that stretched halfway around Esuvia and the cinder cone. The scouts pushed up through the brush, arriving at the shelf. One of the three shouted a warning before a thunderous roar sounded.

A wall of boulders slammed down, careened onto the shelf, and rumbled toward their position. Hanuvar shouted for the troops to scatter, and they took cover behind hillocks and rocks.

Two factors saved them. First, the majority of the boulders missed his people precisely because they had been arranged to cascade down the most obvious access point upon the slope, which Hanuvar had avoided. Second, Calenius could not have anticipated so large a force and hadn't had long to adjust his tactics. The boulders might well have finished a troop of twenty or thirty, but it could not destroy their expedition. While the avalanche smashed fifteen warriors, Hanuvar shouted everyone else forward before the dust had even settled.

More of Calenius' spearmen emerged from another hiding spot and charged onto the rocky shelf to send their weapons raining down.

Two of the scouts had survived the drop of the boulders. One fell immediately, but one, the same bushy-haired Ruminian who'd raised so many objections in the town square, attacked the spearmen with a savage cry, hewing right and left and severing limbs like a hero from legend. His example galvanized the gladiator troop. Some cried they were coming, others called out his name, Lorca, and ran to help.

Hanuvar and his guards followed in the second rank. Antires could be heard muttering good wishes for the mad Ruminian.

The gladiators reached Lorca before he could be overwhelmed, arriving just before two teams of ten emerged from hiding. These were warriors who looked the part, perhaps the best of Calenius' force, let by the fierce Arbatean guard that had guided Hanuvar's first meeting with the wizard. When they clashed into Tafari's troops the blood ran thick. Hanuvar urged his personal cadre back, for he meant to hold them in reserve for the final push.

But a trio of Calenius' warriors broke through the front rank. Hanuvar's guard brought them down, but not before Eshmun took a slash to the thigh. It wasn't crippling, but it left him limping badly, and Hanuvar ordered him to fall back.

With the wizard's forces defeated, a panting Tafari raised his sword on high and let out a victory shout. Of the almost three hundred they'd begun the climb with more than seventy were dead or wounded, but the survivors echoed his cry.

They started around the mountain's rocky shelf, arriving at a point where ancient carved stones led some fifty feet higher to a flattened shoulder where an old ruin stood, obscured in shifting mist.

Ciprion's legionaries had arrived before them and some had dared that climb. Twenty bodies lay twisted upon or beside the stairs. The living were spread along the barren shelf facing away from Hanuvar's people, shields lifted in formation against a stony horror even now plodding forward from the west, occupying almost all of the forty feet between mountain rise and drop-off.

A vast black bull fashioned of volcanic stone shook the ground with each stamp of its hooves. With a start Hanuvar recalled the serpentine bull hybrids he'd observed carved into the huge pictographic stones Calenius had studied. This was one of those monstrous entities brought to a semblance of life, fully twenty feet tall at the shoulder and armed with three horns and a snakey tail. It swung its head into the legionaries. Most swayed clear but two on the edge were clipped in their shields and sent screaming over the side. Ciprion sent his men streaming under its belly for its back legs, led by a shouting centurion, as the creature lashed its whiplike rear. Its open mouth released no sound but the din of swords against it and shouts of warriors filled the air.

Another band of soldiers had readied ropes and cast lassos toward the horns as the huge thing ponderously shifted its long neck once more.

Brave though the Dervans were, their numbers had been cut in half, and fifty soldiers with their handful of gladiators seemed too few. Tafari called his greater force of men forward, shouting for them to ready their own ropes. Every fifth man had carried some in their packs, in case mountain scaling had proven necessary.

Soldiers and gladiators together drove the thing back, the legionaries chopping at the legs with their hatchets while others fought to fasten ropes to the limbs and horns.

Ciprion and a pair of his officers joined Hanuvar. "There's another of the cursed things behind it." Tafari's gladiators streamed past to press their attack. "We're lucky they're so slow." His cheek was bruised and his armor dented, but he looked hale.

"That's a wall of spirits, isn't it?" Hanuvar was looking toward the stairs where the bodies lay, and the upper ledge of rock where what seemed a wall of mist shifted slowly against the wind.

"Yes. Those that didn't die on the stair cracked and ran. And small wonder. The ghosts can tear the soul straight out of a man. Just like you said."

Seeing the two leaders in conference, Tafari pulled back from the earthshaking conflict and joined them, watching silently with Antires, Bomilcar, and Elistala.

Ciprion's gaze settled glumly on the bodies of his dead above. "If he'd wanted, it appears Calenius could have killed us all. There was no defense."

Hanuvar shook his head. "He won't use any more than he has to. He needs them to arrange his bargain and loses one with each kill."

Tafari frowned. "I'm not going to send my men to die to clear those out."

"No one expects you to," Hanuvar said. "I'll go."

"What?" Antires' brows rose in dismay. "No!"

From Bomilcar and Elistala's skeptical looks it was certain they shared Antires' sentiment.

Ciprion's gaze was searching. He understood Hanuvar would not take such a risk without good reason. "What do you know?"

"When Calenius used the spirits earlier they kept well clear of me. They recognized me."

Ciprion briefly mulled that over. "Did they avoid you because you were Volani, or because you weren't the target?"

"I don't know."

"It's too great a risk," Antires said.

"It certainly is," Bomilcar assented.

Ciprion swung to take the captain in, his eyes briefly touching upon those of Elistala. Glumly, he faced Hanuvar and turned over an open hand. "I have nothing better," he admitted. "And the fight has to be carried up there. To Calenius."

"Yes. We must trust to luck, and opportunity in the end," Hanuvar said.

Ciprion nodded.

Hanuvar turned to his allies. "If I get through, be prepared to follow up."

Bomilcar flexed his shoulders. "I'm going too," he said. "If they know you're Volani, then they will know me too."

"And me," Elistala assented.

Hanuvar shook his head. "They might simply have recognized me."

"I'm not letting my general go up there alone," Bomilcar vowed.

Elistala saluted. "Nor I."

"Me either," Antires said.

"You're definitely not Volani," Hanuvar reminded him.

"I've noticed. You said that if we don't stop them, we're all going to die. And Etiocles said that it's better to die among friends."

There wasn't time for debate. He doubted he could talk the playwright out of joining this time, and the end of all was nigh. "Your loyalty is touching, but I will not waste lives. I'll be in the forefront.

If I fall, retreat, and sell your lives more dearly elsewhere. Maybe there's another way up."

"We began explorations," Ciprion offered. "But that's when those monsters turned up."

A cheer roared out from just around the bend where the battle raged and then the smash of rock against rock tumbling down the mountainside, and a tremor. A man's scream of pain followed in its wake.

Wincing in empathy, Tafari thrust a finger toward the stairs and addressed Ciprion directly. "What if there are more forces up there? How can these four handle them?"

Ciprion sounded disappointed that he must explain the obvious. "He will trust to inspiration while we seek additional opportunities." He extended his arm to Hanuvar, who took it, and spoke to him with somber dignity. "It has been an honor. May all our gods watch over you."

A band of injured legionaries, sitting bandaged in the mountain's shadow, gaped in amazement to see the two clasp arms. Hanuvar was unsure how many had been told he was an agent of the emperor. Many might well think him Hanuvar.

He broke the grip. "If this doesn't work, you'll just have to push through the spirits. Every man you have. Maybe in a tight cohort at speed someone in the middle can get through."

"Whatever it takes," Ciprion agreed. "Good luck, my friend."

Tafari held a fist out parallel to his chest and twice struck above his heart, a Nuvaran sign of respect. Hanuvar bowed his head to him, then considered Kalak and pointed him to Antires with the word "guard." The Herrene's eyes widened in surprise when the dog walked to his side. "See that he gets down safe if I don't make it," Hanuvar told his would-be chronicler. Then he started up the stairs, Bomilcar and Elistala following in single file. The dog, as ordered, paced beside Antires.

The steps had been carved so long ago that they were scarcely visible through dirt and weeds, and portions of the exposed black stone were spider-webbed with old cracks.

A trail of pale phantasmic men and women broke free of of a misty mass to glide down the stairs for them. Hanuvar breathed out slowly to steady himself. Bomilcar tried to push past, but Hanuvar stiff-armed him. "No."

He removed his helm, stepped over a legionary staring with

sightless eyes into the darkening sky, and walked around another lying face down. He advanced as if to greet the spirits, hand raised.

Down came the ghosts, their transparent feet passing above the steps.

These were the people of Volanus. Many of the women wore the traditional garb of his people, their legs hidden in layered skirts, their curling hair arrayed with jewels. Some held to memories of themselves on their best days. Other's images had been shaped by the moment of death, and bore signs of ghastly burns. Among those who looked down on them from the highest stair Hanuvar spotted one with the top of his head sheared off. In the front rank was an older man whose face and hands were burn withered.

Hanuvar paused two thirds of the way up, only six steps below the spirits. His hand still raised in greeting, he addressed them in their shared language. "People of Volanus, I am Hanuvar Cabera. Let me and mine pass, and I will set you free."

They did not halt, but swept on toward him. They were but five steps out, then four. "We come to aid you," he tried.

The mournful, set expressions of the phantoms did not change, but the armored soldier in front stopped two stairs up to regard him with unblinking, transparent eyes.

Below, Kalak whined a warning. The distant sounds of battle were strangely muffled.

Hanuvar patted his chest. "Look upon me! I am Hanuvar! And I am one of you."

The burned man drifted down beside the soldier and stretched a hand toward Hanuvar. Though his senses recoiled at the thought, Hanuvar extended his arm, and the chill of the grave touched him as the spirit's palm pressed to his.

Nothing he had ever done could fully have prepared him for this moment, looking up into the eyes of the dead of his people. Every hair upon his arms and neck stood upright. His heart hammered, and he fought panic, the instinctive need to run from the unknown and the wrong and the very face of death. But he could not break—if he did, he would not just fail, he would lose all that mattered beyond himself.

The spirit lowered its hand. Its gaze, vacant before, grew somehow more alert. Curious.

"I was too late to help you in life," Hanuvar said, looking first to the burned man, then to the soldier, then the matron just behind them. "But we will aid you now. Let us pass."

It might be that they could not, that Calenius held too great a hold upon them. It might be that they were nothing but mindless slaves.

But he held out hope, for the spirits fixed their gazes upon him, as if they had awakened to understanding. One of the women touched her face. The man in armor moved his mouth and Hanuvar recognized the shape of the syllables he formed.

He was saying Hanuvar's name.

Kalak bounded up, panting, wriggling past Hanuvar's companions and stood at his leg, growling.

Hanuvar put a hand down, telling him to silence.

The ghosts paid no attention to the mastiff. Hanuvar's name was then visible on other mouths, spreading one to the other until all repeated it. He did not hear them, but he felt them, deep in his bones. They called to him. No longer did they look frightened, or vacant, but determined.

Their voices rose in what would have been a chant to shake the trees, although to human ears it was nothing more than a whisper of wind.

They parted for him and the dog, and they started up. Behind came Bomilcar and Elistala and Antires, the Eltyr softly saying a prayer to Tasarte again and again while the captain swore almost reverently. Antires, ever watchful, said nothing at all.

The wall of spirits closed up behind them, following them forward, but the way before remained open.

The dead paced to either side as they climbed the final steps. Hanuvar saw boys and girls of varied ages, and old men, and young women. Some wore carpenter's aprons and one wore a wedding dress, stained with ashes. One man he recognized as a lecturer at the university. Hanuvar raised his hand in greeting, but the man's recognition, the individual spark in him and all the others, seemed dull. Very little of their will or sense of individual function remained.

Yet they had retained hope for something better, and they held to faith in the man who had once led their city, and whose name they now called. Some of the ghosts seemed to be restraining others for whom the wizard's directives were too strong.

Hanuvar arrived at the top step. A wall of shifting spirits stretched dozens deep all along the mountain's edge. Surely these were more than just those slain in the aftermath of Volanus' fall. Might that black stone contain the whole of his fallen people? Hanuvar felt the entirety of their regard upon him, an icy hand upon his spine.

Ahead lay an outcropping of rock, flat and relatively even, and upon it stood a decrepit temple of black stone unearthed beneath the mountain's cone, rising into the darkening sky. Roof and pediment were crumbled to ruin, and square columns stretched heavenward, pitted with age.

Stepping down one of the five grand steps leading to its interior came a massive figure with dark red hair and cold, cold eyes. Dull gray armor ribbed his chest, and his deadly straight sword hung at his side. He breathed heavily, as though wearied, but he raised his hand in greeting.

Hanuvar advanced, his people behind him, his hound at his side, the ghosts of his people ringing all. A tremor shook the ground.

Calenius' descent had revealed a squat stone pillar near the temple's front, the height of an altar, where a dull amber orb the size of a skull lay upon a crimson pillow, beside the ancient curved horn he'd taken from the mountain. "I knew that you would challenge me, if you lived." Calenius laughed, shaking his head. "You really are remarkable. You remind me of myself."

Hanuvar did not halt. "You said you would release my people. But you meant you would trade their souls."

Calenius scoffed. "You judge me? I've spent millennia finding a way to save my people. What have you spent? A year? Two? How can your pain compare with mine? How can these thousands compare with the hundred thousands of mine?"

Hanuvar halted eight feet out. "You're not trying to save your people. They're already gone. You're trying to make yourself feel better. Was it you who brought them down? Your magical experiments?" He saw from big man's scowl that he'd judged right. "So now you'll slay more, to assuage your guilt? How many centuries did you spend wandering before you finally decided to act by destroying more lives?"

The ground rocked. Below them the legionaries and gladiators cried out in dismay, and the ringing sound of metal on stone echoed distantly. Calenius' gaze swung south and Hanuvar permitted a look himself. One of the distant sister mountains of Esuvia had released a cloud of black smoke, laced with lightning bolts.

"The end is near," Calenius said. "Just as it happened with my people."

"Because you, and they, pushed too greedily without heed of the the consequences?"

"We did. But surely you cannot fault us for seeking knowledge."

"That's not what I fault you for."

Calenius crossed powerful arms over his massive chest. "One last time I offer this. Come with me. Bring these people, if you want. You would work at my right hand. A man of your gifts would flourish in my time. Your own is so backward. My people were builders. Dreamers. Had they not perished, we might now be sailing among the stars."

"You don't seek just to delay me, do you?" Hanuvar asked. "You talk to justify. To convince yourself you're on the right path. Are you?"

Calenius snarled. At the same moment Hanuvar's throwing knife was streaming toward him, and Hanuvar himself charged. Bomilcar and Elistala let out battle cries and hurled their spears. Antires ran forward, his spear before him, and Kalak surged ahead of all.

With almost contemptuous ease Calenius watched the flight of the weapons and sidled to the right as the spears rose in their arc. Hanuvar's knife he caught upon an armored forearm.

Kalak reached him a few steps before Hanuvar. By then Calenius had drawn his blade. He had cast no spell, but the weapon burned blue from within.

He caught the leaping dog by the throat and lifted it, slavering and kicking, at the same time slicing out with the shining blade. Calenius deflected Hanuvar's strike on his bracer and immediately returned a cut of his own. Bomilcar interposed his shield, but the weapon sheared through its upper third, the sharpened edge of which slammed into the captain's armored shoulder and set him spinning.

Calenius flung the dog at the charging Antires. His legs were tangled by the beast and he fell over him with a grunt. The dog yelped and staggered upright.

Calenius smiled in sheer delight. Here was a man who thrilled to the battle. He leapt down with a mighty sideways slash. Hanuvar did not try to intercept that stroke. He slid away.

Elistala rushed in and scored a slash across the wizard's armored shoulder that set him back just as Kalak darted in once more. Calenius' great sword swung at him. The dog ducked. Hanuvar took the opening and cut into the sorcerer's upper arm. He nearly had his head taken off for his trouble; the gleaming sword point swung past his eyes as he threw himself backward, sending shooting pain up his ankle.

Elistala rushed in as the swing finished. Her strike bit the edge of the big man's armor, but Calenius spun and drove the pommel of his sword into the Eltyr's face, staggering her. Bomilcar had flanked quietly from the right and had probably thought himself undetected, but the warrior wizard pivoted to send his blade down across the dent in the captain's shoulder armor and deep through his body. Gasping, Bomilcar sagged, and his life's blood spurted from the terrible wound.

Hanuvar's stomach sank.

The dog snapped at the big man's ankle. Hanuvar delivered a stroke that should have struck Calenius' chest, but his adversary twisted and the blow slashed armor below his armpit instead. A knife had appeared in Calenius' off hand and he sliced Hanuvar's forearm. Before he could stab again Antires interposed himself with a competent spear jab. Calenius sheared the weapon's point off and Antires flung the pole at the wizard before backstepping to draw his sword.

The Herrene's action had given Hanuvar time to reach for a different weapon, though he did not yet pull it. That the grip was weakened on his right was a worry for another moment.

Kalak bit deeply into Calenius' calf but stayed a moment too long. The big man's sword tore into the dog's side and sent him sprawling. Elistala reached to her belt for a shining metal disc.

The sorcerer must have been expecting that all along. He hurled his knife. Elistala, veteran warrior, lowered her head so it would not take her throat and the blade drove into her chin and helmet clasp before falling away, splashing blood with it.

But she had thrown the disk, and Calenius shouted out a spell at last. The golden plate disintegrated into lovely motes. While Antires swept in from the right Hanuvar tossed the true restraining circle Calenius had tried and failed to wield against the metal guardian. Study had shown him the tiny depression on its side. He had pressed it, and thrown, and now it caught the big man in the legs the same way a similar circlet had tripped the mechanical centaur thing at the ruined bridge. The golden lines snared the wizard's powerful limbs and felled him like a tree.

Within the temple a bright blue pinpoint of light sparked into existence, then flamed into a tall archway, as though a doorway was being sculpted in the air.

Hanuvar moved closer, but Calenius was hardly helpless. He had rolled and lashed at Antires, who tripped backward as he flung himself out of the way. The glowing blade scored the stone where the playwright had stood. Hanuvar stepped on the wizard's sword only to face another knife. From where Calenius had pulled it he did not see, but it was in the big man's off hand now, and it drove deep into Hanuvar's calf, on his already injured leg.

He snarled as he took the blow, and swung hard against the big man's helmed head.

Calenius twisted his neck so that he did not get struck at the most powerful point of the swing, but the blade still lodged into the helm's edge and bit into the scalp beyond.

That stilled the big man at last.

Hanuvar called to Antires. "He has small gold discs in his left side pouch! Apply them to the injured!"

He bent to grasp Calenius' sword. Even coated with the blood of Hanuvar's allies the weapon was a thing of beauty, shining from within, unmarred along its perfect edge.

Limping on his bloody leg, Hanuvar reached the pedestal where the globe sat with the horn. He only glanced at them, searching the ground for his true objective. And there, in the midst of a hexagram of ash arranged in complex symbols, he found the black stone.

Hanuvar broke the hexagram's outer edge with a booted foot, then the inner, then plodded to the center and sank to a knee, wincing against the pain. He stared down at the black stone that anchored the spirits of his people, and beheld a shifting radiance. He lifted the sword.

Behind him he heard a weak, guttural cry as he lifted the sword. "No!"

But Hanuvar raised the stone in the palm of his injured right hand, trying not to trouble himself over his clumsy grip. He lobbed the stone into the air, then struck it full force with the great blade.

At the moment of contact the sword blazed brilliantly from within. The stone cracked once and then splintered into thousands of shards that rained against the temple floor. The sword itself flared more and more brightly and Hanuvar released it as he continued his swing. It spun away, lighting the area with its growing light. Sensing danger, he threw himself sideways from the sorcerous hexagram. The sword struck the black wall of the temple, and then melted with an almost human shriek of metal.

The air around him filled then with phantoms, rising skyward. His people, freed of the spell that had prisoned them. Their faces were no long contorted by anguish, but incandescent with yearning. Those who'd remembered only their final ruined moments had been rendered whole.

In the distance, radiant red streams of lava flowed down the face of the far mountain, for Esuvia's second sister had erupted. Half of its cinder cone was blasted away and roared into the sky, a plume of black smoke boiling toward the heavens.

At the sound of footsteps beside him Hanuvar pushed up. He was weak, dazed.

So should Calenius have been, but he loomed over Hanuvar like an avenging demon, a spear in one huge hand. Of the restraining band there was no further sign. He'd torn his helmet off. The scalp above his right temple bled freely and lips were curled back from his teeth. The ground shuddered, and a distant explosion rent the air. Antires was tending Bomilcar; Elistala rose from where she'd bent over Kalak's still form.

"You've ruined centuries of work!" Calenius snarled.

"I freed my people, and stopped your spell."

"Fool. All you did was eliminate the coin I meant to pay Tondros. The spell can't be stopped. I already cast it. The portal's just opened."

"You can stop it."

"With what?" Calenius roared.

"You're the wizard," Hanuvar said. Calenius still stood with spear poised but did not yet strike. Above, the final phantoms faded into the night. Beyond, Bomilcar had roused weakly from Antires' ministrations, propped upon a single elbow. Elistala advanced with her sword ready.

"Back, woman," Calenius snarled. "I can end him in a single thrust."

Again the ground rumbled. Elistala halted her progress.

"You did this because you wanted to aid your people," Hanuvar said. "And yet you would have made others die in their place."

Calenius shook his head as if experiencing the final disappointment from him. "If I had changed time, none of this would have happened. None of it would have mattered, because the suffering would never have taken place!"

"Are you sure that's how it works? Do you think Tondros would take payment in souls if they were to vanish after you traded them? I see in your eyes you've thought of this before. But you haven't wanted to reckon with it."

Beyond Elistala, Ciprion led the first rank of Dervans onto the plateau.

"Warn them back," Hanuvar urged her. Though somewhat doubtful, she moved away.

Hanuvar got his good leg under him and rose, slowly. Calenius still watched, expression clouded with shifting anger and grief, and a new emotion, doubt.

"You've fooled yourself, Calenius." Though Hanuvar's voice was soft, his tone was intent and certain. "You've wanted this so badly you've forced yourself to believe it. You already destroyed one people. Do you want to be remembered for destroying another? Is that your legacy?"

Calenius responded in like tones, shaking his head in disdain. "What does that matter? I've waged battles and wars that sent tens of thousands to their deaths."

Hanuvar understood that sentiment well. "You can pretend that you're a man beyond morals, but I have seen you practice fairness. Kindness even. I have seen you honor your word. Time and again you offered me a chance to live."

"That was weakness." The big man's teeth showed and his hand tightened around the spear. "Clearly, I should have made sure that you were dead."

"You think yourself beyond affection but what has all of this been for except affection? You loved your people, and blame yourself for their end. It drives you on. I understand. There is nothing you can do for them now, though. Their souls are long since passed. Do you think Lady Death would return them to you?"

Hanuvar saw the big man's hands flexing ever so slightly in their grip, and pressed on, saying things he had scarce admitted to himself. "Any day I could board a ship and start for the colony I've founded. I would be acclaimed and honored the moment I stepped ashore. But I don't know that I can go home, any more than you. I had a part in the death of my city. I made mistakes, and nothing I ever do can fully atone for them."

"I do not mean to atone. You and I are beyond such things."

"Are we? Then the dead should be beyond us too. For it is the living who need our help. The people in the land below this mountain have done nothing to you. But because of you they will be buried in ash and stone. Is that what you want?"

Calenius' eerie blue eyes stared intently to his own, and then he looked away.

The ground rattled beneath them and Esuvia sent a plume of smoke into the air.

"There is one thing I might yet do," Calenius said. "Bide here."

He turned, exposing his back. Hanuvar might have struck, but let him retreat to the shining portal.

Antires came to his other side. "Bomilcar's wounds have healed but he's very weak," he said. "He lost a lot of blood. I brought you a part of the final disk. Your leg looks terrible."

"My arm is worse." The leg had been struck in the muscle; something more vital had been injured in his arm.

Antires spoke with quiet regret. "Elistala tried to save Kalak..." his voice trailed off. Elistala now knelt beside her captain helping him to drink, while Ciprion quietly ordered his soldiers into an encircling position. Hanuvar shook his head to him, advising him to wait, and then, almost against his will, looked to where the faithful brown mastiff lay unmoving on his side.

Hanuvar tried to gulp down the lump in his throat. He watched the big man stand before the shifting blue archway. Calenius lifted the horn from the pedestal, raised it to his lips, and blew.

Blue light filled the archway, and the suggestion of something writhed within it. Suddenly a man's shape emerged, standing taller even than Calenius, and oddly elongated. The movements of the being were disjointed, slow one movement and rapid and jerky the next. It wore only a skirt over its red loins.

Hanuvar could not fully take in its features, for they were brilliant as a bonfire's heart. He could not see if it was beauty or something else entirely that glowed within it.

A voice rang out from the being, though Hanuvar did not understand its ringing language.

Calenius answered in kind.

Antires pressed the disk into Hanuvar's good hand, and he lifted it to the seeping red slash upon his arm. The magical object, whatever it truly was, had been partly dissolved, as though some thief had ground down a sliver from a coin. But he applied it to his arm and the limb tingled. A soothing warmth spread down and the skin sealed. It did not complete its transition, for a scar remained, rather than the clear skin that had come with Calenius' healing. He tested his fingers and something still was off, for the grip of the bottom two lacked strength. Still, they moved, and perhaps the injury would improve.

Calenius' arm swept wide and then pointed south, toward the volcanoes. The entity's voice rang on.

Elistala bent to tend his leg. Ciprion arrived at his side, a mixed band of legionaries and gladiators close at hand. Tafari was near but did not draw closer.

"How badly are you wounded?" Ciprion asked.

"I'll live. Feeling a little dizzy," Hanuvar added.

"What did you say to Calenius, and what's he doing?"

"I talked him into stopping the spell."

Ciprion raised his heavy eyebrows in surprise. "I thought he was going to destroy us all."

"So did he."

Ciprion stared at Hanuvar, then surveyed the area around the temple. "He killed your dog."

"That dog deserves a hero's funeral," Hanuvar said quietly.

His Dervan friend seemed to register Hanuvar's depth of feeling on the matter and grunted meditatively. "I'm sorry."

"Did you finish off the stone beasts?" Hanuvar asked.

"We did. We tripped both right off the mountain side." Ciprion pointed to the blood leaking from the bandage Elistala applied to Hanuvar's wound and was about to speak, but fell silent as Calenius faced them. The being still waited behind him.

The big man motioned Hanuvar forward.

Elistala knotted the bandage, already half soaked through, and looked up to her general. "This needs to be sewn."

"In a moment." Earlier he had scarce noticed the wound, but with the excitement of combat fading it was difficult to put any weight upon the limb at all. He limped forward, trying not to stare at the shifting godling. Its very presence filled him with dread. It did not belong here, in this world, and Hanuvar did not belong in its presence.

"I've made an arrangement," Calenius said stiffly. "The moment I give the word, he will halt time, a little. Only around the volcanoes themselves. Because of... my actions to summon the energy, they will still erupt. But I've bought you two days, and hopefully that will be enough."

In one hand Calenius had cradled the amber globe. He passed it across to Hanuvar. "I want you to have this."

He took it in his good hand, aware of swirling clouds within, and the image of a street, and high towers, and people walking along a flowered lane.

"My people recorded memory stones, of times and places. To have Tondros take me to the proper place, I had to know the proper time."

"That's what you were searching for in the tunnel."

"Yes." He pointed to the globe. "I want some part of our people to live on, at least in memory. The images within may at least inspire yours to greater heights."

"You don't want it?"

"I must go. I am the bargain. One man of lengthy life span isn't nearly as enticing as thousands of souls, but I'm not without some value." He shook his head to Hanuvar's questioning look. "There was no other way."

The ground shook. Something close by cracked like a thunderbolt.

"What will happen to you?"

"I shall serve for a hundred years." The hint of a smile brushed the big man's lips. "It may be instructive."

"It may be terrible."

"Yes. Go, Hanuvar, before I change my mind."

This time Hanuvar offered the parting words he had always hesitated to speak. "Fare well, Calenius."

"Live long, Hanuvar. Find your people and lead them home."

Calenius turned without further word. He raised a hand to the entity and spoke to it, head held high.

A heartbeat later the ground rocked...

And then suddenly the tremblor ceased, in midshake. Hanuvar, still staggering, teeth gritted against the pain in his leg, looked up, thinking to see the mountain explode above them, but all was still.

A moment later one of the Dervans cried out that the lava had halted, and Hanuvar turned his head to observe the long stream down Delania's cone stopped halfway along the mountainside, glowing with lethal energy but no longer advancing. The warriors muttered in wonder.

By the time Hanuvar had returned his gaze to the shining archway, it was closing shut. Of Calenius and Tondros, he saw no sign.

"So I don't entirely follow," Antires said. "Calenius was going to sacrifice us all, and tried to kill you, but then he saved us?"

"It's complicated."

"Obviously. I was kind of hoping you could explain."

"He remembered his humanity," Hanuvar said tiredly. "Or maybe I just reminded him too much of himself. We can't stand around talking now, though."

"You look as though you can barely stand."

"There's that. But we have to get down off this mountain. You heard Calenius. There's but two days to evacuate the entire region."

Ciprion was already dictating to a soldier writing upon a papyrus clipped to a small slate. He sent the man running as Hanuvar limped up, and motioned some others back. "We'd best get that leg treated. I've a medic standing by."

"Thank you. I need to be out of here. I've never been more exposed. Sooner or later people will wonder whether I really was pretending."

"Yes."

Antires lifted his arms in consternation. "But it shouldn't matter. Your bravery should earn you the emperor's gratitude! You've saved hundreds of thousands of lives." He reconsidered. "By the gods, you saved everyone here for miles around!"

"He has," Ciprion agreed. "And in a just world, he would be honored above all. But that is not what would play out."

"Why not just tell all?" Antires asked.

"Then the emperor will know that all of us deceived him," Hanuvar explained. "Not just me, but Izivar, and Ciprion." The betrayal alone might inspire tireless efforts to track them down.

Antires frowned, but understood.

"I'll get you down the mountain," Ciprion said. "I don't think you're up to walking far in any case."

"No."

"And where will you go?"

"To find more of my people, and my daughter. I've learned at last where she is."

Ciprion's smile was genuine, heartfelt. "She lives?"

"She does, and is well."

His friend clapped Hanuvar's shoulder. "I'm happy for you." His smile eased. "There's much to do. I've many questions about what happened, but you can tell me on the way down." He turned from him and shouted for a medic, a graying, alert fellow who dashed up to him. "Give this man the finest of care," he said. "He's a highly valued warrior for the empire."

Hanuvar leaned against Antires to help him to sit; the grizzled combat doctor knelt beside him while Ciprion strode off, sent one messenger running with orders to arrange the withdrawal, and dictated further orders to his secretary. In a moment, Hanuvar had no other concern than focusing against the pain. He looked up over the doctor's dark curling hair and up to Antires and Elistala, frowning, and up past the cone of Esuvia and onto the carpet of stars.

Somewhere, beyond the skies, beyond time itself, Calenius was the prisoner of the god of time. Death might have been better for him. And somewhere, in the lands of the death goddess, more of Hanuvar's people were free.

Here in the living realm his daughter lived, and he would see her before too long. There was more challenge to their reunion than that, for she had apparently set her course on a mission of vengeance. But for now, he was content.

※ ※ ※

Hanuvar was in worse shape than he let on. He had lost a lot of blood and Ciprion insisted he be removed by litter, then sent his fleetest messengers on with his suggestions to the emperor, who'd observed the battle from a distant hill, under the protection of his praetorians. Another man was tasked with galloping north with commands for the oncoming legion.

By the time we arrived at Apicius the population remnant was already in motion, in fairly orderly fashion. Enarius had ably taken charge of the evacuation, putting all carts and wagons to use, and deploying all but two of the available boats and ships. One was the emperor's bireme, and the other was Izivar's ship.

With the excuse that Decius had been too badly injured to consult that evening, Ciprion kept Hanuvar separated from a grateful emperor, who was kept busy arranging for the safety of the surrounding settlements in any case. Hanuvar departed with Izivar, her staff, and a small number of the gladiators. And me and Ishana, of course, along with Eshmun and Elistala and Bomilcar, he too borne on a litter.

The rest of the gladiators stayed on in service of the emperor, under command of Tafari, both to help spread word of the evacuation and to see that law and order remained in force and that supplies and conveyances were fairly distributed. You might think it strange that Enarius should trust rebels with this, but the emperor was shorthanded, and so he sent out teams of soldiers bolstered by the newly freed men, who were said to have served with distinction.

Two full days and one full night they had before all three of the volcanoes erupted again. One cast lava, one blew ash. Esuvia itself expelled only the latter, and one full side of its cone collapsed, taking the ancient temple with it. Between the three of them, around a hundred miles of farmland were devastated and four villages utterly destroyed, but owing to the advanced notice the vast majority of the inhabitants escaped alive. The only recorded deaths were among those too stubborn to leave. Much of Apicius itself was buried in ash, apart from a narrow triangle from the town square down to the harbor. Izivar's home was completely destroyed.

Enarius and his staff remained in place until almost the last instant, and his efforts on behalf of the people inspired not just gratitude but an affection that rooted so deeply the people of the region today still speak reverently of him.

In the days after, the emperor kept to his word and awarded citizenship to the gladiators and slave allies who marched up Esuvia. Decades later a pair of them made it into the senate, as you may have heard. Their leader Tafari departed eventually for his homeland, where he rose to a position of prominence, although he returned later in life as an ambassador known for his sagacity.

You probably know that Aquilius was summarily dismissed, just as Enarius had vowed. The kindly emperor permitted the revenant legate to retain one of his villas, but appointed an outsider to oversee the revenants and report upon all of their activities. Metellus would have loved to have been involved with this, but the records about his embezzlement Aquilius provided were damning, and a final straw for Enarius, who had grown more and more dissatisfied with his conduct.

Still believing Metellus had actively risked his life twice to save him, Enarius did not officially punish him over the extensive evidence of corruption, but sent him to the frontier. There, he thought, Metellus might put his talents to better use, or at least acquire the seasoning needed to become a better man.

Enarius acted in good faith, but it is not always true that one kind act begets another, for his clemency was eventually to have dire consequences.

As for Hanuvar, he spent much of the next day in Izivar's company, alone in their cabin. We rendezvoused with Bomilcar's vessel, and together we sailed north for Selanto, where we would shortly send the final Volani of Tyvol out from our harbor. Other voyages still lay before us, but we paused, ever so briefly, to give thanks, and to care for our dead. We built a pyre on the shore and lay the cloth-wrapped dog upon it. And then, while a trumpeter sounded the last call, we set fire to the wood, and sent him blazing into eternity.

—Sosilos, Book Seventeen

Afterword

ANDRONIKOS SOSILOS

Among several challenges in crafting this volume for publication, one proved most persistent: locating an appropriate preamble.

Being intimately familiar with this portion of *The Hanuvid*, for it had been one of my favorite sections since my youth, I knew there was no part in the work where my great-great-uncle stepped outside the narrative to introduce Hanuvar's entry into southern Tyvol. There were occasional transitions between the smaller "books" into which the old scrolls divided *The Hanuvid*, but because Antires had presented all of Hanuvar's Tyvolian campaign as a continuous narrative he had never really stopped to assess matters upon Hanuvar's arrival in Apicius.

I sought amongst the fragments of earlier drafts of *The Hanuvid* that have been passed down through my family, and poured through Antires' surviving letters. While there were promising and even revealing moments, none was ideally suited for my needs. It seemed I would be forced to draft a preamble of my own, and while I thought myself capable of imitating Antires' prose I was loath to do so, for I very much desired to let his own observations stand as the connective threads between each volume of this modern edition.

It was my wife who provided the solution. Her memory is superior to my own, and she recalled seeing amongst Silenus' papers a letter Antires had once sent in response to her query seeking perspective on Hanuvar's state of mind before his encounters with Calenius and the revenants. My wife's recollection proved entirely accurate—such a letter not only existed among Silenus' own archives, it almost perfectly suited my needs. And so I adopted it, altering the letter in only a few places to remove references to Silenus' inquiry, and to add occasional linking text from another of Antires' letters when unrelated paragraphs needed to be excised.

Those familiar with the original *Hanuvid* were likely surprised by the events that took place within the theatre of Apicius. Antires wrote of them in detail but referred to them only in passing within *The Hanuvid* itself, for he had excised them from the work before ever sharing it. He seems to have believed that to include an adventure of his own smacked of self-aggrandizement. In this he erred, perhaps being too close to the events to see how important both he and Izivar had become to the saga as a whole. He certainly thought it necessary to introduce Ishana into the narrative, given her coming importance, but did so only in passing, probably concerned that his romance with her, too, drew too much attention from the subject of his work. I think Hanuvar would have disagreed and told him that many of his greatest victories could not have been accomplished without his friends and allies.

In any case, I added Antires' personal account of the events of that day and threaded it into this new *Hanuvid* with a few small changes to Antires' closing narrative, and I feel it makes the work more cohesive. Because Silenus had never read these pages, I attempted to elucidate points I thought she would have found worthy of comment.

As always, if my own efforts have failed to please, blame not the story, but the teller, who seeks only to bring *The Hanuvid* to life for a new generation.

Acknowledgements

Once again I am grateful to Toni Weisskopf and all the other fine folks at Baen for their support of, assistance with, and faith in Hanuvar, and to loyal friends and family for their help in honing this book. Sydney Argenta, Chris Willrich, Kelly McCullough, and Bob Mecoy provided their usual insightful guidance, suggesting many fine lines and solutions to plot knots, and John C. Hocking and Darian Jones proved ever-reliable sounding boards, thread tweakers, and MacGuffin innovators. Scott Pearson and Joy Freeman provided crucial last minute assistance, as did the clear-eyed Bruce Wesley and the supremely patient Leah Brandtner. The incomparable Shannon Jones pulled me back from staggering into dozens of pits of my own design. Again and again she noted points that lacked clarity or that required deeper consideration and better wording, and put in long hours of careful study into every moment of Hanuvar and Antires' exploits. I shall forever be thankful to her for the love she has shown this work.

Some of you likely noted similarities between Calenius and the singular creation of the brilliant Karl Edward Wagner. I hope that Mr. Wagner would have enjoyed this homage and not found it too far beyond what he might have imagined for his own character.

My other book dedicant was neither a master of horror nor a writer and editor of heroic fiction. And yet Mary Dolan left a mightier imprint upon me than KEW. Her single book—slightly altered upon rerelease under a different title—remains my favorite fictional depiction of Hannibal of Carthage. (George Zebrowski's short story, "The Number of the Sand," is a close second.)

Ms. Dolan fully perceived the kind of mind and personality that can occasionally be glimpsed behind the historical accounts, and then presents Hannibal with such clarity we seem momentarily to be in his company. If *Hannibal of Carthage* (also reprinted, confusingly, and with an inaccuracy in its title that I can imagine irritated Ms. Dolan, as *Hannibal: Scourge of Imperial Rome*) is not entirely successful as a novel, I can't fault her book overmuch, for the moments with Hannibal elevate the rest. I admired many fine phrases throughout the text, and even adapted one of them—"learn how to please yourself and let others envy your happiness"—into advice Izivar offers Enarius.

If you ever wish to have some insight into what Hanuvar's campaign against Tyvol might have been like during the Second Volani War, Dolan's novel, Harold Lamb's biography of Hannibal, and the equally fine biography of Hannibal by Ernle Bradford would get you a lot of the way there.